LOOK AWAY,

A NOVEL BY

LOOK AWAY

BEN HAAS

SIMON AND SCHUSTER · NEW YORK ·

Manufactured in the United States of America

This book is for my mother and father.

PROLOGUE

You could see them in the courthouse square of every little Southern town, then, in the spring of 1932—the dispossessed. With
stunned eyes in unshaven faces, they lounged in ragged overalls and
worn-out shoes on the courthouse steps or on the benches around the
inevitable bronze Confederate soldier, ashamed and bitter in idle-
ness when they should have been breaking the steaming black loam
of the low country or the thick red clay of the uplands, assaulting the
land and impregnating it with cotton. But they no longer owned any
land; the mortgage weevil had eaten it.

Most of them had always been proud men, and independent men.
And in their time they thought they had fought everything their stern
and ruthless God, their sly insidious Devil, could throw at them.
They had fought drought, the slow disaster of the undropping bright
ball of sun fixed seemingly forever in the hard, bright arch of the
sky, while cotton plants withered and dried. They had fought unending torrents of rain, gushing for days from sag-bellied clouds,
hammering the cotton plants into the mud and washing precious topsoil through a thousand eroded conduits to the sea, drowning the
fields and drowning hope. They had fought the hail that came marching through the summer afternoon like an army trampling down the
crops; and always, every season, they had fought as a matter of
course a hundred different tough-rooted, hard-stemmed, ineradicable
enemies like Johnson grass and wire grass and Jimson weed and

cocklebur. They had fought the boll weevil, too; and they had thought then they had met the deadliest enemy of all.

But the mortgage weevil could not even be fought, and that was what filled them with terror and despair and a spreading, communicable, taut-nerved hysteria. The mortgage weevil was a more subtle devourer, and there was no dusting, no cultivating, no countermeasure that could destroy it. Gnawing silently in the musty, terrible dimnesses of a thousand banks and countinghouses, it did its work in secret. Only when the sheriff arrived with his incomprehensible papers, signs and eviction notices, did its ravages come to light. After that, the auctions began: this mule, that shotgun, the bedstead on which the ole woman had borned all the children—and they could only stand in sick incomprehension as what their lives had amounted to was knocked down to the highest bidder for a pittance they never saw. And with the past, the future had been auctioned too, so that now, landless, cropless, creditless, their children scabby and rubber-limbed with rickets, their women dried into gaunt, nervous, juiceless sticks, they could only sit, baffled by yesterday, afraid of tomorrow, survivors of an accident they still could not understand, hoping that a miracle would fall upon them, some savior manifest himself in a second coming to make them men once more.

They sat for a long time as the panicked North sucked the paltry capital it had invested back to its own terrified heart, drying up the thin veins and arteries of life-giving money that had weakly nourished the South. Everything went—cash, mortgage paper, land titles—leaving nothing for extensions, waiving of interest payments or re-financing, leaving neither land nor the credit these people who lived on borrowed money from crop to crop needed to buy seed and fertilizer. They sat, whittling and rolling occasional cigarettes with grudging care for every crumb of tobacco; and presently, no matter where in the state of Muskogee they had forgathered, they heard a sound in the distance, the backfire of an automobile.

It was always the signal for the music to begin, the thin, high whang of old-time fiddle playing, coming from yon side of town, at first so faint they thought it was only another manifestation of the hunger-buzz in their ears. But then it came closer, definite, real, strong and cheerful, almost the sound of hope. They raised their heads and looked at each other with questioning eyes, and then they began to pat their feet. The car backfired again, loudly and deliberately; the music was a cascade of stirring, lanky rhythm now, and then the cavalcade pulled into the square.

It was always led by a Dodge touring car with the top down. There were banners on each side of it and across the radiator.

HOKE MOODY FOR GOVERNOR
VOTE FOR HOKE, THE POOR MAN'S FRIEND

Behind the Dodge came a fire-engine-red Terraplane roadster, and when it appeared, the Negroes, huddled on their side of the square, would murmur softly and fade away like black mist, for the roadster carried six men all robed and hooded in white and it bore the legend on each flank: THE KU KLUX KLAN FOR MOODY.

Next there would be a Model-T Ford, backfiring clownishly every few feet, making the mules that pulled the wagon at the tail of the train jerk their heads and jingle their chains. The musicians rode in the wagon box: a leathery, long-necked fiddle player, a short fat man with a guitar, and a blind banjoist. They played like men fighting bees, filling the square with the twanging skirl and rhythm of their old-time music, and the men in the square arose almost as one and flowed forward to form a crowd, heads lifted and something gleaming in their eyes that had not been there before, despair forgotten for the moment. When the music ended with a wild *shave-and-a-haircut! two bits!* they whooped and applauded.

Then, in the following silence, a man dismounted from the touring car. He was not tall, but he had a body like a section cut from an oak tree, thick and solid beneath a plating of flab. His head was almost too large for his body, and his lank brown hair had a way of falling across his deep-set eyes. Smiling at the crowd with teeth that showed a touch of gold, he shoved his way through gently until he reached the wagon. Then, nimbly for all his bulk, he hoisted himself up the wagon wheel, planted himself in the wagon bed, and stared out over the crowd, arms raised, deep-set blue eyes shining. He held out his hands in a slow, dignified gesture as of benediction, and the noise among the farmers died.

He waited long enough for the crowd to have to hold its breath in expectation. Then, in short, jerky, forceful sentences, thick with the slur and elision of the South, he spoke.

"Hard times, ain't it, friends? Hard, hard times. . . ."

"Yeah, man! You said it!" the crowd chorused back.

"They call it a *De*pression!" His voice rang out like the clang of a hammer on an anvil. "But I call it the judgment of the Lord! Not on you good people, you God-fearin, Bible-readin, hard-workin salt of the earth! Not on you—but on your leaders. You know who I'm talkin about?"

"Yeah, Hoke!" somebody yelled. "Powell Bradham!"

The speaker whirled, pointed toward the man in the crowd. "Who that said that? You, Charlie Collins? Was it you, Buck Hillis? Whoever it was, my friend, you know you done spoke the everlastin truth! Powell Bradham—him that sits up there in his big office in the capital, him and his rich, fat-bellied, nigger-lovin friends—I'll tell you now, and you better listen good. There's a wrathful God up in heaven, and it's Powell Bradham that has drawn his fury down on this land—same as a lightnin rod draws lightnin! It's Bradham and his Yankee-Wall Street-Jew-Catholic-liquor-drinkin friends that have brought down God's judgment on us all—and we deserve it, for lettin him wallow so long in his trough up there in Hannington, him and his Gadarene swine of henchmen! It's our fault, it's our responsibility—and we deserve what we're gettin now for closin our eyes to Bradham and his evil, Godless doins. But now the cry has gone up through the land, the cry that should have been raised years ago—*How long, oh Lord, how long! When wilt thou deliver us from the wilderness?* Well, I'll tell you"—he thrust a finger forward at the crowd in a fierce jabbing motion, his big head bobbing, his mouth open as if gasping for air—"I'll tell you! God helps them that helps themselves! We'll be delivered when we git up off our hams an stand up on our hine legs and deliver ourselves! We'll be delivered when we throw the rascals out and scourge the money-changers from the temple! We'll be delivered when Powell Bradham and Willis Hilton and all their evil crew are driven into the wilderness themselves and there's a government in Hannington that will take the poor man, the one-gallus, one-mule farmer—like you, like me—to its heart! That's when we'll be delivered—when we drive Powell Bradham out and not before!"

The men in the crowd stood tensely, alert, listening carefully. The voice of the man in the wagon soared on, exhorting, prayerful and contemptuous by turns, traveling the rise and fall of two octaves, striking into them with words like daggers, plucking at their souls with hope and deliverance and making them vibrate with its resonance. He did not hammer at them long, not much beyond ten minutes, but when, sweat-soaked, hair flying, he raised himself to his toes, flung his arms wide, and howled with a wild organ note that brought chills to their spines, *"And I say, scourge them from the temple!"* a breath went up from the crowd, an upward-rising sigh of catharsis, and then a wild shrieking whoop of agreement and approbation that shattered the momentary heat-laden silence of the square. And the man in the wagon stood for a moment with head bowed as if in prayer, and then he raised his head and looked at them, beaming, grinning, sweating, and at that precise instant the fiddler raised his bow and the guitarist bent forward and the banjo picker crashed a chord; and suddenly the noon was full of the swirl and thunder and trumpet blood-stir of "Dixie," and the crowd went wild. . . .

Powell Bradham, Governor of the state of Muskogee, stood at the window of his office and looked down at the convict gardeners working on the capitol grounds two stories below. The room was tense with the silence of waiting, and he could feel the concentration of eyes on his back, the separate and unyielding stares of the men who had come here to tell him that they were betraying him, selling him out.

Standing there, marshaling his thoughts, he felt anger and disgust, but not directed at the other men in the room. These emotions were directed at himself. He had served two terms as Governor of the state, had held Muskogee's political structure latched in his fingers like the reins of a well-trained horse for fourteen years. He had received those reins from the hand of his father, who had in turn plucked them from Bradham's grandfather's grasp. What enraged him now, literally griped the bowels within him, was not that he was being betrayed, but that after all that experience, all that training, all the inherited and acquired skills, he had made a rankly amateurish miscalculation that had put him in a position where he could be betrayed. He despised stupidity and ineptness, and he was as merciless with them in himself as in his subordinates, his family or his friends.

Now he turned from the window, a tall man with a handsome, bony face, his dark hair winged with gray at the temples, his carriage military and full of the pride and arrogance that had been the Bradham mark for generations. For a moment his anger was too great to contain, and it unleashed itself harshly.

"Trash!" he grated. "Hoke Moody's nothing but Hampton County trash, and I will not deal with him! Do you hear me? I will not deal with him!"

The big room, ancient, high of ceiling, with walls of tan plaster, an oaken wainscot and a massive marble fireplace, was silent; and Bradham let his eyes move defiantly from face to face of the men sitting across the desk from him. Even if they had come here to deliver an ultimatum, he thought with grim satisfaction, they were still afraid of him. He could see it in their expressions.

St. John Butler, president of the vast complex of Butler Mills, plant after plant of which sprawled across the high, red Piedmont plateau, broke the silence by clearing his throat. His voice was deferential, apologetic. "Powell, you don't hate it coming to this any worse than we do. But we've talked it over, and we don't see any other way out. Either we deal with Hoke Moody or we're going to get hurt— and hurt bad."

Wiley Ginsburg stood up, short, blue-jowled, softly handsome. His father had been Jewish, but Wiley was a member of the Episcopal church, ruler now of a statewide chain of department and variety stores. There was less inclination to placate Bradham in his tone. Bradham wondered if Ginsburg were not really the moving force in this junta.

"Powell, you've let us down. For years we've worked together, and some of us with your father before you. We put up the money, we let you handle the politics, run things your own way, we were pleased, the state was good to do business in. But now you've put us between a rock and a hard place. And the time's come when we've got to speak up. I know all about that pride of yours, 'proud as a Bradham,' that's a saying in this state. But I'm speaking for us all when I say, pride or no pride, you either make a deal with Moody for us or we make it ourselves."

The flare of anger Bradham felt this time was not self-directed; but this kind he could keep in check. He kept his face carefully expressionless, as Wiley Ginsburg remained standing as if not quite sure himself whether or not he was through. Slowly Bradham lowered himself into the chair behind his desk, deliberately making them all wait for him to speak.

Pride, he thought, the word contemptuous in his brain. What would you know of pride, the Bradham kind of pride? Bradhams were governors of this state, Ginsburg, when your grandfather was wearing a skullcap and walking from house to house with his peddler's pack on his back. . . .

No, he thought, Ginsburg could not understand. St. John Butler, maybe; Harris Lesesne. Those two out of the five were from families old enough to know what pride meant. And to know the meanings of the other words, too: duty, honor, obligation. Archaic words, now; obsolete, unless your family had lived by them for so long that they had been ingrained into the very texture of your being. As had another word—Muskogee. . . . Bradham, Muskogee, the family name and the state name were almost synonymous, for the two of them were so interwoven that not only their origins but their fates had to be identical. A Bradham had commanded troops against Cornwallis; another had led the state into the Union; still another had led it back out again. A Bradham—his own grandfather, by God!—had fought carpetbaggers, Radical Republicans and a Federal occupation to rescue the state from Reconstruction rule. His father had fought the mob of trash and red-necks calling themselves the Farmers' Alliance and the Populist party. And that was how the state had come down to him, not only an inheritance, but a trust. And he had followed the Bradham tradition scrupulously and with pride—the tradition that only Bradhams and their designates had earned the right to govern, that only they could be trusted to protect the state they had created and had preserved from assaults from without and within; that it was not only his right and his privilege to do so, but that it was his obligation, too. So much devotion, so much sacrifice and blood woven and dyed into the skein of Muskogee's history, and himself the recipient, the guardian of it all, and now—now here stood this little Jew peddler saying *pride or no pride.* . . .

Still, he kept the anger latched down. He was in a tight place, the worst he had ever been caught in. Anger would not help him now. After all, he *had* made the blunder. Why didn't I crush Hoke Moody when I had the chance? he wondered. I should have stomped on him like a snake—

Aloud he said, "All right, Wiley. We'll leave my pride out of it for a little bit. But I'll remind you, I've never lost an election. Never. Not in my whole political career. Neither did my father or my grandfather. Now"—his voice dropped, scathed Ginsburg—"the first time we have a little opposition, and you come in here yelling calf rope.

Wanting me to hand this state over to Hoke Moody and his rabble lock, stock and barrel, just pass it over to the trash, the poor whites, without even a fight! Damn it, don't you see? Moody's trying to split us. But if you'd just get some starch into your backbone, we'll—"

"Crap." Ginsburg's voice cut across his brutally. "Moody's going to be elected and you know it. You can't succeed yourself, and that would be the only way we'd have a prayer of stopping him. Then, to top it off, you go pick as our candidate a dickeybird like Willis Hilton. All right, he makes a good figurehead. But what we need now ain't a figurehead—we need a *candidate!* Somebody that could go out and fight Moody on his own terms. Instead, we got a nobody, a nothing!" He chopped the air disgustedly with his hand.

St. John Butler leaned forward, a very thin, bony man in his early forties, with deceptively gentle eyes.

"In ordinary times, Powell," he said quietly, "it wouldn't have mattered. But these aren't ordinary times, and you've never had opposition like Moody before. This state's full of desperate people and Moody's using their desperation for all it's worth. And it's working— he's pinning everything that's wrong right squarely on us."

"I know what he's doing," said Bradham harshly.

"Sho." Butler's voice stayed soft. "Of course you do. The thing about it is not to argue among ourselves but to work out a plan of action. Now. Moody has come to Wiley and me and offered us a deal. He's not sure of his own strength yet. He knows that we've got the money and that we could hurt him plenty, even if he could hurt us worse. So he wants to form a coalition. All right, so he wants to be on top and run things, and if we join up with him, we'll have to eat a lot of dirt. But that's better than being frozen out completely, which is what will happen if Moody gets elected without us. And I don't know about these other gentlemen, but that would be something *I* couldn't afford. I'm stretched like a bob-wire fence right now. To have Moody in this office, with a grudge against me and nobody on hand to hold him back—well, that's something I'd hate to see happen. And I'd do just about anything to keep it from happening."

Bradham leaned forward. "Including selling Willis Hilton down the river."

St. John Butler's brown eyes did not waver. "Including doing whatever has to be done," he said.

And somehow that was the moment when Bradham knew that he

was defeated. He had never tasted defeat before and he found, to his amazement, it was far worse than he had dreamed it could be. It was a scald inside him, a bitterness so great that he could hardly contain it, shame and humiliation that racked him like an ague. He, and he alone of all his lineage, had been proved incompetent to discharge his trust. He looked down at his hands before him on the desk and was startled to see that they were trembling slightly.

He realized now that he had known from the beginning that it would end this way. These men were afraid—as terrified as any dispossessed farmer sitting in a courthouse square. They had fortunes to protect, and they knew that if Hoke Moody became Governor against their opposition he would turn on them and their fortunes, slashing like a weasel in a henhouse. But Moody had given them this one last chance to join him, and nothing he, Bradham, could say or do would stop them. For they no longer trusted him to protect them. And there was no use in lecturing them on what a Moody government, what the end of the Bradham dynasty, would mean to the state. They were not interested in the state. They were interested in survival.

So now they had given him a choice. He could act as their negotiator, he could deal with Moody and be their representative in the coalition, a subordinate to the one man whose origins and philosophy he most despised, he could do that and cling to a tatter of power—or he could wrap pride, honor, and duty about him like a toga and go down to defeat with banners flying, fighting alone and without backing. That was his choice. He could lose—or he could betray Willis Hilton, betray the state, betray the words he believed in . . . and survive.

Patiently, they waited for him.

Bradham looked from cold face to cold face. He was sweating; his palms were clammy with perspiration. He saw in their expressions the knowledge that haunted him—the knowledge that if he divorced himself from them and fought on his own, they would have to break him. And it would not, he knew, be difficult for them to do it. He was stretched, financially, like a thread himself. He owned a thousand-acre plantation, but last year's five-cent cotton had turned it into a disaster. He owned a logging camp and sawmill and timber rights to half the enormous Kenoree Swamp, forty miles from here—but those interests, too, had become ratholes down which money disappeared from sight. He had long ago quit paying the loggers, but they would neither leave nor stop cutting timber. Maniacally convinced that as long as they worked, they were entitled at least to be fed, they went on lumbering, piling up logs that could not be given away. And because they refused to quit working, he was, somehow, in a manner beyond his comprehension, obligated to keep on feeding them, so that the whole thing had become a farce of which he could not make head nor tail. Everything in Bradham screamed for him to tell them all to go to hell—that he would fight Moody single-handed if it came to that. But the knowledge that it would mean his ruin, politically, financially, totally . . . he was surprised, horrified, that he could not make his mouth utter the words.

"If we're going to deal," Ginsburg said harshly, "it's gotta be quick. If Moody ever gets wise to how strong he really is, he'll tell us to kiss his ass."

Before Bradham could find an answer, there was an interruption. The double doors of his office swung open; the round, handsome face of a boy of ten appeared in the crack. He had Bradham's gray eyes, Bradham's strong nose. "Daddy," he began, "can I—"

Bradham spoke with irritation. "Not now, son, I'm busy." At that moment, a dark hand touched the boy's shoulder and pulled him backward. A soft but exasperated Negro voice said, "Come along, Cary, didn't I tell you not to bother your daddy?" Bradham caught a flash of a starched white uniform. "Let's us go along home."

The boy's head reluctantly disappeared. The Negro voice said, "I'se sorry, Mister Powell, he—"

Bradham's voice had no anger in it when he spoke again. "All right, Amy. It's all right. Just take him on home. Then send the car back."

The doors closed. Bradham stared at them for a moment.

"We'd like to have you represent us with Moody," said Butler, his voice breaking into Bradham's thoughts. "If you will, we'll give you our backing the way we always have. But we've got to know, Powell. You've got to tell us now—will you or won't you?"

Bradham slowly turned his head and looked at them. His hands were not trembling now, and he no longer felt defeated.

I had forgotten him, he thought. I had forgotten Cary. . . .

And he had forgotten, too, he realized, that honor lost could be redeemed. That if he was very careful, very clever, and very, very patient, whatever he yielded could be recaptured. That he was not the last Bradham, that there was still the instrument God and his loins had given him. All at once he no longer cared about the present; his mind flew ahead into the future. It would take time, but if he lived, if Cary lived . . .

When he spoke, his voice was clear and steady, and there was no longer any contention in it.

"All right, St. John. I'll do whatever you people say. Tell Hoke Moody to come and see me, and I'll make our deal."

BOOK ONE
1946

1 By the time he had finished breakfast in the diner, the train was six hours out of Washington, headed south, and Cary Bradham knew that Muskogee could not be far. Everything now was poignantly familiar—great fields of half-grown cotton, with leaves the color of new currency, springing from rich black dirt; dark, slow, haunted and secret-looking guts of water colonnaded with towering, feather-headed, moss-festooned cypress; occasional hamlets whose oak-shaded streets were already empty of life in the morning heat; warped privies, grassless yards, fluttering clotheslines and flimsy shacks of outlying Negro settlements; and, where the track sometimes paralleled a road, the slow amble of unurgent mules pulling rickety wagons while drivers dozed with lines held slackly. Cary had expected to feel excitement, but the almost sexual pleasure which gripped him as the train hammered him toward home came as a surprise.

He shifted restlessly on the prickly plush seat, a tall young man of twenty-four in the rumpled uniform of an Air Force major. His face, beneath close-cropped brown hair, was strong, bony, and deeply tanned, but, despite the pragmatic confidence of the seasoned officer in his bearing, four years in service, eighteen months of combat flying in B-29s, had not entirely burned away a certain capacity for enthusiasm that he himself knew was immature, almost childish. On the whole, though, he was glad that he had retained it. Certainly, he told himself, aware of his own sentimentality as home drew near, he was glad that he had got out of the war as lightly as he had; suppose he had wound up like Burke Jessup?

Remembering Burke, his lean face turned thoughtful, almost mournful. The poor bastard, he thought. He had stopped over in New York especially to see Burke, who had written that he would be there on leave from the Army hospital; and they had sat in the bar of the Astor Hotel and consumed an incredible quantity of bourbon. But even the whiskey had not softened the shock of seeing what the war had done to Burke, who had been one of his closest friends since childhood. The prematurely bald, pale and crippled infantry captain, grossly overweight from inactivity, had borne no relation to the hard, agile Burke of prewar days.

He knew that his sentimentality had allowed his pity for his friend to be written plainly on his face as he had watched Burke hobble across the lobby, leaning awkwardly on the two canes. And Burke had not missed it as, with no preliminary of greeting, he dropped, breathing heavily, into the other chair and laid his canes across the table.

"They call me Little Goody No-Feet," he had said wryly. "And you can wipe that expression of careful obliviousness off your face and relax. I zigged when I should have zagged, and a Kraut shot hell out of my feet with an eighty-eight; and there's no use for you to sit there on pins and needles all night worrying about saying something that'll make me burst into tears."

So Burke still had his courage, anyway. Cary was glad of that: he saw now that Burke would need it all. He felt a little better, though it was still hard to look at Burke, and both of them got drunk as quickly as they could. Finally, like two men walking cautiously toward a meeting in the middle of a tightwire, they approached their old complete confidence and trust in one another and he was able to look at Burke again.

"So where do you go from here?" Burke said at last, thickly. "Home?"

"Yes," said Cary. "Home."

"You're a lucky bastard," Burke said.

"I know it."

"No, I don't mean because you didn't get shot up. I mean because you can still go home."

"What are you talking about?" Cary sat up straight, frowning. "You can go home, too, when they turn you loose from the hospital."

"Can I?" Burke raised his glass and looked at it. His froglike face was sardonic. There were beads of sweat on his forehead. "I doubt it."

"What are you talking about?" Cary said again. "You mean you aren't coming back to Hannington?"

"Not if I can help it." Burke took a swallow of the drink.

"Why not?" Cary was both disappointed and a little indignant, but he was discounting Burke's determined tone a little, too. Burke was unsettled, that was all; besides, he was drunk. "Of course you're coming home."

"I could if it was still home, but it's not home. Oh, it is to you, sure, you haven't changed a bit. You can't hardly wait to get back and hear them loyal ole slaves singin' welcome-home spirituals to the young massa as he stands on the v'randa of the great house. All right, that's fine. But it's not for me. First place, I don't have any slaves or any veranda. Second place, even if I had, you couldn't drag me back to Muskogee with a team of mules."

"What the hell's wrong with Muskogee?" Cary's voice was angry.

"I'll tell you what's wrong with it." Burke wagged a finger. He was very drunk, but his eyes still focused, and they were intent. "It's a goddam desert island, that's what's wrong with it."

"You're nuts."

"No, I'm detached. Now. I can see it for what it is. Muskogee. The whole damn South. Just an island sitting there in a great big ocean of time, and everybody on it stranded. And content to be that way. Off in the distance, maybe, they can see the mainland, see the shore. But they never want to go to the mainland and they never want anybody from the mainland coming to them." He drained his glass. "Well, I'm on the mainland and I'm going to stay there. If I didn't learn anything else from the war, I learned that there's a great big world out here, with forces operating in it and things happening in it, things the people back there can't imagine—or, if they can, that they'd rather not think about. Hell, no, I'm loose now. Maybe this"—he pointed toward his feet—"is the price I've got to pay for being loose, but I'm free and I'm gonna stay that way. Anyhow, they wouldn't want me back. I've been on the mainland so long that I smell like the mainland now, and they wouldn't want me around."

"You're not even making sense."

"Oh, I know I'm not, to you. That island out there in the time-ocean . . . you're one of the royal family of it. Maybe not a king yet, but anyhow a prince. You'd be a fool not to go back; you would have been a fool to change. But me, I'm just one of the peasants anyhow—they'll never miss me." His face was sweating profusely now and he rubbed it with both hands. "Jesus," he said in another voice, "I'm drunk. Do you wanta help me back to my own hotel?"

So he had put Burke to bed, trying hard not to look at the feet after he had taken off the special shoes, had covered Burke gently, and had set the tag end of the bottle he had found in the room where Burke could reach it in the morning without getting up. He stood over Burke for a moment, looking down at the sweating, flabby, unconscious face, feeling oddly mixed impulses of grief and affection; and he had thought: I don't care what he says. He'll be back . . . he's bound to come home. There's no finer place in the world than Muskogee. . . .

The long, stirring hoot of the whistle brought Cary out of a half doze and he sat up, immediately wide-awake. His excitement rose to a crescendo as he saw that they were really coming into Hannington now. The train clattered along a high railroad embankment, and from the window he could see below the acres of little board shacks jammed close together in blocks marked off by narrow, unpaved streets—this was Little Hammer, the largest Negro district . . . and wasn't that shack yonder where Lucy and Houston Whitley lived? Then the train had rushed past and now there were the forlorn but painted houses of the Mill Hill lintheads, better kept but somehow more desolate than the shanties of the Negroes, and, hovering over them, like an enormous, dirty hen brooding scabrous chicks, the great, blue-windowed, grimy brick hulk of the Hannington Spinning Mill. Then there were the high, smoking chimneys of the fertilizer factory and the cottonseed oil mill; the lesser industries; a spread of railroad yards fanning out ahead, and the porter entered the aisle of the car. "Hannin'ton. This here Hannin'ton."

Even before Sherman had burned the city and it had rebuilt itself from the ground up, Hannington had been not only the capital and largest city of the state, but a railroad hub, and in the rebuilding no expense had been spared on the station. Nor had it been altered since the late eighties: what drew toward them now was a vast, frescoed, and grimily tasteless mausoleum of red brick. A clot of people waited under the long shed that fronted it and Cary strained his eyes but could not pick out his parents. He arose, a dryness in his throat, an odd fluttering in his upper belly. He was home. . . . He wiped his hands along his pants legs and went to the vestibule, where the porter stood over his Valpak, and waited tensely while the train, snorting and banging, inched to a halt.

"Watch yo' step, watch yo' step," the porter said.

Cary swung down to the pavement beside the car. Immediately he was bathed in shocking heat, the airless shimmering radiance from concrete, the brutal slam of the sun above. It felt good. He pressed a half dollar into the porter's hand and bent to scoop up the bag.

"Cary!"

It was a cry, in his mother's voice. Then she was hurrying toward him in an awkward feminine run, handsome face contorted, arms already outreaching. She was a tall woman, who had aged gracefully into her mid-fifties, only plating her body with a thin layer of middle-aged flesh; when she was not crying as she was now, traces of her once-exquisite beauty could still be seen, though for the most part it had been transmuted only to a pleasant, unworried gentleness. He was her only child and the bond between them was a strong one, and there was a tightening in his own throat, a burning in his eyes, as he felt the soft wetness of her cheeks against him and the squeeze of her arms around him. He held her closely for a moment; and then, when he raised his head, he saw his father.

In panama hat and neat seersucker suit, Powell Bradham stood tall and straight behind the woman. It was as if the years had flung themselves against him like waves against a rock and had retreated after only minimal erosion; the hard core of the man remained undamaged. Time had leached the last of the color from his temples, had deepened the lines in a tanned face that, even though it had lost the ready humor and the vulnerability of youth, could have served as the model for Cary's own, and had spotted and veined the backs of his big hands. But otherwise, at sixty, he seemed to have defeated time. He stepped toward Cary and put out his hands, and his strength, undiminished, encircled Cary for a moment. As he felt the brush of his father's lips on his cheek, Gary swallowed hard and trembled a little. He loved his mother, but love was not the proper word for what he felt for Powell Bradham. It was more akin, he thought, to what preachers must feel for God.

Then Bradham released him and stepped back, his eyes appraising, measuring Cary already. He seemed to be pleased; he smiled and said, "Son, it's good to have you back. You look fine." His voice lost a bit of its steadiness as he added softly, "Welcome home."

"You must be starved," Irene Bradham said, sniffling.

Before he could answer, another woman's voice screamed, italicizing the name, *"Cary!"* He turned, startled, and then his heart sank as he recognized the blond girl running across the pavement toward him, mouth wide with excitement, breasts jiggling under her blouse. For God's sake, he thought wearily, couldn't she even wait for me to get home to Mercy Street?

No, he thought, of course she wouldn't. . . . He had known Mary Scott Butler all his life, and for most of that time had fought as best he could the pressures from all sides that seemed determined to push the two of them together. He had been maneuvered into being her marshal when she made her debut at the last Debutante Ball held in Hannington in 1941, when she was seventeen, had been forced into dating her a few times before and after that, but the army had rescued him before the pressures could increase. She had written him regularly while he was in the army and he had replied at about the ratio of one letter to her every six, but she had never taken the hint. Her letters had been like her conversation, crowded, chatty and inane. But she was, after all, St. John Butler's daughter and no matter how much he detested her, he had to observe at least a certain ritual friendliness, for the sake of both their families if not for hers. That she made no secret of the fact that she had been in love with him since she was fifteen touched him not at all.

Now he tried hard to keep the weariness—disgust was too strong a term—that her presence always inspired in him off his face as she ran up to him and embraced him. "Oh, Cary, you're home." She had the round, pale, blue-eyed face of a kitten or a doll, a snub nose, full red lips. She smelled as he remembered her, of White Shoulders perfume. Dutifully he put his arm about her and kissed her. He was surprised at how soft her lips were and how good they felt; surprised, too, of being conscious of the pressure of full, resilient breasts against him and of being physically stirred by their pressing; but then, it had been a long, long time since he had had a woman, and she had filled out. He offered no resistance as she took his hands and backed away and looked him up and down with eyes that shone. "He looks so *good,* doesn't he, Aunt Irene?"

"He certainly does," Irene Bradham said softly.

Cary said, trying to keep his tone neutral, "Mary Scott, it's good to see you," and then he gently but with firmness withdrew his hands from her grasp.

"What about me, boy?" a masculine voice said. "You got a hello for me?"

Cary turned, warming with genuine pleasure. "Uncle Hoke! How're you doing?"

"Pretty good for an old man." Hoke Moody thrust out a hand and Cary took it. It was plump, but surprisingly hard. With his other hand, Moody squeezed Cary's arm. "Boy, it's good to have you home in one piece; how are you, all right? Those little yellow polecats didn't do you any meanness, did they?"

"Not a bit, Uncle Hoke. But I did them some." He was surprised by how little Moody had changed, too; time seemed to have touched him even less than Bradham. His blue eyes still spilled warmth through the magisterial steel-rimmed glasses he wore as he looked up from much lesser height at Cary, and his face was still ruddy and firm-fleshed. He still smelled of talcum power and shaving lotion, just as Cary remembered him from childhood. From the time he was ten or eleven, Hoke Moody had been a frequent visitor at the Mercy Street house, and though Cary knew they were no blood kin, he had a nephew's affection for the senior Senator from Muskogee.

He was a little surprised by the coolness of his father's tone. "I didn't know you were coming down, Hoke."

"You didn't think I'd let ole Cary come home from the wars without putting in an appearance here to greet him, did you?" Moody put an arm around Cary and squeezed. "The good Lord never saw fit to bless me with a son, so I've just had to make do with Cary, and I appreciate the use of him, Powell." He laughed. "Anyhow, Mary Scott wanted to come, but she was too shy to come by herself, so I told her I'd carry her. St. John's out of town." His arm slid away and they all stood there in silence for perhaps three seconds, just looking at each other in the bright sunlight.

"Oh, Cary, I'm so glad you're home," Mary Scott said with a concern that irritated and embarrassed him. "I do hope you'll—" She broke off, just short of asking him to hurry and call her. Cary said nothing, and Powell Bradham shifted a little.

"Well, I reckon we'd better get this boy on home. Y'all come along with us."

"All right," Mary Scott said eagerly, but Hoke Moody touched her arm. "No, not right now. We won't intrude on your reunion—will we, honey? We just came to say hello. Now we've got to run along. We just had to make sure Cary got here safe and sound."

Mary Scott looked downcast but not defeated. "You got here just in time, Cary. They just opened up the pool out at the club; I know how you like to swim."

"I'm sure you and Cary will get in a lot of swimming together this summer," Irene Bradham said, smiling. "Cary'll be calling you soon, just as soon as he gets settled, won't you, Cary?"

There was nothing else to say but "Sure. Sure, I'll call you . . . ah, tomorrow, Mary Scott."

She brightened at that. Hoke Moody pulled her away with a little more forcible touch. "Come along, honey, we've got to go now. Cary, again, welcome home. Powell, Irene, y'all take it easy." He led Mary Scott off across the pavement, earning Cary's gratitude.

"She certainly is a nice girl," Irene Bradham said fondly. "And she thinks the sun rises and sets in you, Cary. You ought to be very proud of having such a *nice* girl think so much of you."

"Yeah," Cary grunted. "I guess so."

Powell Bradham turned. "Dayton."

The uniformed Negro chauffeur seemed to materialize out of nowhere. He was in his thirties, very black, grinning.

"Hello, Dayton," said Cary.

"Hidy, Mr. Cary. Mighty glad to have you back." Dayton took the bag and they moved toward the car.

"Lucy's got all your favorite things for dinner," Irene Bradham bubbled. "She's been like a cat on a hot griddle all day. I'll bet she's asked me a thousand times, *When Mr. Cary's train git in?* She's put the little pot in the big one and stewed the dishrag. . . ."

They drove down Main Street, and it had not changed either. The three white movie theaters, Woolworth's, the McClellan and Kress stores; Ginsburg's; The Hub; Dabney's Hardware; and the handful of eight- and ten-story office buildings that took Hannington out of the small-town class and made it a city—they were all there. Even the leisurely people on the sidewalks were the same—coatless businessmen; slouching, ambling farmers in overalls and khakis, the mark of their calling the sun-reddened webs of wrinkles on the backs of their necks; and the Negroes—of course the Negroes, always the Negroes—dark faces swirling in and out of cheap stores or clustered at bus stops, calm with an immemorial serenity and patience or flashing suddenly bright with laughter. The Negroes—they made up forty per cent of Hannington's hundred thousand people, and it was good to see them; they were the ultimate symbol of the South, of Muskogee, of home; they made him know he was back where he belonged.

Then they had come to the end of Main, and Cary saw ahead of them the capitol building. It sat in the center of a broad, grassy square —a huge Greek revival structure of solid granite and white marble. Despite the massiveness of its dimensions, there was beauty and grace in the soaring reach of its great fluted columns and the frescoed scrollwork of its portico and balconies. The lawn surrounding it was a flawless, close-shorn emerald green, shaded by tall oaks and swamp poplars, accented with the dark shiny green of magnolias. The state flag, a cross of white stars against a blue field, fluttered from a staff atop the dome. From poles on either side of the front walk, which was guarded with old siege guns and stacks of rusty iron cannonballs, flew two more flags—that of the United States of America and the deep, blue-barred red of the Confederacy. Facing both banners with his long gun at high port stood a bronze Confederate soldier twenty feet tall, mustachioed face alert and truculent, pigeon droppings running down his cheeks like tears. The high steps of the capitol were flanked by two exquisitely carved marble statues, one of Apollo and one of Pallas Athena. Sherman's artillery had bombarded the capitol during the battle for Hannington, and a ball had carried away Athena's head. The devastation wrought by the Yankee guns had been deliberately left unrepaired, and the chipped steps and headless statue were listed in the state guidebook as tourist attractions.

Though his father had not held public office for nearly fifteen years, Cary felt sharp nostalgia for the musty, high-ceilinged rooms of the capitol. He had played up and down the worn marble stairs of the interior, so ancient their treads had been shuffled concave by countless feet. He had craned his neck to memorize the intricacies of the bas-relief that circled the ceiling of the rotunda under the dome. For him the capitol had been the place his father worked, and in a way he would always feel as if it belonged to them as much as their own house on Mercy Street.

After that, it was not far to Mercy Street. Cary leaned forward on the seat of the car in anticipation, and when they finally turned the last, crucial corner, he smiled as he saw the grove of oaks and pecans and hickories on the knoll, the big house gleaming whitely through their foliage from the center of a vast, sloping, flawless lawn.

Powell and Irene Bradham had built the Mercy Street house in 1924 after Irene's father died and she inherited his money. It had all been country then, but—perhaps because of the Bradhams—the area had become fashionable and had built up just before the stock market crash until it was full of imposing homes. But the Bradham place still dominated them all.

It had been constructed in the then-fashionable Moorish style of stuccoed brick and red tile roofing. Countless windows gleamed above countless balconies; behind an urn-finialed wall ran a large, flagged veranda. Flanking the high front steps dozed two large, muscular, cast-stone sphinxes. The overall effect was of startling ugliness and unexpected beauty stunningly intermingled; and Cary's pride matched his mother's own as she squeezed his hand and said, "Here we are."

Dayton stopped the car and they got out, Bradham assisting his wife with old-fashioned courtliness. Cary went ahead up the steps, and, with Dayton following with his bag, entered the wide front door.

With his parents crowding in behind him, Cary stopped in the foyer and drew in a long, savoring breath of home. What he breathed was the odor of care, order and luxury; of deep, soft carpets and fine draperies that kept out the sun; of ancient, honestly built, scrupulously polished furniture; of family china, silver, and tradition. A huge mirror in an antique gold-leaf frame hung on one wall; from the other stared down the handsome, bearded countenance in oil of his great-grandfather, a brigadier's star on the collar of his gray uniform jacket. The resemblance to Powell Bradham was remarkable.

Irene Bradham touched Cary's arm lightly. He turned to see a conspiratorial smile on her face. "Lucy's in the kitchen," she whispered. "Why don't you tiptoe out and surprise her?"

Cary smiled and nodded. He turned left and padded through the big dining room with its shining, huge crotch-mahogany sideboard and table. Gently he eased open the swinging door into the wide pantry, making no sound. Beyond, in the kitchen, Lucy stood at the range with her back to him, intent on cookery. She was a short woman, and so thin that her crisp blue uniform ballooned about her narrow torso. Her gray hair, sparse and frizzy, stood out from her head in countless little spiraling twists. She was humming to herself in a low, mellow voice, and she did not hear Cary as he eased up behind her. He stopped six inches away, leaned forward, and, with his mouth close to her ear, said, "Lucy, I'm starving plumb to death."

Lucy went rigid for a half second; then she whirled, arms flying wide, hands uplifted, dark eyes huge in the lined and leathery brown map of her face. Her mouth dropped open, gums blue and stubbled with yellow teeth. Cary saw two streams of water spring forth from her eyes and course down her cheeks. "Bless Gawd," she said in a voice that trembled, "de boy done come home safe," and then she threw herself into his arms.

He could feel her bones as he clamped her tightly against him. Old Aunt Amy had begun the raising of him, but Lucy had finished the job, and his emotions were nearly the same as when he had embraced his mother.

Then she pulled away and stepped back, eyes shining wetly. "Lemme look at you. Lawd, you lookin good, you sho in this world growed up. Only, you's so *skinny!* Don't they feed you none atall in dat army? But we'll fix dat, never you mind."

"Sweet-potato pie. They tell me it's the best thing for skinny folks, Lucy."

"You'll sholy have it! Dere's two cookin right dere in de oven dis minute. Oh, you's lookin *so* good! Thank Gawd you didn't go and git yourself shot up er killed fightin over dere. Miss Irene? Miss Irene! Us got to do a feedin job on dis boy. Us got to put some flaish on his bones. But don't he look good? Ain't it grand to have him back? Ain't de Lawd been good to bofe us?"

"He has indeed," Irene Bradham said quietly from the doorway.

Then, for the first time, Cary remembered that he had not asked anybody about Huse. His keen interest rang in his voice. "Lucy, where's Huse? Is he all right? Has he got home yet?"

A different pride etched itself on her face. "Yassuh, Houston done come home. Ain't doin anything right this minute, but de Lawd sent him back to me, same he send you. Right now he driftin around, sorta seein where he at. He over dere a long time, Mr. Cary, he a truck driver in de Quawtamasta. It take a while before he git hisself sorta circulated back into dis sassiety."

"Well, be sure to tell him I'm home. And tell him one of these

first days soon I aim to get him and go out to The Place and fish the
swamp like we used to. Tell him I said that."

"Yessah, I tell him tonight, first shot out'n de box!"

"Cary," his mother said, "your room is just like it was. We haven't
touched a thing."

"Fine. I'll run up and wash and change. That sure was a dirty
train." Then he remembered that he hadn't asked Lucy about her
other sons. Not wanting to hurt her feelings, he turned to her again.
"Lucy, how're Bish and Robert?"

She was obviously pleased that he had asked. "Oh, dey fine.
Needer one didn't go off to fight, you know. Bish doin very well. Got
his own place of business now, run a undertakin parlor." She did not
say what Robert was doing. Probably nothing, Cary thought with a
touch of sympathy for her. If there ever was a nigger not worth the
powder and shot to blow him to hell . . . He said, "Call me when
dinner's ready," and went back through the house to the stairs.

His father's voice halted him as his foot touched the first tread.
"Cary."

He swung around. His father stood in the double doors of the
room he called his office. Now that he had taken off his hat, Cary
could see that his hair had gone completely silver. With his face as
deeply tanned as it was, the gray hair was becoming to him. "Yes,
sir," Cary said.

"Come on in."

"Yes, sir." Cary followed Bradham through the double doors into
the study. It had always been Cary's favorite place in the house, possibly because even after he was grown, he was allowed in it only
in the presence of his father. Like all the rooms in the house, it was
large and high of ceiling. Three of its walls were lined with bookshelves, most of their contents old and leather-bound, inherited from
Bradham's father and grandfather. There were few new volumes;
Bradham was not a great reader and Irene's book-club novels were
on shelves in the living room. One large section of the shelves was
occupied by six sets of tall volumes in uniform binding, four to a set,
published by the State Archives and History Department. Cary knew
by heart the gilt lettering on their backs: *Speeches and Papers of
Harvey L. Bradham, 1884–1888,* and another set, *1892–1896.
Speeches and Papers of Brandon Bradham, 1908–1912* and *1916–
1918* (a two-volume set; Cary's grandfather had died in office). And,

of course, *Speeches and Papers of Powell H. Bradham, 1920–1924* and *1928–1932.*

The center of the room was occupied by Bradham's big mahogany desk, orderly but not meticulously neat. There were a couple of worn, deep leather chairs, an old leather-covered divan, and two gun cabinets full of rifles, pistols and shotguns. Over the mantel above the fireplace was a cavalry saber in an ornate scabbard; the men of his battalion had presented it to Powell Bradham's grandfather when he was their major.

Cary saw that there was a bowl of ice, a pitcher of water, a bottle of bourbon and two glasses on a tray on his father's desk. Powell Bradham gave his son a smile that was almost shy, a little hesitant.

"I know it's pretty early in the day," he said. "But I thought an occasion like this deserved a drink. What do you say?"

Cary grinned in reply, feeling pleased and warm and very close to his father. "I say yes."

Bradham poured, added ice and water and handed Cary a glass. "I'm glad you're back son. Here's to you. You were a good soldier, did your duty honorably, and I'm proud of you."

Cary felt his cheeks burn, but he did not protest with any false modesty. As a matter of fact, those had been his aims, the ones he knew his father would have required of him, and he was aware that his father had not spoken the words lightly. He drank; and the bourbon was fine, mellow, silky, and rich.

Powell Bradham lowered his glass with a faint tinkle of ice. "It's special stuff I've been saving for exactly this occasion." He sat on the corner of his desk, and Cary dropped to the arm of a chair. For a moment neither of them spoke, while Bradham looked at his son as if taking inventory of what he had become. The silence was not uncomfortable; Cary had known it many times on fishing trips, hunting expeditions, or simply during the long rides to The Place, the plantation, forty miles away, that had been a Saturday morning ritual for his father and himself, their stolen opportunity to be together free of hovering females.

Then Bradham said, "Well. Now that you're home—have you got any special plans?"

"Plans?"

"I mean, about what you want to do. To be. Still aiming to get your law degree?"

Cary frowned. "Yes, sir, I guess so."

He thought his father relaxed a trifle. "Good. I didn't know if you might have changed your mind for some reason." He went behind the desk and opened a drawer. Something flashed through the air, and Cary caught it, opening his hand to see a pocket checkbook.

"You'll have about sixty days between now and time to go back to the University. I opened an account for you. There's five hundred dollars in it. Have yourself a good time for the next sixty days. You've earned it."

Cary was touched. His father was not a free man with money; and he was aware of the significance of the gift. "You don't have to do this," he said. "I've got quite a bit of back pay and terminal leave."

"Save it. Later I'll discuss some good investments for it with you. In the meantime, have your fun with this. Just be careful, that's all I ask."

Cary slid the checkbook into his shirt pocket. "Yes, sir. Thanks. Thanks a lot."

Bradham smiled. "Well, what's first on your agenda, now that you're back?"

"I don't know. I think I'd like to get out in the swamp. Why don't we get Huse to paddle for us and take a fishing trip just like we used to?"

Bradham nodded. "As soon as I can get loose. But you don't need me, so don't wait."

"All right. I'll get Huse and he and I'll go in."

Bradham nodded. "If he'll go."

"What do you mean, if he'll go?" Cary frowned. He could not conceive of Houston Whitley not wanting to go fishing with him. They had been making such expeditions together for years. If Burke Jessup had been his best white friend, Huse had certainly been his best friend among all the Negroes he had known, and quite possibly, when you came down to it, he and Huse had been even closer, perhaps, than he and Burke. "What do you mean, if he'll go?" he asked again.

Bradham shrugged. "I don't know whether he will or not. I haven't seen him since he's been home—he hasn't even bothered to come by and pay his respects. All I know is that a lot of these young Nigras are coming home totally ruined by the war, with a lot of wild notions in their heads and not worth shooting. I'm just saying, don't be surprised if Huse turns out to be one of them."

"Oh, not Huse," Cary said. "I know him too well for that. Huse
will be all right."

"I hope so," his father said, and he turned to the bottle again. "I
don't guess a little sweetener would hurt," he said with a touch of
slyness, "since this is a special occasion and dinner will be a while
yet. Pass your glass."

2 "Why, you dumb black bastard, who the hell do you think
you are?"
  This time he felt no rage. He had seen it building in the
face of the white man, had known it was coming, warned by the nar-
rowing eyes, the thinning mouth, the reddening face and the slow,
tensing curl of fingers. So, unsurprised, he could keep his own face
impassive; he only turned the folded newspaper so the man could see
the advertisement again.

That made the warehouse manager's face redden to a darker
shade. He leaned across his desk in the glassed-in cubicle at the
corner of the vast truckline warehouse. "Don't you wave that thing
at me," he snapped. "I know what it says. And it don't say we're
lookin for any niggers."

Houston Whitley kept his voice patient. "I can do the work. I have
a high school education and I can type."

The white man just stared at him. "Boy," he said at last, hoarsely,
"you are talkin yourself into more trouble than you can talk yourself
out of. I'm givin you just one minute to git your big black ass outa
here. I ain't got no time to mess with crazy niggers."

Houston Whitley knew he was expected to look at the floor and
smile and apologize now. He did not. Careful to keep any vestige of
mockery out of his voice, he said quietly, "Yes, sir. Thank you anyhow." Then he turned and walked through the echoing dimness of
the warehouse. Sweating Negroes shoving loaded hand trucks nodded
as he passed them. He threw the newspaper into a trash barrel. On
the loading platform, a chain of Negroes passed boxes of heavy
freight into delivery vans backed up there. They were too busy to
speak. Huse jumped off the platform into the bright sunlight of the
truck park. It was so much like a Quartermaster motor pool that he

felt briefly as if he were catapulted back a few months in time, only, of course, here all the drivers were white.

He strode through the gate and turned along the sidewalk toward downtown. He was not tall, but a lifetime of hard work with his body had given him powerful shoulders, a big chest, biceps banded and plated with muscles, narrow hips and hard thighs. He still wore his uniform with its staff sergeant's stripes and rocker. He had hoped that it, along with his service ribbons and the ruptured duck, would help in the experiment he had been conducting. But he knew better now. He lifted one hand and looked at the back of it, the color of rich chocolate. The uniform was not going to help. Nothing was going to help.

Blalock had told him that. Blalock had warned him, in that conversation under the lifeboats on the troopship, the day before landing in New York. He and Blalock and Jerry Martelli, a white infantry private from Brooklyn, had been playing three-handed pinochle. Then Blalock, Huse's closest army friend, a tall, ginger-colored corporal from Georgia, had turned the conversation away from women. "Well, it won't be long now. Come tomorrow, we'll be back in the ole U.S.A." He paused. "Huse, I been thinkin. Why don't you and me re-up?"

Huse looked at him in surprise. "Re-up? Man, you crazy?"

Blalock's laugh was self-conscious. "I might be—a little. But not half as crazy as I would be to go back to Jawjuh."

"Get him," said Martelli. "He's found a home in the army. Man, you're off your rocker. My achin back, there ain't enough money in the world to pay *me* to re-up in this lousy friggin army. I'm through with eatin chickenshit from every jerk that thinks he's better'n me 'cause he's got a lousy stripe or a lousy bar."

Blalock smiled at the intense young soldier. "You don't like bein a private in the army?"

"I'd rather be dead."

Blalock nodded. "Well, I'll tell you," he said at last, still smiling. "If you don't like bein a private in the army, don't you ever try bein a nigger in Jawjuh." He waited a moment for the surprise on Martelli's face to fade. "I been a private all my life," he said. "Till I got in the army. And they done promoted me to corporal." He turned to Huse. "What about it?"

"No," Huse said. "No, I reckon not."

"How come not? Gret Gawd, man, you from Muskogee. That ain't no better'n Jawjuh, maybe worse."

"I know," Huse said. "Just the same, I think I go on home."

"Man," said Blalock, "you got holes in yo' head for sure. You a staff sergeant. That's mo' rank'n you'll ever hold in Muskogee."

Huse toyed with his cards. "Maybe so. And maybe not."

"What you mean, maybe not?"

Huse did not look at Blalock. "We been away a long time," he said slowly. "Maybe things have changed."

Blalock just laughed explosively.

Huse raised his head. "All right," he said. "Maybe they ain't. But if they ain't, they goin have to."

"How come they got to? Where you git that stuff you been drinkin, man?"

Huse searched for the words he wanted. "I been gittin it out of newspapers," he said. "And magazines. And off the Armed Forces Radio. And out of I. & E. lectures."

Blalock said a contemptuous obscenity.

Huse felt a throb of anger. Whether at Blalock or at himself for his own foolishness, he did not know. He chopped the air with his hand.

"Look," he said. "They come and got me for this war, didn't they? They took me and said, all right, Houston Whitley, get your ass out there and fight. They give me a carbine and they say, any white man gives you trouble, you shoot him—long as he ain't on our side. How come I do all that? I ask. And they say, you got to do it. Get out there and fight to be free. When this war's over, they say, whole world goin to be free."

"Yeah," Blalock said. "Yeah. All right. You get back to Muskogee, you lemme know how free you are."

"Listen," said Huse. "You was with me when we made that run into Buchenwald; you saw too what I saw there. You saw some our officers breakin down and cryin when they got opportunity to see there what men had done to other men. I saw one captain cuss for five minutes straight, tears runnin down his cheeks, and then turn his face up to the sky and swear out loud to God nothin like that ever goin to be permitted to happen again. And he no Yankee, he a Southern man. Now everybody knows it, knows what happens when one race goes to put another race all the way down. They had to look at it and see it and learn from it, and everybody swearin it'll never happen again. *Promisin,* man . . . and those promises don't come from nowhere, they come down from the very top!"

"Yeah," said Blalock and he took out a pack of cigarettes. "Only one thing you overlook."

"What that?"

"All this freedom talk. All this sayin none of them concentration camps ever goin to happen again. Just one thing you forget. Them people in them camps *white,* man. That why everybody so upset. Nobody make any promises if they black—it just that they *white.*"

"No," said Huse tautly. "No, it just that they people. That's what this whole thing about, everybody know that now."

Blalock's face was sardonic behind its veil of smoke. "So what you figure on? You figure you go home to Muskogee, the white mayor of the town goan come out and welcome you home? He goan say, Howdy, war hero, what about eatin dinner with me and my wife an' little girl tonight? That what he goan say?" Suddenly his gingerbread countenance went twisted and furious. "Like so much shit," he said harshly. "He goan say, Nigger, watch where you walk. You takin up too much room."

"They promised—" Huse began.

"Promise! Promise, shit! They want to get you suckered into where you don't mind gittin killed for 'em, you think you gittin killed for yourself. That's all they promise anythin for."

"That's your idea—"

"And yours? What's yours?"

Huse was silent for a moment. Then he said, "My daddy was a sharecropper. So was his daddy before him. And *his* daddy was a slave somewhere. None of 'em could read and write, none of 'em ever been out of the state. I born a sharecropper, too. I done my time in the cotton fields. I can plow and I can pick with the best of 'em. By all rights, I ought to be a sharecropper now, not able to read, not able to write. But in my time, in my twenty-four years, I managed to get me a high school education. Maybe that ain't much, but it's a lot in Muskogee, white or black. And in my time I been a soldier and I held some rank and I seen half the world—England, Italy, France, Germany . . . I as different from my daddy as my daddy was from the African great-great-whatever-he-was they brought over here outa the jungle. I ain't what I want to be yet, but I'm a lot more than it look like I would be when I was born. If I can do that in twenty-four years, maybe in another twenty-four I can be a lot more than it look like I goin to be now. And maybe I'll have some children someday and maybe they'll be as different from me as I am from my daddy."

Blalock just looked at him, sneering.

Huse threw down his cards. "I goin home," he said. "And I goin to walk like a man. I goin to ask for work that I can do that pays a fair wage, and I goin to make my own way and try to better myself. That's all I want, all I aim to do. Just be a man."

"You goan git yourself killed, too."

"No," Huse said. "Maybe not. Even if it ain't changed yet, enough people like me walk up and ask for what they are entitled to, not no more, not no less, it going to change. You wait and see."

"All right," Blalock said. "I'll do that. And if you ain't been buried, you write me a letter and let me know how you make out."

Some letter, Huse thought bitterly, striding along the sidewalk under heat that was like hot oil spilling over him. Some letter: Dear Blalock. You were right. Nothing's changed. Nothing ain't going to change. I was wrong and you were right. As ever, your nigger friend, Houston Whitley. . . .

Well, he'd tried, anyhow. Tried until he was worn out with trying, exhausted with a weariness that was not physical. Not everyone he had asked for a job had been as truculent as the warehouse manager —some had at least left him a shred of dignity—but in the long run it all amounted to the same thing. Despite the uniform, the stripes, the service ribbons, despite his patience, determined courtesy, and careful diction, when they looked at him, they refused to see a man standing there.

Dispirited, he stopped at a corner. Behind him he heard the gutty thunder of an approaching city bus. Fishing a dime from his pocket, he waited patiently while the bus, like a blue-and-white monster that had spotted him, slowed and nosed over to the curb. When it was still, its doors hissed open gustily. Huse climbed the step, dropped his fare into the box. A couple of white men standing in the aisle moved aside so he could go through to the rear where the Negroes sat, and he nodded thanks at them as he started toward the back.

The bus driver's voice halted him. "Wait a minnit, black boy."

Huse turned. The driver was a short, bull-shouldered white man in his early thirties, a lank string of black hair hanging from under his pushed-back cap. His eyes were blue and narrow, his pale lips stretched in an ugly smile. Recognizing him, Huse was apprehensive. This was a driver he remembered from before the war—Bobo Merchant, and he had a reputation for meanness.

"Yes, sir," Huse said.

"You go around to the back and git on," the driver said.

His hard blue eyes glinted with sardonic amusement. He sat in an attitude of hopeful tension, one blue-shirted arm leaning on the wheel. Huse could see the broad, dark stain of perspiration under the armpit.

"Well, boy." Merchant grinned. "Didn't you hear me?"

"Yes, sir," Huse said. Carefully numb inside, he walked toward the front door, swung down and started for the rear. The doors were open, the bus engine idling. Huse grabbed a handle and swung up on the back step. At that instant, the doors sighed and rolled shut so close to his face that their rubber bumpers almost caught his nose. He heard the sound of shifting gears. Then the bus's engine roared and it started forward. Huse slammed a hand against the doors. They did not open, and now the bus was moving faster. Cursing, Huse dropped back to the pavement. He watched the bus, excreting a cloud of vile black smoke from its tubular anus, roll on down the street until it was out of sight.

"Goddam you," Huse said to it. "Oh, goddam you." He was trembling. He climbed back on the sidewalk and just stood there for a moment, shaking with anger. Then, savagely, he took out a cigarette and began to walk on toward town.

It was an hour later when he swung off another bus at the end of the line where the pavement stopped just above Little Hammer.

Little Hammer was separated from downtown Hannington by a rind of dilapidated white neighborhood composed of big houses that were old and shabby and very tired, like the dregs of white people who lived in them—the snuff-dipping crones, the hopeless old men sitting eternally on the porches; the towheaded, mucus-smeared and ragged children who grubbed in dirt in the narrow yards; the gaunt young men with service-station grease on their hands and the stringy-haired young women perpetually swollen with pregnancy. At the edge of this rind was the hollow where poor white and Negro merged, and here Negroes lived in the same kind of crowded, ancient Victorian warrens inhabited by the whites—houses fallen on evil days and cut up into an incredible number of rooms and apartments. It was to one of these that Huse now turned—the only one that had seen paint in a decade. In its tiny front yard hung a large tin sign on a post: WHITLEY FUNERAL PARLOR.

Huse walked through a narrow alley to a back yard littered with stacks of old lumber and rank with weeds; a black, dilapidated hearse was parked in the narrow drive. He climbed back steps spongy with rot and pushed against a back door whose upper glass had been blanked out with a sign, ill-painted: PRIVAT. KNOCK BEFORE EN- TERENG. It yielded and he went in without knocking.

What had once been the kitchen of the house was now furnished as an office, with a battered desk and a couple of file cabinets. The kitchen table remained, along with sink and cabinets and icebox. As Huse had expected, Bish and his young assistant, Riley Murray, were sitting at the table. But he had not expected the white man sitting with them. "Excuse me—" he blurted.

The white man jumped to his feet, cramming a brown paper bag that looked as if it might have contained a sandwich into his pocket. "Damn it—" he said. He was tall and angular, his face red, his cheeks webbed with the blue of broken veins. He had a huge, blade-shaped nose and a thin, nervous mouth. He wore a shabby brown suit. "I told you to lock that goddam door," he rasped at Bish.

"S'all right," Bish said, arising. He was shorter than Huse and broader, squat and powerful, his head big and bullet-shaped, his nose flat, lips thick. His suit was much newer and neater and more expen- sive than that worn by the white man. "This here my brother. Don't need to worry about him."

"I don't give a damn who he is," the white man said. "I don't need him in here." He started toward Huse, and Huse tensed. But the white man went by and put his hand on the doorknob. "I'll be back by here next Thursday," he said and went out. When the door had been pushed shut behind him, Bish laughed softly.

"You give the lieutenant a bad turn."

"Lieutenant?"

"That's Lieutenant Harper. He on the fo'ce."

"Policeman?" Huse turned to look at the closed door.

"Detective lieutenant."

"What he doing here?"

Bish grinned. "What it look like? Come around for his weekly cut." He went to a cabinet, got down a glass, poured whiskey in it, and handed it to Huse. "Have a drink." Huse took it and went to the icebox and chipped off a piece of ice.

I mighta known, he thought, as he added water at the sink. He had been pleased to come home and find Bish's luck so good, pleased that in only four short years Bish had been able to graduate from his job as porter-bellhop-pimp at that cheap little hotel on upper Grade Street to a good legitimate business like this. He snorted lightly, laughing at himself for his own stupidity. A policeman's cut. That would mean the numbers or women or after-hours whiskey, or maybe all three. . . .

Bish jerked his head at Riley Murray, and Riley went out through the front part of the house, closing the door behind him as Huse dropped into a chair.

"That why I need you here," Bish said, sitting down too. "I got so many int'rests need lookin after. I ain't but one man, cain't do it all myself. Now, I ask you again, come on in with me."

"No," Huse said. The whiskey was beginning to loosen the tautness within him. "No, I ain't for gittin mixed up in nothin got any white policeman involved in it."

"Who say you got to? Who ask you to?" Bish's eyes were keen with intelligence and drive. "I got a undertakin business here needs runnin. You could take that off my hands. Give me mo' time for my . . . other affairs."

"No, thanks. I've seen enough dead folks. I've seen just about all the dead folks I want to see."

He could sense the exasperation in Bish's voice and how Bish was fighting to keep it under control. "You could make good money at it, damn good. You run it for me, you can keep most of the profits. I use it mo' for a front than anythin else."

"It just ain't exactly what I lookin for," Huse said slowly.

Bish leaned forward, his face sardonic, thick lips curling. "Well, jest what the hell are you lookin for?"

Huse was silent a moment. Then, in a burst of bitter honesty, he said harshly, "I don't know."

Bish made a snorting sound through his flat nostrils. "I didn't hardly think you did. But I can tell you what it is."

Huse sat up straight. "All right," he murmured. "You tell me, then."

"You lookin for some way you can shuck outa that black hide of yours," Bish said slowly, evenly, his face completely serious now. "Some people use skin whitener and ashes. You tryin to use gettin you a downtown job that ain't nigger work. And you ain't got no more chance of doin it than if you was to use skin whitener. Or try to make yo' shadow cut loose from you. You colored. You got to reelize that first of all and go on from there."

Huse felt a spur-gouge of anger. "You think I don't reelize it?"

"Hell, no, you don't. You ain't never." Bish's voice was measured; he was choosing his words carefully. "Ever since us growin up out there on ole man Bradham's plantation, ever since that white boy, Cary, take a shine to you and want you to play with him. That the time, from that minute on, you ain't satisfied with your color no more. Look what happen. You git all sorts ideas playin with that white kid. You decide you wanta go to school. You findangle old man Bradham and Papa both into lettin you go. Then, when you gone as far as you could go in that country school, you talk Papa and ever'-body into movin into Hannin'ton so you could go to the colored high school. And that sure tear things. Mama got to go to work in that ole bastard's kitchen. Papa got to dig them pipeline ditches and that motherfucker Sam Deal make him go down in that big, wet ditch when it been rainin fo' days and make him dig and the bank cave in on him. I got to go to work, only job I can git is pimpin and runnin for white whores in that little ole dirty hotel. And Robert—he just a little baby and you in school and all us workin, and nobody to tend to him 'cept a neighbor, and he runs loose like a wild buck and grows up mean as a snake and chain-gang bait if there ever was any. All that, so you can git your high school degree. Because you figgered that high school degree was goin to whiten your skin or shuck you outa that black hide. And now, after ever'body in the fambly make sacrafices, Papa dead, Robert nothin but a worthless bum, you been overseas, seen places nobody in this whole fambly got any idea of, Yurrop, all that—now, you come home—and, by damn, you still don't know what you want, you still can't think of nothin but tryin to run so fast yo' black hide can't catch up with you. Well—"

"All right," Huse said, voice full of anguish. "All right. So I caused it all—"

But Bish had read the pain on his face, it seemed; and Bish's voice gentled.

"All right," he said. "I ain't puttin you in the dozens jest to be mean. I jest tryin to make you see. You want to be treated with respect. You want white folks to treat you with respect. Well, you can git 'em to do it, but not the way you goin after it. You tryin to come up on them from the wrong side, from their goodness. That like tryin to mount a mule from the right hand. You got to come at them from the other way, from their meanness and greediness. There's two things that when people want 'em bad enough ain't got no color. One of 'em's a woman's twat and the other one's money."

He slapped his hand on the table. "You got your high school degree, your white-boy friend; it all I can do to read an' write my own name and I never played with no white. But you can't even git a job workin for a white man except like a animal, while I got a white detective lieutenant drinkin my whiskey, sittin at my table. And doin his damnedest to keep me happy. You know why? Money! Me nor you neither ain't ever goin to sit at the white man's table, but you git enough money an' The Man will come and sit at yours. You show 'em how they can make a profit or git their rocks off and they mighty respectful. They don't care what color you are if they got a hard on or they want some dough. I'll tell you now, I got better connections in this town, know mo' people, draw more water, than a sight of white folks. I got all any nigger'll ever git, and I can show you how to git it, too. Well? What you say? You goan come in with me?"

Huse closed his eyes. He felt too burned-out, too numb with weariness and fogged with drink, to think. "I consider it," he said tiredly and got to his feet, anxious to get out of here.

Bish grinned. "You do that. I sho' need you. I'da had Robert in here with me long time ago, 'cept I can't trust him. I reckon you know he cut up Shad Plummer last winter. He'da been on the road gang right now if Mama hadn't gone to ole man Bradham and he got him off. That Robert crazy; they goan put him in the eelectric chair one these days."

"Let's hope not." Huse sighed. "I gotta go. Thanks for the drink."

Bish came to him and clapped a big hand on his shoulder. "Forgit it. You need any money?"

"No, I got my musterin-out pay."

"Need any, jest say so."

"Thanks. You comin to see Mama tonight?"

"No, can't make it tonight. I tied up."

"She goin to be disappointed. Been nearly a week."

"I git by there soon as I can," Bish said with a trace of irritation. "I can't sit an' listen to her but so much, she drives me crazy with all that church talk."

"Okay, then, I see you." Huse went out and down the spongy steps and through the weedy back yard.

Now he descended into the place called Little Hammer. He walked slowly down the slope of a washed, chuckholed and dusty street. The old Victorian houses at the head of the hollow gave way to pathetic board shanties of two to four rooms, paintless, teetering on wobbly brick piers. Gaunt dogs and fever-eyed, scabby cats drowsed in the apathy of constant hunger beneath them. Landlords found the houses cheaper to let fall apart and rebuild than to maintain; and here steps had collapsed, there shattered windows were blocked with cardboard. Junk of all kind—broken toilet seats, tangled wire, old lumber, anything of putative value that could be hauled home—lay where it would fit, conserved against the possibility of use or trade or the opportunity of charity toward a neighbor.

The air down here was full of the raw stench of poverty, which was also the stench of overflowing privies. There was no running water; a single hand pump in the open served three or four dwellings with water for cooking and washing. Thickening the smell was the broad, slow, tar-colored stream called Molasses Creek that oozed through jungled banks behind the hollow. Used for community dumping, it carried also much of Hannington's sewage in its sludgy open flow; in the late evenings, a cool, pale, lovely mist that reeked intolerably of ordure arose from it and filled the low ground.

Somehow the poverty, disorder and chaos of Little Hammer seemed unreal to Huse now. He had seen people living like this overseas in the rubble and devastation of bombed and destroyed cities. But there had been no war here and he was no longer able to understand how such a place could exist where no bombs had fallen or shells ripped in. He knew the economics of it, knew that white men considered nigger housing the best real estate investment in any Southern city. Knew that these hovels were thrown up unhampered by the enforcement of any building codes, and that because there was no other place for Negroes of ordinary means to live, they were always jammed full, though the rent was outrageous. And though once he had taken it for granted, had assumed it was just the way people lived, now it seemed unreal. That it could be allowed even to exist in a country which had no war to blame it on was something he could not quite really believe or comprehend. . . .

He came to the tiny four-room house in which they had lived ever since they had moved to Little Hammer when he was thirteen. It was too early for Lucy to be home, and the house was empty and very hot. As he edged through the worn furniture and pathetic bric-a-brac, mostly Bradham castoffs, with which Lucy had filled the small living room, rotten floorboards sagged under his feet and his tread shook the whole house on its crumbling piers.

In the tiny bedroom where he slept alone now unless Robert decided to come home for a night, he threw himself on the bed and shielded his eyes with an arm from the long slant of afternoon sun. He was sticky and sodden with sweat, but it was too much trouble to go down three houses to the pump to wash.

It was wasted, he thought, all wasted. Robert's corruption . . . his father's death . . . his mother's years of servitude to the Bradhams—the things that had been the price of his education, his yearned-for high school diploma, which might, perhaps, get him a job cleaning septic tanks.

I'm a fool, Houston Whitley thought, I'm a goddam fool.

He swung off the bed suddenly, fists clenched and beating against his thighs. I ain't goin to let them, he thought savagely. I ain't goin to let them trap me in here. Somehow I got to do somethin with myself. Somehow I got to—

And then he remembered Cary, and he let out a long, shuddering breath and sat down on the bed, rubbing his hands together nervously.

Cary, he thought. That's it. I almost forgot Cary. When he gets home, I can always go to him. He ain't never failed me yet; he won't fail me now. He knows I ain't just another nigger. He knows what I can do. He'll help me. . . .

The thought of Cary made him feel better. Suddenly he no longer felt so alone, so trapped, so helplessly penned. As hope returned to him, he calmed, and after a while he lay down on the bed and this time he was able to drift into a fitful sleep.

Lucy's coming in awakened him, and the first news she had was that Cary was back, and that he had asked about Huse right off and said he'd be by soon to get Huse and go fishing.

I knew it, Huse thought, all right now. You see? He ain't forgot me, not even after four years. No, sir. Not old Cary.

"That's sure good news, Mama," he said.

3 The first time Cary Bradham had seen Houston Whitley was in the early spring of 1932, when Cary was ten. That must have been at the very depth of the Depression, but he had no recollection of its having touched his life. People—grown-ups—talked about hard times, but the phrase meant nothing to him. The routine of the Governor's mansion in which they lived went on as it had for the past four years, and Cary could not remember then even having been aware of the hardship and gray despair that lay across the land. On the morning when the Whitleys came to The Place, he had been merely bored, because it was raining and because his grandmother had dozed off in the middle of the story she was telling him.

He had ridden down to The Place from Hannington with his father as he did every Saturday morning, savoring the pleasure of being, for the hour and a half that it took to make the drive, the focal point of his father's attention. He had pulled the lap robe warmly about him, had snuggled up to his father, and listened as the older man talked, telling wondrous tales of war and hunting, spilling the masculine lore which Cary craved and which his mind licked up as a kitten licks up milk. And while he listened, he looked through the windows of the back seat of the chauffeur-driven Willys-Knight and watched the drenched and desolate country, untilled and forlorn, slip by. There were, first, the high, red hills of the Piedmont plateau, every gully running with a liquid the color of blood, ground flowing downhill and lost forever. Then the land flattened out and they approached the immensity of the Kenoree Swamp, fifteen miles wide and thirty miles long, its wilderness of virgin timber wet black and smoky gray this cold morning. They skirted the swamp, and then they were in the coastal plain, the land here as flat as if it had been machined, a rich, black sandy loam, the fields broad and endless, separated by rows of gaunt, rain-darkened pines. Past Troublefield Crossroads, the store and the high iron flank of the cotton gin, and then onto the sandclay road that led to The Place, the family plantation, the family home, the umbilical cord that bound them both to the land and to its history.

According to his grandmother, the main house of The Place had burned in early 1865, not because of Sherman's depredations, but from a faulty flue. The old house had been a mansion, but by 1870, when the family rebuilt, no one was building mansions any more. So what they put up instead was the immense but simple two-story frame farmhouse, with porches running around three sides, so that there was always shade, no matter the angle of the sun. Its only inhabitant in 1932 was Miss Jenny, his father's mother, who had been a little girl during the War and who had seen the soldiers, blue and gray alike, and had never lost her hot, dry hatred for the Yankees, nor her scathing contempt for them. But time had shriveled her to a tiny, birdlike figure in rocking chair and shawl, and not even her hate, which rang in the stories she told Cary, imprinting itself on some sensitized and unused portion of him like light on photographic film, could keep her awake very long at a stretch. By midmorning she had drowsed off, so Cary pulled the shawl up about her shoulders and went to sit on the porch swing and listen to his father and Mr. Jake Lily, the plantation manager, talk mantalk.

It was still raining—a leftover winter rain coming in March, gushing from low clouds the color of a pencil smudge. The rain hammered on the tin roof and rolled from the porch eaves in a continuous, unbroken sheet. The dooryard was drowned in water, an awesome lake of it; and only the tops of old rows were visible above the brimming furrows of the outlying fields, last year's cotton stalks standing as black and awry along their spines as the bristles on a worn-out brush. Cary pushed the swing and puffed his breath, pretending its vapor was cigarette smoke, while his father and Mr. Jake squatted against the front wall of the house—men always squatted, it seemed, when they talked farming business—and when he could make no sense of what they said, he yawned and watched the rain some more, marveling at the growing expanse of the lake in the dooryard, feeling a delicious dangerous thrill as it widened.

That was when he saw the wagon.

At first it was hardly visible through the slanting wall of rain, and he was not sure he had seen anything at all. But when he looked again, there was no doubt that he had seen it—a wagon drawn by a single mule, just turning into the head of the long drive, coming toward them between flooded fields like a tiny boat adrift on a huge lake.

Cary pointed. "Hey, Daddy, look there."

His father and Jake Lily stood up, squinting.

After a moment, Jake Lily spat. "Hell," he said, "just another bunch of croppers lookin for a place to light. Hafta turn away three or four famblies ever' day." Mr. Jake was a small, fox-faced man who managed somehow always to maintain exactly two days' growth of beard. He turned up the collar of his dirty canvas coat, lined with sheepskin. "I hope they're niggers. Niggers go when you tell 'em to, but whites git mad and stand and argy. I don't mind turnin away niggers, but it's damn hard to tell a white man you ain't got anythin for him."

"I don't want any white croppers on this place," said Bradham positively. "They're nothing but trouble."

"That's a fact," Lily said. "Independent as hell, and always give you a argument come settlin-up time. Niggers work about as good and a lot less trouble; their furnish amounts to less, too. Jest the same, a nigger's a nigger and white's white and it's hard to tell a white man—" He broke off. "That's a right good mule," he said.

It came now at a brisk trot, head up despite the rain. A man and a woman rode the board seat of the wagon, and the wagon box seemed to be full of household goods, draped with an old and sodden patchwork quilt in lieu of a tarpaulin.

Then the mule was splashing into the yard with a jingling of chain. "Whoa," the driver said and pulled it up in the shelter of a live oak. A Negro, he wore a soaked and dirty fedora, a sodden black suit coat out at the elbows, overalls faded almost white and clinging soddenly to his thighs. The woman was shapeless, hunched in a thick army overcoat, her head shielded by an old black wicker summer hat shaped like a beehive.

The man handed her the lines and climbed down over the muddy wagon wheel. He sloshed toward the house, careful to take the path and keep off the grass. When he reached the steps, he climbed the first three of them and halted, just outside the splashing cascade of water that rolled from the eaves. "Mawnin!" he yelled.

Jake Lily jerked his head. "Come on up here!"

"Capn, I wouldn' wanta drip all over yall's po'ch."

"Come up!" Bradham snapped in a deeper voice, more authoritative.

The Negro plunged through the water and gained the shelter of the porch, gasping and wiping his eyes. Then he raked off the dripping hat and bobbed his head, first at Bradham, then at Lily. "Mawnin, Capns." He saw Cary. "Mawnin, young Capn. How you?"

"Mornin," Lily grunted. Then there was silence.

The Negro shifted uneasily, "Sho gittin *some* rain," he said.

"Too much," growled Lily.

"Dat a fact. But maybe it let up befo' long." Again there was silence, except for the drum of the downpour. The man turned his hat around in his hands.

"I 'quired up at de sto' at Troublefield. Dere was a man up dere say you folks might have room for somebody else to crop on sheers."

"No," Jake Lily said. "Sorry. We all full up."

For a few seconds the man's smile did not change. Then, though it remained fixed, hope faded from it like dye washing out of cloth. "Aww," he whispered dully, "is dat a fact?"

"You might could try on down the road—" Jake Lily began. Something in the Negro's face made Cary uncomfortable. There was a vague, uneasy stirring at the pit of his stomach. He got up from the swing and walked to the porch railing and looked at the parked wagon.

The woman was still hunched, only the smoke of her breath proving that she lived. The mule was snorting water from its nostrils, rubbing its head against its leg to clear its eyes. Steam vapored in the cold air above its back. Water dripped from the stringy corner of the quilt where it hung over the side of the wagon.

Then Cary blinked. For the quilt hunched itself up in the center as if it possessed a life of its own. At first he thought the slant of rain between himself and the wagon had played a visual trick. But then the hunch began to move. Slow and ungainly, it traveled from the center of the wagon to the sideboard, and then the edge of the quilt lifted, and from the rind of darkness beneath it three pairs of eyes, marvelously wide and white, stared at Cary with apprehensive curiosity.

Startled, Cary met their gazes. And as he did so, two pairs of the eyes disappeared quickly, as if fleeing from their own audacity. Only the center pair remained, big and unwinking and curious.

His father must have seen it, too, for he heard his father say in disgust and fury, "You got children in that wagon? Hauling them around on a day like this?"

Cary turned back to the grown-ups. His father's face bore a withering look. Bradham believed in working men and stock to their limits; but he would never tolerate useless abuse of either; it was unthrifty and an affront. Cary waited for the Negro to drop his head and shrink away.

He did not. His eyes did not even shift. "Yassuh, Capn," he said quietly. "My chaps in dere. What I suppose to do wid 'em? It been yestiddy mawnin since dey had anythin to eat. I suppose to hole up somewhur an' lissen to dem cry fo' food, jest so we-unses can stay dry? Nawssuh. I go out and look fo' a place I kin earn some rations fo' em. Maybe everybody else hole up on account of de rain, maybe dat my chance." He paused; his voice was intense when he went on. "Me and my wife, we good workers. My oldest boy Bish and de middle one, Huse, dey make good hands, too. De least 'un, Robert, he ain't big, but he kin fetch and tote. I knows how to make a cotton crop, I owns my own mule, and I kin put fo' hands in de field. Seem lak dere ought to be a place somewhurs fo' a man like me, or sumpin done gone mighty bad wrong. Anyhow, I determine to find it, rain er no rain. I got chilluns to look out fer, I ain't use the rain as no excuse not to look out fer 'em." Only now did he drop his head, his voice going flat. "I reckon I try on down the road," he said.

Cary watched his father's face. Bradham's eyes had narrowed thoughtfully; the double creases in his high forehead meant he was thinking. He looked from the man to the well-conditioned mule, stamping in the rain. "Wait a minute," he said.

The man raised his head. "Yes, Capn?"

"Governor," Jake Lily snapped. "This here's the Governor of the state you talkin' to."

"Gov'ner," the man said, in amendment.

"Who'd you crop for last?"

"Mista Jawge Graham, over in Barnett County. But bank done fo'closed his land, won't put in no crop dis year."

"How much cotton you make?"

"Made seven bales on seventeen acres, Cap—Gov'ner. Coulda done better, only he short me on de fertilizer."

His father looked at Jake Lily. The plantation manager's foxy face worked indignantly. "Dammit, Gov'ner, you jest been raisin sand with me about cuttin costs. Besides, we ain't got no land—"

"We've got that fourteen acres other side of the creek."

"You know that ground's worn out. You couldn't raise a fuss on it. Them fourteen acres wouldn't even pay a man's furnish."

The Negro was looking at Bradham with carefully restrained hope. During the silence, which Cary somehow found unbearable, Cary turned to look at the wagon again. That single pair of eyes was still watching the tableau on the porch, alertly and unblinking.

"I know," Bradham said at last, harshly. "But we'll let him try, anyhow."

Cary watched them again. Lily's shoulders rose and fell in helpless disgust. "Don't come barkin at me when it's time to balance the books."

"We might as well plant everything we've got," Bradham said. "Either we make it this season, or we don't make it at all." His voice was rough as he addressed the Negro. "Listen. I'm giving you fourteen acres up yonder. It's bad land, all cottoned out, and you'll have to hump to make anything on it. And by God, I expect you to hump. There's a house, I don't know what kind of shape it's in, and plenty of sawmill slabs to burn. You'll get seed, what fertilizer I can afford, and rations through ginning time. You'll use your own mule. Generally I give a man with his own mule fifty-five per cent, but this is a losing proposition. You get forty per cent, take it or leave it. We keep straight books and we'll have no argument. This is Mr. Jake Lily; he runs this place. You'll pay attention to him or you'll be off so quick it'll make your head swim. Well?"

Cary saw the man's eyes go wide and his mouth sag. He was trembling visibly. "Capn, Gov'ner, my Gawd, dat be fine, dat be fine, thank you so much—"

"Don't thank me, you'll work your butt off for your furnish. Jake, give 'em rations from the house until they can get on books up at the store. Now," he snapped at the Negro, "go get your young-uns in out of the rain."

"Yes, *suh!*" The Negro whirled, ran through the sluice of water and out into the yard.

"Hold on!" Bradham's harsh voice halted him.

The Negro turned, his face going slack with sudden dread. "Y-yassuh, Gov'ner?"

Bradham walked to the edge of the porch. "What's your name?"

Cary saw the fear seep away; the Negro's eyes lit with relief. "My name Otis Whitley, Gov'ner!" he called back through the sound of water. Then he ran through the rain to give the news to the huddled woman on the wagon; and when Cary looked again, the eyes had disappeared and the quilt had dropped.

Now, as he reined in his horse on the crest of the hill overlooking the big house of The Place, he was remembering all that instead of listening to the constant stream of inane chatter pouring from Mary Scott Butler on the little sorrel beside him. This was his second morning home, and what he had really wanted to do was to get Huse and go down in the swamp and catch some bass, but somehow, between Mary Scott and his own parents, he had been maneuvered into taking her riding instead.

". . . And I was just shocked when Julie Caldwell announced her engagement to Don Temple, because everybody knew that Julie had been writing to Burke Jessup all during the war and everybody expected when Burke came home, you know . . . and I said, I said it frankly, I didn't mince any words with her, I said, Julie, I just don't understand how you could do a thing like that to Burke. And honestly, you never saw anybody look so ashamed of herself in all her life. She looked just like she wanted to *die*. Because I told her, Julie, I like Burke, and you could look all over this whole wide world and you wouldn't find a cuter boy than Burke Jessup. But she wouldn't listen, and I hope Burke didn't take it too hard because—"

"Burke Jessup's not cute now," Cary said harshly, unable to keep the irritation out of his voice.

"What?" She looked at him with round blue eyes, small, full lips slightly parted.

"I said Burke's not cute now. His feet got all blown to hell by a German shell, and he's a permanent cripple. Maybe," he said with dry brutality, "that had something to do with Julie's decision. If she was looking for cuteness, she could write Burke off her list."

"My goodness, I knew Burke was wounded, but I didn't know it was really that bad. Anyhow, I think that just makes it worse, don't you? I mean, if a man goes off to fight for his country and he gets hurt doing it, it seems to me the least his girl could do would be to have the decency not to just make his hurt worse. I mean, if it had been you, suppose you and I were . . . were engaged, do you think I would have done a thing like that to you? Not that I'm your girl or anything"—she laughed tinnily—"but suppose I was, well, I would certainly have had the decency not to upset you any worse than you were already upset by pulling a dirty trick like that. I think that if a girl admires a man and loves him, it doesn't seem to me that just because he's been hurt a little bit she ought to feel free to just throw him over like that. I'll tell you, if I'm ever engaged to any man, one thing he can depend on, I'll stick by him no matter what. If *we* were engaged, you wouldn't want to think that I might throw you over just because—"

Almost frantically determined to staunch that flow of words, Cary put his horse into motion. "Come on," he said, "let's ride down."

She was not a very good rider, and, as he had expected, the necessary concentration on maintaining her seat cut off her chatter. But, watching her from the corner of his eye, he could not help but notice that her very lack of rhythm with her mount produced a sensual vibration of her body that was ripely attractive: joggle of plump breasts, ripple of plump thighs beneath the whipcord of the jodhpurs.

Knock that off, he cautioned himself. You make a pass at her and it would be a Federal case. She's just waiting to get you maneuvered into some kind of corner anyhow. His mouth curled wryly, and he focused his attention on the view of The Place they had as the horses went down the rise.

It stretched out almost endlessly below him, fields and pasture, dotted here and there with unpainted tenant cabins weathered to a pure silvery gray. His father had been talking about tractors, but so far the ancient and familiar sight of man and mule harnessed together down the rows in mutual, straining effort persisted. In the distance the beginnings of the Kenoree Swamp made an intense, smoky green line against the sky. Cary felt, for the moment, an utter peace settle on him; he loved this land, this country, this place; and it was good to be back. He thought about Burke Jessup's drunken refusal to return; and he pitied Burke briefly.

But, then, Burke's life had not been as closely tied to this soil, this region, as his own. The Governor's mansion was part of his heritage, and the urban life on Mercy Street; and the oily, steel smell of a B-29's pilot's compartment, that, too was part of it now. But most of all, when he remembered his childhood, he thought of it as a Saturday morning, with himself and Houston Whitley and sometimes Burke roaming the fields and pastures and woods of The Place, exploring its creeks and the swampy guts that edged into it from the Kenoree, hunting, fishing, and camping. Of all his heritage, this was the part most truly become part of himself grown; and he could understand the fierce love of his father, who had grown to manhood here, for these acres and knew now why Bradham had guarded them so jealously when all around him homeplaces had gone on the block during the Depression.

"Come on," he said; "I'll race you." And he put the bay into a canter. Behind him, Mary Scott said despairingly, "Oh, Cary," but she tried. The horse eased into a gallop without trouble; Cary felt the wind in his face, heard the thunder of hoofs on a wooden bridge across a creek, and then, on the other side, nearly to the house, he pulled up and waited for Mary Scott.

When they reached the stable, he dismounted and gave Mary Scott a hand down. He was surprised at how intensely and immediately affected he was by the soft yield of the flesh of her waist under his palms as he gentled her awkward dismount; and her back came up against his chest for a moment as she touched the ground, her rump against his thighs, and he caught a perfume in her hair that he had not noticed before, something muskier and more sensual than he had expected. He turned loose of her quickly, thinking, Jesus, I'm set on a hair trigger. . . .

A lanky colored boy ambled out of the stable. "Walk 'em about five minutes before you water 'em, Parson," Cary ordered, and he and Mary Scott walked toward the house and the car parked in front of it.

As they approached the house, Cary ran his eyes over its scabby weatherboarded flanks fondly. His grandmother had long since been buried in the family burying ground; she had died in 1937, and the house was empty now, after nearly eighty years of habitation. He saw that, like a body from which the will to live is gone, it had begun to rot underneath, in corners, and in secret places. Something ought to be done with it, he thought; and he turned toward the car.

"Cary."

Mary Scott's voice halted him. She was standing beside the front steps.

"Yeah?"

"Did you know I haven't been through this house since I was a little girl? I hardly remember anything at all about it. I'd love to see the inside of it again. I'll bet it's full of all the loveliest antiques."

He frowned. "I don't know. Just the family junk. I think everything that's any good has been moved to Mercy Street." But her words had stirred in him a desire to go inside. "Do you really want to see it?"

"I'd love to, if we've got time."

"Well . . . okay. If the key's where it's supposed to be." He went to the steps. "Come on."

She chattered as they climbed to the porch. "I remember it as real big, the rooms just enormous, and so dim and spooky, and it had a funny kind of smell, and I met your grandmother and I thought she was such a nice little old lady . . ."

"Yeah," Cary said. He fished in a crack beside the front door, found the key and unlocked the old-fashioned, glass-paneled door. "Come on in," and he held it open for Mary Scott.

The house's hall ran all the way through, dim, broad, and high of ceiling. It was uncarpeted, and the floorboards were six inches wide, of worn, rich pine. Cary shut the door behind them, its little bell, designed to ring when a butterfly handle was turned, jingling faintly; and it was like sealing themselves in another century.

Mary Scott moved closer to him. "My goodness. I'd forgotten how big and old it really is."

The figured wallpaper had aged until all its color had turned the shade of tobacco juice, and it was cracking and bellying out from the old plaster above the white wood wainscot. The house smelled almost swampily musty from its long closure; mingled with that was the ineradicable pungency of drying wood and generations of log and coal heating fires. Mary Scott's perfume was peculiarly noticeable and somehow anachronistic.

Something, catching their sound, scurried raspingly across the attic floor overhead, clearly audible through the ceiling. Mary Scott's intake of breath was sharp; instinctively she huddled against Cary.

He laughed. "A squirrel," he said. "Look, there's one room I want to see first. Then I'll show you the rest." He shoved open one of the doors that fronted into the hall. "This is my grandmother's room. When I was little, she used to sit there"—he indicated a padded cherrywood rocker—"and tell me stories about when she was a little girl during the Civil War and Reconstruction." Mutedly, he laughed, remembering the almost eerie bitterness in the reedy voice of the gentle old lady. "God, she hated Yankees. To her they were lower than niggers. I remember when I was six years old, she quit telling me stories and wouldn't start again until I learned to sing two verses and the chorus of 'Dixie.' " Unconsciously, he sang under his breath, *"In Dixie Land where I was born in, early on one frosty mornin'—"*

Nothing had been changed in the room. The rocker was still positioned before the cold, soot-blackened fireplace; the enormous tester bed, its four posts eight feet tall, was made up, canopied and counterpaned, a comforter folded across its foot. The crayon portraits of his grandparents stared down from the wall, the woman young and pretty, but severe in a high-collared dress; the man stern and competent and bearded. Cary moved across the room and touched the cherrywood rocker. It tipped back and forth easily. "Look away," he muttered, "Look away, Dixie Land." For a moment the room was full of the ghosts that had stalked her stories, blue ghosts vile and despoiling, gray ghosts gallant, prideful and courageous, to be admired, honored and unforgotten. Suddenly he felt a new, strange kinship with the gray ones; he had had his own war now, and their exploits took on a new dimension in the light of that. . . .

"That's a lovely rocking chair," Mary Scott said, her voice oddly crass in the hush of the room.

Cary looked at her. She was standing before the huge fireplace as if warming herself at its dead, black gaping mouth. The physical tensions that had been building in him all morning were suddenly sharp and imperious. She was, undeniably, lovely and vital against the death and dust of the room. For a moment his eyes met hers, and then he flickered his own away, not wanting her to see what was there. He did not want any encouragement from her at all, or he might do something foolish, something damned idiotic, get himself into a mess he did not want to be in. . . .

But she was already coming over to where he stood by the chair. With an artlessness that he knew immediately was deliberate, she seemed to be intensely interested in the chair. She rocked it, stroked its arm. She was very close to him, and he smelled the life of her perfume in the midst of the scents of decay. She half turned her body; and the softness of her breast touched him with definite pressure. The room was very quiet; somewhere outside in the morning a chicken began to cackle, but it seemed miles away, centuries away.

Later he knew that she had planned from the beginning that it should happen like this. But he was not even thinking then, as he seized her and pulled her around tightly against him, breasts flattening on his chest, and kissed her. He saw her wide eyes, something flaring in them (later he knew it was triumph) and then they shut and her lips were moist and soft under his, and after a moment the tip of her tongue came exploring his. He felt her hands on his back, excited; and suddenly and in the same instant, the excitement flared high in both of them; and he felt her mouth open wide. There was a certain amount of surprise in him. He had kissed her before, but never like this; he had not known she could kiss like this. If he had known it—

After a minute, he pulled his mouth away. She was looking up at him, and instead of speaking, she craned her face toward him for another kiss. He bent again, holding her this time so that his hand could get to her left breast. He seized the fleshy weight of it, and her hand came up to cover his, but instead of trying to pull it away as he had expected, she pressed it tighter. Embraced like that, Cary beyond any reason or discretion now, they felt the edge of the dusty bed strike their thighs. Then Cary pulled her down on it.

They rolled there. He got her shirt unbuttoned and slid his hand inside it, and she made no protest. He was impatient with the guarding fabric of the bra, strained it as he tried to get his hand under it. Mary Scott seized his wrist, then shoved it away. She sat up, her face very white, and her mouth very red against the paleness. "Wait," she said, and then she was unfastening the shirt. She took it off, and he saw that her body was very white, very smooth and desirable. Her hands went behind her back and tugged at the fastening of the bra. It came loose and she dropped it on the shirt, and she was naked to the waist. Cary's mouth went dry as he stared at the full, slightly dipping curves of her breasts, and then he pulled her to him again and began to kiss her, not on the lips, but on the throat and the breasts and the upper body; and she moaned, her body tensing and writhing.

He was past any thought, any hesitation, now, with the taste of her flesh and the smell of it (she had used the perfume under her breasts, too); and his hand fumbled at the latch of the jodhpurs. He got them open and thrust his hand deep inside, and she made no protest about that, either, but shivered under his touch.

Then he could be satisfied with nothing short of ultimate access to her, and he thought: She wants it, she wants it as bad as I do. . . . Confidently he sat up, began tugging at the jodhpurs. For a moment he thought she was going to help him. Then, shockingly, she rolled away, pushing his hands loose, stood up off the bed and seized her shirt, shielding her breasts with it.

Cary felt blood burning in his face and a savage hammering urgency in his body. "Mary Scott," he rasped, ashamed of himself for the abject pleading in his tone. "Mary Scott, please . . ."

But, incredibly, she was moving back across the room, turning away from him. He saw her hands fasten the back snap of the bra between her shoulder blades, and then she turned back. He had a glimpse of the haltered roundness of her breasts just before she slid into the shirt. "Cary," she said. "Cary, darling."

The word jarred him, like cold water thrown on him, but it was not enough to quench the fire. He got up, reached for her, but she twisted, eluding him, smiling. "Cary—" She struck down his hand. "Please, now, don't be . . . we both got carried away. You know I never let anybody do anything like that to me before. It was . . . it was wonderful, but we can't, I mean, you know—"

"Hell," he said and reached for her again, but when he caught her, he saw that her lower lip had begun to tremble and that her wide, blue eyes were moist.

"Cary—don't . . ."

He could not fight her tears. They were enough to quench him. His hands dropped away from her shoulders.

"All right," he said dully.

Her shirt fully buttoned now, she came close to him, the points of her breasts touching him, and kissed him quickly and chastely on the lips, her hand touching his cheek. "Thank you, Cary, darling. I—you're so nice, so sweet. I knew you'd help me. . . . It's not easy for a girl, either. Not with somebody like you. If the man doesn't help the girl look out for herself . . . You know I never did this with anybody else—you believe that, don't you?"

"Yes," he said, his own voice sounding very far away to him. "Yes." He heard it go on, with a faint incredulity that it should proceed without his volition, at the demand of his body but not his brain, saying what, an hour ago, he would have sworn he would never have voiced. "All right, I'll try to look after you. But . . . can I see you again tonight?"

Something flared in her eyes (again triumph, but he did not recognize it then) and her answer came quickly. "Yes, of course. That would be lovely." Then she took his hand and tugged at it. "Come on. Let's go, now. I . . . I don't trust either of us if we stay here any longer."

"Mary Scott—" Desire rose in him once more and he tried to hold her back.

Her voice sharpened. "Cary. Please. Come on. Take me home. And we . . . can see each other again tonight."

4

Hoke Moody had taken off his coat and loosened his tie and propped his feet up on a leather-covered hassock. He held a good cigar between the thick fingers of his right hand and a glass of bourbon-and-water in his left. Even when he was relaxed, as he was now, his voice had a deep organ tone that caught the attention and fixed it. "This country," he said, "thinks all it has to do now is sit back and relax. We built the biggest army in the history of the world, the most powerful fighting force man ever imagined, and now, by God, we're tearing it to pieces just as fast as we can, without even a thought of Russia sitting over there, just waiting for us to weaken ourselves so she can jump. People think we can trust Joe Stalin. Well, I'll tell you this, United Nations or no United Nations, the only way to make a goddam Communist trustworthy is to carry a damned big club and make sure he knows that either he walks the straight and narrow or he gets frammed. I'm concerned, I tell you, I really am, but there doesn't seem to be a thing in the world I can do to stop it." He looked at Cary, who sat in a chair across from him, a drink also in his hand. "What do you think, boy?"

Cary shrugged. "You're the Senator, Uncle Hoke. I'm nothing but a lousy Air Force major on terminal leave. I didn't get paid to think, I just got paid to fly."

Moody chuckled. "Now, that's a good devious answer, ain't it, Powell?"

Bradham had been silent during the quarter hour they had been relaxing here in his study. Now he said sharply, "Cary's not devious. He just hasn't had time to get his feet on the ground."

"Sho," Moody said easily. "That's just what I'm trying to help him do." He sipped from his glass. "Actually, our troubles with Russia are likely to be the least of it. I'm expecting troubles here at home, right here in Muskogee, that'll make our troubles overseas look like fleabites."

Cary frowned. "What kind of troubles?"

Moody shifted himself upward in the chair and looked at Powell Bradham. "Troubles like the ones we had after the first war. First of all, a lot of soldiers coming home with all sorts of radical ideas. But the worst thing, last time, was the niggers that had been in the army. They come back all charged up with a lot of crazy horseshit and we just had to hammer them back under control. There's people laugh at the Ku Klux Klan nowadays, but I'll tell you this. When I was Grand Dragon of the Klan in this state, back around the mid-twenties, we earned our keep straightening them coons out. And it's gonna be worse this time because the Klan's faded out, and even if it wasn't, it couldn't operate like it did."

Cary nodded, faintly surprised. Vaguely he remembered hearing something about Hoke Moody having been a Klansman once, but he had never realized that Moody had been its top leader in the state. Cary had seen the Klan only one time, had only the faintest memory of them—a band of white robed and hooded men parading Main Street on Confederate Memorial Day along with the American Legion and soldiers from Camp Mason. But that had been years ago, before Hoke Moody had become Governor, even, while his father still held office. Since then, Moody had served four years as Governor and had gone on to the Senate. Now, in 1946, his brother Dale, a few years his junior, held the Governor's office. But it was known that Dale Moody was only a figurehead. Hoke Moody and, Cary thought proudly, Powell Bradham were the real rulers of Muskogee.

"Maybe things won't be so bad this time," Cary said mildly. "After all, this isn't the twenties."

Moody's face had lost every semblance of humor; it was deadly serious. "That's what I'm trying to tell you," he snapped. "This time it's going to be worse."

"How come?" Cary was startled, his interest engaged by Moody's sudden, bitter intensity.

"Because," Moody said harshly, "this time it won't only be the niggers. This time it'll be the niggers *and* the Federal government."

He arose, went to the bottle on the desk, poured more whiskey into his glass. His blue eyes glittered through steel-rimmed spectacles as he turned to Cary, the glass wagging in his hand.

"It's the same array of forces we had against us back in Reconstruction," he said. "I've been where I could watch it build up. I've had a ringside seat up there on the Hill, but nothing I could do would stop it. This government has swollen to enormous size. Under the pretext of the war emergency, it's gathered into its hands powers and prerogatives that don't belong to it, and it's got no intention of turning 'em loose or giving 'em back. It's run now by all those left-wing liberals and half-assed Yankee college professors Truman inherited from Roosevelt, the anti-lynch and FEPC boys—the new carpetbaggers, I call 'em." His voice was contemptuous. "And those buzzards have just been waiting for this war to end, so they can go on with their next campaign. What they want to do is to abolish the rights of the sovereign states, make the Federal government allpowerful, and then do what they failed to do back during Reconstruction. Make the South over into their own image." His voice had begun to soar, as if he were making a campaign speech. "Because they don't believe this is a republic any more, a federation of sovereign states. What they want to make it is a complete democracy, the kind of democracy that brought Athens into paralysis and down to ruin. That may sound wild, but I know those bastards. None of 'em ever worked a gang of niggers in their lives or turned a row behind a hard-tailed mule, but that don't stop 'em from knowing all about it. They've been trying to mongrelize the South and put it under nigger domination for a hundred years, and they're never going to let up. Looks like the only way they'll be happy is when we're all one great big mongrelized mulatto family, with Washington telling us when

to get up and when to go to bed. And that's the battle Muskogee has
got ahead of it—and not only Muskogee, but every other state that
gives a damn about its integrity. They'll threaten us, they'll bribe us,
and they'll seduce us. But no matter how nice and sweet they sing,
they're every bit as dangerous as any Yankee that ever marched with
Sherman. They got one aim for this country, the United States of
America, and that's first to turn it socialist and then to turn it Communist, and they know goddam good and well that they can't do
either one, until they conquer the South. The South, Cary"—he
slammed his hand down on Bradham's desk—"the South—because
it's the one part of the country that still clings to the old values, the
old traditions, the things that made this country great. They think
it's in their way and they've already made up their minds that it's
got to go. And how do they plan to do that? Well, it would be
mighty nice, wouldn't it, if they could put the nigger up alongside
the white man and give him an equal vote and train him to vote their
way? That would work out real good, in a state like this one, where
nearly half the population's niggers, or in Mississippi, where they're
more than half, wouldn't it?" His voice died abruptly, and he took
a long swallow of his drink. Before it was fairly down, he wiped his
mouth with his hand and said quietly, "But, of course, we ain't going
to let 'em do it."

Cary could not help being caught up in Moody's own excitement.
Raised in an atmosphere thick with politics, he had given politics
little thought in the past four years. All his mental and physical
capacities—and his emotional ones, too—had been focused on learning to fly and flying, on making war and winning, on killing and
keeping from getting killed. But he saw immediately the significance
of the problem Moody had presented, and saw it in the same frame-
work as Moody. After all, he was a Muskogeean, too, and a Southerner.

Still, it seemed a little incredible that the problem could be that
severe, that much a matter of life and death. He stood up and went
to the whiskey bottle on the desk. "How are we going to stop 'em?"
he asked, perhaps a bit more flippantly than he meant to, and with
more emphasis on the *we*.

Moody stared at him, his blue eyes almost unbearably keen and
searching. Then, abruptly, his mouth spread into a wide grin, showing
yellow teeth. He turned to Bradham.

"You were right, Powell," he said. "He's a chip off the old block. Did you hear that *we?*"

Slowly, Powell Bradham got out of his chair, his big frame towering over Moody. There was none of Moody's rant in his voice when he spoke.

"What Hoke has said," he told Cary, "is, by and large, true. It's the same battle we've been fighting for over a hundred years. For all we know, it may keep on for another hundred. We're all as much a part of it as your great-grandfather was. No Bradham can *not* be a part of it."

Cary felt an odd prickle, a chill that traveled up from between his shoulder blades to the short hair on the back of his neck. He was moved by the quiet strength of his father's face, and the pride and determination in his father's voice.

"There is no way to be an American without roots," his father went on. "You have got to believe in the place you were born and grew up in, in the manners and customs in which you were raised, before you can believe in America." His big hand, liver-spotted, spread itself on his desk. "The most important thing is to be a Muskogeean. After that, to be a Southerner. Because we may be the only true Americans left. We are the last people who think as the men who wrote the Constitution thought, the last people to see America as they saw it. That's why we have to prepare to defend ourselves. Not only for our own sakes, but for the sake of the entire country. The South built this country and ran it for a long time. It's up to the South to keep its principles from being perverted and watered down. It's up to us, because we're the only pure and unmongrelized segment of America left."

Moody cut in. "The white, Anglo-Saxon Protestant American built the United States. We're the last of the breed left. The North is a Jewish-Catholic hodgepodge. The West is tainted with it too. We're like an army, surrounded." His blue eyes bulged. "But, by God, we'll fight. We'll fight and we'll never surrender. We're not going to be socialized and we're not going to be mongrelized. Not ever, do you hear? Not ever!"

His organ tones vibrated in the silence that followed, deep and strong enough seemingly to stir the air. Then he and Bradham were both looking at Cary without speaking.

That chill was still plucking at Cary's spine. He looked from one of them to the other.

"All right," he said. "I believe what you say. How could I keep from believing it?"

Bradham let out a gusty breath. Moody seemed to relax, and he smiled.

"We didn't know," Moody said. "We didn't know what ideas might have been put in your head in these past four years or how you had come to think."

"My ideas?" Cary hesitated. He had never tried to formulate them. He had what he had inherited, what had been bred or hammered into him: family pride and self-respect and a love for his state and his country. Maybe even some honor and a sense of duty. But those were words that could not be voiced, because they somehow became tarnished when they were spoken, like precious metal exposed to air. His father could say them and come off all right, but they were not words he could ever use aloud. His father was of a generation in which it had been all right to say the words; he was not.

But he could feel them. Just as he could feel the presence in the room now of all those other Bradhams, the generations of them who were also part of his inheritance. One thing he had been taught; being false to himself was betraying them. And it was as if they were watching him now, the whole proud host of them; they were almost real, men who had spilled their blood and had their flesh torn and spent their fortunes for that tangible and yet ephemeral thing they had loved and which he was supposed to love too: Muskogee. He could feel every one of them looking at him, generations focused in the searching, proud gaze of his father, himself only a link in the chain of history they had hammered out and of which he, Cary, was the final terminus and which he could not sever. "My ideas?" he said again. Because he was not used to being confronted with a need to articulate all that forthrightly and without shame, to listeners who would not be embarrassed for him, he found his vocabulary inadequate. "What do you want me to do? Just tell me what you want me to do, and I'll do whatever I can."

The two older men looked at each other, and then they both relaxed and sat down, Moody leaning forward, grinning, swishing his drink around in the glass.

"Well," Moody said, "your daddy and I have run this state together for nigh on to fourteen years now, and we've done a pretty good job of it. But nobody lives forever, Cary. Not even Powell Bradham. Not even Hoke Moody." He chuckled. "Not that I don't aim to give it a pretty good try."

"Yes, sir," Cary said.

"We're getting old," Moody went on, suddenly dead serious. "I'm fifty-seven, your daddy's sixty. We have to plan ahead. Now. I know sixteen years seems like a powerful long time to you, but to your daddy and me it's just a snap of the fingers. Every morning when we get up and listen to our joints creak, we're reminded how fast time goes by." He sipped from his drink.

"Sixteen years from now, Cary," he said, the organ voice vibrating, "you'll be forty years old. That's old enough to be the Governor of this state."

Cary clamped his hands tight around his glass, feeling no surprise, only a confirmation of what had swirled in his mind. The immediate logic, the rightness of it, was unmistakable. "I see," he murmured.

"I don't have any children," Moody said. "I don't know why; I guess it's a judgment the good Lord has visited on me for my sins of omission and commission over the years. But that doesn't mean I don't aim to see this state left in good hands when Gabriel leans down and hollers, Come on, Hoke—let's go! It's got to be left to somebody. And that somebody has got to be a fighter. And he's got to have something he believes in enough to fight for it." His eyes narrowed. "Your daddy and I have talked this over, Cary, and we've come to the conclusion that that somebody ought to be you."

He paused.

"I'll admit," he went on, "I had some second thoughts. You may not be fully aware of it, but there was a time when your papa and I were fighting like two young bulls in a pasture. It took a long time for us to convince each other that we were working for the same things in different ways. But we've worked in double harness long enough now to settle our differences and see eye to eye. We have come to rely on each other, and now we also rely on you."

He passed his empty glass to Bradham. It was an offhanded, completely imperial gesture, but as Moody went on, Bradham arose and refilled it without comment. Cary's eyes swung to his father and then back to Moody.

"I know it doesn't seem like to you," Moody said, "that you'll ever be forty. That sounds like it's old as God, right now. But the time will come, maybe a little sooner, maybe a little later. And you've got to start preparing yourself for it now."

Bradham thrust the glass at Moody and cut in, his voice harsh. "You'll have to go back to the University and on through Law School. That you've already planned on. Then, when you graduate, we'll start you out easy. Maybe public prosecutor here in Hannington. After that, the Legislature. Then a term as Lieutenant Governor and president of the state Senate. When you finish that, you'll run for Governor."

"It will be like training for a track race," Moody said. "Politics is total. You can never lose sight of the objective. Everything you say, everything you do, counts toward the end. Sometimes what you say, what you have to do, is not what you'd rather say or rather do, so it's not easy, it's no bed of roses. So we thought now was the time to tell you . . . ask you, I mean. Because everything from now on counts."

Then the room was silent, as they waited for him to speak.

He looked at his father, and then he looked at Moody, and he got to his feet and said quietly, "Thank you."

Hoke Moody grinned broadly. He heaved himself erect and went to the bottle on the desk. He looked at Bradham jubilantly. "Fourteen years ago," he said exuberantly, "neither one of us would ever have believed this possible, would we? Now. Now, I'm going to pour myself some more of your whiskey and we will drink to—"

"To the state of Muskogee," Bradham said quietly.

Moody blinked his eyes. "Yes," he said. "Sure. To the state of Muskogee."

5

Waiting for Cary, Houston Whitley set the coffeepot on the kerosene stove in the kitchen and lit the flame underneath. It was only seven o'clock in the morning, but his mother had already gone to work; she had to catch the quarter-to-six bus to get to the Bradhams' in time to make breakfast. He had the house to himself, as he sliced streak-o'-lean bacon from a hunk of cellophane-wrapped, grocery-store side meat and shoved the biscuits Lucy had left for him in the oven to heat. He worked quickly and deftly, his spirits high with expectancy, for he was eager to see Cary again, and the more he thought about it, the more he felt certain that Cary could help him.

They had, he remembered, always helped one another when they were children. If it had not been for Cary, for the help he had given Cary and the help Cary had given him, he would never have made it even to the little one-room schoolhouse, Burnt Stump School, two miles from The Place. Surely, if there was one person in the world he could talk to honestly, one white man who would understand and not expect him to pussyfoot, who would listen and then act, that would be Cary.

The meat began to sizzle in the pan. Huse shoved it back and forth idly, his mind not on it at all, his mind slipping back through the years, to the time when they had come to The Place. . . .

The house Bradham had given them on the fourteen acres was no better and no worse than the kind of house Houston Whitley had lived in all his life. Its walls and floors were of a single layer of warped and gray-weathered boards. It contained two rooms, one used as the kitchen and his parents' bedroom, the other a front room in which he, Bishop, and Robert shared one bed. A previous tenant had sealed the walls against the wind with a layer of glued-up newspapers, but the wind had ruptured the calking of paper along each crack and left it peeling.

Nevertheless, that first night, the house had seemed a haven and the warmth of its fireplace a blessing. Huse remembered how he and Bish and Robert, their bellies full of meat, bread and molasses for the first time in days, had lain before the fire. Bish dozed like a drowsy animal, and Robert, five years old, was sound asleep, snuggled against Huse's flank like a puppy against its littermate, his thumb in his mouth. After a while his mother had entered from the other room, bent deftly and strongly to scoop Robert up in her long, thin arms. Huse remembered how the little boy's head had rolled against her breast, though he did not waken. Remembered Lucy rubbing her cheek against the black-wooled roundness. "He plumb wo' out," she said and laid him on the sagging iron bed against the wall. She did not undress him, but pulled a tattered blanket over him and bent and kissed his cheek. "Yall let him have de middle, where he stay warm."

So, with the fire and a full belly and shelter, everything should have been all right again, and he should have been able to drowse like Bish or sleep like Robert. But he could not. He did not seem to be able to get out of the wagon.

They had been in it for three endless days, ever since he and Robert had been baffled by the sudden loading of the furniture in the wagon and the leaving, without announcement or preliminary, of the cabin on Mr. Graham's place that had been their home since Huse could remember. That had been upset, confusion, and apprehension enough, but the wagon had been worse. He seemed still to be able to feel the cold, wet misery of the drenched cave under the quilt, the distress and gripe of hunger and the worse distress of hearing Robert crying with it, not stopping no matter how much he was cuddled, tickled or soothed.

The apprehension had grown into fear, and the fear into a kind of dull terror. *What if Papa can't find nothing atall for us to eat?*

It was the first time he had ever realized that his father was vulnerable and not all-powerful. But now he had seen too many times the reflection of his own fear, his own helplessness, his own distress, in the man's eyes, despite the calm, rocklike confidence of his manner. And something had happened to Houston Whitley in the wagon; a knowledge for which he was not yet ready came to him, and his world changed frighteningly, enlarging, full of unknown menaces and haunted by vague fears. That was why he was still awake and nervous while his brothers slept. They had not seen the change in the world that he had seen; warmth and full bellies were enough for them. But not for him. He could not get out of the wagon; he wondered if he ever would. . . .

But after he met Cary, the new world he had entered seemed far less inimical.

That had been on a bright Saturday morning a week later, when his father had sent him to the creek that wound through the pasture low ground to try to catch a mess of fish. A few catfish on his stringer an hour later, drowsing in the sun, he had been brought awake by a voice from the bank above him. "Hey, you got my favorite fishin' place."

He turned, at first startled and then afraid. A white boy about his own age, but taller, stood on the bank above him, a lock of dark hair curling over his forehead, his legs beneath his short pants seemingly very long from that perspective. He held a cane pole and a can of worms, and he did not look pleased.

Huse scrambled to his feet. "I sorry." His heart was pounding with embarrassment and fear of the unknown. He had never had anything to do with white people, except to speak in passing to Mr. George Graham or his grown sons, but from the time he could remember, he had been rigorously drilled in courtesy toward them and had had hammered into him the knowledge that he must never come in conflict with them. The white man's word and wish were law, as God's word and wish were, and could be disobeyed only at as much risk.

So he did not want to make the strange white boy mad. Never having been around one, he had no idea what a white boy might do, how he would react. He groped frantically for his pole and stringer. "I move," he said.

But when he lifted his stringer with the catfish on them, the white boy said, "Hey, wait." Then he scrambled down the bank to the ledge where Huse had sat. He was not quite as tall as Huse had thought, once they were face to face.

The white boy pointed at the string of catfish. "Hey, where'd you git all those?"

"Cotched 'em."

"Outa here? What'd you use for bait?"

Huse was startled at the white boy's ignorance. "Chicken guts."

"Chicken guts?" The boy looked profoundly surprised.

"Sho. Chicken guts de best catfeesh bait dere is."

"No kiddin'. Where are they? You got any extra?"

"Sho. I got plenty." Huse squatted and unfolded the torn waxed-paper bread wrapper that held his bait. He gestured to the livid mess thus exposed. "Help yo'self."

The white boy bent to look; then he straightened, face contorted, throat working convulsively. He turned away. "Gee, they stink," he said thickly.

Huse could not suppress a grin now. "Sho. Worse dey spoiled, better dey are." Used to the odor, not even noticing, reflecting that white boys sure had weak stomachs, he sliced off a stringy piece with his pocketknife. "Here, lemme have yo' hook."

A little shamefacedly, the white boy passed the pole, and Huse slid the bait on the hook carefully. He folded up the waxed paper and laid it aside. "Now," he said. "You try dat, see if dey don't bite."

"Okay, thanks." The white boy sat down on the bank beside Huse and cast his hook out. He no longer seemed interested in Huse's going away, and Huse sat down, intrigued by this first close contact. He de boss man's son, Huse thought, pleased to have been noticed by any-one of such rank.

They sat quietly, watching their corks. After a while the white boy asked, "What's your name? I ain't seen you around here before."

"I name Houston Whitley. We-unses just come last Saddy."

The white boy looked at him keenly, with heightened interest. "Hey, I bet you were in that wagon. You know—"

"Dat right. I see you upon de po'ch."

"I bet it was you peepin' out, then."

"Sho."

"Boy, you looked funny under that quilt. Couldn't see nothin' but your eyes. You looked like—"

Huse nudged him. "Hush," he said quietly. "You got a bite."

The white boy turned back to the creek. His cork was jiggling. Then it went all the way under. The boy might not have known much about bait, but he was a good fisherman. He was not a heartbeat too early or too late when he smoothly raised the pole.

They both stared incredulously at the way the poletip arched. Then the white boy let out a yell. Swinging inshore at the end of his line was the biggest catfish either of them had ever seen.

Flopping fiercely, it landed on the bank, and Huse saw at once that the white boy was afraid of it. So was he—it was over two feet long. But he acted before he thought, moving quickly, deftly seizing it in the right place so the sharp bones in its fins could not jab him. The weight of his pocketknife made a dull *thunk* as he slammed it down on the fish's head and the stunned fish straightened out, tail twitching feebly.

Quickly he removed the hook and ran the fish onto his own stringer. Then the two of them knelt over it in awe.

The white boy raised his face. "Gee, I never caught a fish that big before." His eyes were huge, his countenance awed and glowing.

"Me needer," Huse said. Their eyes met over the fish then, and something warm arced between them; and from that moment on they were friends. They fished together the rest of the morning, and when it was time to go, Huse was startled and overwhelmed with gratitude when Cary told him, "You go ahead and take the big one. It was caught on your bait."

"Naw, I couldn't do dat. You cotched it."

"That's all right. I don't need it. I want you to have it. Go ahead."

"Dat sho is fine," Huse said, his heart full of warmth and liking. "Dat sho is mighty nice of you." He thought how pleased his father would be when he brought home such a fish, what a fine meal it would make.

"Look," Cary said, "I come out here every Saturday. Meet me down here next Saturday, will you? Bring some more chicken guts. I got a twenty-two rifle. I'll bring that and we can fish and have some target practice."

A .22 rifle! Huse had never fired a gun. "I'll try," he said yearningly. "I mought hafta work in de field."

"Naw, you won't. I'll tell my daddy to see you get off. I'll be right here next Saturday. Meet me, don't forget."

"Okay," said Huse, "I does my best."

Cary had been as good as his word. After that, by special dispensation from Bradham, Huse was free on Saturdays to play with Cary. Or any other time Cary wanted him during the summer. They roamed, fished, explored, and in the fall and winter, they hunted squirrels with Cary's .22. They both loved the outdoors, their personalities meshed perfectly; and within a year they felt so close that it seemed nothing could ever separate them. . . .

Huse forked the bacon out of the frying pan and laid it on a plate. The biscuits were ready, too, and he sat down to eat.

He had learned, of course, as he grew up, that there was nothing unusual about their friendship. In the country, colored boys and white played together naturally. It was only after they had moved to town that he and Cary had begun to drift apart, since, obviously, Cary could not come down into Little Hammer to play and Huse could not go up to Mercy Street.

But that did not matter. What mattered was that nothing had ever undermined the groundwork they had laid in those early days. Cary's friendship had given Huse a sense of security, a sense of having a protector, that he had needed badly exactly at that time.

And that he had needed worse, he thought, mopping a biscuit in some molasses, after the death of Mason Jar.

Thinking of Mason Jar, he laid the biscuit down, his appetite vanishing for the moment. Mason Jar, tall, black as a lump of coal, so black he shone blue in the sun, a laughing giant . . . and Mason Jar, standing there beside the highway, waiting, no longer laughing, just waiting for what he knew had to come. . . .

Mason Jar was not his real name. His real name was Jesse Mangum, and he was Otis Whitley's first cousin. He and Otis had grown up together on the same plantation, played together, drifted apart later. Because neither could read or write, Otis had not known Jesse was working at Bradham's lumber camp in the swamp until Jesse, hearing of the coming of the Whitleys through the grapevine that spread its runners through the whole colored community, materialized at the cabin.

Huse had worshiped Mason Jar from the beginning. The man had enormous strength; he stood over six feet, his shoulders were tremendous, his forearms as big around as Otis's thighs. But his smile was wide, easy and warm, lighting his eyes; and when he played with the children, his hands and voice were gentle.

He was gentle, too, with his wife Thelma, whom Huse came to love almost as much. She was the handsomest woman he had ever seen. She was childless, and work and birthing had not dried her up as Lucy had dried. Her skin was as black as Jesse's, but her face was the aquiline one of an Indian. She was almost as tall as her husband, large of breast and buttock and narrow of waist; and she walked with a lithe, catlike grace, barefooted.

The Whitleys saw a great deal of Jesse and Thelma that summer, for, with work slack at the lumber camp, they visited often, and, knowing their need, the Whitleys shared what rations they had with them, no word of invitation or thanks passing either way. In return, Jesse and Thelma made two more hands in the field, hands badly needed for wresting a cotton crop from the thin, eroded and worn-out soil of the fourteen acres. Huse would never forget the mellow reach of Jesse's voice, singing in the heat-suspended stillness of a July afternoon . . . *I axed my capn for the time of day . . . He thowed his watch away.* . . .

They did not know Jesse had another name until one afternoon when they all rode together in the wagon to the store at Troublefield.

Going to the store was always an event. The store was a wondrous place, big and cool and dim, full of fantastic luxury, rows of canned goods, stacked piles of clothes, guns, ammunition, fishing tackle, tools and harness, seed and fertilizer, and, most enticing of all, the long glass candy case crammed with ant-crawled penny candy. A visit to the store meant a penny sucker each for the Whitley children, and the choice between orange, red, green and purple was always agonizing and thrilling.

Riding back in the wagon afterward, Huse sat on Jesse's lap, licking the diminishing sweetness of the sucker. "Uncle Jesse, how come everybody at the sto' call you Mason Jar?"

He felt Jesse's body go strangely taut. Jesse's voice was flat. "White man gimme dat name."

"Hush, boy," Lucy said. "Don't be so curious."

"It all right. I don't mind tellin. It de man what run de loggin camp, white man named Roy Moody, stuck dat name on me. Dey's a lot of Moodys in dis part, but dat Roy Moody, he de meanest of de whole shootin match. He run dat loggin camp jest like a chain gang. And when he been drinkin, he ain't fit to be around." Jesse spat over the side of the wagon.

"One day him and a bunch of his rowdies up at de sto' drinkin and I come up and do my business and fixin to leave when dey call me over to where dey sittin in de shade. I could smell de white whiskey dey been drinkin fo' I ever come nigh 'em.

"Ole Moody say, 'Jesse, I done made a bet. I bet dese boys a nigger big as you could drink a whole pint Mason jar of cawn likker in one swaller and go on about his business. But dey swear it knock you flat. I tell 'em they crazy, you never even feel it. I bet 'em a dollar apiece you can do it.'

"I say, 'Now, Mr. Roy, you knows I ain't no drinkin man.' An' he laugh an' say, 'Go on, never seed no nigger wouldn' drink when he could git it.' Den he rotch around and holds up a pint jar full of somethin clear, look like cawn likker all right. He say, 'I got five dollars ridin say you kin do it.'

"Dat when I knowed I couldn't git out of it. He got eyes like a wildcat, dey turn yellow when he mad, and his hand in his pocket. I knowed if he pull his knife, I hafta kill him and I don't want that to happen, so I stop fussin and say I give it a try. He take de top off de jar and say, 'Now, hole yo' breath so you git it all down in one big swaller.' And dat exactly what I do, hole my breath and tip dat jug up and drink it all down; and den I suck in my wind and next thing I know, I sicker'n anybody ever been befo' in dis world."

He paused. "Wasn't no cawn whiskey in dat jar," he went on after a moment. "He done fill dat jar wid kerosene."

"Fo' Jesus!" Lucy breathed.

"Dey think dat de funniest thing ever happen. Ole Roy Moody jest roll on de ground laughin. Dey all waitin for me to git sick. Mon, I sick all right, but I ain't let dem see it. I jest kinda grin reel cool an' say, 'Dat sho' good drinkin likker, Mr. Roy. Much obliged,' and walk off biggity as a jaybird. Soons I outa deir sight, I stick my finger down my th'oat, heave up, den run for water and fill my belly and throw up, do that two, three times to wash me out. Never *been* so sick. Seem lak it take all my stren'th. I sick the whole next two weeks, and tryin to work out in de woods. Ever' time he see me slow down, ole Roy Moody walk up and grin and say, 'Whatsa matter, you need another Mason jarful to keep you goin?' Den he start callin me Mason Jar, other white folks hear it, think it funny, they pick it up, too. Since dat time, nearly everybody call me Mason Jar."

By that time they were at the logging camp on the edge of the swamp. Somehow Huse would always link the horror and outrage he had felt at Jesse's story to his first sight of the camp—the wide clearing shaded by a few tall pines, the semicircle of boxlike shanties where the loggers and their families lived, the mule barns and pens, and the twilit swamp brooding darkly only a few paces beyond. It was nightfall then, and after they had said goodbyes and Jesse and Thelma had entered their shanty, Otis had turned the wagon around and started home. Than a sudden glare of incoming headlights, the *oogah-oogah* of a Model T's horn. The car had stopped after forcing the wagon off the road. Huse got a glimpse of a thin, feral face, beardy and with hating, dangerous eyes. "Who you?" The voice was thick with liquor. "What in hell you doin down here?"

Before Otis could explain, the man stuck his head out. "You git yo' black ass outa here and don't come back! Don't need no mo' niggers in here than I done got!" A jeering, maniacal laugh, the car roaring forward, backfiring so the mule jumped, and Roy Moody was gone.

And maybe, Huse thought, that was the night it started. . . . He still had no appetite and he stared down at his plate. Maybe that was the night. . . . The white man alone in his shack in the hot, airless dark, the liquor working in him, and probably too the bitter knowledge that he was hated, despised, not only by the Negroes whom he worked but by the white man who had hired him to work the Negroes. Roy Moody, sweating, in the shanty that was no better than Mason Jar's, and dirtier, full of liquor and lust and the desire to prove again that though they thought him scum outside, down here in the swamp his white skin made him king.

So that when he had worked himself up to whatever drunken pitch it took, he roused himself, crossed the clearing, and slammed unannounced into Mason Jar's house, wanting Thelma.

Mason Jar would have killed him if Thelma had not stopped him. "Don't you see?" she must have said. "It don't matter. What he wants don't amount to anything. It won't make any difference. But if you kill him, then we both lost, then everything ended."

So that Mason Jar had stood raging silently outside in the dark, while inside his own house Roy Moody took his wife. And afterward, Thelma had tried to quiet him when he cried in dry, gasping rage.

"It all right. It don't 'mount to nothing. It don't touch me, not the part of me loves you. Please. Don't you see, there ain't no way to help it?"

And how many times must she have said that to him again? Each time, perhaps, when she brought that lithe, sensual blackness of her body back from the white man's cabin to find him nearly insane, each time it happened during the long stretch of the hot summer that made the cotton grow so good. With something building inside Mason Jar, swelling until it could not be contained. So that she had to say over and over again, "I love you. It don't matter. I love you. If I don't do it, he liable to kill you. But you can't kill him, because that would be like killing yo'self. I hate him, I despise him. But how else I goan save us, now he got this craziness in his head?"

But whatever she had said, it was not enough. Nothing could be enough, even though he knew that what she said was true. So that the time must have come when Jesse looked at his own black skin with rage against it and hatred for his impotence under it. When at last, crazy with frustration and outrage and shame, his mind had warped enough to decide that she was lying now, that his blackness revolted her, and that despite her words, she had been captured by and loved, hungered and yearned for Roy Moody's whiteness.

He had changed; and the Whitleys watched the change descend on him, watched him seal himself up inside himself, never laughing any more, no longer singing, just walking about in dumb, unending misery. Until he could bear it no longer. Until the time came when he had got a five-gallon can of kerosene and crept across the clearing and poured it on the walls of Roy Moody's cabin one night while the two of them were inside. And then, perhaps crying, or perhaps not crying at all, had struck a match and thrown it against the oil-soaked wood, and had turned and run while the weathered, dried and seasoned pine exploded like a bomb. Had locked himself in his own shack and covered his head with a pillow and cried while the roaring flames lit up the very swamp and crackled in the night.

Immediately, a quiet, solemn fear settled over the entire country-side. Huse would never forget the horror of it, a horror worse even than his grief at the inexplicable death of Thelma. When darkness came, the Negroes in the scattered cabins across the plantations were tense and jumpy, listening, waiting, fearing. The children caught the fear without knowing its reason, and it was worse for them, with no rein on their imaginings.

A week of that tension, the air across the county charged with it, like the sullen electrical quiet before a thunderstorm. A white man had died violently. No one, even the whites, was sure yet exactly how or why. But everybody knew it had not ended. Payment would be demanded, but nobody knew from whom or how much.

Only Mason Jar seemed not to feel the tension, seemed not to be saturated with the fear. He walked about freely, night or day, dis-playing no grief, no jubilance, only seeming to be looking for some-thing.

Huse remembered that he had seen the end of it. Nobody had wanted to go to the store that Saturday, but rations had to be got. There was no joking, no laughing or socializing at Troublefield that afternoon—and no one came near Mason Jar, walking up and down at the edge of the paved road as if waiting for a ride. Huse had wanted to run to him, but his father had gripped and held him. "No," Otis said. "No. Leave him alone."

So Mason Jar, huge, black, erect, stood alone in the bright sun-light that fell on the crossroads, on the store, on the weed-grown rail siding and its parked log cars, on the high, corrugated iron flanks of the cotton gin, on the Nehi signs and the Dr. Pepper signs and the 666 Chills-and-Fever Tonic signs. . . .

And then they heard the automobile.

In the dry hush of the afternoon, with even the July flies having stilled their sawing in the oak trees, they could hear it a long way off. Just a hum, at first, like wind in the telegraph and power wires, but the sound thickening rapidly because it was coming very fast.

"Jesse," Otis called from the porch of the store. "Jesse." His voice was pleading and it trembled. Mason Jar seemed not to hear him. He did not even look around. His giant figure, clad in blue work clothes, barefooted, stood easily and relaxed beside the road.

Then Otis had seized the boys and was trying to shove them into the store. Pressed and pushed, Huse turned only by accident, and that was how he saw it.

The car was in sight now, just cresting a hill. It was a blue sedan, mud-spattered, a Model A with wire-spoked wheels. It came fast, faster than he had seen any car come, past the rail siding, past the crossroads, and then it began to slow.

Mason Jar took a step toward the pavement. Otis pulled at Huse's arm. "Git in here," he said fiercely. "Git in here."

But Huse saw it. The sudden blue gleam of the double-barreled shotgun, the three white faces in the car behind it. The man with the gun was squinting, grinning. Mason Jar raised a hand, almost as if in greeting; then the gun exploded from both barrels. Huse screamed and buried his face against his father's belly. A whoop, a shrill high cry like the yell of a fox hunter, and then the car accelerated, its roar thunderous. The sound rocked the air for a moment, then died to a hum once more, leaving only hot, pine-scented silence; and then it was gone as swiftly as it had come. . . .

6 The car slammed and bounced as it hit the chuck holes in the Little Hammer street. Cary Bradham held tightly to the wheel, but when he passed a bare-bottomed, rotund black child of about four squatting and digging intently in the sand of a tiny yard, he took time to smile. Nothing's cuter than a little pickaninny, he thought, as the baby raised awed, huge eyes in a tar-black moon to stare at the passing car. Then the smile vanished, and his gray eyes went serious. So much had happened in these past few days that he was almost a little afraid of it all.

First Mary Scott. There was danger there, and he was going to have to handle her carefully. Last night had been a repetition of the morning at The Place, only more extended. Parked on a rural road after leaving the Hannington Country Club, they had explored each other further. Eventually, except for her panties, he had stripped her naked, his hands exploring her body without stint, and she had been as aroused as he. She had balked him of the final, essential act just in time; but now he knew that, sooner or later, it had to come about.

And I am either going to have to make up my mind to shake loose from her now, he thought, or take a damned long chance. . . .

What his father and Hoke Moody had told him yesterday afternoon was far less unsettling, but it was beginning to dawn on him just what he was committed to now, and that only made the problem of Mary Scott more vexatious. *Everything you say, everything you do, counts.* He was just beginning to realize that he had, in a measure, relinquished some part of his control over his own life. The end, the objective, would be worth it, of course. He was proud and honored that Powell Bradham and Hoke Moody had chosen him. Still, it was something, it was really something, to walk into fresh from the army.

Well, he'd forget it all for today. He looked forward to the coming hours with almost lustful pleasure. To be reunited with Huse, to spend the whole day leisurely in the sun-and-shadow wilderness of the swamp, fishing—it would be like old times. He had often imagined doing it while he was overseas. He could hardly wait now.

Lucy's house had once been painted green, but now it had weathered to gray. It sat at the bottom of the hollow of Little Hammer, surrounded by carefully tended flowers in every inch of spare space. Zinnias and snapdragons had just begun to bloom in the little beds on either side of the rickety steps, and a hydrangea was in lavender explosion at the side of the house. On the wooden railing of the porch sat several geraniums in rusty lard cans.

Cary parked the car and got out; he climbed the treacherous steps carefully, amusedly aware of secret eyes on him as he did so. A white man in Little Hammer, especially this early, usually meant trouble for somebody; and he could imagine the speculation going on behind all those closed doors. He smiled faintly and rapped loudly on the frame of the screen. There was no immediate answer, and he rapped again, fidgeting impatiently on the porch.

Niggers, he thought with fond tolerance, looking out at the sad, collapsing shanties of the hollow without really seeing them, for he had seen them all his life. Uncle Hoke may be a smart man, but he doesn't know niggers the way *we* do. They're not going to give us any trouble—not if we handle them right. Moody, he thought, had the poor-white outlook, he didn't really know niggers at all, he just hated them, because his people had only been in competition with them, had never owned and been owned by them the way the Bradhams always had, emancipation or no. White trash weren't raised by colored nurses or fed by colored cooks; and poor white boys didn't play with nigger boys as he had played with Huse. It was nothing against Uncle Hoke, but he just didn't understand the intricate pattern of black and white, of obligation and counterobligation, the sense of paternal responsibility, that marked the relationship of his own caste with Negroes. Always, in the South, that had been one way to tell the quality from trash—their attitude toward their darkies. Uncle Hoke, for instance, wouldn't understand his eagerness to see Huse again. . . .

He turned to knock again, but before he could, the screen door opened and Houston Whitley stood in the doorway, naked to the waist, his legs clad in army suntans, his feet bare. His face was lit with the kind of wide grin that Cary remembered, a grin that, flashing infrequently, lit up Huse's face with a kind of radiance.

"Well, I be dawggone," Huse said.

Cary grinned back. There was only the flicker of indecision, and then his right hand thrust out. "Huse, how you doing?"

Another clock tick of hesitancy, and then Huse's hand gripped Cary's, hard. Cary could feel the roughness and strength of it; it scraped his palm as it drew away.

"I'm doing fine. How in the world you come on?" Huse opened the screen and stepped aside for Cary to enter. "I just eating breakfast. Come on in."

The house smelled close and shut up, full of the greasy, woodsy aura that, since his earliest childhood, Cary had associated with Negroes. Huse led him into the little kitchen, where a pot of coffee sat over the flame of a kerosene stove. There was an old wooden icebox, an oilcloth-covered table, three chairs, and clean but ancient linoleum on the floor. A dishpan on a smaller table did service as a sink, and the few items of household china were stacked on a couple of open shelves. Huse jerked a thumb at the coffeepot. "You want a cup?"

Again Cary hesitated. "Sure," he said finally. "I'll drink it while you finish your breakfast." He dropped into a chair, while Huse poured coffee into a cup of thick, white china, spotless but cracked.

The smile was still on Huse's face. "Mama wants to use the same grounds two-three times 'fore she throws 'em away, but I tole her, damn it, long as I got some musterin-out pay, we goin to drink first-time coffee. You want it black, I reckon."

"Still black," Cary said. He was a little startled by how much older Huse looked, how much heavier and more solid, all the round edges of immaturity knocked square by experience.

He held the cup between his palms while Huse stood with hands on hips, looking down at him. "You changed," Huse said. "You look older."

"I was just thinking the same thing about you."

"Uh-huh. I reckon we both entitled to. It been a long time, ain't it?" His face still showed that radiance. "Where they send you—Saipan, wasn't it?"

"Yep. I got stuck there while you were bouncing all over Europe."

"Man, they bounced me all right. I made the Grand Tour." Coming from Huse, those words sounded strange to Cary. "I been shot at in Italy, France, and Germany and maybe some other places I don't remember right now."

"You're lucky. They put me on a rock and I stayed there except when I was flying."

Huse dropped into a chair across from Cary. "I was just thinkin about you whilst I was eatin breakfast. You know what I was rememberin? I thinkin about that time you got snakebit."

"You picked a hell of a thing to think about." Cary grunted.

"That a big turnin point in my life. That snake hadn't bit you, I never would have gone to school." He crammed a biscuit in his mouth and chewed it with appetite. Sweat gleamed on his bare, brown torso; beads of it glistened in the sparse, wiry hair on his chest. It was hot in here, and the kitchen smelled strongly of cold pork grease. "Jesus," Huse went on, "that sure a long time ago." He washed down the biscuit with a swallow of coffee. His voice softened. "I been lookin forward to us goin out like this," he said. "I got to go out back a minute, then we can go. I won't be long."

"Sure," Cary said. Huse went out the back door. When it had slammed behind him, Cary looked down at the cup of coffee untouched before him. He lifted it, but not quite to his lips. He felt something twitch and flop within him: a queasiness. Of course, he thought, Lucy washed this, just like she washes the dishes at home. But he looked at the dishpan on the other table, still rimmed with ineradicable grease. And that damned Robert's bound to have drunk out of it, too, one time or another, Cary thought. No telling what *he's* got. . . . Knowing a kind of mean shame, he arose from the table. It took only an instant to flip the contents of the cup back into the pot. Then he put the cup and saucer back in place before him on the table and lit a cigarette. In a moment the back door slammed again as Huse re-entered the kitchen.

"Lemme put on a shirt and some boots," he said, "and I'll be right with you. If you want another cup of coffee while you waitin, just help yourself."

Even to those who knew it as well as Cary Bradham and Houston Whitley, the Kenoree Swamp was an awesome place. Though Bradham's lumber camp had nibbled at its flank for twenty-five years, its men and mules and single little narrow-gauge locomotive had hardly broken the skin; and the swamp remained a sprawling, untouched wilderness, inhabited only by deer, occasional bears, wild pigs, bobcats, and throngs of coons, squirrels and possums. Its timber was virginal, huge gums, swamp poplars, oaks and hickories soaring high, fighting each other for sunlight and trying to shake off the parasitic vines that clawed their flanks; cypresses brooded in black, unflowing ponds; streams that had never yet been named wound and writhed through underbrush that looked capable of strangling a man. Houston Whitley had always loved the swamp. But now, sitting in the stern of the flat-bottomed boat, deftly guiding with an occasional silent dip of the paddle, he felt a vague unease that had been growing stronger ever since the skiff had been launched.

Maybe, he thought, searching for its cause, it had been the matter-of-fact way that Cary had moved into the bow and left the paddling position in the stern to him, unconsciously, of course, and without the passage of any words. It was, he told himself, foolish to let such a small thing spoil what should be such a good day—and after all, these were the positions that they had always taken in boats. Did he expect Cary to paddle for *him?* Still, he could not help thinking: I wonder if it really for me he want me to come. Or is it because he just needs somebody that knows the swamp to come in here with him? Somebody to paddle the boat, so he can fish. Still needs his little nigger boy to run around with him and make sure he don't get hurt. . . .

Thus, he could not shake off the feeling that it was not quite working. We ain't boys any more, he thought. We grown men, and we been away from each other a long time and now it don't seem like we can quite get together.

They had both tried hard. In the car on the long drive, they had reminisced and squeezed the reminiscences dry. All about The Place, the days of their childhood. But the time came when, that used up, something dropped between them, something strange to them both, a curtain of awkwardness. It was not like it had been in the old days at all.

Maybe it just growin up, Huse thought. Bein a child like runnin through an open pasture, nothin in your way. But growin up like walkin through a thicket, too many things grab ahold of you and tangle you and make it hard to see where you goin. What we got to do is make it through that thicket to where we can get out in the open again. Maybe he ain't even tangled in it at all. Maybe it just me. Maybe I ain't tryin hard enough. He been good to me. If it ain't for him, I never even go to school at all. Besides, I need him now.

He dipped the paddle and turned the boat inshore to the mouth of a smaller creek spilling into the river. He was not even thinking about where he was going; he was thinking of what had happened to him after the death of Mason Jar. . . .

It had been two days after Mason Jar's killing before Huse could eat, a week before he ceased to scream and jerk awake in his sleep. His mind was tangled in a shroud of horror, only the words *Why? How come?* ringing in it over and over, everything else muffled.

But there were no answers Otis and Lucy could give him. It had always been that way: the white man. Life itself, food, the possession of a wife, the sanctity of family—all these were, if your skin was dark, totally within the power of the white man's whim, his greed, his boredom, his anger. Lucy and Otis could not bring themselves to tell him that, but they did not need to. He had just found it out for himself. And the world had changed to a place of absolutely no security at all, where senseless, gibbering horrors and unsuspected dangers ran loose like wolves. The ten-year-old boy could not cope with what he had learned; and he slid deep into depression, walking about now in numbed silence, but with screaming terror locked up inside, always menaced, never without fear.

They had lived on The Place six weeks before Huse had even known there was a school two miles away. When he finally learned the function of the tired-looking building, too large for a tenant cabin, too small for a church, shuttered and empty in summer in its grove of pines, there had been no immediate reaction within him. But when he had learned that it would open in mid-October, after all the cotton had been picked and ginned, something began to grow in him that the death of Mason Jar expanded into an obsession; and it helped him knit his world back together. He wanted to go to school.

Otis, when asked about it, seemed startled. "What you wanta mess wid dat for?"

"I wanta be able to read books like Mista Cary." It was the only reason he dared voice.

"Well," Otis had temporized, "we'll see. It all depend on what de Gov'ner say." He would have let it end there, but Huse kept after him. Finally, one Saturday afternoon, they confronted Bradham together. After his father had carefully gone through the grinning, shuffling, good-humored preliminaries, he told Bradham what Huse wanted.

Bradham's stern face had looked down from great height at the boy; and it was bleak, terrifying. Huse wished he'd never thought of the idea.

"No," Bradham said.

"I—" Huse began. He choked up with disappointment.

"Gov'ner, suh, I ain't aim to argue." That was Otis. "But he do want to go reel bad."

"No," said Bradham again, with more kindness in his voice. "No, it would only be bad for him. Teach him how to raise cotton, Otis. Make a good farmer out of him. Then he'll always be able to make a living. School won't do anything for him but spoil him for hard work. That's why I've got a rule about it."

That should have ended it. But by now Huse was totally obsessed, the refusal only firing his determination. He asked Cary to intercede; and Cary had. "He said no," Cary reported. "And he said he didn't want to hear anything more about it."

But still Huse would not accept it. He had no idea what school was like, what it could give him. He was not even interested in learning. It was only that his mind was trying to save itself, and so it clung to the idea, like a man hanging from a ledge over a chasm.

Then he and Cary had gone one night to gig frogs in the creek. They carried flashlights and barbed, homemade tridents mounted at the ends of long cane poles. Barefooted—against express orders— they waded in the shallow, tepid stream that cleft the pasture, raying their lights on sandbars and in shadowy places under the bank. Sometimes twin white jewels reflected back, unwinking: frogs' eyes. Then, careful not to break the hypnosis of the light beam, which would keep the frog immobilized where it squatted, one of them would stalk the game with his spear. The trident was poised, rammed downward, crunching bone and rending cold flesh. Held aloft, skewered, the frog would jerk its legs, bulge its eyes, unroll the flap of its pale tongue. Then they ripped it loose, killed or half killed it with blows on the head, and dropped it in the dank gunnysack Huse carried.

They had been out an hour and were far from the house, wading quietly in water up to their knees, when Cary screamed. Huse whirled, his light flashing across the creek. He saw the long body of the snake break water and curl around Cary's thigh; then Cary flung himself on a sandbar, howling insanely, and the snake was a quick, shimmering twist of darkness, fleeing the light beam.

"He bit me!" Cary shrieked. "Oh, help, Huse, he bit me!" Tears streamed down his cheeks; his voice was a thin, hysterical gabble of panic. Huse turned cold himself as his light fell on blood welling from the several punctures in Cary's fleshy calf.

Then something clicked in the helplessness of his mind. Mason Jar. Snakebites happened often in logging the swamp. Mason Jar had seen men treated, and Mason Jar had told him once—

"Do somethin'!" Cary howled. "Run git Jake Lily! Run git Jake Lily!"

"There ain't time," Huse breathed. "Dat a moccasin. You might be dead 'fo I gits back."

"Oh, God! Oh, God! Oh, damn!" Cary shrieked. "Oh, please do somethin', Huse!"

"Hole still," Huse said. His hands were shaking; his throat felt dry; but he was surprised at how strangely calm he was inside, now. He dug in his pocket, and then he was opening the blade of his knife, razor-keen from idle time spent in honing. As Cary saw the steel shining yellow in the flash beam, his sobs trailed off.

"W-what you think you gonna do?" His voice was nearly tearless in that moment.

Huse dropped to his knees. "I goan cut you and suck out de pizen blood."

Cary's scream seemed to spiral out of him. "Nooo! Oh, noo!"

"Hush," Huse said. "You wanta die? Hush. I'll take keer of you. Hole still."

Jake Lily drove like a madman into Treeseville, the nearest town with a doctor. Huse rode beside Cary in the back seat, holding his hand. It was the first time he had ever ridden in an automobile, and despite everything else that knotted his insides, he knew wonder at their plummeting speed through the darkness. Bradham met them at the doctor's house, he and his wife, their faces both white as paper. The doctor unwrapped the leg and laughed.

"That butcher job with the knife and that tourniquet did more damage than the snake." He turned to Huse. "Boy, ain't anybody ever showed you how to tell a poison snakebite from one that isn't?"

"Naw, suh," said Huse, a new fear growing in him.

"Look here, Governor. See that horseshoe circle? That snake didn't strike, just bit, chewed. Nothing but a water snake. Been a cottonmouth, wouldn't be anything but two punctures. Damn good thing this little nigger didn't cut a tendon, though, or your boy might have been in real trouble. As it is, he hacked that leg up bad enough. But he'll be all right in a spell, if we don't get any infection."

"Oh, thank God," Irene Bradham whispered, and she sat down, rubbing her face. Bradham patted her shoulder. Then he turned to Huse. "Boy," he said, "you come with me," and he dragged Huse into the living room. Huse remembered that there was a table with a lamp on it, and the lamp's shade was all stained glass with tassels hanging around its rim. In the lamplight, Bradham's face was shadowed and harsh.

"You know how much damage you might have done to Cary with that knife of yours? You could have crippled him for life."

Huse felt himself beginning to tremble all over, as if he had a chill. Bradham looked at him bleakly, silently, for a moment. Then he said, still harshly, but his tone somehow different, "You tried, didn't you?"

Huse just gaped at him.

"You sucked the blood, even," Bradham said. "Didn't you know if it was poisoned blood and you had a cut in your mouth it might have killed *you?*"

Huse swallowed. "I . . . I jes skeered Cary going to die if I don't do somethin' quick."

Bradham nodded. "All right," he said. "What do you want?"

"Suh?"

"I said, what do you want?" There was impatience in the man's voice. "You thought Cary was dying. You did what you could to save him. You're entitled to some kind of reward. What do you want?"

"Reward? What dat, please, suh?"

"Something you get for doing all you can instead of losing your head and running off to leave Cary where he was." The impatience was stronger now. "Something I'm going to give you for trying to save Cary. What do you want? How about a twenty-two rifle? One like Cary's got."

Huse shook himself in disbelief, like a wet dog. "You—you mean one of them repeatin rifles?"

"Yes," Bradham said. "That's what I mean."

Huse licked his lips. He would never in the world have another chance to get something like that. He thought of the good feel of the gun, the fascinating balance and heft. And I could use it on squirrels, he thought, bring home a big mess of squirrels. . . .

He opened his mouth to say yes and was as startled as Bradham at what came out. "Dat be mighty nice," he heard himself say. "I sho would like one. But if it's all the same to you, Gov'ner, suh, kin I go to school after the cotton's all ginned instead?"

The moment that Bradham stared at him seemed interminable. Then Bradham thrust a hand into his pocket. "All right," he said. He crammed a dollar bill into Huse's hand. "Tell Otis I said it was all right. Use that to buy yourself a slate or whatever it is you need." Then he turned and went into the other room. . . .

Now Houston Whitley touched the water with the boat paddle and propelled the boat farther up the creek. "Watch your head," he

said to Cary. "Look out for snakes on them limbs." He was thinking: I suck your blood out, take it into my mouth. You got to help
me now.

Cary ducked his head beneath a low-hanging branch. "How'd you
know I wanted to go to that pond we used to call our Secret Place?"

"I didn't," Huse said. "But, don't forget, I been away, too. And
I wanted to see it again."

"Sure," Cary said. "Isn't this the place where we used to tie up,
right here?" He leaned forward and looped the anchor rope around
a tree root. Huse turned the boat parallel with the bank and against
it, and Cary stepped out nimbly and gracefully. More slowly, for he
had no one to hold the boat in place for him, Huse followed. Then,
together, they climbed the rest of the way up the bank and struck out
through the woods.

7

The place in the swamp to which they had come was one
the three of them, Cary, Burke, and Huse, had discovered
when they were sixteen. Perhaps others knew it; maybe
hounds ran deer here in the hunting season, or swamp-roving fisher-
men and trappers came; but they had never seen any sign that anyone else knew the place existed, and they had claimed it as their
own by right of discovery and gloated over their possession of it in
their youth.

Here a blowdown of several great trees had dammed a slow stream
in a basin in the swamp. The resulting pond was perhaps four acres
in extent, its water perfectly still and exactly the color of polished jet,
reflecting without ripple the images of the cypresses that grew from
its center and the huge hardwoods that shaded its margin. It was a
place of hush and shadow, the only sound the water pouring steadily
over the use-slickened logs, the only motion the sway of the silver
festoons of moss that streamed from every lodgment. As Cary and
Huse approached it now, a white heron, startled, took flight from a
cypress knee in mid-pond, flapping with slow grace toward the
woods, its purity of plumage crystalline against their darkness.

Cary stood motionless on the pond's edge until the heron had disappeared in the forest, and then he looked at Huse. Huse was staring at the woods as if he could still see the vanished bird, and Cary examined in that moment the intent, brown face. It was beaded with perspiration from the trek through the swamp and it looked faintly melancholy. The hairline was high, the skull capped with dark, tight knots, shining now with moisture. The nose was dipped at the bridge, heavy in the nostrils; the lips were thick. The cheekbones were high, the chin round and strong, the eyes shadowed under jutting brows. In the army Huse had grown a small, black mustache which made him look older than Cary, and which Cary somehow found jarring, as if it were a symbol of all the changes that had taken place in both of them.

And there were changes. He could see that now. Could see it in Huse, and could see it in himself. They had changed enough so that something about the day was a little out of register; they were not completely easy with each other. It must be, he thought, that we've run out of talk. But what can I talk to him about? The army? A little . . . but I was a major, he an enlisted man; I a flyer, he a truck driver; I was in the Pacific, he in the ETO; and I am white and he's a nigger. Only, he thought, it would be all right if it weren't for that last. But that's what does it. That's what throws everything out of kilter. If he were white, he could kid me about being an officer; but he knows that wouldn't go, now. Or we could talk about the times we got drunk and the women we screwed. But I can't talk about screwing white women to him, and he'd sure as hell better not talk about it to me if he's ever done it. So what does that leave us?

He felt vaguely, oddly guilty, and he took out his cigarettes and offered Huse one, as if to temper his distress, expiate his guilt. Huse took the cigarette and they sat down side by side on a big, fallen poplar tree and smoked. Huse was silent, and Cary could not shake off that unclear feeling that he himself was somehow in the wrong, somehow responsible for the reserve they both felt. He made another effort to break through. "Incidentally," he said, thinking of the string of bass and bream in the boat, "you can have my share of the fish if you want 'em."

Huse flipped his cigarette. It arched out and upward and landed in the still, leaf-stained water.

"I'll just take the ones I caught," he said.

"You don't want mine?" Cary frowned. He had always, since that first big catfish on the creek bank, given most of his catch to Houston Whitley, saving only a few for himself, which Huse had always cleaned in return for the gift of the others.

"I appreciate it, but no, thanks. That a pretty good mess I got myself."

"You're welcome to 'em," Cary insisted. It was suddenly somehow important that Huse accept the fish.

"I told you, I got enough of my own."

Cary tried to stifle a twinge of anger at the rebuff. "Okay," he said, his voice shorter than he intended. "Suit yourself. I'll give 'em to Dayton."

"Sure," Huse said. "Dayton'll be glad to get 'em."

Then he stood up, walked to the edge of the water, squatted down and looked at the mud. "Big mink been walkin along here," he said. He knelt there a moment, then straightened and turned.

"I'm sorry," he said softly. "It's only that's more fish than Mama and I can use before they spoil."

Cary relaxed, grinning. "Sure," he said. "You did catch a right good mess yourself." Then his grin faded, as he realized that Huse was tense about something, nervous, rubbing his palms along his khaki pants as if they were very sweaty. He frowned. "Say, what's eating you?"

"Nothin eatin me. It . . . it just that I got to talk to you." Cary saw Huse's tongue run across his lower lip. "I need some help."

Cary laughed, trying to put Huse at his ease. "Sure. What's the matter? I thought you'd only been home ten days. You already got some little old gal knocked up?"

He saw the shadow flicker across Huse's eyes and immediately regretted his joke. But all Huse said was "No. That ain't it."

"Good. Then talk away. I'm listening."

"But I mean," Huse said, "I got to talk to you like two men talkin. Not like a nigger talkin to a white man."

Cary felt a sudden uneasiness. He narrowed his eyes and looked hard at Huse, trying to penetrate the mask of that brown face. What am I going to be dragged into now? he thought. His voice was cautious with an instinctive reserve.

"Sure," he said. "You know you can do that."

Huse drew in a deep breath and let it out and some of the tension seemed to flow away with it. "Yeah," he said. "Yeah, I knew it. I knew that if there was anybody I could talk to like that, it bound to be you." He sat down on the log beside Cary. He seemed relaxed now, almost eager. "I knew you'd help me."

"I will if I can. What's the trouble?"

"It ain't really trouble. It's just that I'm lookin for a job."

Before Cary could answer, he raised his hand, went on swiftly. "Sho, I know there's plenty of jobs. I can get all the work I want. Ditch-diggin, brick-carryin, all the thirty-cents-an-hour common labor I can handle. But that ain't what I want. I'm a high school graduate. I want me a better job than that kind, I want somethin I'm qualified to do. There's lots of things I'm qualified to do, but nobody don't seem to want to let me work at them. God knows, I've tried. But every time I ask for a job that's not a job somebody needs an animal to do, people look at me like I some kind of ha'nt. You can hear their brains turnin—what got into this jigaboo? Who he think he is?"

Still not giving Cary a chance to speak, he rushed on. "What I'm askin for is your help, your and the Governor's help. I've done my four years of fightin for this country, took my chances like any other man. That's all I want to be treated like now, any other man. But it seem like what I've done don't count. How come that? Why don't what I do, what I *can* do, count as much as what anybody else does? Do you see what I mean, what I'm drivin at? It ain't really a job I'm askin you to help me about—it's to prove I didn't throw them four years away for somethin that ain't worth a damn that I'm askin you for."

He stood up, knuckling his hands against his thighs. "Hell, I ain't sayin it right. It ain't comin through. But—"

"Huse," Cary said.

Huse's hands relaxed, the fingers going straight. "Yeah?"

Cary stood up, aware that his heart was sinking. He tasted a bitterness of disappointment in his mouth. Powell Bradham had been right. Something had happened to Huse, a kind of insanity. Still, Huse was Huse and somehow his anguish had to be diminished; his claim for help could not be denied.

"What kind of work you looking for?"

Huse took out a pack of cigarettes. His hand was shaking, he fumbled with the pack, spilled two cigarettes, disregarded them. "It don't matter," he said. "The thing is, it gotta be work that *goes* somewhere, that's all. Work that I can do and hold my head up and know that if I do it right, I'll advance. Truck-driverin, I don't mind that if there's some kind of future. Or office work of some sort. I used to help in the orderly room, I taught myself to type. Either, long as it means somethin. I don't consider myself too good to do day labor. But I don't see any call to waste everythin I've learned, all the schoolin I've had, hard as I had to fight to get it."

"I see." Cary walked to the edge of the lake and looked out at the black water. He could not get over the feeling of shock, the sense of betrayal: Huse had put him in an impossible spot, and, goddammit, Huse should have sense enough to see it.

Still, he kept his voice gentle, controlled. "I've only been home a couple of days," he said. "But this is still Muskogee, you know."

"I know. I born and raised here same as you. It my state, too. All I want is—"

"I know what you want." Still Cary's voice was even. And still he did not turn to look at Huse, but stared out across the water. "Have you been to see any of the colored businessmen? Merit Crane and people like that? Have you talked to them?"

"No," said Huse.

"Why not?" Cary let an edge creep into his voice now. "Why ask me for help before you ask your own people?"

He heard Huse's rasping breath behind him. "Forget it," Huse said bitterly.

"No." Cary turned. "No, I won't forget it. We're friends. We always have been. You come to me saying you need help. Then it's up to me to do what I can for you. I'll help you all I can. But there's no use beating around the bush. You know goddam good and well what a problem it is. The place to try for a job like you want is with your own people."

"No," said Huse. "It wouldn't mean anythin then."

Cary frowned. "Damn, you're hard to get along with. I don't see what you're driving at."

"I didn't think—" Huse said wearily. "Oh, shit, forget it."

"I just told you I wasn't going to." Cary felt as if he were caught up in some farce beyond his imagining. Why, Huse is crazy, he thought; he's just plain crazy. What am I going to do with this crazy nigger? How am I going to keep from hurting his feelings, making him mad at me? What a hell of a spot to put me in. . . .

"Look," he went on. "Teaching. You could get a teacher's certificate. Hell, that's no problem. Dad can arrange for you to get one without even working up a sweat. It'll be grammar school, I think you've got to have college for high school, but, hell—"

"Me, Houston Whitley. Teachin second grade. That'd look pretty, wouldn't it?"

"Goddam, what do you want, then? I can't figure it out. Hell, go on to college under the GI Bill. Then you can get a high school certificate. You might even be able to get a job at Wheatley-Tubman."

Huse nodded. "Well, we've used up about all the opportunities right there, haven't we? Still, it doesn't mean anythin."

"You aren't making sense."

"I reckon not." Huse's voice turned brittle and sarcastic. "Lo, the poor nigger. The poor educated nigger in Muskogee. He's got three choices. He can go in business for himself, he can work for another nigger, or he can teach niggers. That's it and that's all of it, isn't it?"

"It sounds like enough to me," Cary said harshly. "What do you want, egg in your beer?"

"No," Huse said, and his dark eyes were unreadable. "All I was lookin for was a vote of confidence."

"A vote of confidence? What the hell do you mean?"

"In me," Huse said. "That I'm a man. In my state. That it's a state. In my country. That it's a country. And in my friend, that he's a friend." He tossed his cigarette butt into the lake. "No vote. Okay, well, it was a good try."

"You know I'm your friend," Cary snapped, "but there's some things I can do and some I can't, and you know that, too; and because I am your friend, I'm going to tell you something, Huse. You can talk to me the way you have and get away with it, but for God's sake don't try it with anybody else; you'd only make more trouble for yourself than you could handle." He squatted, not looking at Huse, picked up a stick and broke it in two.

"What you've been trying to tell me," he went on, "is that you won't be satisfied with anything less than a white man's job. And you know yourself that if I were God Almighty, I couldn't get you one."

He still was not looking at Huse, and there was a silence, and he had no idea how Huse was responding.

Then Huse's voice came, and there was contrition in it. "I'm sorry," Huse said. "I didn't go for to put you on the spot."

"It's okay," Cary said, raising his eyes now. "It's just how things are, you know that."

"Yeah, I guess so. I reckon I just lost sight of the fact that even you ain't all-powerful. You know . . . I used to think you were, a long time back, when we were kids."

"Crap," Cary said hoarsely.

"No, I mean it. And I appreciate your listenin now and bein so nice. I— Hell, I'm kind of upset. Seems like all my nerves laid open, everythin touches against me hurts. Things were bad enough in the army, plenty of trouble a colored man could get himself into. But in a way, it freer, too; at least, there, I know I considered an American, part of somethin, a man good enough for his country to want him. Only, seems like since I come home, I ain't anythin, not a man, not nothin. I reckon it drive me a little bit nuts."

"I know what you're up against," Cary said, standing. The humility, the contrition, in Huse's voice had touched him, had erased his anger and confusion at Huse's demandingness. He felt in control of the situation again, and now he could afford to commit himself.

"Look," he said, "let me tell you what I'll do. I'll talk to Dad about it. I know we can get you something in the state government. It may not be exactly what you want, but it'll be better than common labor. I can promise you that much."

Huse was silent for a moment, but Cary saw a flicker in his eyes that could have been hope. "All right," Huse said finally, and then he smiled briefly and some of the warmth came back into his face. Then he was sober again. "I'd sure appreciate it if you would. I might just as well do like you said. Come down off my high horse and face real life."

"Sure," Cary said. "Now you're talking sense."

"Yeah," said Huse. "Hell, I got to have a job. I—I got to start gettin along better. I ain't doin myself no good this way."

"I wouldn't lie to you," Cary said, "you sure ain't. But don't worry, I'll talk to Dad and we'll get you something." He relaxed; it was as if a thunderstorm had rolled up, then receded without unloosing rain or lightning. "Come on, we've got to get started back."

"Yeah," Huse said, "I reckon so." Then he grinned more widely, and his face lit with a radiance that meant he was all right now. In a different voice he said, "What you want to bet we already got a water moccasin in the boat after them fish?"

"I wouldn't be surprised," said Cary.

As it turned out, Huse was right; a thick, gray snake had crawled into the boat. It tried to slither away when they approached, but Cary shot its head off with the .22 pistol he carried in his belt.

8

Huse swung off the bus at the end of the line, dismounting from the front, ignoring Bobo Merchant's startled, angry curse. This time he did not go into Bish's funeral parlor, but struck off directly down through Little Hammer. The sun was setting: a rank, gray mist already hovered in the low ground along Molasses Creek. Huse's legs moved out in long strides, and within him so many conflicting emotions churned that he could hardly sort them out. There was anger and shame that he had asked Cary for help at all, that it had been necessary; there was guilt and remorse for putting Cary on the spot; there was disgust at his own naïveté in believing that Cary would have some magic answer for him, that Cary was still the all-powerful God who could work miracles; and there was a dreary feeling of hopelessness that bore down on him like a great weight lashed to his shoulders. A small colored girl, not over twelve, stared at him wide-eyed as he approached her where she leaned against a rickety picket fence around a yard. He thrust out the newspaper-wrapped fish. "Here. Take these into yo' mama." Then he strode on.

He came to a side street, turned, mounted a hill; at its crest he emerged onto paving, a street that had been blacktopped once long ago, eroded now into worse holes than the sandclay down in the hollow. The street was lined with rows of honky-tonks, hole-in-the-wall stores, billiard parlors. Saturday night was just getting under way: already the broken concrete sidewalks were clustered with loafing men, the week's hard work behind them, seeking relief now from the tensions of grinding labor, of dirty or dangerous jobs in places no white man would go; relief from too much family and too little money and hope that went no further than to next payday. These tensions had already built to exploding point within them; a little money handy now, they clustered in groups, some laughing, some arguing already in irascibility that might, before night's end, build to rage, assault, or murder; others simply stood and frankly admired the girls in tight dresses who switched with considered effect and much motion of the rump back and forth along the district. The racket from a dozen jukeboxes whanged out into the thickening dusk, raw and jungly in its beat, inviting, arousing, jarring the blood in its channels.

Huse strode past Bittner's Grocery, the signs on the windows registering subconsciously: PIG TAILS . . . SPECSHUL JUST IN—TURKEY NECKS. On the other side of it was a red-fronted building with dusty, barred windows. Its sign read: HAPPINESS CLUB. DRINK COCA-COLA. He pushed open the screen door and came into noisy dimness. Men clustered at a short bar without stools; couples and foursomes sat at the few tables and chairs; a squat, gaudy monster of a jukebox bubbled neon through its varicolored arteries at the rear. The room was funky with smells of malt, urine, fried onions, fried fish, unwashed bodies and cheap perfume layered over sweat. Huse shoved up to the counter, his clamoring nerves crying for unstringing, and waited until the man came. "Gimme a pint, Tarzan."

"Yaiah," said the moonfaced owner of the bar, "come on back," and then to his assistant, "watch things, Romer." Huse followed him to a dark, narrow cubicle in the rear piled high with beer crates. Tarzan fished behind a pile of crates, said, "Fo' dollars is the price now," and held the pint bottle of blended whiskey until Huse paid him. Huse shoved the bottle into his shirt and returned to the front. He sat down at a vacant table in a corner and Romer brought him a glass of water.

He drank surreptitiously from the pint, chased it with water, and shoved the bottle back under his shirt. As he fastened the buttons, a very dark girl, body overblown in a too-tight dress, detached herself from the bar and came toward him. "Ain't you Huse Whitley? Don't you remember me? I Bessie McCall."

"Yeah, Bessie," he said tonelessly and without invitation. He ran his eyes over the sagging twin pillows of breasts, the wide hips, the bare, scratched legs. She had a scab on one shin.

There was a hunger in her eyes. "I talk you outa a drink?" She pulled out a chair. "Sweet Jesus, I sho could use one."

Huse felt a pang of pity for her. "Okay," he said, and he shoved the water toward her. She sat down spraddle-legged, cowlike, and he gave her the pint. She bent, shielding it with her body, and drank long and deeply and sighed and did not bother with the water. Huse rubbed the neck of the pint and drank himself and put it back in his shirt.

"I ain't seed you since we moved away from Berry Street," she said. "Where at you been so long, in de army?"

"Yeah."

Her smile was a fixed, mechanical grimace. Her eyes still showed that craving. "Dat pint ain't goin last very long. Whyn't you buy another? You and me kin have some fun tonight."

Huse looked at her through the blur of whiskey, and even with the alcohol working at his loins, he did not want her. "Maybe later," he said. "Right now, I'd just as soon—" Before he could finish, somebody leaned over Bessie from behind and cupped her breasts in slender, long-fingered hands.

"Hello, sugarlump. You got somethin for me?" A narrow, bulging-eyed young face grinned across her shoulder at Huse. "Well, bubba, you finally decide to cut loose an' act like a natchal man?"

Robert. Like his mother, he was long, thin, and with something graceful, almost elegant, in the way he moved. His yellow polo shirt was open at the throat, his faded blue jeans hugged skinny hips; his thick black hair was marcelled back with grease. Huse saw that he was already a little drunk.

Bessie smiled. "Sho, baby. I always got sumpin for you. You got sumpin for me?"

"Mo'n you'll ever be able to handle," Robert crooned. Then his face changed. "Hit de road, sugar; I'll dig you later. I ain't seen my big brudder for nigh a week."

Bessie pushed his hands away from her breasts. "Don't you go tellin—"

Robert straightened up and looked down at her. Huse thought of the head of a mink or a weasel, something slim and deadly. "I say run along."

Bessie's smirk washed away in fear. She shoved back her chair and got up. As she did so, five men, all young, all varying shades of color, came up and ringed the table. They were stamped from the same mold as Robert, with a delicate, swaggering grace in the way they held themselves, with something lurking and dangerous in their eyes, something bitter, disgusted, and obscene in the sets of their mouths. Huse vaguely knew most of them.

One of them set an open bottle of beer in front of Robert, and they greeted Huse. He answered them. "Howdy, Fish, Lloyd, Billy-Bill; how you doin, Ham? How you come on, Rucker?"

Robert did not even look behind him. "You mullifuckers go on," he said. "I be with you in a minute. Wanta talk to my ole big bubba here."

They were his henchmen, his liegemen. "Sho. We be over at the bar." They faded away obediently and in a cloud of raucous obscenities among themselves. When they had gone, Huse looked at his younger brother, who was smiling at him with that same half-lewd, half-contemptuous twist to his mouth that the others had worn. Then Huse dropped his eyes. He could not seem to make any connection in his mind between this snaky-looking, greasy-haired young man and the short, pot-bellied, moonfaced little brother who had huddled close to him in the wagon in the rain, crying because there had been nothing to eat all day. There seemed to be no link between this Robert and the little boy in the cotton fields of their fourteen acres at The Place, too young to chop or pick, but old enough to run and fetch, hurrying through the rows in lurching, short-legged baby strides, carrying dippers of water and spilling half of every one, laughing, working as hard as he could, trying to be as big as anybody in the field, but crumpled and leaden-eyed with weariness when he rode toward the house at sundown on Otis's shoulders or in Otis's arms. . . .

And what Robert had become was Huse's guilt, too, he told himself, part of it, like the death of his father. He could not bear the thought and tried to thrust it away from him.

Robert tilted back the beer bottle and drained half of it at a gulp. He wiped his mouth with the back of his hand and set the bottle down. "Man, dat good. Well, bubba, you been might sca'ce lately."

"You the one been scarce. Mama worried about you. You *supposed* to be stayin there, you know. Where you been sleepin? In jail?"

Robert whinnied. "Where I sleep? Where you think I sleep? Wid sumpin warm and soft, dat where I sleep."

He leaned forward, the lewd grin widening, his eyelids half covering his huge, veined eyes; and Huse thought for a moment of the frogs he and Cary used to gig. "I kin git you some stuff that's good and warm, too, ole bubba. I mean reel stuff, not like that used-up ole whore back yonder. I bet you ain't had none whole time you been home. Why don't you lemme fix you up? I know a lil ole gal got a thang just like velvet, best poontang you ever had. Whuffo you wanta hang around here like a chicken wid de pip? Go along wid us, have a good time. You dry up and blow away, you don't git your nooky."

Huse stared at his younger brother, feeling oddly repelled, disheartened—and fascinated. Robert's words had struck a response in his loins, had touched a need that was, in part, at the core of his inner tenseness.

"I mean, maybe it ain't like them white gals you bang in Yurrop," Robert went on softly, with a twist of that obscene grin and a wink of a bulging eye. "But it good."

"Who say anythin about white gals?" Huse's voice was hushed, but fierce. "You better quit that talk."

"Sho. But how was it? It like they say?"

Huse stared down at his hands, knuckled into fists on the table. His fingers opened and closed as certain memories stabbed at him. After having been accepted that way, entering the most portentous, deadly mystery of a black man's existence and finding that there was no mystery, that there was only two people together, like any two people . . . No wonder I ain't the same man, he thought. No wonder I don't know what I want. He raised his eyes, talking as much to blank out recollection as out of curiosity. "This gal you speakin of—how far she from here?"

"You ain't answered my question," Robert breathed.

"Naw."

Robert's grin faded in disappointment. "You mean you never—?"

"I mean I ain't goin to answer your question. You think I a damned fool?"

Robert leaned back in his chair and narrowed his eyes. "I don't know what you are," he said with an edge to his voice. "A man like you dat got to do ever'thin de hard way. I don't see de army lightened you up any. Whyn't you relax an' have some fun? You an' Bish both, you two crazy. Bish grabblin for all de money he can git, you lookin for whatever you lookin for, both you thinkin you find somethin that make you free, free like a white man." His mouth curled at the corner. "Shit," he said. "Nobody mo' free dan me. Man, you talk about freedom, I got it locked. You learn to slide wid it, quit fightin it, you got it locked, too. I mean, say you and I both git in trouble. Ole man Bradham, he git me off like dat." He snapped his fingers. "He say, sure; dat Robert ain't nothin but a nigger, what you expect from him? You? He say, let Huse Whitley rot in jail. He educated, he uppity, got pree-tensions; he ought to know better and it teach him a lesson."

Robert leaned forward. "Ain't you see? Blacker you are, mo' freedom you got. Nobody expect nothin from you, you ain't got to do nothin, give nobody nothin. You ain't bound, nowhere, nohow. Stay clear of de white man, walk wide around him, and when you meet him, be all nigger. Den you got reel freedom."

Huse just looked at him, surprised by Robert's perception. Everybody, he thought. Everybody say I'm crazy, going at everything bassackwards. Blalock, Bish, Cary, now Robert—everybody. Maybe they're right. Maybe I am. Goddammit, I'm so tired of thinking. . . .

As if reading his mind, Robert touched his hand. "You come on wid me. That little ole gal make you forget everythin. Come on wid me and de boys—we fix you up first-class."

Huse rubbed the bottle under his shirt. Robert waited, mouth twisted, eyes unblinking. Then Huse felt the taut muscles in his back and over his kidneys relax, the strain go out of him. All right, he thought. I ain't forgot how to be a nigger, either. He stood up. "Let's roll," he said. "I'm long overdue."

So that later there were seven of them ambling down the sidewalk, loud and profane with the first effects of the half-gallon jug of popskull whiskey they had bought. Robert carried it openly under his arm, wrapped only in paper; no law came into Little Hammer unless for a serious cutting or shooting.

Huse had not drunk any of the poisonous popskull; and he had only a couple of drinks of his pint of blended whiskey in his belly. Nevertheless, he felt a peculiar intoxication of his own. The early evening was warm, soft; the dusk intimate and exciting, full of promise. The whanging of jukeboxes spouting race music and jive—their beat stirred his blood. So, too, did the way people moved aside for the group of seven as they plowed along, fiercely arrogant and mindlessly dangerous as so many young bulls. The air was weighted with smells of street dust and supper woodsmoke; frying pork and backyard privies; Molasses Creek and the poignancy of honeysuckle blooming in vacant lots. Huse heard himself singing, not loudly, a bawdy song he had not thought of in a long time:

> Honey, turn your lamp down low,
> Honey, turn your lamp down low,
> If the bed breaks down, we'll finish on the flo'.
> Honey, turn your lamp down low.

Robert chortled. "Man, you jest don't know. This little ole gal, time she git a few drinks of moon, she can really turn it on."

" 'At's what I want," Huse said exuberantly. "Somebody can really turn it on." Maybe Robert's right, he thought; maybe he's had the answer all along. Maybe I ought to quit fighting it, slide with it. Then I'd have it locked. . . .

They were out of the honky-tonk section now; along here there were only rows of tired houses. The sidewalk was a rubble of up-ended slabs, ancient and broken; and there were no streetlights. "You look out, Robbut," somebody said. "Don't you fall an' break dat jug."

Robert laughed. "Don't you worry 'bout me an' de jug. You jest—" At that exact moment he tripped and stumbled. Only Huse's quick grip on his arm kept him from falling on his face.

"Hell," Robert said, regaining his balance. "Wouldn't be surprised if I was drunk. I—" Then he shook off Huse's hand. "Hey," he said. "Look ayonder."

It was not quite full dark, and there was still light enough to see the automobile parked at the curb twenty feet away, and to see the girl in it. Robert drew in a long, slow breath. "Man, man, man," he whispered. "You talk about poontang. Dere's *some* more of it."

The car, a 1939 Cadillac roadster, was parked beside a mailbox. The girl behind the wheel was pressing again and again at its starter; and Huse could hear the dry clicks that were her only reward.

At first Huse thought the girl was white. Then he realized that was not possible—not down here in Little Hammer at this time of night. But, in the velvet twilight, her dress was pale and so were her face and throat and bare arms. As she raised her head for a moment, lips pursed in exasperation, he caught a glimpse of her features in the glow of the dashlight; and his breath hung in his throat. My God, he thought; she's beautiful.

Her attention totally on the car, she shook her head furiously, slamming her foot down violently. Robert chuckled softly. "Here.

Hole onto dis jug." Before Huse could move, Robert had pressed the paper-wrapped jar into his hands and was gliding forward with the silent, predatory grace of a hunting cat. The girl was completely unaware of him until he reached the side of the car. Then she made a quick, inchoate sound of fright and jerked up straight in the seat as his face appeared from nowhere, and his voice said silkily, "Sugar, you havin trouble wid your thing? I jest the man can fix yo' thing for you."

Watching the surprise and terror that crossed her face, Huse acted without thinking. He set down the jar and moved across the broken sidewalk quickly, reaching the car in four strides. Behind him he heard a rising murmur of obscene glee and the shuffle of feet as the others followed him.

Seeing him come, the girl looked from him to Robert and then at the others, her eyes wide, showing white in the darkness. Her hand went to her throat. "Please," she said. Robert was reaching for her chin with his hand. "Please . . ."

"Sugar," Robert said. "You and me—"

Huse looked from the girl to Robert, and something roiled in his belly: disgust with his brother and himself. Then anger, and he stepped forward, his hand clamping on Robert's shoulder. He pulled back, not gently. "Look out, Robert," he snapped.

Robert turned, frog-eyes bulging. "Goddam, look out, your own self—" Then Huse moved between him and the girl.

She had a Caucasian's face, all right. Her nose was straight, small of nostril and perfectly chiseled. Her mouth was delicate, red against the paleness of her face. A white woman's mouth, Huse thought. But she can't be white. No white woman would come down in here unless she crazy. Her hair was the deep black of moonless night, but not coarse; it fell in soft curls about her face and neck. He saw small, rounded breasts pushing the white sharkskin of a summer dress that had not come from any secondhand store. He fought down an impulse to try the same thing Robert had—to reach out and touch her. Instead he made his voice as gentle, as reassuring, as he could.

"You having trouble with your car?"

He was pleased that some of the fear ebbed from her face. "Yes. I mean . . . I don't know what's wrong." There was no Negro intonation to her voice, hardly any ordinary Southern accent, even. "I just stopped to mail some letters for my father and I cut off the en-

gine and when I got back in, it wouldn't start. All I get is this click."
She pressed the starter.

Robert's face had changed now; he was grinning at Huse with admiration for his brother's smooth approach. Huse did not look at
him. "I expect your starter's hung. Move over." He opened the car
door, and, a little to his surprise, she slid to the far side of the seat.

He dropped behind the wheel, turned the key in the switch. He
was acutely aware of a subtle fragrance that must have been her
perfume.

"Dat de way to go, man," Robert said, still grinning.

Huse looked up at him without expression. "Rock the car," he
said.

The others looked at Robert, waiting for confirmation of the order. Robert stared at Huse, waiting for Huse to wink, to grin, to give
some sign. When nothing came, his own grin faded.

He turned to his men. "Sho," he said, his voice harsh. "You heerd
de man, boys. Shake it up."

The others ranged themselves about the car immediately, bore
hard on the fenders, and began to jump up and down. The car swayed
wildly from side to side. The girl grasped the door with one hand;
and Huse felt the sharpness of her nails as she seized his arm with
the other.

Robert laughed again, an ugly sound in the darkness.

"Harder!" he rasped.

Now the wheels came off the ground and dropped back hard. The
girl made a choked sound of fright. "Cut it out!" Huse rapped. "Stop
it!" But his words were lost in the whooping and laughing, and the
car teetered dangerously, almost going over.

"Rock it!" Robert squealed. "Swing it, shake it, but please don't
break it!"

Simultaneously, Huse thought he heard a tiny click of sound from
somewhere in the engine. He pressed the starter down hard. Suddenly the engine roared into life. But the wild swaying went on until
Robert bellowed above the laughter and the motor noise, "Hold it!
Wait a minnit! It goin now." His giggle was shrill. "Ever'body pile
in!" he yelled. "Us all take a ride!"

There was a scramble for the automobile. Huse rammed the gear
shift into low; his foot crushed the accelerator. The back tires
squealed as the car shot away from the curb. He knew a grim satis-

faction as he heard a yell of fright. "Hey! Look out!" Then they were out in the middle of the street, away clean, cool air rushing about them.

The raucous curses and yelling faded behind them. Huse looked at the girl. She sat straight, wide-eyed and tense, wind ruffling silky black hair. He slacked his speed. Was she really as lovely as she looked? And what was she, anyway—octoroon? No, less than that. White—but not quite white.

"I'm sorry," he said harshly, shame touching him that she had to be rescued from his own brother; maybe even from himself if he'd had a few drinks more. He felt dirty. "Don't be afraid, though. I'm not going to kidnap you. I just want to get you clear of them."

"I'm not afraid," she said, and then she smiled. "Thanks. Thanks a whole lot."

He turned the car toward town, anxious to get where there were streetlights and see her in their glow. "My name's Houston Whitley," he said.

"How do you do, Mr. Whitley." Her polite tone was almost ludicrous after the stress of the moments before. "I'm Virginia Crane."

Huse looked at her, startled. "You any kin to Merit Crane?"

"He's my father."

Then Huse understood.

Merit Crane was white, too, only not quite white. His mother had been an octoroon who had worked for Hartley Temple, of the old family that once had owned nearly half of Hannington. Every native of Hannington knew Merit Crane's story, knew that Temple could not acknowledge Merit Crane as his son in public, but, in private, had treated him as one. Crane had received his share of Temple's estate, exactly as Temple's four legitimate children had. Moreover, Crane's half brothers, rather than having repudiated him, seemed almost proud of him, as if he were a tribute to their father's lustiness; Crane could turn to them as sources of capital unobtainable by any other Negro in Hannington. The drops of Negro blood that left hardly any stain at all in his skin had locked him into the colored community of Hannington as if into a prison; but they had not kept him from pyramiding his original inheritance and becoming one of the city's wealthiest men. In addition, because of his unique and impeccable connections on both sides of the color line, he had inherited the position of official spokesman and go-between for the

Negroes of Hannington in their dealings with the white municipal government. Huse stared at Virginia Crane. "What's your daddy doing letting you come down in Little Hammer at night like this?"

She laughed; and he liked the sound of it. "He'd have a spasm if he knew. I took some letters to mail for him this morning and forgot to do it. I just remembered them a little while ago on the way home from Wheatley-Tubman and stopped at the nearest mailbox." She paused. Her voice was earnest when she said, "Thank you again for your help. It's the first time I . . . I've ever had any trouble like that. Usually people let me alone."

Of course they do, Huse thought. Because they think you're white. Nobody would know any different unless you told 'em or unless they saw you in a place like Little Hammer. . . . He hoped she couldn't smell the whiskey on his breath. "It's all right," he said; and he pulled the car over to the curb. They were under a streetlight now; and he looked at her in its brightness and saw that her beauty had diminished not a whit; she was indeed the loveliest woman he had ever seen. He was aware of an odd tightness in his throat, a growing tension in his body. He said, a little hesitantly, "Don't you think I'd better be your chauffeur and drive you home? You wouldn't want the engine to choke down and have that starter to hang up again by yourself."

Her dark brows, sharp as crayon marks against skin that was not even swarthy, drew together slightly. Then she smiled. Her teeth were small and white. "That would be kind of you," she said quietly. "Do you know where I live?"

"Yes, ma'am. You live over in Princeton."

"That's right." Then, as if she had been looking at him appraisingly too, she said, touching the stripes on his sleeve, "Oh, you're in the army."

"No, ma'am. Just got discharged. Just got back from overseas. Europe." He said it with pride, aware that he was cleaning up his own speech, pronouncing his words more crisply and using the correct grammar that Lizzie Blackwelder had drummed into his head in the country school so long ago.

"Europe." There was a yearning in her voice. "When I was a little girl, my father promised he'd take us there someday. I don't reckon we'll ever go, now. But things—people—they're different in Europe, aren't they? I mean, in places like England and France."

"Yes," Huse said, knowing exactly what she meant. "They're different."

She looked down at her hands, folded in her lap. "Hannington's such an awful place. So . . . so provincial." It was as if she were testing him with the last word.

"Yes," he said smoothly. "It's provincial. It's insular."

She raised her eyes and looked at him with heightened interest. He pressed the advantage. "Europe's nicer even than New York. Have you ever been to New York?"

"No. No, I've never been there." She seemed to look past him, at something beyond him, as if she could see all the way to New York. "But I'm going there someday," she said. For that one phrase, her voice had an oddly metallic ring; it stirred something within him strangely. Then, in an ordinary tone, she said, "But I've got to finish school here, first."

"You're at Wheatley-Tubman?"

"Yes. I'm majoring in dramatics."

"I didn't know they taught that there."

"It's not much," she said with a trace of bitterness, "believe me. But it's the best I can do." Again her voice changed. "Are you planning to go to college?"

Huse hesitated. "I don't know," he said. The last thing he wanted to do was talk about his future. It was too unsettled, too chaotic. He shifted gears. "I haven't thought too much about it one way or another." Then he put the car in motion.

Princeton lay on the far side of Hannington, widely separated from Little Hammer by more than the breadth of a city, though it was a Negro district too. It was where the Negro businessmen lived —the really prosperous ones—and the professors and administrators of Wheatley-Tubman College. To Houston Whitley, it was a part of town as unknown as any of the white residential districts; he had passed through it, but he had never been in a house there. Now he took his time about driving across town, in no hurry to have Virginia Crane vanish into a place where he could not follow. She did not seem in any hurry to get home, either. As they talked—about trivial things; since, for instance, there was only one Negro high school in Hannington, they knew the same teachers—Huse began to sense in the girl a loneliness, a confusion, that matched his own. He listened to her with part of his mind, while the rest sketched in the dimensions of her problem. Slowly he began to realize the pathos of it, to understand what it must be like to exist in a limbo like the one she inhabited. She was too white to be Negro, and yet that faint dilution of her blood made her, at least here in Hannington, as much Negro as if her skin were inky black, her nose flat, her lips thick and her hair nappy. Her father's money counted for nothing; her own loveliness and grace counted for nothing—not even the paleness of her skin—so that though most of her heritage was white, she could claim none of the privileges or benefits of it, must play Negro, be Negro, without looking Negro or, he guessed, even feeling Negro. The dimensions of the trap in which she was caught made his own frustrations seem negligible; and he was ashamed. But he was glad, too; for if she had not been trapped, she would have been completely beyond his reach.

She was saying, he became aware, that she wanted to be an actress.

"Like Lena Horne," he suggested automatically.

"No, not like Lena Horne. I mean, she's a singer, mainly. I want to be a real actress, someone who can—" She broke off. "Turn here," she said.

They were entering Princeton now. The houses along here, mostly single-story, were brick or neatly painted frame. Though there was wealth here comparable to the wealth on Mercy Street—in a few instances, at least—these houses had been carefully, diplomatically, scaled not to flaunt any unallowable pretentions. Their lots were not wide, and the place had the look of one of the less prosperous middle-class white residential areas. If there was any ostentation at all, it was in the precision with which the lawns were tended, the profusion of lawn furniture, and, most of all, in the large, powerful and shiny automobiles that sat in every driveway. Huse noticed that these were free of the flapping mudguards, chrome dazzles, flags, foxtails, and other ornamentation lavished on their vehicles by the Negroes in Little Hammer.

"Anyway," Virginia Crane said, after a moment, "I don't think my ambitions are very interesting."

A kind of desperation grew in Houston Whitley. In a few moments she would be home, and then he might have lost her forever; and suddenly he could not bear the thought of that. He heard words tumbling out of his mouth, anxious and unpremeditated.

"They are to me. Listen, Miss Crane—Virginia—I know I look like something the cat dragged in. That's because I've been fishing all day with a white friend of mine, Cary Bradham—he's the son of Powell Bradham, used to be Governor of this state." He used the names desperately, ruthlessly, and saw that she was impressed. "I haven't had a chance to clean up. And those . . . those rowdies I was with. I just bumped into them on my way home." I hope you never find out he was my brother, he thought; because you have got to know I am not his kind. You have got to know I'm not ordinary, not just another nigger. "Look. I'd like to see you again. May I? Please?"

She was silent for a moment. His palms were sweating, making the steering wheel slippery. Then she said, "Up there where the light's burning on the porch. That's where I live. You can stop here and I'll drive the rest of the way."

"Let me see you to your door," Huse said urgently.

"No. No, thank you. Please, stop here and let me have the wheel."

"Yes, ma'am." Huse felt everything within him seem to crumple. He pulled over to the curb, shifted into neutral, and got out.

Virginia Crane slid behind the wheel and leaned on the door. "How will you get home?"

"I'll ride a bus. I don't mind."

She nodded. "Thank you again." She shifted gears, but she did not let out the clutch pedal. In the tiny glow of the dash light, her face was thoughtful. Then she smiled, and Huse tensed and held his breath.

"We're having a drama workshop at Wheatley-Tubman," she said. "In the auditorium, every night, from eight to ten for the next month. It's open to anybody interested in the drama. Maybe you'd like to attend. I'm there every night, except Saturdays and Sundays, of course."

"I—I've never done any acting," he heard himself say foolishly.

She was still smiling; and the smile touched her voice. "That doesn't matter. You can help with the scenery. Monday night, eight o'clock?"

Huse swallowed. "I'll be there," he said thickly.

"I'm glad," she said. "It's lots of fun. Good night, Mr. Whitley." Then the car eased forward. He stood where he was, at the side of the road, watching the red eyes of its tail lights recede, pause, then turn. He saw her enter a driveway five houses down; a floodlight came on; the car door and a screen door slammed; there were voices. Then the floodlight went off. Blinking in the darkness, Huse turned and walked slowly to the corner. He had to wait a long time before an incoming bus stopped to pick him up, but he had lost track of time; all he could do was marvel at how quickly his world had changed.

9 As she always did, Lucy Whitley awakened this morning before first light. She could remember days when getting up had been a hard thing: cold mornings and a weary body craving more warmth and sleep than it could ever get. But it was easy now, for she slept lightly and restlessly. Old age. Funny, she thought, opening her eyes in the dark room, how things swing 'round. When you little, you got so much juice you can't stay down nohow; then you growed and have to arise, and hate to do it; then get old and rest won't come and don't last. So in a whole life, never a time when you can lay abed.

She did not move for a while, but lay there with her eyes closed, listening to the shrill crow and answer of the neighborhood chickens. That Fate Harrison's big ole Plymouth rock, she thought, recognizing the roosters by their voices. And that there Sis Lo Porter's lil ole banty. She liked the ringing sound of roosters at first day; it was a country sound that brought back old times. Her hand moved across the bed, over the lumpy, tenantless mattress; and she felt a sadness not yet burned out, a grieving. Ten years, she thought, and I ain't got used to not finding him there yet.

But she did not want to remember the day they had brought home the news that Otis had been taken to the funeral parlor. When she had gone to see him, there hadn't been a mark on him—the dirt hadn't crushed him when the pipeline ditch bank caved in, had just suffocated him. Fred Mitchell, who had been working alongside Otis and had barely missed the same fate, had told her about it in a dull voice. *Nobody got any business down in dat ditch after all dat rain. But ole Sam Deal, he make us go down in dere anyhow. He say*

*when he chain-gang guard he don't let no niggers loaf, he ain't goin
to now he work for de city either. So we go on in, wid it still drizzlin
and like workin in a swamp. Otis, he talk as he work. Tell me he miss
de country mighty bad, miss his ole mule he have to sell off when
y'all move. But he say it worth it, long as it make his sons better off.
Ole Sam Deal, he come over and stand on de edge of de bank, tell us
cut out de talkin and work. Bank start to cave, he jump back, I look
up, next thing I know, fifteen feet dat red clay comin down on us,
heavy wid water. No time to grab Otis, I jump. I see Otis turn round,
raise he shovel like he fixin to push all dat dirt back. Den it on top
of him, a mountain. It so gummy it take a long time to dig him out
and he dead when we git to him. Dat Sam Deal ain't a bit upset;
when we lay Otis bare, he jest look down at him and say, calm as if
he in church, Well, we done killed us a nigger. . . .*

You start thinkin them upsettin thoughts, Lucy warned herself,
and your nervous stomach goin to start actin up again. With resolution, she threw back the cover and began the task of making joints
respond to her will. All this stiffness another sign of age, she thought.
Time useta be I could chop cotton all day, pat my foot all night at a
jamboree, and never even feel it in the mornin.

Groping in the dimness, she found the kerosene lamp and conjured a pool of yellow light from it. There was some talk of bringing
electricity in down here. Y'all needn't bother yo'selves about that,
she thought. It too costly. Time you buy all them light bulbsies and
burn 'em, run them electric thingamabobs, goin to have to pay three,
four dollars a month just to that light company. Don't need nothing
else us *got* to pay. . . . Because she had been with the Bradhams so
long, she made seventeen dollars a week. That was five dollars more
than the going weekly wage for cooks.

After she had used the slop jar under her bed, she took the lamp,
went into the kitchen, shook the coffeepot, found it nearly full from
last night, and lit the burner beneath it. When the reheated coffee
sang in the pot, she poured a cup and sat down at the table. She
never ate breakfast any more; seemed like it made her stomach cut
up so bad nowadays. But the coffee was good and strong, heavy with
chicory. Outside, more roosters were raising their voices, and they
made her think of the country.

Them had been hard days out there, but look at it one way, they
hadn't been real bad. In the country there was more room and sun-

light, and not so much bad goings-on. That was what had shocked her and Otis both when they had moved to Little Hammer. Not only the way people were jammed up in here, but the just plain sinful, don't-care nasty dirtiness of so many of them. Not that there weren't good people, too, but—

She smiled at herself. Listen at ole homesick you, she thought sardonically. How long you last if they put you back in a cotton field now? You better thank de good Lawd you got dat nice, easy job in that pretty kitchen in that pretty house with all them pretty things. Sho, you had troubles since you come to town, but there trouble in the country, too. Man is born to trouble, no matter where he go, ain't that what the Good Book say? She sipped her coffee.

Farmin cotton such hard work anyhow. Bad enough makin it grow, worse pickin it. The bolls all seemed to spring open at just the wrong height, you couldn't stand up, couldn't bend over, had to keep your back just so all day. The sharp husks gouged at your fingers and after a while your hands were raw from them, and your back achin like a bad tooth, and the sun caught up there in the sky like it had forgotten how to come down.

And the whole time, you worried and helpless. Earth, air, sky and water—they could wipe you out whenever they pleased. Too much rain, not enough; boll weevil; hail; all you could do was work and trust in God's mercy.

Even if you made cotton, you were still helpless. The price could drop, and then you wound up in debt with no smidgen of cash money to carry you through winter. Or if the price was good, you couldn't seem to get straight with the landlord's books—how many times had she heard Otis come stomping in at settling-up time, cursing under his breath, knowing he'd been done out of cash money due him, but, unable to read and write, with no way to prove it. What Otis had hungered after was land of his own. "A man hole title to some land," he used to say, "he can live forever. Because even after he gone, his sons say, *Our daddy bought this land for us.* His grandsons say, *This land come from our granddaddy.* If I could just make me some cash, I'd put it in land."

But, of course, he had never got his land. Land had killed him, though: the caving ditch bank. He had died by land, but never owned any, except what they had finally buried him in—and Bradham had given her the ten dollars to pay for that.

Her coffee was finished now. Time to begin Huse's breakfast. At least I got him, she thought with pride. At least he ain't left me. . . . Bish had no time for her any more and Robert—well, there was nothing she could do about Robert but pray. . . . She went into Huse's room and looked down at the wide muscular man's body of him, sound asleep and naked to the waist. Gently she pulled the bedspread over him and tucked it around his shoulders.

Her face was thoughtful when she straightened up. She hoped the Governor and Miss Irene got back from their vacation up in Tryon, North Carolina, real soon. They'd been away for nearly two weeks now, and all that time Huse hadn't been able to do anything about a job except help out with Bish part time. Cary had promised to see the Governor about a job for Huse with the state, and it had slipped his mind and the Governor had got away before he could do it. These boys that come back from the army, she thought, they sho' are hard to get settled down. Seem like they can't concentrate on nothin, less'n there a girl mixed up in it somewhere. Cary running around with that little Mary Scott Butler, or else she all the time on the telephone to him, and they goin at it so hot and heavy, they better be lookin out or one of these days that gal goin to have a swellin in her belly she ain't goin to want. She out to cotch Cary, and she goin to use everythin she got to do it with, and she goin to be sorry if she don't watch herself. . . .

And Huse. He was getting as bad. He had a girl, too, somebody he'd just met in the past couple of weeks. Been out with her almost every night. And yet he wouldn't talk about her, wouldn't even tell his own mother her name. All he would say was that she was a nice girl, a real nice girl, and that there was no call for Lucy to worry about her being anything else. He got a bad case on her, too, Lucy thought, and first thing I know, he goin to be comin to me and tellin me he married. Then they all be gone and won't be nobody but me. Well, when that time come, it come, it the Lawd's will, like everthing else. . . .

Later she trudged up the high slope of the road toward the bus stop, pleased that the morning was dry, not damp, and that her joints were limbering. A cluster of her neighbors, also bound for work, walked with her, and though she passed the morning's gossip with them, her mind was not on it. She was still caught up in thoughts of the past.

Of all the children, she thought, Huse was most like his father. That drive in him, that wanting something all the time—not just money, not even land, but something bigger, something beyond her understanding. But if it had baffled her, it had not baffled Lizzie Blackwelder, the little brown starved sparrow of a woman who had made the two-mile walk from the schoolhouse to their cabin on The Place that hot afternoon in late May.

Both Lucy and Otis had been a little awed: having a schoolteacher come to call was like having the preacher.

"I've come to talk about Houston," Lizzie Blackwelder had said in her thin, timid voice.

"Yes, ma'am. You look hot and tired. Lemme git you a cold glass buttermilk from de jug we keep down in de well."

"That would be nice," Lizzie Blackwelder said politely. While Lucy went for the buttermilk jug, Robert went after Otis, who was out in the fields. Then they sat on the porch and drank buttermilk and listened while Lizzie Blackwelder talked.

"He's got an exceptional intelligence," she said. "About the best of any boy I've ever taught. In two years, he's gone right on through six grades. Of course, I've done a lot of extra work with him after school. But now I've taken him as far as I can." She rocked in the rickety chair and fanned herself and stared out at the mist of dust suspended in the sunset. She looked tired and nervous and afraid of her own shadow. "But he ought not to be allowed to quit now. Somehow, he's got to go on."

"How?" Otis was leaning forward, his face lit with pride, interest, maybe something more. "How can he go on?"

"I don't know. What he ought to do is to go on to high school. But there isn't any high school for colored. Not in the whole county. The closest one I know of is in Hannington."

"Then how?" asked Otis again.

"I don't know." She closed her eyes as if she were thinking of the long walk back home. "Maybe," she said at last, "you could get a job in town and move to Hannington."

"Move?" Otis sat up straight. "I just put in a crop. Can't move and leave a crop."

"I reckon not," she said. "It was just the only thing I could think of." She seemed to shake off a little of her fatigue; she half turned in the chair to face them both; and for a moment her big eyes glowed, and in that instant Lucy thought, Why, she's a pretty little thing.

"All I know," she said, with a kind of reedy, tremulous fierceness, "is that he ought not to be wasted. You don't know what it's like. I fought my own way through six grades, and then I was balked, couldn't go any further. I know what it's like to—" She broke off. "Don't you see? Most of them, they've already been ruined or they aren't strong enough. They either been hammered down for so long with no advantages that they are like so many mud clods out there in that field; or else there's so much—just *so* much—in their way that they don't have the strength to overcome it. They get a year here, a half year there; the school closes at picking time and planting time, and all they can ever catch hold of is dribs and drabs. It's not their fault, but day in and day out, I'm beating at them and it never sinks in and sometimes I wonder why I— And then along comes somebody like Huse. Not often. Maybe only twice, three times, in all these years. But he's not ruined yet, and he's got the strength it takes. And . . . and it's *important* that he not be wasted. Not just for him, for all of us, for every Negro—" She broke off.

"Excuse me, I'm sorry. I didn't mean to get all wound up. I'm very nervous; the doctor says I've got low blood pressure. But . . . to me this is something very important. That's why I walked all the way over here."

"Yes, ma'am," Otis said. "I hitch up the mule and carry you home in the wagon. But to move—"

"We jest got settled here good," Lucy said, full of apprehension. She looked at Otis imploringly, feeling suddenly menaced, the world shifting under her. He did not even see her; his eyes were staring past her, fixed on something far away.

"We makin a crop here," Lucy went on. "Never lived in no town and don't know nothin about it. Wouldn't know how to find work there, wouldn't—"

"I know," Lizzie Blackwelder said. "I know. I didn't mean to be telling you what to do."

"We jest found an honest landlord, might lay by a few dollars."

"Yes." Lizzie Blackwelder stood up. "Well, I have to be going." But she did not move. Perhaps waiting for Otis to get the mule and harness it.

But Otis didn't. He seemed to have forgotten her. He stood up, too, and walked toward the end of the porch. "Move," he said, not looking at either of them. He took his pipe from the bib pocket of his overalls and clamped its bit between his teeth. It wagged when he talked, unlit, cold.

"How many times," he said around it, "how many times I done been cheated because I couldn't read, couldn't write, couldn't figure. And my daddy befo' me and his befo' him. Move." Then, as if they did not exist, he stepped off the end of the porch and walked around the corner of the house, his head down, already lost in thought.

"Just a minute," Lucy had said. "I'll have him hitch up de mule."

"No." There was desperation in Lizzie Blackwelder's voice. "No. Don't bother him, please don't. I don't mind walking. Goodbye, Mrs. Whitley." Then she had stepped off the porch and was hurrying down the wagon track out to the big road, her tiny, birdlike, shuffling figure dark against the last of the light along the horizon. . . .

That night Lucy couldn't keep her eyes off Huse. She stared at him as if he were a strange child dropped into the house by mistake, one sprung from the womb of another. Her heart was like lead. Later, in darkness, when Huse, Bish and Robert were breathing quietly in the one bed they shared in the other room, Otis stirred beside her. She had thought he was asleep, too, he had lain so silent and so still for so long. He said aloud, but not to her, "After pickin time . . ."

For a moment Lucy did not think she could stand it. Then she moved closer to him, despair turning to resignation, and that to trust as she felt the warmth of his body against hers.

"All right," she said.

Usually, at this early hour, the Negroes had the bus almost to themselves, for few white people had to be abroad at such a time of morning. Seating from the rear, Lucy and her friends and the others who got on at the early stops filled the bus all the way to the four rows of seats in front which were always reserved for whites, and which remained empty for a while. There was much laughter and joking, for this was the club car of servants on their way to work.

But this morning there seemed to be an unusual number of whites out, and before long there were enough of them so that the Negroes toward the front arose and drifted to the rear and stood in the aisle. By the time the bus turned down Mercy Street, Lucy herself had been standing for twenty minutes, and she was glad when it was time to pull the cord. A bus was a mean, bouncy thing to ride any time, and worse when you had to stand.

She traded goodbyes with her friends and got off at the rear door. The step down was a long one and, stumbling as she reached the pavement, she thought with envy of those few lucky ones whose white folks hauled them back and forth in cars or taxicabs, or who lived in where they worked. Still, riding the bus was not without its advantage. Miss Irene paid her a dollar and a quarter for bus fare every week, over and above her salary. By purchasing a weekly book of tickets, she saved twenty-five cents of that, and thus she could count on having Sunday-school money.

When she gained the sidewalk, she stopped and looked at the Mercy Street house, yet unawakened. Its wide, flawless lawn glistened with dew; birds sang in trees and shrubs and bickered and fought in the birdbaths. The house itself was white as purity and its windows shone like jewels where morning sunlight touched their panes. *It so pretty,* Lucy thought as she walked up the drive, a chord within her touched and singing with the loveliness of the place. . . .

Otis had gone to Powell Bradham after ginning time and told him they had to move to town and why. To his surprise, Bradham not only gave him a free discharge from the place, with no unforeseen debts and encumbrances, but bought his mule for a fair price and offered other help. Aunt Amy—family cook and nurse for uncounted years—was finally too old to work. But she would not leave until she personally had trained her own replacement. "He say it solve a problem for him," Otis had reported, still stunned. "Dey got to have somebody reliable to cook, and that ole witchwoman don't want nobody that already know how, that she got to untrain before she can teach 'em her way. He say, if she satisfied with you and you kin do the work, he help us find a house in town and maybe git me a job, too."

Seeing the doubt and fear still lingering in her eyes, he put out a hand and touched her. "Dis may be a better way for a man to leave his mark den ownin land, even," he said in a low, intense voice. "Since our ancestors done been took from Africa, nobody in yo' fambly or mine ever know how to read and write. Since de world began—you know what I mean? Don't you see what a big thing dis may be? Maybe we give rise to a whole new generation, a different generation. And maybe it be worth whatever it cost us. Maybe . . . maybe a man can be remembered by what he do just as well as what he own."

Remembering that, Lucy went to the back door of the Mercy Street house and unlocked the kitchen with her key. She entered quietly and flipped on the light. As always, she had left the immense kitchen and the pantry spotless the night before; and, as always, she felt a thrust of proprietary admiration for its shining order this morning.

Coming here, she remembered, as she took off her coat and hung it in a pantry closet, had been like going to Heaven, or dreaming while you were awake. Not even Otis knew what it had been like for her, and she had never been able to find the words to tell him. "Dey got so many pretty things there" was all she had ever been able to say. But he was a man, and he would not have understood anyhow. To him, a mule, a gun, a hound dog, a crop—these were things of beauty, and he had owned them and had their satisfaction. But she had never, in her life, owned anything beautiful except her children and had never had any hope of it. Then she had been lifted from that world of drab pine boards and dust and sun and grease and tin and rags and put down here. Her eyes shone and her face softened as she looked at the ranked and orderly rows of fine bone china in the kitchen and dining room cabinets, the heavy, ancestral silver service on the sideboard, the deep rugs and carpets and the graceful furniture that years of ownership and care seemed to have made glow with its own inner light. Nobody could have understood how she felt, what wealth she had suddenly come into. Except that old Amy had known. Lucy had seen the moist eyes and the quivering lip of the old woman on the last day of her stewardship; and she had understood that it was not grief at leaving the service of the family, but grief at being deprived of her freehold of all this beauty, of having to re-linquish it to someone else, when it was the only beauty she had ever owned. It had been hers; now it was Lucy's. . . .

It would be a while before Mr. Cary, who was the only one in the house right now, got up and wanted his breakfast, but Lucy busied herself getting things in readiness. Once she paused and looked about the kitchen again, smiling, lost deep in pride. She knew something the Bradhams did not know. They thought all these possessions were theirs. They thought, too, that it was themselves that claimed her fealty. They were wrong on both counts. Everything here was as much hers as theirs—more, for she handled it every day, took time to admire and love it. And though she liked the family, it was the beauty to which they gave her access and not any deep love for them that held her loyalty.

Cary Bradham came down to breakfast that morning with a stomach that felt as if it were packed with cold grease and a pain over his left eye as if an auger had bored into his skull and its bit were still in place. He had got drunk last night, completely, blindly drunk—and all by himself, alone in the solitude of the house, ignoring the frantic ringing of the phone.

She's the one to blame, he thought bitterly, squinting against the pain and mopping water from his eye as he descended the stair. She got us both into this; now she's got to help me figure out some way to get us out. I will not marry her. Goddammit, I simply will not marry her.

Clad only in pajamas, his hair still rumpled with sleep, his face unshaven and grainy, he padded barefoot into the kitchen, where Lucy stood at the range. She smiled at him, all yellow teeth and blue gums. "Mawnin, Mr. Cary."

"Morning, Lucy," he said dully. He dropped into a chair at the kitchen table, his nerves shrieking for coffee. He ran his hand across his face, knuckling at his eyes. When his finger pressed the left eyeball, the pain in his head trebled. He said, "Lucy, for God's sake give me a cup of coffee."

"Yassuh." She took the pot from the stove and poured and set the cup before him. "You not feelin' good this mawnin?"

"I'm not feelin' good this morning."

"I fix you some bacon and eggs; they perk you up."

The thought of food knotted his stomach, brought a bile of nausea into his throat. "No. No, never mind. All I want is coffee."

"Yassuh. But you got to eat somethin or yo' stren'th go down."

"Just coffee, dammit!" He was instantly contrite after the flare; he had never spoken to Lucy like that before. But he made no apology; he lacked the stamina to frame one.

He saw the fleeting pout that crossed her face, and she turned away. "Yassuh." She went to the back door. "I go out and cut some flowers for de table."

He felt relief when the door shut behind her. The coffee was scalding hot, and he did not drink it immediately, but lit a cigarette while he waited for it to cool. He was already smoked out, his mouth foul and his throat raw, and the cigarette made him feel worse rather than better; but he did not put it out.

He stared through the curling smoke at the coffee cup without seeing it.

She had told him yesterday afternoon, on their way back from the club pool. He had noticed that she was strangely silent, her maddening flow of chatter extinguished, and had been grateful for it. He had felt good, loose and relaxed after the swim, and as he drove, the desire for her grew in him. He swung the car off the highway in a few moments, bounced it up a familiar side road, and then pulled it into the shelter of a grove of trees.

It was a fine, bright afternoon, and in the seclusion of the woods there was no sound after the cessation of the engine clatter but the dry, thready buzz of insects. No breeze stirred, and the foliage that surrounded them like a wall was a lush, bright green.

"Well," he said confidently, "here we are again," and he pulled her toward him.

She came without resisting, but when he kissed her, there was no avidity to her mouth, and her lips were cool. His hand sought her breasts and played over them, trying to kindle her, but they seemed to have no effect.

That was when he felt the first dampening intimation that something was wrong. Slowly, reluctantly, he let her go and drew away, and he looked down at the rounded face with its short nose, its wide blue eyes, and its frame of bright hair, with apprehension growing in him. Three days after their first encounter in his grandmother's bedroom at The Place, he had broken down the last barriers of her resistance. It had been worth it. She was not particularly experienced, but her body was so unbelievably lush, and she was so enthusiastic, and his life had been monastic for so long. He had brought a blanket and had spread it on the ground, in the darkness, and she had come to it with him unprotestingly. Her hands, touching his shoulders, had been cold at first; after that, they were never cold again, but always warm and confident.

That had been the real start of the affair, if it could be termed that. It had not kindled anything in him except more tolerance for her vapid company the rest of the time and a desire to have the use of her body for as long as it excited him. With the caution of a pilot threading a plane through an intricate flak pattern, he had managed to avoid having to say any of the usual words that went with that sort of thing, and, to his surprise, she had not pressed him for them or said them either. She had just let him do with her whatever he wanted to, when he wanted to, and had seemed to take a pleasure in it that was equal to his own.

But now, in the airless heat of the midafternoon woods, he began to feel cold.

"Wait a minute," he said. "What's the matter here?"

Mary Scott's full lower lip began to tremble. All at once her eyes were moist. But she did not answer him.

Along with his fear, irritation grew. He seized her wrist. "Mary Scott? Dammit, what's the trouble?"

"Cary, I— I don't know how to tell you."

"Tell me?" His fingers tightened; he felt bone shift beneath them. "Tell me what?"

The silence in the woods seemed interminable. He plainly heard the feathery sound of the breath she drew in, and then her cheeks were wet, her eyes brimming. Her voice was a shaky whisper. "Cary, I— I'm two days overdue."

His hand slid away from her wrist. "Don't be ridiculous," he said harshly, knowing that the words had no tangency to the situation at all.

"I'm not being . . . I mean, it's the truth." She was blubbering now. "I should have begun my period two days ago, and nothing's happened, and I'm always regular as a clock and I'm afraid, I'm afraid . . ."

"You mean you think you're pregnant." His voice crackled in the stillness. He had an odd sense of time suspended, of his world teetering, poised, on the brink of something; his mind raced ahead to the ramifications of the future, recoiled in fear and horror and retreated. It could not be true, it must not be true. "You can't be," he said, as if that would solve everything. "You can't be."

But she was crying now full blast, blubbering, he thought, and along with the sickness in the pit of his belly there was rage, all of it directed at her. He seized her and shook her. "Goddammit, stop that bawling. Two days isn't anything—is it?" Suddenly he was aware of how ignorant he was of the mystical, fatal rhythm of a woman's

entrails. "I've always used— Except that one time. One time doesn't
amount to anything. Hell, you're sick or something, isn't that it?
Isn't it?"

"No," she wailed, and she struck down his hands, "I'm not sick,
I'm going to have a baby, I know I am, and don't look at me that
way. Please, Cary, don't look at me that way, because we've got to
do something. If I don't come through, we've got to do something and
do it quick."

"Dammit, don't talk like that. There's nothing the matter with
you. Take some castor oil or something, isn't that what they do? You
can't be— I've only been home three weeks, for this to happen . . .
damn it, will you stop that crying?"

All his old feeling of disgust for her had come back on him. He
could not imagine now how he had ever wanted her body; he felt as
if the touch of it would sicken him. If she was pregnant, that meant
marriage, didn't it? And to be *married* to Mary Scott—this vapid,
rattling, baby-faced blonde. . . . She'd known it, damn it; she'd
known this would happen, planned on it—it was all her fault. To
have to marry any woman now, to have to marry *her*—he saw all the
shining years of young freedom he was entitled to go spiraling away
like water sucked down a drain, and he was enraged and despairing.

It took every tatter of will he possessed to steady himself, to make
his mind begin to work rationally again. She had thrown herself
against him, burying her face in his shirt, her back heaving with the
strangled cadence of her sobbing, and, automatically, he placed a
hand between her shoulder blades, aware now that he must bring
her back to rationality, too, and that it could not be done by screaming at her. "All right," he said. "All right. If you'll stop that crying,
we can talk about it."

But talking about it had not changed it at all. Whatever was inside
her, whatever he had put there, either existed or did not exist, and
there was nothing either of them could do about it but wait and see.
She had begged, "Cary, please don't be mad at me. It's bad enough
without having you mad at me, please . . . ," the kitten-face flaccid
and red with crying now, and he hardly able to bear looking at it for
the bitterness he felt.

"All right," he had said. "I'm not mad. But—my aching back—to
only be home three weeks and have something like this sprung on

you!" Then, in a calmer tone, "Look, it could still be a . . . a mix-up. You might have a cold or something. There's no point in getting all worked up about it this early. Let's wait a few days and see, and then . . . hell, it'll be all right. It's *got* to be all right." Somehow he managed a confident grin. She sniffled loudly and took out a Kleenex and mopped her eyes.

"If it isn't," she said, "what'll we do?"

"I don't know," he said. "I don't have any idea. All I know is that we've got to wait." And then, savagely, he put the car in gear and spun it out of the woods and back onto the highway, thinking: Please. Please, God. Not <u>her</u>. Not <u>her</u>. . . .

He had been supposed to pick her up that night, but the thought of it made him shrivel inside. He did not even phone her; by that time he had three drinks inside him. He took a bottle of bourbon from his father's whiskey cabinet and retired into his father's office and tossed the drinks down one after the other. When the telephone rang, he cursed it loudly, but he answered it.

"Cary?" Her voice trembled.

Before she could say anything else, he cut in harshly. "Has anything happened? You know what I mean?"

"No—"

He slammed down the phone and whirled and went back into the office and poured another drink. Before he had the glass to his mouth the phone jangled once more, but he did not even look toward it. For the next hour, while the phone clamored at ten-minute intervals, he sat there on the leather sofa, deliberately drinking himself numb, hoping that alcohol would order his thoughts and offer him a solution.

What it offered him was the courage to think about the situation, to assess its dangers and its detriments and to weigh alternatives.

And that was when he knew that, if Mary Scott Butler really was pregnant, he was hopelessly, inextricably trapped.

If she had been any other girl, he might have arranged an abortion. He did not count as obstacles that he had no idea of how to go about finding somebody to perform it or what it would cost. Surely there must be an abortionist somewhere here in Hannington, and if there was, he could be located.

The trouble was that she was not any other girl. She was Mary Scott Butler, daughter of St. John Butler; and he was Cary Bradham,

son of Powell Bradham—and St. John Butler was one of Powell
Bradham's chief political supporters, always had been. If anything
happened, if there were a misstep, if somebody found out or Mary
Scott got sick from it . . . What he and Mary Scott had cooked
up between them in one unguarded night, he saw now, was not just
the messy little affair of an unmarried girl got pregnant. It was the
germ of a major scandal that could rock dynasties.

It could, he saw, create a feud that not only would hurt his father,
but, worse, would ruin any chance he himself had for the governorship Hoke Moody and Powell Bradham had offered him, so far in
the future. Politics is total, Moody had said; that meant that a scandal
today could ruin you twenty years from now, and you had to be
continually on the alert.

The more he thought about it, the more it was like peeling away
the leaves of an artichoke, revealing layer after layer of significance,
perceiving repercussions that would vibrate far into the future. For
himself, he would rather not have the governorship than to have to
marry Mary Scott. But, he knew, it was something his father desperately wanted for him—it was, his father had conceived, Cary's duty
to the state, and, in his father's lexicon, those two words were always
in boldface type: *honor, duty.* Unless he put the same interpretations
on them, weighted them with the same value, he would earn only his
father's contempt; and he did not think he could bear that. The hell
with Mary Scott, yes—but he could not say, the hell with Powell
Bradham.

The phone rang again. He poured himself another drink.

Goddamn her, if she was pregnant, there was not going to be any
way out but to marry her and marry her quick.

"Bitch," he said aloud bitterly. "Bitch."

The telephone died. In the silence he shuddered. He sensed his
father's presence, somehow, very strongly in the empty room; and it
was as if his father had said aloud what he must do. Because he was
a Bradham. Because he was to be Governor of Muskogee.

Because of those two words. *Honor. Duty.*

"Fuck honor!" he said aloud, harshly. "Fuck duty!"

But he knew, even as they seemed to re-echo in the silence of the
room, that what he had voiced was only empty bravado. He was
tangled in too tight a web. If she was pregnant, there was only one
safe way out.

Despair settled on him leadenly, and he poured another drink; the phone rang one more time and that was the last time it rang that night.

Now his coffee was barely cool enough to drink. He raised it to his lips, and its black, taut strength seemed to vibrate along all his nerves. He felt slightly better when he set down the cup.

The back door opened, and Lucy came in with an armload of gladioli, dew still on their swordlike leaves.

"You feelin any better, Mr. Cary?"

His voice was dull. "I guess I'll live, Lucy."

She laid the flowers in the sink and ran cool water in with them. "When de pay boss and Miss Irene git back?"

"They'll be in this afternoon." He drank from the cup again.

"I hope dey done had a nice vacation up dere in dem mountains."

"Yeah," he said. He finished the rest of the cup. "Lucy, pour me some more coffee."

"Yassuh. Seem like they been gone a mighty long time." She came to the table with the coffeepot in her hand. "Mr. Cary?" Her voice was tentative, even a little timid.

"Yeah, Lucy?" He did not look up at her.

"You mind when you and Houston go fishin in de swamp couple weeks ago, you tell him you speak to de Governor about a job for him?"

Oh, for Christ's sake, Cary thought, stress tautening his muscles. Of all the times to have to worry about a nigger that's too lazy to go out and find a job for himself. But, carefully, he kept his voice under control. "I remember. But Daddy got away before I had the chance."

"Yassuh. Only Huse gettin powerful tired of layin around not doin nothin but helpin Bish down at de funeral parlor. He don't much like dat funeral parlor work. You reckon after de Governor comes in today and he git rested, you could kinda approach him about it?"

Cary stubbed out his cigarette in the saucer. It seemed almost ludicrous that life should have to go on in some sort of ordered fashion with disaster looming over him as it did. But he had made the promise to Huse and it had to be kept, silly as it was. What did Huse think his father was going to be able to do, make him chief engineer of the highway department or something? He had not really given it much thought, knowing that no matter what he lined up for

Huse, it would not be enough. That one day with Huse had made him so uncomfortable that he had not sought Huse out again; his friend had changed too much—besides, there had been Mary Scott and her nice, soft little body to preoccupy him. I'd have been better off down in the swamp with Huse, he thought now, bitterly, no matter how uppity and misguided he is.

Aloud, he said, "Lucy, I'll tend to it just as soon as Daddy gets home." He was anxious to be rid of her while he drank the second cup of coffee. "Look, you just tell Huse to come on by here tomorrow evening and by that time we'll know what we can do for him."

"Yas, suh, Mr. Cary, dat mighty nice of you. Thank you a whole lot." She went back to the sink and lifted the flowers out and laid them on the drainboard. At that moment the telephone began to ring, and Lucy reached for a towel to dry her hands.

Cary arose wearily, everything within him seemingly fused into one massive, solid cinder. "Never mind," he said. "I know who it is. I'll get it." And he went slowly into the hall, hoping against hope that this was release from the trap, and knowing that it was not.

10 When she appeared on stage, Houston could feel himself swell with his love for her and his pride in her.

It had taken him by surprise, the thing that had happened the first time he had seen her emerge from the wings of the Wheatley-Tubman auditorium. That had been the Monday night after the Saturday he had met her and after a Sunday spent in an odd kind of anticipatory fog. During that Sunday he had tried to tell himself he was an idiot. . . . You got no business feeling this way about a girl you ain't seen but one time, a girl you never pass more than a few words with. She ain't studying about you, except to be nice to you a little bit to pay you off for keeping your own brother from getting himself in bad trouble. . . . But reason was too blunt a weapon to make any cut in the excitement that had gripped him. He had been at the auditorium early Monday night, resplendent in newly purchased civilian clothes and, unused to their comparative looseness and baggy fit, also feeling that his appearance must be clownish.

She had been there, as she promised, and, expecting the worst, he had been startled and elated by the enthusiasm with which she had greeted him and introduced him to the other members of the workshop, her hand slipped through the crook of his arm in a pleasantly possessive way, as if they were old friends. She had a knack of sociability beyond any possessed by anyone else he had ever known, and she was, obviously, so respected and looked up to by the others present that she not only transferred him into the group without strain, but seemed to have imprinted on the others' minds her own startlingly high appraisal of him as a person, so that he joined it as a respected member from the start, not looked down upon as an awkward amateur. He knew nothing about drama, except for having read some plays, but she seemed convinced he was as *au courant* as anyone else there and not only had them believing it, but had him believing it, too.

So, instead of the excitement he had felt having been crushed, it was soaring in him as he took a seat in the auditorium a few rows back from the stage and watched readings begin immediately. The workshop was dealing with several one-act plays, ancient and written for high school production, dreary and banal even to someone as unquestioningly brimming with euphoria as he was. And, almost without exception, the reading of the lines, direct from scripts, was flat, sparkless, and mumbling.

The auditorium was stifling hot, and the heat was worse because he would not remove his coat, knowing that he had already sweated his shirt into huge dark blotches under his arms. The tie seemed to choke him, and the starched collar, the first he had worn in years, sawed at his neck. But he forgot these discomforts when Virginia Crane began to read, for then something magical happened.

He could not define it nor find words to express it. But there was nothing flat or unimpassioned about her lines. She was as unfamiliar with them as the rest, and she stumbled or lost her place occasionally. But that did not matter, either. For the moment she opened her mouth, the stale air in the auditorium seemed to freshen and come alive, to vibrate and shimmer. It was as if she threw off an aura that filled and dominated the place. He found himself sitting upright, unable to break his eyes loose from her. Everyone else on stage seemed to vanish; all surroundings—the dark, grimy auditorium with its streaked walls, the narrow, bare little stage—no longer noticed, blurred into nothingness. There was only Virginia—electric, startling in her power and grace, so alive that not even her beauty could hamper the spell she wove. The qualities of loneliness and uncertainty he had sensed in her were drowned in the new personality she had become.

It was happening not only to him. He saw everyone else responding with the same intensity; and when at last her part was finished and she faded into the background, it was as if a light had been turned off. He heard a faint, general sigh as of catharsis, and he was aware of a slackening in his own body, a letdown that deepened as the other actors droned on ineptly, some with mushmouthed unintelligibility. Everything after that was anticlimax.

Until the workshop session ended formally at ten. When it was over, there was much good-natured raucousness and intramural joking that went over Huse's head. He saw with despair half the men in the cast clustering around Virginia Crane, and he thought: Now is when I lose her. No one was more surprised than he when, subtly and naturally, she disengaged herself from the rest and wound up at his side again, as if it had been understood all along that, of all the men there, he was the one she was officially with.

And then, with the same grace of transition, they were out of the auditorium and in the cool night air. She still had her arm linked in his as they strolled across the campus to the gate. The buildings of Wheatley-Tubman were all very old and crowded together, and some of them were literally crumbling, but there seemed to him excitement even in their dark bulks, and the sad, worn flats of the narrow lawns were like vast meadows in the night. He heard laughter, and the music of a radio playing somewhere not far away, and he smelled the faint, exciting perfume of her, and occasionally her hip brushed against his, and he thought: There ain't no help for it. I love her.

"Well," she said, "what did you think of your first night at the workshop?"

"I enjoyed it. I enjoyed you, especially. You're the best one they've got."

"That's not saying much." There was no false modesty in her voice. "But thank you, anyway." Then her hand slipped down his arm and grasped his hand, lacing her fingers between his; with this new and special kind of intimacy they went on to the car.

Huse opened the car door for her. "It mighty early to be going home," he said, unable to keep the wistfulness out of his voice.

"I don't know of any place else to go," she said; and he thought he sensed the same wistfulness. He racked his brain. Where in Hannington could you take a girl like Virginia Crane?

He had no idea. There were few places of entertainment even for whites in Hannington. The city virtually closed down after the movies were out at eleven o'clock, except for a scattering of late restaurants and drive-ins, beer taverns and some bawdy roadhouses outside of town. For Negroes, the night, at least on weekends, did not end so early—it rolled on full force far beyond legal hours in blind tigers and honky-tonks, in cafés reeking of fried fish and pork skins and spilled beer, in the "candy shops" and "smoke shops" set up in private homes, really only fronts for whorehouses and all-night bars. But he could no more have taken Virginia Crane in any such place than he could have a white woman. His heart sank.

"Maybe," she said, after a moment, "we could just ride around a while. It's a wonderful night."

His spirits rose. "Sho," he said, "that's a good idea," and she moved over and let him take the wheel.

"I don't understand," he heard himself say later. They were parked in a grove of pines not far from town. He wanted desperately to kiss her, but he was holding himself in check. He would take no risk of frightening her or revolting her.

"What don't you understand?" She was leaning against him, not provocatively, but naturally, as if the touch of his body against hers felt good to her.

His heart hammering almost painfully, he slipped his arm about her. "How come, when you've got all those college boys after you, you pick me to be out with tonight?"

She turned that pale, wide-eyed face up to him; his hand toyed with the softness of her hair. "Because I like you," she said simply. "I liked you right away."

"I still don't understand it. A girl like you, with so many boy-friends—"

"So many boyfriends." There was enough bitter irony in her voice to surprise him. "What makes you think I've got so many boy-friends?"

"Well, you're bound to . . . I mean—"

"Because I'm so light? Because I'm Merit Crane's daughter? Don't you know that scares away more men than it attracts?" Her voice suddenly went harsh. "Lord, I wish I'd been born black as the ace of spades at the end of a corn row!"

Huse tensed, surprised. "What you mean? You're lovely. Why, if you wanted to, you could pass just about anywhere."

She sat up straight. "I know that," she said fiercely. "Don't you think I know that?"

He was silent, realizing he had stirred something in her better left alone.

"So I'm too white for nigger and too nigger for white," she went on, voice metallic in the darkness. "I'm so white that there's no place in Hannington I couldn't go if I wanted to. And I'm so nigger that as soon as they found out who I was, they'd throw me out. Oh, I've tried it. I've tried it more times than you might guess, and I've always got away with it. I've gone to white movies and tried on dresses in the department stores and eaten in some of their restaurants. But it's never any good, it's always spoiled. Because I never know from one second to the next when somebody's going to recognize me, say there's Merit Crane's daughter, and then it doesn't matter how white I look, out I go. I've quit doing it now, rather than risk being humiliated that way."

He caught the agony in her voice and it touched a chord within himself. "I know," he said. "They like to humiliate you. I can't figure it out. I've been trying to, but I just can't. Like me, I came home from the army, had my mind made up I was going to be a man same as any other man, ask for what a man entitled to. But they don't want me to be a man. They got to have somebody they can take out all their meanness on, and that's who they want me to be. I know what you mean exactly. I been feeling for weeks now like I throwing myself against some kind of fence that wall me off from my manhood, can't get through it, bounce back every time. I got one white friend, Cary Bradham; I told you about him. I can talk to him better than any other white man I know of; we played together when we kids. He told me two weeks ago he'd do me a favor, but he hasn't done it yet, and he won't be in any hurry about it, I don't guess. Not even him, and I was counting on him. I know how you feel, all right. Only, I guess it's worse for you." He broke off.

She was silent for a moment. Then she said, with a wry little laugh, "I guess we're both in the same boat, aren't we?"

"Everybody's in that boat."

"No," she said. "Not everybody. Just people like us who know what we're missing, what we're being deprived of. Just a few of us who're not willing to—" Her voice turned hopeless. "Anyhow, it doesn't make any difference. There's nothing we can do about it. Not as long as we stay here." She clasped and unclasped her hands in her lap and stared straight ahead, as if looking at something he could not see.

"I wanted to go North," she said. "That was really what I wanted to do. Not just because I could go in a restaurant up there—but because that's where the theater is. All my life I've wanted to act, to be on the stage. It's like having something inside of me beating, wanting to get out. But I'm stuck here in Hannington, my daddy's only child, the apple of his eye, and he won't let me go, he can't bear to see me leave."

"You could go anyhow," he said. "You're of age."

"No," she said, "I wasn't brought up that way. I've got to have his permission to go. I love my parents too much for there to be any ugliness between us; he'll give me anything I want that he can buy for me right here, but he won't do that . . ."

Huse felt tension go out of him, a kind of fear drain away. "Well, I'm glad you aren't going. Not right after I've just met you."

She turned toward him again. "I'm glad, too," she said. "It's funny, I feel closer to you than anybody I've met in ages." He was looking into her eyes then, and she was looking back at him with the same electric intensity that had arced from her onstage, her face raised and very pale in the moonlight. So he kissed her, a long kiss and one that moved him more than any kiss ever had before, and when he released her, she said, "Oh, Huse, Huse," and held her face up again. After he kissed her that time, she pulled away and brushed back her hair and straightened her skirt, and her voice shook when she said, "I think it's time for you to take me home."

"I'm sorry," he said. "I didn't mean to—"

"No. No, no, don't be sorry. I didn't mean it that way." She put her hand on his arm, laid her cheek against his shoulder. "I didn't mean it that way at all. It's just that I've got to be home by midnight or Daddy will be furious. Please . . ."

"All right," Huse said. His hand trembled slightly as he groped for the switch key. Emotions of so many various kinds that he could not sort one from another boiled in him. The ride back to town with her beside him seemed over in an instant.

He tried to drive her to Princeton himself, but she refused. "No, I couldn't let you do that. Then you'd have to ride a bus all the way home. As a matter of fact, the buses stop running at midnight, don't they? You'd be stranded and have to walk."

"I don't mind," he insisted, but she made him get out at the head of Little Hammer anyhow. She did not, however, drive away immediately. With her face turned up to his, she whispered, "You're coming to the workshop tomorrow night, aren't you?" He was startled by the note of pleading in her voice.

He smiled down at her. "Wild horses couldn't keep me away." Then he bent and briefly kissed her on the lips. Her hand covered his where it rested on the rim of the car door and squeezed. When he raised his head, her voice had a tremor in it. "Good night."

"Good night," he said hoarsely; and he stood for the length of time it took for the tail lights to disappear, watching them vanish. Inside him something new was soaring and swooping; and there was not a touch of fatigue anywhere in his body; it was totally alive and strong. Whistling loudly, exuberantly, he turned and strode quickly and lightly down into the darkened hollow of Little Hammer. If he had not been a man nearly twenty-five years old, he would have run.

It was the first time Houston Whitley had ever really been in love, and he was startled by how it changed him. The apathy and discouragement he had felt for so long vanished. It was not that the reasons for it were any less concrete, but he knew now a wild and arrogant confidence that there was nothing he could not overcome, a boundless optimism, a certainty that he could use his own strength to make his own world. Because, she had told him, she loved him, too.

That first night had set the pattern for all the others. During the day he helped Bish at the funeral parlor, taking as his province all the clerical work, which, until now, had been agony for his unlettered brother. The operations of the mortician's trade revolted him almost as much as the sleazier and illegal sidelines Bish carried on behind the front it provided; but he had still not heard from Cary and he was beginning to think he never would. If he had not had Virginia, he would have been hurt and sullen over Cary's failure to follow through on his promise; but he did not seem capable of being sullen any more. Not as long as he could meet her at the drama workshop every weekday night and then steal two precious hours between ten and twelve when they could drive and talk endlessly and park and he could kiss her and, to an extent, explore her body.

But she would never let him go home with her. Always she made him slip from under the wheel at the head of the hollow and drove back to Princeton herself, though he bitterly begrudged the loss of that last twenty minutes and would willingly have walked back home to gain them.

He stopped just this side of making an issue of that.

"I still don't see how come," he said, "you don't let me take you on home like a man ought to. Just like I don't see why I can't see you over the weekend. What's the matter? Are you ashamed of me or something?"

As soon as he had said it, he was sorry, for the distress on her face was obvious. She took his hand between both of hers, raised it to her lips and kissed it.

"No," she said, "my darling Huse, no, of course I'm not ashamed of you. How could I be ashamed of you?" She laid the back of his hand against her cheek, rubbing it there. "But it isn't that easy. It's going to take time, and we've got to be a little bit patient. If Daddy knew I was serious about anybody, he'd fly off the handle, and it's going to take time to get him used to it. When we do tell him, I want everything to be just right. I want to make sure he can't object to anything about it."

"Like what?"

"Well, he'll want to be sure any man I'm . . . interested in is settled and has got a good job. You know what I mean."

"What you mean is, he wants to see you marry a doctor or a lawyer or somebody like that." His voice turned bitter. "And I haven't even been to college. Only, even if I went, it would take four years. And you think I could wait four years? I'd go crazy."

"So would I." Her lips played over the back of his hand. Before she could speak again, he pulled his hand away and put his arm around her and pulled her to him tightly and with brutal force.

"Damn it," he said harshly, "I love you. That's the main thing.

I love you, and your daddy doesn't have to worry about me looking after you." Then he kissed her. He could feel her body tauten, then relax in his arms, and when he released her, she was breathing hard.

"Oh," she said, "I love you, too. So much. So very, very, very much." Then she slid across the seat. She gave a short, wry laugh. "I still wish," she said, "that instead of being Merit Crane's daughter, I'd been born tar-black in a cornfield. It would be a whole lot simpler. Only . . . only then you wouldn't love me, would you? If I were tar-black and had a flat nose and nappy hair?"

"I'd love you," he said fiercely. "I'd love you any way you were."

"Sure," she whispered, "and I'd love you. Huse. Huse, please, though, give me some time to get Daddy prepared. He thinks I'm still a little girl; he wants to keep me under his wing forever. It's going to take some doing."

There was so much distress in her voice, her pleading was so genuine, that his irritation was lost in pity for her, and in gratitude for her love of him. "All right." He took out a pack of cigarettes and lit one.

"Look," he said, "this job business. If I had a good job, I mean a real good job, not something ordinary, would that speed things up any? Would it bring your daddy around any quicker?"

"It would help," she said. "It certainly would."

"Then I'll get one. I been sitting on my fanny too long waiting to hear from Cary Bradham. I shoulda known better. He's my friend, yeah, but he's my friend just as long as I don't try to climb out of my place, it look like. I don't know where else to look, there's hardly any colored business here in Hannington except the bank and your daddy's outfit, but, by God, there's bound to be something somewhere, and if there is, I'm going to get it. You just wait. I ain't going to let not having a good job stand between you and me. If working in a funeral parlor isn't good enough—and I know it ain't—then I'll get one that is!"

She moved up close to him. "I know you will," she whispered. "I know you can do anything you want to do. Because you're you—you're Houston Whitley. There's nobody going to stop Houston Whitley—not *my* Houston Whitley."

"That's my baby," he said, still full of the flush of his love for her. "One of these days soon, we'll walk into your house and I'll say, Mr. Crane, I want to marry your daughter; and he'll say, why, of course, Mr. Whitley, you're just the man I had in mind for her all along." Then they both laughed and felt better; and he kissed her again.

It was not that easy, though. Huse spent the next two days making the rounds of West Grade, the street that, ghettolike, encompassed all the consequential Negro businesses of the city. Leaving out Merit Crane's enterprises, there were pathetically few of these. It was not so much the shortage of ambition or competence, Huse knew, that restricted the growth of Negro business as it was the lack of capital. The white moneymen of the town would advance gladly loans for bars and grills and taverns, for barbershops and pool halls and service stations, but they were not about to foster any competition for themselves along more serious lines. And, except for the Farmer's and Planter's Bank, those businesses started with Negro capital were pathetically shaky and small.

He had a definite image of the job he had to have now. He did not expect an executive or supervisory position, but he did have to have a white-collar job that at least could conceivably lead to such a goal. He would not have been ashamed to tell Merit Crane that he was a teller in the bank, for a bank teller could conceivably become a cashier or president in time; he would not have been ashamed to be a clerk in Landrum's Insurance Agency or Hollowell's Realty Company, for there would be a future at either place. The trouble was that, for the ten, maybe fifteen, jobs like that available on West Grade, there had already been dozens of applicants. He had a high school education? All right, the high school in Hannington was grinding out a hundred and eighty graduates a year. Of those, maybe thirty or forty went on to college somewhere, finding the only way to salvage their education to be to continue it until they could become doctors, lawyers, ministers, or teachers. The rest of the hundred and eighty ran into the same brick wall Houston Whitley was encountering now; some went North, hopefully; some joined the armed forces, desperately; and some were ditchdiggers and carpenters and common laborers.

He hated the thought of going to Cary again, but there seemed to be no alternative. It would not be easy for either of them: what pride he had left would have to be totally swallowed, and Cary would be humiliated, too, at being reminded that he had, for the first time, let

Huse down. On the evening of his second day of job hunting on Grade Street, he slogged home through the twilight from the bus stop with bitterness rasping brutally inside him. Two men were friends, one had asked the other for a favor; and because the two of them were of different colors—which was the only reason the favor was necessary in the first place—the whole affair was complicated and ramified and degrading for them both.

When he reached the house, Lucy was already there. Before he could even greet her, she spoke.

"Sonny boy, de Governor done come back this evenin. I ax Mr. Cary when he goan talk to him and he say right away. Cary say for you to come by there tomorrow after dinnertime and talk to de Governor about it." She smiled and patted his shoulder. "You know Mr. Cary goan do right by you. He find you a good job."

Magically, Huse felt his despondency sloughing away, hope and confidence filling the void it left. "I mighta known he wouldn't let me down," he said; and then he felt a quick, intense surge of warmth and affection for his mother for handling the messy details of it for him, and he hugged her bony frame tightly against him and kissed her cheek. "Mama, you're the greatest. You don't know what this means to me. If Cary can get me a good job, I'm going to have something to tell you mighty soon that'll open your eyes wide."

"Can't you tell me now?"

"No, ma'am. But if Cary just finds something good for me, you wait."

She smiled. "Awright, Huse. I wait. An' when I say my prayers tonight, I'll ax for everythin to turn out just right. Everythin work out good if you jest trust in the Lawd."

11 For Houston Whitley, the next morning seemed interminable. He had not been able to keep from hinting to Virginia last night that something was on the fire, that it wouldn't be as long as it had been. "Come a few days from now," he had said, "we can stop all this sneakin' around, and you can introduce me to your daddy as a man with a good job that one of the biggest powers in this state helped him get. When your daddy

finds out that Governor Bradham got me my job, that his son one of my oldest and closest friends, it ought to make a little dent in him."

Now, as he swung off the bus near Mercy Street, bathed and neatly dressed in his blue civilian suit, his movements were jerky with excitement. There were so many things Bradham could have lined up for him that he would not have had a chance of getting himself. There were administrative jobs in the state colored colleges—Wheatley-Tubman and Washington Teacher's: they could lead to careers. So could a job in the office at the state asylum for colored; and then there were the local colored hospitals—oh, there was no telling what the magic of Bradham's prestige exercised at Cary's behest could work. Probably there were jobs he hadn't even thought of—oh, not the kind of jobs he'd wanted at first, jobs that had been symbols. What he wanted now was a job that was a reality. He was no longer interested in abstract principles or the outdated slogans of a year ago that he had been fool enough to break his heart believing in. The Houston Whitley determined to get what he was entitled to seemed another, ancient incarnation of himself, now. If he could only get Virginia Crane, the rest of it could go to hell; there was no room for any other yearning in him. If he could come before Merit Crane as a young man just starting out in a good career with the backing of one of the most powerful white men in the state, he could approach Crane on nearly equal terms. But if he had to come before Crane as the employee of a funeral parlor of more than dubious reputation, then he was beaten before he started.

Never, he realized, had he had more at stake than he had this afternoon. Impatience fluttered and beat within him, hope and apprehension warred. He hurried up the long drive of the house. There was no question, of course, of going to the front door. He jog-trotted around to the back and knocked and Lucy let him in.

Her face glowed with pride. "You looks mighty handsome," she said, and she patted his arm.

His throat was thick. "Is the Governor in?"

She nodded. "He's here. I'll go tell him you come."

"He ain't said anything to you about what he's got in mind?"

She shook her head. "Uh-uh. But he did say not to worry, that if you needed a job, he could fix you up."

"Good." Huse rammed his hands in his pockets, then took them out nervously. "Go ahead, Mama, tell him I'm here."

She vanished through the pantry, and he wheeled and paced about the kitchen. The land beyond the pantry door was forbidden country to him; only once had he passed through it. He had been fifteen then, come to do some yardwork around the house, and Cary and Burke had spirited him through it and upstairs to Cary's room to show him a new gun. He had been nearly overwhelmed by his sight of the interior of the Mercy Street house; he had not dreamed such splendor existed. And to think—his mother worked in the midst of it every day. Why, it was like something out of a moving picture show. He grinned fleetingly at that old memory, and then his grin vanished. Time had passed, but he hadn't got any farther than the kitchen and he never would. Well, it didn't matter. If he could get set up with Virginia and settled down, he would lead his own life and let the whites lead theirs and not envy anybody. . . .

Then the pantry door slammed open and Cary entered from the dining room. He seemed surprised to see Huse, as if he had forgotten that he was coming. "Oh," he grunted, "you did get here, didn't you?"

"Cary, I sure appreciate—" Huse broke off, staring at the white man. Cary, he thought, looked rough, tired, drawn. Something was wrong with him. He hadn't gained any weight, might have lost some, and there were dark crescents under eyes that looked dull and worried.

"I sure appreciate it," he finished.

"Skip it. I'm sorry it took so long. But something came up and the next thing I knew Dad was off to Tryon." He seemed uncomfortable, slightly haunted, very fidgety. "Look, I've got to go, got to meet somebody. I'll see you later, huh, Huse?"

Huse frowned. He'd hoped Cary would be present when he talked to the Governor. But he made a wide gesture with his hands. "Sho. See you, then." As Cary went out, he stared at him thoughtfully, wondering: What you reckon has happened to him? He don't look good at all. . . .

There was no time to speculate, though, for the pantry door opened again, and then Bradham was coming through it, followed by Lucy.

"Well, Huse," Bradham said.

"Good evening, Governor, sir," Huse said with careful politeness, standing tensely.

"Cary tells me you've decided it's about time you went to work." Bradham was still vacationing, and though he wore white shirt and tie, he had doffed his coat as a token of his leisure. Huse searched his face for some clue to what was coming up, but Bradham's countenance was like something stamped on a coin, handsome and expressionless.

"Yes, sir," Huse said. "I have been hunting for a good job for quite some time now, Governor, and I don't seem to be able to find anything. I . . . thought that maybe you and Cary could help me."

Bradham nodded. "You know we're always glad to give you what help we can, Huse. But I've just got home from vacation and I haven't had too much time to check around."

Huse held himself tightly reined. "No, sir."

"But I'll tell you what," Bradham went on. "You know where the Department of Property is?"

"No, sir. Where is that?"

"Big red brick building right behind the capitol. Third floor. You go down there tomorrow and ask for Mr. Richard Cresap, maintenance supervisor, and tell him I sent you, and he'll fix you up with something."

"Maintenance supervisor," Huse heard himself repeat. "Yes, sir. Thank you, Governor." But there was an uneasiness rising within him. He hesitated a moment, screwing up his courage. Then he said, "Excuse me, Governor."

"Yes?" Bradham had seemed on the point of turning to go.

"This Mr. Cresap, maintenance supervisor, sir. Could you tell me what kind of work that gentleman hires people for, Governor?"

Bradham's gray eyes met his, faintly startled at first; and Huse tried to make himself look away diplomatically. But somehow he could not do it; their gazes locked for a moment, and he saw Bradham's face flush slightly.

"Mr. Cresap hires people to work around the state office buildings," Bradham said slowly. "Looking after them. Taking care of them. Keeping them clean."

The bitterness Huse felt was instantaneous and total, for he understood now, and suddenly he felt the wrenching conflict of simultaneous impulses toward laughing and cursing. To his own astonishment, his voice was calm.

"That would be janitor work, you mean, Governor, sir? Sweeping up and that kind of thing?"

Still they could not wrench their eyes apart, and Bradham's flush was deepening. "That's right. But the state pays better than most places. You'll get sixty cents an hour, Huse."

Huse drew in a long breath. "Yes, sir, that's twenty-four dollars a week, sweeping floors, isn't it?"

"That's right."

Now the breath went out, and when it left him, he felt himself beginning to shrivel inside. "Governor," he said, still in that astonishingly calm voice, "I thank you very much, sir, but I'm afraid that wasn't the type of work I was looking for."

He heard Lucy gasp, and when her face moved into his range of vision, he saw that it was wide-eyed and appalled.

Bradham's lips curved in an icy smile. "Well, I'm sorry, then, Huse. That's just about the best I can offer you. I was afraid it might not suit you. I was afraid the army might have put some notions in your head that you'd have been better off without."

Lucy's voice broke in, desperately. "Mr. Powell, he ain't mean that like it sound. You know how these soldier boys is. It just take a little time for them to settle down and get their feet on the ground. He go by and see Mr. Cresap first thing in the mornin, I promise you dat."

"It's up to him," Bradham said coolly. "But you'd better talk to this boy, Lucy. He's not going to get himself anywhere around here with the foolish notions he's got. He doesn't seem to know who his friends are, or when somebody's trying to do him a favor."

Huse felt a hot bile of shame and anger roiling high in his throat, and he swallowed hard. He stood there tensely, and then he said, quietly as he could, "I appreciate your thinking about me, anyhow, Governor. Much obliged to you, sir. It was real nice of you." There was no irony in his quivering voice. Then, unable to look at Bradham or let Bradham see his face any longer, he whirled. He could not look at his mother, either. He heard her say, voice reedy with distress, "Son, wait—Huse!" But then he was out the back door. The screen slammed loudly behind him of its own weight.

He ran down the driveway, his face hot, eyes stinging, belly twisted inside. "Janitor!" he said thickly and with fury. "Janitor. Floor sweeper. Ah, God damn them. God damn them all straight to hell, the white bastards!"

He felt as if his face had been forced down and rubbed in ordure. He could not shake off the feeling, or rid himself of the hatred of them for humiliating him that burned like acid, or of the worse hatred of himself for being vulnerable to the humiliation. But when you nigger, he thought brutally, you vulnerable to everything.

He managed to get himself under better control by the time he went to Wheatley-Tubman to meet Virginia, but he was still fine-drawn and bitter, still felt as if his own blackness were somehow something rancid. Looking at Virginia, he thought, not for the first time, what a contrast there was between their colors.

"Look," he said, "we got to cut out tonight. Got to talk. Something's happened."

"All right. I don't guess it will hurt to skip one night. What's the matter, Huse? Darling?"

"I'll tell you in a little bit," he said. "Go make it right with the people and then let's go."

They parked along the curb near Johnson's Drugstore with cups of Coca-Cola in their hands, and Huse told her what had happened. "And Cary my best friend," he said harshly. "He the one person I thought I could count on; but he ain't done anything. He ain't told his father how I feel, what I want. Or if he did, his old man didn't listen." His voice trailed off. "I don't know anything but to keep on working for Bish down at the funeral home." He crumpled his cup in his hands.

She laid a hand on his. "It's perfectly respectable work. Why, one of my daddy's best friends is an undertaker."

"Not like this," he said. "Not like my brother is. But I can make money at it." He turned to her, his voice going fierce. "I can make one hell of a lot of money at it. And that's what I'm going to do. After we're married, if you want to ride around in a Cadillac, by God, you'll have your Cadillac. And we'll buy a house in Princeton, too. And we'll go to Europe when we want to." He tossed the Coca-Cola cup out the window. "If it ever gets fit to go to again." His arm went around her. "Because I love you."

"I love you, too. I don't care if you work at a funeral home. I don't care what you do. I love you . . ."

He did not kiss her. "All right," he said. "Then we might as well get the rough part over."

Her body tensed beneath his hand. "What rough part?"

"Let's go home and you can introduce me to your daddy."

She was silent for a moment. "Huse, I don't—"

"Listen," he said. "The score is all added up now. It ain't going to change. I'm all I'm ever going to be, and we might as well quit putting everything off. Because I can't go sneaking around here and there with you much longer, and this drama workshop ain't going to last forever, and sooner or later you're going to have to let me march up to your daddy and you're going to have to stand there beside me and say—"

"I know," she murmured. She was silent again for a moment; and he was aware that the little throbbing fear deep within him, his own fear of her whiteness, his own basic distrust of it, was waiting for her answer to be finally extinguished. Then her answer came, firmly.

"All right," she said. "Come on. We'll go beard my ferocious father in his den."

The fear flickered and died and then went out, and his love for her was total again, and he pulled her to him. "Let me kiss you first," he said. "For luck."

What was in him as they went up the front steps of the Crane house together was a harsh sort of arrogance, one that now was unwilling to be cowed or broken by anything. He had reached the hard, irreducible bedrock of his life; he knew now that he would be sucked into the web of Bish's opportunistic finagling and illegality and would probably spend his life there, a small-time nigger undertaker and numbers man, with a little after-hours whiskey and some women on the side. It didn't matter. Nobody expected any better of him; he had found that out. Nobody wanted him to do any better, so the hell with it. He would do what he had to do, and he would make money— God, he would make money—and he would use that money as Bish had told him it could be used, to buy the respect of white bastards who would give it to you no other way. He knew exactly what he was now, and nobody was going to be able to chip away at him any more; he had nothing more to lose, and there was no more cause for him to truckle before Merit Crane than there had been for him to truckle before Powell Bradham. What Crane said tonight could make no difference; Virginia loved him and he would have her anyhow.

So he entered the house, which was surprisingly large inside, with a briskness and lack of fear that Virginia could not match. Her hand was cool, a little clammy, as he held it; but his own was perfectly dry.

Huse looked about him at the interior of Merit Crane's house, as Virginia led him through an entry. It was furnished with quiet, tasteful luxury. There were no old, roughhewn pieces of furniture like the family heirlooms of the Bradhams; nothing hand-me-down. Everything was new and in sets and evidently extremely costly. Their feet made no sound on the deep carpets as Virginia led him nervously to the living room.

She moved in front of Huse, who halted in the doorway. "Daddy," she said. "Mama."

The man in the easy chair at the far end of the living room wore a velvet smoking jacket, something Huse had never seen except in advertisements. He lowered the book he held and looked up, and then he set it aside and arose. There was an easy, supple grace in his movements. He was slender, compactly built, not tall, startlingly handsome, his forehead high, his nose straight and finely chiseled, his eyes dark and piercing. He was almost imperceptibly a shade darker than Virginia, his hair a little coarser, sleekly greased down into waves on his scalp, gray at the temples. A straight-stemmed brier pipe clamped between his teeth added authority to a face which needed none. He showed no surprise at the sudden appearance of the couple in his doorway.

"Well, come in, my dear," he said. His voice was soft and each word was so perfectly pronounced that it seemed polished before being released. He looked at the woman on the sofa. "Geraldine, we seem to have company."

Virginia's mother was an older, plumper duplicate of her, quite as light, her hair quite as soft and lustrous. She was smartly dressed, impeccably made up; earrings made little golden glitters as she turned her head. Her brows arched and vee'd.

"I thought you were at the drama workshop," she said, in a soft, polished diction that was an exact copy of Merit Crane's style of speaking.

"I was, but I've brought someone with me that I wanted you to meet, so I cut the workshop tonight." Virginia's voice was just a little short of being certain or steady, and Huse began to realize now just how much she was dominated by her parents.

"Oh?" Merit Crane said; and he came across the room. Virginia moved aside.

"Daddy, this is a very good friend of mine, Mr. Houston Whitley. Houston, this is my father."

Crane's dark, keen eyes fastened on Huse's face for a second;

then, with his left hand, he took his pipe from his mouth and he thrust out his right. It was soft, but strong.

"How do you do, Mr. Whitley," he said, his voice still soft and absolutely noncommittal. "Darling, this is Mr. Whitley. Mr. Whitley, my wife, Mrs. Crane."

"Yes, ma'am. How do you do, Mrs. Crane." He was desperately trying to hone his own diction to match theirs, but he could not get his speech that smooth, and he felt awkward and mushmouthed. The woman did not put out her hand; she only looked at him curiously, nodded.

There was a moment's awkward silence. Then Crane said with a touch of dryness, "Well. Have a seat, Mr. Whitley." He motioned to a fragile antique chair and Huse sat down. He was beginning to sweat, already felt wilted and sticky. Crane took his own easy chair, and Virginia perched herself on the arm of it.

The room was again almost tangibly silent, as the four of them looked at each other. Then, turning his pipe around and around in his hand, Merit Crane asked, "Are you in the drama workshop over at Wheatley-Tubman, too, Mr. Whitley?"

"Yes, sir."

"You are in school?"

"No, sir. I just recently got out of the army. I'm working now."

"I see," Crane murmured, and he slipped his arm fondly and with proprietorship about Virginia's waist. He looked up at her, smiling faintly. "Have you and Mr. Whitley known each other long, pudd'n?"

"About two or three weeks," she said.

Crane nodded. "Well, we're always glad to meet our daughter's friends, Mr. Whitley. Whitley. Whitley. The name rings a bell. Ah, yes, the Whitley Funeral Parlor. Are you connected with that?"

Huse nodded. "Yes, sir," he said, and he knew immediately that his tone was a little too loud, defiant, and defensive. "My brother Bish is the owner of it. I work there."

He did not miss the sudden opacity of Crane's eyes, as if to conceal all reaction to the statement.

"I've heard it's doing very well," Crane said. "A moneymaking business."

"Yes, sir, we're doing pretty good."

Again the room fell silent; Huse wanted to shift on the chair but dared not, fearing it might break. Suddenly, as if with decision, Crane sat up. "Would you care for a drink, Mr. Whitley?"

Huse looked at Virginia questioningly; her eyes were on her mother and he got no help there. "Yes, sir. Thank you."

Crane took his arm from Virginia and stood up. "Darling?" he said to his wife, and she shook her head. "Maybe you'd like to come out in the kitchen with me, Mr. Whitley, and show me how you'd like yours mixed."

"Yes, sir," Huse said with relief, getting up off the chair.

He followed Merit Crane into a narrow but spotless kitchen. Crane opened a wood cabinet over the counter and took from its paneled interior an unopened bottle of bonded bourbon. He broke the seal with a twist of his hand, went to the refrigerator and took out a tray of ice cubes. "We've just had the house done over," he said, as if making idle conversation. "It was so hard to get things done during the war and it ran down so."

"It's very nice," Huse said, "very pretty."

"Thank you." Crane put ice into the glasses, shoved the bottle and a shot glass to Huse. "Water, soda, or what have you?"

Huse carefully poured less than a full ounce. "Just water, thank you," and Crane filled it.

Crane set his glass on the counter and put his pipe in his mouth. Huse took out a cigarette and lit it. He was beginning to realize what a momentous thing it had been for Virginia to bring him here. It was as if she had never before brought home a man who had to be introduced and the entire family were in a quandary about it.

"We're very fond of Virginia, of course," Crane said. "She's our only child."

"Yes, sir, I know that." He took a deep breath. "I'm fond of her, too."

Crane's face did not change expression. "I gathered that. And I daresay she's equally fond of you or she wouldn't have brought you here tonight."

Huse nodded.

Crane turned away, made a thing of stirring his drink a bit more. Without looking at Huse, he said, "I don't want you to think we try to run our daughter's life. Because we don't. Still, she's very young and without much experience in the world, and, of course, we feel an obligation to guide her."

"Of course," Huse said.

"She's a very lovely girl," Crane went on, "if I do say so myself. And, naturally, she attracts a great many men. We, of course, have to be very selective about those of whom we approve or disapprove. It's not only a question of Virginia's welfare; there are other matters to consider. We have a certain standing in the community. Some of the very best blood in Hannington flows in Virginia's veins, you know, some of the oldest and most aristocratic." Now there was an almost imperceptible edge of bitterness mixed with the pride in his dry, flawless voice.

"Yes, sir," Huse said cautiously.

"We're always pleased for Virginia to be interested in nice young men. But, of course, she's still very young, far too young to be allowed to become serious about anyone."

Still Crane was not looking at him. And at his last words, Huse fought down an impulse to whirl this small, suave, confident man around and make him face him. Instead, he said, in no mood to be diplomatic any longer, "I'm seriously interested in her. And I hope she's seriously interested in me."

Crane turned now, at last. There was no expression on his face. "Ah, I hope not," he said. "Not that I have anything against you, but—"

"But—" Huse said; and his anger broke through now. "But what? Good Lord, Mr. Crane, Virginia's twenty-one years old. She's a grown woman. And me—maybe I'm not much, but I've never been in jail and I've got a certain amount of education and I've got a job I can make some money at and I don't consider myself any worse than anybody else. Sure, you don't know anything about me. That's why I asked Virginia to bring me here and introduce me. So you could get to know me. And so I could get to know you."

Crane nodded, his dark brows slanting in an irritation that could not otherwise break through his polite mask.

"That's very honorable of you," he said. "Not all young men would have been so considerate of the feeling of Virginia's parents. I respect that in you, Mr. Whitley. But I don't believe there's really any point in our improving our acquaintance. Because it would be simply impossible for me to approve of any sort of serious relationship between you and Virginia."

Huse stared at him. Why, you cocky, smug little old rooster, he thought, anger and outrage exploding inside his brain. It took every ounce of self-control he had to keep his fists from clenching and raising. You stand there like you God, like you own the world, like you white, he thought, and tell me— Aloud, he blurted, in a voice that was strangled, "I don't follow you. How can you say that when you don't know anything about me?"

"I don't have to know anything about you, Mr. Whitley. You may be one of the finest men in the world for all I know; I daresay you are. But we have certain plans for Virginia, and you simply don't fit into them."

"Why? Why?"

"There's no need for you to raise your voice, Mr. Whitley. We can discuss this like gentlemen, I hope."

"Gentlemen," Huse said. "But you're not even giving me a chance to—"

"It's been my experience that being ruthless at the start of one of these situations, no matter how its distresses me, saves everyone a great deal of trouble and pain later on." Merit Crane took his pipe from his mouth and sipped from his drink. "Just please believe what I say, Mr. Whitley, as discourteous as it may sound and as unreasonable as you think it to be. Just please take what I say at face value, and we'll spare ourselves both a lot of unpleasantness. We're happy to have you visiting here with us tonight, but I'm afraid that we simply can't—"

"Listen, Mr. Crane." His temper had slipped its rein now. First old man Bradham, now this one—what were they trying to do to him? Make him feel like something low, mean, nasty? He could understand Bradham; Bradham was white. But Merit Crane wasn't, no matter what sort of world he had built around himself—if he wanted to prove to himself that he wasn't white, all he had to do was to try to use a bathroom, a drinking fountain, downtown. "Listen. When I said I was serious about Virginia and she was serious about me, I meant we love each other. And you standing here telling me we can't don't show me a thing. You won't even give me a reason and you expect me to—"

"A reason." Crane's voice was almost weary, faintly reluctant. "So you have to have a reason, do you? Hasn't a reason already occurred to you?"

"No," snapped Huse, "it hasn't."

"Then you don't give a damn for Virginia's welfare," Crane said harshly.

Huse stared at him. "I don't give a damn—?"

"It's not only that your social standing is far below Virginia's," Crane went on, his voice staccato now. "Since you force me to say it, Mr. Whitley, there's a reason why you're not suitable for Virginia that was immediately apparent the moment you walked into the room. Now, do you want me to have to put it in so many words?"

"Yes. Yes, by God, if you're going to talk to me like that, you put it into words."

"All right, then." Crane took his pipe from his mouth. His gaze touched Huse's, the two of them looking at each other tensely, but without fear of one another.

"It should be obvious to you," Crane said flatly, "without my having to point it out, that you're far too dark for Virginia."

Stunned, Huse could find no words to answer. Dark. Too dark. But you're a nigger, too! he thought.

Then it was clear to him—all the ramifications of it. Then he understood why that tiny fear had nagged him deep within and would not leave; he had known it all along, subconsciously. Because money, intelligence, love, hard work—none of that could count with Merit Crane. Not all the wealth, all the college degrees, all the culture in the world could earn enough social status to match his here in Princeton unless you were also equally light. That was the one overriding standard. Lightness was more important to Crane than whiteness was even to Powell Bradham. Social cleavages cut vertically as well as horizontally, vertically by color: brown was better than black, ginger better than brown, mulatto better than ginger, quadroon better than mulatto, octoroon better than quadroon, white better than anything, white better than anything. White always better than anything!

"Virginia is so very light," Crane's voice went on, still without passion. "As I said, she has an aristocratic heritage. When she marries, it's our duty to see to it that she marries suitably. Is my meaning clear now? We simply can't settle for anything less."

Huse found his voice now. "Your meaning's clear. Sure, I understand it. I'm too much nigger for your daughter. Is that what you're trying to say?"

"If you want to be that vulgar about it," Crane said coldly, "yes."

Huse stared at him a moment longer with the greatest contempt and hatred he had ever felt for anyone. Then he whirled. "We'll see," he whispered, and he slammed through the swinging door of the kitchen and stalked back to the living room.

It was empty.

He whirled on Merit Crane, who had followed him. "Where is she?"

Crane's lips curved in a faint smile. "I imagine she and her mother have gone to her bedroom to talk things over. Good night, Mr. Whitley."

Huse looked down at him, hands clenching and unclenching. There was no crack in Crane's armor of superiority. His lips were still lifting his mustache in that small, confident smile.

Huse's voice was a bellow that seemed to shake the room. "Virginia! Virginiaaaa!"

There was no sound from anywhere in the house.

Huse drew in a great, rasping, sobbing breath. He faced Crane again, and his mouth opened and shut, but nothing came out. Then he whirled and strode out the front door and into the cool darkness of the night.

12 It had been something of a shock to the boy's mother, and of course it must have come as one to the Butlers as well. Nevertheless, Powell Bradham could not say that he himself was displeased. Not only would he soon have a grandchild—and nobody knew the hunger in him to see the line continued, perpetuated—but this alliance by marriage with St. John Butler was what he had been working toward all along. Another segment of the structure he was slowly and painstakingly building had just fallen into place, quietly, and with its full importance unrealized by anyone but himself, but there.

The women, Bradham knew, would be appeased by the big wedding and the reassuring knowledge that there could not possibly be more than six weeks of time to be accounted for, a leeway that could be comfortably and respectably handled. St. John could be grateful

—and was—that as long as it had happened this way, Cary was the man involved. And as for Cary—well, he was not only getting a beautiful and aristocratic young lady, but he had just put himself in line eventually to inherit one of the largest fortunes in Muskogee, the huge personal capital that he, Bradham, had always lacked, and which, if he had owned it, would have made him invulnerable and virtually all-powerful. He would never be that now, but Cary would; and though the boy seemed faintly touched with bitterness that this had happened, Bradham knew that with the coming of maturity and wisdom, Cary would look back on all this and see that it was the best thing that had ever happened to him.

The only thing to guard against was any tendency on St. John's part to try to suck Cary into the management of the mills. Politics was a full-time job, with the law as its underpinning, and men could be hired to run textile mills. But no man could be hired to be a Bradham and run Muskogee. . . .

"No, goddammit." Hoke Moody's voice broke the linkage of his thoughts with its truculent crackle. "I won't stand for you bucking me like this, Curt. If you introduce that amendment, so help me God, you and your county both will suffer."

"It's a matter of principle, Hoke," the man across the table from him said. They were sitting in white-painted wrought-iron chairs in the wide, pleasant court of Hoke Moody's home, the flank of the high, ancient house casting a cool shadow across them. There were four of them, Hoke Moody, his brother Dale, Bradham and Curtis McKnight. "You can't completely disregard the education of forty per cent of the population of this state!"

"I can if I please to," Moody said brutally. "And I please to." His voice sharpened itself. "Listen, Curt. Get some sense into your head. I've got the Legislature lined up to where it'll go along with this school bond issue. It's taken a lot of doing—eighty million dollars ain't chicken feed. Now you come along with this fool amendment to earmark forty per cent of it for nigger schools. What the hell you trying to do? Kill the whole bond issue dead as a doornail?" He picked up his glass from the table; ice tinkled in it. "What's the matter? Don't you *believe* in education?"

Curtis McKnight smiled faintly. He was lanky, rawboned, gray-haired, with a rugged, homely face and gentle eyes behind horn-rimmed glasses. His hands were immense and capable-looking; his voice slurred with the almost British liquid accent of the coastal plain. Despite the fact that he was a political adversary, Bradham felt a certain kinship with the man. The McKnights were as old a family as the Bradhams, and he and Curt had served in the army together for a while. After the war, McKnight had stayed on in Europe, trying to write short stories or something. The Depression had brought him home to the family plantation over in Washam County, where he'd sold off all but ten acres of the family plantation, keeping only the big house and its immediate grounds. Now he taught English at a small church college and wrote a book of poetry or essays occasionally. Poor as a church mouse, he still had somehow managed to hang on to the virtually hereditary family seat in the state Senate.

"Maybe I believe in education more than you do, Hoke," he said calmly.

"There ain't nobody believes in it more than me! Education brought my daddy out of the piney woods and into politics. Education is what changed my fam'ly, changed me, from the poor old hard-times farmers we was to what we are now, and my papa whopped respect for education into me with a doubled plowline. I may not be able to quote Homer from memory the way you can, but don't you go telling me there's anybody believes in education more than me!"

McKnight's wide mouth quirked, fanning wrinkles about his eyes. "Difference is, Hoke, I believe in it for everybody."

"Crap," Moody said. "Educate a nigger, all you do is ruin a field hand. Listen, Curt, we ain't built any schools since before the war, and we got a hell of a lot of catching up to do. It'll take every penny of that bond issue for us to provide for our white young-uns, and until that's done, I'm not even going to study about the niggers. I'm not going to study about that fool amendment of yours, either, you hear? Confound it, all you're trying to do is stir up trouble."

McKnight shook his head. "No, Hoke, not stir it up. Prevent it."

"What you mean, prevent it?" Dale Moody asked. He was ten years younger than his brother, in his mid-forties, gaunt where Hoke was chunky. His mouth was thin and humorless, and he seldom spoke unless Hoke had given him the cue. When he did, it was with that nasal poor-white whine which his older brother had managed to eradicate from his speech, but which Dale had never lost.

McKnight shifted in his chair, plucking at the worn suit that clung to gaunt limbs.

"Muskogee's still living in 1890," he said. "Not antebellum days, because we don't really have slaves. And not Reconstruction days, because the Negroes walked tall then, maybe too tall. But just about 1890 is the way I figure it. Nothing's changed since then. It's as if time were frozen."

"In 1890," Hoke Moody rapped, "my daddy led the Farmers' Alliance he'd formed against the entrenched state government." He turned to Bradham. "That was your granddaddy, Powell." His gaze went back to Curtis McKnight. "He put the little white farmer and the little colored farmer together into one organization and set out to wrench some kind of decent deal for 'em from the planters that had been running this state and grinding the little man down ever since before the war. And he didn't get that far, Curt." He flipped his fingers contemptuously. "They broke him like a gourd. You know how? They hollered nigger. Like Hitler, they divided and conquered, turned white against black. You talk about 1890, that was the year that broke my daddy's heart. When he got beat, something happened in his head." Moody tapped his skull. "He'd had big dreams for the niggers and whites working together up until then. Dreams of a poor man's paradise, no matter what color he was. He came out of that defeat, that mean, low, mudslingin' battle, a bitter and unstable man, Curt. He came out of it hating niggers, because he'd learned something that he taught me and that I've never forgot, and I ain't going to forget it, either. A nigger on your side is a political liability; a nigger you can be against is a political asset. It's as simple as that, Curt. You're right. That ain't changed a bit since 1890, and that's why you can take your amendment and—"

"I know all about your father and the Farmers' Alliance," McKnight said. "What I was trying to say, though, is that we can't live in 1890 any longer. This is 1946. You've got thousands of Negroes in this state now who've been in service and have seen the world, who've been accepted in other countries not as inferiors, but just as people. Who have come, Hoke, into contact with that most dangerous of notions, the idea of the equality of man. Our war propaganda has drummed on it and even the Negroes are aware of it now. Freedom, equality; they've been let out of the cage. If you don't watch out, they're going to run through this land like tigers."

His voice crispened. "I'm a Southerner same as you. I have some of the same prejudices, bred too deep in me for me ever to be completely rid of 'em. I know the Negroes' shortcomings as well as you do. But I happen to believe that those shortcomings are not his fault, but ours."

He grinned, passing his glass to Moody for freshening; and his grin was sardonic. "Now that you're a Senator, you make much of the danger of the threat to states' rights by the central government. But you're not doing a thing in the world but inviting the Federal government sooner or later to cloud up and rain all over you. These Negroes have changed, Hoke, and the young ones and maybe some of the older ones, too. They'll keep on changing. You can't keep them as unofficial slaves. They'll go North, a lot of them, and then they'll start to figure in the political balance of the country. Others, that stay here, sooner or later will demand what they think they've got coming. Sooner or later, we'll have to give it to them. The question is, do we do it voluntarily and control the situation ourselves? Or do we sit on our butts and do nothing until the political force of Negroes gone North forces the Federal government to move in again and ram something none of us wants down our throats?"

He paused. "That's aside, of course," he said with deceptive mildness, "from the fact that, theoretically, they're human beings and American citizens and entitled to certain benefits enjoyed by most men of that status."

Moody stared at him. "Shit," he said.

"That's not much of an answer, Hoke." McKnight displayed no anger.

"It's about all the answer you're going to get. I ain't worried about Northern niggers. I wish all the niggers would go North. They commit most of the crime and they pay damn little of the taxes. The North is plain-out welcome to 'em any time it wants 'em. And if they think they can run the country from up North, let 'em try it."

McKnight spread his hands in an admission of defeat. "All right, Hoke. I was just trying to save you when judgment day comes."

"Judgment day?" Dale Moody's voice was incredulous.

"I mean a political judgment day. A day when you have to stand up and face your accusers and say, I have acted in good faith."

"Of all the tripe," Dale Moody said.

"Maybe so," McKnight said. He stood up. "But I predict that the time will come when you'll be scratching, tumbling and falling head over heels to appropriate money for colored schools."

Hoke Moody shook his head as if baffled. "Curt, those Confederate ancestors of yours ought to be revolving in their graves."

McKnight smiled. "I couldn't care less," he said in that gentle voice. "Have you ever seen a Chinese tomb, Hoke? The Chinese deposit the bones of their ancestors on an altar and bow down and worship them. But because Negroes went to no schools or one-room schools in the days of my ancestors is no reason for me to feel obligated to let them continue that way in the middle of the twentieth century. I'm not Chinese, Hoke. I'm a Presbyterian. That's a kind of Christian, I think." He looked at Powell Bradham. "Powell, I won't trouble you to carry me back to the hotel. I'll just call a cab."

Bradham arose. "Oh, no. I ran you out here, I'll run you back." He felt oddly anxious to be divorced as much as possible from the Moodys in the eyes of this old friend. This small gesture of consideration and independence was important to him.

"Well, gentlemen," said McKnight, "when you're down our way, come to see us."

Moody stood up, thrusting out his hand. He was grinning. "You come back, Curt. Any time, when you haven't got coons on the mind. Take it easy."

"Yes," McKnight said, shaking hands with Moody. "Let's all take it easy, by all means. So long, Hoke, Dale. Powell, shall we be going on?"

Nowadays, Bradham rarely depended on Dayton; he preferred to drive himself. When they were in the car and rolling toward town, McKnight took out a pipe and a tobacco pouch. "The more I see of Hoke Moody," he said, "the less I understand him. He's a mighty complex man."

"There's nothing complex about him," Bradham snapped. "You ought to know that better than anybody. He's trash. Nothing but Hampton County trash."

McKnight chuckled. "Maybe that's as good an explanation as any. Still, it baffles me. He's carving himself out a truly monumental reputation in the Senate as a statesman. And here at home, he acts like an illiterate red-neck. Only it's not an act. How can a man carry, tolerate, two such opposing natures within him?"

"Listen," Bradham said, "there's only one Moody. And that's the Hampton County one. If you ever forget that, you're in trouble." He was silent for a moment. Then he said bitterly, "He's smart, though. He was smart enough back in 1928 to see his chance to split the party and get big by opposing Al Smith. I should have smashed him then, the way my grandfather smashed his father. I could have done it. But that gave him his foothold, and then, in 1932—well, you know the story."

"I know it," McKnight said, his face serious. "And I think you've done a wonderful job of holding him in check. But I meant it, Powell: either we learn to take a new attitude toward all the things this war is going to result in, or we're in for trouble. Educating Negroes is only part of it. The South has stayed a separate little kingdom of its own ever since it was settled; not even the War Between the States changed that. But there's never been a war like this last one, and there's never been an era like the one we're about to enter. And we're either going to have to quit refusing to learn how to swim, or we're going to drown in events. It's as simple as that."

"Maybe so. But even if I were in favor of your amendment—which I'm not—it would be politically impossible to ram it through. It would start a rebellion."

"There's going to be a rebellion anyhow," McKnight said, looking out the window. "One way or the other, it's going to come."

"Well," said Bradham sharply, "when it does, I'd rather it be a Nigra rebellion than a white one. We can handle a Nigra rebellion. . . . No, Curt, you're ahead of your time. The Nigra hasn't got a better friend than me, you know that. Bradhams have always taken care of their Nigras. But if I were Governor, I'd tell you exactly the same thing Hoke told you, but I think you'd understand it better from me." He slammed on brakes suddenly, as a policeman blocked his entrance to lower Main Street. "Now, what the hell?"

"I don't know," McKnight said. "I hear band music. Some kind of parade."

Bradham suddenly grinned. "Oh, yeah. I forgot. Sweet Daddy Salvation's in town."

"Not that mountebank," said McKnight. He chuckled ruefully. "Well, we've got a ringside seat for the parade, anyhow. Might as well lie back and enjoy it."

The music came nearer, loud and stirring, a band march. A uniformed Negro band crossed the intersection, strutting, brass blaring, marching in perfect cadence and with impeccable rhythm. Behind them came a sea of dark men and women clad in long, snow-white gowns, hems dragging the pavement. They clapped and sang in time to the band music: *Oh, I want to be in that number—when them saints go marching in.* Above them floated a huge banner, blue on white: WELCOME TO DADDY SALVATION FROM HIS ANGELS. Another banner read: SWEET DADDY, WE LOVE YOU. Then another band from the Negro junior high school, its drum major performing marvelous feats with a baton that was a spinning dazzle in the sun, the bass drum booming loudly, as the brass blared: *Every time I get the spirit.* The gospel music crashed and ripped through the summer afternoon infectiously.

Then there was the loud, long blare of an automobile horn leaned on continuously. A motorcade came into sight, new cars all polished to a high gloss, banners on their sides: SWEET DADDY WILL SAVE YOU and PRAISE SWEET DADDY. At the end of the motorcade came a float. It was done all in white, thronged with the white-vestmented figures, their dark faces shining with sweat above their robes. On a dais in its center, bowing and gesturing with almost ludicrous dignity to the crowd, was a small, dark man in morning clothes: a high collar, a long-tailed coat and striped pants. His thick black hair hung in curls and ringlets to his shoulders, his fingernails were fully three inches long, rings glittered in thick encrustation on his fingers spread in benediction and blessing. The banners on the sides of the float proclaimed: COME ONE, COME ALL TO THE TEMPLE OF SALVATION.

"Look at that," Powell Bradham said in deep disgust. "Look at that monkey up there. And look at that crowd he's got with him. He comes to town once a year and cleans these niggers out of every bit of cash they've got, and they eat it up and beg for more." His voice dripped contempt. "And that crowd there—those black 'angels'— that's what you're so damned concerned about. That's what you want to spend the state's good money on. They'll parade down to his 'Temple of Salvation' now and have a big baptizing and talk in the tongues and he'll convince 'em he's God come down to earth, and when he leaves here, he'll leave 'em all broke. And they wouldn't miss it for the world."

The tail end of the parade passed them by now, vividly uniformed men strutting and prancing lithely and with fluid grace in brilliant red tunics, blue trousers, and high shakos, their banner proclaiming:

TEMPLE GUARDS—WELCOME SWEET DADDY. The band music faded
in the distance; the policeman blew his whistle.

All Curtis McKnight said was "If you don't even have bread, the
only thing you have left is circuses."

The Temple of Salvation was an ornate, gingerbread-trimmed
wooden structure painted red, white, and blue; it sat on a rise of high
ground at the rim of Little Hammer, and there was not much about
it to suggest a church—a stranger would have taken it for a house,
even a barn, anything but a place of worship.

Behind the church, a pond perhaps twenty feet in diameter and
five feet deep at the center had been dug and was filled now with
muddy water. Its edges were thronged, jammed, packed, with men
and women in street clothes and the white vestments of the temple.
In the center of the pond, himself shrouded in white, stood Daddy
Salvation, freshly come from New York, the water up to his chest,
sweat rolling down his dark, epicene face, his teeth flashing white in
a wide, perpetual smile. The bands were playing gospel songs, brass
and cymbals almost drowning the roar of many throats; the sound
seemed to vibrate like the heat waves that shimmered between the
earth and the high, achingly blue sky. Daddy Salvation threw back
his shaggy head, bellowed with a deep voice that rolled even through
the band music, "Send the next sinner to be washed in the Blood!"

A laughing, praising shriek went up from the crowd, and a young
girl in white robes waded gingerly out into the water, her face
twisted with self-consciousness. "Come to Salvation, honey!" Daddy
bawled. "Come to life everlastin!" He slogged toward her and took
her hand with his own, his three-inch nails locking over her skin like
the jaws of a trap. "I baptize thee in the name of God, my father, and
Jesus, my brother, and in the name of Daddy Salvation, that you may
have grace, life, and riches untold everlastin!" He pulled her to
him, locked his arms around her breasts, and she and he almost vanished under the muddy surface together. A second later they re-
emerged. A roar went up from the pond bank: *"Praise Gawd!"* The
girl's eyes were wide, white, dazed; a rigid smile was on her face; the
drenched vestments clung to her body as she lurched toward shore.
Daddy Salvation raised his hands. "Send me another sinner!" he
hollered.

Huse Whitley closed his eyes and stood rigidly against the pressure of his mother's hand on his back. "Son, please," she urged, "please go down dere and be washed clean."

"No," Huse said harshly. "Let me alone, Mama!"

"Huse, please, you got to be washed clean in de blood ob de Lamb. You got to be baptized in dat Jurdan water. Huse, it make me so happy if you go."

"No," he snapped again. "I said, let me alone!" He slipped from her touch and turned and shoved through the crowd, away from the pond. He was sweating a river, and his stomach was roiling. He did not know whether it was the whiskey in him, the heat of sky and crowd, or the spectacle he had been watching, but he was nearly sick.

He managed to fight free of the worst of the crowd and leaned against the side of the temple; here there was some shade. He heard the blare of the bands, the whooping, praising and singing; it all blended together in one massive frightfulness that scraped his nerves; he closed his eyes again and sagged there, gasping, his hand clutching the bottle inside his shirt. He'd been a fool, a damn idiot, to come here with Lucy, but she had nagged so, begged so, pleaded. . . .

Then his anger against her abated a little. It had, of course, been the measure of her desperation—nothing else had worked; obviously she had hoped that the hysteria of Daddy Salvation's coming would reach inside him where nothing else could and rip out the sinfulness there and change his life. She had meant well, but nothing, he told himself, nothing would ever touch that place inside him that was like a wound; nothing would ever heal it.

He knew, because he had tried everything. Ever since that one final, incredible night with Virginia.

After his encounter with Merit Crane, he had been so enraged, so stunned, that his mind had failed to function for hours. Only when time enough for him to calm had passed did he begin to think rationally. Then he told himself, It don't matter. I love her, she loves me. She's grown and of age. So it don't matter what they think. All that matters is us.

He had felt the anger and despair begin to slough away, as he went mechanically about his chores with Bish. They can't stop us. I don't care who they are, they can't stop us. . . . He went to the telephone, dialed her number. It rang only twice before a woman's voice that was not Virginia's answered.

"Hello."

"Hello. I'd like to speak to Virginia, please."

"Who's calling?"

"Just let me speak to Virginia, please, ma'am."

"Who's calling, please?"

"Is Virginia there?"

"No, I'm sorry, she isn't." And the phone clicked.

The rage came back. He slammed down the phone and stalked the kitchen-office like a penned lion. When he sat down at the desk again, the work before him blurred, made no sense. All he could think of was his anger and despair. He phoned twice more with the same results.

That night he went to the drama workshop. She was not there. He left immediately and wandered through Little Hammer and back out to the Happiness Club. He drank beer until ten and then went home and threw himself on the bed and welcomed the oblivion of sleep.

The next day was a repetition of the previous one. It was not until the third day that the phone rang in Bish's office and he answered it.

"Whitley Funeral Parlor."

"Huse? Oh, darling, is that you?"

"Ginny . . ." His hand tightened on the phone. "I've been trying—"

"I know. Look, I've got to see you. Tonight. Meet me in front of the auditorium. They've finally agreed to let me go back to the workshop."

"I'll be there." He wanted to yell his elation, his determination, but he kept his voice calm.

"Good. I've got to hang up now. I love you." There was no time for him to speak before the connection was broken.

The rest of the day seemed endless. So did the fifteen minutes before she appeared before the auditorium. But when he saw her coming down the walk toward him, wearing the same white dress she had worn the first night they met, he ran to her, held her tightly; and it was all worth while, everything was all right again.

After a second, she pushed his arms away. Her eyes were wide, her face very pale. "The car's outside the gate. Come on."

As he slipped behind the wheel, she said, "I had to give my word of honor I wouldn't see you tonight."

"Don't talk about it," he said. "Not right now. Just sit there, be by me." He roared the car away from the curb and drove straight to the place where they usually parked. It was dark now, and the woods were cool and quiet. He cut the engine and turned toward her and pulled her into his arms and kissed her; she came against him with a new and special kind of hunger, and he felt a kindling in himself.

When they broke loose, he said, "Ginny, Virginia, it's not going to change anything, is it? It's not going to change anything at all?"

She did not even answer, she just pressed her body against him again and held her face up; and he felt her hand on the back of his neck, digging into the flesh there frantically. Her body sank back on the seat, with his bearing down on it, and he felt the touch of her thigh against his flank, pressing, rubbing. He felt her body arch under his, almost convulsively, and he got his hands under her skirt, touching the rim of the pants there, tugging at them instinctively.

Her mouth broke away; he heard the whisper of her voice in his ear. "Huse, wait, give me a chance . . . open the door." She pushed him away. He opened the car door. She was struggling with the pants. He saw the white flash of her thighs beneath the upraised dress. He ripped at his own clothing and came back to her. Her arms pulled him down.

It was awkward; their hands fumbled together. Then he heard the indrawn gasp of her breath. "I knew they couldn't stop us," he said hoarsely, and he poised his body.

All at once it changed to nightmare. Her arms came up, locking across her, pushing him back, her hips tried to pull away. "Huse, no. No, Huse, no, no, no." Her voice was terrified.

He was too far gone to heed her terror now. "Ginny, I've got to—" He eased his body down gently.

"No!" she screamed, and her voice rang and echoed through the still woods. "No, I can't do it. Don't you understand? *I don't want a nigger baby!*"

Then she was hitting and clawing at him, twisting away from beneath him, and Houston Whitley sat up, the words penetrating his brain with a kind of delayed action, quenching his desire and paralyzing thought.

His hands did things with his clothes automatically. She was sitting up, crying and panting. He stared at her, still frozen. He managed one word. "Ginny . . ."

She covered her face with her hands. "I thought I could do it. I thought it was you I wanted more than the other. I thought . . . right up until then. Oh, Huse, I'm sorry, I'm so damned dreadfully awfully sorry, I'm sorry as I can be, please forgive me, Huse, but I can't, I don't want to, I can't . . ."

She took her face from her hands, drew in a long, shuddering, sniffling breath.

"They finally agreed to it," she whispered. "What I've dreamed of all my life. They're . . . they're sending me away, letting me go to New York, to dramatic school, by myself." Her face was a mask of grief turned toward him. "After you left the other night, we had a terrible argument. I . . . I told them they couldn't stop me, that I loved you—I do love you, Huse, I really do, you believe me—I told 'em I wasn't going to let anything— It was the first time I ever defied them. I wouldn't leave my room after that, I wouldn't talk to them. And then finally, this morning, they came to me and said I could do it. That I could go to New York and study and . . . if I would just go away from you."

He still sat without moving, but emotion was stirring in him now. Comprehension. And with comprehension, a terrible sickness.

He felt as if he were about to cry himself. He said hoarsely, "Ginny. You can't—"

"I didn't know what to do. All my life, the one thing I've wanted, a chance to act—and you—and they wouldn't even have let me if it hadn't been for you, and I do love you, but don't you see?"

"No, I don't." His brain was working now. "Listen, if you want to go to New York, all right, go. I'll go, too. I can live there just as well as down here. You can study and we can still get married and—"

"I thought I could," she said sadly. "Don't you think I thought about that, too? Only—you don't understand, Huse. Neither did I, right up until that last minute just now. But, don't you see? I can go to New York as . . . as a *white woman!*"

Before he could answer, her voice dropped, steadied, and went on with husky intensity.

"Not a Negro any more. Once I'm up there, it's all behind me. Don't you understand, Huse? This is my chance to be free! All my life I've felt I belonged in that world; all I had to do was get on a train to move into it. Now I can. And as much as I love you, I can't take you with me. I thought for a little while maybe I could. I even thought that if I could have you it would be enough and I wouldn't have to go. But when I felt you inside me, I . . . I was so afraid. I could see myself shut back in the same old box. It's not your fault, it's not my fault. It's just that I've got a whole life ahead of me and I can't bear to spend it black when I can spend it white!"

He remembered very little of what happened after that. He remembered that he had begun to laugh and could not stop. And while he was still laughing, he rose to his feet and began to run through the woods. Nigger, he thought crazily, somebody's always making this nigger run. He laughed and ran until he tripped over a log in the woods, and when he sprawled on the cool, wet leaves, he just lay there and laughed until there was no breath in him and his body jerked spasmodically with silent laughter. He heard her voice calling desperately to him, eerie in the night silence; he heard the roar of the car engine at last; he lay there for a long time after it was gone before he at last got to his feet and began the walk through darkness back to town. . . .

The baptizing was over now, and people were filing into the Temple of Salvation, the baptized ones still in their drenched and muddy vestments. Huse tried to avoid Lucy, but she caught him ducking around the end of the building. Her wrinkled face was taut with grief and worry. "Son, please come on inside for the service. It do you lot of good. Daddy Salvation, he a powerful preacher."

She was the only one who could touch him now, who could make any claim on him at all. Slowly, reluctantly, he let her guide him into the hot, dim interior of the temple; she scrooched onto a crowded bench and he sat down beside her.

The temple was richly furnished within, with a red carpet down the aisle and into the chancel, where a white-clad choir of angels had gathered. A piano rang out tinnily and the choir began to sing *Was you there when they crucified my Lord*. Huse felt sweat rolling in rivulets down his flanks, drenching his starched white shirt, though he was coatless. The congregation joined; the church swelled with the rich sound of voices, and when it was over, a hush fell. Suddenly the choir began another rousing song: *Daddy Salvation is the Son of God*. Daddy himself appeared in the chancel, stood on the red-carpeted dais. He had changed into morning clothes again; his hair glittered with plastered grease; he held up his hands over his head like a prizefighter taking applause while the singing, its rhythm infectious, went on, choir and audience alike roaring and clapping hands.

Huse did not sing. His hand caressed the bottle inside his shirt. Desperately, he wanted a drink. God, it was hot in here. Why had he let himself be brought?

Daddy Salvation began to pray. He had a loud, fine voice that reached to every corner of the temple. Huse bowed his head, while Daddy Salvation talked directly to God.

"Lord, you've sent me a fine congregation today. You've sent me down a wondrous bunch of angels. What's that you say, Lord? You say they've found favor in your eyes? Ah, that's fine, Lord, thank you . . ."

The congregation murmured in awe and affirmation all through the prayer. Huse tried not to hear either the murmuring or the praying. He blotted it out with remembering what had happened after that last night with Virginia.

It was not easy to remember. It was a blur of drunken fog and action, of carousing and fighting. Nigger, nigger, nigger, his brain had screamed. They want nigger? Everybody want nigger? Well, I'll give 'em nigger!

He had sought oblivion by trying to get to the core of his own blackness. If, beneath the veneer of education, training, experience, nothing had changed in the hundreds of years since his ancestors had come from Africa, if, within him, there was a savage, naked, painted, a bone in its nose—why, then, let the savage have his chance. It had been, he knew now, the savage who had laughed hysterically that night, the savage that had known all along what a great, sardonic joke it was to try to be anything else. He had plunged into the violent night life of Little Hammer like a man throwing himself into a whirlpool. He made himself a terror, worse than Robert, and exulted in it—drinking immensely, fighting viciously, taking women indiscriminately. Houston Whitley had failed; now let the savage have his chance!

Lucy had been frantic with worry. He had disregarded her. Only her most tearful efforts had brought him here today. Now he was both fascinated and repelled by what he had seen. The savage in him responded urgently to these hysterical, primitive rites. The savage urged him to join, to accept. Then there would be no vestige of anything but nigger left; he could return completely to the womb of blackness, forever safe from the responsibility of his own actions and the hurt and grief that came with it.

Daddy Salvation was preaching.

"And the Lord tells me, Daddy, my son, go down there into Hannington and tell those good people about all the many mansions I got waiting for them in my house. Go down there and tell them that it don't matter what happens to them today, that it's what's going to happen in that great tomorrow that counts. Go down there and tell them that if they can't have a Cadillac automobile on earth, I'll give 'em one in heaven! Go down there and tell them that if they can't find peace and rest down there, they can take it on a feather bed when they get up here. You go down and tell 'em all that, Daddy, my son, tell 'em of my grace and shed it all over them and make them born anew . . ."

It was a kind of chant, and the audience was chanting with him as he chanted and bounced in his shiny black patent-leather shoes. "Lawd, listen! . . . Ain't he won'erful? Praise God, amen. . . . Praise good Daddy . . ."

Huse felt a tightness in his throat. He looked at the sea of sweating, dark, enraptured faces. Something churned in his belly. No, he thought desperately. No, I can't—

He shook himself all over, a long, rippling shudder, like a dog coming out of water. To sink in this darkness, to let this blackness close over his head—it was so tempting and so horrifying. Terror rose in him as he found that, deep within, he was responding to the rolling rhythms of Daddy Salvation's preaching; he was having to think consciously to keep from voicing his own instinctive response. The savage was battering away, seeking complete control; and all at once he was afraid of the savage again.

Collection. Daddy Salvation was making the collection speech.

"And the Lord loveth a cheerful giver. And the Lord loveth pennies. And He loveth nickels and He loveth dimes. He loveth hard money, but He loveth folding money more. He loveth dollar bills and He loveth fives and He loveth tens, and, verily, as ye give, so shall ye have grace."

Angels with collection plates were passing up and down the aisle.

"He say, Daddy, tell them people down in Hannington, tell 'em that their good works and their cheerful giving shall find favor in My eyes. Tell 'em that if there's one thing I despise, it's a stingy giver, for My work on earth must go on. The whole world has got to know that Daddy Salvation has got the secret of grace, so wars can end and oppression stop and heaven on earth come down. And so I tell you, verily, the Lord say *give!*"

Huse saw a dozen work-worn hands begin to tug at knotted handkerchiefs, where small change had been tied in the corners for safekeeping. He saw calloused fingers dip into creased and soft-sweated wallets and take out green money. He heard the angel choir singing; he saw Lucy, her own eyes glowing, fumbling in her pocket, watched with horror as she unknotted her own Sunday-school money that should have gone to the A.M.E. Zion Church, the weekly quarter, hard-saved from bus fare. He heard the singing and the clapping and the shouting and the praising; sweat ran down his face, his stomach roiled; he closed his eyes. So much blackness. . . .

The collection plate was thrust under his nose. It was heaped with a feathery, incredible mound of bills. He heard the clink of Lucy's change as it dropped in.

Fury, revulsion, hate and horror rose in him. He threw up a hand, knocked the plate high. Money went showering. Lucy exclaimed, "Huse!" But he was on his feet now, shaking all over with dread. All this blackness—it was closing in on him, he was being locked in a coffin by it, shut down, smothered; he could not stand it.

Blindly he turned and ran as fast as he could from the church, running again, knowing that he could not stop this time, could not stop running until he was somewhere free of blackness. He broke into the coolness of the outdoors, the fresh air fine in his lungs, and as he came into the bright sunlight, still running, he knew that he would have to run a long way, and that the direction in which he had to run was North. . . .

BOOK TWO
1955-1956

1 By eleven-thirty the little courtroom in the city hall had become intolerably stuffy. Cary Bradham glanced hopefully at his watch. Maybe Judge Mims would call the noon recess immediately after the next case. He sighed, picked up the warrant from the table, glanced at it, and handed it to the bailiff. The bailiff barked a name. "Cletus French!"

The gaunt young Negro who arose from the guarded bench at the side of the courtroom was absolutely black; the sunlight through drawn venetian blinds struck blue gleams from his cheekbones. His wiry hair was long and tousled; an enormous Adam's apple worked in his stringy neck. He wore a filthy T shirt and a pair of equally dirty winter pants far too thick for the season. When he ambled before the bench, Cary stepped to one side; the Negro smelled of vomit.

"Cletus French," said the judge. "Charged with being drunk and disorderly in violation of city ordinance twelve-fourteen. How you plead, Cletus?"

"Suh?" The Negro knuckled at his eyes.

"How you plead?" Judge Mims was a soft-looking old man with a red face and short temper. "Were you drunk?"

"Drunk?" Cletus French seemed trying to decide. "Yassuh, I reckon, a little bit. But I been lots drunker."

The little courtroom rippled with the laughter of the whites who were awaiting trial for traffic offenses. Cary nodded to Dr. Crandall, sitting in the front row, and the doctor nodded back.

"Then you plead guilty," Mims was saying. "Do you have counsel?"

"Counsel?" Cletus scratched his head.

Cary Bradham stepped forward. "Your Honor."

"Yes, Mr. Solicitor."

"Dr. Ralph Crandall is here in behalf of the defendant."

Judge Mims adjusted his glasses. "Oh, hello, Ralph. I didn't see you sittin' out there. You got somethin' you want to say about this boy?"

Dr. Crandall was one of the more fashionable general surgeons in Hannington. "Yes, sir, Your Honor. Cletus is a pretty good boy. I don't know of his having been in any trouble before. I'm sure if you let him off this time, he'll be okay." Crandall paused. "Besides," he added, grinning, "he's my yardman and I got a truckload of fertilizer just been dumped on my lawn out home now, waiting for somebody to spread it. If you can't let him off, I sure hope you'll suspend his sentence, Judge. I ain't exactly a popular man in my neighborhood right now with all that manure piled up."

The court roared with laughter. Even Cletus grinned broadly, as if in appreciation of an excellent joke. After a moment, Mims slapped his desk with his gavel.

"All right, Ralph. But see that he stays out of trouble. Cletus French, a plea of guilty is hereby entered and you are sentenced to thirty days on the roads, suspended on condition that you pay costs of court and violate no law for one year. That's twelve months you've got to lay off the popskull, Cletus, or if you drink it, you better stay at home until it wears off." Mims rapped the gavel again. "This court is recessed until one P.M."

Cletus stood where he was, looking about uncomprehendingly. Crandall came forward. "My God, Cletus, you smell worse than the fertilizer." He squeezed Cary's arm. "I appreciate it, Cary. Come on, Cletus. I'm going to take your fine out of your pay, a dollar a week for ten weeks, you hear? And if you get into any more trouble, I'm going to let 'em shoot you straight onto the roads."

"Yassuh, Dr. Ralph, thank you, suh."

Crandall herded Cletus out. Cary took his handkerchief and mopped his forehead. What I need, he thought, is a good night's sleep. . . . He'd had too much to drink at the Young Democrats' party last night and his head was throbbing, his senses dulled, everything about him remote and foggy. He hoped he hadn't made a damned fool out of himself last night. Well, if he had, Mary Scott—who hadn't been up when he left the house this morning—would tell him all about it when he got home.

He slipped his briefcase under his arm and went through a corridor to the little cubicle that served as his office. About six more months of this, he thought; that's all I can take. If I never see another drunk nigger or cheap whore again, it'll be too soon. Thank God, I'll be out of this rat race and into the Legislature this fall. . . .

He opened the office door and stepped inside, tossed his briefcase on a chair and closed the door; he had done all that before he saw the man sitting behind his desk.

The man had a round, sallow face and was nearly bald. His brows were pale above bright blue eyes. His heavy torso was clad in a white sport shirt, and two rubber-tipped canes were laid before him across Cary's desk. When he grinned at Cary a fan of wrinkles crinkled the corner of each eye. "Hello, chum. How's the jail and bail business?"

Cary stared at him blankly for an instant, and then he yelled with the exuberance he felt. "Burke!"

"In about thirty pounds too much of the flesh." Burke Jessup chuckled, and he leaned forward across the desk, extending a thick-fingered hand. " 'Scuse me if I don't stand up. It's more trouble than it's worth these days. Cary, how in the hell you doing?"

Cary gripped his hand as hard as he could. "Why, you sneaky old sonofabitch. What are you doing back in Hannington? I thought you were workin' on a paper in Philadelphia. Who do you think you are, tippytoeing into my private sanctum like this? God, Burke, it's good to see you."

"Likewise." Burke gestured expansively. "Don't be shy. Sit down. After all, it's your office."

Cary pushed his briefcase onto the floor and dropped into a chair. "Well, what made you decide to visit after all this time? How long you here for?"

"Permanently, I hope," Burke said quietly.

Cary's pleasure deepened. He had not quite realized until this moment how much he had missed Burke, and for how long. A man made only a few friends like that, friends whose personalities meshed exactly with his own, so that there was always a flow of understanding and confidence between them. He had, years ago, depended on Burke for that kind of friendship and had missed it a great deal, especially lately. Maybe some men had wives that filled that need, but, of course, Mary Scott . . . He said, "That's good news. What's the deal?"

Burke took out cigarettes and a lighter. "Well, it seemed about time to take a flyer into free enterprise. Maggie and I scraped the bottom of the barrel and wrung out the socks and raised enough cash to make a down payment on the Kenoree County *Enterprise*." He laughed. "You know the old story—every newspaper man dreams of owning a weekly paper in his old hometown. Well, we decided to give it a whirl."

"The *Enterprise*? My God, I didn't know they were still publishing weekly papers."

"Oh, yeah. Some of them are pretty prosperous. A lot of country people still subscribe to one weekly instead of the dailies. And the *Enterprise* seems to cover Kenoree County like the dew. Old Charlie Fesperman used to be on the *Herald* with my daddy, you know, before he bought the *Enterprise* years ago. He and I have been in touch from time to time." Burke sobered. "Now Charlie finds that he's got cancer. He's an old, tired sick man with no heirs, and so he offered us pretty reasonable terms." He laughed shortly and not without bitterness. "It had to be damned reasonable. Otherwise we couldn't have touched it."

Cary glanced at his watch. "In honor of this occasion," he said, "I think a small libation is called for. Look in the bottom drawer, there."

Burke arched his pale brows, then bent. In a moment he placed a half-empty pint bottle of bourbon and two paper cups on the desk. "Ordinarily," Cary said with a tinge of defensiveness which he hoped did not betray the lie, "I don't touch the stuff during working hours. But a snort before lunch won't hurt—you're going to eat with me, aren't you?"

"Figured on it." Burke nodded. He raised the cup, looked at it with a certain amusement and said, "Here's to whatever." Then he tossed the undiluted whiskey off at a single gulp.

Cary drank his the same way, grateful for the slow, settling calm that flowed along the pathways of his body. He looked at Burke hopefully. "Another?"

"Nope. One shot of hot whiskey at high noon's about my limit. My equilibrium's not too good as it is." Burke slid the bottle back in the drawer for him, tossed the crumpled cups in the wastebasket, and then, with a smooth, fluid motion that bulged his arm and shoulder muscles beneath his shirt, levered himself with the two canes to his feet. Cary restrained the impulse to take his arm as he shuffled toward the door, the built-up shoes making their slow, awkward sound on the plastic tile floor.

Burke grinned over his shoulder. "You can see that I don't attend many square dances."

"No," said Cary, "I reckon not."

When they were settled in a booth in the Main Street Grill, the unpretentious restaurant where Cary usually lunched because it was close to City Hall, Burke said, panting slightly, "Well . . . how is everybody? What's the news?"

Cary shrugged. "No news. Everybody still doing business at the same old stand."

"The Moody-Bradham combine still rolling along like a juggernaut, I take it."

Cary grinned. "I'd say the regime was stable. You know, that was a pretty sneaky trick you pulled, hauling off and getting married without letting anybody know until it was too late. Mary Scott was real miffed at being cheated out of a trip to Philadelphia."

"Sorry. You know if we'd invited anybody, it would have been you. But I didn't feel up to all the whoop-de-do of anything more than standing up in front of a j.p., and Maggie went along with it. I had to save a little strength for the honeymoon, you know."

Cary nodded. "I'm anxious to meet Maggie," he said. "Did she come down with you?"

Burke nodded. "We rented a furnished house—Charlie Fesperman found it for us and we took it sight unseen. It's not much, but it fits the budget. She's out there now, trying to find out where everything is."

"Well, what about you two coming out to the house for dinner and some drinks tonight? Nothing fancy—there won't be anybody there but us. Give us a chance to get acquainted with Maggie."

"Some other time. It's too short notice to put Mary Scott to that much trouble."

"Hell, she'll slice my throat if she finds out you and Maggie are in town and she didn't get first crack at you. I'll call her when we get back from lunch. You won't have any trouble finding the place— we've got a house out on the Shady Branch road, right above that spring where we used to camp when we were kids."

Burke's brows arched again. "You're a country squire, huh?"

Cary shook his head. "There's damned little country left right around Hannington. Didn't you notice on your way in how things are built up? This town's booming, Burke. It went crazy after the war—now it's doubled its size. Better than a hundred and fifty thousand people now—we're shooting for two hundred thousand in the next census. We've got teams prowling around the North trying to persuade the Yankees to relocate their plants down here and—we've got plans to turn Muskogee into a right fair industrial state."

"You're going to have to do something," Burke said. "We sure did see a mess of empty croppers' shacks on the way down. Not just here, all along the line."

"Yep. They're all migrating to Washington and Detroit and New York and St. Louis, places like that. Acreage allotments and mechanization's got 'em. Why, we've lost half a dozen families off The Place ourselves, and we don't even miss 'em."

The waitress arrived at last and they gave their orders.

Burke sipped from the glass of water she had brought. "How are things down here now? Pretty tense?"

Cary smiled, shaking his head. "No, actually they're fairly quiet."

"The Supreme Court ruling didn't stir up a lot of hassle?"

Cary shrugged. "Some. But after all, they backed off from implementing it. Nobody knows what they're really going to try to require of us until they render their decision on the reargument. Besides"— he grinned—"the State of Muskogee doesn't acknowledge that they have ever really ruled anything."

Burke's eyes widened. "What?"

"According to our interpretation, the ruling is clearly illegal. The Constitution gives the Federal government no authority to interfere in a state system of education."

"You mean you're simply pretending that the ruling doesn't exist?"

"That's about the size of it," Cary said. "We're not even participating in the reargument. For that matter, neither are Georgia, Alabama, and Mississippi."

Burke rubbed his face. "Just what in hell do you expect to gain by that?"

"It seemed pretty wild to me at first, too, until Dad and Hoke Moody explained the reason for the decision. But the main objective is to maintain a consistent attitude. Muskogee had no intention of desegregating its schools or anything else, no matter what the Supreme Court says. So, except for strengthening a few of our laws in the Legislature last fall, without reference at all to the decision, we're taking no action. The ruling won't be enforced here because it's contrary to state law and an invasion of states' rights and thus illegal—and that's that."

"You're talking nullification," Burke said, a little incredulously. He shook his head. "It sounds fantastic to me, like all the preliminary maneuvering before the Civil War. Like history repeating itself."

"Listen," Cary said, not unaware of the tinge of disapproval in Burke's voice, "we've spent millions of dollars, just like every other Southern state, to build new colored schools. We've been building 'em like crazy for the past three years. A lot of niggers are going to better schools now than white children have got. In this state, at least, they've got no complaint. They know there's not going to be any integration and they're not pushing for it. All right, so it amounts to nullification of the Supreme Court decision. So what? Even if they come up with some wild, harebrained scheme for complete integration immediately—which they're not; they know what a hot potato they've got—how could they enforce it? Send in Federal troops? Reconquer the South? All right, let them play their political gambit. But there's not going to be any integration in Muskogee and that's that. This is April, 1955, not April, 1865. They're not dealing with a conquered country now."

He broke off, aware that Burke was looking at him speculatively, the makings of a wry smile on his lips. "You sound just like the senior Senator from Muskogee. Do you really believe the world's going to come to an end if the barriers fall?"

Cary was silent for a moment. When he spoke again, he tried to get all the sincerity of what he felt into his words. "Look," he said, "I never thought about niggers until I got home from overseas. Neither did anybody else around here; they were just here and there was a system for taking care of 'em and it seemed to be working pretty good. You know how I used to feel about Huse, how I've never had anything against niggers or anybody else." His voice harshened now, and he pointed in the direction of City Hall.

"But I've been down there in City Court for nearly two years now. Day in and day out, I've seen the parade of burrheads come through there; I rassle with 'em all day long. Believe me, it's been a revelation. I used to think that Daddy and Uncle Hoke were just plain old-fashioned demagogues when they'd talk about what a bunch of . . . of apes niggers were. But now I know that that's because they knew them and I didn't. But I know 'em now. I know 'em inside and out. They'll steal anything that ain't tied down. They'll cut each other up and kill each other in an argument over a nickel. They got no more sense of responsibility, no more morality, than a pen full of hound dogs."

"You sound pretty rough," Burke said thinly. "You sound bitter."

"You should have spent two years like I have. What I've seen down there in court is enough to turn a pig's stomach. Sure, there's good ones, honest ones, clean ones, faithful ones, law-abiding ones. But they're in a damned small minority." He let out a long breath. "I don't have any kids of my own. But even so, I'm not going to see the white children of this state forced to associate with the dirty, uneducated, immoral riffraff out of Little Hammer, learning all kinds of bad habits and vices, picking up all sorts of filthy diseases. There are plenty of white people I don't want to associate with either, and just like I reserve the right not to associate with them, so I reserve the right not to be forced by a bunch of bleeding-heart liberals to associate with undesirable black people. That's just the way I feel." He paused. "What do you think?"

Burke grinned. "I think," he said easily, "that it's a subject I'm not going to get into an argument with you about. Anyhow, I'm not an expert like you. I've been away too long, exiled in the wilderness of the North."

"Yes," Cary said. "I'm curious. Last time I saw you, back in 1946, you were looped to the gills and swearing you'd never come back. And there hasn't been a word about coming home in your letters. What made you take such a notion so quick?"

The waitress brought their food. Burke spread his napkin in his lap. His face was grave.

"Well," he said, "I've watched it all. From the Dixiecrat rebellion in 1948 on. I've watched it build up bit by bit, and now I've got the feeling that it's coming to a head, and maybe I just decided I wanted a ringside seat. Besides, I'm kind of—personally—running out of steam. I need to work at something where I can sort of pick my own gait. The hours on a morning paper are bastardly." He grinned. "Or maybe that's all rationalization. Maybe the truth is, I'm just like a dog with an impulse to go back and pee on his own home post."

Cary relaxed and smiled; all at once there was a reaching out from him toward Burke. "Well, I'm glad as hell you're back," he said softly. "It's been rough going around here without somebody I can . . . sort of trust to blow off steam to."

He saw the understanding in Burke's face. "I mean," Cary went on haltingly, "you know—I'm under such a hell of a lot of pressure all the time. It seems that when I got home from the war they had quite a program laid out for me."

"Yeah. I've been following your career. You haven't missed a lick, have you? And you'll be going into the Legislature this fall."

"That's right. Anyhow, I've kind of got to walk a chalk line all the time. You know . . ."

"Sure. You're a public figure now. It's hard to be your own man."

"That's it, exactly," Cary said, appreciative of Burke's quick understanding.

Burke's mouth twisted. "You want to be a public figure that much?"

"It doesn't matter what I want. There's not any way out of it."

"Why not? You could always tell Hoke Moody to go take a running jump—"

"It's not Hoke Moody." There was a tinge of anger in Cary's voice. "If Hoke Moody didn't exist, I would still have to do what I'm doing. You know that."

The derision vanished from Burke's face. "I reckon so. It's what you might call the Bradham doom." He smiled, changing the subject. "I hope Mary Scott and Maggie'll take to each other. I always liked Mary Scott. Of course we didn't run exactly in the same circles and you were the only link between us. But she could have been a lot more stuck-up on account of her old man's money than she was. Maggie's never been South before and this is all going to be kind of strange and lonesome to her. You reckon Mary Scott would kind of take her under her wing and ease her in to some of these clannish local circles?"

"Hell, yes, she'll be glad to." Cary looked at his watch. "Damn, I've got to hurry. Mims will be reconvening in fifteen minutes. Look, we'll see you and Maggie tonight, about seven. Okay?"

"Fine. We appreciate the invitation. You go ahead now. I've got to spend this afternoon at the *Enterprise* office anyhow. Tell Mary Scott hello."

Once, on this high plateau, he and Burke had hunted doves and quail. Now his house and four others covered its tableland, but of the five his was the largest. Mary Scott had planned it herself and furnished it with a genuine talent for decoration. It was a long, low, graceful structure of antique brick, carefully landscaped and shaded by big pecan trees that were the remnants of an ancient orchard.

Cary parked the car in the garage beside Mary Scott's station wagon and entered the house through the back door. Lois, the young combination maid and cook, was putting a pie in the oven as he went through the kitchen into dining and living rooms and saw no sign of his wife. He did not call her, but went to his den, opened a locked whiskey cabinet there, took out a bottle and returned to the kitchen.

"Where's Mrs. Bradham, Lois?" he asked as he made himself a highball that was deep amber.

"She in de bedroom gittin herself fixed fo' de company tonight."

"All right." Cary took his drink back to the den, removed his coat, loosened his tie, unlaced his shoes. He dropped into an easy chair and propped his feet on a hassock after switching on the television set. He watched the commercial that swam into view on the screen without even really seeing it. What he was interested in was the drink and the loving fingers with which it would caress his body and brain.

He needed it less tonight, though, than usual. Tonight, instead of his usual emptiness, he felt a positive emotion for the first time in a great while—pleasure at the coming of Burke and Maggie.

It was not often any more that he could feel something that could be definitively identified as pleasure rather than the absence of discontent. His feelings, over the years, seemed to have shrunk away from the surface, to have concentrated themselves in a small, inert ball, deep within him and beyond reach from outside, safe, like a creature curled and hibernating in a stump. He could not even really hate Mary Scott any more.

He had gone into the marriage hating her. Hating the entrapment, the deliberate entrapment, that now would cost him the years of youth to which he was entitled. He had taken his revenge upon her by making no effort to conceal his unhappiness, and this had hurt her, and she had taken hers on him by pretending not to notice and carefully continuing to enact the part of the loving wife. After the child had been born dead, the desire for revenge went out of both of them. They began to be polite to each other, and now they had built a simulacrum of a happy marriage, not enough to fool either one of them, but enough to deceive everybody else. It was the only course open to them, because divorce was, in his situation, impossible, and it had never even been discussed. Anyway, for all he knew, she might even have all that was required to make her happy.

For himself, he got along all right now, except that he sometimes worried about the diminution of his sexual desire. From the first enraged moment of realization of his entrapment, Mary Scott's body had become repellent to him and there had been tremendous temptation to be flagrantly unfaithful. But so much was pivoted on him, he was at the center of such a web of plans, its warp and woof extending to such portentous reaches, that his courage failed him when he considered the possibility of disastrous scandal. So there had been only a few casual, almost anonymous encounters and they had been a long time ago. Occasionally, driven by angry masculine pride and determination rather than necessity, he approached Mary Scott, but, more than likely, it would be on a night when there was no spark of any kind in her, and those occasions, dreadful, were now infrequent. As if atrophied from disuse, his sexual impulse was no longer urgent; and that made it easier.

Thus they lived together in a polite and mutually cooperative neutrality, enacting the necessary charade of deep affection in the presence of a third party of any sort (except the cook), and no longer attempting to hurt each other. They had both learned that it was not true that after years of living with someone you must feel either love or hate; they had learned that it was entirely possible to feel nothing.

The drink was half finished when he became aware of Mary Scott in the doorway. She was wearing a robe of pink satin and her yellow-gold hair was pushed up on her head. She had courageously fought her tendency to plumpness to a standstill and was, he thought dispassionately, certainly a good-looking woman. But she stirred him no more than a wax figure might have.

"I didn't know you were home," she said, and she came to him and bent; he saw the swaying dangle of her breasts as the robe gaped, and felt no response. Her lips touched his fleetingly and coolly in a ritual kiss. When she straightened up, she looked at the glass in his hand.

"I'm glad you invited Burke and his wife out tonight. I called her on the phone and she sounded real nice. But please don't get so far along that you're hopeless by the time they get here. You had an awful lot last night. That drinking's not doing you any good."

"I've had a rough day," he said without anger or defensiveness. "Mondays are always bad. I think every nigger in Hannington got drunk or used an ice pick on somebody over the weekend. Did you pick up that bottle of Scotch? You know how Yankees like Scotch."

"I got it, but I don't see how anybody can drink the stuff."

"Well, they like it up North. What are you having for dinner?"

"Sirloin tip roast, candied sweet potatoes, string beans, tossed salad, corn sticks and chess pie."

"Sounds fine," he said.

"You'd better take your shower," she said. "You look awfully sweaty."

"I will. I'm going to have one more drink first."

"All right. I've got to finish putting on my makeup." She turned away. He watched her go, finished the rest of the drink with a quick gulp and got up and made himself another one.

2 "You know," Maggie Jessup said, "for me this is just like coming to a foreign country. Somehow I never got South before. But it's so much prettier than I had even imagined. Everything's so green—and those absolutely gorgeous azaleas!"

Beside her on the living-room sofa, Burke Jessup laughed softly. "See, you're getting the magnolia and mockingbird symptoms already. One more martini and you'll run out and buy a hoopskirt."

She laughed, too. "I guess not. Having to wear a girdle's bad enough."

Seated in a chair a little distance away, Cary looked at her across the rim of his glass, his vision a little blurred by whiskey. Before the Jessups came, he had been wondering, rather brutally, what sort of woman would marry a man like Burke, a man so physically unattractive and helpless. He had imagined some sour New England frostbitten type, driven by fear of becoming an old maid into snatching even damaged merchandise like Burke, or a neurotic working out a penance. He had not expected this.

She was not tall, but she was slender and that helped give her the impression of height. So, too, did the erectness of her carriage; her shoulders seemed never to slump and their straightness emphasized small but attractive breasts that rode high on her body. Her hair was dark brown, with blond highlights in it, and she wore it close-cut, so that it made a sort of softened helmet on her head. Her face was triangular, not beautiful, her cheekbones prominent, chin slightly pointed, cheeks and nose faintly dusted with freckles and teeth somewhat irregular, though white. But her eyes were large and their lashes long, and, a surprising mixture of blue-green, they had a way of looking directly at the person to whom she talked or listened, usually with a friendly warmth and the compliment of complete attention. She would, he thought, be at least as old as Burke and maybe a couple of years older: there were definite crinkles of crow's-feet at the corners of her eyes, but somehow on her they were becoming.

Burke did himself proud, he thought, pleased for his friend, but not without a touch of envy as he looked at Mary Scott, who had seemed immediately to realize she was out of her depth and had taken little part in the conversation after the excellent dinner. Then he brought his mind back to what Burke was saying.

"Huse?" he answered. "Well, I don't really know how he's getting along. The only news I get of him is through Lucy—she still works for the folks. Huse came home from the army and I went fishing with him one time, but he'd changed so I hardly knew him."

"Changed?" Burke looked interested.

"Yeah. You know—his eyes were bigger than his stomach. He came home filled with the usual crap they pick up in the army. Practically demanded that Dad and I find some kind of superspecial job for him. I don't know exactly what he thought we could get him— maybe chief of the State Highway Commission or something. Anyhow, Dad tried to line up a job, but he practically threw it back in his face and after that he took off and went North. Got himself a college degree and married some brown girl and came back, and now they're both teaching in the city school system here, but I never see him any more." He paused, a little surprised and amused by the note of sadness in his own voice. "I reckon it's just as well."

Maggie looked interested. "Huse? He's the Negro you told me about, Burke?"

"Yes," Mary Scott said. "One of Cary's old playmates." There was a faint edge of disgust to her voice.

"He was one of mine, too," Burke said. "We had a hell of a good time, the three of us. But his trouble was—well, I don't know whether you can call it trouble or not. But anyhow, I used to think sometimes that he was about the brightest of the three of us."

"I'd like to meet him sometime," Maggie said casually. "He must be quite a guy."

Cary heard Mary Scott make a muffled noise of astonishment.

"I always get so amused," Maggie went on, "listening to Burke's misty-eyed reminiscences about his dear little colored friend." She was looking at Cary, smiling with a touch of irony. "He makes such a thing of it. I went through school with several little colored children, but I don't go around buttonholing everybody and telling 'em how some of my best friends were Negroes when I was little. They just were. So what?"

The room was silent for a moment. Then Cary grinned, surprised at the insight that had come to him. "Why, honey chile," he said with an exaggerated drawl, "that's how usn prove us is aristocracy. Down heah, if you didn't have a little niggah to play with when you were growin' up, you just weren't anybody. I mean, you were *white trash.*"

She laughed; he liked the sound of it, not shrill, but coming from deep inside her with pleasure. "Oh, so that's it. It's a status symbol. Excuse me." She arose. "Now I understand. . . . May I have another drink?"

While she poured herself a drink—Cary observed with the heightened perception of liquor that Mary Scott would never have got her own so long as there was a man in the room—the cook, Lois, appeared in the dining room arch. "Miz Bradham, dishes all washed and ever'thang put away. It all right I go now?"

Mary Scott arose. "Excuse me," she said, as she went past Maggie to the kitchen. "I guess I'd better check. You know how it is."

When she had gone, Maggie returned to her chair with a curious look on her face. "No," she said, "how is it?"

Burke shrugged, and there was a moment of silence, one of those lulls that fall occasionally over any gathering. Noticing that neither of his guests seemed uncomfortable or made any desperate effort to mend the gap, Cary was pleased. That meant they were enjoying themselves.

Mary Scott reappeared. "Well," she said, picking up the drink she had been nursing for an hour, "she got everything put away all right for once. I declare, sometimes she leaves such a mess I think she does it on purpose. It looks like after two years she'd know where things went."

"She's a lot better than some we've had," Cary said.

"They're all spoiled," said Mary Scott. "Every time I pay her off on Friday I never know whether she's going to show up on Monday or not." She laughed, as if pleased she had finally found something to add to the conversation. "You know what happened one time? I paid her off and then Monday came and she didn't show up. And then she didn't come Tuesday and I couldn't find her anywhere. I went down to where she lives, but everybody there said they'd never heard of her—it's the way they do, you know, when white people come around asking for one of 'em—and anyhow I was just frantic, without help, and I was just about to call the employment agency to get somebody else when, come Wednesday morning, in she prisses big as life and twice as natural just like nothing had happened. Of course I hopped all over her and asked her where she'd been"—here Mary Scott thickened her own drawl to a whining imitation of Lois— " 'Miz Braddum, I gots sumpin to tell you.' "

Her voice dropped to a whisper anticipatory of shock. "I said, 'What is it, Lois?' and she says, 'Well, Miz Braddum, tell you de truth, I done went and got married.' "

Maggie Jessup nodded, obviously trying to follow the anecdote closely.

"So I asked her," Mary Scott said, "I asked her, 'Well, Lois, wasn't this kind of sudden?' And you know what she said?" She paused and then her mockery thickened and there was laughter in her voice as she bent forward. "She said, 'Well, to tell de truth, Miz Braddum, I done already went and got pregnunt!' "

She laughed and Cary slid down further in his chair, smiling thinly, not missing the irony on Burke's face as he chuckled. Mary Scott loved this story, but it only filled Cary with a kind of sickness, considering the circumstances of their own marriage, and his sickness increased as he saw that Burke had obviously guessed long ago why he and Mary Scott had married.

Maggie Jessup smiled politely. She bent forward, arms across her knees. "That happens among white people, too, sometimes, doesn't it?"

Cary sat up straight, cold, but when he saw the shock on Burke's face he knew that Burke had not told Maggie and that the question had been asked in innocence. Mary Scott's countenance had gone blank; then her mouth straightened out primly.

"I know," Maggie went on smoothly, "that some of the girls in the best families in Philadelphia could have made exactly the same statement."

Mary Scott's face reddened. "Well," she said.

Burke Jessup's voice cut in quickly. "I think the point Mary Scott was trying to make is that it's probably a little more common among the colored people down here, sugar."

Mary Scott looked relieved. "Yes. You know half the nigger children are illegitimate."

For the first time that night, Maggie's good humor seemed to vanish. Her face went bleak. "That's a dreadful word," she said.

"What?" Mary Scott was uncomprehending.

"Nigger," Maggie said. "I detest that word."

A silence that was truly uncomfortable fell across the room then. It lasted for perhaps three ticks of a clock. Cary cleared his throat and sat up straight. "Well," he said defensively, "we don't use it to their faces, Maggie. One of the worst whippings I ever got was when I was a kid and called my nurse a nigger to her face. She went straight to my dad and he whaled the tar out of me. Only white trash call them niggers where they can hear it."

"Why call them niggers at all?" Maggie said sharply. "It's not a very pretty word."

"They use it themselves sometimes—" Cary floundered.

Again Burke cut in. "Honey, don't you know that for a Southerner, saying the word *Negro* takes practice? For somebody with a real Southern accent, *Nigra* is actually about as close as they can come without sounding phony. I think they use the word *nigger* more because it's easier to say than as a term of contempt."

"But it is a term of contempt," Maggie said. "Like kike or sheeny. I don't know, I just don't like it. It's a hate word."

Again the room fell silent. Then Burke chuckled, leaning over and patting Maggie's hand. "You've got to make allowances for Harriet Beecher Stowe here, folks. She comes from a long line of ticket agents on the underground railroad."

Cary realized that he was anxious not to have Maggie angry with him. "It's just the way we were brought up to talk," he said calmly. "We can't help it, Maggie."

With great effort, Burke got up and hobbled toward the bar. He poured himself a drink and then turned, leaning against the table for support. Cary saw that Burke was a little more drunk than he had guessed. He was swaying slightly.

"I explained all the rules to Maggie before we started out," he said, his voice ironic. " 'Darling,' I said, 'darling, one thing you've got to learn is to curb your black abolitionist tongue. Once you're below the Smith and Wesson line, you've got to abide by the rules.' " He raised his glass. "Rule number one: Slavery was the best thing that ever happened to the Negro. It took him out of a coconut tree in Africa and civilized him. Rule two: The Southern Negro lives in the best of all possible worlds. He's free, and yet his white folks are still bound to watch over him and look after him. Rule three: There's no finer or more respected person than a good, old-timey nigger who knows his place. And there's no greater abomination than a Yankee-fied, uppity nigger always carrying on about his rights."

"What did I do to bring all this on?" Maggie asked, smiling help-lessly and spreading her hands.

"Rule four: No matter how long they've worked for you, they're lazy, undependable, always get drunk on Saturday night and lay out on Monday. But they always have such funny excuses it's worth keeping them just to be able to quote 'em at parties." He drained his glass. "Them's the rules, sugar. You got to learn 'em if you're going to live down here. Otherwise the Klan will come and gitcha. Ain't that right, Mary Scott?"

His sardonic lecture had completely disarmed and neutralized her. She laughed. "Burke, you haven't changed a bit."

Cary looked at Maggie. "Seriously," he said, "before you get all upset and condemnatory of us unconstructed rebels, you ought to come down to court someday and watch the cases we run through, day in and day out. Negroes are about forty per cent of the population here, Maggie, but they're responsible for about eighty per cent of the crime. The statistics are there, and if you think the statistics aren't true, you come down and watch that miserable parade in court. That'll give you some of the other side of the picture. Or go talk to the public health officer about diseases or—" He stood up. "You know I've heard this stuff debated for years now, and I'm tired of it myself. Can't we change the subject?"

"I think it's about damn time," Burke said. "Come on and have a drink."

"By all means let's change the subject," Maggie said. "Honestly, I didn't mean to offend anybody. And I wasn't condemning. It's only that—you're right, let's skip it." She turned to Mary Scott. "What do they call those lovely white azaleas you've got out there beside your steps?"

When Cary had poured himself another drink, Burke tapped him on the shoulder and by tacit agreement they went together into the kitchen. Burke did not sit down but leaned, swaying slightly, on his canes.

"Well," he asked softly and with apprehension, "what do you think of Maggie?"

Cary grinned and knuckled his arm. "You did fine. I like her a hell of a lot."

Relief was evident on Burke's face. "That's good. She's quite the little fire-eater and I was afraid she might have made everybody mad." He eased himself down into a chair and took a swallow of his drink. "I was just about at the end of my string when I met her, you know," he said quietly. "I thought I never would get used to being—" He picked up one of the canes and rapped it eloquently against the floor. "Man, I had the black dog riding my back for sure. We were both working on the same paper, me a copy editor, she a society reporter. She moved in on me . . . and it all changed." He frowned. "Now we've got everything sunk in this weekly. Jesus, I hope we can make it go."

"Hell, you will if anybody can."

"I don't know; I'm beginning to have second thoughts after spending the afternoon with Charlie Fesperman. He's a nice old guy personally, but the paper's always been about as far right as it can get. All his editorials need to make them paleolithic is to be chiseled in stone. We're going to have to change that . . . somewhat. I don't know what kind of reception we'll get."

Cary was silent for a moment. "I haven't read a copy of the *Enterprise* in a long time," he said at last. "But if you'll take a friendly word of advice, I wouldn't make any changes that were too radical. Not right away, anyhow. I believe if I were you, I'd kind of feel the situation out before I stuck out my neck. I mean, if the way Maggie talked in there is any indication of what editorial tack you're planning to take. Of course it's a free country, and you're free to write anything you want to, but—"

Burke nodded. "I know. But. Yeah, that's something I should have thought more about before I bought the paper."

"It's not me, you understand," Cary said quickly, defensively. "But a paper's pretty dependent on its advertisers, the way I understand it. And the Citizens' Council is mighty strong here in Hannington right now."

Burke looked up at him. "You mean the uptown Klan?" he asked wryly. "That's what Hodding Carter called it."

Cary grinned. "Don't let 'em hear you call 'em that. Just about every businessman in town has joined since a fellow came over from Mississippi and showed 'em how to start a chapter this January. They take it pretty seriously. That's one reason the local colored gentry are lying low, and that the NAACP is just spinning its wheels trying to organize here. A darky that got the Council down on him could find himself in mighty bad straits pretty quick."

"Economic boycott, eh?"

"I suppose you could call it that. It's nothing like the Klan, Burke, even though I understand there's some raggedy-ass bird running around trying to revive that, too, without much success. These people aren't night riders or nigger lynchers. But they're determined to resist this Supreme Court crap, and so it might pay to go a little easy at first."

Burke nodded. "I suppose you belong, too."

Cary felt his face flush. "Well . . . I had to join for—"

"—for political reasons," Burke finished, nodding again. "Sure, I can understand that." He scratched his head. "And I appreciate the advice. Taking it is where the rub comes in. Maggie's got some pretty set ideas about certain things. As a matter of fact"—he looked up at Cary and their eyes met—"so have I. But I'd hate to think things have come to a pass in my own hometown where I couldn't say what I think without being afraid."

"It all depends on what you think."

Burke let out a gusty sigh. "I just think people are people," he said, almost wearily. "And that everybody ought to be allowed to be people. I don't know, Cary, maybe I made a mistake coming back and getting mixed up in this. I'd hate to see you and me staring down each other's throats, for instance."

"You know that's not going to happen," Cary said quickly. "I don't give a damn what you write about me, that's not going to happen." He laughed. "If you ran a daily with a big circulation, maybe I'd feel different."

"But a gnat bite won't worry you. Well, I'm not going to write anything about you if I can help it. Not till I get my feet on the ground, anyhow. I'm going to look around and try to find out the truth, and then I'll decide what I'll write."

"That sounds reasonable," Cary said gently.

"It's always been my failing. Trying to find out the truth. Only trouble is, one minute the truth is hairy and it's got spots; the next, it's slick and it's got stripes; it's a hard thing to hold onto long enough to identify. But I've been after it for a long time; I reckon I'll keep trying." He set down his glass and picked up his canes and heaved himself to his feet. "Now, shall we join the ladies?"

"Yeah," said Cary. "And let's talk about something else. I'm sick to my stomach with this nigger business."

"It was wonderful," Maggie Jessup said, and there was sincerity in her voice. "It really was. Look, Burke and I should be settled by Saturday night. What about you two coming over to eat with us then?"

They were standing in the doorway while the Jessups said their goodbyes. Mary Scott looked regretful. "We'd love to. But I'm leaving for the beach with my mother Saturday morning. We've got a cottage down there we've got to see to getting ready for the summer."

Maggie looked genuinely disappointed. Then she turned to Cary, who had not heard anything about Mary Scott's being gone over the weekend, but was not surprised; probably it had been arranged today and she had not had a chance to mention it. She felt under no obligation to ask his permission before leaving and he made no point of it.

"Then you'll be alone," Maggie said to Cary. "All the more reason for you to come. You'll need somebody to look after you."

He savored the warmth she stirred in him. "Well, I expect it can be arranged. What time?"

"Any time, it doesn't matter. Early enough for a drink first."

"I'll be riding out at The Place Saturday, but I'll be back in by six. Okay?"

"Ole massa riding over his plantation," Burke said with a grin.

Maggie's eyes flared with interest. "You really do have a plantation, don't you?"

"Sort of one. But I just like riding. That's why I'm going. Not to count the slaves."

"Oh, I love riding too," Maggie said wistfully. "I haven't ridden in years."

"Do you? Then why don't you let me pick up you and Burke and y'all come along? We've got plenty of horses."

"Me on a horse?" Burke sneered.

"Hell, you can contemplate your navel. But if Maggie likes to ride, let her ride. The horses need the exercise. I'll show her around Saturday, and after that she can run out there and use any horse she wants to any time she pleases."

Burke looked at Maggie fondly. "Would you like that?"

"I'd love it," she said hesitantly. "If you'd—"

"Okay," Burke said. "Then it's settled."

Mary Scott moved close to Cary. This was part of the ritual, the act they always put on before outsiders, company and newspapermen alike. His part of it now was to put his arm about her. This time he did not do it.

"Thank you so much again," Maggie said to Mary Scott. "Good night."

Cary watched the Jessups walk to their car, Maggie carefully gaiting herself to Burke's excruciating slowness, ready to steady him if he stumbled. When they were gone, Cary closed the door.

"Well," he said tonelessly, still wide-awake and oddly restless.

Mary Scott walked to an ashtray, picked it up, and emptied it into another one. Cary thought how thick and cowlike she looked compared to Maggie.

"She's very nice," Mary Scott said. "But that Yankee accent sure does get on my nerves. And she smokes like a chimney, doesn't she?" She carried the brimming ashtray toward the kitchen. "It's pretty late and you've got to work tomorrow. You'd better be going to bed."

"I'll be there in a little while," said Cary. "But I think I'll have another drink first."

She did not answer as she vanished into the kitchen.

He poured the drink and carried it into the den. He sat down and propped up his feet, but he did not turn on the television set this time.

I would like a woman tonight, he thought, surprised at the definite stirring in his loins. It was the first time he had felt this way in many days. It would be nice to have a woman tonight, he thought.

He finished his drink and went into the bedroom. Mary Scott had already undressed and was lying in her bed asleep. Cary looked down at her for a moment, his face expressionless. Then he took off his clothes, donned his pajamas, and slid into his own bed.

He had drunk too much and smoked too much, and besides the desire got worse. It was a long time before he got to sleep.

3 The name of the school was Washington Heights Senior High, and it was so new that the tang of fresh paint and damp concrete had not yet departed from its walls. As Houston Whitley left the classroom in which he taught American history, his footsteps on the tinted concrete floor echoed hollowly in the wide, deserted corridor.

As he walked toward the school office, he looked at the shiny glazed-tile walls, the ranks of new lockers, the profusion of sky-domes funneling in light from overhead, and he smiled crookedly, comparing this costly, modern plant with the single cramped room —icy in winter, a furnace in spring—in which Lizzie Blackwelder had done her best to teach. Compared to that, this place was fantastic. It was, in fact, fantastic compared even to the dingy old brick pile, condemned for use by whites, in which he had got his high school education.

But he was not deceived by it. It was a whore of a school, luscious on the outside, empty on the inside, promising much, delivering little. They are only going to give you so much, he thought, and then they stop and make you do without the rest, not because they can't afford it, but because they don't want you to get any ideas just because you got a new building. . . . That, of course, accounted for the fact that except for one outdated encyclopedia, there were no books yet on the shelves of the spacious room designated as a library, no power equipment in the shop, no hot water for the showers in the gym and no athletic equipment, no visual aids; the state-issued textbooks all secondhand castoffs discarded by the white schools. They got to be careful, he thought.

He rubbed his palms against his pants legs. I got to be careful, too, he told himself. I got to sit real loose and be real easy talking to old Dr. Haney. I know what it is; it's what Carson Bell said, and it's got around.

He entered the office and leaned on the counter. Miss Zora, the principal's assistant, looked up from her typewriter and smiled. "Good afternoon, Mr. Whitley."

"Dr. Haney wanted to see me after school." Huse grinned. "Maybe I'm going to be kept in. Is he in his office?"

"Yes, sir. Go right in."

He knocked briefly on the frosted-glass panel of the door to Dr. Haney's office and entered. The man behind the desk within was very old, his face long and horselike, his head bald except for a frosting of white fuzz, like an unshaven beard. Dr. Haney, Huse remembered, had been principal of the other high school when he himself was attending it.

Now Haney looked up, gave Huse a fleeting, mechanical smile and said, in his high, rather prissy voice, "Come in, Houston."

"Thanks." Huse stood before Haney's desk with an idiotic sense of guilt, feeling as if he himself were a student up for punishment. The feeling was not lessened by the way Haney leaned back in his chair and focused muddy eyes on Huse through his gold-rimmed glasses; Haney hooked his thumbs in his pepper-and-salt vest. "Sit down, Houston."

Huse pulled up a softly upholstered chair. "You wanted to see me, sir?"

"Yes." Now Haney leaned forward, locking together dark hands that were surprisingly large for so small a man. He was so old that his body trembled slightly, but perceptibly, almost constantly. Huse tried to read the expression lurking in his eyes. Suddenly he knew what it was: fear, almost terror. Dr. Haney was afraid, and Huse knew that it was a fear he had been carrying with him for years; he himself understood it perfectly. Haney was afraid for his job.

"Houston," Haney quavered after a moment, "you know how important discipline is in this school. I have always insisted on the most rigid discipline."

"Yes, sir."

"I mean, not only discipline of actions, but discipline of speech and of attitude."

"Yes, sir, I know exactly what you mean."

Haney's quavering voice drew out each word he spoke almost intolerably. "I understand that one of your students made a remark in class a few days ago that, if it has reached me correctly, could have dangerous repercussions for us all. Do you know what I mean?"

"I think I do," Huse said. I know damn well what you mean, he thought. It scared me just as bad as it scared you. "You're talking about what Carson Bell said."

Haney nodded. "I understand," he quavered on, "that the Bell boy is a very intelligent youngster. But it sounds like he's also a mighty intractable one."

"He says what he thinks, no two ways about that. He's like his daddy that way." Carson Bell's father, Charles Bell, was the minister of the A.M.E. Zion church which the Whitleys attended, and he had earned a reputation in Hannington as a fiery preacher. "But he's a smart boy with a good working mind. It's just that he's immature."

"Yes, you know that and I know it. But what we both must keep in mind is that when a student in my—our—school makes such a remark, it is liable to be misinterpreted by . . . by other people."

"You mean the school board. The white folks."

"Yes. Exactly." The fear deepened in Haney's watery eyes. "Particularly a remark like that—if it has been reported to me correctly."

"What Carson Bell said," Huse murmured, "was 'They called Hitler a fanatic because he kept on fighting a long time after he knew he was beat. How come Robert E. Lee wasn't a fanatic, too, then? How come he's such a hero instead? He bound to have known by the end of 1864 he didn't have a chance of winning, but he kept on fighting and got a lot of people killed. Don't that make him a fanatic just like Hitler?' "

Doctor Haney shuddered visibly. "Yes, that's the way it was told to me." He removed his glasses. "Can you imagine what would happen if that remark got outside the school to the wrong people?"

"I reckon they'd just about lynch somebody," Huse said.

"Quite right. And it wouldn't be Carson Bell. It would be you—because they'd swear he learned it in your class. And it would be me, because they'd swear I encouraged you to teach it to him." A surprising vigor came into Haney's voice. "Houston, the Bell boy has got to be squelched and kept under control. You've got to have a talk with him."

"I already did," Huse said.

"With what results?"

Huse hesitated. "He said he felt sorry for me. Because I was an Uncle Tom."

Haney sighed. "These impatient young men. They have no understanding at all, this generation." He half closed his eyes, as if fatigue were overtaking him, and his voice became a whisper. "I started teaching school forty years ago in Keyhoe County. There was no support from either the state or the county government. I had to beg scrap lumber to build a schoolhouse with, literally beg it and literally build it with my own hands and what help I could get from the parents. Then I had to sell the idea of schooling. Everybody knew the white folks were against it for Negroes, and everybody was afraid. But I got me a group of children together and I went ahead and taught 'em, and when the white folks burned the schoolhouse down, I went ahead and rebuilt it again. That time I had more help. After a while, when they saw we weren't going to quit, the county came along and took over the school so it could control it. It was the first public school for Negroes in Keyhoe County since Reconstruction times . . ."

His voice trailed off. "I was a young man then," he said at last, "and I didn't have sense enough to know what I was up against. But I'm a young man no longer—I'm old and tired. Just the same, I've —we've—come a long way. When I think of my old building and then look at this . . ." His voice was almost tearful. "We didn't get to where we are by mocking the white man and making smart remarks about people like Robert E. Lee that he worships. We got here by negotiating and compromising and pleasing, and I think what we've managed to get speaks for itself. I don't want any smart-alec boy jeopardizing it, either. I want you to talk to Carson again,

Huse. I want you to make it plain to him that I simply will not tolerate such remarks. White people will show no more respect for us if we show none for them. And you tell him this—that if I hear him use the words Uncle Tom in this school, I'll see that he's expelled."

"Yes, sir."

Dr. Haney's mind seemed to detach itself; he was no longer talking to Huse. "These are dangerous times, dangerous times; everybody wants to change the old ways overnight. And I've only got until the end of this semester, and then I am to retire. And my pension is all I'll have to live on, and I'll not see it all ruined by an upstart—" He turned back to Huse as if suddenly remembering that he was there.

"That's all, Houston. Just make sure you have a good talk with Bell and report back to me. And, for your own sake, guard against letting any more such remarks be made in your hearing, do you understand?"

Huse stood up. "Yes, sir," he said. "I understand."

Later, driving home, Huse tried to shut Carson Bell out of his mind. He's got to learn, he thought. Like I had to, like everybody's got to. There's no other way out, unless you want to slice your wrists with razor blades.

He had come close to that, too, in his time. Before I got sense, he thought. Before I found out if you can't get what you want, be satisfied with what you got. . . .

When he had fled North as blindly as a runaway slave, he had possessed no clearly formed idea of where he was bound or what he would do. But he remembered Harlem from furloughs in New York, and he had no intention of living there. Vaguely he planned, in the promised land, to live the way a man ought to live, that was all.

But he had to compromise immediately. His army savings had dwindled, and when he found out what rents were, he wound up boarding with a family named Travis in Harlem. They were good people, originally from Georgia, and he shared a room with their oldest boy.

Promising himself it was only temporary, he immediately sought work. Confidently, neatly dressed, watching speech and manners, he answered advertisement after advertisement. He never quite got past the barrier of startled secretaries. There had always been "some mistake." Nobody called him nigger; usually they called him "sir." But the mistake was always there, and he finally realized that he had made it in not mentioning his race in letters or phone calls of application.

He began to feel that he was playing a wild and eerie guessing game, one in which no one would admit to seeing his color, but, instead, confronted him with debilities and shortcomings of different natures—defects he had not known he possessed. Soon he began to understand why weariness, bitterness and cynicism were even more deeply etched in the dark faces here than those at home in Little Hammer. These people had sought a promised land and found none, only a different one. In the South, they had at least known who and what they were; here they had to ascertain their status through trial and humiliating error, dwelling in a kind of foggy limbo, not sure what was permissible and what not, which taboos were enforced and which waived; it was not long before Huse, with horror, was able to recognize the effects of having no fixed identity at all.

He saw it in the young people, clotting the corners, idle, hardeyed, in gangs, making for themselves a collective identity they could not find individually, belonging to their gang and to their turf. He saw it in the wild zoot suits, the desperate attempt to proclaim through dress, *I am somebody*. He saw it in the explosive violence in the cheap bars and grills, in the stunned, withdrawn eyes and faces of drug addicts, in the hopeless slump of the shoulders of old people sitting on steps and fire escapes and roofs at twilight. And he saw it in himself, as the world seemed to be losing its hardness and texture and tangibility.

He got a part-time job, helping in a small grocery store on 128th Street. It felt good to work at something, even that. But still there was a crater in the bleak lunar terrain of his emotions, or, more aptly, a draining abscess that he did not dare touch with memory. Somewhere in the city was Virginia Crane. But not in Harlem, of course. He was possessed with a need to roam the streets downtown and search the crowds, hungry for the sight of her, hopeful that here, on different ground, everything might be different.

All this stressed his personality this way and that, so that it might

have ripped like worn paper if it had not been for Della Marfield. . . .

She came into the grocery store one afternoon for a pound of
dried pinto beans. Small, slight, her skin a soft smooth chocolate,
she was not pretty, but her eyes were large, calm, yet with something
vivid in them. They attracted him, and when he learned that, incredibly, she too was from Hannington, their friendship was sealed.
The loneliness in each of them reached toward the other, seeking
contact and making it.

Somehow she had scraped up money enough to go to New York
University. Later she hoped to be able to return to Muskogee, get a
master's degree at Wheatley-Tubman, and teach. Teaching was her
obsession, the desire and need to do it the only source of aggression
and drive within her otherwise modest and rather shy person.
"Somebody's got to go back there and cut away the underbrush in
the wilderness and let some light in." The way she said it, it did not
sound portentous or overblown, just determined.

And it was she who had kept at him until at last she had given
him some focus for his life. Almost without any volition of his own,
he found himself at N.Y.U. too, financed by the GI Bill of Rights.

She had given him focus, but she could not heal the abscess. She
was no Virginia Crane, no pale fire in moonlight; there was no
electricity, no fire, when he touched her flesh or kissed her. She was
only a short, plain, quiet brown girl with a great deal of iron somewhere deep inside her. But she was good for him and he came to
depend on her.

Together they began an exploration. Panaceas, sovereign reme-
dies for being Negro, had never been in short supply anywhere. New
York was brimming with them, ranging from beauty parlors offering
skin-whitening treatments to the more subtle and complicated solution Ralph Lansky put forth to Huse.

Ralph Lansky was white, but he seemed to regret the fact bitterly.
He was a tall, shambling young man, big and rawboned, with a
knobby face, tightly curling red hair, and dark, intense eyes. He was,
at least theoretically, a writer of short stories, and he had a sparsely
furnished apartment, two rooms and a tiny kitchen, not far from
Washington Square. But he haunted Harlem, somehow completely
identifying with Negroes and acquiring thereby a sort of protective

coloration, their tolerance if not their acceptance. They did not trust him, because they had learned by hard experience that no matter how Negro a white man tried to be, there always came the final moment of revelation when whatever gain he expected for himself became clear. There always had to be a gain—maybe the use of Negro women without the necessity of rape or payment, maybe a chance to unload a little heroin, maybe the fulfillment of some deep inner need for abasement. Whatever it was, sooner or later it would be revealed, and, they were sure, it would always be at cost to the black man.

But because he knew their customs and their cant so perfectly, because he made no overtures to their women, Ralph Lansky had earned slightly more than the usual measure of confidence. Moreover, he was, for Huse and Della, an entree into a wholly new world —the world of relaxed, colorful, and intellectually stimulating weekend parties until two in the Village. They were helplessly flattered and pleased when he invited them to the first one, and they enjoyed it immensely. The little apartment was jammed with white and black, there was a startling amount of liquor, and, most of all, intense hours of endless discussion about everything—writing, art, politics, women. It was a heady new experience for both of them, this easy mingling combined with coruscating intellectuality, and they orbited around Ralph Lansky for months.

He made no secret, of course, of the fact that he was a Communist, but he made no effort to convert anybody else—not at first. Huse and Della drank his liquor for months before, finally, things were somehow arranged so that they wound up at his apartment, along with two or three other young Negroes, after all the other guests at that particular party had gone home.

It was late and they were all a little drunk, and Lansky sat in the middle of the living room floor like a guru, and then the revelation came. Fierily, he made a plea for them to join the Party. It was their only solution—under the crushing hand of capitalism, they would never be allowed to rise, to exploit their own potentiality to the fullest. Only in a classless society could the Negro ever expect to be fully accepted as a man. Lansky was an impassioned, persuasive speaker; by now he understood their psychology perfectly; there was not a grievance, even the ones of which they were hardly aware themselves until he touched upon them, which he did not pinpoint and for which he did not offer a solution. He even managed, by implication, to point out to the men that within the Party no racial distinctions were made when it came to sex, and that there would be ample opportunity for them to enjoy an unprecedented freedom in their relationships with the women members, including the white ones. But he was not crass about that; he offered that bait subtly, along with all the rest—an end to economic and social discrimination, an end to grinding poverty, an end to shame and humiliation, an end to always being down and never able to get up.

Huse and Della listened closely; once Huse looked at Della and saw her mouth curving faintly in a smile. He recognized that set of her lips: the core of her expression was contempt.

An echo of it rang inside himself. No less than any of the rest of them, he hungered for change, for release, for a chance. But something about the world Ralph Lansky postulated filled him with revulsion. He had read Karl Marx and some of Lenin; he had read Koestler, too, and the daily newspapers, had seen in newsreels the reality of the Berlin airlift. It was not Marx's utopian vision that revolted him, but the intellectual dishonesty of Lansky, his subjugation of his own reason to ideology and doctrine. To Huse it seemed an even greater abridgment of freedom than he himself had ever suffered.

He listened patiently to all that Lansky said. He promised glibly to think about it. Then he and Della left and never went back. Huse's disgust with Lansky was not only for his ability knowingly to mouth falsehoods and warp facts, but because he had proved himself like all the other whites. He, too, had been seeking the gain and had made his pitch for it.

After that, he gave serious consideration to only one other panacea. A strange new sect called the Black Muslims was beginning to conduct meetings in a storefront temple on Lenox Avenue. Della was completely uninterested—Huse attended a few meetings by himself.

It was not their religion that attracted him; it was the demands they made of converts. A new Muslim renounced his former name and began a new existence. He was required to follow a rigid moral code, emphasizing chastity, the sanctity of family, cleanliness, honesty and thrift. He renounced gambling, gluttony, alcohol, and promiscuity—and at the same time, he renounced meekness. He was a Negro, and he was to be militantly proud of the fact and guilty of sin if he showed subservience to the whites. Huse found the idea of twenty million Negroes practicing the Muslim doctrine of morality and self-respect fascinating; what a force such a group could become, what a breakthrough from despair it would be! But as he attended more meetings, his enthusiasm waned and a revulsion began to grow in him. Once the truths had been said and the virtues preached, they were drowned in a continuing flood tide of oratorical hatred. Like Nazis in reverse, the Muslim leaders hammered constantly on the theme of the master race—only their master race was black.

There was no pussyfooting in the Muslim doctrine. "Black," they roared, "is the blessed of Allah, and white is the color of the devil. You are the chosen! All evil is white! The white man has set dogs on us, hanged us, raped us, robbed us. But the day will come when the slaveholder will be devoured by his own hounds, the hangman hanged by his own rope, the rapists' women forfeit, the robber robbed! Christianity has kept you on your knees before the white man too long. Allah tells you to get up off your knees, hate the white man as he hates you—an eye for an eye, a tooth for a tooth . . ."

Huse could not deny that the virulent, unmincing oratory struck surely a deep emotional chord within him, touched a wild and primitive lust for vengeance. The aim of the Muslims was clear: if they could not destroy white society, they would withdraw from it completely and absolutely and fight it if it encroached upon them. As rabble-rousing, it was appealing, on a brutal, unsophisticated level, with the added advantage of being completely untainted by any white participation or manipulation. But intellectually it was irrational, even paranoiac, certainly dangerous. Huse rejected it finally, but not without ambivalent feelings.

And then the discouragement settled over him again. There was no quick and easy solution, and apathy and despair once more glazed his faculties. Oxlike, he plodded through his studies, making fair grades.

When he lagged, Della bolstered him as best she could. "There isn't any answer," she kept saying. "Except everybody doing everything he's capable of. And believing."

"Believing what? You sound like the *Reader's Digest*."

"No. But believing that you don't own yourself. That you've been given more than most others, and that it only came through the sacrifice and suffering of a lot of people, and that you can't throw yourself away. There's not going to be any all-of-a-sudden Great Getting-Up Morning. You don't plant a bean seed and go out next morning and pick a mess of beans. But the seed will grow if somebody plows the ground and waits. And there's not one plow that'll break the ground except everybody learning as much as he can and teaching it to everybody else he can. I'm sorry, I didn't mean to sound put-out with you, but you know how I feel."

So it went for an aimless year. And during that whole time, there was not one moment, asleep or waking, when he was entirely free from the memory of Virginia Crane. He knew that Della was in love with him; he knew that he liked and admired her and that she would make him a good wife. But the memory of Virginia was a captivity that bound both will and emotions and would not let them go. He could not, even now, relinquish hope entirely, though he knew that it was foolish and the source of constant anguish. . . .

Then one night he and Della sat in the balcony of a theater, watching a play that had opened a few weeks before to good reviews. It was, for them, a major event, the expenditure of so much of their slender funds at once thrilling, frightening, and festive. But Huse felt betrayed; to him the play seemed poor, the money wasted. He was watching the second act with only half his attention when Virginia Crane appeared onstage.

Immediately, magically, the play and audience came simultaneously alive. Huse stared incredulously, looked at his Playbill, saw the name Virginia Marshall listed there. Then something twisted and wrenched within him and it was all he could do not to cry out. He sat there in enthralled pain throughout the ten minutes she was onstage; and when she moved confidently into the embrace of an actor—a white actor—and smiled up at him amorously, her loveliness was heartbreaking, even at that distance from the proscenium.

The actor bent his head to kiss her, and Huse was on his feet without volition. His hand crunched Della's wrist so hard the bones slid under his grasp. "Come on," he heard himself rasp hoarsely, "this show stinks. Let's get out of here." And before she could resist, he dragged her down the stairs and out onto the street.

They had walked from Forty-fourth Street to Times Square before he began to slow.

"Huse! Darling, what's the matter with you?" Her voice trembled with a combination of outrage and concern.

"Nothing," he snapped. "It was just a rotten show." He began to walk swiftly once more and she had to trot to keep up with him. On the A train back to Harlem, he startled her by proposing; and they were married two weeks later.

That had been five years ago; but it seemed at once an eternity and yesterday. An eternity because he could no longer make any connection in his mind between the man he was now and the man he had been then. He had an identity now: He was Houston Whitley, a competent teacher, a settled man of thirty-one; together he and Della had a combined income of fifty-six hundred dollars, more than many white families in Hannington; and there was no longer any anger in him. He knew now what he could and could not have, and he knew how to get along with what he could get and be satisfied with it, how not to regret what was beyond him. He knew now that there would never be any moments of excruciating passion in his life, any bold and defiant challenging of fate; there would be only the slow, calm steady flow of ordered life, the maturity in which wisdom always won over passion. Forty years from now, he would be a Dr. Haney in a Dr. Haney's office, with a Dr. Haney's concern for security and a Dr. Haney's abhorrence of people who rocked the boat, and the prospect did not bother him in the least.

He had it made now, as long as he did not upset the careful, delicate psychic and economic balance he had achieved, if he just gave it time to thicken and harden until it was the strongest part of him. Once that had happened, he would, at least, be out of the wagon, be out of it forever, and that was all he wanted now, to stay out of the wagon.

But as he drove the battered old Ford through Princeton toward the newly developed area on the outskirts where he and Della lived, he passed Merit Crane's house. He tried hard not to look at it and was almost, not quite, successful. The agony that went through him was as quick, as wild and bitter, as it had been six years before; and it took him several minutes of steady concentration on the road before it passed.

4 The development in which the Whitleys lived had been designed for the growing number of moderately prosperous Negroes, their only alternative to the squalor of Little Hammer or the expense of Princeton. Built by one of Merit Crane's companies, the rows of houses in swampy bottomland beside a stream were little better than asbestos-shingled cheeseboxes on narrow slices of ground. But they were the first pieces of real estate that most of their owners had ever held title to; and pride of possession was reflected in the neatness of the lawns and in the flowers and shrubs banked in every available space.

The Whitleys lived in the exact center of a block in the lowest part of the development. Parking his car in their short drive, Huse decided not to discuss his talk with Dr. Haney with Della. He did not feel up to debating the rights and wrongs of the matter with her tonight.

She taught the third grade and got home before him. As he entered the house, he could smell a delicious combination of aromas that meant she was busy with supper. He sniffed appreciatively and started toward the kitchen to tell her hello and get himself a drink. But a voice said from the corner of the living room, "Hey, ain't you even goan stop and speak?"

He turned, and his face went grim. Robert was sprawled in a chair, a copy of *The New Yorker* incongruous on his lap, his long legs, clad in ragged, filthy jeans, stretched out before him, his toes waggling from the slits in the ends of his shoes. He grinned at Huse and hoisted himself straighter in the chair and laid the magazine aside.

"I like to look at them ad-vertisements," he said. "I'd sho like to jest sniff one of dem white ladies up close. I bet they smells mighty good."

He was in his late twenties now, but he looked older. His face was lined at the corners of his mouth; his teeth were going bad and one of the front ones had turned blue. His eyes were bloodshot. Huse closed his eyes for an instant, detesting this Robert, trying to wish him out of existence and conjure back the little boy who had slept between him and Bish so long ago.

"All right," he said at last. "What you want now?"

"Nothin much. I jest missed you when you come to see Mama last night and I got lonesome for you. Co'se, if you could spare about ten bucks, I'll pay you back next week."

Huse snorted. "Yeah, I'll bet." But he knew he would give Robert the money, even though Robert owed him probably two hundred borrowed that way, even though he could not spare it and it would leave him short. He did not even try to lecture Robert. It would have been like trying to persuade a weasel to turn vegetarian. Robert was what he was; and he himself had played his part in making him that.

He pulled out his wallet. "I ain't got much in the way of cash. Let me see how Della's fixed." He went into the kitchen.

Della turned from the stove. She had gained weight in the past year, but her face was still plain and placid, and there was understanding and a kind of sympathy in her eyes. Huse lowered his voice. "How long has he been here?"

"He was sitting out front when I got home."

"He wants to borrow ten dollars. I've only got four in cash. Have you got it?"

She did not utter any of the protests or objections to which she was entitled. "I think so. Let me look in my handbag." She went into the bedroom, returned with a ten-dollar bill and placed it in his hand. "I'll have to cash a check tomorrow to get more grocery money."

"Thanks." Huse strode back to the living room. "Okay. Here you are."

Robert unfolded himself out of the chair. "Much obliged." He doubled the bill and slipped it in his pocket. Up close, he smelled foul and unwashed. "That's mighty kindly. I'll pay you back next week sho. Well, I got business to tend to now. If you ain't goin to offer me no drink, I'll be goin." He winked at Huse. "Got a little deal cookin for tonight."

"So long." Then Huse said, helplessly, "How'd you get out here?"

"Rode the bus fur as Princeton, walked the rest of the way."

"How you going to get back?"

"Same way, I reckon."

"Get in the car," Huse said wearily. "I'll ride you up to the bus line."

Robert grinned. "Now, that's what I call service."

As Huse drove uphill, out of the bottomland, Robert looked out the window. After a while he murmured, "You know, it pretty down in here."

"Yeah," Huse said, surprised by the wistfulness in his brother's voice.

"You know," Robert went on, almost as if talking to himself, "I can still remember when us lived out in the country. I remember how dat lower field useta look like it stretch out to all creation. And Daddy used to look like he was tall as a tree. Funny how big things look to you when you little, how little they git when you big." He turned toward Huse. "Got a cigarette?"

Huse handed him a pack. Robert shook one out and dropped the pack back in Huse's lap. With the cigarette between his teeth, he said, "You ever go back out to 'at ole place?"

"Not in a long time," Huse said.

Robert was silent. "Man," he said at last, "you couldn't git me out in one of them cotton fields now with a shotgun at my back."

They had reached the bus stop. Huse pulled over to the side of the street. "I'll let you out here if you don't mind. Della will be waiting supper."

"Yeah," said Robert, "much obliged." He flipped a hand in farewell as Huse turned the car around. Driving away, Huse saw Robert in the rearview mirror, leaning against a telephone pole, the cigarette cupped back inside his palm. He looked solitary, almost forlorn. I should have given him a coupla more cigarettes to last him until he gets to town, Huse thought.

When he reached home again, he was buoyed by the sight of a familiar sedan parked before the house. He grinned, his melancholy slipping away, and cut his own engine.

As he entered the front door, a dapper man a few years older than himself, with a sharp, handsome, light-tan face, emerged from the kitchen, drink in hand. "Hi, man!"

"Hi, yourself, man!" Huse thrust out his hand enthusiastically. Jeff Marfield was Della's brother, a lawyer with an office down on Grade Street. His financial help had made Della's college education possible. "Where you been so long? Ain't seen you in a coon's age."

Della emerged from the kitchen with a drink for Huse. "I'll have supper ready in a few minutes. Jeff, you'll stay and eat?"

"I got to run on home. Just thought I'd come by and let you know I wasn't dead." Marfield dropped into the same chair Robert had occupied. "I've been out beating the bushes trying to organize a statewide membership campaign."

"How is it going?" asked Della, sitting down beside Huse on the sofa.

Marfield grinned ruefully. "Like trying to carry water in a sifter. It's the National Association for the *Advancement* of Colored People, but I'm beginning to wonder if anybody really wants to get advanced. Everywhere I turn, everybody scared to rock the boat." He took a sip of his drink. "I go to the business and professional men; they say, *No, man, I can't afford to get my name on that list.* I go to the ministers—them, of all people, who ought to be working with me—and I get, *My concern is with the Gospel, not with worldly things.* If Christ had felt like they do, he'd have lived to a ripe old age. Then I go out in the canebrakes and the cotton fields and I try to round up support there. But those poor people—they just like oxen hitched to a wagon, and talking to them just like talking to oxen. They don't understand, they don't comprehend, they got no frame of reference even to *think* about rights in. And they so bound up in debt and peonage, they least of all can afford to antagonize the whites."

"That's a shame," murmured Della.

"I told you," Huse said, unable to keep a certain gloating out of his voice. "I told you, you're beating your head against a brick wall."

"Well," Marfield said a little harshly, "I got to keep on beating. Time's running out on us. What's next Monday—May thirty-first? We're expecting the Supreme Court decision on how to implement school integration then. The white folks have been laying mighty low for the past year, depending on their lawyers to block any real decree of enforcement from the Court; but if the Court actually points its finger and says, *You have got to integrate,* I don't expect them to lay low any longer. The Court has told us what we're entitled to; now it's going to tell us how to get it, and once we've heard that, we're not going to lay low, either. We're going to—"

Huse stood up. "You're going to get a lot of niggers killed or hurt," he said brutally. "That's what you're going to do." He turned, gesturing, his voice rising. "Why can't you get it into your head that you're beat before you start? We're all beat, there ain't no help for it. We're sewed up tight, like kittens in a bag, and there ain't no way to get out. You talk about how folks won't support you. Well, I don't blame 'em. What do you do, really? You pussyfoot here and piddle there and lawsuit and lawsuit and lawsuit, and nothing *real* ever comes out of it. You go out here and get everybody mad at you and get nothing more to show for it than if you stayed home and minded your own business."

"We'll have something to show next Monday. We'll get in gear then—you wait."

"Next Monday," Huse sneered. "You think God's going to turn everybody white next Monday?"

Marfield grinned, unruffled. "It'd be a bigger joke if He turned everybody black."

"Well, He ain't going to do either one, and neither is the Supreme Court. You wait and see. If they'd really meant for Negro children to go to better schools, they'd have wrapped everything up in one ball to begin with instead of piddling around for a year trying to figure out some way to sugarcoat their decision so it would satisfy everybody and wouldn't cause any real change in things. And what's happened in that year? The white folks have had time to mobilize. They know they've got the power and they've gathered it together. This White Citizens' Council—it's got every white man that can scrape up the two-dollar membership fee in it, and any time they want to, they can cut your water off, man. They can fix it so you can't borrow money at the bank, so you can't buy bread at the grocery store, so you can't get a job dumping honey outa septic tanks, even. They got it locked. And if that ain't enough, there's always the Ku Klux Klan ready to take you out and work you over. That year's time gave both those outfits a chance to come to life and grow. That's all it did. Now what you want is for everybody to go in with you and buck a lock at the board."

"If we get a favorable decision, it'll be enforced one way or the other. If we have to go through every court in the land."

"Court," Huse grunted. "That's all you think about, court. It's some kind of magic word with you. Don't you know the white folks can out-court you, too? Do you really think the Moodys and the Bradhams are going to miss any chance to law you plumb to death? I'll bet you ain't even got any Negro children lined up to apply for white schools yet, anyhow—have you?"

"No. But we will have by fall."

"Sho. And a kid applying for first grade in a white school will be grown and working before his case ever gets settled. That is, if white folks ever *let* him work."

Marfield shook his head. "Man, you *are* sour, aren't you?"

"Nope. Just realistic. You and your Court decision already made things hard enough for me and Della. We used to have tenure— now we've got to negotiate a new contract every year, so they can fire us any time they don't like the way we talk, and us with no recourse. On top of that, you keep on the way you're going and we won't have any jobs at all. You integrate all these schools, you think they're going to use colored teachers to teach white children? Man, you're trying to law us plumb out of business."

"Please," Della said plaintively. "Please, don't you two fuss so."

Jeff stood up. "We're not fussing." He smiled. "We're just debating. Huse is good for me; I like to hear him go on that way. He epitomizes everything I've got to work to overcome. Self-interest, apathy, just plain frazzled-out discouragement." There was no rancor in his voice. "Someday I'm going to bring him into the fold, and when I do, I'll know we're on our way to winning."

"That'll be the day," Huse snorted. "I ain't about to cut off my nose to spite my face."

"Sure, sure," Jeff said. "Well, win, lose, or draw, I'm having some folks in at my house Monday night after the decision's been announced. If it's a strong one, I aim to get drunk to celebrate. If it's weak and namby-pamby, I aim to get drunk to drown my disappointment. Louise and I'd like to have you and Huse there. Okay?"

"Next Monday, that's the thirty-first. Yeah, that's all right. We'll be there. And whichever way it goes, I'll get just as drunk as you do. Fair enough?"

Marfield laughed. "If that's all the support I can get out of you, yeah. See you then. So long, sis. And keep your fingers crossed."

Later, at the supper table, Della seemed to be thoughtful. Huse could feel her eyes upon him as he ate, and he did not attempt to meet them. They ate in silence.

She's a good wife, Huse thought. It ain't her fault I don't ever seem to be able to let myself go with her completely. It ain't her fault I can't get rid of Virginia. I wish—

"Huse." Della broke the silence.

"Yeah?"

"I was just thinking. We really ought to join the NAACP, even if we aren't active in it. After all, it must be embarrassing to Jeff when he can't get even his own sister and brother-in-law to sign up."

Huse laid down his fork. "Look," he said, "don't you start in on me, too. You've got to make up your mind. We scraped through N.Y.U. and then we came home for our masters' at Wheatley-Tubman because they'd rather hire graduates of Negro colleges inside the state than people with Northern degrees. We wore ourselves out, you baby-sitting and doing daywork and me on that construction gang to pay the way. All right, now we're through all that and doing what you always claimed was the only thing we ought to do. We're teaching. Now we can join the NAACP and prance around yelling about rights and freedom and get fired, or we can keep our mouths shut and go on teaching. But we can't do both. If you really want to, we'll join. But you better be prepared to go back to washing white folks' dirty dishes and I better figure on hauling mortar in a wheelbarrow again. I'll leave that up to you."

She was silent for a moment. "I guess you're right. Anyhow—" There was something odd in her voice.

"Anyhow, what?" He asked it gently.

All at once she smiled. "Anyhow, it's not only ourselves we've got to think about now."

Huse stared. "What?"

She looked both pleased and frightened. "My period never did come last month. After I got out of class day before yesterday, I went to see Dr. Gantt. He called me this afternoon; the test was positive."

For a moment it seemed to Houston Whitley that his brain ground completely to a halt. He felt his stomach knot with a spastic reaction that had nothing to do with gratification, that was instantaneous dread. "A baby?" he heard himself whisper banally. "A baby? You're going to have a baby?"

She nodded, still smiling with a pleased smugness that infuriated him. "That's what Dr. Gantt said."

His brain raced. A child—that was the last thing he wanted. A final abridgment of his freedom, the slamming of the last door of the trap. A child—and he would be bound to Della always then, by his own conscience, bound forever to this half existence of affection without love, of sex without passion or catharsis, of pretending, eternally pretending. . . . And the economic catastrophe of it too. If Della had to quit work, if they lost the two thousand a year she brought in—

All that in an instant while she smiled at him, and he tried to quell the bitterness within him and fabricate a reaction that would not tear both of them apart. He heard himself saying, temporizing, playing for time, "But how? We've always been so careful. I don't even remember a time when I didn't use—"

"There was a time," she said. "You woke me up in the middle of the night. Don't you remember that? I don't think either of us was really awake until it was all over."

Huse rubbed his face. "But that was so close to the time you usually come around anyhow."

"Well, it just happened," Della said, and then her face lost the smile; it was a round, cautious brownness with questioning eyes. "Huse," she said quietly, "aren't you pleased? Don't you want a child?"

"I—" He gathered his faculties, unable to be cruel enough to speak the truth. Suddenly he realized that they looked at this from exactly opposite poles: to a woman a child was a beginning; to a man it was always an ending. He stood up. "Of course I do," he said very softly. "I was just so taken by surprise. Of course I want a son. Why didn't you tell me sooner, before you went to Gantt?" He came around the table. "It's wonderful," he said, desperately trying to keep from sounding hollow. "It's absolutely wonderful. Have you— have you told Jeff?"

"No, of course not; I wouldn't tell him before I told you."

He tried to put spirit in his voice. "Then we'll announce it at his party Monday night." He bent and kissed her and held her with as much tenderness as he could muster; and it was deception, all deception, and he hated himself. But it seemed to work; he felt her relax in his arms, and then she laid her head against his chest.

"I guess, really," she said, "I was a little afraid to tell you. I didn't know how you'd react."

"Don't be a fool," he said, alarmed and surprised at her perception. "Don't be a fool, I'm tickled silly about it."

"It'll be a boy," she said quietly. "I know it will. And I've already got a name picked out for him, if you approve."

He held her more tightly, staring at the muddy, water-painted sheetrock wall of the dining room rather blankly. "What's that?"

She stroked his arm. "I thought we'd call him Otis," she said.

5

On May 31, 1955, the Supreme Court of the United States delivered its long-delayed opinion on the question of relief of discrimination in public education. . . .

The concrete-block building six miles out from Hannington on a secondary road had once been a store and service station; now its dirt driveway was littered with rubbish and shards of glass from its broken windows. Stubs of pipe and tubing protruded like unligated ends of severed arteries from a concrete island bereft of pumps. The night wind rustled the surrounding weed fields, whispered in the heads of the gaunt pines about the place, and set the one remaining cold-drink sign to swaying, squeaking and banging where it hung, bullet-riddled, from a single nail on the side of the building.

Inside, the partitionless common area of the store was jammed with men and lit by the glow from electric light bulbs in sockets mounted on a rude cross of two-by-fours at one end of the room. Before the cross there was a rickety table serving as altar and lectern. On it lay a Bible open to the twelfth chapter of Romans, an unsheathed cavalry saber bought from a mail-order antique firearms house and a gallon jug of water used for "purifying" initiates. These items rested on an American flag used as an altar cloth; more prominently, a huge Confederate flag was fastened to the wall behind the cross.

The man in Klan regalia—the crimson peaked hat and crimson robe of a high official—who stood before the altar had a weathered face deeply lined with years and hard living. His eyes were a glittering blue; his mouth was short and traplike. His voice rose and fell in harsh, jerky, nasal tones; not a good speaker, he was an impassioned one. Watching and listening from the ranks of the two dozen men assembled, Bobo Merchant, the bus driver, hatless, but himself wearing the white robe of a Klansman, was stirred. Full of the warmth of belonging—and of two drinks of white corn whiskey just before the meeting—he was deeply grateful to Red Hanna for recruiting him. By God, this was just the outfit he had been looking for—and what Sam Deal, old-time chain-gang guard, veteran Klansman, and Grand Dragon of the American Klan in the state of Muskogee, was saying was exactly what he had hoped he would hear.

"This is jest the beginnin," Sam Deal rapped out. "This is jest the start of the nigger-New York Jew plan for gittin their hands on the fair bodies of our Southern white women. Oh, they got it all laid out—can't you see it now? The big nigger bucks in the schools with our innocent young girls. Buck niggers and white girls dancin together, that black, horny, diseased, dirty body rubbin up against that fair, unspoiled white one. That's their plan, that's what they want. They don't care nothin about schoolin—what they want is a chance to git next to our women. First it'll be the schools. Then it'll be the cafés, with them dirty niggers leavin their germs on the plates and dishes and glasses white men got to eat and drink out of. And it'll be the movie shows and the taverns—and then the livin room and then the bedroom. Ever'whur that white women are, that's whur they want to git themselves. They ain't but one thing they want, and all the rest of it's jest a smoke screen. What they're after is to rape and sedooce and violate the fairest, most innocent, finest creation of God's hand—the Anglo-Saxon Southern white woman!"

A kind of rippling murmur went through the Klansmen, a sound like the one the wind made in the pines outside.

"And who's to stop 'em?" Sam Deal's voice did not soar. He asked the question as a schoolmaster might have. "Who's gonna stand between the dirty niggers and their vile intentions? The Supreme Court? Hell, no. The Federal government? Hell, no. It's all dominated by dirty Communist Jews that want to see the Anglo-Saxon Protestant white man brought down to destruction and his blood polluted and black dirty niggers lovin up his women. I'll tell you who's to stop 'em! It's us! The one organization *dedicated* to the protection of Southern women an' our Southern way of life! The one organization that they're all ascared of—that's made 'em tremble in their boots ever since they come down here after the War and tried to set the nigger up on top and didn't git away with it. The one organization that can't be corrupted by the dirty New York Communist Jews and the Communists in Washington and the Jew Court with its Frankfurters and its Warrens and its traitors like Hugo Black that used to be a Klansman himself. And you know what that organization is? I'll tell you what it is! It's us! It's the Knights of the Ku Klux Klan— and if nobody else will save the South, we'll do it just like we've done it before!"

Against the murmur, with discernible words this time. "God, that's tellin 'em! . . . You goddam right."

Sam Deal held up a red-swathed arm. "Now, this organization don't believe in violence—you all know that. But we believe in protectin the South, and protectin our women and protectin our children and ourselves. Now, tonight, what we're gonna do is serve notice, give warnin, of that. We ain't out to hurt anybody tonight. But we're gonna show the niggers that we're here and that we mean business and that if they keep on with their foolishness, it's at their risk. I don't want nobody hurt, unless somethin happens you got to defend yourself. But when we're through tonight, ever' nigger in Muskogee will know that the Klan is watchin 'em. Because what we're doin here is goin to be done all over the state. Come tomorrow mornin, everybody'll know that the Knights of the Ku Klux Klan is vigilantly on guard!"

He broke off. Then he said, "Now, before we leave to carry out our assignments, I'll ask your Kludd to pray for us all." He stepped aside, motioning to another red-clothed figure behind him.

As the bulky figure of the chaplain stepped forward—he was, Bobo knew, a preacher from some Primitive Baptist church out in the country—Bobo shifted restlessly. He was anxious to join his team and get on about the business.

The Kludd bowed his head, still covered with the scarlet dunce cap, and began to pray.

"Gret Heavenly Father, we ask yo' blessins on these, yo' servants. Help us to stand firm again the fo'ces of the godless that want to undermine all yo' good wuks . . ." His voice droned on.

With head bowed, Bobo tried to bridle his impatience. He had been a Klansman for a month now, and he had begun to doubt that they were ever going to do anything, especially when he had learned that the Klan he had joined was not the one his father had belonged to.

There had been, somebody told him, three different sets of Klans. First the one after the Confederate war, the one that had saved the

South from the niggers and carpetbaggers and chased the Yankees home. Then the one that had been revived in 1915 by an Atlanta preacher and organizer named Col. Bill Simmons. That had been the Klan Bobo's daddy had joined—what was now called the "Old Klan." It was the Klan that had spread across the country like wild-fire in the 1920s, under the leadership of a man named Evans who was its Imperial Wizard, becoming a true invisible empire, not only in the South but in the North and Midwest as well. It had kind of petered out during the Depression, Bobo understood, and back in 1944 when the Federal government had hit it for nearly three quarters of a million dollars in back taxes, it had dissolved to avoid payment.

He had been depressed to learn that the American Klan, which he had joined, was not a national organization. But since the "Old Klan" had dissolved, a dozen different independent Klans had sprung up in its wake. The American Klan was one of these, competing with others for membership and prestige. During the first month of his membership, it had been kind of dull, Bobo thought, and he had not been too happy about his investment of a ten-dollar initiation fee and twelve dollars for first-month dues. But now it sounded like some excitement was coming, and he drew himself up with pride at being one of the last-ditch defenders of Southern womanhood, the patriot-ism and sense of crucial responsibility he felt sending a good mascu-line tingle throughout his body.

As the Kludd's voice droned on, Bobo cocked his eyes up at the Stars and Bars. To him it was a symbol of a terrible wrong for which adequate revenge had never yet been gained. Actually, never having got past the fifth grade, he was a little foggy about the details of what had happened; he knew and had been taught to revere the names of Jefferson Davis and Robert E. Lee, and to despise the names Grant and Sherman; and there were three important places—names fixed in his mind—Fort Sumter, Gettysburg, and Appomattox. Otherwise, his knowledge of the conflict was a blur of heroic impressions which, without realizing it, he had gained from motion pictures—*Birth of a Nation; Old Judge Priest; Gone with the Wind* . . . and there was one with Shirley Temple. Once the South had been paradise, but then the arrogant, hateful Yankees had swarmed in with overwhelming numbers and spoiled it and turned the niggers loose, and— He choked up with rage and hatred just thinking about it.

The Kludd's country voice said amen and ceased. Sam Deal

stepped forward again, and at his side was the Exalted Cyclops, ruler of this Klavern, this chapter. Carl Prevatte—he drove a laundry truck during the day—raised his hands. "All right. You teams know what you've got to do. Git with it—and report back here by midnight."

The two dozen men murmured and filed out of the building to the parked cars at its side. They opened the trunks of five cars and into each they rammed crosses made of cheap pine lumber wrapped with oil-soaked burlap. Carefully they tied a red flag on each pointed stem projecting from the trunks.

Red Hanna, the Kleagle, hatchet-faced and with hands that always shook perceptibly, caught Bobo Merchant's arm. "Hey, Bobo. You got any of that moon left under the front seat?"

Ordinarily Bobo would have been evasive; Red was noted for never buying anybody a drink himself. But tonight he felt united with Red Hanna; they were comrades, bound together on a mission of importance and danger. "Yeah," he said expansively. "Come on, we'll have us a good long drink before we start to rollin . . ."

Jeff Marfield's house in Princeton was a neat story-and-a-half brick dwelling on a rise of ground. His living room was double the size of the one in the Whitleys' house and tonight it was packed with guests. Marfield himself was a little drunk as he stood in the center of a knot of people with glass in hand.

"Didn't win?" he said loudly. "What you talking about? We've been winning ever since the end of the war. The armed forces have been integrated. In 1947 they outlawed the white primary. We've got Negroes into law schools and universities in three or four states— and the District of Columbia and some of the border states have already begun desegregation. And then the 1954 decision and now this—it's a trend, man, and nobody's going to stop it now. We've got the law of the land on our side. Win? Of course we've won. All right, so the decision didn't call for absolute and complete immediate integration. It says they've got to move with speed, don't it?"

"Deliberate speed," Houston Whitley said. He had taken several drinks, but somehow they seemed not to affect him at all. He was, instead of being morosely drunk, morosely sober. "What's that? Deliberate speed. You tell me what it is. And all that stuff in there about taking into consideration local conditions. You may think you've won, but I'll tell you right now, it's they who've won. They can keep you tied up in courts for the next thirty years." Disgusted, he turned away from the group. He had read the decision carefully in the evening newspaper, which had printed its short text in full. He could not see what Jeff had to be jubilant about. To him it seemed that it had been designed only to allow pretext for indefinite delay.

A huge man in a dark suit, rawboned and nearly six feet four, followed him out of the group. "You don't sound very optimistic, Huse." This was Charles Bell, minister of Mt. Olive A.M.E. Zion, which the Whitleys attended, and the father of the headstrong, mercurial Carson Bell whom Huse had reprimanded not long before. Bell was coal-black and bald as an egg and his long face was so homely that it was both powerful and attractive. "You don't sound like you believe anything's been accomplished at all."

"I don't," Huse said grimly. "I can't see where it's going to help anybody one bit. All it's going to do is cause more trouble for the Negro than anything since the Civil War. I'm sorry, but I know old man Bradham who runs this state. I know him pretty well, and I know *he* ain't going to give a Negro anything. I'll make you a bet, preacher. I'll bet you that five years from now there's still not a single Negro student in any white school in this state." He paused. "When the Court handed down its decision in 1954, Jeff was just like this. Expecting the millennium overnight. Now he's expecting it again, but it still ain't on its way. Long as white folks got a breath in them and a cartridge left, it never will get here."

"You shouldn't be so bitter," Bell said. "You sound as if you don't believe in law at all. You sound as if you'd favor violence."

Huse laughed shortly. "That's the last thing I'd favor. You know who always gets the short end in a race riot. No, I'm just saying that nothing's changed and that nothing's going to change."

"Old calamity howler still howling, huh?" asked Marfield as he came up. "Preacher, you ever see such a negative personality?"

Bell smiled. "I'm afraid Huse is suffering from the sickness of our time. Disbelief in the ability of God to change the hearts of men."

"Disbelief in the Supreme Court to change the hearts of men," said Huse tersely. "Or any court."

Marfield's voice was nettled. "Well, have you got any better suggestion?"

"Reinhold Niebuhr once wrote," Charles Bell added, "that the

Negro would never receive his rights until he forced the white man to give them to him, but that the Negro could never achieve those rights through armed rebellion or violence. I fail to see any middle way except through the courts, myself. The courts and prayer. I refuse to despair, Huse. The heart of man does change. Look at India. Look at what Gandhi achieved. It took him years, but he changed the hearts of the English and helped win independence for his people."

"I'm familiar with what Gandhi did," Huse said.

"Well, I'm not, entirely," Jeff said.

"You should be," said Charles Bell. "Without an army, without even recourse to the courts, without even so much as a weapon, Mohandas Gandhi helped obtain India's independence by mobilizing civil disobedience, passive resistance. I've often wondered if, really, we shouldn't emulate the Indians and use that tactic. It was effective for Gandhi both in South Africa and in India."

Huse shook his head. "It wouldn't work. Negroes aren't the mystics that the Indians are. Who's going to let himself be jailed at the mercy of white people for a principle? Martyrs have gone out of fashion. Besides, Gandhi represented a majority; his followers outnumbered the whites. We're a minority."

"All right," Jeff said sharply. "Then it's the courts. Even if it means 'the insolence of office and the law's delay.' " His voice crackled. "The main thing is, it's got to be something. And people have got to work for it, not sit around moaning that nothing will really ever change." He swept his arm in a gesture that included the entire living room. "You're not the only one," he said bitterly. "Sometimes I feel like a voice crying in the wilderness. Look at 'em." There was an edge of contempt in his tone. "The great American middle-class Negro. The hardest person in the whole world to get off his can and into action. He isn't scrubbing floors or out chopping cotton any more, and he's forgot how bad off some people still are. He's so afraid somebody'll mistake him for a field hand, he stays as far away from reality as he can. Everywhere he turns, he gets slapped in the face, but he refuses to acknowledge that he feels it. Long as he's got his big Cadillac and can drink cocktails instead of 'smoke' and brag about how much he lost at poker and see his wife's name in the society column of some little two-bit Afro-American newspaper, he's happy in his dreamworld as a pig in a tater patch."

Huse felt anger in turn. "All right. But you put yourself in my place. Everything I've got's dependent—flat-out dependent—on staying in good with the white man. I've got a wife and I'm going to have a kid to support and—"

Jeff's face changed completely. "A kid?"

"That's right. Della's going to have a baby."

Jeff's face lit with an enormous grin. "Well, I be damned! Man, why you wait so long to say it? My little baby sister gonna be a mama! That's some news! When's it going to happen?"

"Relax," said Huse dryly. "At least eight months."

"Hot damn! I'm gonna be an uncle!" Jeff stepped clear and his voice bellowed above the chatter. "Hey, everybody! Listen to me! I got an announcement to make!"

"Abraham Lincoln just signed the Emancipation Proclamation," somebody gibed.

"Naw, he's just entered himself in the first grade at a white school," somebody else said, laughing.

"No, this's something bigger than that." Jeff strode across the room and embraced Della. "I just got some good news about my baby sister! The Whitleys are expecting a blessed event!"

"Jeff, for goodness sake." Della looked down at the floor.

"Don't you for-goodness-sake me, woman. This is the best news I've had in years, except for the Court decision."

People crowded in around Della. Charles Bell put his hand on Huse's right shoulder. "May God's blessing be upon you both," he said in his deep voice.

"Thanks," Huse said acidly.

Bell smiled gently. "This is going to be the greatest adventure of your life, Huse. When you see that child lying there beside its mother, that helpless babe, you're going to understand the story of the Nativity in a way you never understood it before. The child will bring you closer to Jesus Christ and closer to God than you have ever been. You don't understand that now, but you will when it happens. You'll lose yourself and then find yourself, the way Jesus did, your only concern for that one you've got to watch over, just like His concern for us." He strode over to Della. "When I pray for you now, I'll include the new life."

"Thank you," said Della quietly.

Huse turned away. He still could not stifle his bitterness, his sense of being totally trapped now into a finality of imprisonment. And he felt also a sense of outrage—that this demand should be made on him now, the responsibility foisted on him, to rear a child into a life of futility, of dead ends and blank walls, and still somehow be expected to have enthusiasm for the prospect, to be excited and positive about guiding a new life through a world that was nothing but a dirty trick.

He turned toward the table where Jeff had set out whiskey and mixer. Maybe a really big drink would shake off that depression, mitigate that foreboding of doom. Maybe—

The explosion seemed to jar the house.

A woman screamed. The roar of a car outside split the night. Then the men were running for the door.

Huse and Marfield reached it first, with Bell just behind.

"Stay back!" Huse snapped. "Damn it, y'all stay back." He thought of Mason Jar, recognizing the double thunder of two shotgun charges fired at once. As he wrenched open the door, spent bird shot pattered down from overhead.

For a moment they all halted in the doorway, staring, their faces firelit.

It was Huse who broke the silence.

"You see?" he grated savagely. "You see? Didn't I tell you? Nothing has changed, nothing at all!"

And he pointed at the bright yellow flame of the cross burning on Marfield's lawn.

6 With a glass of iced tea in one hand and a thick book cradled in his lap, Burke Jessup sat in a rocking chair on the front porch of The Place. A glance at his watch confirmed what he had already guessed from the sun; it was four o'clock, and Maggie and Cary should be riding in any moment now. He hoped they would hurry.

From the porch he could look out across a landscape glowing with the muted colors of Southern autumn. In pastures that had once been cotton fields, the chunky red rectangles that were white-faced cattle moved placidly. It was, thought Burke, a beautiful land and, where it remained unraped, a fertile one. And, he thought, it's like a cocked pistol ready to go off.

He had taken pleasure in riding about it with Maggie this summer, showing her with a proprietary air this country that was his. Contacting stringers and correspondents in the little lost and forlorn communities about the county—places with grainy frontier names like Wildcat Fork, Possum Walk, Caney Mill and Drowning Run— he had been struck again by what a genuine frontier country the South remained. "Basically," he told Maggie, "it hasn't changed since the Indians were driven out. If old Andy Jackson himself reappeared in the flesh at one of these country stores, he'd feel right at home talking to the loafers. Oh, he might be a little puzzled by their attitude toward the Federal government, but soon as he found out what caused it, likely he'd join them in it."

He could tell that she was becoming fascinated with it herself. He showed her the boxlike little Negro churches set down in the most astounding wildernesses, and the pathetic graveyards behind them, where graves were decorated with bits of colored glass and tinted patent-medicine bottles and old automobile tires painted white. He showed her the farm and plantation great houses, most of them a far cry from the mansions of movies and historical novels, but still with a certain impressive grandeur to their generous wings and porches sprawling wide and graciously in groves of oak and magnolia and bamboo and crape myrtle. She saw, too, the homes of country Negroes, the croppers' and renters' shacks set down brutally in the direct sun of a shadeless, limitless field, a sea of cotton washing up to the very doorsteps; or hidden shyly in a hollow of tangled vine and brush along some forgotten wagon trace.

Then, in sudden jarring contrast, they would round a bend and find in what was last month's wasteland the steel skeleton of a giant new factory rising overnight out of brush and mud like a massive, rectilinear mushroom. The crowded, union-strangled Northern industries had found out about the cheap land, resolutely unorganized labor and low taxes of the South. Magically, chosen communities were transformed from sleepy country hamlets to sprawling complexes of dreary, treeless housing developments, supermarkets, filling stations, country clubs, flying services, and all the other stamped-tin and pressed-plastic accoutrements required to cope with the money-spawning monsters welcomed into their midst. Hannington itself had become the focus of expanded or new regional sales offices as the new industries created new markets; and around its outskirts bull-dozers and graders prowled and devastated, leveling whole forests and rolling up topsoil like a rug to provide housing for the hosts of neo-carpetbaggers arriving daily by Eastern.

But this yeast of change had not yet been working long enough to leaven the essential plain mixture of the state, and, thought Burke, their behavior for the past several months, during which he had personally observed it, had been completely traditional. Up until the Supreme Court's implementation decision, Cary's calm confidence that nothing the Federal government could say or do would ever put a Negro into a white school—or any other white enclave—seemed to have been shared by everyone. With certainty that their lawyers and their legislators and their own monolithic opposition would cause the Court to vitiate its ruling, they had stayed unconcerned. There had been no strife, no violence, no bitterness even; it was as if the original 1954 ruling had not even existed.

The second ruling had changed all that. It was as if the Court's words had to be repeated before realization came that they really meant what they said. Suddenly the people—the individual people, the back-country farmers, the mill hands, the clerks and the professional man—all felt personally threatened. They began to look at their Negro farmhands or yardmen or cooks with new eyes, seeing exactly the same surface that had presented itself before, but for the first time wondering what really lay below the impenetrable cork layer of submission, of courtesy and of easy laughter. Behind the yard-man's eyes was he coveting the housewife as his rightful due? What was that in the face of the nurse as she changed the baby—resignation or hatred? Suddenly the whites realized that they had no idea what went on in the secret councils of the Negroes—every surface emotion of the trusted retainer seemed to have its mirror image.

What was causing that reaction, Burke thought, was conscience. No white—including himself—could say his conscience was clear; even the best-willed had thoughtlessly or in the custom of the country dealt out a share of abuse. So long as the recipient of that abuse seemed to accept it willingly, even with love, as a dog might accept a kick without feeling the injustice of it, conscience had remained quiet. But now had come the realization that none of them knew how the Negro really accepted the abuse, and the thought that he might feel hatred or, worse, contempt for his abuser was intolerable. In whatever measure, Burke thought, each deserved that contempt, in that measure had he reacted now; in that measure he knew the excruciating diminishment of his own ego, or even physical fear.

So that now the determination to strike first was spreading across the South. It manifested itself in the revival of the Ku Klux Klan, still mainly ineffectual, still officially disavowed by most state governments. More strongly it showed itself in the tightly knit groupings of the better classes into the Citizens' Councils. And what alarmed Burke was the rapid diminishment of middle ground and the depletion of the reservoirs of genuine good will that had existed between the races under the old arrangement. You could feel it in the air, he thought—that tense, electric contempt for rational measures and the suspicion that fed it. It was as if a slow, contagious insanity had contaminated the air with invisible spores; and now they were lodging and taking root.

He did not like to think about what that insanity would do to him. He had no fear of catching it himself, and that, he knew, could very well be his doom. For its growth could be too easily measured by the decline in the fortunes of the *Enterprise* over the past six months.

Maggie had not been easy to restrain; she had seen the hovels of Little Hammer, the poverty, the growing brutality of police and courts, always callous toward Negroes and with less fear now of the check of public opinion. Characteristically, she had wanted him to use the paper as a cudgel with which to lay about among the oppressors.

But he had resisted that. No one could understand better than he the tragedy of being helpless, of having to live at the mercy of the good will of others, and nobody valued more the drive toward independence and the ability to walk alone. All the same, he knew the South—and Muskogee, especially—too well to have any hope of furthering revolution by advocating it, and he tried to explain that to Maggie.

"Neither court orders nor preaching at 'em," he told her, "is going to change these people overnight. The way they feel is bred too deeply in them. This is going to have to be an evolutionary thing. All we can do—all anybody who doesn't pretend to be God can do—

is to plead for people to attack the problem in a constructive way and try to bring some beneficial order out of it. I'm sorry you don't think I'm being radical enough, but I'm trying to work in the realm of the possible, and I have to call my shots as I see them. You haven't been down here long enough to understand how mixed with love all this hatred and suspicion is. If the love can just be aroused and appealed to without bringing out the hatred—"

He tried to explain to her that the love really existed. So many whites had been raised by Negroes, tenderly; so many Negroes had received white bounty and help in return. Though the Negroes had borne more than their share, there had been sacrifice on the part of each race for the other. Long before the Supreme Court decision, such organizations as the Southern White Women for Elimination of Lynching, and its outgrowth, the Fellowship of the Concerned, both made up of white Southern churchwomen, had fought for the elimination of vigilante violence against Negroes and for more just treatment of them in the courts.

"They went to law enforcement officers and made it plain to them they were more interested in justice than in having men burned alive, hanged, or mutilated to protect their chastity. And they showed up in courtrooms at the kind of sordid trials no respectable women had ever attended before; they showed up in bunches and they didn't say anything; they just sat there watching, taking in everything their menfolks were doing and giving them private hell later on if the trial wasn't fair. I'm not saying they reformed Southern justice single-handed, but when judges and jurors realized that their own women were keeping tabs on them, there was a change. And there's more of that spirit than anybody realizes, if it doesn't get squeezed out by the extremists on both sides. And I'm not going to be one of the squeezers. I'm going to be just a plain old ordinary moderate, doing what he can to inject a little reason into the whole situation."

But, he reflected dourly, if Maggie thought he had not been radical enough, there were others who thought he was too radical. *Either you are with us,* the advertisers had begun to say, *or you are against us.* The middle ground was shrinking, and the paper was feeling the effects of that. He and Maggie tried to conceal their concern from each other and pretend that everything would be all right as soon as the first reaction was past, as soon as emotions cooled and reason prevailed, but both of them knew there was very little margin to allow for the setbacks they were having in the meantime. Still, there was, of course, no question of watering the paper's policy further.

Burke looked down at the book in his lap. It was *An American Dilemma,* a massive survey of prejudice in America by a Swedish economist. He grimaced, thinking that it was not so much a book as a time bomb. It had been published in the early 1940s—but its explosive effect had been truly felt only when the Supreme Court had cited it as one of the bases of its 1954 decision. Now he closed it with an angry snap.

"American, hell," he grated. "A Jessup dilemma." He wished Cary and Maggie would come on back; they had been out long enough, and he was irritated with them for leaving him by himself so long. But he forgot his self-pity when he saw the plume of dust on the long driveway leading into The Place and then the battered old Ford that raised it. Somebody was coming; and automatically he reached for his canes, for he always felt very helpless and vulnerable in the presence of anybody else without them.

7 Maggie Jessup put the big bay horse at the jump with full speed. There was the inevitable moment when she was sure it was taking off wrong, but that was a part of almost every jump and she urged it confidently with her legs. She felt the bay gather and leap; it soared high and cleanly over the board fence; she caught it up with the bit as it landed, let it have another twenty yards, and reined it in. It had been a splendid jump, and she was exultant, glad that Cary had been there to see it.

"Fine!" he yelled, and he put his own mount around to gather distance. She watched him come, saw him take the gray up and over with tremendous control and grace, bring it down and check it and canter toward her. She watched them come, man and horse, with an almost esthetic pleasure in the picture they made, powerful and perfectly matched. She felt quick gratitude once more toward Cary for arranging it so that she could ride every Saturday; with things on the paper going from bad to worse and Burke becoming subtly more and more withdrawn and morose, it was the high spot of her week, the one period of restoration she allowed her overstretched nerves. Then she looked at her watch, gasped in horrified guilt as she realized that they had left Burke alone far too long, and said as he came up, "My goodness, it's almost four-thirty."

He brushed a lock of thick, dark hair away from his forehead. "I reckon we'd better be getting on back," he said. "But I lost all track of time. You're getting to be a better rider every day."

"Not like you," she said honestly.

He shrugged his shoulders. "You want to see somebody handle a horse, you ought to have seen my father in his prime. He used to steeplechase at Tryon and Camden."

Maggie nodded; she had got used to his always measuring his own qualifications against those of his father. There was something almost infantile in his worship of the older man and vaguely it irritated her. But what was it Burke had said? "Down here, honey, it's as much who your father is as who you are. Maybe more."

She thought of her own father. He had not been tall and powerful and handsome and impressive and courtly like Powell Bradham, whom she had met twice now, but she thought he had probably been a great deal easier to live with. He had been field engineer for a construction company and home only infrequently, but when he was there his short, thick presence had seemed to light the house magically. No, she thought, I wouldn't exchange my childhood for his. Nor my father for his, either. At least he let me learn to think for myself. . . .

As they rode across the pasture, the sun was very hot. To their right a creek fed a low spot, a marsh—a savannah, she understood they called it—where water always stood and the grass was tall and green; small white herons strode among the rushes spearing frogs. Maggie took a moment to admire them. Then she asked, making conversation, "Did you know Burke's father?"

"Not too well. He worked on the morning paper here, kept crazy hours. He was always asleep in the morning and went to work in the afternoon. I hardly ever saw him. Where Burke and I got to be buddies was in school; we were in the same room from the third grade on." He paused. "I reckon you know that Burke's daddy shot himself when Burke was about fifteen. I never did know why, though rumor had it . . . well, it was something about a woman. He wasn't a big man, not the kind you'd look at twice, and the few times I ever saw him, he always looked nervous and absent-minded, like his thoughts were running two days ahead or two days behind."

"I knew it," Maggie said, "but Burke's never discussed it with me to any extent."

"Burke's had it rough," Cary said. He sighed. "Of course, everybody has, I reckon."

"Yes," she said gravely. "I suppose so." This was another thing she had learned to expect in Cary: a certain melancholy that settled on him at odd moments.

He reined in, as they topped a rise, and pointed toward a tractor maneuvering across a distant field, dragging a disc harrow behind. "Look there," he said. "I can remember when we worked all this land with mules and drag harrows. We had about twice as many tenants then as we do now. And cotton allotments have been cut back so much we're not cultivating half the land we used to. Even down in our lumber camp in the swamp, we're using power saws and bulldozing our roads, and we snake our timber out with tractors instead of mules. Logging more than we ever did and with fewer people. I reckon that's one reason for all this damfool agitation. We used to keep the Nigras so busy they didn't have time to raise Cain." Looking toward the house, he raised himself in his stirrups. A strange car was parked in the driveway, a dusty old Ford, sun glittering dully on its dirty chrome. "Looks like Burke's got company," he said. "Let's see who it is." He put his horse into a gallop and she followed.

When they clattered into the yard in front of the house, Maggie saw that there were two people, both Negroes, standing before the car, talking to Burke, who was on the porch. The man was blocky and muscular, his head very large, his shoulders very wide; he was about Burke's age and wore a neatly pressed blue sport shirt buttoned to the neck and an old pair of slacks sharply creased. The woman beside him was small and rather shapeless of body, obviously well along into pregnancy. She wore a flowered summer dress, was a little lighter than the man, and had an open, pleasant face that immediately impressed Maggie with its gentleness.

Cary reined in his horse. Maggie saw his mouth drop open slightly for a moment, then snap shut. All at once he was grinning.

"Well, I'll be damned," he grunted. "Houston Whitley!" Maggie sat up straight in the saddle, looking at the couple with new interest.

It was a name that she had heard over and over. So this was the Houston Whitley of the wild and boastful tales of Burke's and Cary's childhood exploits. This was the "little nigger boy" who somehow had been responsible for forming much of the attitudes of two white men toward his race. Maggie watched Cary keenly as he dismounted and strode forward.

He stopped half a dozen paces away from Houston Whitley, and Maggie saw attitudes of tension make the bodies of both men rigid for a moment as they looked at each other without speaking. Then Cary relaxed. "Well, Huse," he said, "it's good to see you. It's been a mighty long time." But she noticed that he did not put out his hand.

Houston Whitley seemed to relax too, then, and his wide lips curled in a smile under his mustache. His voice was deep, his diction far more crisp, less slurred, than that of Cary. "It's good to see you." There was another moment of silence; then Houston Whitley went on. "I don't believe you've ever met my wife Della. Della, this is Mr. Cary Bradham."

The woman smiled shyly. "How do you do, Mr. Bradham?"

"Hello, Della." Cary said it perfunctorily and turned back to Huse. "Well, what brings you out here? You decided to go back to cotton farming?"

Houston Whitley was still smiling. "Not exactly. But I did get a little homesick. In all the time Della and I have been married, I never have brought her out here to see The Place. We just took a notion to come this afternoon . . . I hope we're not intruding."

"Hell, no, you're not intruding," Burke said heartily from the porch. "Maggie, swing on down and come meet these people. This is Houston Whitley I've told you so much about. Huse, this is my wife, Mrs. Jessup."

Maggie was already in the act of dismounting; now she came forward. "Hello, Mr. Whitley," she said and thrust out her hand. She was watching Cary's face when she did it and took a quick, perverse pleasure in his look of surprise.

There was less pleasure in the obvious embarrassment in Houston Whitley's eyes as he took her hand. "Mrs. Jessup," he said, and he did not hold her hand long. "My wife, Della."

Maggie said carefully, "Hello, Mrs. Whitley," and put out her hand again. Della Whitley took it slowly, smiling with that same shyness. Her palm was rough, hard.

"Hell," Burke said from the porch, "don't y'all stand out there where I have to yell. Come on up here on the porch. We've got a lot of old times to talk over."

Cary nodded, and they went up on the porch. Maggie went to Burke and he put his arm about her for support. She closed her eyes for a moment; it was good to touch him, good to be embraced by him. Cary was saying, "Well, what have you been doing with yourself, Huse? I hear you're teaching now."

"Yes, sir. I teach at Washington Heights and Della teaches at Atterbury Elementary."

Maggie felt a growing irritation with Cary. Did he have to be so pompous, so patronizing?

"Well, we've built you some nice schools. They ought to be good places to work."

Houston Whitley's face was expressionless. "Oh, yes, they're fine."

"I'm glad you got settled down. You had me worried for a while way back yonder, you remember?"

"I remember." His gaze dropped; he looked down at his feet, and one of them automatically made a shuffling motion in the dust. "Yes, we're settled very well, thank you." He paused for an uncomfortably long moment. "Well, this is very nice, but I guess we'd better be going. It's getting pretty late. I thought we'd drive as far as we could up to the old house—you know, the one we used to have up yonder. Della wants to see it and . . . I kind of wanted to have a look at it myself."

"It's empty, about fallen down," Cary said. "We're not working as many hands as we used to." His face softened then and his voice turned warm, losing its stiffness. "Go ahead, Huse, look around as much as you want to. It's been a long time, hasn't it?" He slapped Houston Whitley's upper arm lightly with his open hand. "Those were the days, weren't they?"

Houston Whitley's expressionless face creased in a faint smile. "We had some good times."

"You remember that time we went into the swamp against orders and got lost? And how I shot up all my twenty-two bullets signaling and we were sitting there crying and that big black man—what was his name?"

"Mason Jar," Huse said.

"Yeah, Mason Jar. He heard it and came and walked us out of the swamp and never told anybody about the mess we were in?"

"I remember it," Huse said. "I remember it very well."

"Yes, sir," Cary said. "Good times." And then he sobered. "Huse, watch out for yourself, you hear? Stay out of all this trouble people are stirring up."

"Don't worry," Houston Whitley said. "Trouble is the last thing I'm looking for." There was an awkward pause and then he bowed slightly toward Maggie. "Well, it is very nice to have met you, Mrs. Jessup. Mr. Burke, it's sure good to have you home. Come along, Della, we'd better hurry. Goodbye, all. Cary, tell Mr. Powell and Miss Irene I said hello." With Della smiling and bowing slightly too, they turned and went down the steps and got into the car. It started with a loud roar of faulty muffler, making the horses fidget, and then, as Della waved, moved slowly past the house.

Cary watched it go, and when he turned to Burke and Maggie, she saw that his face was thoughtful and touched once more with that melancholy. He sat down on the rail, as if suddenly tired, and seemed completely oblivious to both of them.

Maggie turned to Burke and put her arm about him. "You'd better sit down," she said. "You've been standing up too long and you'll be all worn out."

8 The summer had not been an easy one for Houston Whitley. Knowing that Della could not resume teaching in the fall and that he could not possibly meet his financial obligations on his own three-thousand-dollar salary from the city school board, he sought a summer's work and found it with a roofing crew. He spent the blazing days spreading caldrons of pitch atop the roofs of new buildings, and the work burned him down hard and lean. He took a grim satisfaction in holding down his part of the job and being indistinguishable from the other laborers in the crew in speech or attitude. The hard work seemed to cleanse something within him that had gotten soiled and flaccid over the years, and except when the foreman forgot his name and called him "boy" he was rather proud of his ability to handle himself in this world with which he had almost lost contact.

In the meantime, Della was not having an easy pregnancy. Her feet and ankles had swollen painfully; she felt the heat severely, though she did not complain, and seemed always to be half drugged with a kind of dazed exhaustion, which, when it broke for short periods, was replaced by irritability. It was a rough summer, but it would have been even worse if it had not been for Martha Lacey, their neighbor on the right.

She was a comfortable-looking widow in her sixties who had somewhere learned to read and write a little, but had no formal education. There had been no time for any, even if it had been available during her youth, which it had not. She had lived most of her life in Little Hammer, striving with the responsibilities of raising and supporting two daughters and a son on her earnings as a maid. She rarely spoke of that struggle, but Huse did not have to imagine it—such situations were common in Little Hammer. There would have been long nights spent sewing or ironing for white folks to earn extra money; the desperate accumulation and hoarding of each penny and the sick feeling of helplessness when it was spent and no more was to be had; meals missed and house unwarmed, children crying, children shivering; spare hours spent scavenging for bottles along the highways to be redeemed for deposit or for coal along the railroad tracks; dark midnight hours of hopeless wondering and fervent praying about how to meet massive challenges with no resources. Martha's life was written in the calluses of her hands, in the bad teeth that had never known a dentist, in eyes weakened by years of wearing dime-store glasses. But she had done what she had set out to do, and done it alone and proudly. No, not alone, either, she said. "De good Lawd was lookin atter me. He make a way where dey ain't no way. Come time when I say, 'Lawd, how much longer fo' I rest?' He say, 'Martha, you jest take one step mo'.' And I take dat one lil step an' den He gimme stren'th to take anudder one, and somehow I makes de grade."

The two daughters were married now, one living in Washington and the other in New Jersey. The son was dean of men at Wheatley-Tubman and lived in Princeton. His prestige would have been damaged by allowing his mother to continue to live in Little Hammer, but having her living with him in Princeton would have been even more embarrassing—she was too "old-timey." So he had bought her the house in the development and made the payments on it; the rest of her support she earned herself, still doing daywork to eke out a minuscule Social Security check.

After all those years of sacrifice for others, she seemed unable to break the habit, and now she focused all her instinctive concern on Della, fussing over her like a hen with one chick. When Huse was home, she made a to-do over him, too; both of them came to lean on her and she had never failed them.

He was glad she was waiting for them when they came home from the trip to The Place. That, he knew now, had been a mistake. It had tired Della too much and it had left him oddly restless and melancholy. He wished that Cary had been either one way or the other with him—either wholly the reserved and patronizing white man or else completely relaxed and friendly. Now he was forced to think once more about Cary, to worry the implications of his attitudes as a dog might gnaw at an old and meatless bone. It was not that he expected to see Cary again any time soon, but somehow Cary's attitude toward him was a mirror in which he was trying to see himself, and he found himself analyzing over and over every speech of Cary, every word and action, to see what it told him about Houston Whitley. It did not tell him much, except to make him aware that he was still capable of a kind of grief at the loss of the bond between himself and the white man; he wondered if Cary ever felt that kind of grief too. Probably not, he decided.

Or maybe the grief was for something else. The shack in which they had lived during those days was nearly fallen down now, a rotted hulk of leaning boards. But it had been haunted with ghosts. Treading slowly and cautiously on the uncertain floor of the two small rooms, trying not to fall through the decayed and sagging porch, he had almost felt the presence of Otis, had almost been able to see him loafing on the porch in the twilight, tired and relaxed after a day's work, pipe in mouth, maybe holding the small, weary, round and uncorrupted Robert against him. Had been acutely aware of the presence of another self that had belonged to him, of a Houston Whitley who could never have imagined the Houston Whitley he had become now and who reproached him from the shadows. The place stirred too much in him; they did not stay long, and when they reached home both of them were on edge, Della from physical weariness and he from the stress of descending into the valley of the past.

Martha came over as they were getting out of the car and offered to fix their supper, and they were both grateful to her. While she stirred about the kitchen, Della went into the bedroom and lay down to rest. Huse found the tag end of a bottle of whiskey (he could not afford it often now and hoarded it carefully when he had it) and made himself a massive drink. He went into the living room, turned on the television set and dropped into a chair, clinging to the glass as if it were a life raft.

The screen flickered until an image coalesced. Huse sipped his drink and stared at it dully and without comprehension. An announcer's oily voice said, ". . . *Radiance,* the hair spray of the stars. And now, from Hollywood . . ."

Suddenly she was there. "Hello. I'm Virginia Marshall. Let's face it—hair can be a problem. Especially when you're on location in the Mexican desert, as I was with Terry O'Rourke in filming our great new picture together, *Two Across the Border . . .*"

The drink shook in Houston Whitley's hand. He felt its chill soak through his pants as some of its contents sloshed over the glass's rim. He wanted to spring up and cut off the set—no, kick it into oblivion. But he did not; he sat there in helpless, fascinated agony, as she looked through the glass directly at him, talked directly to him, just as lovely, just as heartbreakingly beautiful, as she had been nine years before.

" . . . remember . . . *Radiance,* the hair spray of the stars . . . "
She smiled, friendly, yet intimate; her voice pierced him, and then she was gone. He bent forward, one hand over his eyes.

He stayed like that for a moment, his body trembling slightly, and then he swallowed half the drink at a gulp. He gave a long, shuddering sigh, got up wearily and went to the set and turned it off. With the glass in his hand, he went to the front door and stared out at the gathering darkness.

While he stood thus, headlights came down the street and stopped in front of his house. He was pleased, relieved, to see Jeff Marfield get out of the travel-battered Oldsmobile and come up the walk. He held the screen door open.

"Hello, man." Jeff, as usual, was dapper and impeccable. "Am I interrupting your supper?"

"Nope. Haven't eaten. Come on in; I think I've got one more drink in the bottle."

Jeff shook his head. "Don't really want one. Where's Della?"

"We went out in the country today. She's frazzled out. Resting in back. Martha Lacey's cooking supper."

"Good deal. I'd like to talk to you about something if you got a minute. Need a favor."

"Sure. Sit down."

Jeff did so. As he laid his hat on a table beside the chair, Huse sensed that he was oddly embarrassed about something. "You sure you don't want a drink?"

"No, I reckon not." Marfield squirmed in the chair a bit, lit a cigarette, his sharp, usually good-humored face serious. Huse sat down in another chair near him.

"Well," said Jeff as if postponing whatever was on his mind, "you all ready for school to start?"

"I reckon so."

"You got a new principal over there at Washington Heights this year?"

"Not yet. Old man Haney's due to retire, but they haven't found a replacement for him. He's staying on for a while until they do."

Jeff nodded, his face sardonic. "I don't reckon it's easy for the white folks to find as tried and true and tested a Uncle Tom as old Dr. Haney."

"That's a pretty snotty way to talk about him," Huse said, a little startled to hear himself defending Haney. "He was dodging lynching bees trying to set up some education for colored folks before you were born."

Marfield nodded. "I know. That part of it I respect him for. But they broke him and he sold out to 'em and now he's worse than no man at all. I've heard Carson Bell, Charles's boy, talking about him. He's scared of his own shadow."

"Carson Bell's a troublemaker," Huse said disgustedly.

"I wish I could lay my hands on about fifty thousand trouble-makers just like him," Jeff said. "I'd make the white folks sit up and take notice. No, Carson's not a troublemaker. What Carson is, is the prototype of a new breed of Negro. One that's grown up in prosperity of a kind, one that's had time to learn and study and think, one that's had a chance to get a fairly reasonable education without having to hammer all the strength out of him to do it. He's the first generation of it—the fruits of what little improvement we've been able to bring about so far. And I'll tell you now, there's going to be a stir among the white folks when they see how many Carson Bells are arising."

He ground out his cigarette. "But I reckon that's neither here nor there. I said I came to ask a favor of you. But I'll swear, I'm a little ashamed to do it."

"No need for you to be. You know I'll do anything I can."

Jeff nodded. "Well," he said a bit hesitantly, "I'm in a kind of funny fix. I hate to ask you to do it, but I wonder if you could buy a car for me."

Huse stared at him. "Huh?"

Marfield grinned without much humor. "Well, I've banged around so much in that old wreck of mine that it's plumb wore out. Engine needs a complete overhaul and the transmission's about shot. I've been putting a little money aside as a kind of sinking fund to make the down payment on a new one, and I figured now or never. But the damnedest thing—when I went out to try to buy one, I ran into trouble. Nobody would finance one for me."

Houston Whitley looked at him for a second or two and then grinned. "I ain't even going to say I told you so."

"I know, I know. Anyhow, it's this White Citizens' Council. I'm the only NAACP official around here they can really put a finger on. So now nobody'll approve my credit. I mean, not on any kind of note. These old boys from the country can come in with ten dollars crop money and a junk pile on wheels to trade and walk out with a Cadillac. But not me. I've tried the banks and every finance company in town. Man, I'm poison." He paused. "So I thought that if I gave you the money, maybe you could go down and buy the car for me and tend to the financing. We could work up some kind of side-note deal to protect you and I'd give you the payment every month. Then, when it's paid for, you could sign it over to me."

"Hell, I ain't worried about any side note. I'll do it for you, if they'll approve *my* credit. It isn't too hot right now with Della's money out of my income."

"Don't worry, they'll okay anybody they're sure don't belong to the NAACP. Maybe it's a good thing you didn't join—otherwise I'd be walking."

Huse was serious. "You know this is liable to be only a sample, don't you? Things can get a lot rougher."

Jeff rubbed his hands together. "Well, there's no use trying to put a good face on it. They *are* rough."

"How so?"

"Well, these white folks have made damned sure the word gets out. You join the NAACP, you're right smack in the middle of a boycott. You aren't going to work, you aren't going to borrow money, you aren't even going to find a grocery man that will sell you food. Of course, our membership rolls are secret—that's the only thing that's saving us—but I hear tell they're going to try to introduce a bill at the next Legislature requiring us to make 'em public. If they do, we'll fight it in court."

"You can't beat 'em. I've told you that."

"Oh, I wouldn't be too sure. We're not entirely without friends, I mean white friends, right here in Muskogee. Only it's not much easier for them—maybe worse in some cases. But just for instance, there's a white preacher here in town, I wouldn't tell you his name, not that I don't trust you, but you've got no business knowing anyhow. And then there's the people in the Muskogee Council on Human Relations, Mr. Curtis McKnight and a bunch of others."

"Council on Human Relations? What's that?"

"It's an interracial group, whites and colored together working for improvement of things, just like they work together in the NAACP, only this is all Southerners. It's a kind of offshoot of the Southern Regional Council, which is the same thing on a larger scale down in Atlanta. There are white people working for us, but they've got to go slow too."

He lit another cigarette. "Don't worry about the NAACP, it'll get along. It's the other outfits that are going to suffer, the little improvement organizations that are all-Negro here in Hannington, for instance. I don't know, they've never amounted to anything anyhow. Right this minute we've got maybe a half-dozen different committees and organizations here in the Negro community, over and aside from the NAACP, but they never have been anything but jokes and I guess this pressure will about paralyze them completely. They never have worked together anyhow—they'd rather hassle among themselves than really stand up for their rights."

He stood up. "Anyhow, they aren't going to scare us off and they aren't going to starve us out. We'll keep on hacking away. Huse, I sure appreciate you agreeing to do that for me. I'll run by sometime this week with a check for what I've got to spend. Tell Della I said hello and look after her real good; she's the only sister I've got. Well, I've got to go. Louise will be waiting supper."

"Sho," Huse said, and he watched Marfield leave. As the lawyer strode down the front walk, Huse saw that despite his protestations of confidence, his step was slow and his shoulders were bent as if in discouragement.

9 Senator Hoke Moody leaned back in his chair, lit a cigar, and used the interval while the match was against the tobacco to let his eyes range over the other five men seated at the long conference table in the room adjoining the Governor's office. At sixty-two he was heavier and softer than he had been in the days when he campaigned against Powell Bradham from the back of a wagon, but, he told himself, his mind, if anything, was better. When a fox got older, it got smarter. And Hoke Moody could not help thinking of himself as a fox and looking with a certain contempt at all these . . . these rabbits grouped around him.

If they were not rabbits, he would not have been able to maintain his iron control over them. He despised them for allowing him to do that, despised their weakness and their inability to see things clearly and as a whole, as a fox must do when the hounds gather. Especially Powell Bradham—it was for him that Moody felt most contempt. Look at 'im, Moody thought, the inner workings of his mind phrased always in the Hampton County jargon of his youth. He's like one of them terrapins somebody carves the date on his shell and a hundred years later somebody else finds him wandering around in the same woods. Right now, if you were to give him a gray uniform with some gold braid on it, a slouch hat and a sword and flag to carry, he'd start raising a battalion.

And Cary, he thought, is just like him. No wonder the old breed can't stand the gaff any longer. They pass that blindness along from one generation to another. But he'll make a good front man when the time comes, and that's all I need him for. . . .

His eyes shuttled onward to his brother Dale, serving his second term as Governor. The contempt he felt did not diminish much. He knew his brother too well. Dale was mediocrity, proved mediocrity. He was too young to have known their father well, to have been influenced by him in the earlier days, before he had turned harsh, an embittered bigot. All Bradham could think about was honor; all Dale could think about was how much he hated niggers. He was rendered as blind and ineffectual by that and as easy to control as the Bradhams.

Still, Dale was not without his use. Hoke Moody was a statesman now, with a national reputation to preserve. Flat-out rabble-rousing in a senator had come to be unpopular; get tainted with the tag of being another Bilbo and your usefulness was over. So he, Hoke, had to watch himself. Dale, though, made a good surrogate, a go-between with the mass of common voters. Dale was so much like an ordinary red-neck in his reactions, for that matter, that in himself he was a useful barometer; he summed up all their vices and virtues, and his own attitudes epitomized theirs, so that he was in reality a sort of living one-man Gallup poll.

Moody's eyes flickered on past his brother to Dale's twenty-four year old son, Mitchell. Now there, he thought, losing all his contempt, is a different case. Mitch and I are gonna do a lot of business someday. He saw in Mitch an amalgamation of his own qualities with those of his brother. Mitch had his father's sharp country face, but he owned also a keen intelligence, a drive and a ruthlessness that must have come directly to him from Cole Moody, traits Dale had always lacked. When Cary Bradham's term is up, Moody thought, Mitch will be old enough and ready, and I'll have the boy well trained then. If I'm going to have any real heir, Mitch will have to be it. . . .

The fifth man was Milton Fanning, the Attorney General of the state. Fanning was a nothing, but he would be the next Governor when Dale's term was up, one of those caretakers Moody found it necessary to use: a puppet, to be manipulated.

Moody blew smoke and rolled the cigar in his mouth.

"I don't see," he said at last, "that we need any real fancy program in the Legislature to cope with this integration crap. The more we can keep the state as a legal entity out of it and let the Citizens' Councils and the like carry the ball, the better off we'll be. At the same time, we've got to do something—the people expect it." He grinned. "I hope those niggers realize they've given us the best political issue we've had in years. All these new factories coming down, bringing in a bunch of Yankee Republicans, Eisenhower making inroads with his damned popularity, this integration fight is the best thing that could have happened. It gives us something to rally the people back to us with, so the Republicans can't get a toehold." His voice turned crisp.

"Anyhow," he went on, hoisting his bulk up straight, "I see just a few limited actions in the Legislature. I'd like to see a bill go through giving the Governor the power to close all schools if any schools are integrated. That'll make the white folks think twice about throwing any weight behind the niggers. Secondly, I think it would be a mighty salutary thing to see a bill passed that would require foreign corporations doing business in the state to make their personnel rolls public. That would put a crimp in the NAACP—no nigger's going to join if he knows everybody can read his name in the papers. And one last thing—I believe we ought to have a complete purge of the voting registration rolls and a new reregistration. We've let too many nigger voters get on the rolls and I think we'd be better off without 'em." He took his cigar from his mouth. "I don't see much else needs doing. Anybody got any other ideas?"

Dale Moody rubbed his face, turned. "I told you about that talk I had with Sam Deal." He looked at the others. "Sam Deal came to me and said if we'd knock the anti-mask law off the books, or at least agree not to enforce it too hard, he can get the Klan built up enough so that no nigger'll dare step out of line—"

"Well, we ain't going to accommodate Sam," Moody said briskly. "If a nigger gets out of line, he'll get a knot jerked in him all right, but it'll be a legal knot." He grinned thinly. "I'll admit it sounds attractive to sort of deliver an invitation to the Klan to go out and cut the balls off a few black bucks just to make an example. But we ain't. We'll clamp down on the Klan tight as we clamp on the niggers. That may sound strange coming from me, but this new Klan ain't my old Klan, and I don't feel a damned bit of obligation to it. Moreover, that's the image the whole country has got of the South— a bunch of Klansmen stringing up niggers from every tree. It'll just hurt us, not help us. Hell, I don't care if Sam and his crowd go out and burn a few crosses. It'll make people feel better and it won't do any harm. But you can pass the word to him and pass it emphatically. Anything rougher than that and their ass'll be in a sling."

He consigned the dead and mangled cigar to an ashtray. "Anything else?" He watched them for a moment or two, the contempt returning. They were, he saw, all afraid of him, each in his own way. He smiled. "All right," he said. "I'll leave y'all to work out the details. Keep me filled in." And he stood up to indicate the meeting was over.

Cary Bradham walked beside his father through the rotunda of the capitol, neither of them speaking. Both of them, Cary knew, were rankling a little with Hoke Moody's high-handedness. Cary, now that he was in the Legislature and so had been taken into the councils of the mighty, was just becoming acquainted with it; he looked sideways at his father, wondering if Moody had been like that all these years, and, if so, why his father had endured it.

They came to the main doorway, stepped out onto the topmost of the high steps, and there Powell Bradham halted for a moment. He was looking up at the blood-colored flag with its two diagonal bars, watching it snap in the sunset breeze. "It'll soon be time to take it down," Cary murmured, pausing beside his father.

"Overnight," Bradham said. He was silent for a moment. Then he said, "I wonder how much longer we are going to have to fight them."

"Sir?"

"How much longer are they going to keep on trying to destroy us? Will we have to fight for the next hundred years, too?"

"You mean this is the same war," Cary said, aware of an eerie touch along his spine and the back of his neck.

"Of course it's the same war. Haven't I told you that all along? It's lasted a hundred years; will it go on another hundred?" Bradham's mouth was a thin line under his mustache; his medallion profile was limned against the reddening light. Cary thought: He looks just like the portrait in the hall. He leaned against the decapitated statue of Athena and waited until his father was ready to go. Two convicts were taking down the flags now and his father would not move until that was done.

Then Bradham said, "Come on," and went quickly down the steps. They walked together to the parking lot. Bradham stopped at the rear bumper of his Cadillac. "Get in and sit with me a minute," he said.

Cary looked at him questioningly and then they got in the front seat of the car together.

When he had closed the door Cary had a sensation of *déjà vu;* he remembered—and something in his father's attitude made him feel like—the small boy who had ridden beside his father to The Place every Saturday morning. He smiled faintly and lit a cigarette, waiting for Bradham to speak.

"If it would further Hoke Moody's political progress," Bradham said at last, harshly, "he would get himself elected president of the NAACP. He's an opportunist, nothing else. He's never been anything but an opportunist."

This was the first speech Cary had ever heard against Moody from his father, and the bitterness of it startled him. He sat up straight. "Sir?"

Bradham looked at him, gray eyes swirling angrily. "Moody really cares no more about the welfare of this state than he would a chess pawn. All Moody cares about is Moody." He rubbed a big hand over a clenched fist. "You heard him in there, dealing out his orders like God Almighty."

"Yes, sir," Cary said quietly.

"Sitting there as if he owned—" Bradham grated. "Telling me and you—" He broke off, seemed to get a grip on himself. "All right," he said. "For now. Cary, there's something I've got to tell you."

Something in his voice touched Cary with excitement. He shifted on the seat. "Yes, sir."

Bradham was staring out the windshield with eyes focusing on nothing. "In 1932," he said in a dry voice that was like the crackling of dead sticks, "things fell out so that I had to form this coalition with Moody or be completely unseated from any say in the government of this state. I was left no choice except to do that. Up until now, I reckon you've figured it was fifty-fifty; sometimes I even tried to persuade myself that it was. But, of course, it wasn't. Moody had the whip hand and it was him on top and me—" His mouth twisted. "I had to submit myself to that white trash's authority. Just as we had to in there today. I didn't do it because I wanted to or for any personal gain, either. I did it because I had to do it for the state; I had to keep a Bradham in the government to keep the white trash from running wild."

He paused. "I had over twenty years of it," he went on finally. "But what made it worth while, what sustained me, besides knowing that if I wasn't there Moody would have everything his way—what I was always planning ahead to was you."

"Me?" Cary said it softly, the excitement quickening.

"Did you think that because I was defeated in 1932 I had quit fighting? Did you think I planned to stand aside and let Hoke Moody found a dynasty, take over this state for the Moodys forever? By hell, no! I love Muskogee too much for that." He turned to Cary, his eyes glittering. "But I let Moody think that. I let him believe I was whipped and that I had come to heel. I served him loyally for twenty years, made myself as useful to him as I could. Do you know why I did that? Do you know now?"

Cary said nothing.

"All right," Bradham said. "Moody has promised you the governorship. He's convinced that it's safe now, that he can control the Bradhams as he thinks he controls everything else in the state. It's exactly what I've been working for twenty years to make him think. His promise to make you Governor—he's used that as bait for years to keep me in line and prides himself on his cleverness. He thinks he can use you, a Bradham, make you Governor, make you take his orders, and then step aside gracefully when he's ready to hand over power to that mink-faced nephew of his. That's what he thinks."

He stopped again for a moment, breathing deeply as if he had run a long way. "It hasn't been easy for me," he said at last. "Only my knowledge of my duty to the state has kept me at it. It's not going to be easy for you, either. But we have both got to be patient and clever and wait our chance. Let Moody make you Governor, and then—"

Cary was staring at him. "You mean that all this time you were planning for me—" His mind groped, trying to comprehend the ramifications of this. Suddenly so much was clear to him, a hundred different questions answered, a hundred curiosities satisfied. His breath went out in awe. "You want me," he whispered, "to let Moody make me Governor and then turn on him and take the state away from him."

"You will," his father said. "You've got to. Don't you see? Moody's trash. He has no integrity. He has no principles of his own.

He'll make a stand now, but he can't be trusted to stand. When it suits him, he'll yield. He doesn't care about Muskogee, he doesn't care about any of the things *we* care about. All he cares for is power for himself—and to pass along to Mitch." His voice harshened. "This battle's just starting, this next hundred years. And Bradhams are not going to sit by while Moodys lead. Do you understand?"

Cary nodded, and as he looked at the set features of the determined old man who was his father, he felt a rush of affection and pride that clogged his throat and made it hard to speak. His father had sacrificed twenty years for him. Least psychologically equipped for it of all men, his father had willingly endured the humiliation of playing second fiddle to Hoke Moody, of being one of Moody's understrappers, not for his own personal gain, but for him . . . and for Muskogee. Never before had he realized just what a tremendously courageous man his father was.

He said thickly, "I understand. I understand exactly."

His father's eyes probed his own. "Well?"

Cary sought words. "You know I'll do my best. You know you can count on me."

It was all he knew to say; but when he saw the relief and pride and love on his father's face, he knew that it was enough.

His father touched his hand with his fingertips and then drew the fingers away.

"So you must be very careful," he said. "Never buck Moody and always do exactly what he says and pretend butter wouldn't melt in your mouth. And after the Legislature, then Lieutenant Governor next, and after that, then your time will have come."

He turned around in the car and grasped the steering wheel. "You have one advantage I've lacked," he said. "You'll have St. John Butler behind you all the way. Count yourself lucky that you have Mary Scott for a wife. It'll make it easier, much easier all around." He seemed to have relaxed. "We'll talk more about this later. Here comes Hoke. Your mother will be waiting supper on me." He slapped Cary's thigh with a big palm. "Good night, son. Lord, I feel better than I have in twenty years."

Cary said quietly, pleased that his father was pleased, "Good night, Dad. And don't worry. We'll make it work out just exactly like you've planned." He slid out of the car and shut the door. Feeling somehow taller, oddly charged with strength and power, he walked toward his own car. He passed Hoke Moody striding short-legged across the parking lot and flipped his hand.

"Good night, Uncle Hoke," he called, and was surprised at the warmth and respect he was able deliberately to put into his voice.

Moody waved back. "Good night, son. Give Mary Scott my love." Then he was walking on toward his car, where a uniformed chauffeur lounged. Cary turned for a moment and studied the short thick figure bobbing through the dusk; he was sizing up the enemy, and the enemy did not look so formidable.

10 He had bought the car for Jeff Marfield, but now he wondered if it had not been a mistake. There was a sick knot of apprehension in him as he entered the Law Building downtown and waited until all the white people were in the elevator before he got on. It must have something to do with the car; it must be connected with it in some way. Why else would Cary Bradham summon him to his office?

He had been jarred when Martha had given him the scrawled message last night: *Mr Kery Bradom say offss ten ohclok.tomar.*

"Did he say what he wanted?" he had quizzed Martha.

"Uh-uh, he jes' say be sure to be there."

Be there, Huse had thought. Not can you be there, not will you be there . . . just be there. The imperial summons. And trouble afoot, sure as shooting. It had to be the car; it was the only thing he could think of. And now, dammit, he wished he'd never stuck his neck out for Jeff.

He had hidden the message from Della; she was in bad enough shape as it was without something else to worry her. But suppose Cary were calling him in to tell him that he was going to be fired for helping out the NAACP's state president? He couldn't hide that. And where would he get another job, and the baby coming on? Suppose he was boycotted completely the way Jeff had been? Dammit, he thought savagely, emerging from the elevator and turning down the hall, I'll never stick my neck out again—not for anybody!

He found the door all right: *Bradham & Bradham, Attorneys.*
His hand was so sweaty that it slipped on the metal knob as he
turned it. He entered an outer office occupied by two secretaries,
and as he closed the door behind him, another door opened and
Powell Bradham emerged from it with a sheaf of papers in his hand.
Huse had not seen him in years; he was startled at how the erect
form had begun to bow. Bradham's face looked narrower, as if the
flesh were evanescing from beneath the skin, leaving lines and
wattles. His eyes flickered curiously over Huse without recognition,
and Huse said, "Good morning, Mr. Powell. I haven't seen you in
a long time."

Bradham said without smiling, "Oh, it's you, Huse. I didn't know
you at first. Hello." He turned to one of the secretaries, his back to
Huse, and bent to confer with her. The knotted apprehension in
Huse deepened at that cool dismissal; it was a bad portent.

The other secretary looked at him with suspicion. "Yes," she said
tersely, "what do you want?"

Huse swallowed. "My name is Houston Whitley; Mr. Cary Bradham sent for me."

She nodded and picked up a phone. "Mr. Cary, there's a Nigra
man named Whitley out here says you sent for him." She put down
the phone. "You can go in," she said tersely. "Through that door
there."

"Thank you, ma'am," said Huse, bobbing his head carefully. He
took a deep breath, went to the door and opened it.

Cary Bradham's office was large but Spartanly furnished, designed
for work. Except for a few hunting prints on the plaster walls, it
was bare of ornamentation. Cary sat behind a desk heaped with
papers. "Hello, Huse," he said, his face expressionless. His gesture
indicated a straight-backed chair across the desk. "Sit down."

"Yes, sir," Huse said, easing himself into the seat. "How are you,
Mr. Cary?" He had put the "Mr." on in exploration. He waited to
see if Cary would tell him to drop the formality but Cary did not.
Huse's apprehension did not lessen.

Cary leaned back in his chair and lit a cigarette. He looked at
Huse through the curling smoke for a moment before he spoke.
"Well, did you show your wife everything there was to see out at
The Place the other day?"

"There wasn't much to see," Huse said. "Old house about fallen down."

Cary nodded. He looked at Huse for a moment more with a peculiarly penetrating expression of appraisal, as if he were trying to read Huse's mind. Huse tried not to fidget, looking back at Cary obliquely. He saw that the years were beginning to flesh out the basically massive structure of Cary's head, gray his temples slightly.

Then Cary's voice crackled at him. "Huse, how do you like teaching at Washington Heights?"

Oh, Lord, he thought; here it comes. "I like it right well," he said shakily, trying hard to keep the panic out of his voice, hating himself for feeling panic at all.

Cary leaned forward, elbows on his desk. "You think if Dr. Haney was to leave, you could take over as principal?"

Huse knew that his mouth opened and shut twice without any sound coming out. He felt an odd collapsing sensation within, as apprehension crumbled, relief grew. "Principal?" He managed the word at last; it squeaked ludicrously.

Cary was grinning more broadly. "Well, Haney's overdue for retirement. You see, after I bumped into you out at The Place, I got to thinking about old times and wondering if there wasn't something I could do for you to help you out, your wife having a baby coming on and all. Well, as state Senator from this county, I draw a little water here and there, so I got to checking around and found out they were looking for a replacement for Haney but hadn't been able to find anybody . . . reliable enough. So I told the school board I thought I knew a pretty good man, and they suggested I talk to you about it."

"Well, now, that's mighty nice. I don't know what to say . . ." He felt a warm, genuine gratitude toward Cary, a kind of rich pleasure that Cary had thought of him, that those early years had meant something to Cary as well as to him. Worry sloughed away. The job would be a godsend—it would mean at least a thousand more a year.

"You don't have to say anything," Cary told him. "It's not settled yet." He leaned forward. "The main thing, Huse, is that they need somebody they can trust. Somebody who can take a mature view of things—you know what I mean?"

Some of the pleasure went out of Huse. This was not entirely a token of friendship, nor any recognition of competence, then. What they need, Huse thought, what they're hurting for, is an Uncle Tom they can be sure won't turn into a Nat Turner. All right, he thought. You give me that principal's job, I can scrape and shuffle as good as the next one.

"Yes, sir," he said, choosing his words carefully. "I know exactly what you mean. Well, I'll tell you exactly how I stand. I don't hold with all this race foolishness. I don't see anything wrong with separate but equal. Washington Heights is a fine school; it cost a lot of money. No reason why colored children can't get as good an education there as anywhere else if they just apply themselves. Me, I don't see any call for people stirring up all this trouble. Looks to me like my race would be better off if it quit hollering about integration so much and buckled down to using what it's already been given."

Cary's grin was wide now and full of satisfaction. "I hoped you'd feel that way. From what Burke told me of the conversation between you and him the other day, I gathered you did—and Lucy said so too. Now. If I make a recommendation, I'll be sticking my neck out. I'd sure be upset if it got chopped off, you understand?"

Huse made his face grave and sincere. "Cary, you know if I had that job I wouldn't do anything to put you on the spot. People have been hammering at me from all sides, join the NAACP, join the Urban League, join this, join that. I've told them all to go take a flying leap." He thought of a master stroke. "I told 'em I got too many good white friends to go around stirring up trouble for 'em."

Cary nodded. Then his face turned businesslike. "All right, Huse, I think you've got the right idea. I believe I can arrange it. Just the same, I wouldn't broadcast it around if I were you until it's official. You'll be notified as soon as the board takes action. I'll try to get the biggest salary increase out of them for you that I can. They need a man there they can depend on. If he turns out to be dependable, I don't think he needs to worry about getting paid what he's worth."

"I don't know how to tell you how much I appreciate it."

Cary's face softened, relaxed for an instant. "It was my pleasure. We needed a man, and I'm glad you're it. Just don't let me down."

"You know that's the last thing I'd do," Huse said in a voice as sincere as he could make it.

"I know," Cary said with complete trust; and then he stood up.

Huse arose too. "Thanks again," he said, noting how Cary almost visibly swelled under his gratitude, wondering if one of the main reasons white men kept the clamps on wasn't so they could experience the peculiar glow of dispensing largesse to their inferiors. Suddenly he was afraid of what he might say if he didn't hurry up and leave. He quickly mouthed another obsequious goodbye and went out.

There had been last night the problem of hiring a substitute for today whom he had to pay out of his own pocket; it had seemed the ultimate irony to have to pay someone to hold down his job while he went to get fired; but he did not begrudge the expenditure now. He left the Law Building walking on air, buoyed by the knowledge of his own vindication. Let Jeff Marfield sneer at him; his policy of keeping his mouth shut had paid off.

Since he had the substitute, he was free for the day. He was a little surprised to find that he felt no impulse to go straight home and tell Della the news, but something held him from it. Moreover, by the time he reached his car, some of the elation had begun to drain away, and he was beginning to feel inexplicably guilty.

Hell, he told himself, what's the matter with you? Man, you've just made a big step up and here you are beginning to mope like a sick chicken. Goddammit, cut that out; what you ought to do is celebrate.

The thought of that made him feel better; with sudden resolve, he drove through town to the row of honky-tonks on the edge of Little Hammer. He pulled the car to the curb in front of the Happiness Club and went in.

Except for one or two shabby and unwashed morning drinkers, it was deserted, and its emptiness in the morning light was depressing. He ordered a beer and drank it quickly, trying desperately to restore his exhilaration.

But it did not work, nor did the second one he drank, nor the one after that. He felt bloated and there was a terrible taste in his mouth when, at last, he slid off the stool. And, for some reason, he still did not want to go home, but there was no other place to go.

Martha Lacey was busy in the kitchen making lunch and Della was sitting at the table when he came in. Since she had been unaware of the conference with Cary, her eyes widened in her puffy face. "Hello, darling. What in the world are you doing home?" Apprehension clouded her gaze. "Is anything wrong? You're not sick?"

He tried to put the exultation he had originally felt into his voice; but it seemed to him his tone was brassy and false. "Fartherest thing from it! No, I came home to tell you the good news."

"Good news?"

"I got a surprise for you." He sat down at the table, smiling what he hoped was a delighted smile. "Last night Cary Bradham called and wanted to see me. I went by there this morning and we had a nice talk." His voice got loud. "You're looking at the new principal of Washington Heights."

"Well, Lawd-a-mercy, 'at's mighty fine," Martha Lacey said immediately and enthusiastically.

Huse said, "Thank you," and looked at Della. "Well, aren't *you* going to say something?"

For a moment, surprise had made her face vacuous. Now she said, her voice matter-of-fact, "What about Dr. Haney?"

"Haney's retiring; I'm replacing him."

"I see."

Her lack of enthusiasm jarred and irritated him. "Well, for God's sake, is that all you can say? I get a promotion, finally make principal, and all you can say is, I see?"

"No, I think it's wonderful, I really do. I'm very proud of you." But her voice sounded forced.

Baffled, Huse frowned. "You don't sound like it."

"I said I was proud."

"Yeah." He slid into angry depression, sullenness. "All right, thanks."

An odd tension filled the room. Martha ladled food onto two plates and set it down before them. "I reckon I better git on home," she said quietly.

"Oh, no, stay and eat," Della said automatically.

"Thank you, but I got some mendin to do. I come back directly and do the dishes. Now, don't you go troublin yourself about 'em, you hear?" She waddled out the back door.

"All right," said Huse bitterly when she had gone. "What's eating you? I come home with what I *thought* was good news and I get looked at like I was bragging about robbing the poor box in some church. What's the trouble?"

"I told you, nothing," Della said. But she laid down her fork.

"Yeah, nothing," he said caustically.

She bowed her head. "I'm sorry. I know you're excited. I didn't mean to be a wet blanket."

"Then how come you are one?"

She said nothing for a long time. Huse grated, finally, "Hell."

Della raised her head and her eyes were moist. "Huse, I am sorry. It's just that . . ." Her voice trembled. "I don't know. It seems such a waste. I never thought when we got married that someday you'd . . . you'd come home bragging about being another Dr. Haney."

Huse stared at her for a clock tick. Then he slammed the table and jumped to his feet.

"Damnation!" he bellowed. "You're just like that brother of yours. All you can think of is to see how bad you can put me on the spot! Because I got more sense than either one of you, because I know how to work the white folks around to my own benefit. That's all you two can think about, race, race, race, race. You'll use anything you can to make me look like a damn fool because I've had my bait of this race stuff and I won't fall for it any more!"

"That's not true," she said quickly. "It's just that neither one of us wants to see you prostitute yourself—"

"Prostitute myself?" he roared. "Jesus God, how can I keep from prostituting myself? Every nigger since the days of Ham has had to prostitute himself to live!" He slammed the table again. "It's easy for you to sit there and criticize. You've got to bear that child, that's all. But I've got to feed it and support it and figure out which way to teach it to go to stay alive in this world. I've got to make bricks without straw, unless I can talk the white folks into giving me some straw. I don't know where else to get the straw I need; they got all the straw there is. I didn't ask you to get pregnant, I didn't want to bring a kid into this world—but as long as I'm stuck with it now, by God, don't you come whining around me with this race crap." He saw her face going ashy; he tried to stop himself, but he could not; the words raced on, spilling out as if he had to purge himself. "Ain't no kid of mine going to beat his brains out against a brick wall. *My* kid's going to get along the easy way and I'll save him all the pain I can—"

Della was shoving back her chair, her face contorted, stricken. Her lips moved twice, three times, before he caught the words. "You hate having the baby, don't you?"

"Yes!" he heard himself roar. "Yes, damn it, I hate having it. I got all I can do to look out after us without—"

He broke off. She was wheeling away from the table. She stood there a moment; he saw her throat work, and she placed a hand across her swollen abdomen. "I'm sorry," she whispered. "Oh, God, I'm so sorry." And then she was lumbering awkwardly toward the bedroom.

11 So now he had all he knew he was ever going to get. A principal's job paying four thousand a year, a wife for whom he felt affection, even love, but no passion, and a child coming to bind him forever to the sterile pattern. It was not what he had dreamed of in those long, hot afternoons in Burnt Stump School after all other students had gone, something in him beginning to vibrate and expand as Lizzie Blackwelder cracked, at first timidly, and then with reckless abandon opened the door to a world it would have been impossible to discover alone. It was not what he had so proudly and confidently brayed about to Blalock on the troopship coming home. Nor did it have any relation to the glittering future he had made up while he held Virginia Crane in his arms.

But it was all he had and all he was ever going to get, and, by God, he vowed, he was going to hang onto it, such as it was. Let them call him Uncle Tom. Let them call him anything they wanted to. He did not care what they called him. He knew what he had been through to achieve even this much and what it had taken out of him, and he was not, he told himself, ashamed of it.

Not even when they brought Carson Bell before him, early in January.

The English teacher and advisor to the staff of *The Washhite,* the high school paper, Lillian Trumbull, came to him nervously one day after school. She was a rabbit-faced woman of thirty, the color of butterscotch. "Mr. Whitley," she blurted after she had shut his office door behind her, "I've just got to have some help with that Bell child. He's getting completely out of control."

Huse leaned back in the chair that had belonged to Dr. Haney. "Well, now, Mrs. Trumbull, are you telling me that you can't control your students?" He knew exactly what she meant, but he did not want to make it easy for her; she was the type that, once given sympathy, would have brought all her troubles to his doorstep immediately, no matter how minor.

Not that he believed her troubles with Carson Bell were minor. Charles Bell's strong-willed son was editor this year of *The Washhite,* and Huse could imagine what a challenge to him that must be.

"It's not his behavior," Lillian Trumbull said. She licked her lips nervously. "It's . . . it's his utter lack of cooperation. You can't talk to the boy without his taking everything you say and twisting it around so . . . so it makes you sound foolish your own self. But the main thing is what he keeps trying to put in the paper. All sorts of foolishness that if anybody ever got ahold of it, there's no telling how much trouble it would cause. I've taught in this school system for five years. I know."

Huse felt himself assailed by a kind of weary anger directed against young Bell. If the kid's as smart as he claims to be, he thought, he should have got the message from that session I had with him last year. His voice was crisp. "All right, Mrs. Trumbull. What kind of thing does he try to slip into the paper on you? Nothing," he added, "would surprise me about that boy."

She fished in the pocket of her skirt and handed him a folded sheet of typing paper. "I found this in the material that went to the printshop with the other copy for the next issue. You'll see that it doesn't have my initials on it. It's just God's grace that I caught it before it got set up and maybe printed."

Huse unfolded the sheet and read the typing on it. Obviously it had been intended as an editorial.

"I okay all the copy," she said as he let his eyes skim down the page. "But the students are responsible for all proofreading and printing. It *could* have got in the paper and spread all over town if one of the printing students hadn't noticed it wasn't okayed and brought it to me."

"Second-class students," Huse read aloud. "School authorities claim that though Washington Heights is a segregated school its facilities are 'equal' to any white school in town. Our principal and faculty may swallow this line, but we are of a different generation and our eyes are clearer. Ask any student—are the library shelves in white schools nearly empty of books? Do white students have to stand in line to use one beat-up old set of 1938 encyclopedias for reference? Do white students have to take showers after gym in cold water in the middle of winter? Were the white high schools unable to field their football teams this year until parents of students took up a collection to buy necessary uniforms and equipment? Next time somebody tells you that Washington Heights is equal, ask them, equal to what? Come on, Mr. Principal. Our parents pay taxes too. If we're going to be penned up here all by ourselves like we all had the itch, at least squeeze some money out of the 'white folks' so we'll have something to show for our three years in Washhites besides 'the sniffles' from cold showers. We're citizens too!"

Huse nodded and laid the paper aside. He kept his voice perfectly controlled, despite the reaction that sickened him for a moment and the cold fury that followed it. This, he knew, had been a deliberate attempt to get him. If it had got printed and had fallen into the hands of the superintendent of schools, or the school board— He closed his eyes a second, and then he said quietly, "It a good thing you caught it. Is Carson still in the building?"

She nodded. "I thought you'd want to see him, so I made him stay and wait."

"Good," said Huse, and his voice was cold. "I think you'd better tell him to come in. I want to talk to him . . . privately."

"Yes, Mr. Whitley," she said; and she arose with the rigidity of vindicated virtue and went out.

Carson Bell was a tall, neat, slender boy, quite as dark as his father. He entered Houston Whitley's office without fear, sullenness, or contrition. If anything, there was defiance, maybe even contempt, on his face.

"Close the door behind you, Carson," said Huse, still in that carefully controlled voice.

When young Bell had done that, Huse let him stand for a full moment before his desk before he spoke again. Then he picked up the sheet of copy paper and handed it to Bell.

"Did you write that?"

Carson glanced at it briefly. "Yes, sir," he said.

"And tried to slip it into *The Washhite* without Mrs. Trumbull's okay?"

"Yes, sir," the boy said promptly.

Huse let out a long breath. He had known Carson well enough not to expect the boy to try to lie out of it or to attempt to shift the blame. But he had expected Carson to show a little fear at being caught. There was none, however: the black, purely African, face was as passionless and void of expression as if carved from oiled and polished wood. Huse's anger deepened.

"All right," he said. "You've been editor of the paper for over a semester. You knew it was against the rules. Why did you try it?"

"Because I thought it needed to be said." Carson Bell's voice was rather high-pitched. "Because it's the truth."

"How do you know it's the truth?" Huse rapped back at him instantly. "What do you know about white schools? Have you ever been in one?"

For the first time uncertainty touched Carson Bell's face. "No," he said. "And I'm beginning to think I never will be. But I'll bet you they're better than this one."

"How do you know that?" Huse pressed mercilessly.

"Because they're white!" Carson snapped. "And the whites always give themselves the best of everything and the colored always takes the leftovers."

Huse did not give him even an instant to get balance. He flung out an arm.

"You remember the old school you went to before they built this one? This new building cost nearly a half a million dollars. Do you call *this* a leftover?"

"No, sir," Carson Bell flung back instantly. "But we're using leftover books and leftover everything else, and whatever it is, we don't get it until the white boys are through with it."

Anger thickened in Huse, but he kept his voice controlled, and he met Carson Bell's eyes, though he suddenly felt a strong urge to look away.

"So," he said, aware of his own sophistry, "you wrote a sneak editorial about a lot of things you really don't know anything about."

"I know all I need to know—"

"An editorial," Huse went on quietly, "that could have cost me and Miss Trumbull our jobs. You know that, don't you? I'm responsible to the school board for everything and everybody in this school, including that paper. You could have got me fired, Carson. Is that what you wanted to do? Get me fired?"

He saw Carson's tongue come out and lick his lips. "They wouldn't have fired you," Carson said; but he had not thought about that until now and suddenly his voice shook. Huse felt pleased at having him on the defensive. He bored in.

"Oh, wouldn't they? That shows how much you know about it, Carson. In times like these that editorial would get me and Miss Trumbull fired like that." He snapped his fingers.

"I don't believe it," Carson said. "Anyhow, I didn't mean to—"

"What you did or didn't mean has no bearing on the question," Huse rapped. "All that interests me now is seeing that you get the proper punishment."

Carson Bell set his jaw and said nothing.

"We've been over this ground before," Huse went on. "We had this out last year, and you were warned about causing trouble of this sort. I told you then, Carson, there is no room in Washington Heights High School for a maverick. This is a school for people who want to study, not people who come here to see how much trouble they can stir up."

Carson chewed at his lower lip and kept silent.

Huse leaned back in his chair. "I could expel you," he said. "I could expel you for the rest of the school year."

He waited for the fear to cross Carson's face, but it did not come. How much, Huse wondered in a moment of savagery, will it take to break him? Then, quite suddenly, all his anger drained from him and he was left enervated, feeling dirty and ashamed and with a desire to get this over with as quickly as possible and wash his hands of it. Not only because it was a messy situation—after all, Charles Bell was his friend as well as his minister. But because, too, he saw in the slender, unafraid boy standing before him something that he did not want to look at, something that caused him a pain he refused to define to himself.

"But I'm not going to," he said. "As it happens, your father is one of my very good friends, a man I respect and admire. To expel you would hurt him more than it would you."

Something flickered in Carson's eyes. "Don't worry about my father," he said.

"So for your sake, I'm giving you another chance. You're off *The Washhite,* of course, effective as of now. And you're on probation. One more offense and out you go. I mean that, Carson."

"Yes, sir," the boy said. He did not flicker a muscle.

"Remember everything I've said to you," Huse added. "Don't force me to have to drop the block on you."

"Yes, sir," Carson said again.

Huse was suddenly very tired. "All right," he said. "You can go now."

"Yes, sir," Carson said, and he turned and went out, his back very straight.

When the door had closed behind him, Huse let out a long, whistling breath. He slumped back and put his hand over his eyes, pinching the bridge of his nose.

"Ahhh . . ." he said.

Behind his closed lids, the image of Carson Bell's eyes danced. Large, expressive—and overflowing with a quiet, absolute contempt.

"Shit," Houston Whitley said softly, and he got up and went to the window. Some boys were playing football on the frostbitten grass of the yard.

Why? he wondered. Why should I stand here and feel guilty about doing my duty? Why should I feel embarrassed to be with Della or Jeff? Why should I feel like . . . like a pimp or a whore?

He had felt like that ever since he had moved into this office. They had all made him feel like that—Della, Jeff, Charles Bell. The only one who didn't nag him was Martha Lacey. Damn it, you'd think they'd accord him a little respect. He'd come up the ladder, he had a good job; why did they all look at him like that?

He watched Carson Bell walk across the yard, head down, shoulders bent. He drew in a deep breath.

"I'll expel a thousand Carson Bells," he said aloud, "if I have to."

They talked, Jeff and Della and some others, about the younger generation being a new breed of Negro. As if it were somehow sanctified, as if it were entitled to more than any other generation.

But what about us? he thought. What about us other generations? After we've scrabbled and shuffled and begged and brownnosed, aren't we entitled to something too?

He had that out with Jeff Marfield last night, in the Whitleys' living room, in the most heated argument they had ever had. "You don't want to rock the boat," Jeff had stormed; "nobody wants to rock the boat."

"Maybe that's because we'll all be better off if the boat ain't rocked. Things are quiet now. Why can't they stay that way?"

"Stay that way, man? My God, they can't!"

"How come?"

Jeff whirled, pointing to Della's swollen belly. "That's how come. Because there's little babies being born every hour, every day. And time's running out. We already frittered away the heritage of God only knows how many babies by not rocking the boat. How many more are we going to deprive?"

Huse had found himself getting angry. "Listen," he snapped, "you been living with it so long, you don't know dream from reality. Dream is everybody free—reality is living when you aren't and know you aren't going to be. You talk about my baby—well, let me tell you something. I'm going to teach him what reality is. I'm going to teach him it don't do you any good to ram your head against a brick wall. It took me thirty-two years and a lot of grief to learn that, but it's going to be the first thing I'll teach *him!*"

Marfield looked at him a moment, almost as if he were seeing him for the first time. Then his lip curled.

"Reality. You wouldn't know reality if it walked up and bit you. I'm not the one living in a dream. You are." He paused. "You've got a warm house and a job with a little prestige and a little money and you think it's real. Well, let me tell you what's real. Little Hammer's real. People going to bed hungry and getting up hungry and wondering where the next meal's coming from. Little kids chattering their teeth with cold and old folks dying with pneumonia 'cause they've got no heat. Young-uns that ought to be in school— only they've got no clothes, no shoes, no book fees, no lunches, no anything, and both their parents working and them growing up wild as razorback hogs. That's reality. And all this you've got here"—he gestured—"is the dream."

Before Huse could interrupt, he went on.

"Because you just dream it belongs to you, when the white man is just letting you use it. You're Houston Whitley. You're a high school principal. You've got a college degree. You've got powerful white friends. But that's all a dream, too. Because all this can vanish to-morrow if the white folks want it to. You can be jailed tomorrow without charge or bail. You can be beat up, shot, hanged, gassed, electrocuted, castrated like a sheep or framed and put in prison, if they take a notion to, and none of this makes any difference if they take that notion. So it's not real. Nothing's real that doesn't come to you because you're a man. You can be here today and back down in Little Hammer tomorrow and Della and your baby with you—and it won't matter how good an Uncle Tom you are if the fashion in Uncle Toms changes or a better one comes along. You've got a lot of thinking to do about what reality is, my friend." And he had picked up his hat, kissed Della, and stalked out.

All I know, Huse thought now, watching the boys scrimmage on the field, is that I don't know of any other way of hanging on. I—

His phone rang. He turned to the desk and picked it up.

It was Della; her voice sounded strange, both frightened and eager, if that was possible, and as he listened to her words he forgot Carson Bell.

"Huse? Darling, I think you'd better come on home. My water broke this morning, and now I'm beginning to have pains. I've already called the doctor and the hospital, and Martha Lacey's here with me, but I think you'd better come quick. I don't think this is any false alarm. I wouldn't be surprised if by tomorrow morning you're a father . . ."

BOOK THREE
1956-1957

1 Nazareth General Hospital was not far from the railroad tracks, and every hour or so the thunder of a passing freight literally shook its ancient bricks in their crumbling mortar. It was the only hospital for Negroes in Hannington; built in 1922 under the auspices of the Episcopal diocese, a small wing added in 1940, it was cramped and obsolete. The Negro population of Hannington had nearly doubled in the past ten years as dispossessed field hands drifted to town, and now it operated under a tremendous strain, short of everything—space, staff, equipment and money. Its doctors were not allowed staff privileges at any other hospital; neither were they eligible for membership in county and state medical associations. Huse had been vaguely aware of the place's shortcomings, but they had never been so forcefully rammed home to him, so much a matter of his own concern, as they were now. He paced the tiny, cramped and grimy cubicle at the end of the second floor hall impatiently, a rising disgust combined with the apprehension already within him. Once he paused to crush underfoot on the dirty linoleum a cockroach that had crawled from behind a baseboard. Then he stooped and, with a matchbook cover as a trowel, scraped up the carcass and threw it into a trash basket.

"You jest wearin yourself out for nothin," Martha Lacey said from the chair in which she sat. "All that walkin back and forth ain't goin to bring that baby here no quicker."

"I know it," Huse said. He looked from Martha to a short, black man in blue jeans, slumped in a chair, asleep with a magazine spread across his face. How can he do it? Huse wondered. Then he glanced at his wristwatch for the tenth time in the past ten minutes.

He forced himself to sit down in the rickety chair beside her. Looking down the corridor, he saw lines of white-shrouded beds, the people in them asleep. There was the rasping sound of multiple snoring, and someone groaned and turned over. Huse ran his hand over his face. "Martha, it's past midnight and you've got to go to work tomorrow. Let me call a taxicab and send you on home in it, like I did Mama."

"Naw, that's all right," she said. "I stay a while longer. I kinda feel like Della belong to me too, a little bit. I done nurse this baby this far along, I stay at it a spell longer. Kinder got my hand on the plow now."

"Does it always take this long?"

Martha laughed, her vast bosom heaving. "Lawd, with the fust one, you never kin tell. We might be sittin here this time tomorrow, still waitin."

In this hole? Huse thought despairingly. He stared glumly at the black streak that fanned out across the wall above the waiting room register.

Martha's voice was less amused now, more sympathetic. "You jest got to be patient," she said. "Jest be patient and trust and pray. I been prayin every night for Della. Pray for you too."

Huse looked at her in surprise. "Pray for me?"

She nodded. "It ain't easy for a man, neither. New life comin along, he got to pick up a bigger load and carry it." A train whistle blared; a train rushed by, filling the room with thunder, drowning her voice. The clacking rushing roar of boxcars went on for a long time. Huse saw patients half rousing themselves in the hall beds. At last its racketing faded away. Martha continued as if there had been no interruption. "It hard enough for most men. It harder for you."

Huse looked at her keenly. "How come you say it's harder for me?"

"You already pulled too many different ways," Martha said. She seemed to be staring into distance. "Most men, they don't have to choose but one thing, either work or go hungry, that's all they got to worry about. People like you, like Mr. Marfield, you got a whole lot of other choices to make too. It different from the old times. Nobody expect you to choose, try to exert any free will back then. The Lawd hand you somethin, you take it and that all. Most men still go like that; you don't. You worry and discontent yo'self about all the choices you got."

Huse was startled by her perception. At last he said very quietly, "It's not easy to figure out which way to go."

"I know," she said. "But somehow somethin, somebody, maybe de Lawd, come along and give you a nudge sooner or later. It jest take time. Don't worry, honey. A little time and your path come clear." She let out a fluttering sigh and settled her squat bulk back in the chair. "It sure hot in here. We mus' be right over the boiler room."

He did not realize that he was asleep until somebody shook his shoulder and awakened him. Martha Lacey's voice was low and urgent. "Wake up, Huse. Here come that Dr. Gantt."

Huse sat upright, blinking, rubbing a face greasy with a night's wakeful sweat. Blurrily he glanced at his watch and was surprised to see that it was nearly six o'clock in the morning. He had slept for nearly three hours. The last he remembered was Gantt advising him to go home; nothing was going to happen for maybe as long as eight hours yet. But Martha had not let him do that. "Them doctors don't know everythin. Jest the time you think nothin's goan happen, that's when a woman hauls off and has that baby."

Now Gantt must have come back to the hospital while he slept, for here he was emerging from the hall in white hospital clothes, a white cap on his head. He was tall, handsome, suave, and he was smiling, though his face looked tired.

Huse sprang to his feet. "Paul?"

"Well, she pulled a sneaky one on us." Gantt grinned. "I get home and take off my clothes and soon as I get stretched out, she hauls off and does it. You've got a fine baby boy, Huse, and Della's in good shape—lots better than I dared hope for. Congratulations." He thrust out his hand.

Huse took it numbly. "Bless God," Martha said softly.

"She's kind of doped up," Gantt went on, "but she's conscious enough so if you want to go in— She's in Room 210. Be a little quiet, there are two other patients in there with her."

Huse was suddenly weak with relief. All at once fatigue caught up with him crushingly. "Thanks," he heard himself mumble inanely. "Thanks a lot."

"It's all right," Gantt said. He tapped Huse's arm and went out. Huse turned to Martha. "You . . . you come along, too."

She smiled, showing snaggled teeth, and shook her head. "Naw. There's a time for company and there's a time when company don't do nobody any good. You go ahead and see yo' wife and baby. It just about time for me to go to work now. I think best thing I kin do is go catch a bus and ride on out to my white folkses. I'll be early, but that'll gimme a little time to fix me some breakfast. Don't forget to call your mama now soon as you through with Della. Maybe if you don't mind I can ride over here with you tonight and see the little baby."

Before he could muster enough wits to protest, she had waddled away down the corridor. Huse stood where he was for a moment longer, strangely reluctant to move. It had come now, this period to, this ending of, one phase of his life and it was difficult to move toward acceptance of it.

He and Della had managed to patch up all the fabric they had shredded the day of his promotion. She had apologized for her unnatural attitude toward his step upward, had certified her genuine pride and pleasure in it; he had, in turn, pointed out in what anger he had denied his wanting a child and used that as an excuse; he had not really known what he was saying, she had goaded him. Of course he wanted the child. . . .

But he still did not. Even now he could feel coming on him like the closing pressure of an enormous hand a moment of black, bitter letdown; partly it was fatigue, but partly too the knowledge that another portion of his already tenuous control over his own existence was gone. There was also guilt for having been so resentful when convention demanded he be weightless with relief and joy and pride; he conceived of himself as a monster, but there was nothing he could do about the feelings that held him.

A little numbly he turned at last and picked his way along the corridor crowded with beds full of sleeping patients.

The door to Room 210 was partly open, and he edged through it hesitantly. There were three beds in it. A night lamp burned by one. Somebody was snoring. Huse walked into the lamp glow and looked down. "Della?" he whispered.

Her hair was in disorder; her face against the pillow looked gray and tired and old. When she slowly opened her eyes, they were glazed with drugs. But she smiled. It was a smile of total satisfaction, unlike anything he had ever seen on her face before.

"You got a little boy," she said thickly. "A little Otis Whitley."

"Fine," Huse said.

"I hope you like him." She closed her eyes. "Please like him."

He made himself take her hand. It was flaccid and damp; there was no strength in her fingers as she curled them around his palm. "You know I'm going to like him," he said in a voice of deep reassurance.

"Yes," she whispered. "He's perfect, they say. We're mighty lucky."

"Are you all right?"

"I'm all right," she said groggily. "It was you I worried about."

"Me?"

"Poor you. Waiting out there so long. No sleep. You must be mighty tired."

"I got some sleep," he said. "You need some too." He disengaged his hand and then bent and kissed her on the forehead. "You better rest." He was anxious to get out of the stuffy little room.

"Yes," said Della softly. "I'll rest. You go see your son."

"Sho," Huse said. He kissed her again and she closed her eyes and he edged back out into the corridor. Somehow, when he was there, he felt more lonely than he ever had before in his life, more cut off and isolated from everyone.

His son. The words had no real meaning for him; he could not muster impatience or even curiosity. He walked slowly down the hall toward the crowded nursery and moved to a space between the beds of two patients before the big glass window. The nursery was packed with wicker baskets of dark babies, a tired-looking aide moving among them. Huse rapped gently on the window. It took her a long time to thread her way to the door.

"Whitley," Huse said quietly, so as not to waken any of the patients in the hall. "My name's Whitley. I'd like to see my little boy."

She nodded, closed the door, and he watched as she coursed among the baskets like a bird dog working a broom-sedge field. Finding the right one, she scooped up its contents in a blanket and came to the window. She stopped before Huse and opened the blanket.

Huse stared at the dark and wrinkled bit of human flesh, so small, mouth gaping sparrowlike in a thin cry, withered little fingers opening and closing. He did not know what he had expected, but he had not expected this. While the child had been inside Della, he had thought bitterly of it as an inimical, menacing presence. But there was no menace in this. He put out a hand and touched the glass.

The nurse smiled, tiredly and mechanically. Her mouth formed soundless words that he could read. "It's a fine boy."

"Yes," Huse said. "Yes, he looks fine, all right."

The nurse folded the blanket, and he turned away from the window. Oddly, he was not particularly tired as he threaded the length of the corridor. The elevator was not working; he went down to the lobby through a badly lighted stairwell in which the air smelled stale and unchanged. The rail seemed to leave a coating of greasy dust on his palm. In the lobby a sleepy student nurse drowsed behind the ancient wooden switchboard; she did not look up as he went through the front door into the predawn darkness outside.

He walked slowly toward the small parking lot where he had left his car. He got into it and drove down into Little Hammer and knocked at Lucy's door. He felt oddly numb, and his mind did not seem to be working, as if it were too tired to assess the significance of what had happened this morning.

When Lucy, in a tattered robe, opened the door, there was a question on her face. Huse heard himself answering it. "You got a little grandson, Mama. A little Otis Whitley. He and Della both doing well."

Her face lit with a purely female radiance. "Now, ain't dat wonderful!" she said. "Oh, dat's fine!" And then, with concern, "Son, come in outa dat cold befo' you catch yo' death."

He followed her into the narrow kitchen, where coffee bubbled on the stove. She asked him questions, wanting to know every detail of the night; he answered them mechanically as he took off his coat and sat at the table. He realized he had forgotten to ask how much the baby weighed. She seemed to think this was a crucial oversight.

She poured him a cup of coffee; it was sharp and bitter—yesterday's grounds. She put the pot on the stove and came to sit opposite him at the table, where her own coffee was cooling. Her eyes played over his face with a kind of warmth he had not seen in them for a long time, and she said, her voice positive, "Otis. Wid a name like dat, he bound to grow into a mighty man."

Huse looked at her, setting down the cup. "Was Daddy a mighty man, Mama?" he asked quietly.

Her eyes seemed to look beyond him, into a limitless distance.

"Yeah," she said. "He was dat." She was silent for a moment. "If he hadn't been, you be behind a plow out dere on De Place right now, croppin on sheers. But he bound dat not goin to happen. First he thought he would git some land for y'all. But den yo teacher come to talk, and he decide dat maybe land wasn't de answer, learnin was. Maybe we give rise to a new generation, he say. He a man dat think about things like dat all de time. Not about himself, but about his young-uns."

"I see," Huse said. He closed his hands tightly around the cup, squeezing it.

"Determined always you goan have it better dan him. He a farmer all his life, he despise town and town ways. But we come, because he say we hatter do it for you."

"Sometimes I wish he hadn't," Huse heard himself say, with a bitterness that surprised even him.

"Don't you talk like dat," Lucy said sharply.

"But it killed him," Huse said.

"A man got to die sooner or later. He say dat. Better he accomplish somethin before he go. Maybe it worth it to him." She stood up and went to the stove and freshened her coffee. "One thing sho, dis Otis goin to be different from de udder one, lead a different life, a better, easier one, like you. You kin thank yo daddy fo' dat."

"You think it's such a better, easier life?" said Huse harshly.

She turned, the cup poised. For the first time that he could remember since becoming an adult, she was angry with him.

"I ain't goan listen to you sittin dere feelin sorry for yo'self," she said. "I ain't goin to listen to you sayin yo daddy wasted ever'thang he did. You better off dan he ever dream of bein. An' it up to you to see dat your boy better off dan you. If you don't, maybe yo' daddy did waste hisself, an' I ain't goin to think dat."

Her eyes snapped as she looked at him, and Huse met them only briefly before he turned his head. He pushed back his chair and stood up. "When you're ready," he said, "I'll run you over to the Bradhams'."

Her voice softened. "Naw," she said. "I got a ride dis mornin wid John Hampton. He workin on Miz Cardell's yard, down de street. You been up all night, you bound to be tired. You go on home and git some sleep." She came to him and touched his cheek, smiling.

"I hope Cary comes by de Mercy Street place today. He sho be tickled when he hear you got a little boy."

"Yeah," Huse said. Suddenly he put his arm around his mother, squeezed her bony frame, and kissed her. "All right," he said. "If you're sure you got a ride. I'll come by tonight and take you over to the hospital to see your new grandson."

"I kin hardly wait," she said. "I know he's a fine 'un."

He went down the rickety steps of Lucy's house and to his car. The coffee had helped, but he was still so tired that his whole body shuddered with fatigue. He paused with his hand on the door handle, then realized that he was too wound up to go home yet. He turned away from the car and, hardly of his volition, began to walk down the street, through the dawn that was breaking over Little Hammer.

In the slowly graying darkness, the bright orange squares that were windows looked deceptively warm and cosy. But above them there were more than a few chimneys from which no smoke curled upward, and Huse shuddered, remembering what it was like to run out of fuel on a day like this. In Little Hammer the margin of survival was so narrow that such a day could be a crisis, even a disaster, for it was cold as iron now and would stay that way. Inside those smokeless houses despairing adults would go shivering about their chores; children would stay huddled under blankets or be sent to a neighbor's fire, and there would be the sick and weak, old and young, who would not survive the damage they sustained when the heat ran out. . . .

He strode along faster, his feet slipping on the frozen ruts. The sun climbed higher, and its light struck the winding, glassy surface of Molasses Creek, gilding the frost on piles of garbage, glinting on the rims of ice inshore. Huse saw people shuttling back and forth, hunched in miserable anticipation or hurrying back to warmth, between the dwellings and the awry outhouses behind them. There was the ring of axes chopping kindling; in one back yard two bundled women poured hot water over a frozen hand pump; from here and there came the protesting grunt and thunder of old cars being started, or the rachitic whine of those that refused. He passed a man staring perplexedly under the hood of a rusted hulk; as he went by, he heard the man cursing in bitter hopelessness: another disaster for which there was no margin.

A door slammed; a boy in his teens appeared on the porch of a house, carrying a dead rat nearly as large as a house cat. With a gesture of repugnance, he flung it into the street, the limp, clubbed body flopping on the hard ground near Huse. Huse stared at it; he had almost forgotten how much worse the rats were down here in winter than in summer, when they came into the houses for warmth. He kicked the rat aside and walked on, feeling only a curious numbness that seemed to have solidified within him, and through which no other emotion could penetrate.

He was moving downhill; the road led him into a part of Little Hammer called "the Swamp." This was where the dregs settled; there was no place lower to go. Houses in here were mere wooden shells, without any pretense of care or maintenance, windows gone, doors missing, some whole structures nearly falling over, but still inhabited. Frozen garbage and unspeakable human waste littered the yards; as Huse passed one house, a frowsy, sullen man lurched onto a porch and vomited loudly and greenly on the ground. The vomit steamed in the cold; the man wiped his mouth, stared at Huse threateningly, and disappeared within a doorless opening.

Huse averted his head and walked on. The drive, the nervous restlessness within him, had dissipated now; each step had become an effort; but still he felt no impulse to return to the car. He wondered why. It was as if he were looking for something down here, but he had no idea what.

He climbed out of the Swamp and finally gained the poorly paved street at the top of the hollow along which shuttered honky-tonks— as sordid and yet pathetic in their promiseless emptiness as old whores sleeping—made two ranks. He strode along the deserted sidewalk, on past the place where he had first met Virginia Crane, and turned back down into the hollow.

Something was happening inside him now as he walked; that numbness he had felt ever since he had emerged from the hospital was beginning to break; there was a fermenting within him. He did not know what it was; he rubbed eyes gritty with sleep and circled back through Little Hammer toward his car.

He passed through the flowing procession now of men and women headed for the bus stop. They streamed out of the shanties, all bent over as if to shield and conserve the warmth within them, and they were not joking and laughing in this morning's cold.

Chilled himself, he stopped in the lee of a house and lit a cigarette; the smoke tasted harsh and rasped his throat, but it seemed to help dispel the cold. He stood there, watching the flow of people, hearing a baby cry inside the house behind him. Something was happening inside him, and it was beginning to happen strongly, but it was still amorphous and beyond identification. He was aware that his hand was trembling as he took the cigarette from his lips and put it back again.

Then he saw the children.

They were bound for school; and there were not many of them, because school was too expensive a luxury. But he watched those there were as they joined the exodus toward the bus stop or cut across the yards for the half-hour walk to the grammar school. Parents who took enough interest to send them saw that they were as clean as possible, but interest alone, or hope, could not provide enough warm clothes. The cold must have struck some of them viciously through garments so threadbare and tattered they could have been little more than lace against the wind; there was, too, the easily identifiable pinch of hunger and malnutrition on many faces. And yet they were laughing and shouting with the unquenchable exuberance and optimism of the very young as they scattered themselves along the street, and if they were daunted by the brutal weather they did not show it.

Huse watched them go, and suddenly he was sick with pity for them, because he knew what was bound to happen to them. There was no hope for them; their spirits might survive the cold, but they would not survive the realities they would face later. He raised his head and looked toward the hospital on the rim of Little Hammer in the distance, black smoke from its chimney palling the sky. Whatever it was moving within him grew stronger, more urgent; but still it had no form or name. He stepped out into the wind and began to walk swiftly toward his car. Maybe, he thought, it's always like this when a man's first son is born. It's like I'm seeing things with somebody else's eyes.

He got in the car, started the engine, and was about to roar out of Little Hammer, in a hurry to get home, in a hurry to have whatever this was in him come to its fruition so that he could be rid of it. But he changed his mind. Instead of gunning the car, he opened the right-hand door and said to a knot of cold-pinched men and women trudging by, "You folks get in. I'll give you a ride up the hill."

Finally, he was home. The house seemed very large and empty. With that curious tension inside him, he stood over the welcome heat from the floor furnace for a moment, and then he went into the kitchen. He realized suddenly that though he was too unsettled to be hungry, he needed to eat, and he found bacon and put it in a frying pan and slid bread in the oven. He wished Della were here; he wanted to talk with somebody about the way he felt, about the strangeness that had come over him. Something inside him that had been tied down for a long time seemed to be trying to break loose.

He turned the bacon in the pan, took an egg from a carton. "Damn it," he said; it was like chasing something in a dream, feeling what he felt and not being able to say what it was. "Damn it, I—" The telephone rang and he slid the frying pan off the burner, went into the hall, and picked it up.

"Hello," he said absently.

"Huse, dat you?" It was Martha Lacey's voice; and it was trembling. He stiffened, focusing his attention.

"Yeah, it's me."

"How Della and de baby?"

"Fine. Just fine."

"Dat's good." There was a pause. Suddenly Martha's voice rushed into his ear, frightened and confused. "Huse, I'm in de jailhouse and I don't know nobody but you to come git me out."

Huse rubbed his face. "The jailhouse?" he asked vacantly.

"Yeah, I been arrested." There was a sob in her voice.

Huse just stood there for a moment, unanswering. In that instant, whatever it was that had been at work in him slid into place; he felt outrage. Not just at whatever it was that had happened to Martha. But at what had happened to all of them. To his father, to Bish and Robert; to Mason Jar and Thelma; to himself and to the people in Little Hammer. And most of all, outrage at what must happen, inexorably, to his son.

But his voice sounded abstracted, even casual. "Martha, what for?"

"It . . . it happen on de bus. I ridin to work after I leave de hospital, and de bus full wid colored so I sit about halfway down front in de white folks' seats. So tired I doze off. Next thing I know, a po-liceman shakin me. Bus done filled up wid white people and he say de driver tole me to move to de back and I wouldn't do it. Driver say I cuss at him. Huse, you know I wouldn't cuss at no-body." She sounded on the verge of tears, as if that accusation were the worst of all. "Anyhow, dey finally let me call somebody, and I afraid for my boy Geoffrey to know his mama been arrested, Geof-frey so funny, so I thought . . ."

Huse closed his eyes, shaken by the anger that roiled through him. Still his voice was calm. "Now, don't you worry, Martha. I'll be right down there and get you out. Just be easy in your mind, don't say anything to anybody, and wait quietly."

He could hear the relief in her voice. "Oh, I sho hope you will. I declare, I never been in no jail before, I'm plumb ashamed."

"No," Huse said evenly. "No call for you to be ashamed. It *them* that ought to be ashamed." He drew in a long breath. "Now, don't you worry, I'll be right there. Goodbye."

He hung up the phone and stood with his hand on it for a moment. Then he shook himself all over, as a dog might, coming out of water. The anger he felt now was no longer vague or diffused, but clean and sharp and focused, and his hand was steady and sure as he picked up the phone with a decisive motion and dialed Jeff Marfield's number.

2 As he drove through traffic, Jeff Marfield's face was half serious, half amused. "Now, you let me do the talking. Way you look, if you open your mouth you'll spit fire and we'll all wind up behind bars." He grinned. "You're beginning to see the light, huh, sinner?"

"It ain't a damn bit funny," Huse growled. "A fine old woman like Martha. Been up all night with me, helping me sweat out that baby, and then trying to go straight to work and next thing she knows, some ofay flatfoot is hustling her into a police car."

"I know it's not funny," Jeff said, his grin fading. "I'm not laugh-ing at what happened. I'm laughing at how mad you were when you called me. Man, that telephone wire must have been glowing like a hot iron." His voice became more serious. "You see now what I've been talking about all along. If it can happen to a woman like Martha, it can happen to anybody—you, me, anybody. We've been through all this dozens of times while you were sitting on your can. The Ministerial Association, the Hannington Businessmen's Association, the Associated Democrats and the Bethune Women's Club. They all got together, along with the NAACP, and sent delegations to the bus company petitioning 'em for courteous treatment. Every Negro organization in town has been represented. And they just laugh at us. Hell, they know they've got us by the balls. No matter how rough they treat Negroes, they know they're not going to lose any business. They know the Negroes couldn't get along without the buses." He threw out a hand. "What can we do?"

"I don't know," Huse rasped, still in the grip of the rage that had held him ever since Martha's phone call. "But they can't be let get away with this. Have you been to the city authorities?"

Marfield laughed bitterly. "Hell, yes. But they don't pay any attention either. Negroes ain't voters." He paused. "The NAACP is formulating a plan for legal action, now that we've got the school decision out of the way. We'll bring a test case eventually . . ."

"Eventually, hell! Legal action, hell! Somebody ought to teach those bastards a lesson right now!"

"Man, you are wrought up."

"You're damn right. If it had been anybody but Martha, a helpless old woman that had been up all night trying to do a friend a favor—"

"Martha," Jeff said harshly. "What's so sacrosanct about Martha? Why is she better than anybody else? This has been going on for years. Where have you been, so busy brownnosing white people you couldn't see what was happening? Why?"

"All right," Huse snapped. "Get off my back."

"I'm sorry," Jeff said wryly. "It just galls me to hear you raising so much hell now when you've been quiet so long; you had to wait until your own ox was gored, didn't you?"

"That ain't it," Huse said. "Not all of it." He drew in a deep breath. "All right," he said, "I've got it coming."

"No, I was too rough on you." Jeff's voice softened. "You haven't had anybody to worry about but yourself up until now. It makes a difference, don't it?"

Huse didn't answer for a moment. Then he said, "Yonder's a parking place. Right there."

City Hall was an ancient red brick building, its dingy interior cramped and redolent of dust, tobacco and humanity. They climbed narrow wooden stairs to the police headquarters on the second floor and came out into a large room walled off by a counter. Behind it, a bald-headed, gum-chewing policeman with sergeant's stripes on the sleeves of his blue winter shirt looked at them suspiciously. He leaned on the counter without speaking, his jaws moving rhythmically, his bulging eyes sweeping them up and down with distaste and unveiled insolence.

"Awright," he said, after he had made the wait long enough.

"You have a woman here named Martha Lacey," Jeff said courteously. "I'm her attorney and I'd like to arrange bond."

"Oh, you would, huh?" The officer straightened up and went to a file cabinet. He came back with a handful of cards through which he shuffled. He seemed not to be able to find the right card for a long time. At last he said, "Oh, yeah, that's the fat ole gal cussed the bus driver. Ole woman like that oughta know better." He chewed for a moment. "Violation of the public transportation ordinance, disorderly conduct, and resisting an officer. Three charges, bond set at twenty dollars a charge, that'll be sixty dollars."

"All right," Huse said. He took out his checkbook.

The officer looked at it. "Cain't take no check."

Huse stared at him. "What do you mean, you can't take a check?" he rasped angrily.

The policeman's eyes went hard. "Nigger," he said, "when you talk to me, you keep your voice down and you say sir, you hear me?"

Jeff laid a hand on Huse's arm. "Excuse me, sir, but you can call the bank and verify the check." His voice dripped mollification.

"I ain't calling no bank," the policeman said. "You bring sixty dollars cash in here, you can have her." He turned away.

Huse stood tensely. Marfield shook his head, jerked it toward the door. "Come on," he said quietly. "Let's go to the bank."

When they were on the street, Huse exploded. "Of all the goddam bastards!"

"All right, calm down, somebody might hear you. When you've

had as many dealings with the white law as I have, you'll get used to it. Look, you've got new responsibilities. I'll make the bond."

Huse shook his head. "No," he said harshly. "No, I'll make it. I'll make it myself."

Jeff looked at him curiously and nodded. "All right," he said. "If it's that important to you."

The desk sergeant counted the money and slid it into a drawer. He signaled another patrolman and gave him instructions. Then he turned away and sat down at a cluttered desk behind the counter.

Jeff said, softly and courteously, "Excuse me, sergeant."

The sergeant put his feet on the desk and leaned back. He did not appear to hear.

"Excuse me, sergeant." Jeff's voice rose, but it was still easy and courteous. "But I believe we're supposed to have a receipt for the bond?"

The sergeant took out a toothpick and began to pick his teeth.

"Sergeant," Huse said harshly. "Sergeant, we'd appreciate a receipt for the bond money."

Slowly, insolently, the sergeant turned in his chair. His eyes half lidded, he got up and came leisurely to the counter. "What's your name, boy?"

Huse gripped the edge of the counter. "Houston Whitley," he said, with perfect control and only the faintest touch of contempt, "sir."

The sergeant's mouth hardened. He misspelled the name when he scribbled it on the receipt form and handed it to Huse. "Whitley," he said, and his eyes met Huse's. "We'll keep it in mind."

"Yes, sir," Huse said thinly. "Please do that, sir, by all means."

The sergeant turned away. Jeff looked at Huse and shook his head in a cautionary manner. They waited several minutes, with Huse afraid to speak for fear he could not control what he would say. After a long while a door opened at the far end of the narrow room and Martha Lacey shuffled in, a patrolman behind her.

"Okay, auntie," he said. "You can go now. But you got to be in court next Friday, nine o'clock."

"Yes, suh," Martha whispered. She waddled across the room, dabbing at her eyes with her handkerchief. Her face was an ashy gray.

Huse came to her quickly and put his arm about her. "All right, Martha. You're going to be all right now."

"I ain't never been 'rested before." She was sniffling. "I so ashamed."

"Nothing to be ashamed of," Jeff Marfield said. "You didn't do anything wrong. Don't you worry, I'll take care of you in court." As they went down the steps, his voice went cold. "What bus driver was it, Martha? You know his name?"

She was still sniffling. "It dat Bobo Merchant."

"I thought so," said Jeff grimly. "They're all bad, but he's the worst of the whole shooting match. He's a sadist, loves to harass Negroes. We've had more complaints about him than the rest of them put together."

"Well, somebody ought to harass him," Huse said roughly. "Come on, Martha. Here's the car over here."

All the way home she kept telling them over and over again how it had happened, as if she could not really believe it herself. When she had caught the bus at the hospital, the rear seats had already been filled with Negroes, so she had taken a vacant one just forward of the middle. She hadn't meant to nod, but she must have fallen into a rocklike sleep of utter exhaustion. The next thing she had known, she was being shaken awake by the policeman and the bus driver. "I don't even know whether dey axed me to move back or not fust. If dey did, I was sleepin too sound to hear. If I'da heard, I'd sho have moved. I don't want no trouble with white folks."

Huse saw her into her own house and insisted that she go to bed and get some rest. She was still crying and it took several minutes to calm her. Meanwhile, Jeff called her employer on Huse's phone and told the white woman who answered that Martha was sick. "She was real nice," he reported to Martha. "She say she was mighty sorry and for you to hurry up and get well."

That seemed to calm her down, as if it had been one of her major worries. After she had eaten toast and drunk coffee, she promised to nap, and Huse and Jeff went next door to the Whitley house.

There was still coffee on the stove. Huse poured two cups and put them on the kitchen table. He stared at Jeff before he sat down and said, "Well, what are you aiming to do about it?"

"Go to court, plead not guilty."

"Is that all?"

Marfield raised his eyes from the cup. He leaned back. "What else you want me to do? I've already told you, we've protested to the bus company and the city until we've run out of breath."

"Then get some more breath!" Huse snapped. "That old woman sat up all night trying to do a kindness. Then she falls off to sleep like any human being would and—"

"She ain't a human being," Jeff cut in quickly and sarcastically. "She's a nigger." He paused. "That little boy born this morning," he went on in a softer voice, "your son, my nephew—he isn't one either. He's just a nigger, too."

"He is if somebody doesn't do something," Huse said coldly.

"That's what I've been trying to tell you." There was no mockery in Jeff's voice. It turned serious. "All right," he said. "I don't know what else can be done. But I'll call Charles Bell and see if we can't use his church for a meeting. We'll get the different groups together and talk it over. I don't know if it'll do any good; they've been scared to death to open their mouths for the past six months. But you're right—this is a special kind of outrage, the kind that might get their blood up and get some sort of action." He cocked his head, looking obliquely at Huse with half-lidded eyes. "You planning to be there?"

"Hell, yes. What you think?"

"I didn't know what to think." Jeff made a gesture. "You've talked a long time about how getting mixed up in anything like this would put your neck on the chopping block. You haven't been principal of Washington Heights hardly three months yet, not long enough to get your chair warm. I just want to make sure you don't rush into anything too hastily. After all, you've worked hard to get where you are and you've got a clean record so far. And now you've got a new responsibility."

"I know," Huse said. He stood up and walked to the sink and stared out the window above it into the back yard, where Della's yesterday's wash, painfully hung before her water broke, still flapped whitely on the line. "I know what responsibilities I've got."

He paused. "I'll be honest with you," he went on, and it was as if he were talking to himself, not to Jeff. "I didn't really want this child."

"I could sense that."

"I didn't think—I don't think—that this is the kind of world anybody ought to bring another child into, not a child with dark skin." Huse rubbed the back of his neck. "But the boy is here now," he said crisply, "and I have already named him after my daddy. And whatever he was, my daddy was a trying man. He never gave up trying, always trying for us to have it a little bit better than him, to be a little more man. It was that trying that got him killed. Now how can I be less of a man than my daddy was? Now I got a boy, too; I got to be trying. I don't see any way around it."

"All right," Jeff said quietly after a moment. "As long as you go into it with your eyes open. It's a long, hard, lonesome road, God knows, and it's uphill all the way. I don't reckon any of us would try it if it wasn't for our children." He stood up, too. "Well, let me see if I can get hold of Charles Bell. Maybe something will come out of this, maybe it won't. But it's just like you said. We got to be trying."

The meeting started at eight o'clock in the sanctuary of Mt. Olive A.M.E. Zion Church. It was one of the largest and oldest Negro churches in Hannington, actually purchased from a white Methodist congregation that had moved away as Little Hammer had threatened to engulf it. The sexton had built a fire in the furnace and closed off all radiators except those in the sanctuary, but it was still uncomfortably cold as the representatives of the various Negro groups filed in.

Standing beside Jeff Marfield, Houston Whitley was introduced to those of them he did not already know. He had spent most of the day in an exhausted sleep and had awakened to find most of the hot bile rage drained away, replaced instead by a strangely determined sense of purpose. He had bathed and dressed and taken Lucy to the hospital to see her grandson. He had looked at the child again himself, and had felt himself respond directly to it this time: there had been within him the beginnings of pleasure and of pride. He had not told Della anything about the events of the day. All he told her was how much more he valued the child than he had expected to. She had held his hand and said, "I knew you would. I knew all along." For that moment they had been closer perhaps than they ever had been before in their marriage. Then he had left, taken Lucy home and come directly to the church.

Most of the Negro ministers of Hannington had been invited to the meeting by Charles Bell, but not more than a third of them had responded. There was bare representation from the various denominational groups; no more. Huse pondered this: he did not see how any effective united action could take place without full cooperation of the Negro clergy. They were the most influential single group in the life of the community. For the Negroes, even the middle-class ones, their church was their main fountain of hope, the focus of their social life, and the only organization that satisfied their yearning to belong somewhere. Ministers were looked to not only for spiritual guidance, but for day-to-day temporal guidance as well.

"What's the matter with the preachers?" he whispered to Jeff. "Where are they?"

Marfield's mouth quirked. "Same place as everybody else. Home, keeping out of trouble."

Some of Jeff's associates in the NAACP came; there were the officers of the Hannington Associated Democrats, a political organization; quite a number from the Bethune Women's Club, a social group. And there were the emissaries from the Hannington Community Relations Committee, which was supposedly the official liaison between the white and Negro communities. Huse stiffened when Merit Crane, his face set and businesslike, only his mouth smiling greetings, came in as head of the latter group. Dapper, exuding power and confidence, he shook Huse's hand with only a flicker in his eyes to betray that he had ever seen Huse before.

When the thirty of them present were ranged on the front pews, Charles Bell arose and opened the meeting with a prayer.

"Our Father in Heaven," his organ voice rolled out across the room, "we are gathered here tonight in Your name to seek the means of righting injustice and bringing all men closer together in brotherhood and fellowship. Lord, we have turned the other cheek, as Thou hast commanded; and we have loved our enemy as ourself. We have been patient and forbearing and have remembered that the meek shall inherit the earth. But, Lord, we are only men, Thy children, the clay modeled by Thy hands. We have walked for a long time with our heads down and our shoulders bowed. Our spirits are sore, and our patience runs thin. If there is bitterness of spirit in us, take it from us. If there is injured pride and the lust for revenge, cleanse us of that. But if there is in us the desire to confront Evil, Injustice and Intolerance where we find them and wrestle them to defeat, then, oh God, multiply our strength and our courage, strengthen our will and our determination. Give us wisdom and good will and crown our purpose with success. In Christ's name we ask this. Amen."

A chorus of *amens* arose from the pews. While Bell had prayed, Huse obliquely watched Merit Crane sitting in the pew in front of him; the very sight of the man stirred remembered anger and a guilty sense of loss. I have got to forget all that, he told himself fiercely. Especially now. But he knew he was helpless to.

Jeff Marfield arose and faced the group. "I think most of you are aware of the outrage that occurred early this morning," he said crisply. "But for the benefit of those who aren't, I'll recount the details." Briefly, but in a voice that crackled with harnessed indignation, he told what had happened to Martha Lacey. "Of course," he concluded, "it's only one in a long series of such incidents. And it won't be the last unless we firmly do something effective. We have negotiated with the bus company and the city until we're out of breath, and all they do is laugh and allow the bus employees to abuse us as they see fit. It's intolerable that they be allowed to continue. The Supreme Court has acknowledged that insofar as schooling is concerned, we're entitled to all the rights and benefits of any other American citizen. I don't see why the same thing doesn't apply to the city buses. We've got to stick up for our rights. Some way has got to be found to bring this situation to a head and rid ourselves of it once and for all." His eyes swept over them. "The chair now invites comments and suggestions."

Merit Crane had been listening attentively, nodding his handsome head. Now he cleared his throat and stood up. "Mr. Chairman."

"Mr. Crane."

Crane turned and smiled at the others, his face suddenly glittering with charm. "Mr. Chairman, ladies and gentlemen," he said in that precise, musical voice of his, "I think we're all agreed that we are truly faced with a difficult situation here. I propose that, rather than going to the bus company again or to the Public Utilities Commission, we appoint a committee to draw up a list of grievances and requests for redress of them. I would then be happy myself to lead a delegation to present this to my personal friend, Mayor Cameron, with the strongest insistence that some redress be given us."

There were a few thoughtful murmurs of approval from the audience. Huse sat rigidly, fists clenching and unclenching, Crane's smooth blandness already sticking in his gorge. Then he was on his feet without realizing it.

"What good will that do?"

Crane's smile moderated itself, but he did not lose his composure. "It might do a great deal of good," he said quietly. "I have had the opportunity to negotiate with the city authorities on a number of questions. When approached properly, I have usually found them willing to meet us halfway." His voice took on an edge. "Certainly nothing will be accomplished by confronting them with a blundering and ill-considered ultimatum. I know those people of old. You can't just walk up to them and say, 'Here is what we want. You give it to us or else.' "

Huse stared at him coldly. "Why not?" he said.

Crane shook his head patronizingly. "Mr. Whitley, meaning no offense, but your inexperience in handling matters of this sort is showing. I have been negotiating with the city fathers for twenty-five years. I know exactly what we can and cannot expect from them."

"So do I," Huse said. "Nothing. That's what we can expect."

"Maybe you have some better suggestion," Crane said icily.

Huse stood motionless for a moment. Then he slid out of the pew and came around front. He faced the group, ran his eyes over that sea of dark faces, most of them intent, some of them approving, some frowning, some frightened already and wishing they were out of it.

"I don't know that I've got any better suggestion," he said. "All I know is what Mr. Marfield's already said—that the subject's been talked to death already. Seems like if they were going to give us anything, they've had plenty of chances to do it. Seems to me they don't intend to give us anything. They just don't care. So I don't see what there is to be accomplished by drawing up another petition." His voice began to ring. "Why should we have to keep going to them with our hats in our hands anyhow? Aren't we their best customers? White people don't ride the bus much, they've got cars. Why, if it weren't for us Negroes, that bus company would go out of business in a month. So why—"

280 · LOOK AWAY, LOOK AWAY

"That's dangerous talk," Merit Crane sliced in sharply. "If the white people hear you talking boycott, there'll be even more trouble."

Huse opened and shut his mouth once, without speaking. He turned and looked at Crane. And then something clicked in his brain. Boycott. He had not even been thinking of that, but—

"They boycott us, don't they?" he said quietly. "Every day you can read in the newspapers about where some Citizens' Council big-wig has spouted off with a warning. And there are Negroes in Han-nington hurting from boycott right now. You don't believe it, you ask Jeff Marfield!" He whirled to confront the crowd. "Why not a boycott? If every Negro in Hannington would agree to stay off the buses, even for just one day, that would hit the bus company a lot harder than some little old paper petition."

A murmur went up from the others, half assent, half fear. He heard the words "No, too dangerous."

Crane's face was serious and his tone was angry. "Young man, I've had more experience than anyone else in this room in dealing with the white authorities. I can tell you right now, even if you could get up some kind of boycott, you'd stir up the worst hornet's nest we ever had in this town. There'd be trouble you can't even dream of."

"Trouble!" Huse snapped. "That's what you're afraid of, isn't it? That's what you always think about—avoiding trouble. Because you've got it made like no other Negro in Hannington. And you don't want anybody to rock your boat!"

"Huse!" Charles Bell said quickly, his voice monitory.

There was fury in Crane's eyes. "I didn't come here to be insulted by an upstart! I came here to offer my services as negotiator. If they're not required—"

Bell placed a hand on his shoulder. "Merit . . ." He thrust a finger at Huse. "Personalities bandied around will accomplish less than nothing. Am I correct in that you're proposing we organize some sort of boycott of the buses?"

"If they can boycott us, why can't we boycott them?"

The room was absolutely silent for a moment. Huse saw that Crane had regained his composure. When he spoke at last, it was as if he were lecturing an obtuse child. "Young man, one of the first things one learns in negotiating, in business or in the field of civil rights, is to respect the other fellow's strength and not make any wild threats you can't back up. I realize you're inexperienced, so I'm happy to make you a present of that maxim. You say, why can't we boycott the buses? Very well, I'll tell you why. Because it would hurt us worse than it would hurt them, that's why. Very well, suppose for the sake of argument everybody agreed to stay off the buses for one day. How would people get to their jobs? And people who don't show up for work—especially when it's because they've been mixed up in something like this—very often get fired. A lot of us are dependent on favorable relations with the white community for our very livelihood. I should think you yourself would be acutely aware of that, Mr. Whitley."

"I am," Huse snapped. He drew his finger across his throat. "I'm also up to here with being treated like some kind of dog instead of a man on two legs."

"Amen!" a woman in the audience ripped out. Again a roll of sound arose, whether in support or opposition Huse could not tell.

"Order, please . . . order." Jeff Marfield's voice rose above the hubbub and quelled it. Then he went to Charles Bell and whispered something. Bell nodded, whispering in reply.

"Not that we're offering such a boycott in the form of a motion," Jeff said, turning back to Huse. "But just for the sake of argument, let's consider the complications involved. If such a boycott were organized, it would have to come quick before the whites could take reprisals that would break it up. Today's Friday. Suppose the boycott were set for next Monday. First of all, how would you get the word around? Unless every Negro in Hannington participated, it wouldn't be worth the risk. How're you going to spread the word?"

"I don't know. I hadn't thought about it . . ." Huse's voice trailed off, his brain racing. This idea had seized him more strongly than he had at first realized. He knew that maybe it was crazy, visionary—but if it was not, if it could be made somehow to work . . .

"Look," he said at last. "We could spread the word first of all through the churches. Couldn't every preacher in town be given an announcement to read at Sunday service? Maybe some of them could even work it into their sermons. That would get nearly everybody, right there. And . . . and why couldn't we get some notices printed or mimeographed or something and see if we couldn't get volunteers to go around and pass them out to catch the ones who miss church?

You know how everything spreads on the grapevine in this town. If the preachers would help us, we could get the word around."

He saw Charles Bell nod. Then Bell said, "All right, we'll grant there's a chance that it would work—if we could get total cooperation of the clergy." He grinned ruefully. "That's another matter that would have to be worked out, but we won't go into that now. Suppose the word does get around. Then what about all the people with jobs they've got to get to on Monday? How're you going to get them to work on time, so the white people won't have an excuse to fire them?"

Huse was startled at how swiftly, how competently, his brain was working now; it was as if all the details of this had lain fallow in his subconscious, were now being brought to fruition without any conscious mental effort on his part. He was as awed as anyone by his ready answer.

"Car pools," he said. "That's one way. There are a lot of Negroes without cars, granted. But there are a lot of them with cars, too, more than ever before. If every neighborhood or church congregation would get together and organize car pools—if we could get everything on four wheels to run, no matter how ramshackle it is— we could haul a lot of people. And maybe—" Another suggestion came boiling out of his mind. "Maybe we could get the five colored cab companies in this town to cooperate. Maybe for just one day they'd haul passengers around town at reduced rates. They wouldn't lose any money because they'd have so many more riders. Couldn't a committee be formed to contact them?"

Bell and Marfield looked at one another. Before either could speak, Merit Crane said in a voice boiling with rage, "You know what you're going to do? You're going to have the jailhouse full of Negroes on Monday, that's what you're going to do!"

Huse swung toward him. "Why? What laws will we have broken? There's no law says people *have* to ride the bus. They can't arrest you for not riding the bus."

"No," Crane snapped. "But they can harass you. And people will fight back and get themselves arrested—or hurt." He laughed shortly and harshly. "Don't worry, young man, they can find plenty of pretexts."

Huse nodded. "I won't argue with you about that," he said. "But suppose we do our best not to give them any pretext. Let them harass us. If we accept it without fighting back, what can they do to us then?" He felt every muscle in his body tense itself; he was aware of something glimmering in his mind, half formed or half remembered. Then he heard it come out. "We'll offer passive resistance," he said.

"What do you mean, passive resistance? Clarify yourself."

"Just what I say," Huse replied slowly, ordering his thoughts, choosing words. "We've lived with oppression for years in the hope that someday it would disappear. But instead of that, it only gets worse. It seems to me that the time has come when we owe it to ourselves—and, most of all, to our children—to fight back. But how? With guns, with violence? We don't want that and couldn't win even if we did. But there's another weapon we can use. It's the same one Gandhi used in India. Passive resistance." He turned to Bell, questioningly. "Charles? What do you think?"

The tall minister was silent for a moment; and during that time Huse saw, with excitement, a kindling begin in his deep, intense eyes. "Why not?" Bell said at last; and he turned to face the people in the pews.

"Gandhi's people used passive resistance the way armies use rifles. It might work for us."

His voice sharpened. "I think there's merit in this idea of at least a one-day boycott. But it won't be feasible unless it's carried out nonviolently. And that's what Huse is driving at. Remember the words of Jesus, 'love your enemies.' We will use the power of love."

"Love," Merit Crane said incredulously. "What's love got to do with it? Love conquers all?"

"It'll avert violence on our part," Bell said crisply. "That much, at least—if we use it properly. Christ said it; Gandhi put it to work. You must love the man who wrongs and oppresses you. Hate's destructive, love's constructive. You must love that man so much that you prove your love for him by resisting the wrong he does and forcing him to turn from it." He turned to Crane, and his voice was dry. "We preach it every Sunday morning and all you folks listen to it. If we can't apply it now, then something's bad wrong somewhere."

The silence in the room was impressive when he broke off. Crane shifted uncomfortably. "I'll tell you again, you'll get a lot of people arrested."

Charles Bell looked at him and nodded. "Maybe so. But if those who are arrested submit with love, if the rest of us remain united with them and offer ourselves as well—what will they do then? If we're all prepared to go to jail for principle, can they arrest us all?"

"They can try," Merit Crane said bitterly; and a murmur of fearful assent went through the group. All this talk of going to jail had frightened them.

Suddenly a woman, thin, plain, very dark, arose from her bench. This was Sarah McLain, a delegate from the Bethune Women's Club.

"I think the Reverend Bell and Mr. Whitley are right," she said in a voice that quivered with emotion. "I think the time has come when we have got to stand up and be counted. And if it takes going to jail to show that we won't stand for the kind of subhuman treatment we've been getting—well, then, I don't want to go to jail, but I will. And I won't fight the policeman who takes me there, either." She paused and smiled. "I'll love him. That ought to convince him to turn me loose."

A titter went through the crowd. She had broken the momentary tension of fear. Her voice turned serious as she went on.

"I think we should give this boycott thing a try. I think if it's prepared and carried out properly, like Mr. Whitley has suggested, it will work. But I don't see why it's got to be limited to one day. It looks to me like if we're going to do it, we might as well do it right."

"You mean a longer boycott?" Bell asked. "A week?"

"I mean a boycott," she said, " for as long as it takes for them to meet our demands. A year, if necessary. Or forever if it takes that long."

"Ridiculous!" Merit Crane snapped. "Have all you people gone out of your heads? A year—"

Now there was, suddenly, wild confusion. Others arose from the benches, debating with each other, yelling at those who held the floor. "It's too dangerous." "Why not? It might work." "I'm tired of being treated like dirt." "White folks won't let you get away with anything like that." ". . . hasn't got a prayer of bringing it off." ". . . been kept down long enough!" Their voices swelled in confused tumult, until Charles Bell's deep tones overrode them.

"Order, please, order!"

As they quieted, he held up his hands. "Mrs. McLain . . ." He gestured to her to come forward, and when she did he whispered to her. She listened intently, head cocked, biting her lower lip and nodding. Then she went back to her place.

"Mr. Chairman," she said, "I'd like to offer a motion."

Charles Bell held out his hands for silence again. "Mrs. McLain."

"Mr. Chairman, I motion that all Negroes of Hannington be asked to observe a one-day boycott of the buses on next Monday. And I motion that a mass meeting be arranged at some convenient place Monday night to allow the citizens themselves to vote on whether they want to continue the boycott further or let it drop. And I motion that all Negro organizations and churches of Hannington be asked to participate in the boycott."

There was a moment's silence.

"You have heard the motion," Charles Bell said finally. "Do I hear a second?"

Houston Whitley drew in a long breath. "Second the motion," he said.

"The motion has been made and seconded," Bell said briskly. "All in favor signify by raising your right hand."

Huse stood quite still for a moment, his arm at his side. All at once he realized exactly what he had done, what he had set in motion here, and for the first time he rationally comprehended the cost to himself. It meant his job, it meant the destruction of the whole structure of life and prosperity he had built up so far, it might even mean Little Hammer again . . . or it could mean worse: physical punishment, jail. What got into me? he wondered sickly. What in the world ever led me to—? He fought down the impulse to yell, Wait! Wait! It's all a mistake, I didn't mean to start this. Merit Crane's right, we've got to negotiate.

But it was too late. Already hands were coming up, a tentative few at first, but then a quickly augmented forest of them. And as he watched them rise, the terror drained away from him as quickly as it had come and something took its place. He was aware of an upwelling of power and purpose that infused his whole being, seeming to come at once from deep within and from without, and he was no longer afraid; and then quickly and with resolution he raised his own hand.

Jeff Marfield counted quickly and silently. He nudged Charles Bell.

"Nays," Bell said.

Merit Crane thrust up his hand. There was a substantial number of other hands raised in the crowd. Again Jeff counted, said something aside to Charles Bell.

Bell waited. The hands came down. Deliberately Bell let silence drag out for a moment. Huse felt tension in the large muscles of his back; his palms were sweating.

"Ayes," Bell said, "eighteen. Nays twelve. The motion is carried."

Merit Crane let out a long breath. He looked down at the floor. "All right," he said, his voice shaky with suppressed anger. "It's Mr. Whitley's show. Where does he propose to go from here?"

Huse's mind had anticipated the question. "It seems to me we'll have to appoint several committees. The ministers present to contact the other ministers of their faith in town. Another committee to contact the taxi companies and obtain their cooperation, and to deal with any organizations not represented here tonight. A committee to prepare and distribute some sort of printed notice. And supervising all these committees and setting policy, it seems to me there ought to be some sort of board of directors or steering committee. I suggest that nominations for the steering committee are in order."

"Will you put that in the form of a motion, please," Bell said.

"Just a minute," Merit Crane said. He walked back to the pew on which he had originally sat and picked up his hat. "I don't care to be associated with this. I don't care to be associated with it at all. I'm sorry, gentlemen, but I think it is all very harmful and foolish." And he turned and walked out.

Before he had reached the end of the aisles, Huse, afraid others might follow suit, spoke loudly. "All right. I motion that nominations be made for a steering committee composed of one member from each of the organizations represented here."

Somebody seconded the motion. Then Sarah McLain arose again. "Mr. Chairman."

"Mrs. McLain?" Jeff Marfield said.

She looked at Huse, and her eyes were shining with excitement, determination, and perhaps a vision of the future.

"Since this whole thing is his idea," she said, "I nominate for president of the steering committee Mr. Houston Whitley."

3 Houston Whitley rubbed his eyes with thumb and forefinger, massaged his temples with his palms. Then he put his forearm on the table and pillowed his head on it. Brilliant blue and red lights of fatigue danced behind his closed lids.

Then somebody was shaking him awake. Jeff Marfield stood over him grinning, a cigarette dangling from his lips, his shirt collar open and his tie pulled down. Jeff's own eyes were bloodshot with fatigue. "All right, Sleeping Beauty, wake up. There's still work to do."

Groggily Huse sat up. He yawned. "I didn't even know I was asleep," he mumbled. He looked at his watch; it was four-fifteen. Why, he thought, I wasn't out but three or four minutes.

Still, even that much rest had helped. After the selection of the various committees the night before, they had gone immediately to work. As they explored ways and means, the ramifications of what they were attempting slowly revealed themselves; they could see just what an immense task they had ahead of them. "Because," Huse had emphasized, "it's got to be just as unanimous as we can make it. If it's only partly effective, we're whipped before we start."

It was well past Friday midnight into Saturday morning when he had made that statement. Marfield by that time had been melancholy with fatigue. "If they don't pull together any better on this than they do on anything else, we'll never make it, then," he had grunted.

But just then Huse was running on nervous energy, borne along by a wild, inner excitement, a growing sense of purpose. "Well, this is going to be different," he had snapped. "If they don't care enough to do this, then they're all hopeless anyhow—and they might just as well repeal the Thirteenth Amendment."

It had been three o'clock Saturday morning before he had got to bed, nearly five before he could unwind enough to sleep. He had tossed restlessly, trying desperately not to think of his own concerns, not to wonder how he would stay alive, what he could do to earn a living, when word of his participation in this, as it inevitably must, reached the Hannington school board. When it was over, he knew, he would have to take Della and the child and go North again. No school system in the South would hire him after this.

He tried not to think, either, of the slenderness of his bank account; it would be nearly totally obliterated when he had finished paying for the baby. He tried not to yield to the temptation to carry on an inner debate with whatever it was in him that kept saying over and over again, hollowly, *Fool. Fool.*

At last he had slept. But he had been up at eight again, had drunk gallons of coffee, somehow managed to get to the hospital to see Della and the baby for a few moments. Looking at the child—it was astonishing how it had changed, unwrinkled, plumped out, in just two days—the voice within him subsided; it did not say *fool* again.

When he got to Mt. Olive Church, he found that Bell and Marfield had preceded him. They had set up headquarters in the meeting room of the church and Carson Bell was serving as messenger. With no time to waste, Huse immediately had plunged into a whirlpool of work.

By noon, two-thirds of the ministers had agreed to go along; by twelve-thirty they had the cooperation of every colored taxicab operation in town: passengers would be hauled for the same fare it cost to ride a bus. Charles Bell continued to work to persuade the reluctant minority of ministers; Jeff busied himself with the transportation committee, contacting car owners and evolving a scheme of pickup stations and a shuttle service; two Negro-operated filling stations offered gasoline at cost to all participating cars; Sarah McLain was rounding up volunteers to distribute printed notices around the Negro community and forming them into teams; the telephone rang constantly; and in the midst of all the uproar, Huse had finished redrafting the text of the notice which would be carried by hand and had turned it over to a girl volunteer to be typed and mimeographed on the church machine. During the long day, the church had thus seethed with activity, and Huse was surprised at how many volunteers simply wandered in and asked for a task, any task, to which they could turn their hands. He began to feel a certain optimism, a sense that what had begun as an ephemera was fleshing itself out as practicality.

Now as he tried to grope through the fatigue that had clamped down on him, Charles Bell came over and sat on the end of the table. His face was as lined and weary as that of a huge, black bloodhound.

"There are some of these ecclesiastical knotheads," he said disgustedly, "who simply refuse to go along. I don't know what to do about them."

"Forget 'em," Huse said. "If they won't, they won't. This is a free-choice operation. Anybody who sticks out his neck does it of his own volition."

"Well, except in one or two cases they don't amount to much anyhow," Bell said. "We've got the majority consenting at least to make the announcement. Last night after everybody left, Carson and I worked up and mimeographed a short dissertation on the theory of passive resistance and nonviolence; I've got Carson delivering a copy to every minister he can reach now in the hope that they'll build their sermons around it, or at least mention it. It seems to me it's one of the keys to the whole operation. We're taking an enormous risk, you know, when you back off and look at this thing. This could just as easily result in a race riot as a boycott, if the whites get ugly enough." He looked at Jeff. "You've had more experience than I have at this sort of thing. How do you think they'll react?"

Marfield laughed shortly and ground out his cigarette. "Like a bunch of turpentined hound dogs," he said.

"That bad, eh?" Bell's face was lugubrious.

"When the shock wears off. The main thing is to hope this takes 'em by surprise. That'll give us a chance to see how it's going to work and build up some momentum before they can organize countermeasures. But if this thing works and the mass meeting decides to go on with it, they'll do everything they can to make life miserable for everybody involved in it." He lit another cigarette though the smoke from the last one had barely cleared his lungs. "If it turns out to be a long-range proposition, we're going to have to put together a more substantial organization than we've got now and find some capital to keep it going. There'll be arrests; and we'll have to form some sort of pool of property or money for bail-bond purposes; we'll have to have a full-time office and supervisory staff. But, of course, that's all in the future. The main thing now is, will the people go along?"

"I think they will," Bell said slowly. "Many of the ministers have told me they're sure their congregations will. We've suffered under this . . . this cock-crowing white supremacy long enough. Everybody's tired of it, been tired of it a long time. But until the Supreme

Court spoke up, nobody ever thought there was really a chance of doing anything about it. Now there's a different spirit, a kind of optimistic determination. People are beginning to feel that it's now or never. I know how much the NAACP's done, Jeff; basically its legal work is responsible for providing a climate this new spirit can bloom in. I know how discouraged you've been about public apathy, but I think you're going to find this is different. This is something that can capture the imagination of everybody. Lawsuits, legal questions . . . they baffle the man in the street and fail to stir him. But injustice on the buses . . . that's something he can grasp. Now he's got a chance to figure personally in an attempt at progress, register his own indignation and resentment firsthand. I don't think he'll pass up the opportunity."

"I hope not," said Jeff. "We'll sure be left standing here with egg on our face if he does."

A panting adolescent girl carrying an immense sheaf of paper dropped it on the table beside Huse. "Here's the first batch of notices, Mr. Whitley. Two thousand. We're running off five thousand more."

Huse scooped three off the top. "Get these out to Mrs. McLain and tell her to get her volunteers on the road. There's no time to lose." He passed copies to Marfield and to Bell, and the three of them scanned them:

STAY OFF THE BUSES MONDAY, JANUARY 23.

Negroes have been subjected to the worst kind of treatment on the city buses for a long time. The bus company refuses to give satisfaction. Now another Negro woman has been arrested and jailed for violating the Jim Crow law.

Don't ride the buses anywhere Monday. If you have to go to work, take a taxicab or walk or share a ride with someone. Register your indignation with your feet!

There will be a mass meeting Monday night at 7:00 at Mt. Olive A.M.E. Zion. Be sure to come for further information.

"I tried to keep it as simple as I could," Huse said. "I wanted everybody who laid his hands on it to be able to understand it."

"It looks all right," Jeff said.

Huse arose. "Then I suggest, if we're wound up as far as we can go here, that we all get on our walking shoes and grab a handful and start toting them around. It's doggone near five o'clock, and there's a lot of ground to cover. Charles, you've got a sermon to write. Will you tend the store for us?"

Bell grinned. "Gladly. Good luck. If you're not back tonight, we'll see you in church tomorrow."

"We'll be there," Huse said. As he started for the door, Carson Bell came in. He looked drawn and weary, too.

"Hello, Carson," Huse said. "Aren't you about ready to take a break?"

The dark, fine head came up and shook itself. "I can go a while longer." Then Carson looked down at the floor. "Mr. Whitley?"

"Uh-huh."

"I—" Carson fidgeted. "I'd like to beg your pardon," he said all in a rush, raising his head. "I—well, I had you tagged as some kind of . . . some kind of old-timey Uncle Tom. I thought you were scared of your own shadow. I was wrong and . . . well, sir, I apologize."

Huse said gravely, "No need for apologies, Carson. But thank you, anyhow." He thought, You don't know how scared I still am. I'm about as scared as I've ever been in my life. If this could have happened when I was your age, when I was full of piss and vinegar and there wasn't anything in the world that could scare me . . . He clapped Carson on the shoulder and edged by him. What was it Jeff had said? *Give me fifty thousand Carson Bells.*

Huse allowed himself a fantasy, fifty thousand Carson Bells marching together against the bus company and the city, demanding justice. Instead, he thought wryly, what we've got is a bunch of nervous, sore-footed middle-aged coots like me that all the spunk has already been burned out of. All we've learned is how to endure; that's the only thing we know that Carson doesn't. And maybe we've learned that too well. . . .

He entered the sanctuary, where Sarah McLain was distributing leaflets to volunteers. Some were already departing with handfuls, others were waiting for a fresh supply. Huse was surprised to see among them many ministers and businessmen. He nodded to one of the preachers he knew. "Hello, Reverend Walworth. You going to help us pass out papers? What about your sermon for tomorrow?"

The Baptist minister was an old man, bony, gaunt, and gray-haired. He smiled; and there was something gleaming in his deep-set eyes as he tapped the pile of notices he held. "This *is* my sermon for tomorrow, Brother Whitley. Now you'll excuse me; Sister McLain has given me a big chunk of country to cover. I must be on my way."

"Good luck," Huse said, and watched the old man limp up the aisle toward the door. Thoughtfully he walked over to Sarah McLain. "Sarah, you need another pair of legs?"

She looked harassed but competent. "Need all of 'em I can get. We're running way behind. The mimeograph machine broke down. Got seven thousand of these things to give out between now and Monday morning." She seized a handful from a stack and thrust them at him. "Here."

"What section you want me to take?"

She unfolded a city map marked up in crayon. "Nobody's got this part yet. I'm kind of reluctant to send the young-uns down in there." It was a gerrymandered section of Little Hammer, contorted to encompass most of the honky-tonks and rougher areas; it included, Huse saw, the Swamp. Sarah McLain laughed. "I'm going to send some of the preachers down in there, too. There's a few of 'em I know that need the education." She brushed her hair back from her forehead and her face turned serious. "Mr. Whitley, something's happened since yesterday, did you know that? Even the people that were lukewarm last night have showed up down here today to tote notices. There's something—" She made an inarticulate gesture with her hand. "There's something working here. Something that I never saw before. It's like when you mix the yeast in a batch of bread dough and all of a sudden it comes alive. A lot of people know Martha Lacey; she's been around Hannington a long time. And they know she's never done anything but good. You can . . . can feel the outrage in the air. I swear, I believe the white folks are going to rue the day they ever laid hands on her." Then her voice turned crisp. "Get on out there and go to work. Time's awasting."

Even though it was only six o'clock, the kitchen of the Whitley Funeral Parlor was a scene of activity. Two or three couples, already drunk, giggled and pawed each other around the table or the sink, as Riley Murray sold bottles or poured shots of after-hours whiskey, the liquor stores having closed a half-hour before. Traffic was beginning to build to the hall stairway which led to rooms above, and in a room just off the kitchen a poker game was already in progress.

Bish stared at the notice, his thick lips working as he tried to read it. Finally he lowered it, and he frowned as he looked at Huse. Bish was getting fat, grossly fat; the tight-stretched skin over round cheeks shone in the yellow light of the overhead fixture. He thrust the notice back at Huse. "What kinda shit is that?"

"It's no shit at all; it means what it says," Huse said crisply.

Bishop shook his head as if baffled. "You gone clean outa your mind? What you tryin do, ruin yourself forever? You know what's gonna happen when the white folks get ahold of this thing and find you mixed up in it?"

"I got a pretty good idea." Huse looked straight into Bish's eyes. "Now, you going to let me pass this around in here or ain't you?"

"Good God, no. Ole Harper or somebody come in here an' find one of them things layin around, they'd be hell to pay and no pitch hot. I don't know what got into you, but I know one thing. You git them things outa here and you git 'em out right now. I ain't goin to have 'em layin around here and take a chance of ruinin the connections I done spent so long buildin up."

Huse felt his lips go tight with exasperation. "Dammit, Bish, don't you care about *anything* but money?"

Bish picked up his drink from the table and took a swallow of it. "No," he said. "Now you take them things away from here."

Anger flared in Huse. "I'll be damned if I will. I'm going to pass 'em out. Everybody's got to know about this." He coolly turned away from Bish and took a step toward the room where the poker game was going.

"Riley," Bish said. With surprising speed he moved around in front of Huse and blocked his passage.

Riley Murray set down the bottle and came over to stand beside Bish. Years had thickened him, too; he was a powerful man now, and there were scars on his face that told of violent encounters.

"Don't make me git rough with you," Bish said tautly.

Huse looked from him to Riley Murray. This was his first stop and he still had a long way to go. He read the determination in his brother's eyes and he knew there was no way he could get past Bish.

"All right," he said quietly, "I got a lot of other places to hit. I can't be held up by trouble with you." He turned away and started for the back door. A girl in a tight red dress was leaning against the sink counter, her arm about a drunken man nuzzling the base of her throat. "Hey, mister," she said as Huse passed, "what you got there? You runnin some kinda contest?" She snatched a notice off the stack.

"Stay off the buses," she read, slowly and haltingly.

Bish strode to her. "Give 'im that back."

She pressed it against her breasts. "Go 'way, I wanta read it."

The man raised his head. "What is that, buddy? Come on, gimme one."

"Sure," Huse said loudly. "They're free. Anybody wants one can have one." Two other couples in the room had been watching curiously; now they came forward. He peeled off a stack of leaflets and thrust them into the hand of the man who was holding the girl. "Pass these around," he said, and as Bish came toward him he went quickly out the back door.

After that, there was the slow, grinding work of going from house to house. He knocked on doors, and when people came he handed them the leaflet, and if they gave him time he explained briefly what it was all about. But this made slow going, and by eight o'clock the pile of notices was only slightly diminished. So wherever he could, he began slipping a notice under the door or into a mailbox if there was one. As he progressed deeper into Little Hammer, it became a business not without risk. Sometimes when he climbed a darkened porch there would be a truculent challenge from within; perhaps the door would swing open and he would be confronted with dangerous, not infrequently drunken, suspicion.

But what surprised him was how many of the people he encountered had already heard about the Martha Lacey incident. How many of them made the same comment: "It about time somebody teach 'at damn bus company a lesson." How many of them carefully folded the notice and put it away in a pocket and thanked him instead of crumpling it and discarding it. Even as his legs began to tire and his stomach rumbled for the supper he would not take time to give it, his inner weariness had lessened. As Sarah McLain had said, something was working here.

He descended into the last-ditch jungle called the Swamp. He saw a fight building in the middle of the rutted street; saw the gleam of a knife blade and one gladiator turn and run, the other chasing. There came, from the rotten, collapsing hovels, a thready inner hysteria of carousing audible through the walls. Drunks lurched up and down steps, staring at him with truculent suspicion.

But he did not miss a house. At the last and worst of them all, he recognized the thick-bodied woman who appeared in the doorway: Bessie McCall, who had lived near them on Berry Street, had grown up with him. He had not seen her since the night years ago in the Happiness Club. She did not recognize him; she was swaying, her muddy eyes unfocused. "Who dat? We havin a party. You cain't come in lessn you got yo' own likker." Behind her he saw an old woman, withered, a snuff brush protruding from her mouth, rocking in a chair in a corner; a child of about three, naked, sat on the floor near her feet, screaming; there was the rock-'n'-roll whang of a radio, and a man and woman danced past the door, very close together, shuffling, the woman's hips moving in a circular motion, the man's hands cupping her buttocks.

"Here," Huse said, and he thrust three leaflets into Bessie's hand. "What th' hell?" he heard her grunt; and he wheeled quickly and jumped off the porch, eager to be out of this place.

It was nearly midnight when he reached the Happiness Club, nearly out of leaflets and promising himself this would be his last stop. The place was jammed with people, rancid with smoke and sweat and spilled beer, raucous with noise and profanity and drunken laughter.

He had intended just to circulate through the crowd passing out leaflets, but people were so jammed that it would take forever. He pulled out a vacant chair from an occupied table, and began to hammer its legs against the floor with all his strength.

The thunderous noise quenched the uproar; the gabble died away into a silence of surprised curiosity as he kept on pounding. When he saw the proprietor, face set in anger, edging toward him, he stopped hammering and used the chair to climb to the center of the nearest table, squarely between an indignantly startled couple.

His voice was a bellow: "All right, everybody listen! Stay off the buses Monday! Don't ride the buses Monday. They've arrested a poor old woman who went to sleep and didn't move back when they told her to. They put her in jail and charged her with disorderly conduct and resisting an officer. We're going to teach 'em a lesson. Nobody is to ride the bus Monday! Walk to work or share a ride or take a cab. The cabs will haul you for the same fare you pay the buses. They've made fools of us long enough—let's show 'em that we're tired of it! Go to church tomorrow and your preacher will tell you all about it! Take these notices and pass the word along. Stay off the buses tomorrow and come to Mt. Olive Church to the mass meeting Monday night! We're going to teach somebody a lesson this time!"

Just as the proprietor was about to grab for him, he climbed down. "Read this, friend," he said, handing the man a notice, and he dropped another on the table on which he had stood.

There was a touch on his arm. He turned to look into the dark, slackly curious face of Robert. Robert's breath smelled of cheap whiskey. "What you up to now?" Robert asked thickly, and he took a notice. "Shit, I can't read this," he said. "Somebody read it to me."

The girl at the table was already reading it aloud. Robert listened intently. Others were crowding up now, curiously, and taking notices from Huse's hand. A murmur swelled in the room as they were read aloud. When the girl had finished reading, Robert's face broke into a slow grin.

"Is that really de straight stuff, man?"

"It's straight," Huse said.

"Hot damn!" Robert said. "We goan have some action now!" He reached in his coat pocket and brought out an old Iver Johnson Owl's Head revolver. "I bought me a new pistol jest in time!"

Huse turned on him savagely. "You put that goddam thing up."

"But, bubba, dem white folks gonna be mean if you do this." He put his hand on Huse's arm. "Look, whut about dis? You wanta teach dat bus company a lesson, me and de boys can lay for some of dem drivers and work 'em over a little bit. Carve a couple of 'em up, dey'll change deir tune."

"Dammit," Huse said, "no! This is going to be a nonviolent boycott. Don't you go—"

"Nonviolent? What you mean, nonviolent?"

"I mean nobody's going to try to get rough with white folks, no matter how rough they get with us."

"Shee-ut. You mean us ain't goan git a chance to do no fightin?" His lips twisted. "You ain't goan teach white folks no lesson dat way. Only thing they goan understand is dis here Owl's Head or cut a

few of 'em up wid a knife. You ain't goan make 'em be nice to you
no other way."

"If you cause trouble," Huse said thinly, "so help me God, I'll
do everything I can to help the white folks put you on the chain gang
or in the big house. I mean that, and you better listen to me. And
you better spread the word to the rest of your bunch. Anybody that
causes trouble, fights or cuts or shoots, every Negro in Hannington's
going to help the white folks put him under the jailhouse. You pass
that word along."

Robert's face went mean and ugly. "Who the hell you think you
are?"

Huse stared at him coldly. "I'm the man that's running this thing,"
he said slowly and evenly, "and I mean exactly what I say and you'd
better remember that."

Their eyes locked for a moment, and then Robert said huskily,
"Shee-ut," and he turned his head away. He slouched off, headed
for the bar.

Everybody in the Happiness Club was concentrating on the notices. People crowded around Huse, firing a battery of questions. He
tried to answer them all, as swiftly and meatily as he could. But he
realized, disheartened, that he was so tired his brain would no longer
work; he was not really making sense; and when he at last went out
into the cold, he felt as if he had done nothing at all tonight except
confuse people instead of enlightening them.

Driving home, he looped by the church and saw that lights still
burned in the sanctuary, even though it was nearly one. He parked
his car and went wearily into the church. Sarah McLain and Carson
Bell were picking up crumpled leaflets from the floor. There was a
thick stack of them on one of the pews, undistributed, and Huse's
heart sank as he saw them.

"Well, I got rid of all mine," he said. "How'd the others do?"

Sarah McLain rubbed her face. "We didn't do so good," she said
in a voice thin with fatigue. "A lot of them brought a bunch of theirs
back. They went as far as they could go, but they just wore out before they could get rid of them all." She pointed at the undistributed
pile. "I figure we gave out about half as many as we planned on."

"That's rough," Huse said. "I'll swear that's rough. That means
that we only got to half as many people as we counted on reaching."

"There just wasn't enough time or enough help," Sarah said.

Carson Bell's voice was apprehensive. "What do you think this'll do to the boycott, Mr. Whitley? Do you think it'll kill it?"

"I haven't got any idea," Huse told him wearily. "It sure won't help it any." It's not going to work, he told himself as he pitched in to help them get the sanctuary clean. It can't possibly work. All we're doing is stirring up a lot of trouble and not accomplishing anything. Maybe I should have listened to Merit Crane. . . .

But the next morning there was an incredible stroke of luck. The jangling of the telephone jerked him painfully out of sleep, and Jeff Marfield's voice said with a throb of excitement, "You seen the newspaper?"

"No. Just woke up."

"Go get it, then."

He did. He carried it back to the telephone from the stoop and unrolled it. Headlines seemed to leap at him: NEGROES PLOT BUS BOYCOTT. And beneath that, squarely centered in the middle of the front page, was a reproduction, word for word, of one of the notices that had been distributed the night before.

Huse came wide-awake. "Well, I'll be damned," he muttered sickly. "The white folks have got hold of our plans. Now the fat's in the fire."

"In the fire, hell." Jeff laughed. "Man, they've just done us a favor. How else could we get the word around? Now everybody will see it."

"By gosh," Huse said slowly, "I believe you're right." Still holding the phone, he read the front-page editorial beneath the notice.

The Free Press has learned that certain elements, probably led by outside agitators, are encouraging the Negro community of Hannington to boycott the city bus system tomorrow.

Hannington has always enjoyed an excellent relationship between the races. Now, apparently, the NAACP and other Communist-inspired troublemakers have decided for their own selfish purposes to create discord and turn the colored community against the white.

Such tactics are bound to fail. We are sure the Negro citizens of our

city will not support them. And we urge the authorities to use all neces-
sary means to deal with the outsiders who . . .

There was more, much more, including a virulent attack on the
Supreme Court, but Huse laid the paper aside.

"So now I'm a Communist outsider."

Jeff laughed. "Don't worry. If they got the notice, they know who
you are. They've got me and Charles Bell and you and everybody
else pinpointed. But they're not going to acknowledge that the movement is locally led. If they did, they'd have to admit there's a reason
for it."

"I'd like to know who squealed."

"We'll never be able to pin that down. It could have been Merit
Crane, it could have been—"

"Yeah," Huse said gustily. "Yeah, it could even have been my
own brother."

"Well, it doesn't make any difference now. The main thing is,
they've solved a problem for us. We don't have to go out and pound
the pavement again this afternoon with notices."

Later that morning Huse sat in church and heard Charles Bell
preach.

"Shadrach, Meshach, and Abednego," he thundered. "The children of the Lord, beset, outnumbered and captive. And when they
were forced into the fiery furnace, they didn't struggle, for they believed in the love of God. And sure enough, the angel came into the
furnace with them and shielded them—and when they emerged un-
harmed, their enemies bowed down to them, and it was a triumph
of love . . ."

It was a fine, bright, cold Sunday. After church he went to the
hospital. Everybody there would know now, he reflected, and Della
would know, too.

She did. When he sat down beside her bed, he was aware of the
eyes of the other two occupants of the room fixed on him with a
kind of awe. There was something of the same expression in Della's
eyes. "Why didn't you tell me?" she asked immediately.

"I didn't want to worry you. Just having had the baby and all."

"Worry me? *Worry* me? You think I wasn't already worried,
thinking I was married to a Dr. Haney? Wondering how I could have

misjudged my husband so badly, wondering if I was going to have to fight to keep my son from being raised a . . . a man without self-respect or courage?" She took his hand. "Oh, Huse, I'm less worried now than I've ever been in my whole life."

"But you don't understand the ramifications. This will likely cost me my job. And us with a new baby on our hands."

"Don't you worry about that," she said quickly. "Don't you worry about the baby and me. Don't you worry about anything but what you've got to do right now."

When he left the hospital, he felt stronger and less apprehensive, and he was surprised to find himself whistling as he walked across the parking lot to his car, pleased that it would be only a couple more days before Della and the baby could come home.

He spent the afternoon at the church, working frantically to make sure that every conceivable loose end was tied up. The atmosphere there, he thought, was exactly like that in an army outfit before it moved up on the line. There was resolution, but also a grim awareness of reality. Everyone knew now that this was no lark, that the determination of the whites that the boycott should fail probably was as great as theirs that it should succeed. And each of its instigators had to look ahead into his private future, knowing that he was from now on a marked man, a pinpointed target for all the subtle or brutal reprisals that could be brought against them.

Sarah McLain summed it up wryly. "Now I know how the signers of the Declaration of Independence felt. It sure is an all-gone feeling."

Despite the work in which they were swamped, the afternoon seemed interminable. When Huse got home at twilight, the house seemed forbiddingly empty. He made himself a scanty supper and had just settled down with a drink when the phone rang.

He picked it up. "Hello?"

A strange voice said, "Nigger, you know you're asking for a funeral, don't you? You'd better call off this crazy business, or you going to wind up hangin from a telephone pole with you on one side and your balls on the other. You've been warned, you black bastard. The K.K.K. only warns once." The phone clicked.

Huse lowered the receiver. He looked at the telephone and tried to grin. But he did not feel like grinning at what he had just heard. Instead he went into the bedroom and whisked from a bureau drawer a Colt army automatic he had smuggled home from overseas years before. He thrust it in the waistband of his pants, surprised that he did not feel at all foolish. Then he looked at the phone again.

"All right, you shit-ass," he said again. "You come and try it now."

As if in answer, the phone rang again.

Huse hesitated, then picked it up. "Yeah?" he said harshly, bracing himself for the tirade he expected to follow.

"Huse?" The white man's voice was familiar. He groped in his memory; before he could identify it, the voice went on. "This is Burke Jessup."

Huse relaxed. "Burke, how are you?"

"I'm okay. I hope you can say the same. Listen, Huse, keep your eyes open. Your name has been mentioned in connection with this boycott. It seems that Merit Crane is kind of jealous at having somebody horn in on his specialty of race relations. I believe he's done a lot of talking to the city authorities about what's going on."

"Yeah," Huse grunted disgustedly. "We figured it was him . . . or somebody."

"Well, I don't know if you're really mixed up in this thing or not, but if you are, walk a chalk line. If you so much as burp in a no-burping zone, they're going to drop the block on you." He paused. "I just thought I'd pass the word along . . . for old times' sake, you know."

"I appreciate it," Huse said. "I really do, Burke. But isn't it kind of risky for you to call me up?"

Burke laughed. "You mean, am I going back on my own race? Well, as a matter of fact, hell, yes. Or to put it a little more accurately, I happen to think that if you can bring this thing off, it'll be a salutary lesson for all concerned. But for God's sake, don't let it degenerate into violence. Make your people leave their shooting irons and their switchblades at home."

"We hope they will," Huse said.

"Look, Huse, there was another reason for my calling you. It happens that I'm the local stringer—correspondent, that is—for the Atlanta bureau of *Tempo*. I called the bureau chief and he's interested in the story. By the same token, I thought it might be helpful to you to get the whole affair aired in a weekly news magazine as big as that one."

Huse hesitated. Then he said slowly, "I don't reckon it would hurt any."

"Can I ask you some questions, then?"

"Sure, fire away."

"Is this just a one-shot affair, or will it be something long and extended?"

"We haven't decided that yet. The people will decide that tomorrow. If the boycott works, if they come to the mass meeting and want to keep on with it, why, it's their decision."

"I see; you're playing it all by ear."

"That's right."

"The paper charges that outside influences have helped inspire this. What about that?"

"It's a damned lie. This is an action originated by local Negroes to seek redress of local injustices. I started the thing and I'm not a member of the NAACP or anything else. I'm just a man that got his bellyful and decided to do something about it."

"So it's all-Negro, eh?" Burke said thoughtfully. "That makes it kind of unique, doesn't it? Most of the activist Negro organizations have white members, too. I haven't heard before of any purely Negro organization moving like this." He chuckled. "Not since Nat Turner's Rebellion, anyhow."

"This is not going to be any Nat Turner's Rebellion. It's going to be carried out in the spirit of love and without violence. If there's any violence, it won't come from us. Every Negro minister has explained that to his flock. This is purely going to be an operation of passive resistance."

"Suppose the whites get violent with your people?"

"We hope that if they do our people will refuse to return the violence. We refuse to allow ourselves to be drawn into the sin of hate and bloodshed. All we want to do is turn our white friends' hearts away from that same sin." He broke off. "Burke, I'm talking too much too soon. I'm sorry."

"It's all right. Except that I will say that you're really playing a long shot. You're gambling against human nature."

"No, we're gambling on our knowledge of the Negro's determination to have justice and on our belief that he's willing to suffer to get it. After all, he's used to suffering and not fighting back. A little more suffering, a little more enduring that returns some tangible benefit—he is prepared to undertake that." He broke off. "Listen, Burke, you seem to have all the inside dope from your end. Where did you get it?"

There was a pause. Then Burke said drily, "Where do you think?"

Huse let out his breath. "Cary," he said after a moment, wearily.

"That's right."

Huse hesitated, hating to ask the question. "How does he feel about it?"

"I rather imagine," Burke said slowly, "that he'll get around to telling you that in person, Huse."

For a moment Huse battled with grief and a sense of loss. "Yeah, I guess he will."

"As for me," Burke said, "about all I have to add is, good luck."

Huse was aware of an odd thickening of his throat. "No other white man ever wished me that before," he said, unable to keep his voice from betraying how deeply he was touched.

"Maybe you never gave one a chance to," said Burke. "You might be surprised at how many of them do before you're through. Well, thanks, Huse, and good night."

"Good night," he said; and he hung up the phone slowly. He wondered if he had talked too much to Burke. But he did not think so. He could remember when they had been children, Burke had always been mediator if any dispute arose between himself and Cary; and Burke had always been just. No, maybe it was possible that Burke was on his side.

"You've got to trust somebody," he said aloud; and then he went into the bedroom. He was unbuttoning his shirt when he heard a car pull up in front.

He had not realized he was so tense; but his reaction was instinctive. He jerked the automatic from his waistband and worked the slide, sending a round into the chamber. He was not expecting anybody at this time of night. He latched the safety in place and with the Colt in his hand padded in socked feet toward the living room.

There were footsteps on the concrete walk now. Huse stood tensely, out of the light, thumb on the safety of the gun, finger curled around the trigger. He held his breath.

A fist rapped hard on his door.

"Who is it?" he called sharply.

The fist hammered again. Huse edged to the door.

"Who is it?"

"Cary Bradham." He recognized the voice. "I want to see you."

Huse felt a weakening of his knees, an unknotting of tense muscles. He looked down at the gun in his hand with something like panic. Then, moving very swiftly, he eased it under a sofa cushion and went to the door.

Cary's overcoat collar was turned up against the cold, and his face was red with it. He rubbed his hands together as he stepped into the warmth of the room.

Huse closed the door behind him. "Hello, Cary," he said quietly.

He was a little surprised that there was no anger or outrage in Cary's voice. "Hello, Huse. I'm glad I didn't get you out of bed."

"No, I was just going to get undressed."

"Good. I'd like to have a talk with you."

"Sure," Huse said. "Let me take your coat."

After he had done so, Cary dropped into a chair. He lit a cigarette, and Huse noticed that his hands shook slightly. "Can I get you a drink?" Huse asked softly.

"No, thanks," Cary said. "I can't stay but a minute or two."

"Aw, that's too bad," Huse said; and now he realized that the moment had come which all along he had dreaded more than anything else. This was the one cost of the whole affair that he most begrudged paying. Cary had gone out of his way to do him a favor, had stuck out his neck for him—and he had betrayed Cary, cut the ground out from under him in the most drastic way. If he had been Cary, he would have been ragingly angry. But all he could see in Cary's eyes was a kind of hurt, a grief even, that matched his own. That made it all the worse.

"Huse," Cary said at last, "I've come down here to ask you to call this thing off. Our source of information says you thought it up and you're directing it. So now I'm asking you, for the benefit of everybody concerned, to stop it while there's still time."

Huse found that he could not look at Cary. "I'm sorry," he said. "I can't do that."

"Why not?"

"In the first place, it's gone too far. It's out of my control. In the second place, it's something that has to be done."

"Why? Why does it have to be done?" Suddenly words burst from Cary in a hot flow. "Dammit, Huse, if you had a gripe, why didn't you come to me? You know I'd have been happy to go to the authorities with you and try to straighten things out. You know if you'd only come to me first I would have—"

Huse shook his head. "Would you?" he asked. "Tell me the truth, Cary, would you? Would you really have been happy to go before the city and act as your nigger friend's advocate? And not just for me, but for all like me? For all similarly situated, as the Supreme Court says? For all the poor goddam coons and spades that have been treated like dirt for years, for all the shines and jigs and little nigs in this town that never have had a goddam chance? Would you *really* have been happy to be our advocate, Cary?"

Cary was silent for a moment; then he blew out a long puff of smoke. "It's not too late," he said. "If you'll call this thing off, I can still save your job for you. And I'll go to see Sam Deal with you and you can present your grievances."

Huse closed his eyes, fighting back the temptation to consider that. "No," he said. "Don't ask me to."

"I did you a favor," Cary said, and now there was a trace of bitterness in his voice. "I did it because . . . because we've known each other for a long time and . . . I wanted to do something for you. I didn't expect to get it rammed back down my throat. I thought maybe when I came here and asked a favor in return—"

"Please," Huse said, and he could hear the imploring note in his own voice. "Please don't use that on me. Anyhow, don't you see? I couldn't stop it even if I wanted to. How you going to stop maybe ten, twenty thousand people that have had somebody's foot on their necks for years and now they're tired of it?"

Cary stood up. "Is that your last word?"

"I don't know of any other word I can say."

Cary nodded. "All right. If I didn't know you as well as I do, I could make all kinds of threats, but they wouldn't do any good, would they? Okay, Huse. Well, I guess you know your job's gone."

"I was going to call the city school superintendent and resign first thing in the morning."

Cary looked at him curiously. "I suppose the NAACP or the Communists will pay you enough to live on?"

"Yeah," Huse said with bitterness. "Yeah, they pay me a fortune. I'm independently wealthy, that's how come I can afford to do this. You might as well understand, Cary, nobody's paying me a thing, no Communists, no NAACP, nobody. I'm doing this because I've got to. And I've got no idea of how I'm going to live."

"That's too bad," Cary said. His face was unreadable. "You ought to at least get something to make it worth your while. Because if you go ahead with this, they'll smash you."

Huse looked at him keenly. *"They?"*

Cary's chest rose and fell as he sucked in a long breath. "We," he said.

They stood there for a moment looking at one another. Then Cary turned away quickly, put on his coat and went toward the door. He put his hand on the knob, then halted. After a second he turned back.

"Huse," he said. The pain in his eyes was clear now.

"Yes," Huse said tautly.

Cary stood there for a second or two. "Nothing," he said at last, and then he opened the door and went out. He did not slam it, but closed it quietly and firmly behind him.

5 The cold dawn wind had a cutting edge as it whistled down the building-walled canyon that was the main street of Hannington. Standing on the corner of Main and Kiscoe, the transfer point for all crosstown bus riders, Jeff Marfield and Houston Whitley drew back instinctively into the lee of a storefront.

"They ought to be coming along any minute now," Jeff said. "It's after five o'clock."

"Yeah," Huse said.

"I feel like a virgin bride," Jeff went on. "I know something's bound to happen soon, but I don't know whether it's going to be good or bad." He stepped out of the storefront and looked around the intersection. "One thing sure," he said as he stepped back in. "There's nobody waiting for 'em here now. Except those cops."

Huse nodded. On each corner of the intersection stood a patrolman, billy club dangling from his wrist. The one on their corner had accosted them as they came up. Before he could speak, Jeff Marfield had quickly told him, "We just waiting for a bus, officer."

The policeman had grinned. "That's right, boy. If you want to ride the bus, don't you be afraid to. Nobody's going to bother you."

"Yes, sir," Jeff said. "That sure is nice to know." Somehow the rumor had started that roving goon squads of Negroes had been organized to keep other Negroes off the buses by force. Huse and Jeff both took a certain wry pleasure in watching the policemen shiver in the knife-edged wind for nothing; the radio had said that officers would be posted at all major bus stops, including those in the Negro sections.

Now Huse said, "There never is anybody on these corners until the first buses get here. It doesn't mean a thing." Then he gripped Jeff's arm. "But look yonder. Maybe that does."

A single car moved down Main Street. It was old and dented and its muffler roared loudly. And as it passed, they could see that it was packed front and back with Negroes.

"Well, there's a few that got the word anyway," Jeff muttered, an undertone of excitement in his voice. "Now if everybody just—"

He broke off as they heard the guttural roar of a bus somewhere down the street. Almost immediately its twin sounded like an echo from the opposite direction.

Huse suddenly realized that his mouth had gone dry, that his whole body was attuned as it had used to attune itself before he drove into a combat zone. He seized Jeff's arm and they moved out of the storefront toward the corner.

From both directions now, buses were coming toward them, huge blue-white monsters in the gray morning light. Then they were snorting to a halt at the corners. The interior lights clicked on; the doors hissed open; people began to dismount.

Exactly two passengers got off the bus that towered over Huse and Jeff. Both of them were white.

"Come on," Jeff said, and he started across the street to the other corner. Four passengers were getting off the bus there. And they were white, too.

Jeff and Huse halted in the middle of the street and looked at one another.

"It's working," Jeff said quietly and with great thankfulness. "Praise be to God, it's working. Each one of those buses would normally carry forty or fifty colored."

Houston Whitley rubbed his eyes. "I never really believed . . ."

he whispered. "I didn't honestly think . . . ." Suddenly every muscle within him slackened; he was weak-kneed with a mixture of elation and relief.

They gained the opposite corner. Huse recognized Bobo Merchant climbing down out of the bus. He and Jeff eased behind the jut of a building. The wind whipped to them tatters of the colloquy between Merchant and the policeman.

". . . don't know what's got into all the goddam niggers. . . . Every goddam sidewalk full of the sonsabitches walkin, but none at any of the stops."

"Fuck 'em," they heard the patrolman say. "Let 'em walk. I hope they freeze their goddam asses off."

"Me, too. It's a relief not to have to bother with the black bastards."

"It's a goddam relief for us not to have to bother with you, either, you white bastard," Jeff Marfield said thinly.

"Come on," Huse said. "We've got to get our cars in operation." He was about to move out of their shelter from the wind when he saw two Negro men slouching up Kiscoe Street toward the intersection.

"Hold on a minute," he said. "Let's see what happens." And he dragged Jeff into the lee of another darkened storefront.

With collars turned up and caps pulled down over their ears, the two laborers shuffled past. Huse watched them closely. He wanted to see exactly what they would do. It was quite possible that they had not heard about the boycott at all, or if they had, did not understand it.

But as they reached the corner, it was obvious that they understood one thing—the policeman with the billy club before the entrance to the bus. Huse stifled delighted laughter as he saw the two Negroes stop short, staring. Then they bobbed their heads, hesitated, and faded around the corner, away from the buses, in the direction from which they had come.

They stopped close enough for Huse and Jeff to hear their puzzled conversation.

"Whut you reckon 'at white po-leeceman doin out dere in front dat bus?"

"Beats me. Must have somethin to do wid all dat bus trouble we been hearin about dis weekend. Maybe ain't no niggers allowed to ride dem buses anymo'."

"Mus' not be. Look, dere another cop on yonder corner."

"Well, if 'at ain't a hell of a note. How them white folks expect us git to work if we cain't ride buses?"

"Dam 'f I know. But I ain't goin to mess wid 'em. I'd druther walk den mess wid dem po-leece. One time I got drunk an' dey 'rested me an' beat me so bad I couldn't work for a week cause when dey hit me in de stomach I puked on one of 'em's unifawm."

"Well, I be John Browned if dat ain't a case. Shit, come on, we got a long walk ahead and we goan ketch hell for bein late."

Jeff Marfield stepped out of the storefront. "Hey, you fellows," he called softly. "You want a ride to work? Come on, I'll carry you."

They stared at him. "Who you? Whut's goan on here? How come us cain't ride de bus? Whut dem white folks up to dis time? We got to be out at de fert'lizer plant by six."

Jeff grinned broadly. "Don't worry, I'll get you there. And I'll explain it all to you on the way."

Huse drove around town as if in a dream. The committee had estimated that given sixty per cent effectiveness, the boycott could be called a success. But as nearly as Huse could tell, the boycott was a hundred per cent effective. Even the Negroes who had not got the word or who had planned to disregard it were frightened away from the buses by the policemen at every stop or the motorcycle escorts that accompanied each bus through the Negro sections as protection against the nonexistent goon squads.

And as daylight fell on Hannington, the sidewalks were clogged with walking Negroes, though cars darted from one location to another, picking up loads that made their springs sag. Huse himself drove frantically all morning.

Once, with a full car, he passed a string of four Negro women trudging along the sidewalk. He pulled over to the curb. "I've got a load right now, but if you'll wait here, I'll be back in a little while and give you a ride."

The tall, dark, strong-looking woman who seemed their spokesman shook her head. " 'At's all right. It won't hurt us to walk a little bit. Seem like it might feel good to walk, knowin us walkin for our rights."

Huse tried hard to think of something to say; there was nothing. "Yes" was all he could manage, and then he put the car in motion again.

The bony, ancient woman crammed beside him in the front seat nodded. "Walkin for freedom," she said softly. "Lookayonder, 'at's what dey doin. I remember my grandma tellin me how she did de same thing back endurin de Yankee waw. How she an' granpappy an' all de young-uns took off from ole marster's place an' walked two days an' two nights lookin fo' de Yankee army so dey could be free. Now people doin hit all over again. Sho is curious how de worl' turns, ain't it?"

It was like that all day. The bus stops stayed empty; the sidewalks stayed full. College students thumbed rides; people with cars kept them crowded; even mule-drawn wagons loaded with passengers could be seen on the streets.

Houston Whitley had never been so deeply moved. "These people," he said, his voice full of awe as he sat with the other members of the various committees in the church to make plans for the mass meeting that night. "These people. Who would have thought it?"

"Surely the spirit of the Lord has descended on this town," Charles Bell said. "And in all this, not one incident, not one stone cast in anger, not one inflammatory insult. Surely God has walked the streets today."

"Just so long as He hasn't ridden the bus," Jeff Marfield said with a smile. Then his face went serious. "All right," he said. "We've got it. Now what are we going to do with it?"

Sarah McLain said, "It looks to me like we've showed the white folks what we can do if we take a mind to. And my heart goes out to all those poor old women forced to walk. Don't you think this one day of it's enough to make our point? Don't you think they'll listen if we present our demands now?"

Charles Bell nodded. "You may be right. It's certainly been a very impressive demonstration. But I don't see how we can even hope to continue it past today. We simply don't have the facilities or the financing to—" He turned to Houston Whitley. "What do you think, Huse?"

Huse stood up, walked to a window and looked out. Even as he watched, a bus, completely empty, roared past on the unpaved street. The bus driver was making this round purely through habit now; he could not have slowed for a passenger even if there had been one.

"I don't think it's a decision for us to make," he said. "Maybe we've made our point, maybe we haven't. If we haven't, it would be criminal for us to stop if we could continue. But every man jack of us here owns a car of some kind. We're not the ones who ride the buses, and who'll have to walk if we keep up. And it seems to me that they're the ones who ought to have the say-so."

"What you're suggesting," Jeff Marfield said, "is that we wait until the mass meeting tonight?"

"That's right. If nobody comes, we have our answer. If a lot of people come, they can make the decision for us. I don't see any other way to do it."

"That's pretty risky," Jeff said. "Sometimes without strong leadership things like this can just dwindle out."

There was a crackle in Huse's voice. "I don't see anything risky in letting the people make their own decision. Not people like the ones we have seen today."

"Praise the Lord," Sarah McLain said, "that's the truth."

"Okay," Jeff said. "Then we'll be guided by the mass meeting. But if the answer is yes, go ahead, we've got to be prepared. This thing can't be handled on just a catch-as-catch-can basis. There'll have to be some organization. Some provision will have to be made for financing—and proper handling of the finances. Some provision will have to be made for working out a long-range program."

"We've got a pretty good setup," Huse said.

"Not good enough to make this thing work indefinitely." Jeff picked up a briefcase and laid it on the desk in front of him. "I've done some preliminary work on this," he said, "and I've got the charter and bylaws of an organization laid out that should do the trick. I'd like to have you look them over and give me your comments." He passed out several copies.

Huse sat down and picked up the carbon Jeff had shoved toward him. "The Hannington Civic Betterment Association, huh? That's an impressive name."

Jeff smiled tightly. "This is liable to wind up being an impressive organization."

Huse studied the charter silently for several moments.

"What it really does," Jeff said, "is to solidify our present setup and make provision for expanding it. We have got to have a legal entity like this to protect the whole enterprise. Otherwise we'll all be up on tax raps and heaven only knows what else."

"Yes, I see you project collecting dues," Charles Bell said.

"We've got to have financing from somewhere. Provision is made to receive dues and voluntary contributions. We're going to have to have a full-time director—he's got to be paid; he can't be expected to work for nothing—and there'll be telephone bills and office expenses and . . ." He grinned. "And most probably bail bonds."

"Ugh," Sarah McLain said.

"My suggestion is that if this meets with the approval of the steering committee, the committee elect a slate of officers, including the permanent director, and submit the whole thing to the mass meeting tonight for ratification."

There was a moment's silence while they studied the articles further. Then Sarah McLain laid down her copy. "I'll agree on one condition," she said.

"What's that?" Jeff asked.

"That Houston Whitley," she said, "serve as director. And I think this salary of fifty dollars a week is far too low. It should be at least sixty-five."

"I'll go along with that," Charles Bell said promptly. "What about it, Huse?"

He shook his head. "No," he said. "No, I couldn't do it."

Jeff Marfield looked at him quickly. "Why not? I know the salary's not much, but it would replace a little of what you've already sacrificed, and maybe later—"

"No," Huse said sharply. "The salary's all right. But I'm not taking any handout from this thing; I can go somewhere and get a job. Besides, I'm not competent to handle this on a long-range basis. I don't know anything about this kind of work. You're the expert in that, Jeff."

"Yeah, the expert," Jeff said bitterly. "I've been working for years to get people to follow me and they ignore me. Then you come along and snap your fingers and they flock to you. I don't know why, but you've accomplished more in one weekend than I have in a decade.

And as for the salary being a handout," Marfield went on, "man, some handout! You'll work harder than you've ever worked in your life. And you'll take more risks. Don't worry, you'll earn your salary —and twice over. Nobody's giving you anything."

"Please, Huse," Sarah McLain said urgently. "I know it'll mean sacrifices on your part. But you're the force behind this whole thing. Without you, it'll collapse."

Huse stared at them, looking from one face to another. He did not want the post; it was the last thing in the world he wanted. His wants were to get Della and the baby safely home, and as soon after as possible to leave Hannington. He was finished here, no two ways about that, and there was no alternative to going North, or maybe even West, for he had been wondering about California. Anywhere, so long as he could find a job, construct some kind of life, and try to content himself with what he had. . . .

But looking at Sarah McLain and the others, he saw the impossibility of that dream. There was something in the eyes of each of them; he did not understand it, but it was as if each of them saw in him some quality that they lacked and needed to be complete. A faint shiver touched his spine.

"All right," he heard himself say. "If it means so much to everybody. If the mass meeting is a success, I'll accept." He paused, and then his voice hardened. "But there's one thing. . . . If I put my hand to this plow—why, then, I'm going to push it just as far as it will go."

They had hoped for several hundred people at the meeting; five thousand came.

A traffic jam had developed by six o'clock. By six-thirty the area was crawling with policemen. They were disregarded; the crowd that filled the church and overflowed into the street outside was quiet and orderly.

Some of them had come in jam-packed automobiles. Some of them had walked long, weary blocks. None of them had ridden the buses. But one way or the other, they were there.

"Look at them," Charles Bell whispered, as Huse, Bell, Jeff, and Martha Lacey prepared to enter the chancel. Tears were streaming unashamedly down Bell's cheeks. "Look at what God has done."

"Preacher," Huse whispered, "I don't know what to say to all those people."

Bell squeezed his arm. "Don't worry. The Lord will give you words."

Huse closed his eyes. He was shaken and awestricken. He had never imagined anything like this. He could not have; it was totally without precedent. Never, so far as he knew, in the history of the Negro race in America, had so many Negroes gathered in orderly fashion to express a yearning for the end of oppression. And they were all looking to him. They were all looking to *him*. . . .

Somebody had found a public address system somewhere. Speakers had been set up outside so that those who could not squeeze into the church could hear. Around the periphery of the mass of dark humanity that fanned out for blocks from the church entrance, television cameras had been set up, flashbulbs were going off. Somehow reporters had got into the church and were standing against the walls down front, and more television cameras were operating in the aisle.

"Well," Jeff Marfield said, his voice taut, "it's that time." He gave Huse a slight push, and all of them strode out into the chancel.

A murmur went up from the crowd. " 'Ere they are! Praise Gawd, we gonna hear sumpin now."

Charles Bell held up his hands. The murmur stilled itself. "Let us pray," Bell said.

"Our Heavenly Father," he began, "this day you have worked in us all . . ." His voice rolled on, rising and falling with sonorous tones. "We cried for help in the wilderness and you came to us. . . . You have strengthened not only our spirits but our legs and our feet. . . . Bless the words that are spoken here tonight and the actions that are taken. . . . Give us wisdom to choose the right and stand steadfast for it. . . . Hold our hands from violence against our fellow men, of whatever color, and fill our hearts to overflowing with love for enemies as well as friends . . ."

When he had finished, Jeff Marfield introduced a shy, embarrassed Martha Lacey. The audience arose spontaneously, applauding. When the long ovation had died, Martha's face was wet with tears. She faded back and sat down ponderously on one of the folding chairs that had been put in the chancel.

"And now," said Jeff simply, "I would like to introduce the man who set this movement in action: Mr. Houston Whitley."

There was applause. It was prolonged, echoed thunderously, re-echoed as it was taken up by the crowd outside.

Huse stood quietly behind the lectern. He was not even thinking about what he was going to say now. And he was not in the least nervous. He felt no surprise at that. There was humility in him as he looked out over the crowd, but there was, too, a new sense of strength and power of a sort he had never before known. He felt capable. Not optimistic, not exultant. Just capable.

At last the room was silent.

"Friends," he said, and he listened to the feedback of his own voice from the speakers outside and was surprised at how deep and clear it was. "Friends, all of us in our time have walked many long and weary roads, and no matter how far we plodded, how many twists and turnings we came to, how many bends we rounded, most of those roads have led us nowhere. That was because each of us walked his road alone. But today we have walked together. Today we have set out on one more journey. This may be a long road, too; it may be uphill and full of holes; the dust may choke us and the sun beat down upon us and there may be snares and pitfalls in our path. But we are used to walking by now; we are used to enduring, and it may be that if we keep straight on, never turning aside, never pausing to rest, and always, always walking together—it may be that this road will lead us out of the wilderness in which we have roamed so long . . ."

He could hear his own eloquence floating back to him in the hush that gripped the crowd; and it was eloquence, too, true eloquence, but he was not surprised at that either now.

His voice went on, calm, deep, and full of authority; it seemed not to be his voice at all, and yet he felt as if for the first time he was using his true voice. He recounted the story of what had happened to Martha Lacey and all that had followed it. He had gathered an exhaustive history of indignities suffered by Negroes on the buses; one man, he reminded them, had been shot and killed by a policeman called by the bus driver in an argument over a fare; another, a blind man, was being led off the bus by his wife when the doors had closed prematurely and the bus had started. His leg trapped, the man had been dragged for a block and severely injured. Those were things that had happened: facts. He enumerated them coolly and without hysteria.

"And we have endured all this," he said. "We endured it patiently and in the hope that the perpetrators of these injustices would themselves right these wrongs. But they have not, and now we are tired. We are tired of being oppressed, tired of being victimized, tired of being humiliated, tired of being treated unjustly. We are worn out with all that, and no one can blame us if at last we say to our oppressors, 'Stop! Enough!' "

There was heavy applause. He waited until it died. Then he told them about the organization of the Hannington Civic Betterment Association. He read off its slate of officers. "Later," he said, "you will be read a resolution. If you approve the resolution, the protest will continue until the conditions set forth in it are met by the bus company. But . . . maybe you will not approve the resolution. Maybe you are tired of walking . . ."

"No! No, no!" It went up as a shout.

"Then we will continue to walk. For though we are a patient people, we cannot be patient with anything less than our freedom as American citizens and as children of God. If we are patient with anything less, our patience will be no longer a blessing but a curse, not a virtue but a vice, not good but evil."

Behind him he heard someone whispering to Charles Bell. "The police are making us turn off loudspeakers. White people over across the hollow complaining."

"Turn them off," Bell said wearily.

Huse felt a flare of anger; it was about to slip into his voice, but with a sudden thrust of fear, he caught it in time.

"But there will be no anger in our protest," he heard himself say with urgency. "There will be no violence, no hatred, no lawlessness and no disorder." He gestured to the television cameras. "There will be room in our hearts only for love and determination that our love will rescue those who would commit injustice from their own sins. The eyes of the city, of the state, perhaps the nation and the world, are focused on us here tonight. They will remain focused. Let us so conduct ourselves that when we have come to the end of the road, when we have won our nonviolent battle, when there is liberty and justice for all, white or colored, it can be said that here a Christian people using the power of Christ began to lay the foundations of a new America. And, my friends, until that day comes, we'll keep our walking shoes on and stay on the freedom road!"

There was tremendous applause as he bowed slightly and then sat down beside Martha Lacey. It went on and on, in waves, from outside as well as within the church.

"Huse," Martha said, "oh, you done grand," and she squeezed his hand. "I wish Della coulda been here."

Huse said nothing. As the roaring swelled, he felt dazed.

At last it calmed. Then Jeff Marfield read the charter of the Hannington Civic Betterment Association. "And this," he told them, "is the resolution we shall present to the bus company." He began to read:

" 'The Negro citizens of Hannington, united in the Hannington Civic Betterment Association, will continue effectively to protest the unjust conditions existing in the operations of the city buses, and we shall stay off the buses until the following requests are agreed to by the bus company:

" 'One. All riders are to be seated on a first-come, first-served basis, regardless of race or color. White people shall seat from the front to the rear and Negroes from the rear to the front and there will be no lines of demarcation or reserved seats. No rider shall be asked by the bus driver to give up his seat.

" 'Two. In view of the large percentage of business given the bus company by Negro riders, qualified Negroes should be employed to operate buses serving sections that are predominantly Negro.

" 'Three.' And this is extremely important. 'There will be no difference in the service rendered Negroes from that rendered whites, and no difference in the courtesy shown to Negroes from that shown to whites. Bus operators are not to be allowed to use insulting and abusive language to Negroes.' "

He paused for a long moment. "You have heard the resolution and our proposed means of implementing it. Now, the decision is yours. Will you support the protest? Will you support the Hannington Civic Betterment Association? Will you walk for freedom?"

The church was hushed.

"All in favor," Jeff Marfield said, "will now stand up."

There was a shout and the sound of many bodies in motion and then, like a single sprawling organism in convulsion, the entire audience stood.

Marfield's voice rose above the clamor.

"Then it is so ordered. The protest will continue until we have won."

6 Emerging from the cramped, dark and musty interior of the *Enterprise*'s littered office into an April twilight warm with east wind and golden with the last of sunlight, Burke Jessup felt like a mole scrabbling out of its burrow. Forgetting for a moment the unrest that had dogged him all day, he balanced on his canes, drew in a great breath of spring-warmed air, and raised his head until he could see, above the tops of the low buildings that lined Snelling Street, the breastlike roundness of the upper part of the capitol dome and the state flag that fluttered there against the sunset.

I have got to get out more, he thought. I have to get more fresh air and some kind of exercise. This is the time of year when we ought to be getting out into the country somehow. Maggie, too; she needs it worse than I do. I wish I could talk her into riding again.

But he would not be able to, he thought, as he turned and began to hobble the half block to the intersection of Snelling with Main. She had too much pride. She would not use Cary's horses when Cary himself had been avoiding the Jessups for months.

Cary's easing away from them socially had hurt Maggie, even though Burke had understood it and tried to explain it to her. "He can't afford it," he had told her, trying to make her see. "Not the way things have been since this boycott began. Cary's a politician, honey; he's got a political future to look out for. And right now any association with us would be poison."

But the logic of it made no impression on Maggie. It was not her kind of logic. With Maggie it was always all or nothing. When she gave her love, it was unconditionally, until hell froze over; and she gave her friendship and her enthusiasm with the same totality. Expediency was a term she had never understood and never would. "I had thought he was braver than that," she had said. She was not bitter about it, only disappointed.

Now he had reached the intersection, and he stood at the corner for a moment watching the diminished flow of pedestrians. This was a sight he always liked to see, one that usually restored and refreshed him. Most of the people who went by were Negroes; they were still walking. Despite everything the city had been able to do to them, they were still walking.

He liked to watch their faces as they passed. Maybe he only imagined it, or maybe they still did wear that special expression they had worn at the beginning. It was pride in adversity—a compound of determination and serene confidence and self-respect, and he thought he could see it alike on the countenances of old and young. The young swung by strong and laughing and joking and raucous, hardly even noticing the demand on their energy; the old shuffled along painfully, with creaky joints and bent shoulders, each step an individual, calculated sacrifice and matter of concern, but old or young, none showed any signs of quitting, and watching them always made him feel a little less sorry for himself.

He knew what they had been going through. He had followed the progress of the boycott carefully, had even been involved in it himself in a minor way, since his story in *Tempo*—or at least the story for which he had gathered the data—had been the first public notice of it nationally. Since then, of course, it had become a *cause célèbre: Time, Life, Newsweek,* all the press associations—for a while Hannington had swarmed with their reporters and photographers and researchers. It had taken them a little while to realize not only the drama but the significance of what was happening here, but now the Hannington boycott was a national issue.

The city, of course, had not taken it lying down. It had responded exactly as Burke had guessed it would. At first there was arrogant confidence, manifested by Mayor Cameron's announcement that no consideration would be given to any demands by Negroes until they ceased "coercion." Daily there was assurance in newspaper editorials and from high officials that the boycott was on the verge of momentary collapse: Negroes, it was explained, simply lacked both the organizational ability and the drive to continue a united effort for long. An angry pronunciamento from the Citizens' Council had demanded that all Negroes participating in the boycott be fired from their jobs.

The Negroes kept on walking. Or using the car pools that had been so thoroughly organized that they functioned almost as a public utility. If there was anything wrong with their organizational ability, it did not show in the way the car pools worked. Nor had Burke seen any break in their united front that would indicate lack of drive. And as for mass firings—well, the entire social and economic fabric of Hannington for centuries had been inextricably woven out of the availability of their cheap labor. The white middle-class housewife had declined to become a martyr to her sense of racial outrage; she was not going to do her own heavy cleaning or nursemaiding or cooking to teach the Negroes a lesson. Nor were businessmen, whose enterprises were built on underpinnings of cheap black muscle, going to yank the foundations out from under their profits.

When it became evident that the boycott would not collapse of its own weight, the city had at last offered to negotiate. The negotiations had been secret, but Houston Whitley had described them to Burke for the benefit of *Tempo*.

"There was Mayor Cameron and Sam Deal and the city councilmen and a couple of men from the bus company. We presented our demands, and for a while it looked like they were willing to go along with us, especially the bus company men. But then that Sam Deal put his mouth in. Just about the time the mayor was saying that the demands didn't look unreasonable, Deal says, 'You know what's going to happen if you give in? These niggers are gonna go around bragging how they beat the white people down, and then where'll we all be?' " Huse had laughed shortly. "That killed that. You should have seen everybody back away."

It was surprising, Burke thought, how Huse had changed. No, perhaps he had not changed at all. Maybe that potential for leadership had been inside him this whole time, thwarted, frustrated, for lack of opportunity. Whatever the explanation, he seemed to have grown, physically, mentally and morally. There was no trace of the self-pity or feeling of inferiority that Burke had sensed in him that day at The Place. He was a man just coming into the realization of his full powers, and, as such, he would have stood out in any society, white or dark, as a powerful and yet self-contained personality, one that had not yet reached its full potential but was steadily mounting toward it.

Maybe it was the support that had poured in from across the country that had strengthened him. "That one article you got printed about us," he told Burke, "sure started a flood tide." The Civic Betterment Association had small offices in a run-down building on Grade Street now; Huse had gestured toward two girls opening a pile of mail on a table. "We're getting letters from every state in the Union and from overseas, places far away as England and, of all places, Germany. Even got one in from Singapore yesterday and quite a few from Tokyo. And do you know what? A lot of 'em are from white people. From white people even here in the South."

He had paused. "And the contributions," he said, and there was a touch of awe in his voice. "They're what have saved us. They're coming in large and small, from everywhere. Negroes in Atlanta and Birmingham and New Orleans. White people there, too." He grinned. "Not many of 'em, though. Lots in the North, however. Anyhow, all of them sending money. Maybe a quarter some old mammy in Alabama's saved, maybe fifty dollars from somebody in Connecticut or New York. But we couldn't last without 'em. Do you know that we've managed to buy fifteen new station wagons to use in the car pools? And there's money left over—enough to operate on. It's like . . . like the manna that God sent down to feed the Hebrew children." His voice had crispened. "It's all being properly accounted for, too."

Anyway, Burke remembered, watching the stream of pedestrians slowly begin to ebb, the negotiations had been a Mexican standoff. And when they had come to naught, the city had turned hard and ugly and had cracked down.

The Negro cab companies were told that under city ordinance they could not operate at reduced fares. An expanded police force harassed the car-pool drivers with a blizzard of traffic violation tickets, brought in Negroes who walked as vagrants and loiterers. Through the city's influence, liability insurance on the car pools had been canceled by the company which carried it; the Civic Betterment Association had been forced to reinsure through Lloyd's of London. But what was worst of all, Burke thought, turning away from Main and hobbling back toward the office, was that the city's attitude had served as notification to the white trash that the season was open on Negroes.

They were always there, he reflected, in any city—Hannington, New York, London or Podunk. Always just below the surface, like the evil, tough-hided, needle-toothed and valueless garfish that lurked in the weeds of the swamp lakes. And, like the gars, destroyers, spoilers, with nothing but their own bodies as eventual fertilizer to contribute to the world. In Hannington, in the South, they were the mudsills of society, with no one, not even the Negroes, beneath them, and this enraged them and they tried to climb in the only way they knew, by forcing someone else under them. Their minds worked at the flickering levels of those of predatory animals, but they lacked a predator's courage.

Still, there were times when they were useful—when their votes could be bought for elections or when terror was useful, for they were good at terror—and the city government had decided to use them now. It let them roam the streets in bands of drunken punks, attacking Negroes when they found the courage. It let them harass Houston Whitley and the other leaders of the boycott with threatening scribbled letters signed "KKK" and with obscene phone calls that kept up day and night, as if in planned campaign. It let them parade in their Klan robes through the Negro sections, as nearly thirty carloads of them had done last night through Little Hammer. And their very presence, violent, unpredictable, unleashed, had built an air of tension in the city that today was almost tangible. There was fear on both sides today, for the scum had been turned loose and given a free hand, and nobody could be quite sure what would come of it. It was hoped that they would stir the Negroes to violence and justify more arrests and reprisals, but so far that had not worked. Not even when the Klan had paraded last night.

In the old days, Burke knew, a Klan parade would have meant the bolting and shuttering of every Negro house for miles around. But it had not been that way last night in Little Hammer. As the carloads of hooded men had driven down into the hollow, a strange thing had happened; lights had been turned up in every house, doors opened, and soon the porches were thronged with Negroes. None of them said anything; they just clotted the porches and the sides of the street and watched the Klan go by. There were perhaps a hundred and fifty Klansmen. There were thirty times that many Negroes. . . .

The sun was going down now; it was getting dark. He would be glad to get back to the *Enterprise* office. Instead of the break leaving him refreshed, his mood had changed once more and now he felt a kind of black despair, and he was anxious for the reassuring sight of Maggie.

When he came in, she was on the telephone. "Yes, Mr. Dabney," she was saying. He noticed that her fingers, white with strain, were knotted around a pencil as if they would break it. "Yes, Mr. Dabney, I realize that. But I don't see how—" Her voice shook a little. "All right, sir. If there's no way I can make you change your mind. Yes, sir." She hung up. Unaware of Burke's presence, she dragged her hand across her face. Then she said, shortly and tersely, an obscene word.

He shoved through the swinging gate in the railing that walled off their meager editorial offices. "That, I take it," he said, with a sinking feeling in his stomach, "was Mr. Dabney."

Maggie swung around as he dropped into the chair behind his desk. "You are so right." He knew the cost of her wan smile. "Dabney's Hardware is no longer one of our advertisers."

Burke nodded. "The editorial?"

"The editorial."

"Hell," he said bitterly. "Maybe I shouldn't have written it."

Maggie stood up. She's aged, he thought, noting how thin and drawn she looked. Just in our one year down here, she's aged so much. Suddenly he hated Hannington for that.

She came over and sat down on his desk where she could draw his head against her breasts. "Listen," she said, "it was a damn good editorial. And I wouldn't trade it off for a dozen Dabney accounts."

Burke closed his eyes; the warmth of her breasts was comforting; he could hear the beating of her heart. He had thought about the editorial for a long time before he had written it. He had not wanted to write it, and he had tried every way he knew how to talk himself out of writing it, but he had known all along that he would have to do it.

What had finally triggered it was a speech at a Citizens' Council meeting he had covered. The speaker was a lawyer and a founding member of the Mississippi Councils, the original ones. Burke and Maggie had listened to him with growing disbelief; his speech was smooth, well thought out, literate and persuasive.

It was also bigoted, slyly obscene, and, it became apparent as he proceeded, vindictive almost to the point of derangement.

They had heard a great deal of such stuff in the past several months, but there was something different about this speech. As the man ranted on, Burke did not feel the usual sad contempt mixed with a grudging admiration for sincerity and willingness to fight even if outnumbered. Instead, this time, he began to be aware of a fear, a slow, insidious horror, a gray dread that deepened as the speech continued. When it was over, there was a rising ovation; the members of the local Council, the bankers, the lawyers, the doctors, the substantial merchants—they scrambled to their feet and applauded wildly.

Burke and Maggie hurried out. When they had gained the cool sanctuary of the March night, Maggie shuddered. "God," she grated, "I thought the Nazis went out with Hitler."

Behind them they could hear the applause continuing. Burke gulped in great breaths of air. His stomach was queasy; he felt as if he had been exposed to something noisome.

"Listen to them," Maggie whispered in awe. "Listen to them clap in there."

That was when he knew he was going to have to write the editorial; and he knew too that if he did it would probably ruin them.

They were close to ruin already. Long ago he had taken a stand in favor of honest negotiations in good faith with the Hannington Civic Betterment Association, had pointed out that simple courtesy cost nothing and would go a long way toward solving the problem of the boycott. That had not seemed radical to him; but the rest of Kenoree County apparently considered it so. Their circulation had eroded away to not more than half its original count; their advertising had dropped below the break-even point. To write the editorial that he knew he must write would be to administer his own *coup de grâce*.

But a pattern was becoming clear to him now, and the speech at the Council meeting had suddenly brought a lot of things into focus. He could see now what was happening, and he was genuinely terrified by it. Its significance spread far beyond the racial issue.

It was as if the lights were going out in Hannington, as if they were slowly being extinguished over much of the South. A gray twilight of fear was settling down, and already creatures of darkness were beginning to show themselves, as if they had patiently lain in wait all this time until enough murk had settled so their true shapes could not be discerned.

Now they had the disguise they wanted. Transforming themselves into Southern patriots or defenders of the Constitution, they began to spread their infection. Because of them, men weighed their words before they spoke and trembled lest they be misunderstood. Because of them, Southern newspapers must judge the cost before they printed truth. Indeed, some of them were themselves editors or publishers, just as others were crackpots running mimeograph machines in shabby upstairs offices. But whether high or low, what they said was being listened to; they were gaining a strength beyond the justification of their numbers, as they tapped the vitriolic pool of hereditary animus against the Negro and sent its acid streams coursing also at Jew, Catholic, nonconformist, intellectual, and at the very structure of the first ten Amendments to the Constitution they pretended to defend. They were Typhoid Marys of paranoia; perhaps they would have been ludicrous if those they came in contact with had not been so susceptible to infection or if they had been without precedent. But they had not been without precedent: the constant ache in Burke's shattered feet and legs reminded him of that.

He was perhaps more afraid of them than he had ever been in the war, for he was helpless now, physically and financially. But his hatred and horror of them was greater than his fear, and he could not help fighting them with the one pitiful weapon he had left.

So they were finished now. He knew it and Maggie knew it, but neither of them would say it.

After a while he straightened up and she slid off the desk and bent and kissed him, and he patted her on the fanny.

"Come on," she said, "let's go home and have a drink. It's late."

"What about bringing me a couple of cans of beer and a hamburger from around the corner and then you go on? I'm going to quit talking about that article query to the *New York Times Magazine* and go ahead and write them tonight. They haven't had a really good piece yet on what's going on down here, not in depth." He started to add, "And we can sure as hell use the money," but she already knew that.

"No," Maggie said, "I'd rather wait here. I don't like to leave you alone and I don't want to be alone either. I'll find something to do while you do that."

"Suit yourself," he said. "Then make that four cans of beer if you've got any change."

He watched her go out, and he no longer felt discouraged as he admired the erect grace with which she carried her trim body. He loved her very much. What the hell. As long as he had Maggie, he'd make out.

7

Sometimes he wondered if she didn't talk so much deliberately, just because she knew how it rasped his nerves. He had long ago perfected a technique of not hearing her, even when she was directly across the table from him; he could switch off his mind and still make all the appropriate answers required. They were not much; all she needed was a listener, not a responder. A cigar-store Indian would probably have served as well as a husband.

But tonight he did not seem to be able to switch off his mind, and all her aimless chatter scraped directly on its exposed surfaces, and he thought he would go mad. After dinner he made himself a huge drink; he had deliberately stinted on the meal to leave room for it. But somehow the alcohol only made him more vulnerable, not less. And there was no escape from her, no Maggie and Burke to fly to.

". . . and Daddy asked me if I didn't want to go along with him and Mama, after all, I haven't been to New York since last fall, but I told him I'd have to talk it over with you first, but I knew you wouldn't mind. It'll only be for a couple of weeks; Daddy's going to stay on but Mama's coming back after a couple of weeks, she's especially anxious to get to Black, Starr and Gorham because she wants to match Grandmother's antique sterling gravy ladle and give it to Aunt Jessie for her birthday, if they can do it, but it shouldn't take more than two weeks if they can do it at all, which I doubt, I think the thing was handmade and I don't believe they hand-make a single piece of silver like that any more. And then of course there're my summer clothes to get, but I don't have to go much of anywhere but Saks for those, they've got the cutest pool outfit, I saw it in the *Times Magazine* . . ."

"Yes," he said. "All right, okay."

But she went on, and he was sure she was doing it deliberately. His mind scuttled around inside his head, searching for escape. He quickly drained the glass and stood up.

"Look," he said, "I've got to go back down to the office for a while. I don't seem to be able to relax; I might as well work. This damn Legislature, the stuff piles up, you can't get anything done."

"With that great big drink in you?" Mary Scott laughed. "I'd hate to see any work you turn out tonight."

"It just sharpens my wits when I'm tired," Cary said defensively. "I'll only be a couple of hours."

"Well, all right, go ahead." There was no rancor in her voice, no hurt at being left alone. She knew she had him anyway, had him good, had him better than she had ever had him. Dammit, he thought, why did Burke have to go off the deep end with that damned paper of his?

It was good to be outside, free of her mouth. The car was like a haven when he got in and closed the door. He backed out of the garage and paused in the driveway for a moment, feeling the warm spring wind play on him, something ancient and musky in it, something deeply, vaguely stirring. Then he backed the car the rest of the way out and began to drive; but he drove aimlessly, not toward his office.

He had no intention of shutting himself up there and working tonight. Not if he had to drive around all night until he was sure she was in bed and asleep. In the silence behind the steering wheel he could feel his nerves slowly begin to unwind.

For a while he tried not to think of anything, but it was no use. Maggie kept coming into his mind. Not Burke, just Maggie. He could trace mentally the outline of every part of her face, could conjure up for himself the look of her eyes when she had just made a successful jump, and she was completely and totally alive in a way that spilled some of her life over into him and made him a little more alive too.

But, of course, she was forbidden. She and Burke too. Powell Bradham had issued that proscription as soon as Burke's first editorial about the bus boycott had appeared.

"I know his little old paper doesn't amount to a hill of beans," Bradham said. "But you can't take even that risk. Not with people feeling the way they do now. You can't get tarred with that kind of brush. Oh, I know he's your best friend. But not even that counts now. Not if we're going to do what we aim to do. Until you're in that chair up yonder"—he had gestured vaguely toward the capitol—"you can't afford a single misstep that Moody could turn and pin you with if he found out what we're up to."

And he had agreed readily enough, then. In fact, he had decided, his father could ask him to climb a greased flagpole bare-assed, and he would agree. As long as his father was with him, as long as his father's eyes were upon him with that lambent love and pride. It would only be later, after he came down off the flagpole with a sore tail that he would begin to wonder: Was this trip necessary?

For a while his sense of mission, of unity and identity with his father, had compensated for the loneliness. But tonight it seemed as if nothing could compensate for it. The hunger in him for the sight of Maggie, the sound of her voice, her presence close, was brutal. If he could find some pretext to touch her, that would be even better. Just to touch her in an ordinary way, give her a brief, friendly kiss of greeting, put his arm about her in an affectionate way. Nothing any more complicated than that, for he knew he could expect nothing more; he knew too well her commitment to Burke and that she would carry it out to the letter. But in the torment in which he had been living almost since the night he had met her, he had learned to make do with very little.

And now, since January, he had not had even that. Goddamn Houston Whitley, he thought bitterly. Goddamn him and his bus boycott both. I hope all those niggers walk their feet off.

Probably, he thought, they would, if they were waiting for the city to give in to them. He knew too well how little chance of that there was. Hoke Moody had issued ironclad instructions. The Legislature was considering new laws now that would be aimed specifically at boycotts of this nature wherever in the state they might occur. All those niggers are going to accomplish, he thought, is to wear out their shoe leather and keep me from being able to see Maggie.

He knew his father was right, of course. Even he was surprised by how bitter feelings were in Hannington, how great the outrage across the state. It would be political suicide now to even have someone like Burke Jessup for a friend. And his father had selflessly worked and schemed for too many years for him to take a chance of blowing the whole thing.

But when he had quit thinking and truly saw the road for the first time, his hunger and loneliness took him to the street on which the Jessups lived.

As he drove by their house, he saw that it was completely dark and the car was not in the driveway. He was at once disappointed and relieved. Both of them were probably still at the office. Well, that took care of that.

Since he was not going to work, he had no particular reason for going downtown. But he turned the car in that direction anyway. He had driven several blocks before his own intention clarified itself; and then he knew that he could stand it no longer; he had to see Maggie and he was headed for the *Enterprise* office and to hell with the consequences.

There was plenty of parking space on Snelling at this time of night, and he pulled the car to the curb close to the *Enterprise* office. He was gratified to see that lights still burned inside, though it was after nine. For a grown man in his thirties to feel this way, he thought as he got out, was absurd, ridiculous. He was like a high school freshman with a crush on a senior girl, unable to resist capering around so that she would notice him, building wild dreams that even he knew had no tenuous connection with reality.

They would probably give him the freeze anyway, he thought, trying the door and finding it unlocked. And he deserved it. He wished he had a drink to bolster his courage.

He stuck his head inside the door. Maggie was at one of the two desks behind the rail, clipping a newspaper. Burke was at the other, hunched over a typewriter, cigarette dangling from his lips, his face screwed up in concentration.

Cary said with false heartiness, "Anybody home?"

Both of them jumped and turned and stared at him, and then Burke's face broke into a slow grin.

"Well, lo," he said, "the lost is found. Come on in, scarceness."

"Where in the world," Maggie said with severity, "have you been keeping yourself?"

Apparently they were not angry with him, maybe even glad to see him. He relaxed.

330 · LOOK AWAY, LOOK AWAY

"The Legislature's in session. It's my busy season. It's kept me
tied up."

"Well, pull up a chair and sit. I think there's a can of beer left,
but it's probably hot. What's new in Marse Robert's army?"

"We're going to charge if Longstreet ever gets here and Stuart
comes back with the cavalry. What's new in the scalawag-and-carpet-
bagger department?"

"Oh, we're still boring from within," Burke said, handing Cary a
can of beer and an opener. He leaned back in his chair and looked at
Cary searchingly. "I suppose you've come to lecture us about the
editorial."

"What editorial?"

"What editorial, he says." Burke's voice was sardonic. "Didn't
you get your copy of the *Enterprise* today?"

"I didn't see it." Cary frowned, feeling apprehensive. "I don't
think it usually comes until Wednesday." There was no humor in his
voice now. "What have you gone and done this time?"

Maggie handed him a paper. "See for yourself."

Cary unfolded it and began to read; and as he read he felt a
sickness growing inside him, not because of what the editorial said
but because of what he knew having printed this would do to them.

"For God's sake," he said at last, laying the paper aside. "Did
you have to publish this crap?"

"I keep asking myself that," Burke said, "and the answer keeps
coming up yes."

"Don't you know . . ." Cary tried to keep the grief out of his
voice. "Don't you know what this is going to do to you?"

"We've got a pretty good idea," Maggie said thinly. "We've already lost our last big advertising account this afternoon." Her voice
trembled. "That's what I like about the South. It's so nice and free
down here."

Cary turned toward her with an anger that was not meant for her.
"Do you expect the best people in this town to enjoy being called
Nazis and Fascists?"

"We didn't call them that."

"No, but you sure as hell implied it. You—"

"Cary, listen." Burke's voice was unusually hard as he cut in.
"Did you hear that speech that bird from Mississippi made? And all
those nice fat-bottomed businessmen giving him a rising ovation?"

"No, I didn't hear it, but—"

"Then you should have," Burke said, and his face was grim. "The speech he made would have done Goebbels proud, and those people lapped it up. Don't you see, it was what they wanted to hear? The same old master-race, final-solution doctrine all over again, wrapped in a Confederate flag." His voice crackled. "It's history repeating itself, and I don't mean German history, I mean Southern history. A minority of sonsabitches so crazed on the nigger question that they're perfectly willing to take away everybody's rights to settle it their way. They don't teach it much in Southern history books—maybe you don't know about it—but here in Muskogee, in a lot of other states down here, long before the Civil War, it had already got the same way. It could cost a man his life or his property even to suggest that slavery might not be the divine plan of God. There were plenty of Southern white men lynched in the 1850s for daring to suggest that, and if you don't think the wheel's turning full circle, you just take a look at our account books. Oh, the lynching's a little more subtle now, but it's happening." He paused.

"I'm scared of totalitarianism, Cary. I'm scared of it and I hate it. But if it ever gets a foothold in this country, it will be right here in the South. Because the majority was intimidated by this hysterical minority. This is the logical spawning ground, Cary—you can look back at history and see that. This is the place with the guilt of slavery on its conscience that it's never really been able to justify; this is the place with an ancient grudge against a whole race of people; this is the land of dissent at your own risk, the land of the Ku Klux Klan and the closed ballot box and the egomaniacs who once took half a country to an absurd war and whose progeny boast of it." He ground out his cigarette.

"It's a fine country, a wonderful country, a beautiful one, and it can hypnotize you. If you were born here, you're bound to love it. And yet, if you have any sensitivity at all, there's so much in it that you've got to hate, too, and be afraid of. . . . We're all suffering from schizophrenia and we're never going to be cured until we get rid of our nigger fixation. Once we do that, God knows, we've got everything else it would take to make us great. I don't want to be a goddam martyr. I just want to be left to live in peace and make a little money. But that's what everybody was saying in 1855, and that's what they were saying in Germany in 1937 and—" He broke off. "Oh, hell," he said, "this isn't getting this piece of work finished." He reached for another cigarette. "Do me a favor, will you, Cary?"

"What's that?" Cary said. He was looking hard at Burke, wondering if Burke were quite sane. It's his legs, he thought. That's what it is. He says they hurt him all the time. That's enough to get anybody this hysterical. . . .

"Maggie's had a long day and she's bushed. And I've got to get this thing I'm working on finished tonight. What about taking her home? I'll come along in a little while, when I'm through here."

"No," Maggie said quickly. "I'll stay."

"You will not," Burke said. "You're beat now. And I'll be beat by the time I finish this. One of us has got to be reasonably fresh and able to cope in the morning, and I doubt if it'll be me." He smiled and patted her hand. "If I don't get this damned thing finished and in the mail, I'll toss and turn all night. You go along; this big old Fascist here will look out for you, won't you, big old Fascist?"

Cary could not control the sudden leaping inside him at the thought of being alone with Maggie. Just to have her by him for a while without the distraction of Burke. "Sure," he said, trying to keep any unseemly eagerness out of his voice. "I'll take just as good care of her as a Fascist can."

"I don't like to leave you by yourself," Maggie insisted to Burke. "Especially when you're tired."

Cary did not miss the sudden flare of anger that crossed Burke's face briefly. "Dammit," he said irritably, "I can manage. I'm a grown man, even if—" He broke off. "Sorry," he said quietly. "You run along with Cary, honey, and let me finish this. I'll be okay."

Maggie stood hesitantly for a moment, and then, without enthusiasm, she said, "All right. But try not to be any longer than you can help." She turned to Cary. "Let me get my coat."

As he drove her toward home, slowly as he could, she was tensely silent. He tried, desperately, to break her down with jocularity that rang hollow. When she did not respond, his distress and sense of loss grew. At last he quit joking and said very seriously, "Maggie, what's the matter? Do you hate me or something?"

"Don't be ridiculous," she said tiredly. "Of course I don't hate you."

"I thought maybe because I had been tied up for so long and hadn't been around, or because I . . . I'm on the other side, don't see eye to eye . . ."

"What's the matter?" she said with a trace of asperity. "Got a guilty conscience?" Then her voice softened. "No, Cary, I don't hate anybody. I just feel like I'm shut up in some kind of madhouse, that's all. I'd just like to get out of this madhouse and back to some kind of sanity before I go as mad as everybody else."

"I guess to an outsider it does seem kind of weird."

"Yes," she said, "I guess that's a good word for it." And then she was silent again. She was, he could sense, utterly drained, utterly discouraged. She had a right to be, he thought, with quick, fierce compassion for her. With a cripple for a husband, a cripple who didn't have any better sense than to cut off his nose to spite his face, who could have had it easy if he had only used some sense. . . . He realized that he had fallen into the habit of thinking of Burke with a kind of duality. There was Burke the friend; but there was also a Burke whom he was beginning to hate. Not for his politics, but because he owned Maggie completely, possessed something which Cary envied him, and because, owning it, he was incompetent to care for it. That Burke was a barrier, an obstacle, a stumbling block in the way of—

Now they were at the darkened house. Cary stopped the car and got out and opened the door for Maggie. He took her arm, helped her up over the curb. They paused on the sidewalk. "Well," Cary said tentatively. He dreaded the next second in which she would turn away and leave him.

"Oh, come on in," she said with a mixture of weariness and courtesy, "and have a drink." Her voice softened a little. "I don't think I want to sit by myself right away anyhow."

He hedged. "Well, I wouldn't—"

"Don't worry. The neighbors aren't speaking to us anyhow." She started up the walk and he fell in alongside her eagerly.

No matter how often he saw it, something about the Jessup house always depressed Cary Bradham. It was in a section of town that was almost run-down, but not quite, a small, shingled bungalow with a tiny yard. They had rented it furnished and the furniture was like the house and the neighborhood—fair value once for what it had cost, but now shabby and tired with age and usage. He hated Maggie's having to live in a place like this. Only her touch, he thought as she unlocked the door and they entered, saved it from being totally a horror—she had contrived a little individuality with a few prints and imaginative arrangement of furniture. As she turned on the living room light, Cary saw that as usual the room was overflowing with books the tiny shelf space was inadequate to hold.

Maggie made a helpless gesture. "I don't know where they all come from. I put them up and they seem to slither back out. I think we suffer from a malady called book ooze. God, if we had all the money we've spent on books and magazines, we'd be solvent. Thank heaven there's not a single good bookstore in this town; it's saved us a fortune." She gestured to the sofa. "Sit down. I've got to powder my nose and then I'll fix a couple of drinks."

"I'll do it," he said. "I know where everything is."

"No," she said, "I didn't do the supper dishes last night or the breakfast dishes this morning, and I don't want you to see my dirty kitchen." She disappeared down the hall.

Cary dropped to the sofa and thumbed through a magazine without seeing it. The house still smelled of this morning's frying bacon. He was aware that his heart was hammering, his palms sweating. He felt a wild and dangerous resolve growing in him, that he knew he must resist and knew that he would not. He threw the magazine aside, shifting restlessly on the sofa, and lit a cigarette.

It seemed an eternity before Maggie appeared with the drinks. She gave him his, dropped into a chair, and put her stockinged feet up on a hassock. She sipped from her glass and closed her eyes for a moment. Cary took that unguarded moment to look at her closely.

He was right, she had aged. Most of her makeup had rubbed off; the lines were deeper at her eyes and there were creases at the corners of her mouth; in the glare of the lamp beside the sofa he could see every freckle and a few scattered blemishes on a skin no longer smooth with the tautness of youth. She was not, in that moment, what could be called a beautiful or even a pretty woman, and yet somehow that only increased his want of her. He cursed silently Burke's stupidity for letting her come to this, even as he knew that in reality Burke had not. It was her nature to exhaust herself at whatever she undertook.

It was all he could do to stay on the sofa and not go to her. She pinched at her eyelids and sighed and drank again and opened her eyes and raised her head and smiled. "Now," she said, "maybe I'll live."

"I hope so."

"What have you been doing with yourself? Where have you been all this time?"

"I told you, that Legislature's a bitch, once you get tangled up with it."

"It's a bitch, all right," she said bitterly. Then, "Let's not start that again, though. How's Mary Scott?"

"As usual." His voice was harsh.

Time passed. It was agony to sit there passively, trying desperately to concentrate on small talk. Actually, she did not demand much of that. She seemed too tired to talk a great deal, but he began to sense that she was glad to have his companionship and in no hurry for him to leave. That excited him a little, though he knew it was only because she was nervous tonight and perhaps a little afraid to be alone. She would not need him once Burke was home.

Finally their carefully nursed drinks ran out. Maggie stood up, looking at her wristwatch. "It's after ten-thirty. I wonder how much longer Burke is going to be."

"I guess he'll be along in a little while."

"I know, but I can't help worrying. His legs are giving him so much trouble these days and I always feel like . . . like I've gone off and left a child when I leave him." She laughed shortly. "Don't you ever repeat that. The worse things get on the paper, the touchier he gets about being . . . you know."

"Crippled," Cary said harshly.

She looked at him in some surprise. "Yes," she said evenly. "Crippled."

"It must put a hell of a burden on you," he went on recklessly, "having to look after him like that."

He was puzzling her. She said, "He looks after me, too, in a lot of ways." As if to put an end to that, she picked up their glasses and turned her back. "I'll make us another drink," she said, and she went through the tiny dining room into the kitchen.

Cary stood there for a moment, rubbing his palms along his trouser legs. He could hear the rattle of ice trays. His heart was beating almost painfully and his throat was dry. Then, as if moved by something beyond his volition, he went into the kitchen.

It was a mess, a clutter of stacked dishes still unscraped. Maggie was at the sink, running water into his glass. She looked around, startled, as he came in.

"All right," she said, cutting off the faucet and turning. "So you couldn't resist seeing what a foul housekeeper I am. Aren't you glad you're not married to *me?*"

Cary moved up to her, towered over her, looked down at her. "No," he heard himself say quietly.

Her eyes widened and something stirred in them, and she was silent for an instant, and then she held out the glass. "Here's your drink," she said.

He took it, but he did not move and he did not quit looking at her; and suddenly he knew, as she looked back at him without expression, that if he kissed her, she would not resist.

"Thanks," he said, and then he clamped her with one arm and pulled her to him. He was not startled but was relieved when she came easily, and then he bent and fastened his mouth on hers.

She moved against him tightly; he felt the pressures of her body. Her mouth opened under his; she slackened for a moment, letting him hold her. He opened his eyes for an instant, saw that hers were closed, and as excitement grew in him, he kissed her with a franker sexuality.

And then she pulled away, not wrenching, just pulling firmly, stepping back, her face very white, her breasts rising and falling under her dress.

"Well," she said bleakly, "I guess that's par for the course. After all, I am your best friend's wife. So it had to come, didn't it?"

Cary took a step toward her. There was a peculiar sound in his head, exactly as if he held a seashell against each ear; it drowned out all thought.

"You liked it," he heard himself say thickly.

"Of course I liked it," she snapped. "What do you think I am, made of iron? But that doesn't mean I want you to do it again." She turned, pushing him aside, not gently, and went past him back into the living room carrying her drink. He stood indecisively for a moment and then followed her. At the wide opening between the dining and living rooms, he halted.

She had sat down in a chair and had lit a cigarette and now drew on it in short, nervous puffs.

Cary said, "I'm sorry, Maggie."

"I know you are," she said tonelessly. "I am, too. If I were just built that way, we could have ourselves a ball, couldn't we?"

"I didn't expect that."

"Sometimes I wish I were built that way." She crushed out the cigarette, though it was only half smoked. "It must be fine to have your fun and not worry about your conscience. Well . . ." She shook another cigarette out of the pack.

Cary said quietly, "I didn't kiss you just because I wanted some fun, Maggie."

"I didn't think you did," she said. "You'd be a fool to risk Burke's friendship just for some fun."

"Yes," he said.

"I'd be a fool to risk Burke for anything," she said.

"I know," he said with objectivity. "In a lot of ways, I'm not much stacked up alongside Burke—especially from your viewpoint. I don't fool myself about that."

She stood up and now her bleak face relaxed into a smile. "You have your points, Cary. I hope we can still be friends. That's a good round cliché, isn't it? But—" She was rubbing her hands together. "It's getting awfully late. I wish . . . Burke would come on. I'm worried about him."

Cary emptied his glass and set it on the dining room table. "I'll drive back down to the *Enterprise* office and herd him home. Then I guess I'd better get home myself." He went to the front door. "Good night, Maggie."

"Good night," she said.

He felt very good as he drove back downtown to Snelling Street. Something within him had unknotted itself; he was unburdened. At least Maggie knew how he felt; the awful ordeal of pretending to her was over. It would never go any further, he knew, than it had tonight, but even this much had cleared his mind. Each of them knew where the other stood, and somehow that was a gain. He felt closer to Burke, oddly enough, as he turned into Snelling Street, able to face him now without that terrible impatience to sweep him aside and take Maggie. Because he knew he had no chance with Maggie. So, in a way, the issue was settled.

The *Enterprise* office was dark; apparently Burke had finished and gone on home. Cary drove on past and turned into Main. Just around the corner he saw the lights of a shabby café and beer joint. On impulse, he parked the car and went in. Except for a drowsy counterman, it was deserted. He went to the pay phone and called Maggie. "I guess he's on his way home," he said. "The office is dark. Has he got there yet?"

"No," she said. "Not yet. But he'll be in in a little while, I guess. Thank you again, Cary."

"It's all right," he said, and he hung up. He did not want to go home. He went to the counter and ordered a cup of coffee and took a long time drinking it, not really thinking about anything. When he had finished, he went back to the pay phone. He did not know whether he was genuinely concerned about Burke, or whether he just wanted to hear Maggie's voice again.

"This is Cary again," he said when she answered. "He's home now, isn't he?"

"No," she said, and her voice was trembling. "No, he isn't."

Cary frowned, and now he was concerned. It was foolish, Burke could take care of himself, and yet— "Look," he said, "I'm still downtown. Where did y'all leave the car this morning?"

"We got to the office late. All the parking spaces were filled. We parked it in the lot down next to the railroad station."

"All right, I'll go down and see if it's gone. He may just be having a last beer before everything shuts down."

"I hate to put you to the trouble—"

"It's not any trouble," he said, his voice soft. "If his car is gone, I'll know he's headed home. Otherwise, he'll be in one of the places around here or near the depot. So if I find him, I'll give you a ring and we'll have a beer together and I'll send him on."

"Thank you," she said. "Thank you so much, Cary."

He hung up and went out of the café. The *Enterprise* office was located in a shabby area of town, a section of pawnshops and beer joints and sad little offices at the top of grimy, narrow stairways, where sad or furtive people did sad or furtive things to earn a marginal living. The railroad station was only a block away, and Cary left his car where it was and briskly began to walk.

8 After Maggie and Cary had left together, Burke Jessup turned back to the typewriter. As he struggled with a prospectus which, he hoped, would lead an editor to authorize him to do a finished article, he was aware of a sense of desperation. Long ago he had sold a few magazine articles, but except for the stuff he had fed *Tempo,* he had not tried any free-lancing since coming to Hannington. The paper had demanded all his energies; besides, until the bus boycott, there had been little in Hannington to use as material. He knew that, largely as a result of his own initial efforts, the boycott had been over-reported now, but maybe, just maybe, there was room somewhere for a few thousand words of background, inside information, on it, and on the response of the whites to it.

Because its acceptance immediately was so crucial to them—the *Times Magazine,* he vaguely remembered, paid about three hundred dollars top—he wanted the article query to be perfect, and it took a long time to finish it. Even then he know it was a long way from perfect, but it was as good as he could make it, fatigued as he was. He was stiff and aching when he arose from the typewriter, balancing himself on his canes, and his movements were slow and uncertain as he turned out the lights and locked the front door.

There was a mailbox on the corner at which there would be an early-morning pickup, and he dropped the letter into it with a sense of both relief and discouragement. It was a hope, but essentially a forlorn one. That seemed to be the only kind of hope left to him any more, but it was better than nothing.

He maneuvered around the corner onto Main. The single block to the railroad station seemed a forbidding distance. When he saw that the Elite Grill was open, he was unable to resist the temptation of a cup of coffee. So he lumbered inside, legs aching, and managed to gain a seat at the counter. Except for himself, the counterman, and two men drinking beer in a booth, the place was empty.

The counterman was fat, with a nose like an owl's beak and thick, hairy arms, bare beneath his T shirt. He knew Burke: the Jessups often ate in here, for it was cheap and the servings were large. "Workin late tonight, Mr. Jessup?"

"Yep, Fred, I had something I had to finish up. Black coffee, please."

Fred drew a cup and set it before him. It was too hot to drink. Over in the booth, the two beer drinkers were getting loud.

"I tole 'at sonbitch he better let Evelyn alone. He thinks I won't cut 'im, he better not mess around her. I ain't afraid of doin time, I done time before."

Burke turned and looked at them. Garfish, he thought. One of them was squarely built and had the limpid eyes, the slackness around the mouth, of the alcoholic. The other one was skinny, raw-boned, towheaded, with full red lips. A heart with a dagger on it was tattooed on his forearm, beneath his rolled-up sleeve.

" 'At's right," the alcoholic said encouragingly. "You cut 'im. I hope you cut 'is goddam guts out."

Burke turned back to the counter. "Nice people," he said in a low voice.

"Bums," Fred said tightly. "God, the bums you git in a place like this."

He drew himself a cup of coffee and lit a cigarette and leaned on the counter.

"I read your paper today," he said. "Read that editorial you wrote."

"Oh," Burke said, bracing himself. "What did you think of it?"

"Lot of good stuff in it," Fred said, surprisingly. "There's a lotta these big mules in town got the idea ain't nobody got any right to live but them. This always has been a town where the little man gits treated like dirt, don't matter what color he is. Of course, you understand I ain't sayin I want anybody to come along and set niggers up alongside of me. But you got to hand it to them niggers, they got guts."

"Yep," Burke said, "they sure have."

"I told my old lady the other night, I halfway hope them niggers will make that bus company knuckle under. It would serve some of these big-assed businessmen right, teach 'em a lesson."

Burke looked at Fred keenly. "That could be right dangerous talk around Hannington, couldn't it?"

"Well, I don't talk like that to everybody. A man's got to make a livin, you know, and God knows they make it hard enough for you as it is. But you wouldn't have wrote that editorial if you didn't feel the same way." He laughed deep in his chest. "Besides, ain't no-body going to bother *me*."

Burke sipped his coffee, wondering how many more like Fred Earnhart there were in Hannington, in the South. People with an essential sense of fairness, but, like the Christians of early Rome or disguised infidels in an armed Islamic camp, afraid to speak until some brother had given them a secret sign.

He felt buoyed, a little more optimistic. "Well, I believe the Negroes are going to win. I happen to know Houston Whitley—he's the head of this whole thing. And if what he tells me is the truth, they're going to be just like a snapping turtle—they're going to hang on and not let go until it thunders."

"This Whitley—for a nigger, he must be quite a guy."

"For anybody, he's quite a guy," Burke said. "Hell, I knew him when he was a little raggedy-ass kid out on a plantation. He and I used to play together. His daddy was an ordinary sharecropper. And Huse pulled himself up by his bootstraps, got himself a college edu-cation—he gave up a good job as a high school principal here to take this thing on. I can't help but pull for him. I don't happen to think the world's going to come to an end if Negroes get a decent break. It might be the best thing ever happened to the South." He realized that in the lightheadedness of fatigue his voice had risen until it was almost shrill, and he lowered it. "But they've still got a fight ahead of 'em."

Fred sipped his coffee. "Well," he muttered in a low voice, "I'll tell you just how I feel about it. There's some niggers I wouldn't mind associatin with, and there's a hell of a lot of 'em I don't want to have nothin to do with. And I feel just the same way about white people." He dropped to a whisper. "I'd rather sit next to a clean nigger on a bus than one of them lintheads back yonder in that booth, I'll tell you that. I don't want nobody forcin anybody on me, black or white. I'll pick my own friends, and how I pick 'em is my own goddam business."

Burke had finished the coffee. He slipped a dime on the counter. "That's fair enough," he said. "Well, I'm beat, Fred, I'm going home. See you tomorrow."

"Yes, sir, Mr. Jessup. Take it easy."

Maybe it was the coffee, maybe it was the conversation with Fred; anyhow, the parking lot no longer seemed so far way. Main Street at this time of night was deserted; he was glad of that, because he was always afraid on a crowded sidewalk. He dreaded the thought of being knocked over and then pitied.

Like a goddam beetle on its back, he thought. He let out a long sigh. He had almost forgotten what it had been like to be whole and strong, to be able to run, to climb, to kick—or to make love to a woman without all sorts of delicate and embarrassing arrangements and makeshifts.

And that, he told himself, was the worst part of it. Not to be able to be a whole, complete man in bed. Always to feel that you were not so much a man making love as you were a baby being tended to. Maggie, he thought with returning bitterness, had certainly short-changed herself in that department when she had married him. And it was odd that she did not seem to mind, for he knew that there was a deep strain of violent sexuality within her.

It was a dirty trick, he told himself, for me to ever let her marry me. But I wanted her so much. But what have I been able to give her? Not a goddam thing. Not a decent living, not any security, not even any real satisfaction in bed. And yet, she never bitches. Even though we both know she'd be better off without me.

She should have married somebody like Cary, he thought. Somebody who could have given her everything. They would have been good for each other—Cary could have given her security and she could have educated him, knocked some of those case-hardened hand-me-down ideas of his out of him. Maggie is just the girl who could have done it. . . . If I had any consideration for her, he thought, his spirits reaching bottom again, I'd go ahead and do what Dad did when he found out he'd reached the end of his rope, when he woke up one day and realized he was trapped by what he was and declined to be trapped: I'd blow my damn brains out and give her a chance while she's still got some time left.

And then he realized with disgust—he was halfway down the block now—just how sorry for himself he had been feeling. That was something he detested, and, full of self-contempt, he straightened up and reached out farther with the canes. The hell with that noise, he thought. If I think I've got it rough, at least *I* don't have to live with Mary Scott.

He laughed sardonically at that and forced himself to move along more swiftly. He had hit bottom and rebounded. None of his problems was insoluble. After all, they weren't chained to Hannington. So the paper was flubbing, so what? So you took your kick in the teeth like a man and you told Hannington to go to hell, and you went back North and you and Maggie both got jobs on a good daily and you settled down with a little security and the knowledge that you'd had your fling. The main thing was not to get bogged down in self-pity. A man could get so he couldn't see the woods for the trees. That was what had happened to his father, bogged down by debt, by the knowledge of his own mediocrity, by a hopeless affair with another woman. And yet, it could all have been straightened out, bit by bit and inch by inch, if the old man hadn't panicked and lost his perspective.

He had almost reached the railroad station, and he quit thinking now and gave all his attention to getting down the curb, across the wide street and up the other side. There was a wide, dark parking lot between the station and the express warehouse that flanked it, and he felt a little uneasy about having left his car there for so long. Station and warehouse were both deserted this late, and the car would be a sitting duck for anybody who wanted it badly enough. Although, grinning, he could could imagine the consternation of an automobile thief confronted with the special controls the VA had financed.

As he made the far side of the street and climbed the curb, he glanced back the way he had come. He was a little surprised to see two men crossing the street not far way, in the middle of the block. He thought he recognized them, the square-set man and the lean one, the two drunks in the café, bound home now, he guessed, to some shabby boardinghouse or mill-hill hovel beyond the station.

He reached the parking lot and turned into its asphalt expanse. It was unlighted and so deep in shadow that he could not even see whether the car was there or not. He moved more slowly now, groping carefully with the canes. You'd think the railroad company would put some lights out here, he thought.

He heard a train blowing somewhere in the distance. He heard the shuffle of his own built-up shoes and the tiny whispers of the rubber tips of the canes. He heard the footsteps of the two men on the sidewalk, heard them talking in low, thick tones, but he could not make out any words.

He was anxious to get through the darkness to his car. He felt helpless and vulnerable in a place like this. If he were whole, he would not have given it a second thought, but— He tried to move across the asphalt more swiftly.

Then he halted.

The voices had ceased, but he could still hear the footsteps of the men. They were unrhythmic, as if the men were very drunk. He turned, saw the outlines of them against the lighted street. And then he realized that, instead of passing the parking lot, they were coming into it too.

Something lifted the short hairs on the back of his neck. A quick, senseless fear contracted his entrails. Of course it was just two drunks taking a shortcut, but . . . He began to walk as swiftly as he could —but still with excruciating slowness—toward where his car was parked at the far end of the lot.

But the steps were coming at double the pace of his own. They were very close now, and he saw he was not going to make the car. He told himself that there was really no reason to feel this panic, to feel at bay, but he turned in the direction of the sound of the steps and clamped his hand on one of the canes in a different manner, so it could be used as a weapon.

He stood very still, holding his breath, waiting for them to pass by.

But they were not going to pass by.

He heard one of them say, "There's th' sonbitch."

Then they were coming up to him, two darker shapes in the darkness.

Burke felt cold all over. God, he thought, if I only had two good legs. Then the fear was replaced with anger. He shoved himself erect on the canes, bracing on one, gripping the other one so he could swing it if he had to.

He could see them halting, facing him, five feet away. "Yeah . . ." one of them said gustily.

Burke was pleased with the calm strength of his own voice. "All right, boys. What can I do for you?"

They did not answer him directly. But one of them said, "Let's git the fuckin nigger-lover," and they walked up very close to him, very slowly.

"You fuckin nigger-lover," one of them said harshly. "You love them fuckin niggers, don't you?"

"All right," Burke said savagely and he started to raise the clubbed cane. At that moment one of them giggled and the other cane went flying out from under him.

Like a beetle on its goddam back, he thought bitterly but without despair as he landed hard on the asphalt. He could see them standing over him. "Help!" he yelled, and he lashed futilely with the cane he still held. "Help!"

"Won't do you no good to yell," a voice said. "This is what you fuckin nigger-lovers got comin to you."

The brogan toe caught him in the ribs with terrific impact. He doubled, writhing, as the other cane was snatched away from him. A foot caught him in the back, directly on the spine, and he tried to scream, but only a strangled squeak came out. Somebody stumbled over his feet and the agony was worse.

"Kick the goddam shit out of him," he heard one of them grate from what seemed miles away. "Kick his fuckin head in." He tried to cover his face with his hands, but he was too late. A kick with terrible force smashed into nose and mouth and jaw, and his throat filled with blood.

Then they were both kicking him everywhere and all he could feel was rage at not being able to arise and kill them, at having to lie here and let them kill him instead, and then, even in the blackness he saw the foot poised above his face, saw it come down stomping; it blotted out everything and then he felt and thought nothing more.

9 As soon as it was apparent that they were going to win, the bombings started.

Many of the forty-odd pickup stations for the car pool had been set up in churches.

In one night three of these and the home of Charles Bell were dynamited. The churches were empty at the time, and the Bells were eating supper in their kitchen when the front of their house was suddenly blasted inward. It was fortunate that none of them had been in the living room, for the dynamite must have made it a hell of shattered glass and flying wood.

As soon as he heard about it, Huse drove flat-out to the Bells'.

Bell lived not far from his church—which had also been blasted—in one of the more prosperous outskirts that had come to rim the back side of Little Hammer. Already an immense crowd had gathered, a murmuring, ugly throng of Negroes, buzzing with outrage like an overturned hive of bees. Bell, tall, dark, outwardly unruffled, was standing before them on the shattered remains of his porch, desperately trying to make himself heard. "Please, please," he was calling. "Please, everyone calm yourself." Beside him Huse recognized two white men, Mayor Simon Cameron and Chief of Police Meston.

Huse tried to shove through the crowd. A policeman grabbed him, thrusting a billy club into his stomach. "All right, nigger, jest you stay back."

A dark giant in overalls beside them put his face close to the policeman. "That's Mr. Whitley to you," he snarled. "An' you let him by." His hand was across the bib of his overalls as if he were holding something beneath it; Huse was certain he saw the outline of a pistol.

The policeman said nothing, but the billy club dropped away. Huse put his hand on the arm of the man in overalls. "Brother," he said, almost fiercely, "remember—we return violence with love."

The big man's eyes were lambent, savage with anger. "I got a thirty-eight I'd like to love somebody with."

"No," Huse said intensely. "No, you want to ruin everything? Remember what you've been taught. Remember the mass meetings."

Weekly mass meetings—always attended to overflowing—had been held ever since the beginning of the boycott, their primary purpose to indoctrinate, hammer into each individual consciousness, the concept of nonviolence.

Now, looking into the eyes of the big man with the .38, Huse felt that everything for which he had striven was delicately balanced on the edge of disaster. This was not, he knew, the only armed man in the crowd, or the only one embittered with killing rage. His hand tightened on the man's arm.

"You have got to believe," he said. "You have got to walk like Christ."

The big man's eyes met his, still swirling with rage. "The bastards," the big man said throatily, and he swallowed hard. A kind of shudder racked him. "All right," he said gustily. "All right." And he turned away.

Huse pushed on through the crowd, which recognized him—he was known now by every Negro in Hannington. When he gained the shattered porch, Bell turned to him, face taut. "You talk to them. That's a powder keg out there."

"Tell them to disperse," Mayor Cameron said. His voice was shaky. He was tall, saturnine, bald; and right now he appeared very frightened. "Believe me, whoever did this will suffer for it. We'll not have this sort of thing in Hannington. I never— Tell them that and tell them to disperse. We don't want bloodshed."

Huse looked at him levelly for a second. "You announced you were going to get tough. What did you expect after you said that?" Then he turned back to face the crowd.

They knew he was up there, and they were watching him, and the air was almost crackling with the electricity of their arousal. Every word, he knew, had to be right; a single wrong one could turn Hannington into an abattoir. There was not an inch of leeway for mistake.

He mustered all the force and persuasiveness of a voice now well trained by much speaking. "My friends, give me your attention!"

The crowd was silent.

"Above all, we must not lose our heads. A terrible wrong has been done here, but we must not compound it. I implore you, if you are carrying a weapon, take it home immediately. If you do not have one, do not seek to get one. Let us rid ourselves of all weapons of vengeance but our love. Remember the words of Jesus: *Love your enemies . . . pray for them that despitefully use you.* If we attempt to live by the sword, we will perish by the sword. We will continue to love our white brothers regardless of their misguided deeds; only by that love can we change them, not with weapons. Let us not forfeit all our gains; let us not forfeit God's blessing by yielding to hatred. Let us all go home now and pray in thanksgiving that preacher Bell's family was spared. I ask you, please, disperse. Go to your homes."

For a long moment, there in the darkness lit by the floodlights of police cars and fire trucks, the crowd was silent. Huse did not know whether he had won or lost.

Then a man's voice shouted, "Amen." Another took up the cry, and another. Somebody else yelled, "God bless you, Houston Whitley." Then, slowly but definitely, there was a surge of movement; they were dispersing.

Huse was aware that his face was drenched with cold sweat. He watched them go, somehow managing a smile all the while, but his knees were weak when he finally turned to Cameron and Meston, the police chief.

Cameron said, "Whew . . . that was close." His voice regained a trace of its old asperity. "Whitley, you did a wise thing. We could have had a race riot. Now, let me tell you something. This city is going to make every effort to apprehend these bombers. We'll even post a reward if necessary. We're not going to tolerate anything like this from anybody, white or colored."

"That's very reassuring," Huse said without a trace of sarcasm. "Would you like to see some of the threatening notes preacher Bell and I have received? Maybe they'd give you some clues. You might start with known members of the KKK."

"Listen," Meston said. "Don't you try to tell us how to handle our business."

Huse turned to him. "All right, Chief," he said calmly. "But I will tell you one thing. If you don't want violence tonight, you'd better see that not a single policeman goes into the Negro sections. Not on foot, not in squad cars. These people want to be nonviolent, but they're only human, and if your men go down into Little Hammer I won't guarantee anything. I can't be everywhere at once."

"I'll be goddamned if I'll have you try to tell the police department where—" Meston's florid face twisted with rage.

Cameron put a hand on his arm. "All right, Chief." He looked at Huse. "It's a reasonable request. We'll keep the police out of the Negro sections tonight." He hesitated. "Again I'd like to say I'm sorry about this. I had no idea—" As if he could not force any further apology out, he turned and stepped down off the ruined porch. "Come on, Chief," he said, and they walked across the splinter-strewn yard to a police car.

When they had gone, Bell rubbed his face. "The angel of the Lord has sure been with me and mine tonight," he said in a trembling voice, and he leaned against a slanting post as if his knees had given way. He put his hand over his eyes. After he had stood like that for a few moments, he straightened up. "Huse, look out for yourself. I'm surprised they didn't try to get you. You're the one they really want."

That had been a tense night, but both sides had kept their parts of the bargain, and the next morning the danger of mass violence was over.

Huse had remained awake nearly all night; even after he had finally gone to bed, he could not sleep. With Della restless beside him, he lay tense; his stomach knotted every time there was the sound of an automobile anywhere in the street outside. Once one roared past the house and he held his breath, but nothing happened.

Della lay tightly against him; Otis wheezed gently in the crib in the corner. Della put her arm about him and clung to him. He could feel her breath on his shoulder.

They had, he thought, been very close during these past several months, closer than ever before in their marriage. It was not just the increased pressures on them that had strengthened the bond; it was that he no longer was borne down so by guilt. He no longer imagined disappointment or silent condemnation of his inadequacies and cowardices in everything between them. He himself was never quite free of a sense of wonder at the power that infused him; until all this began, he had never been intensely religious, but so much had happened to him, he had accomplished so much, that he had come to believe, as Bell insisted, that they had all been touched with the hand of God. In codifying the nonviolent doctrine, he had delved more deeply into both philosophy and theology than ever before; he concerned himself with the dynamics of love. He had already known the Greek word and definition for the force he had mobilized: *agape,* the basic, essential and abundant love that existed as part of every unwarped nature, having nothing to do with either friendship or desire, a selfless, generalized love great enough to encompass even enemies. It was the reverse side of the coin of hate, and, he was beginning to understand, quite as universal and powerful a force: Christ had managed to call forth enough of it to found a religion, Gandhi enough to free a nation. If he could somehow evolve definite, measured techniques for using the force of love, he saw available to him a novel and tremendous weapon, one the opposition had no field manuals on defeating.

He moved Della's arm and turned over and put his own arm about her. Her warmth was comforting. Briefly he wondered what sort of life he would be living now if he had married Virginia Crane. The pang came as usual, but it was not so sharp now, and it was lost in the thought that he must get Della and Otis to some place of safety tomorrow. If they had come after Charles Bell, they would come after him, too.

At last he slept. The next morning, when he went out on the stoop to get the paper, he saw something peculiar in the shrubbery that grew by the front wall of the house. He went down the steps and walked around to take a closer look, and then his flesh turned cold. It was twelve sticks of dynamite bound together in a bomb that had failed to explode.

The police, of course, did not catch the dynamiters, any more than they had caught the man or men who had stomped Burke Jessup to death. Huse installed floodlights on his house, and his neighbors volunteered to take turns standing guard at night; Bell and Marfield took the same measures. Over her protests, Della was sent with Otis to live with her aunt in North Carolina.

The bombings had left their mark on Houston Whitley. He fought a terrible inner battle that he knew he must win if the boycott was to continue. Every nerve and fiber of his being flamed with hatred and the desire for revenge. He knew that merely to control the hatred, the cry of vengeance within himself, to suppress it and dissimulate before the people to whom he talked of love, would be ruinous. His sincerity was the impetus that kept the movement going. It could not be compromised.

So for nearly two days after Della had left, he was sunk deep in battle with himself. He had to face the question: Did he really believe in the power of love? Did he really believe in nonviolence? Could he love his enemies—even when they tried to bomb his wife and child?

It was a struggle that racked him, leaving him burned-out and hollow inside. He went to Charles Bell with the problem, found that Bell was doing battle with the same aspect of his own humanity. They lent each other strength; at last Huse emerged from the ordeal convinced that he had won, that he had purged himself of the ability to hate. To decry wrong and injustice, yes; to oppose it, yes; even to hate it as a fact. But not to hate the people who perpetrated it. The final test was when he addressed the weekly mass meeting. Again he talked of love and nonviolence to the people, and he found himself believing what he said, found no trace of insincerity in himself, and saw that he impressed and moved them as always. So he had won that struggle, and he did not think he would ever have to fight it again.

But in the course of it another kind of knowledge had come to him, too—an awareness of the likelihood of his own early death. He was a marked man, and sooner or later they would get him. It was not an easy thing to live with. A sniper, a bomber, a hit-and-run assassin—there was, really, nothing to prevent any of these from getting him any time someone took the notion. Conceivably it might even be a member of his own race—for not all of them were proponents of the boycott; besides the minority indifferent to it, there was a smaller minority who, because of fear, self-interest, or wounded pride, opposed it savagely. Merit Crane was one of these; his own brother Bish another.

He had already fought battles with this latter minority. They were not stupid, and they had tried to undercut him or smear him in a dozen different ways. But somehow he had always managed to turn their attacks and to retain unquestioned leadership.

Meanwhile the bombings continued, fortunately with no casualties. At last, though, the dynamiters made a mistake, and one of the few white ministers who had dared speak out against the anarchy into which Hannington had been plunged was badly slashed by flying glass when his manse was bombed.

Immediately a reaction set in; the city was aroused by this offense against a white man in a way that it had never been by the bombing of Negro homes and churches, and the wave of revulsion that swept through it redounded to the benefit of the boycotters. Even the rabidly segregationist papers were appalled; for the first time they, along with influential businessmen, raised their voices, setting limits to the terror. More white ministers found courage to speak up in their pulpits.

Now, after almost a year, Huse took hope that the end was in sight. The opposition seemed to be running out of steam; the bus company was unashamedly begging for relaxation of the city ordinances. Even the obscene and threatening phone calls, which had become a part of his daily life, tapered off a bit. Perhaps, he dared think, there was daylight ahead.

The police took him just as he came out of Little Hammer after a visit to Lucy.

It was dark. As he gained the paved street in his car, he saw head-lights pull out of a driveway and fall in behind him. He was afraid. He had two choices. If it was thugs, assassins—and it easily could be—he should speed up, try to outrun them. If it was the police, he should slow down, drive with the greatest care to commit no traffic violation.

He made his decision and slowed down. The headlights slowed, too, and stayed behind him for a block as he drove through the poorly lighted shabby rind of white dwellings that rimmed this edge of Little Hammer. Then the headlights speeded up; the car swung alongside, bearing hard toward his right fender; he was dazzled by a sudden spotlight beam and pulled over to the curb.

The three policemen who jumped out of the car were all big men. One of them blocked the right door, two others ran around to the left. As Huse took the keys out of the switch, the door beside him was yanked open. A big hand seized his arm and pulled, dragging him sprawling from behind the wheel.

"All right, Whitley," one of them said. "You're under arrest." His hand was on his pistol holster. "Turn around and lean against the car and put your hands behind your head."

"You mind telling me the charge, officer?" Huse asked in as mild a voice as he could manage.

"Goddamn you, turn around." He was whirled and slammed against the car. Somebody grabbed his arms and pulled them up and behind so that his hands crossed over the back of his head. "Now stand like that." Then he was being frisked, hands slapping every pocket.

"He's clean," somebody said.

A cop grabbed each arm, hustled him around his own car to the police car. One of them held the back door open while the other shoved him in. He landed heavily on the seat as the third patrolman got in from the other side.

Then he was crowded in the middle between two cops. Each one of them seized a wrist; he felt the cold iron and heard the click of closing handcuffs.

"I repeat," he said sharply, "what is the charge?"

"Shut your goddam mouth, nigger," one of them said and pushed him back against the seat. The driver was behind the wheel now, and the car began to roll.

To go to the police station at City Hall, it should have headed straight downtown. Instead, when it reached an intersection, it turned sharply to the right.

The coldness of fear within Huse deepened. Surely they wouldn't— He said huskily, "Where are you taking me?" He waited until he was sure his voice would not tremble. "This is not the way to the police station."

"Maybe we wanta ride around a little bit first," the one on the right said. The one on the left laughed shortly.

Their route brought them to the southbound highway. They halted at the intersection; then the car swung into traffic, headed away from town.

"I demand to be taken to the police station," Huse said angrily. "I demand to know the charge against me and be allowed to call my lawyer."

The one on the left laughed. "You sure talk a lot, don't you?"

They drove two miles south, then swung off the main highway along a narrow paved road that ran through farming country. Or what had been farming country: it seemed to have all gone to weeds and scrub oak now. There was little moon. The occasional house they passed was dark. Once Huse heard the hollow bell-like voice of a baying hound challenging them from the roadside; somewhere far away a cow was calling agonizedly for the services of a bull.

Then even these country sounds died away as the car headed sharply downhill; and now there was nothing but the towering blackness of swamp forest on either side.

Huse had not spoken since they had turned onto the highway. He was trapped and he knew it; words would do no good. They were taking him out to kill him.

The headlights picked up the iron-pipe railings of a narrow bridge. The car swung off the road onto the shoulder and stopped. "This all right?" the driver said.

"This is fine," one of the policemen in back answered. "I've fished this river—it's good an' deep here. All right, coon, let's git out." He opened the door and dragged Huse across the seat.

They were going to kill him and yet he did not hate them. He was impressed by that, pleased with it. His knees were weak, but he could stand. He thought regretfully of Della and Lucy; probably it would be a long time before his body was found out here in this remote spot; he himself grieved for the agony they would undergo. Deliberately, he drew himself up straight, sucking in great gulps of night air, filling nostrils and lungs with the earth smells he had always loved: water, forest, dew, grass, all the distillations of the wilderness in which they stood.

Then he was shoved roughly toward the bridge. He was forced up against the iron railing. Below him he saw the black, unreflecting waters of a deep swamp river. He thought of Emmett Till, the boy in Mississippi who had vanished, later found drowned, wrapped in chains. It had taken a long time for his body to come to light.

"Now you can beg if you want to," a cop said harshly from behind him. "Go ahead, coon, you got any begging to do, now's the time."

Huse forced himself to stand erect. "I have no begging to do," he said. "But if you'll give me time, I'll pray for you."

"Shit," somebody said from behind him.

One of the policemen was very close to his back now. His voice was soft, full of mockery. "That's a deep river down there, ain't it, nigger? How'd you like a midnight swim? You're a goddam important nigger—you reckon if you was to go over this bridge you could walk on that water?"

"That's what he tells all the niggers he can do," somebody else said. "Let's see how big a liar he is."

They were silent for a moment. Every muscle in Huse was tense. He closed his eyes and began to pray without sound. He said the Lord's Prayer. Below him he could hear the quiet gurgle of the water. Independently of his spirit, his back muscles and something at the base of his skull seemed to be in a panic of their own, waiting for the tearing pain that he knew was bound to come.

He finished the prayer. "For ever and ever, amen," he said under his breath. Why don't they go ahead and do it and get it over with? he thought. Now I lay me down to sleep, I pray the Lord my soul to keep. . . .

A hand seized his arm. "All right, nigger, let's go." He was yanked around, facing the patrol car again. They pushed him toward it, and he stumbled, suddenly about to collapse with relief, legs watery, bowels and bladder threatening to relax.

One of the policemen laughed. "By God, he was scared white, wasn't he?"

"Hell, if he could be white he'd stay scared all the time," another one said, and they shoved him into the car, which seemed a sanctuary now. They turned the car around and drove toward town. He had never been as glad to see any place in his life as he was to see City Hall when the patrol car finally pulled up behind it.

It was the first time he had ever been in jail. The charge, he found when he was booked, was doing forty miles an hour in a thirty-five-mile zone. The time of arrest was given as fifteen minutes before the booking, so that on the records there would be nothing to indicate the long ride into the country. Then they shoved him upstairs and into the bullpen, which was full of Negroes.

Some of them were members of the Civic Improvement Association, who had been arrested that evening in what was apparently a wide sweep. But there were also the usual drunks, knife-fighters, vagrants and sneak thieves. There were no beds in the bullpen; the inmates were expected to sleep on blankets on the floor. There was a single toilet; its flushing handle was broken off and it was clogged brimful.

When Huse was recognized, the others clustered around him, some in awe, some in hope that they could attach themselves to him, others in supplication. He said nothing about his ordeal in the country; if word of that spread, he knew, it would inflame the boycotters, increase the already huge burden of outrage they must balance, endanger nonviolent resistance by that much more. Finally an end to the uproar his admission had caused came when the jailer appeared. "All right, goddammit," the jailer said. He was an immensely paunchy white man with a round, red face, gray hair, and yellow, snaggled teeth. "Shut that goddam racket up."

Huse pressed against the bars. "I demand to be allowed to phone my lawyer."

"I said shut up, nigger," the jailer said. He turned and walked away.

Somebody touched Huse's arm. A short, bent, very dark Negro in ragged clothes crouched before him. He smelled of some unusual alcohol—Sterno or paint thinner, or the violent concoction called "smoke."

"Better be quiet," the bent man said. "Ole Minton, he's *mean*. He'll git some of his boys to kick yo' teeth in, you give 'im trouble."

Huse looked down at him and then, for the first time, smiled. "Thank you for your advice," he said, and he went over to a corner of the cell and sat down. It would not hurt him to spend a night in jail. It would give him a certain prestige, in fact, And it was, he reflected, a lot better than being at the bottom of a swampy river. . . .

Jeff Marfield found him the next morning and made bond for him. Huse did not tell him all of what had happened, either. It was something he would always keep locked within himself. But if they had meant to frighten him into giving up, their tactics had backfired. Instead of weakening him, the ordeal had strengthened him, tempered him as fire tempers steel. He knew now what it was like to put his life on the line for a belief, and knew that he could do it. The haunting fear of his own imminent death lifted and never came back.

He pressed the boycott with renewed vigor. A week of that, and then he received a call from Mayor Cameron asking him to meet with officials of the city and of the bus companies at City Hall.

When he hung up the telephone, he felt like shouting, but he did nothing to disrupt the routine of the office or raise false hopes. Nevertheless, somehow he was already certain that they had won.

Ten days later, television cameras whirred and reporters crowded forward as Houston Whitley, Jeff Marfield, Sarah McLain, Charles Bell, and two other members of the organization boarded a blue-and-white bus marked "Special" at the corner of Main and Kiscoe. It was immediately obvious to Huse that the driver behind the wheel had been carefully picked for this public ceremony of peace. He was young and spruce in his uniform, and he looked intelligent. Nevertheless something flickered in his eyes as they dropped their fares in the box; for a moment his face was set. Then, almost painfully, it racked itself into a smile.

"Good morning," he said, and the words did not sound too forced.

"Good morning," murmured Huse, at the end of the file. He smiled back at the driver and dropped his fare into the box.

"Thank you," the driver said.

"You're quite welcome," Huse said. Then, as the driver put the bus in motion, he joined the others in the block of forward seats that, until now, had been legally and traditionally reserved for whites.

BOOK FOUR
1963

1 It did not often sleet in Muskogee, but it was sleeting now, a steady rattling slash of icy pellets against the windows of the magnificent old walled house belonging to Hoke Moody. When Cary parted the fine wine-colored drapes and looked out into the courtyard, the ground was powdered with white and the sky was a low, sullen cast-iron gray. He could feel the cold radiating inward from the windowpane, and he shivered and let the drapes fall together. He hoped this wouldn't take long; he wanted to get back to Maggie.

The drawing room was furnished very much as it must have been a hundred years before: Moody had bought the contents of the house along with the house itself, purchasing at one swoop all the trappings and apparel of aristocracy, as if his intention had been to buy a heritage. There was a fire in the great Italian marble fireplace, and the men were ranged around it on settees or in rocking chairs. No central heating system yet devised could thoroughly warm the two and a half stories of great, sprawling rooms with their lofty ceilings frescoed and medallioned with plaster ornamentation, and the fire felt good.

Cary went to a tea cart that sat behind the men and poured himself another drink. Moody, directly in front of the fire, swathed in a quilted dressing gown, was talking. He was seventy-four now, and of late his bull voice seemed to have shrunk, withering to a rasped squeak.

"Listen," he was saying, "I know that damned bunch out there. I've dealt with 'em, and I can tell you right now, they'll send troops in here just as quick as they did to Oxford. They don't want to; they'd sooner take a lickin' than have to, with what they've got ahead to get through Congress and knowing it's got to get past me. But from the standpoint of votes, they've just about written us off anyhow. If they can git the nigger vote in the big cities, they'll figure it's worth it."

"We can interpose—" Powell Bradham began. He was older than Moody, seventy-six now, but he needed no dressing gown to keep him warm. The years had extracted the meat and the juice from him, but the big frame was still there, and the gray eyes were not fogged with any senility whatsoever.

"Interpose." Hoke Moody's laugh was short, breathy, contemptuous. "For God's sake, Powell, interpose. They've knocked interposition down in Louisiana; they've knocked it down in Mississippi. It's a goddam dead issue. Interpose . . ." He laughed again; the laugh turned into a cough and he choked and spat into the fire.

Bradham shook his head, turning on Moody a face that looked more than ever like a hawk's. "It's not a dead issue," he said angrily. "It's the core of the whole thing, the constitutional question. That's got to be our defense; that's what we've got to keep throwing back in their faces. The question of constitutionality—we've got to make everybody see how our rights are being invaded. The nigger doesn't make any difference—one nigger in the University's not going to make it fall down and I'm not concerned about him. But I am concerned about fighting 'em every inch of the way on states' rights."

Mitch Moody, Hoke's nephew, was sitting on a hassock directly beside the fire. He swung toward Bradham, his sharp face impatient. "For God's sake, Mr. Powell, don't you understand English?" He stood up, looking at them all, trim, slender, well tailored, his back to the fire.

"States' rights," he said, in a voice almost as nasal as that of his father, Dale. "There isn't any more states' rights so far as the Federal courts are concerned, and we'd be wasting our time worrying about that. What we've got to think about is the corner we've painted ourselves into."

Like a teacher making a point, he wagged a forefinger. "We've hung on these past five or six years because of one thing and one thing only, and that's because we promised there'd never be any integration in Muskogee—never!—and we've kept that promise, except for the city buses. There's not a single nigger in any white school in this state; we haven't integrated a single lunch counter. We're clean, and that's where our power lies. Every time anybody has challenged us, like Curt McKnight and his crowd, we've been able to beat down the challenge. Nobody is going to take this state away from us unless he can prove he can do a better job of maintaining white supremacy—and so far the job we've done is perfect and nobody can pick a hole in it. But if we let this damn nigger into the University, then we're shot. We swore it would never happen, and now we crawfish. That makes us vulnerable."

Hoke Moody nodded. "You've put your finger on it, Mitch. On the one hand, we knuckle under and let the nigger in and it's going to cost us a hell of a lot of votes. On the other hand, if we don't, we're going to have those boys in the Justice Department down on us like a duck on a June bug, bayonets and all. And even my connections won't stop 'em when push comes to shove."

"I'm not worried about the bayonets," Mitch snapped. "I'm worried about the votes."

Hoke laughed, no longer a deep chuckle but a cackle. "Now you're talking, boy."

Mitch's face was flushed; his eyes glittered. "This nigger. This Bell. Has he been checked out thoroughly? If we can find something that would disqualify him . . ."

"We went through all that when he first submitted his application," Cary said wearily, as if he were addressing a not very bright child. With ten years in politics behind him now, including a successful campaign for Lieutenant Governor, he was in no mood to be tolerant of the younger Moody's arrogant self-confidence, his brash contempt for the opinions of others. Besides, he thought, someday I am going to have to fight him. . . . "He's clean as a whistle. Honor student. Preacher's son. You can't blackmail him and you can't scare him. We've turned him inside out at every hearing."

"Well, it was a thought," Mitch said, showing no retreat. "There's still bound to be some way to wiggle out." He turned. "Colonel Whipple, we haven't heard from you yet. You got any ideas?"

The lanky man on the settee looked at them one by one. He was in his late fifties, his face bony and sun-bronzed, his hair close-cropped and gray. His eyes were startlingly blue, and there were fans of wrinkles at their corners. Though he had come with neither a big hat nor high-heeled boots, he gave the impression of a man who would be at home in both.

"Well," he said, his voice a slow drawl, "I don't know for sure if it's in order for me to speak yet. What about it, Senator?"

Moody nodded. "Sure, Terry. You said you had a piece to say. Well, say it."

Col. Terence Whipple stood up, well over six feet. He thrust big hands into his hip pockets. Cary paid close attention; he had been wondering about Whipple's presence here. Whipple had been introduced only as a retired army colonel; apparently he was a friend Moody had made on the Armed Services Committee.

"Well," he said, "I appreciate the Senator lettin me sit in on this. I know it's a highly confidential meetin, and, of course, I'll honor that confidence after I leave. But I'm sure y'all realize that the problem y'all are facin now is one of more than local interest. And copin with it is exactly what the organization I'm president of is set up and financed to do. That's why I contacted the Senator's brother and offered my services."

Dale Moody, who was sitting next to Whipple on the settee, turned to Hoke, and then to Powell Bradham. "You people listen to this," he said. "The Colonel's come up with something that might do a lot of good."

"I reckon most of you have heard of the Constitutional Legion," Whipple went on. "We originally organized in order to be able to repel the armed invasion of this country by Russia or the United Nations. Our members are given military trainin with standard military weapons, are taught guerrilla tactics. But after Oxford, Mississippi, it looks like before we worry about Russia and the United Nations, we got to worry about invasion from Washington." The drawl was leaving his voice now; he was speaking with military crispness.

"Now, as soon as we found out about the Supreme Court orderin that Bell nigger into Muskogee University, my people over in Texas authorized me to draw up a plan of resistance. That was the trouble in Oxford—nobody really had any sort of plan worked out, and a wonderful opportunity was missed. If we'd been allowed to take charge at Oxford, you wouldn't be havin this trouble you're havin right now."

Cary said, a little impatiently, "All right, Colonel. What is your plan?"

The Colonel looked at him with those bright blue eyes. "I'm comin to it, sir, I'm comin to it," he said amiably.

Then his voice sharpened again. "Briefly, gentlemen, my plan is this. The first part of it depends on you. Mr. Bradham here has suggested interposition. I submit, gentlemen, that the doctrine of interposition is not dead. And that it can be very useful to you. I don't see how you can yield to these Jews that are tryin to ram that nigger down your throat without puttin up some kind of fight, even if it's just a show for your electorate. You interpose the constitutional sovereignty of the state of Muskogee between the Federal government and the University. Of course the courts will knock it down, but at least all the people will know you've tried. Then . . . then you warn the Justice Department that if they go ahead and put the nigger in school, there will be violence, but you'll try to control it with the state police."

His long, thin mouth quirked in a slight grin. "All right. Now your skirts are clear with the voters and with the Justice Department. And now this is where the Constitutional Legion comes in."

He paused, his eyes sweeping them one by one.

"I, gentlemen, can promise you the assistance of as many as five hundred armed, trained citizens from outside your state. These men will resist the nigger's entry into the school by riot and violence. They will be from half a dozen Southern states, but none from Muskogee, so that you are always in the position of being able to disclaim them. There will be rioting, gentlemen, that will make Oxford, Mississippi, look like a ladies' tea party, and in the course of it I can assure you that the nigger will get killed."

He was smiling almost happily.

"The Federal government will send in troops. My men will oppose them. We will not hurt any of the soldiers, not any more than we have to." He paused. "But I do not intend to yield until a Federal soldier has been forced to kill a white man."

He stopped speaking, and the room was absolutely silent, with every man in it looking at him as if hypnotized.

His voice vibrated. "Think of it, gentlemen. A Southern white man killed—in plain sight and unmistakably—by a Federal soldier trying to put a nigger in a school. Think of how it would mobilize the entire Deep South. It's the one thing that's been lackin in this situation so far. Think of how it would put an end to indecision, to all this wishy-washiness and fear of resistance." Now his voice was harsh. "I promise you gentlemen, if just one Southern white man could be killed by a Federal soldier over a nigger, there wouldn't be enough Federal troops in Christendom to put another nigger in a white school anywhere in the Deep South. And with the nigger killed, too, there'll never be another one foolhardy enough even to dare to try to bust his way into a white man's school."

Cary stood almost frozen by the tea cart, the half-empty glass in his hand. He looked at Whipple incredulously.

"You'd deliberately get one of your own men killed?"

Whipple's face was quizzical. "Is there a man in this room that wouldn't be willin to die to stop this Jew-Communist-United Nations conspiracy? My men, sir, are Americans, and they are Southerners. They are willin to lay down their lives before they will submit to tyranny."

Hoke Moody said quietly, "Fix me another drink, will you, Cary?" He was rocking, his chair moving with a slow, steady rhythm.

Powell Bradham cleared his throat. "It's a drastic prescription," he said. "But you're right in one respect, Colonel. It would mobilize the South." He struck his thigh with one bony, spotted fist. "By God, it would put some starch into a lot of backbones that have been willing to sell states' rights down the river!"

Cary's eyes shuttled to his father. His father was standing very straight, his face set. Whipple was smiling at his father, as if in appreciation.

Cary set the whiskey bottle down so hard the sound of it brought all heads but Hoke Moody's around.

"It's a lot of damn foolishness!" he said.

Whipple's eyes turned cold; he took a step forward. "Sir," he said.

Cary moved toward the group, handed Moody a glass. "I said it was a lot of damn foolishness." Deliberately he made his words precise, distinct. "And it would ruin the state of Muskogee."

Whipple's eyes locked with Cary's. "I fail to see any basis for that statement, sir. No Muskogeeans need be connected with it."

"Horseshit," Cary said. He chopped the air with his hand. "Do you think if you start a riot at the University our people are going to keep out of it? Hell, man, you don't want to start a riot, you want to start a civil war."

"It may come to that eventually," Whipple said evenly.

"I thought you were a Regular Army officer," Cary said. "A career soldier that took an oath—"

Something flickered across Whipple's face. "I'm retired," he snapped. "And I'm well out of it. A soldier no longer has the right to speak his mind. The civilians in the Pentagon are all tools of the UN. A patriot doesn't dare open his mouth."

"So that's it," said Cary coldly. "They forced you to retire."

"Nobody forced me to do anything! Besides, Mr. Bradham, if I recollect correctly, there was another U.S. Regular who was forced to choose sides in a similar situation. His name was Robert E.—"

"Well, hello, General Lee," said Cary caustically. His tone was biting. "Lee resigned his commission. Have you done that yet, Colonel?"

He turned away from Whipple and faced the others without waiting for an answer.

"We've got to use some sense in this situation. Right now we've got teams roaming the North, trying to bring industry down here. We need that industry: cotton's shot, tobacco's shot, this state's going to be on the financial rocks if we don't get something in here besides textile mills. And I say that as a member by marriage of the Butler family. I know: textiles are all we've got now and they can't carry the load alone. Not with the foreign competition we've got, Japan and Hong Kong—"

"And who built up that foreign competition?" Whipple lashed. "Don't you know that was part of the whole plot? To impoverish the South and bring it to heel? This country did it with its foreign-aid money. It's all part of the big picture, the conspiracy—"

"I don't care who built it up," Cary snapped. "If it's part of the conspiracy, then it's just as important to fight that part of it by getting other industry down in here as it is to fight the part of it that wants to put a nigger in college. If it's a conspiracy, we're striking just as much of a blow for liberty by ruining their plans there as we are by blocking that nigger. This state, the whole South, can't fight without resources. We tried that once before, remember? And it didn't work. As long as we're broke, we're never going to draw any water, but when we get nice and fat and rich, we can make a hell of a lot of people listen to us. If we go raising hell at the University and make a national scandal, we haven't got a prayer of bringing any new mills, any new money, in here. And that's more important than one nigger in a college."

"*You* may think so," Dale Moody retorted. "But that one nigger could be the lever that would upset our whole applecart. We've gone too far to back down. If we just roll over and play dead, none of us may ever hold public office again. We'll be tagged as a bunch of cowards by every voter in Muskogee."

"Not if we play our cards right. You know the University well as I do. There's a dozen different ways that nigger can be pressured out once he's in. He won't last two weeks anyhow, so why raise Cain about letting him in? Look at Autherine Lucy in Alabama. It didn't take the University of Alabama but a month to find grounds for expelling her back in 1956. We can have that nigger in and out again long before election day and nobody getting hurt."

His father spoke. "But the principle of states' rights will have been infringed one more time, and they'll be congratulating themselves on having weakened it just that much more—"

"I know; that galls me as much as it does you." He paused; his voice slowed. "But regardless of that, I say we'd be fools to let Colonel Whipple and his army set foot inside this state when the nigger goes to register."

Whipple's face was very white beneath the tan. "I was under the impression that of all the Southern states, Muskogee was the home of the most fighting blood."

Cary looked at him squarely. "Colonel, I'm not a Regular, like you. But I spent four years in the Army Air Force. You're welcome to examine my record—or maybe my father's before me. Or the record of any other Bradham. I don't think we need you to tell us what fighting blood is . . . or patriotism, either. And back when I was soldiering, a man didn't draw the pay of the United States Army and plot against it at the same time—not even retirement pay—and still call himself a soldier."

"Sir, I will not stand—" Whipple took another step forward.

Hoke Moody raised a hand. "All right, all right," he said in his shrunken voice. "Both of you, ease off. We'll have none of that." He rocked for a moment. Cary could not see his face, but he heard Moody let out a wheezing breath.

Then Moody's voice was conciliatory. "Colonel, we appreciate the offer you have made, and you can tell your backers in Texas that. But I'm afraid we're going to have to decline it. I reckon Muskogee better try to kill its own snakes without bringing in any outside help. We'll figure out something; we'll put on some kind of show for the voters. But it looks like when push comes to shove, we'll have to let the nigger go to school for a while until we can arrange to kick him out. Thanks anyway, Colonel."

Whipple looked down at Moody. "Very well, Senator," he said thinly, his face taut. Then he raised his head and looked at Cary again.

"Young man," he said, "I shudder to think of the fate of Muskogee if everybody's as soft on Communism as you are. If there are many like you, the Reds and Jews and niggers will have this state in their pocket before you can say Jack Robinson. I trust that there are not." He picked up his hat from the settee and strode past Cary, who stood rigidly, to the door. There he paused.

"Thank you for your time, gentlemen," he said. "If you change your mind, remember, the offer remains open—not only in this crisis, but in the others that are bound to come. If we can be useful to you any time, just holler. We'll be waitin to hear from you— because you can't give here without givin there, and you can't give there without givin somewhere else—and pretty soon you'll wake up and find you don't have a damn thing left to give. Before that time comes, we hope to hear from you. Good day." He opened the door and went out.

When it had closed behind him, the room was silent. Cary went to the window, saw Whipple emerge into the courtyard, cross it, head bent against the sleet, and exit through the iron gate to the street. He turned back, shutting the drapes.

"That man's crazy," he said. "He's dangerous-crazy."

Nobody answered him.

"A private army," Cary said. "Somebody ought to do something about him."

"I don't know whether he's as crazy as you think," Mitch Moody said, and he spat into the fire.

"Whether he's crazy or not," Hoke Moody said, "I don't want him in Muskogee. Sure, he had it all planned—and it might work out just like he said. But I got one rule, and I'm not going to break it on account of a nigger or anybody else—and that's that nobody runs this state but me. I'm not going to have anybody come in here and ask me to give him authority to raise as much hell as he sees fit and let the situation get out of my hands. When something happens in this state, it'll be because Hoke Moody wants it to happen, not be- cause some oil king in Texas wants it to. And that's that."

2 A half hour later, Cary and his father stood in the splattering sting of whipping sleet on the sidewalk next to Powell Bradham's automobile. The older man's overcoat collar was turned up, his hat pulled down; otherwise he seemed to ignore, be impervious to, the weather.

"You took a chance in there this afternoon," he said, and his voice was not pleased. "Suppose Hoke Moody had wanted to go along with Whipple? You'd have isolated yourself."

"I'm sorry," Cary said. He had expected this reprimand and there was resentment of it in his voice. "But my belly's a little too weak to stand a man like Whipple." He tried to turn his face away from the sleet. "You and I have been shot at by people like him in our time."

"I'd go easy on comparisons like that if I were you," Bradham said. "At least Whipple's willing to act. Hoke Moody will just sit there and let them put that nigger in. Expediency, that's his only God. He doesn't care about Muskogee; all he cares about is what's good for the Moodys. If he thought the voters would let him get away with it, he'd sell this state down the river and knuckle under to Washington tomorrow if they made it worth his while."

"I don't doubt that," said Cary.

"Now, our plans are too important for you to go taking chances. We're getting close to home now. Just a few more years and we'll have this state back in our hands and run it like it should be run, and then there'll be one state in the Union to serve as a model for others, anyhow; one state that'll stay sovereign and manage its own affairs. That's too important—I've worked too long and hard—for you to jeopardize it with any kind of loose language that might make Moody suspicious of you. You can't get elected without him."

"Just the same," Cary said sharply, "I'm a grown man. My God, I'm forty years old. When I get ready to speak my mind, I aim to speak it, just like I did today."

"Don't be a damned fool!" his father snapped. "What's got into you, anyhow? That woman must be—" He broke off; his face softened. "I'm sorry, son. I had my say about that. I'm not going to mess with that part of your life. You'll have to realize for yourself how dangerous that could be to you." He looked at the pavement for

a moment. Then he raised his head and smiled faintly and clapped
Cary on the shoulder. "I know it's been a long haul, son. Longer
for me, even, than for you. Bear with me a spell more. That's all I
ask. Will you do that?"

Cary felt some of the tension drain from himself. He smiled back
at his father. "I've come this far," he said. "I reckon I can go a little
farther."

His father tapped his arm. "That's the spirit. Now, you get in out
of this sleet before you catch your death of cold." He opened the
door of his own car and slid into the back seat. He leaned partway
out. "When are you and Mary Scott coming over?"

"Soon," Cary said. "Later this week."

"Well, don't be too long. You know your mama."

"Yes, sir, I know her. We'll be there."

His father smiled. "All right. Be careful driving home, son, in all
this bad weather."

"I will," Cary said. He shut the door and moved back as the
chauffeur eased the car away from the curb and out onto the icy
street. He stood there for a moment in the sleet, and then turned to
his own car nearby.

But he was not going home. That, he thought, as he slid in behind
the wheel, is the last place I intend to go. Not as long as Maggie is
waiting for me to come to her. . . .

Hannington was so unused to ice and snow that the smallest flurry
threw the whole city into a mixture of exhilaration and panic. The
state offices had closed as soon as the sleet had begun, and Maggie
had driven straight home to her apartment.

The building in which she lived was not a pretentious one, nor was
it in a very good section of town. This was a concession to Cary; he
seemed to feel more secure with her living here where he would not
be likely to bump into anyone who knew him. She did not mind: she
had carefully arranged for herself a life of utter simplicity, almost
austerity, and the place was good enough.

From the third-story window at which she was sitting now, she
could look down into the yard of the big but run-down house next
door. Watching the sleet batter the broad, glassy leaves of a magnolia almost directly beneath her, encasing the slick greenness in a
thin armor of ice, she thought: I hope it keeps up. I hope it sleets

for a long time. She had a hunger for real winter that had grown more imperious every year.

She remembered how Burke had hated the Northern winters and had wondered at her love for them. A faint grimace of pain crossed her face at the thought of him: even after seven years, his image would spring unexpectedly into her mind with startling clarity, and she could almost hear the easy, biting humor of his speech, with its ineradicable drawl. He was still a constant presence in the pattern of her life and always would be. But she did not think he would have disapproved of the way she lived now. She could imagine him saying, "Sure, you're entitled to somebody. And I'd rather it was Cary than anybody else. You might do him some good."

Or maybe that was just rationalization, part of an elaborate structure of excuses she had erected in her mind. For it had taken a lot of rationalization for her to become the mistress of another woman's husband.

There had been no thought of that at first. On that night when Cary had offered to look for Burke, she had waited with growing uneasiness, a sharp, almost childlike hunger for Burke to hurry and come. It had been a long time since anybody but Burke had kissed her like that; a very long time since anyone with the vitality of Cary had done it, and she felt menaced by her own unexpected response. She wanted the sight of Burke to bring her emotions into balance, to reassure her.

But instead of Burke, it was Cary who had come again, very late, and when she saw the paleness of his face, the grief and dread in his eyes as he stood uncertainly in the doorway, she knew. He told her anyway, as gently as he could, told her how he had found the body in the parking lot and the manner of Burke's death, and when she wanted to rush to where they had taken the body, he stopped her.

"It wouldn't do you any good to see him like he is," Cary said miserably; and he stood firmly against her ever looking at Burke again. She supposed she was glad he had.

She had wanted to tear her garments and her hair and keen; she could see why women did that now. Instead, she just sat numbly on the sofa.

"Goddamn them," Cary said. "If I could just get my hands on them." His voice was full of agony; she remembered that he had loved Burke, too. But her pity for him was lost in the rage that suddenly welled within her, and then, at last, she was screaming.

"He had to come back!" she screamed. "He loved this place so much and insisted on coming back. All he wanted to do was make it a little better, help it to see some truth—and what did it do to him? It kicked him to death! Oh, I hate— I hate—" She became incoherent. Cary just stood helplessly, waiting for Mary Scott, whom he had summoned, to come.

Mary Scott was all sympathy and eagerness to help. She assumed responsibility for the funeral arrangements, displaying the indecent pleasure some women feel in such circumstances. She drove Maggie almost insane; her misguided officiousness was nearly the worst part of the ordeal, and when it was finished and Burke had been buried beside his father and mother in the Methodist cemetery, Maggie despised Mary Scott. Not only had she been condescending; through lack of organizational ability she had bungled a simple funeral, making it an undignified and hectic social event, refusing to be deterred by Maggie's protestations. Furthermore, Mary Scott had been scandalized when Houston Whitley came by to pay his respects and Maggie invited him into the house. "It's all right to talk to them on the porch," she had whispered, wide-eyed with shock, to Maggie. "But not to invite them in, big as anything. Especially that one. *Him,* of all people."

As a matter of fact, Huse, with delicacy, had not wanted to come in, but Maggie had insisted. She took a revengeful pleasure in the uncomfortable, outraged silence of the white visitors in the living room when she introduced him with exquisite courtesy.

When they had withdrawn from the others, she could sense the genuine grief within him. "Mrs. Jessup, I valued Burke more than . . . than any other white friend I ever had. He was a fighter. It will be a long time before we see his like again." Instinctively he took her hand. "He was a *man,* Mrs. Jessup," he said, and immediately released it.

That was the first thing anybody had said about Burke that made any sense. Her gratitude was very real when she said, "Thank you, Mr. Whitley."

"Huse," he said. "If I can ever help you, call on me, please do." He was just turning to leave when Cary came into the dining room where they stood beside the coffin. He saw Huse and stopped short.

"Hello, Huse," he said after a moment.

"Hello, Cary."

They looked at one another for a space of time. "We'll miss him, won't we, Cary?" Huse said at last, quietly, and then he was on his way to the front door. Cary turned, watching him go, his face very pale. He raised a hand in a halting gesture, dropped it, and that was all.

Burke's GI insurance paid their debts and left a little over, but there was still the problem of the *Enterprise*. Maggie thought about trying to continue it herself . . . pick up the banner from the hand of the fallen, she thought wryly, and charge on into the cannon's mouth. But she had had enough of lost causes. "I'm going home to Philadelphia for a while," she told Cary. Her aging mother lived there with Maggie's uncle and aunt and had been too feeble to attend the funeral. Now Maggie yearned to see her own family, to get clear of this nightmare world and flee to sanity.

There was anxiety in Cary's voice. "But you'll come back, won't you?"

"I don't know," she said. "We'll see."

She stayed in Philadelphia three weeks. And it was sometime during that period, after the first sharp grief began to dull, that she realized she would have to go back. Somehow payment had to be extracted from Muskogee, from Hannington, for what they had done to Burke. She was not going to let them get away scot-free, to gloat, to think: *Well, that's one more nigger-lover we sure taught a lesson to. . . .*

To let that happen, she believed, would be monstrous, an obscenity. The anger in her and the hatred she felt for Muskogee were terrible, racking her, and she would not let them get away with it.

Now, sitting at the window, she wondered if there had not been an element of rationalization in that, too. How much of impulse to return had truly been the desire to avenge Burke and how much the knowledge, even then, that she and Cary were not through with each other yet?

Anyhow, she had come back and had finally managed to dispose of the *Enterprise* to a retired newspaperman from South Carolina who would have no trouble fitting into the community. Cary, of course, was immediately on hand to help her in every respect. It was he who had found the paper's buyer, and he who got her the job in the Department of Archives and History. In fact, everybody was exquisitely nice to her now, as if to say they bore no hard feelings and hoped she didn't. What she felt, she did not let show.

She had not been there long before she realized how foolish she was to have returned. There was no way to strike at a city, at a state. The people here had been hammered at for years by the rest of the country with no perceptible effect, defeated in war, humiliated in peace, laughed at, excoriated, preached to and entreated; and nothing had changed them. She was not going to change them either.

When that realization hit her, she was depressed and lonely and began to drink a little too much. She had been drinking a little too much that night when Cary had come to her apartment, six months after her return.

She was surprised when he knocked at her door; it was after ten. But she was glad to see him; the loneliness had been very bad that night.

"Hello," she said. "What are you doing out and around at this hour?"

He smiled, but she could see he was tense. "I was working late at the office. Just thought I'd stop off and check up on you."

"Well, come in," she said, "if you don't mind the mess. You know what a sloppy housekeeper I am. Would you like a drink?"

He nodded. She was a little surprised at how her heart was beginning to hammer beneath her breasts. She made the drink quickly. They used to mourn a year, she was thinking. But I don't believe I could stand another six months. . . .

"You stay here too late," she said, passing him the glass, "and Mary Scott will be sending out the bloodhounds."

He stared at his drink sourly. "Mary Scott doesn't give a damn how late I stay out."

"A very tolerant wife."

"Yeah," he said. He raised his head and looked at her directly. He drew in a deep breath. Then the words came out in a rush. "She doesn't give a damn because she doesn't give a damn about me and she knows I don't give a damn about her."

She had sensed that for a long time, but had never heard it put into words. She said nothing, just looked at him.

He raced ahead, as if wanting to get it all out before it dried up. "It wasn't my idea to marry her in the first place. She . . . let me get her pregnant."

"How inconsiderate of her," said Maggie cuttingly.

"She knew what she was doing. She wanted it to happen. She'd been trying to get her hooks into me for years, and she knew there wasn't any other way she could do that. I used to think it was because she was in love with me, but now I know different. It was because there'd never been a Governor in the Butler family before, and she wanted to be a Governor's wife. Not Cary Bradham's. Just the Governor's." He paused. "You know I *am* going to be Governor."

It was such a pathetic attempt to impress her, to remind her that he *was* somebody important. "Yes," she said.

"That's why I don't get a divorce. Because it would ruin my chances. You know how straitlaced people are down here." He sighed and drank. "Ahh, hell," he said.

"If you don't like living with Mary Scott," she said, "why not give up the idea of being Governor? Sounds fairly simple to me."

"God," he said, "you don't know." He stood up, walked to the window and looked out into the night.

"It's not that easy," he said finally. "Not when you're me. I was raised to be Governor the way a racehorse is bred to run. I don't have any choice in the matter."

"Why not? You could just bow out."

He laughed shortly. "Yeah. After my father's spent twenty years setting it up for me."

"So that's it," she said, with a perception the whiskey had lent her. "Mary Scott, the governorship, and your father. Or—no Mary Scott, no governorship . . . and no father."

"It's not like that," he said. "I can't explain it to you. But it's just that there's something I've got to do. I mean, it's something it's my duty to do, don't you see?"

She looked at him curiously. "Are you serious?"

"Of course I am."

"I see," she said. She did not undervalue the effect a sense of duty could have on a man. Burke's had got him killed. She felt more respect for Cary; his dilemma seemed more explicable. "I've never heard of anyone whose duty it was to govern a state."

"Not just to govern." He was silent, as if he were not sure he wanted to say what he said next. "But to take this state away from Hoke Moody and his crowd."

Maggie sat up straight on the sofa, unfolding her legs. "Take it away from Moody? But I thought—"

"Yeah, that's what he thinks, too. That I'm his man." Cary turned. "He took Muskogee away from my father in 1932. My father's knuckled under to him ever since then, so that Moody would think we were both his men. It's the only way I'll ever get elected. But when I get elected—" His face grim, he set down his glass.

"Like two children fighting over a football," she said, fuzzily intrigued by the idea. "Like it was personal property to be passed back and forth."

"My family built it. We're entitled to run it. We know what's best for it."

"Ah," she said. "And what's that?"

"To keep it a sovereign state," he said harshly. "To preserve the principles it was built on."

Her voice turned bitter. "Complete," she said, "with people who kick people to death."

He strode over to her, took her hand and pulled her to her feet. She thought how strikingly handsome he was with the frost of gray at his temples: a picture-book man, and with no more substance. "Maggie," he said hoarsely, "don't be like that." He put his hand on her waist.

That was when it came to her that she had found what she had sought and despaired of finding. She almost laughed aloud at the way it popped into her mind—fantastic and perfectly logical. But she did not. Instead, she moved closer to him and tilted her head back; he kissed her and she quit scheming then and let him kiss her; she was terrifically aroused; this was a whole man and her strength would not have to serve for two.

Afterward, she had lain on the bed, her head in the crook of his arm, and had thought: Now I am the mistress of the future Governor of Muskogee. And again she almost laughed aloud. What a fine wry trick it would be, what a trick that Burke would have appreciated, if she could completely capture Cary and gain power over him. And change him, strip him of all those inherited beliefs and secondhand ideas and send him to the governorship that way and thus also change the state! And, she thought, I could do it if I tried. Nobody has ever touched him, nobody ever tried to shape him but his father. So why can't I—?

What she had not counted on, though, was that within a few weeks she herself would fall deeply in love with Cary. That, she supposed, was where she had miscalculated.

A small child, muffled to the ears as against a blizzard, ran out of the house next door and fruitlessly strove to roll a snowball out of half an inch of sleet. Maggie smiled in gentle amusement and sympathy.

First of all, of course, there had been his body, thickening a little now, but a dynamo of strength compared to Burke's, capable of matching her own not inconsiderable desire. But there was more than that, she found as she knew him better. He had a gentleness and a generosity that she had suspected but had not been sure of, a lack of egotism startling in one with his background, and a saving ability to laugh at himself. Most of all, his need and love for her were genuine; they were hard claims to deny and had trapped her into a love of her own.

Now they were comfortably settled into a relationship that had endured for seven years without interference from anyone. She did not have all she wanted of Cary, but she knew she had all she was ever going to get, and even that much was too important to jeopardize. Thus, she had not changed him after all: every attempt had resulted in a bitter conflict and she had given it up. The joke, she thought wryly, was on her.

Then she heard his familiar tread in the corridor outside. She sprang up with an eagerness that had not abated over the years. "Look out, you'll get wet," he said, as he entered with hat and overcoat glistening, and she came to him.

"I don't care," she said; and as he bent and kissed her, she put her arms about him; the ice felt good. "I was getting worried about you."

"We had quite a conference," he said, getting out of the wraps.

"About Carson Bell?"

He nodded, smiling with faint irony. "You can simmer down. Your little nigger's going to be allowed to register. It may not be any fun for him, but we'll let him get away with it. There was a bird at the conference wanted to do everything but start another war to keep him from it, but I talked 'em out of that."

She looked at him in surprise. "You?"

"Me," he said. "I must be getting soft in my old age." He grinned slightly. "Or else I've been corrupted by my Yankee mistress." His face sobered, and he put his arms around her. "I wish to hell sometimes I hadn't been born a Bradham," he whispered with intensity. "Or that I had the guts to tell everybody to take the Governor's office and ram it." His eyes were cloudy. "Because time's running out for both of us, and this isn't enough for me. Damn it, I wish we could just—" He broke off. "The hell with it," he said at last, wearily. "Let's go to bed. I'm cold. Maybe you can warm me up."

3 "Now, remember," the instructor said. "If you're by a wall, always lie with your back to it. If there isn't any wall, lie with your back on the ground. You wanta protect your kidneys. A kick in the kidneys or on the backbone can tear you up worse than almost anywhere else. So keep your back protected. Put your legs tight together, and draw them up to protect your belly. Hunch your shoulders and put your hands over your face to protect your eyes. You aren't going to be able to cover yourself completely, but you can keep them from doing too much damage if you hold yourself in the right position. Now, let's see everybody try it."

In what had once been the gymnasium of a now-defunct military academy in Washam County in southern Muskogee, the twenty-five volunteers lay down on the floor. Each of them drew himself up into a fetal position, knees and chin almost touching. The instructor, a burly man in white slacks and T shirt, walked among them.

"Get them legs together, son. Keep them heels in. Don't let 'em kick you where it hurts. . . . That's good, boy. . . . No, not on your side, on your back. They can paralyze you for life if they can get to your backbone."

Beside Houston Whitley in the doorway of the gym, Curtis McKnight nodded. "You've got it down to a science, haven't you?"

Huse grinned. "Well, we've had a lot of practical experience in the past six years, Curt."

McKnight sighed. He was showing his age; his body was bent and he walked with a cane. "Yes," he said in that soft, low-country voice of his, "that you have."

Huse took his arm. "If you've got time, I'd like to show you the rest of the layout."

"That's what I came for," McKnight said.

"Well, you've earned the guided tour. You don't know how much we appreciate your negotiating the lease on this building for us."

"Forget it. I've got to do something to earn my keep since I got too old to sit in the Legislature. All I can do is see that you're unmolested in Washam County and occasionally write a magazine piece."

"It's right smart," Huse said. "Right smart." They went down a corridor, and he opened another door. It was a school classroom, complete with desks. Quietly, unobtrusively, they stood at the back and watched.

The students in here were both young men and young women, and not all of them were Negroes. The instructor was a young white man, not over twenty-three, in khaki shirt and blue jeans. Facing him was a short, stocky Negro man of not over the same age.

"It's not as easy as it looks," the white man was telling the class in a mild tone. "It takes a lot of practice. After all, we're only human. Except you, you black ape," he snarled, and he whirled on the Negro and spat directly into his face.

The Negro man rocked forward on the balls of his feet, a clenched fist coming up. The white man slapped him, hard enough so the sound of palm on cheek rapped soddenly through the room. "Nigger," he sneered, "black stinkin nigger."

The Negro's fist was cocked; then it dropped to his side. Even as the white man spat into his face again, he set his feet solidly on the floor and his hands unclenched. But his eyes were cloudy with genuine anger and humiliation.

"What's the matter, nigger, you afraid to fight?" The white man slapped him again, harder.

The Negro just stood there, rigid, head raised. He closed his eyes for a moment, and when he opened them they were calm and free of the rage that had made them opaque a moment before.

Suddenly the white man grinned and put his arm about the Negro's shoulders and faced the class.

"You see? It's just as much physical as it is mental. You've got to break the chain of reflexes. George here knew perfectly well I was his friend. But his first reflex was to clobber me just the same. If you forget just one time, if you don't break yourself of that habit of hitting back, you can start a full-scale war and ruin a whole movement with the wrong punch at the wrong time. You have got to practice until body and mind are both coordinated in nonviolence."

Again Huse led McKnight out into the corridor. "Every one of these people we're training here," he said, "will go out and train others. Just like the people in the Better Citizens Schools project. Are you getting tired, Curt?"

"I can manage a while longer," McKnight said.

"Well, if you get tired, let me know." Huse walked slowly down the corridor. They had nearly reached its end when he opened another door.

It was another schoolroom. Its desks were occupied by both Negro men and women, and most of them were well along in years. A young, exceptionally pretty Negro woman stood at the blackboard.

"Always be sure," she was saying, "to write the numbers very large." With a piece of chalk, she wrote:

$$\begin{array}{ccc} 4 & 5 & 6 \\ +4 & +4 & +4 \\ \hline 8 & 9 & 10 \end{array}$$

"By keeping the number combinations in order," she continued, "they are learned much more quickly. Remember, no matter how well you know this material yourself, you are teaching people who may have had no formal education at all. Don't rush through. Don't take anything for granted. Be sure they all know one step before you go on to the next one."

Huse and McKnight left the room. "Come on, let's go to my office," Huse said, "and I'll have them bring us some coffee."

"Fine," McKnight said. "I used to be able to hunt birds all day long; now the old legs give out mighty quick."

As they turned a corner and went slowly down another corridor, Huse said, "Most of the students in the Better Citizens School are elderly people, retired people who have plenty of time and who've volunteered their services to become teachers. From here they'll go out and form classes in their own communities."

"I don't understand," McKnight said, "why somebody hasn't done this long ago."

"Fear," Huse said promptly; "you know that. Just like you know that nearly half the older Negroes are for all practical purposes illiterate. If a Negro knows how to read and write and figure, he's a lot harder to take advantage of and deprive of his rights. White folks, well aware of that, put every obstacle in the way of the older generation getting any education that they could. I know; I went through that with Powell Bradham, myself. I had an awful time convincing him that I ought to be allowed to go to school. He swore it would spoil me."

McKnight grinned. "From his standpoint, I guess it did. Old Powell—he's the last of a dying breed."

"Well, his breed can't die too soon to suit me," Huse said crisply.

"Don't condemn him too harshly," McKnight said. "He's the product of a system, just like the illiterates you're going to try to teach. Once you were given a role in that system, you had no alternative but to play it to the hilt. Once you were given a niche to fill, white or black, it was mighty hard to break out of it. I know, I tried."

"And you did."

"But it wasn't easy. If a few things had gone the other way for me, I reckon I could have been a Powell Bradham as easily as I could have been a Curtis McKnight."

"Well, I'm glad they didn't go that way." Huse opened a door marked MR. WHITLEY. His office, which he used only on his regular visits here, was small and simply furnished. He motioned McKnight to a chair and crossed to another door. "Miss Dennison," he called to a secretary in the room on the other side, "would you mind bringing Mr. McKnight and me each a cup of coffee?"

"I'll be happy to," she said and sprang up from behind the typewriter. Huse closed the door and turned back to his desk. A pile of large, yellow, paperbound pamphlets on it caught his attention. "Well," he said, "I see the new Better Citizens workbooks have come from the printers." He handed McKnight one and took one himself and sat down behind his desk, thumbing through it.

His Better Citizens Schools program was financed by several major foundations. It had been his own idea; he considered it quite possibly one of the most important he had conceived in the past half-dozen years. Every two weeks a cadre of volunteers, all expenses paid out of the foundation grants, came in to be trained in the techniques of teaching. After that, without pay, they would go out into the Little Hammers and the lonesome back country of the South and organize classes of their own. Even now, in Muskogee, in Alabama and Mississippi and parts of Georgia, the task they undertook was not without risk: though grudgingly granting it to the younger generation under Federal pressure, the whites were not anxious to see education brought to the oldsters.

The workbook through which Huse leafed had been carefully composed to give Negroes the broadest possible education in the fundamentals of managing their own everyday affairs. Its large type was like that of a child's primary-grade workbook, and, indeed, the first several pages were devoted to the alphabet and simple words for practice writing and spelling. But almost all the spelling words had some direct tangency to civil rights: *attorney, better, citizen, district, election,* on through to *habeas corpus* and down to *voting, witness, yearly* and *zone.*

There was a section on handwriting, with huge sample letters and space to practice them. Then followed such exercises as the filling out of mail-order blanks, of money-order blanks, and the writing of simple correspondence. After that there was elementary arithmetic, and here again the practice exercises served a dual purpose: *Twelve students are arrested sitting-in at a lunch counter. They are fined $50.00 apiece. What is the total amount of their fine?* There were sections on Social Security and how it functioned, and on politeness and good manners. There was a brief but clear and complete section on the American governmental system, stressing the importance of the free ballot.

One of the largest sections was a history of nonviolence and an explanation of its principles. A reading supplement contained biographies of illustrious Negroes: Crispus Attucks, Harriet Tubman, Frederick Douglass, Mary McLeod Bethune. There was a supplement on how to plan a voter registration campaign, including steps for a block party. The book concluded with the lyrics of a dozen of what had come to be known as "freedom songs."

Curtis McKnight laid his book aside. "Somehow," he said, "I find it hard to comprehend that today, in 1963, the latter half of the twentieth century, here in America, a great mass of adults must still be taken by the hand and led like little children into the management of their own affairs. The plight of these people touches me; the reason for it angers me; the waste of it saddens me."

"It is touching," Huse said. "If you could see the expression on the face of some old man who has been a sharecropper all his life, who, knowing he has been cheated, still has had to take whatever pittance his landlord says is due him because he himself can't even add and subtract—if you could see the expression on the face of such a man when he realizes at last he can manage his own affairs, after maybe fifty or sixty years of exploitation, see how much taller he stands— If I accomplish nothing else, I hope I'll have paid for my space here on earth with this adult-education program."

"I daresay you've paid for your space," McKnight said dryly as the girl brought in the coffee. He thanked her, smiling. "This is already quite a different world from what it was seven years ago, and you've done your share to make it that way."

"Well," Huse said slowly, "I've tried. Lots of what I've done hasn't been done intentionally. It's more like something outside myself forced me into it. Originally, after we won the boycott, all I wanted to do was get a little rest."

By that time, he had already become perhaps the best-known Negro in America. News of the boycott's success put his picture on front pages, even those of papers that were his staunchest enemies. The television networks had given his triumph national airing. And whether he wanted to be or not, Houston Whitley was suddenly, in the public eye, one of those folk figures that spring larger than life unexpectedly from American soil. Hero to many, villain to others, he was swamped with a flood of congratulations and denunciations not only from across the country but from around the world.

Still, despite the fact that they had won, there was no sudden transformation of human nature, no immediate flood of sweetness and light. No sooner had the prayers of thanksgiving died away at the last mass meeting than the bombings flared again; they were to continue sporadically for years, senseless, unpredictable and vicious, though miraculously without casualties. There were scuffles on the buses between whites and Negroes, but in every case but one the whites were adjudged the aggressors. An outbreak of sniper-firing, as vicious as the bombings, occurred: the buses were peppered, though nobody was hurt, and at the height of it they were taken off the streets completely. Huse's heart sank at the prospect of another long battle to force them to run again, but within a week they were back in operation. At last, except for the bombings, the violence simmered and died; a pattern of accommodation was achieved, and the fight was over. By that time he was running only on nervous energy.

Nobody but himself and Della realized the extent of his exhaustion. For nearly a year he had forced himself to be more than human, to be militant without vindictiveness, ambitious without personal ambition, angry without giving violent vent to his rage, menaced without any move to protect himself. Only a deeper faith in God than he had believed himself capable of, a stronger devotion to Christ, inspired and strengthened by the miracle that he himself had helped to work and had witnessed, had sustained him this long. Not even that faith could mitigate the terrible enervation that hit him when it was all over.

He was too tired even to plan. Several colleges and universities had made him excellent teaching offers; he had signed a contract to write a book about the boycott in particular and nonviolence in general. He was in demand for lectures and speeches. For the first time in his life, there was the prospect of complete financial security. He yearned for that, and for quiet, for safety, and for the lifting of the huge burden of responsibility he had borne so long.

But Marfield and Bell would not let him alone. "Don't you understand?" Jeff hammered at him. "You've started a snowball rolling downhill. It's getting bigger and bigger; we've got to keep it rolling; we can't give up now." They were in Huse's living room; Jeff slapped the mass of letters and telegrams he had taken from a briefcase. "There are half a dozen cities want to organize Civic Betterment Associations and asking for our help; leaders all over the South are beginning to stir, because suddenly the rank and file are pushing them. You've waked the people up, you've given them hope. You've shown how they themselves—not just the lawyers and the experts and the professional race men—can strike a blow for their own self-respect. What was it Shakespeare said? *There comes a tide in the affairs of men that, taken at the flood*— The Negro's tide is rising, Huse; you can't just let it come in and go out again and sit idly by."

"Idly by?" Huse's voice was angry. "Have I been sitting idly by? But I'm frazzled out, I just— Anyway, why me? Why does it have to be me? You and Charles know all the techniques, you're much better organizers."

"Because you're the symbol," Bell said gently. "You're the charismatic man to whom the people look. You're the one who has their admiration, their faith and confidence. We could lead them, instruct them, yes. But we couldn't inspire them. And without inspiration, none of it would work. We understand your weariness, Huse. But our whole race is weary. Still, with God's help, we've got to keep on. All of us. . . ."

"I don't know," Huse said, and he rubbed his eyes. "I just don't know . . ."

"It'll be different from the boycott," Marfield said excitedly. "We won't have to run a shoestring operation. I've got inquiries in here from three different big foundations wanting to know if you plan to continue in civil rights work and offering to discuss plans of support. I've got pledges from all sorts of local organizations. I've got dollars and quarters and nickels and dimes from people so far out in the boondocks they have to pipe the sunlight in, from people that dollars and quarters and nickels and dimes don't come easy to. We can get the financial support; we could charter a new organization to work on a national scale, with chapters in every city where there's a large Negro population . . ."

"Wouldn't we be competing with the NAACP?" Despite his weariness, there was interest in Huse's voice.

"No. If we would, I'd say just to throw all this support over to them. But they're already pledged and committed up to their ears in school desegregation. And they're geared up to work through the courts, not on the buses or in the streets. They've got their function— legal action. We'll have ours—direct action, nonviolently. There's a need for each."

He leaned forward, put a hand on Huse's knee. "It's now or never, Huse. It's make or break—and it's all in your hands. What do you say?"

It had a pretentious name: *For Racial Equality Everywhere*. But it shortened down very dramatically to FREE, and drama was not an inconsiderable part of their stock-in-trade.

It was a nonprofit organization, its membership composed not of individuals but of affiliate organizations. Its structure was rather complicated: Houston Whitley was president, Charles Bell executive director, Jeff Marfield treasurer and legal counsel. Marfield retained his membership in the National Association for the Advancement of Colored People, but resigned his office in it, after having arranged for a replacement. An executive board, composed of members from affiliates across the South, was theoretically responsible for making policy; rarely, however, did it contest or question the proposals the officers set before it. The board was elected by delegates from the affiliates, the number of voting delegates based on the amount of each affiliate's contribution to FREE, up to a maximum amount. There were, also, various committees with individual responsibilities.

FREE was completely nonsectarian, and because of the fact that the churches were natural lenses through which Negro energy and action could be focused, a majority of the executive board was composed of ministers.

FREE's objectives were set forth bluntly in its charter: through nonviolence, the complete integration of the Negro into every aspect of American life, financially, socially, and politically. After much soul-searching, Huse and his associates pushed the doctrine of nonviolence one step farther, and civil disobedience when necessary also became a stated policy of FREE.

Huse saw no alternative to this if the organization was to be effective. The legal system of every Southern state was a skein of restrictive laws aimed at Negroes, most of them passed in the last decade of the nineteenth or the first decade of the twentieth century, bitter reaction to the excesses of Reconstruction. Now, as the white South mobilized to resist the Supreme Court's ruling and the new, militant spirit stirring among Negroes, it wove new strands into that skein: again there was a spate of discriminatory lawmaking, aimed either at preserving segregated schools or at restricting boycotts and picketing. Huse foresaw the necessity of having to break such laws repeatedly, but nonviolently, and of being prepared to take the consequences.

Another area in which he was determined to buck the whites head on was that of voting. Until shortly after the end of the Second World War, Negroes had been kept from voting by the device of the Democratic white primary. When that had been struck down by a Federal court, the states retaliated with the use of elaborate liter-

acy tests. These were waived for whites, but administered painstakingly to Negroes by registrars who were the sole judges of an
applicant's passing or failure. Few Negroes passed, only those known
to be "safe." Another reaction to the Supreme Court decision on
segregation had been the discarding of the old registration lists in
most states and complete new registrations. Even the "safe" Negroes
failed to pass that time around, so that when FREE was formed,
there were fewer Negroes registered to vote in the South than there
had been ten years earlier.

To Huse it seemed that all other measures were merely attacks on
symptoms; the disease of discrimination could not be totally cured
until Southern Negroes had free access to the ballot. He made that a
major objective of FREE and set up a special department to attack
the problem.

FREE was a going operation from the start; the world into which
it sprang was the world of Little Rock, of sit-ins and freedom rides
and picket lines. Events came so swiftly and FREE was so deeply
involved in all of them that it seemed to Huse he lived in a sort of
frantic blur of crises and emergencies and opportunities. Afraid lest
the increased determination of the whites choke off the new spirit he
discerned among the Negroes, he whipped from city to city across
the South, spreading the doctrine of nonviolent action, helping implement bus boycotts, and in the process attaining a towering stature
matched only perhaps by a Georgia minister named King. He was
jailed several times; once he was beaten while in jail. He had been
shot at twice; miraculously, the assassins had missed.

And he had tapped, too, a new and unsuspected reservoir of
energy and determination among the Negroes—the college students,
who spontaneously had originated the sit-in technique and spread it
across not only the South but the nation. Though they turned to
FREE for advice, they formed their own organizations, too, and not
only Huse but the whole country began to realize that over the past
decade an entirely new breed of Negroes had grown to maturity.

All this expenditure of pride and energy and determination and
treasure had not been without effect. Crack after crack appeared in
the massive façade of segregation—a dime-store lunch counter here,
a chain restaurant there, a bus-station waiting room somewhere else.
But for every gain there had been strengthened resistance. The Citi-

zens' Councils lost prestige as they seemed impotent to stem the tide; to fill the vacuum even more radical organizations sprang up. Once more the South seemed to consider itself a nation at war: there were a thousand quick spurts of violence that a decade before would have been the signal for white and black to be at each other's throats. But now the Negro, at least, would not be provoked; he had learned that violence could gain him nothing and lose him everything. He did not want revenge; he wanted progress, and he went about achieving it with careful pragmatism.

"But I'm not deceiving myself," Huse told Curtis McKnight. "All right, so we've integrated a few lunch counters, so now there's a Negro sitting in the Georgia Legislature, a few studying in white schools and colleges. Just the same, we've only scratched the surface. At the rate we're going, it'll take another thousand years. We can't wait that long. We've got our troubles, too. An organization like this one depends on movement, and if we don't move, we fall apart. Pariston, particularly, hurt us."

It pained him even to think about that—his first full-scale failure. The city was a small one, perhaps thirty thousand, in the southwest corner of the state. Nearly half its population was colored and lived under absolute segregation. Confidently, Huse had determined to make a model town, a showplace, out of Pariston, and he had mustered an all-out attack—voting registration drives, sit-ins, school integration suits, picketing, boycotting. He had thrown the book at Pariston—and Pariston had thrown it right back at him.

The city absolutely refused to yield. Architect of its resistance was its police chief, Clancy Moore, a keenly intelligent man with a face like leather and a mind and wit as tough. With monolithic backing from the whites, Moore simply arrested and jailed every Negro who broke any law whatsoever, until he had immense wire pens filled with them. With equal precision, he took into custody the whites who drifted into town bent on fomenting trouble. He was harsh, but he scrupulously avoided brutality; and he was the rock upon which the wave of Huse's and FREE's prestige almost broke itself.

At the end of six months, Huse had no alternative but to admit defeat and withdraw. He had accomplished nothing except the depletion of FREE's treasury and the resources of the Negroes of the town to pay fines or make bond for the hundreds of arrested Negroes.

The state's news media made certain that the fiasco was well publicized, and Huse had not failed to note the sharp decline in contributions since then, along with a tapering off in new membership.

"We've sort of been in the doldrums ever since then," Huse went on. "But it's not so much the money or the prestige I'm worried about. It's the pattern that was set. Moore, in a kind of perverted way, turned nonviolence against us and beat us with it. If others learn that technique . . ."

McKnight's face was serious, his voice urgent. "You mustn't be discouraged. You're going to have more defeats than this before you're through. If you falter, it'll be another hundred years before anybody dares try again." He relaxed and smiled. "Don't worry; there aren't enough Clancy Moores to hurt you. The kind of discipline and intelligence he showed is still a pretty scarce commodity among your opposition." He stood up. "Are you about ready to go back to Hannington?"

"Yes, sir. Any time you're ready to leave. I'll drop you off at your place."

"Bad weather for driving; I wish you'd stay and spend the night."

"I'd like to mighty well," Huse said. "You give me a lot of strength, Curt. But I've got to get back. Day after tomorrow, Carson Bell's bound for the University. There's a lot to be done, and I want to be on hand for whatever help I may be able to give."

"Yes, of course," said McKnight. "Tell Charles and his family my prayers are with them."

"I'll do that," Huse said soberly. "I reckon they'll need all the prayers they can get."

4 Carson Bell awakened in the warm room lit by the sun that had melted the sleet which had fallen two days before; and he lay there drowsily for a moment or two before he remembered this was the day.

Almost immediately his stomach knotted with apprehensive anticipation, and he threw back the covers and leaped out of bed, a tall, slender, very dark young man of twenty-three. He went to the window and looked out; there were several cars parked on the street outside. A glance at his wristwatch told him that it was seven-thirty: why hadn't they waked him up?

He had bathed the night before; now he dressed quickly but carefully in the clothes his mother had laid out for him: the neat brown suit he had bought at Ginsburg's last week—they hadn't let him try it on, but fortunately it fit perfectly—the quiet tie, the shoes shined until they glistened. He was very hungry, and he could smell breakfast smells as he opened the door into the hall and heard voices in the kitchen and living room; but he doubted that he would be able to eat anything the way his stomach was twisted.

Well, old boy, he thought wryly, standing in the doorway, this is it. You asked for it, now you're going to get it.

He realized now as he went toward the kitchen that he had never really expected this day to come. Maybe if he had known how he was going to feel when it did, he would not have started the whole thing. Two years before, at the end of his junior year at Wheatley-Tubman, he had gone to Jeff Marfield and Houston Whitley. "That college," he had said, "is a farce. The place is falling down. They got no budget, they got no instructors, they got no anything. How'm I going to get an education in a place like that?" He wanted to be a doctor, and he was seriously concerned about the deficiencies, the gaps and omissions, in what he was getting; but he was mad, too. He was mad because he was a Muskogeean and he could afford the tuition and there was a fine university only forty miles away and it might as well have been on the moon. "I want you to help me," he had said, "transfer to the University of Muskogee."

The first thing they had tried to do was talk him out of it. He understood the reason why, now. They were testing his determination, his dedication. They knew what he had not realized—just how tortuous a path he was attempting to choose, and what dangers lurked along it. But nothing they could say altered his decision one jot, and at last they had yielded.

"It's out of our line," Jeff Marfield said. "It'll have to be an NAACP show. But I know they'd love to crack the University, and if you're sure . . ."

"I'm sure," he had said.

He had not told his parents until after he was certain he could get the help he needed. When he did tell them, his mother stared at him for a moment, and then she began to cry. His father's face was first astonished, then set, and then, finally, it broke into a slow, quiet smile; and Carson saw the pride in his father's eyes. "All right, son, if you're sure you want to do it."

Then two years. Two years of legal battles, of applications and reapplications and entrance exams and transcripts and lawyers and courts. And last October, just as the whole matter had finally reached the United States Supreme Court, the eruptive, violent, savage hell of rioting at Oxford.

That had frightened them all. Even his father had suggested, tentatively, that he might want to reconsider. His girlfriend, Elizabeth Quinn, begged him to give it up. He himself would have liked to back out, but he was not going to do it. He wanted too much out of life to back away now. He could see every day, around him, in movies, on television, what rewards the world held for the educated, the cultivated, and the bold; he saw no reason why his skin should be allowed to lock him off from those rewards. He did not feel second-class. He felt as intelligent, as strong, as clean, as deserving as anybody. If he was going to be denied the use of his capabilities, he did not want to live anyhow.

So he would not give up; a Supreme Court justice had at last canceled the final of many stays delaying the enforcement of the injunction against the state, requiring that he be admitted, and the day he had never quite believed would come was finally here.

He went into the kitchen. His mother was at the stove, his father and the three white men drinking coffee at the table. "Good morning, everybody," he said, trying to keep his voice light and casual. He went to his mother and kissed her. "Mama, you let me oversleep."

The Assistant Attorney General was a big man in his late thirties; he looked as if he might once have been a football tackle, which was true. His brown eyes were very sharp, very alert; his hair had thinned to a few wisps across his skull.

"I suggested that, Carson. We don't have to be at the University until eleven." His lips curled. "You'll need your rest."

"All right, Mr. Reisenbach," Carson said. He liked the big man: Reisenbach seemed to radiate confidence. He sat down at the table and his father shoved the morning paper toward him. Huge black headlines leaped out at him: BELL TO ATTEMPT TO REGISTER TODAY.

"Attempt," Carson said. "What do they mean, attempt?"

"Don't worry," said Reisenbach. "You'll register." He sipped from the coffee cup. "Washington talked to Hoke Moody and his brother early this morning. We've been assured there'll be no interference. Dale Moody's guaranteed the state police will keep order."

"A Moody's guarantee," Charles Bell said bitterly.

Reisenbach looked at Bell quickly. "I don't say it'll be any picnic, Mr. Bell. But once Moody's given his word to the Department of Justice, he'd better keep it if he knows what's good for him. We're not going to let any tinhorn hand us another Oxford." He seemed to relax a little. "It's all worked out. We're not going to contradict anything he says about how much pressure we were prepared to bring. He can tell as hairy a story as he wants to, to the voters. But Carson will register. You can be assured of that."

"But only two marshals," Bell protested. "It doesn't seem enough."

"Either two are enough or we'll need troops. We arrive at the campus at eleven o'clock, while the students are in class. The whole thing will be over by noon, before any crowd has a chance to gather. We want to do it as quietly, as unobtrusively as possible. If there's trouble, we'll withdraw. A proclamation has already been drawn to Federalize the National Guard if necessary; it can be done and we can be back with guardsmen if we have to by nine tomorrow morning. Moody knows all that; he knows we'll do whatever we have to do and that he doesn't have a chance. So I'm sure two marshals will be enough."

"I hope you're right," Bell said uneasily. Suddenly he slammed the table with his open palm and stood up. "By heaven," he roared, "it's Satan's own scandal that an intelligent and well-educated American youth in the latter half of the twentieth century has to have a guard to go to college in his own state!"

Carson stood, put his hand on his father's arm. "Easy, Dad. Simmer down. . . . What's all that racket out front?"

"Whitley and Marfield are trying to hold off the reporters and television boys while you eat your breakfast," Reisenbach said grinning as Charles Bell dropped heavily back into his chair.

"Do I have to face them?"

"It wouldn't hurt," Reisenbach said. "A little television publicity never hurt any cause, Carson."

"But I just gave them an interview last night."

"They're insatiable." Reisenbach arose. "Well, I'm going to

check in while you eat." He left the kitchen and went to the phone in the hall and dialed a number which Carson knew tied him into a direct line to Washington. He talked very softly, but in clipped, precise tones which sounded strange to Carson's ears: a Yankee accent. Occasionally he laughed with easy confidence as if he considered this a lark. Carson tried hard to concentrate on the huge platter of ham and eggs his mother had put before him, but he found he could get down only a third of it. While he drank his second cup of coffee, he ran his eyes over the paper.

MOODY SAYS WASHINGTON THREATENS OVERWHELMING FORCE, he read.

Governor Dale Moody last night issued a statement in which he said that the state of Muskogee had exhausted every avenue of resistance to the registration of Carson Bell, of Hannington, at the University of Muskogee today.

"We are at the mercy of the same overwhelming force used against the broken South in the dark days of Reconstruction," the Governor said. "Further resistance could mean only violence and bloodshed, and, since I have been advised that the administration is prepared to Federalize the National Guard, could result only in pitting Muskogeean against Muskogeean. Accordingly, I have instructed the trustees of the University to allow the Negro to register and have ordered the state police to mobilize to prevent violence either against the Negro or against the students of the University from the Negro's armed guard."

The governor promised that this was only the first phase of a concerted program his administration is preparing to maintain segregation at the University. "We have lost a battle," he conceded, "but the war is a long way from being over."

Reisenbach came back into the room. "Everything's still under control," he said. He rubbed his big hands together. "If you're through breakfast, Carse, why don't you go out and talk to the TV boys?"

He had never known time to possess such a quality. He imagined that time must possess the same quality for a soldier just before a charge. Each minute seemed to stretch out interminably, and yet, by some strange duality, to be all too short. He made a brief statement to the clamoring reporters and television cameramen and came back inside. Reisenbach sat on the sofa, chatting easily with Houston

Whitley and Jeff Marfield; apparently they were old friends. His mother followed him up to his room and helped him go about the completely unnecessary business of rechecking his suitcase. After a while his father came, too. While they were in the privacy of the room, they prayed together. Then Elizabeth Quinn called; she was near hysteria. He calmed her as best he could, but the effort it took set his own nerves more on edge. He looked at his watch countless times. He tried to imagine what would be waiting for him at the University. He could not. He tried to strike up a conversation with the two burly marshals, but they seemed reluctant to talk, as if they spoke only on orders.

It was only fifteen minutes until time to leave when Houston Whitley came into the kitchen where Carson was drinking his fourth cup of coffee. For the moment the two of them were alone, and Whitley sat down across from him, grinning faintly.

"Don't forget to go pee before you leave," he said softly. "It's agony to fill yourself so full of coffee you're about to explode and then everybody's watching you and there's no chance to pee."

Carson grinned, and a measure of relaxation came to him.

"Words from a professional," he said.

"You know it," said Whitley. He paused, lit a cigarette. Then he leaned forward. "There's something you've got to remember," he said.

"What's that?"

"They're more afraid of you than you are of them."

Carson arched his brows. "Yeah," he said. "Afraid I'm gonna grab one of their blond coeds and haul her off into the bushes."

"That's part of it, but that's not all of it," said Whitley. "All unjust men are afraid of just men. All cowards are afraid of courage. So it isn't that they hate you; they fear you. And it's easier to forgive them for being afraid than it is for hating." Reisenbach was coming into the room now; Whitley went on quickly. "I don't want to sound like Polonius. But remember what I just told you. And . . . your outward appearance is important. If you smile too much they'll think you're either servile or patronizing; if you're too reserved, they'll think you're stuck-up and contemptuous. Be easy, be relaxed. And for crying out loud, keep your sense of humor and show it from time to time. It's a tall order, I know, but it can make the difference— "

Reisenbach said, "Carson, it's time."

Carson Bell sucked in a great breath; it seemed to go into his stomach instead of his lungs. He stood up.

"Yes, sir," he said. "Just as soon as I go to the bathroom."

In the car, he was surprised at how calm he was. Sitting beside Reisenbach, who drove, the two marshals like a load of carved idols in the back seat, a string of press cars and television trucks following them, he stared out at the winter-bitten landscape of the Piedmont, flooded with bright, cold sunlight possessing a quality of hardness. It was as if he had never seen it before; it had a lunar quality of novelty and everything was very vivid: vignettes, disconnected but sharp, oddly graven on his sensibilities like paintings in a gallery. A pair of shaggy mules standing with their heads over a barbed-wire fence, watching traffic like spectators at a race. A roadside service station and café with a big placard out front: WHITE ONLY. The stark network of a big oak's naked branches against the washed blue of the sky. He wondered why everything he looked at had such a strange impressiveness; then he knew. A last look, he thought; and all at once he was afraid again.

"The thing I don't like about this country," Reisenbach said in his clipped, jovial tones, "is that there's no skiing. What do people do in the winter down here, Carson?"

The question irritated him. "I don't know," he said tersely.

Reisenbach laughed. "I'm going to have to find out," he said. "It looks like I'll be spending a lot of time down here in the fall and winter for the next few years."

He sobered then as Carson did not respond, and reached over and slapped Carson's thigh. "Don't worry, boy," he said. "You're going to be all right."

"Uh-huh," Carson said, nodding.

Then they were coming into Chesterland, the college town. It was full of fine old houses; Carson saw a colored maid sweeping a front porch, a yardman working on an immense, tree-studded lawn. Suddenly there was a scream of sirens, and two motorcycle policemen pulled out of a side street and fell in ahead of the convoy.

Reisenbach cursed softly, then smiled crookedly. "The welcoming committee. So everybody will be sure to know we're coming."

Carson did not answer. The sound of the sirens abraded his

nerves. He felt as if his entrails were rubber bands, like those used for power on the model airplanes he had used to build, as if the sound of the sirens turned a crank somewhere that would wind everything within him tighter and tighter; he could envision the knots forming in his twisted viscera. He clung tightly to the briefcase on his lap that contained all the necessary papers for registration. Reisenbach had overlooked no detail: "They'll be careful to lose the file with your transcripts and other stuff. So we'll just have a copy of everything ready to give them."

They approached two enormous stone pillars, the entrance to the campus. Beyond, Carson could see great stone buildings, massively venerable, widely spaced on impeccably tended greensward. He contrasted the clean order here, the quiet loveliness, with the crumbling, makeshift, shored-up ugliness of Wheatley-Tubman. His original sense of outrage about the neglect of the Negro college returned; he felt better.

"Well," said Reisenbach wryly as they turned between the pillars, "I see your eminent Governor has kept part of his promise, anyhow. But he has certainly reneged on the rest of it. No outsiders were supposed to be allowed on the campus."

There were state police cars parked everywhere along the narrow streets. Helmeted troopers, billy clubs dangling from their wrists, were posted like sentries at intervals. Behind them on the lawns there was a thick scattering of people—mostly young white men in late teens or early twenties. As the sirens screamed their arrival, white faces turned, the crowd surged forward to the road, stopped behind the barrier of police cars. Carson saw pale features contorted, mouths open; he knew they were yelling. Many of them were waving small Confederate flags.

"Punks," one of the marshals said from the back seat. His name was Vickers. "Those aren't college kids. They let the punks in."

"Yes," Reisenbach said thinly. "They're punks all right. The old double cross. And Dale Moody had better hope his troopers control them. Because if they break out, I'll burn him a new one."

As their car moved along, very slowly because the escort had slowed, the crowd seemed to roll up behind it. Carson saw strings and clots of people detach themselves, begin to gallop across the campus toward the Union Building where he would register. He was afraid again; not the queasy apprehension of the unknown, but the raw, immediate physical fear of present danger.

"Jesus," Vickers said when they turned the corner. "Look at that mob."

In the parking area before the Union, which was a large Greco-Roman building with impressive columns, humanity swarmed. It made a wall before the steps, across the asphalt, onto the grass. Like outriders around a herd, state police circled its perimeter. Sirens dying, the two motorcycles pulled over to the curb.

"Well," Reisenbach said. He seemed secretly happy about something. "Well. Aha." He drove the car very slowly straight toward the crowd, smiling faintly.

The mob turned to face it, formed a phalanx before it. Carson saw again, almost incredulously, those contorted faces, those waving flags; and now he could hear the noise. "Ahh, nigger, nigger, nigger," they were chanting, or so it seemed to him. There were other words, other slogans, but they all contained that word and it was all he heard. "Nigger, nigger, nigger."

Reisenbach leaned on the horn. The bumper was near the knees now of the first rank. Carson saw a wall of jackets and blue jeans and Wellington boots and tennis shoes, and sharp faces and round ones, clear and pimply ones, and eyes all wide and mouths all open and hands flying in obscene gestures. Defiance and hatred, a convulsion of it, a seething of it. Reisenbach did not slow. "Move, you punks," he said happily.

They heard police whistles blowing then. Belatedly the state police were advancing on the crowd. The members of the mob directly in front of the car were pinned for a moment; the car was almost on them; their hatred changed to a kind of panic as Reisenbach failed to stop. Then the crowd surged and shifted and rolled away in waves, forming an open lane with ranks on either side, and the police moved to hem the demonstrators in and keep them from shoving forward.

The noise was like a waterfall, a liquid surge of it continuously spouting from all those throats: *Yaaaaniggeryaa fuckniggeryaabas-tardyaablackbastardyaanigger* . . .

Reisenbach cracked his window. "Captain!" he bellowed.

An officer of the police strode over, put his florid face near the window. His cheeks were mottled with little blue veins. His eyes, opaque, flickered to Carson and then back to Reisenbach.

"Who's responsible for this?" Reisenbach snapped. "Governor Moody promised all outsiders would be kept off the campus!"

There was no expression on the officer's face. "Far as I know," he said loudly, "these are all students."

Reisenbach cursed softly and rolled up the window as the captain turned away. He sat behind the wheel a moment, slapping his thighs thoughtfully. Then he turned to Carson.

"They're not going to do you any physical harm," he said. "I'm pretty sure of that. But we don't have to try it. All I have to do is phone the Department that in my judgment it's too risky and we can be back here tomorrow morning with an escort of troops." He paused. "It's up to you."

Carson sat rigidly for a moment. He looked at the seething ranks of hate-filled faces. He could feel the hate pouring from the mob in tangible waves; he was more afraid than he had ever been in his life. None of these people had even seen him before, yet they were focusing all the hatred they owned on him, and he had not known until now the dreadful terror of being the object of such hatred.

Then he remembered what Whitley had told him: "They're more afraid of you than you are of them."

It did not seem possible. He looked down at his hands, at the dark, almost black skin on the backs of his hands. This is how they used to feel when the lynchers came for them, he thought. And they never had an assistant attorney general and two marshals to stand with them. . . .

His own voice sounded strange and as if it came from far away, and from somewhere he found the ability to smile faintly as he looked at Reisenbach. "If we don't make it with two marshals," he said, "we might not even make it with troops. I'm ready if you gentlemen are."

Reisenbach grinned and patted his thigh again. "That's the boy." He signaled to the captain, who came back with an imposed-upon expression on his face.

"We're getting out of the car," Reisenbach said crisply. "Keep this mob back." He turned to the marshals. "Ryker. Vickers."

The marshals got out of the back. A roar went up from the mob. Slowly Carson got out, fell in between the marshals. They walked around the car and toward the steps of the Union, Reisenbach falling in alongside.

The crowd surged forward; the police gave them slack, then halted them. Carson was looking down a long lane of bodies that ran to the steps and up them to the portico. He was aware of a jumping, writhing blur of faces on either side of him, aware of the bobbing signs and waving flags and the tide of obscenity and hatred that spilled from all those mouths. But he knew the only way he could get down that gauntlet without breaking was not to look at either side, to keep his eyes fixed straight ahead.

That was the way he walked, with his head high and his eyes to the front.

"Steady," Reisenbach said, for now the crowd was throwing things. An egg splashed in front of Carson on the pavement; something whizzed by his head. A paper bag splatted by his foot, broke and oozed; it was full of human ordure. He stepped over it and went on.

He was no longer afraid. He saw now that the police must have their orders. He could be insulted, but he could not be harmed. This part of it was all a show, deliberately staged for the television cameras spaced around the campus.

Now the crowd had begun to sing. It was not jeering or taunting; it was just singing, a deep, intimidating chant.

> Oh, we'll hang the black nigger to a sour apple tree,
> We'll hang the black nigger to a sour apple tree,
> We'll hang the black nigger to a sour apple tree,

It did not end; it just went on, over and over; but he was climbing the steps now, and then he was inside the Union, and a gray-haired man, portly, pale-faced, in a gray suit, confronted him. Doors closed behind; the sound of the mob was sealed off; it was like having achieved sanctuary, and Carson swallowed hard and tried to stiffen knees gone watery.

The gray-haired man said, "You're Carson Bell?" His voice was neither friendly nor unfriendly.

"Yes, sir," Carson said.

"I'm Dr. Breathwaite, the registrar. We've been expecting you. Come this way, if you please."

Reisenbach let out a long, gusty breath. "Well, we made it this far," he said; and for the first time Carson realized that Reisenbach had been scared too.

He had thought that once he was registered and admitted, the worst part of it would be over.

It was not; it had only begun.

That was the longest, loneliest day he had ever spent in his life. Reisenbach stayed until he was registered and assigned a dormitory room—by himself, at the end of a hall, without a roommate. Then Reisenbach wished him luck, told him to keep his courage up, and left. There was anger in him, and Carson guessed that he was going directly to the capitol. That left Carson with the two marshals, Ryker and Vickers. They were not talkative; they were as impersonal as a pair of robots, and Carson found himself wondering if, shorn of their official capacity, they would not have rather been with the mob than against it. He had no fear that they would not execute their duty, but he had no sense of their executing it with enthusiasm. They would stay with him until he felt assured of safety and asked them to leave, and though he was glad of their protection, he was not looking forward to their company.

He attended an orientation session for newly registered students. No one sat near him and the marshals. He was assigned an adviser, who looked scared to death about the whole thing. At one o'clock he and the marshals found the cafeteria and ate lunch. A hush fell over the place when they entered; by the time they had been served and found a table, the hush had become a low, sullen murmur. He did not look around him, only concentrated on the food, but he could feel the stares of curiosity and hatred. He could not eat much; and he was glad when they were out of there.

There was nothing to do after lunch, so he and Ryker and Vickers strolled the campus. It had been cleared of the mob by that time, and most of the police cars were gone too. It seemed to him a breathtakingly beautiful place now that the ugliness had been swept from it, perhaps the most beautiful place he had ever seen. There was over it now an air of peace and serenity that seemed to fall with the bright winter sunlight of afternoon.

When they passed other students, Carson would occasionally nod. No one ever responded: again, uniformly, those stares of curiosity and hatred. His heart sank; loneliness and bitterness bore in on him. They went back to the dormitory room where cots had been set up for the marshals. Carson lay down and tried to nap, while the marshals read paperback novels they had brought with them.

Lying there on his bed, his arm thrown across his eyes, he began to wonder seriously if he could go through with it. A great, cold despondency settled on him, chilling his soul through and through. The loneliness was crushing. If it was going to be like this—not just today, but on and on, for months, for two years . . . Panic rose in him. This was more than he had counted on. He was in far over his head. If he had only known it would be like this before they had spent all the money on him, invested all the time and effort and hope in his now-childish-seeming show of bravado . . .

He did not sleep very well, and the afternoon was endless, and then it was time to eat supper.

He dreaded entering the cafeteria. By this time the panic within him was worse, though he was careful not to show it. Silently he was cursing himself for a fool, an idiot. You had to show off, he berated himself, had to be a big shot.

They went into the cafeteria. Again that hush. Carson tried to keep his head high, but he found himself looking at the floor most of the time. The pressure of all those hate-filled eyes on him was nearly intolerable. He did not want anything to eat; he felt as if he could never eat again. I can't do it, he thought sickly. I just can't do it. I'll have to tell them I didn't know how it would be. . . .

He and the marshals found seats at a long table. Immediately the other occupants arose and carried their food away. Somebody said, "I never ate with a nigger and I ain't startin' now." Somebody else, a few tables away, began to sing, softly, "We'll hang the black nigger to a sour apple tree . . ."

Carson kept his eyes on his plate. No, he thought. No. They can't expect me to—

Then there was an uprise of sound in the cafeteria. It was a chorus of booing, without warning, loud and raucous. Carson looked up in surprise, and then he laid down his fork, staring.

Two people were coming slowly across the wide aisle that had been left around him and the marshals: a boy, probably not over nineteen, white, with a bloodless, set face and fierce, pale eyes behind heavy glasses; a short, rather wide-hipped blond girl in sweater and plaid skirt. They both carried trays.

Carson tensed; the marshals raised their heads and laid their hands on the table. The booing swelled to thunder.

The boy and girl came straight ahead. Then they paused at Carson's table. Carson looked up at them and they looked down at him, and then the boy smiled. "Hello," he said in a voice that he could not quite keep from quavering. "Do you mind if we sit down and eat here?"

Carson kept on staring at them, unable to speak.

"We'd like to," the girl said. She was smiling, too.

Suddenly his paralysis broke. Swallowing hard, he got clumsily to his feet. "Yes," he said. "Please sit down." And as they pulled out chairs, he felt something slump within him; all at once the panic drained away.

The booing was still going on, and somebody was pounding a table, but Carson did not hear it for the moment. And then the world seemed to swim back into focus, to gain reality once more, and suddenly he was all right. The fear was gone, the loneliness broken, and he had his courage back. He had not been an idiot after all. He dropped into his chair, smiling and acknowledging introductions he did not even hear. What he was thinking was, I'm going to make it.

As he picked up his fork again, all at once he was ravenously hungry. I can do it now, he thought, as he began to eat, at the same time trying to make conversation. The sound of his own voice was reassuring; the sound of their voices even more so. Yeah, he thought. As long as I'm not completely alone. . . .

5 "Well," said Jeff Marfield, "at least Carson's in there and maybe he'll even stay there." He tossed the newspaper aside with a wry grin. "Listen to the whites. You'd think the end of the world had come. Score one more for the NAACP."

They were sitting in Houston Whitley's private office in FREE's central headquarters suite in an old building on Grade Street in Hannington. Like the rest of the layout, Huse's office was neither large nor pretentious. He and Marfield were relentless in their efforts to hold down overhead and to avoid any charges of waste or mismanagement of funds. Although FREE had active affiliates in every Southern state and a number of border and Northern states, the head-quarters functioned with a paid staff of only fifteen, making up in dedication and willingness to work around the clock what it lacked in numbers. Huse's office did have an inexpensive carpet on the floor, and there were autographed portraits of prominent Americans, white and black, on the walls; otherwise it was devoid of ornamentation.

With a gesture of disgust Huse pushed at the immense pile of papers that had accumulated for his attention on his desk. "Yeah," he said. "But that doesn't help us any." He slipped a document out of the pile. "Look at it. Membership and contributions both going down just like an elevator. We've got to do something to put FREE back on its feet. If we don't, we're going under."

"I've pushed the membership drive as hard as I can," Marfield said. "But we haven't got much to talk about, that's a fact—and everybody and his brother is out trying to lay hold of every penny they can get their hands on and every name they can get on their membership rolls. SNICK, CORE, the Southern Christian Leadership Conference, the NAACP, all the local organizations in every city—man, even the Black Muslims down here recruiting, opening temples. They're combing the black ghettos like rabbit hunters in a broomstraw field, and every time they jump some poor little old diddiebop, they all open up on him at once. I don't mean there's not a mess of people haven't joined anything—you know the big majority is still sitting on its hands waiting for somebody to pass 'em freedom on a silver platter—but everybody that is going to join has already been collared. It's like when I was a little boy and we used to buy maybe two tons of coal a winter. We'd start with the big pieces, but we'd wind up sifting the dirt for little chunks no bigger than your thumb by the time that ton was used up. That's what we're down to now, sifting."

Huse nodded. "Well, we've got to do two things. We've got to persuade a lot of people that they're better off putting their money in FREE than anywhere else, and we've got to get those people that're still sitting on their hands up off 'em and into action." He got up and strode to the single window of his office and looked out at the barroom directly across the street from their headquarters.

"On the plane back from Washington yesterday, I came up with a couple of ideas. I don't know if they're going to work, but if the board will go along I'm going to try 'em out." He rammed his hands in his hip pockets. "I'm going to hit Hannington just like we did Pariston. Only harder."

Behind him he heard Jeff Marfield draw in a startled breath. "What? Man, you must have lost your mind."

Huse turned. Marfield was shoving back his chair, standing up. "Pariston," he said feelingly, "was bad enough. It near about ruined us. But Hannington—good Lord!"

Huse's voice was crisp. "Why not? It's still one of the most segregated towns in the whole United States. All we've got here is the buses. Sit-ins didn't make a dent. Schools still segregated. No wonder people have no faith left in FREE when it can't even change its own headquarters town."

Jeff shook his head. "That's all well and good. But we're in no shape to bite off anything like that right now. Sure, I agree we need something to get us back on the track. But why not pick an easier place to crack, maybe something in the Piedmont Region of North Carolina or middle Tennessee, somewhere we could be fairly sure of winning? Then, after we get a little victory under our belts and gain some strength, we could think about Hannington."

"No," Huse said. "I've figured it all out. It's going to be Hannington next."

He smiled slightly; he could almost read Marfield's mind. Jeff was a good, faithful administrator, but he lacked imagination. That was why he had been no great shakes as an organizer for the NAACP. He was Huse's right hand here at FREE; he was fiercely dedicated, energetic and experienced. But he had that one fatal blind spot. And, more and more, Huse had come to see that only imagination and daring would accomplish anything. He had spent two months analyzing the reasons for their failure at Pariston and trying to learn the lesson implicit in it; now he thought he had grasped the nub of it, and he was ready to put what he had learned to the test. But Jeff would think—

"Sam Deal," Jeff said harshly. "Is that why?"

Huse grinned. "Maybe."

Now there was real anger on Jeff's face. "All right. So you've got a score to settle with him about your daddy. But if you try to use FREE to settle it, you'll ruin us!" He made a savage gesture with his hand. "Why do you think Deal quite the Public Utilities Commission? Why do you think they ran him for police commissioner and saw to it that he won? I'll tell you why—because they know he's the meanest damned white man they've got in this town. Because he'd rather see a nigger shot than eat his dinner." His voice dropped. "I'm just as anxious to crack Hannington as you are. But now isn't the time. We got to get strong again after Pariston first."

"Hannington isn't Pariston," Huse said easily. "And Sam Deal isn't Clancy Moore."

"You're damned right," said Jeff tautly. "Deal can muster force that makes what Moore threw at us look like rose petals."

"Let him throw it," Huse said evenly. His voice went hard. "This is *my* town," he said. "Houston Whitley's town. This is where the whole thing started. The people know me, they know what I can do, they've got experience in going up against the city. I'm not going to fart around with half measures any longer. If I can't break Hannington, then I'm a fraud and I ought to quit."

Jeff stared at him. "So that's it."

"That's what?"

"The newspaper headlines have dropped off, haven't they?" Marfield's voice was caustic. "You haven't had your picture on the front page anywhere in weeks. And that's hurting you, isn't it? So you'll throw FREE against impossible opposition just to prove to everybody that you're still the daddy of 'em all."

"Do you really believe that?" This was something else Huse had expected, a charge he knew he would have to overcome before he could implement his plans.

"What else can I believe? Either that or your grudge against Deal. It doesn't make sense to risk the whole future of FREE, maybe even of the nonviolent movement, taking it into the wrong fight at the wrong time."

Huse looked at Jeff unwaveringly. "I *am* the nonviolent movement," he said at last.

Marfield got to his feet. "No," he said, and there was pain in his voice. "No, don't say that. You're not the movement. The movement is people. It's the first slave that ever took off North in the dark of the moon, trying to dodge the patterollers. It's students at Tuskegee building their school with their own hands. It's a family in a white-supremacy jungle like Clarendon County, South Carolina, exposing their little boy to the danger of being used as one of the desegregation test cases. No, don't tell me you're the movement. It started long before you were ever heard of. It *was,* before there was a Hannington boycott or a Houston Whitley either."

Huse chose his words carefully. "Maybe so," he said. "But right now, here, in this moment of time in this country, I *am* the nonviolent movement. At least as far as the public at large is concerned, the people we depend on for support. It's my name they know; and as long as my name makes headlines they know the movement is alive and that we haven't changed our goals one bit. Everything we've done so far, publicity helped us do, and when we didn't get the right publicity, like in Pariston, we failed. That's why we're going to hit Hannington next. Because there are headlines in it and we need the headlines, and if I know Sam Deal, he'll fall all over himself helping us get them."

Jeff Marfield looked uncomfortable. He dropped his eyes, and he was silent for half a minute. "All right," he said at last. "But I hope you know what you're doing. Because if we fail in Hannington, we may never get another chance."

But it was not as easy as he had made it sound, Huse discovered. Jeff was right: the people were afraid of Sam Deal. His very presence as police commissioner meant that the city had thrown away all the rules, that now the old pro was in charge, the get-tough man. There were still Negroes in Hannington who had done their time in chain-gang sweatboxes at the order of Deal, Negroes who could remember the "cat," the whip with the twists of barbed wire in the ends of its multiple lashes. They had spread the legend of Sam Deal, just as had every other Negro who had ever come in contact with him in the career which had carried him slowly up the ladder from one political-handout job to another. He was hated, yes, bitterly hated; but he was feared even more.

So that almost immediately, even after he had convinced his own reluctant board, Huse saw that the support he would have in this enterprise would be nothing like the support he had enjoyed during the boycott. The boycott had built itself around a single incident, an outrage that had come at exactly the psychological moment and provided a rallying point. There was no such incident now, and fear, apathy and discouragement lay over the Negro communities of Hannington like a pall and seemed to paralyze all action.

He would have a small, hard core of regulars, of those capable of understanding what was needed without having it concretized for them in some blood-stirring example. Most of them were younger Negroes, the majority students at Wheatley-Tubman. Compared to what he had been able to mobilize during the boycott, even to the group he had headed in Pariston, it was a pathetically small cadre.

Then there was the overwhelming problem of financing. FREE's treasury was in precarious shape. Huse knew how much money such a campaign as the one he had plotted could devour. Once it was under way, once he had managed to stir the public imagination, contributions would come—or so he hoped. But he could not even get it under way unless he could find the financing.

So he turned once more to the agencies which, over the past several years, had supported the bulk of his efforts—the large foundations. Few of them had publicized the grants they had given him: in many cases there were commercial tie-ins which could have been injured by boycotts in the South. Ford had already undergone such a boycott in some areas for grants to the NAACP from the Ford Foundation, though the boycott had not proved particularly hurtful. Still, they were a cautious lot; in addition there were now other organizations besieging them for support in the same field. But he had been first; the name Houston Whitley carried its own prestige, and he managed to wangle a small grant from one of them. It was not as much as he had wanted, but it would have to do.

There remained, then, only the final detail of getting Della and the children out of Hannington. Otis was seven now, a stocky, alert boy with a joyous sense of humor; there was also Terri, aged four, thin and indefatigable.

Huse had bought a fairly modest house in Princeton. He had tried to persuade Lucy to come and live with them, but she had declined, insisting on remaining in the house in Little Hammer. Not long after the boycott had begun, Powell Bradham had let her go; the action had wrenched both her and the Bradhams. "Miz Irene cried like a baby," she reported, "and Mr. Cary, his eyes was full of water." But, of course, that had been part of the penalty; there would have been no way for a Bradham to explain why a Whitley should continue to work for him. Whitleys had embarrassed the Bradhams enough as it was. Since that time, Huse and, to a greater extent, Bish had contributed to her modest support, and Bradham had made arrangements for her to draw Social Security. It had cost Bradham money; nothing had ever been deducted from her pay and he had had to pay both his accumulated contribution and hers, but he did it.

Huse sat in the living room of the Princeton house now while Della put Otis and Terri to bed. He had been chain-smoking tonight and had had two drinks, and he was in a restless mood; nothing seemed to occupy his attention. He was geared up completely for the start of the campaign. Until that began, he lived in a halfworld.

After a while Della came into the room. The years and the better living had thickened her; she was on the verge of getting fat. She was panting when she sat down in a chair—panting and smiling.

"That Terri," she said. "She's a case. She says she wants a polar bear for her birthday."

Huse smiled faintly. "I'm afraid not. We aren't geared up to accommodate polar bears. They're too white."

Della chuckled. Then as she saw the serious expression cross his face, her own face became serious too. "I reckon you want us to leave again, don't you?"

"I think it would be a good idea if you went back to North Carolina for a while."

She sighed. "I guess so. But I sure do hate to go off and make you stay by yourself. When you get into these things, I feel like I ought to be here too."

Huse fought down a slight edge of irritation. Fourteen years, he thought. After all that time, I should feel like I can't live without her. . . . He knew exactly how fortunate he was to have a wife like her, realized with perfect clarity that it was she who had salvaged him from confusion and despair that might have left him one of the blank-eyed, degraded derelicts that had horrified him in Harlem. And yet, despite all that, his capacity to love her still was not total; there was a compartment in his emotions that walled off a vitality that would have completed his love for her. He had tried vainly to force it open but he could not. Only one person could have access to that, even after all these years. . . .

"I know," he said, and his twinge of guilt made his voice gentle. "And I like to have you here. But it's too dangerous, especially for the kids. And you know I can't accomplish anything when I'm worried about y'all."

"All right," she said. "But I hate to take Otis out of school with just one month to go and have to transfer him into another school up there. It doesn't seem fair to him."

"Well, you can tutor him as well as anybody if he comes up short."

"Yes," she said, and she sighed again and got up and came over to where he sat. She went around behind him and put her hand on his forehead and pulled it back against the ample softness of her bosom. "But you be careful," she said softly. "You're the only husband I've got. Don't you let anything happen to you." She paused; he felt her lips brush the top of his head. "I love you."

He closed his eyes. "I love you, too," he said, and there was a touch of pain in his voice. He knew she would think it was caused by the prospect of parting, but actually it was there because he only wished that what he had said could be true without reservation, that the ghost—magically unaged—he saw on movie screens and sometimes on television would cease its haunting of him.

6 The Negroes came out at two o'clock on a fine, sunny April afternoon, and when they came, Sam Deal was waiting for them happily.

They had submitted their demands to the city four days earlier. Complete integration of all business establishments and restaurant facilities, public parks, playgrounds, swimming pools. The city was to hire a number of Negro policemen proportionate to the Negro population. Business establishments were to hire qualified Negro employees. Public schools, which had been held inviolate for nine years, were to be desegregated. . . .

When Sam Deal had seen the demands, he had been very pleased. He had been a little afraid that the city would try to keep him under wraps and waste a lot of time negotiating with the niggers. But there was no basis for negotiation in their demands—it was just "This is what we want or else," and what they wanted was the world with a fence around it, and it would have been political suicide for the mayor or anybody else even to have suggested negotiation.

So now, as he had hoped they would, they had turned to him and he was in charge. Behind him was all the power of a city of over a quarter million; backing that up, all the power of the state. For word had come down from Dale Moody, and thus presumably from Hoke: Stop them. If you've got to arrest every nigger in Hannington, stop them. And if you need the state police, just holler.

But Sam Deal had no intention of calling in the state police. Hell, no. He had spent a year training the city force for just such an occasion, and he wasn't letting anybody horn in on his show. . . .

Now, as he stood waiting with Chief Meston in front of the capitol, at the end of Main Street, he thought with pleasure: By God, this is jest like old times. Only thing missing is that I can't turn the boys loose yet. . . .

By boys, he meant his Klansmen. He was no longer Grand Dragon of the Klan; he had been advised to resign when he was made police commissioner: with the reputation the Klan had, a thing like that could cause a lot of stink. So he had severed his official connection, but they still turned to him for advice. Right this minute there were two representatives of the Muskogee Klan in Atlanta at a general meeting of the various Klans of the South. That Georgia attorney, the one with the fine old Southern name, was a smart cooky and an old-time Klansman. He was making real progress in trying to pull all the scattered Klans back together, unite them in a single, strong invisible empire, the way they'd been back in the twenties when Sam Deal had first joined. It looked like he might do it, and Sam Deal hoped he would and had advised his boys to go along with anything reasonable. He shared the Georgia lawyer's vision: he, too, wanted to see the Klan regain its old-time strength, become the power in national affairs that it once had been. And, he thought, that could happen if the niggers kept it up. People were tired of these Citizens' Councils that just sat on their butts and talked and threatened and did nothing, and they were beginning to think more about the Klan nowadays. Hadn't the Georgia Klan pulled nearly five thousand people to a rally outside the city limits of Albany last year when the niggers were acting up down there? Why, that was more people that had been at a Klan rally in thirty years, and it was a real good sign.

But for right now, he had to keep the local boys out of this action. The Klavalier Klub, the inner circle of loyal Klansmen entrusted with the actual punishment of people who got out of line—the ass-tear committee, it was usually called, or the wrecking crew—why, those boys were just itching for action. And there were some people from Nacirema, the fellows who had been to bombing school, back up here with their dynamite, but he'd had to restrain them, too. The time wasn't ripe for that sort of stuff—not yet. The people had to get a bellyful of the niggers before they'd stand for it; so Sam Deal had promised his boys action—but not now, only when the right moment came.

He looked proudly at the forces he had arrayed. The niggers had announced their intention of coming up Main Street, of marching on the capitol to demonstrate and then to sit in on the capitol steps and the city hall steps and at all the restaurants. They had applied for a parade permit—which, of course, had been turned down—and had said they would come anyhow. Which suited Sam Deal fine, for he had plenty of men and dogs and fire trucks to handle them. Seventy policemen, armed with guns and riot sticks and tear gas grenades and gas masks. Every tenth man had on leash a German shepherd dog, trained to a fine hair for this sort of work, big brutes with handsome silver-brown coats. In addition, there were the fire trucks, three pumpers spaced so their hoses had a field of fire covering the last block of the approach to the capitol. He and Meston had made a real study of riot control and had learned the worth of fire trucks, though they had never been used in Hannington. Hit a man with a squirt from a fire hose and it was like slamming him with an enormous fist.

In addition, the city jail was as clear and empty as they could get it. Only the worst offenders had been picked up in the past several days: Sam Deal wanted to leave as much room for niggers as he could. He figured if he packed them in like sardines, he might accommodate as many as two hundred.

So everything was ready, and he was happy. He didn't know when he had felt so good—not since the old chain-gang days. Back then he'd had a nickname among the prisoners—though he'd still been in his twenties, they had called him Old Shoot-'em-up, had even made a song about him. He closed his eyes for a moment, hearing it in his mind as it had been sung by the gang on the Cullahoochee farm, his last assignment in the prison system, before he'd wangled the better job of pushing niggers for the city construction forces:

Old Shoot-'em-up with his ten-gauge gun,
Look out, boys, don't try to run,
Swing 'at hammer, swing 'at maul,
Old Shoot-'em-up bang you
Jest to see you fall. . . .

He thought about how it had been back on the prison farm. The sweating, glittering, naked torsos in rows in the field, or cutting timber in the woods. Himself with the cradled shotgun and the saddle horse, and the leather whip he kept latched to the saddle. The knowledge of power, absolute, complete power, that in his hands was life or death, all those men in the field at his mercy. . . . He had never been a very big man; rations had been slim when he was growing up on the rented farm in Hampton County. The nigger sharecroppers who were furnished by the planters ate better than his folks did. So he had stopped growing at about five feet five, and he had always felt too short, until he went to work at the prison farm and they gave him the shotgun, the horse, the whip, and all those niggers to drive. Since then he had felt as tall as anybody.

Now, at fifty-seven, still wiry, still bouncy with a small man's energy, still with an ever-present quid of Brown's Mule tobacco in his jaw, he waited restlessly, an electrified bullhorn dangling from his hand. He looked at his watch, surveyed the ranks of policemen and the waiting fire trucks again, and said impatiently, "Dammit, I wish they'd hurry up."

Meston, towering over him, did not seem so enthusiastic. "While we're waitin," he said, "let me have my boys run those bastards off. Goddam Yankee troublemakers." He pointed to the television trucks at the curbs and the clots of newspapermen with cameras dangling from their necks who lounged on the capitol lawn in easygoing, parochial groups. "Sonsabitches just like buzzards. Every time somethin happens they circle in, and damn' if I know where they come from."

"Niggers tipped 'em off," Sam Deal said. His voice was high, almost shrill. "No, we can't arrest all of 'em. But if any git in the way, no use being particular with 'em." He spat a long stream. "I hate the bastards bad as you do. But maybe it won't hurt if some pitchers of this do git in the paper. It'll make a lot of niggers stop and think before they git too big for their britches."

Meston growled something and went off to check his men. Sam

Deal waited. He had already talked to the reporters. He had told them that he would do his duty, that any nigger that broke the law was going to wind up in jail. "We cain't have two kinds of law," he had said, rather proud of the thought. "We cain't have one law for white folks and another law for niggers. We enforce the law strickly and impartially." It would look good, he thought, in print.

He took his plug of tobacco out of his coat pocket and bit off a hunk to freshen his chew. A flashbulb popped, startling and irritating him; he turned to confront a smiling photographer. "What the hell's the matter with you?" he rasped. "You never see a man chew t'baccer before?"

"Just a good human-interest shot, Commissioner," the man said.

"You git your ass over there on the grass and stay outa my way or I'll see you git a human-int'rest shot." He squirted tobacco, narrowly missing the man's brown-and-white shoes, and laughed as the man jumped back hastily. Then he heard the siren down the street, and he turned around, lifting the bullhorn and standing expectant and ready, for that was the signal that they were coming.

They came marching up the sidewalks on both sides of the street, four hundred of them, men, women, and even some children who had cut school and tagged along or who had never been in school in the first place. They moved in orderly files, trying hard not to take up all the sidewalk, and as they came, they sang. The song they sang had a haunting melody; it had been an old hymn and now it was, since it had first been sung during the sit-ins in Raleigh, North Carolina, the theme song of the Negro civil rights movement, if it had one.

> We shall overcome,
> We shall overcome,
> We shall overcome some day . . .
> Deep in my heart, I do believe
> We shall overcome some day . . .
>
> We are not afraid,
> We are not afraid,
> We are not afraid today . . .

The voices swelled above the honks and derisive blares of the horns of automobiles in the street.

> Deep in my heart, I do believe
> We shall overcome some day . . .

Houston Whitley marched at the head of the right-hand column, Jeff Marfield at the head of the left one. There was no hesitation, no indecision or fear in Huse now; he felt normal, completely himself, a man in the slot in which he belonged. He could hear the song rising in that militant and yet mellow fervor with which his people sang; he could hear the shuffling and tramping of feet behind him; in white shirt and neat blue suit he marched proudly, shoulders back, head high. In front, at the end of Main, he could see the alabaster gleam of the capitol dome, the flag whipping on its rod.

> We'll walk hand in hand . . .
> We'll walk hand in hand . . .

This was what he had been born to do; this was why he had been created Houston Whitley; this was what it all added up to: the wagon, Cary, Bradham, Mason Jar, Burnt Stump School, Lizzie Blackwelder, even Sam Deal, Bish, Robert . . . he could see the pattern in it now; it was one reason he believed in God. Each random part, only a mischance at the time, fitted neatly into one cohesive, guided whole: he had no fear; he felt protected. That was the sum of his religion, that out of all the disjected parts a coherent whole had emerged, and that it was not anything he had done himself, only the force of a great hand pushing him. . . .

Horns all along Main Street blared now; white people snarled curses from under the canopies and in the entries of the stores; nobody heard them.

> The Lord will see us through,
> The Lord will see us through . . .

They believed that, Huse knew. So did he. Too many times, with nothing else to fall back on, they had had to throw themselves on His mercy. He was not remote from them; the relationship was an intimate one. They had depended on Him for a long time now; and that was part of their strength, too, maybe the mainstay of it. . . .

Now they had almost reached the end of Main. The capitol was in full view. He saw the American and Confederate flags whipping with vivid brilliance in the afternoon sunlight. He saw the parked fire trucks, but did not fully comprehend them. He saw the police and their dogs and helmets and clubs, and he comprehended them precisely. He saw, too, the television cameras and the reporters and newspaper cameramen, and he was gratified; and he raised his arm in a signal and the two streams of marching Negroes converged now, moving out into the street and forming a column of fours.

It was a different song they were singing:

> If I had a hammer, I'd hammer in the morning,
> I'd hammer in the evening all over this land.
> I'd hammer out freedom,
> I'd hammer out justice,
> I'd hammer out love between my brothers and sisters
> All over this land.

> If I had a bell, I'd ring it in the morning . . .

He saw the police forming ranks, sunlight glittering on the white helmet liners and on the white dome of the capitol. He heard whistles blowing; he heard shouted commands. He called above the singing, "Come on. March on!"

> If I had a song, I'd sing it in the morning,
> I'd sing it in the evening, all over this land.
> I'd sing out freedom,
> I'd sing out justice . . .

Meston's burly figure was coming forward, a hand held up, exactly like an Indian fighter approaching an oncoming tribe. He strode up to Huse.

"Whitley," he said.

> Well, I've got a hammer, and I've got a bell,
> And I've got a song to sing all over this land . . .

"Chief," Huse said.

"Tell these people to go home. Tell them to go back where they come from. You've got no parade permit."

"Constitution guarantees freedom of assembly, Chief. Can't argue with the Constitution."

> It's the hammer of justice,
> It's the bell of freedom,
> It's a song about love between my brothers and sisters
> All over this land.

Now there was quiet, as the song ended.

Meston said, "Go home, dammit. I ain't goin to tell you twice. Disperse."

"No, Chief," Huse said.

He saw Sam Deal waiting in front of the capitol, pacing back and forth with the bullhorn in his hand.

"We're going on up yonder," he said, and he started forward.

"All right," said Meston. "Suit yourself. You're all under arrest." And he turned and strode hurriedly back toward the end of the street.

The columns marched on.

"All the way to the capitol steps!" Huse yelled, turning.

The word went down the line. "All the way to the capitol steps!"

Police and dogs: a wall before them. Fire trucks on either side, bracketing.

Huse's heart hammered; his pulses throbbed with exultance. They were almost at the end of the street now; he could see the individual expressions on the faces of the police, could see the dogs straining at the leashes, wondered why white men's dogs always hated Negroes, thought: No, we aren't going to win today. But we are going to start winning.

Sam Deal put the bullhorn to his mouth, and his amplified voice thundered out over the street. "Give 'em water!"

Suddenly Huse comprehended the fire trucks. He saw nozzles pointed at them like cannons' mouths. There was that much time: then a pile driver hit him in the chest, knocked him off his feet and sent him rolling across the street, gasping for air against the flood of water.

He hit the gutter, the stream hard on him, battering. He tried to get up and it knocked him down again. He was drowning in the gutter, water so hard against his face he could not breathe, a single hose for him alone, slamming, and he got to his hands and knees and it rolled him over on the grass of the lawn.

He heard screaming and shouting behind him. Suddenly the water pressure eased, but only on him; the hose had turned on the others. Hoses knifed through the ranks with their spray, scattering people like ninepins. But not everybody was off his feet, though Huse saw the lighter ones, the girls and the very young, go rolling ahead of the driving white columns. The heavier men were fighting ahead. He heard somebody yell, "All the way up to them steps!" He sat up, dripping, gasping, gagging with the water he had swallowed, and watched the crowd surge forward.

Sam Deal's voice bellowed, "Let them dogs out!"

The dark wall against the white one, and then the dogs leaping forward. He saw one grab at a Negro's thigh; he saw a cameraman crowding forward, squatting, camera outthrust like a weapon. Then the spray hit him again, and he rolled back under the hammer fist of water, and the dogs and cops were moving into the crowd with billy clubs, and the crowd was breaking, shattering against that wall of resistance, and he scrabbled across the grass, trying to get out of range of the fire hose and finally made it, water breaking on him uselessly as he gained the shelter of a gardenia bush. Somebody yelled, "Dammit, don't break down all the shrubbery!" and he clambered to his feet.

His columns were broken, fragmented, flooded, men and women huddled against curbs and storefronts as the fire hoses played on them, the dogs surging forward and fending off the advance of those not hit by hose streams. Photographers were snapping pictures endlessly; he watched one of those go down, too, under a not-accidental twist of a hose. He backed away, looking at a scene of utter chaos, but a scene recorded: if things went as he thought they would, that was what was important, a scene recorded. Then the ranks of police were moving forward, making arrests, Sam Deal yelling through the bullhorn, "Collar 'em! Collar 'em and book 'em!" A pair of white-helmeted policemen moved toward him. He stood there waiting, dripping. Then hands seized him: "Come on, Whitley, you're under arrest." And, still with water pouring down him, he allowed himself to be led away, counting the day a complete success.

7 It was the beginning of the Negro revolution. The dog had the Negro by the thigh: virtually every newspaper in the nation carried that picture, and perhaps that alone was responsible. In America an American citizen had sought his rights; they had put the dogs on him.

Among those who had been in Pariston, there was a story, perhaps apocryphal, that during the demonstrations there a small Negro boy had marched up to Clancy Moore.

Moore had put his hand on the boy's head and smiled down at him. "Boy, what's your name?"

And the child had looked up and said, "My name's Freedom."

So the story went, Moore had lifted his hand.

"Go home, Freedom," he said.

That was what the picture seemed to say. *Go home, Freedom.* It convulsed the country, in indignation, shock, horror—and approbation.

In Hannington and across the South the Negroes came out. They were arrested. They were crammed in jail. They sang and clapped so their jailers could not sleep at night; and when the jails were full and they were crowded into war surplus barracks, into fairgrounds buildings, into barbed-wire pens, still they sang.

They sang, while they clapped:

> Woke up this morning,
> With my mind stayed on Freedom,
> Woke up this morning,
> With my mind stayed on Freedom.
> Hallelu, hallelu, hallelu, hallelujah . . .

In Danville, in Louisville, in Chattanooga and Asheville they gathered and they demonstrated. In Raleigh they stood before a movie theater, while hundreds of arrestees in the jail across the street sang and clapped; and they lifted their voices in an improvised spiritual:

> Go down, Moses,
> Go down to Raleigh, North Carolina,
> Let me in the show . . .

They came out in Charlotte and Durham; in Greenville, Columbia and Charleston; in Hannington, Pariston and Brandonville; in Rome, Atlanta, and Albany; in Jacksonville, Gainesville and Cocoa Beach; in Montgomery, Birmingham and Gadsden; in Baton Rouge, Shreveport and New Orleans; in Clarksdale, Greenville and Jackson; in Dallas, Denton and Houston. In all those places and in many in between the Negroes came out.

It was the picture that had done it—the freedom-seeking man

and the leaping, snarling dog blocking his way. The picture brought them out in the North, too; and suddenly they were marching in Brooklyn and in the Bronx; in Philadelphia, on Chicago's South Side; in Detroit. They marched from Lenox Avenue in Harlem to Auburn Avenue in Atlanta.

Their watchword was *Freedom Now*. They attacked on every front. They picketed movie theaters. They sat-in at restaurants and in hotel lobbies. They marched before department stores. They waded in at beaches and swimming pools. On highways, interstate routes along which a traveling Negro could drive for five hundred miles without finding food, a bed, or a place to void his bowels, they hit the way stations, the chain restaurants and motels.

Sunday mornings found them entering churches. In some they were received and welcomed; in others they were allowed in and ignored; at many they were arrested. White ministers preached sermons: some hammered out Biblical reference after reference designed to prove that segregation was God's will; others spoke for law and order; and a number preached, without weaseling, the brotherhood of man. Of the latter—those who urged that their own churches be open to all—many, especially in the Deep South, had pulpits shot out from under them by enraged congregations, or themselves resigned in anguished disgust.

In the first ninety days of the demonstrations, over ten thousand Negroes were arrested. They went to jail happily, singing a paraphrased gospel song:

> Have you been to jail?
> Yes, mah Lawd,
> Will you go again?
> Yes, mah Lawd . . .

They offered themselves for arrest, begged for arrest, were determined to reduce to absurdity the policy of arrest, to show up the bankruptcy and hypocrisy of those communities which could respond only with arrest before the whole nation and the world. Filling the jails as they did, they plunged many a municipal budget into deficit; and some municipalities retaliated by setting outrageous bonds.

The crosscurrents were many: though it had been the use of dogs in Hannington that had stirred the outcry, dogs were used in Chicago with little notice. When state laws requiring segregation were found unconstitutional, many states repealed them in order not to prejudice the prosecution of demonstrators. Thus, a sitter-inner who had been arrested for trespass under a segregation law had been arrested illegally; as soon as the law was repealed, he could be arrested legally on the complaint of the property owner. The repeal of the segregation laws aided in the fight to maintain segregation.

Houston Whitley, his hands full to overflowing with FREE's total involvement in all this, was gratified. He had gambled and the gamble had paid off. He had counted on Sam Deal for the brutal resistance which he had known was the only thing that could again arouse public fervor and support; and Deal had not let him down. Now Huse again commanded immense national prestige, and FREE's membership rolls and coffers reflected the publicity that accompanied his every pronouncement or action. He turned over details of the Hannington project to Marfield, instructing him to keep maximum pressure applied, and desperately attempted to fulfill the requests for advice, encouragement, and leadership that poured in from cities large and small, North and South.

In most of these cities a pattern emerged. First of all, in revulsion and protest at what had happened in Hannington, and inspired by it as well, the hard-core cadre of workers who had hung on in each community came out in demonstrations. Usually these were the young people, the students.

The first demonstrations always took the authorities by surprise; on the first several nights there would be massive arrests, crammed jails. But by that time the fever had spread, and the demonstrators kept on coming.

Then, as the demonstrations continued, the apathy that had settled over nearly every colored community began to break. Streets became clogged at night with carloads of curious Negroes who had come downtown to see what was going on. They drove slowly by the picket lines or the singing, shouting crowds, staring with big eyes at the neat young students ignoring the catcalls and incitements of hordes of white toughs. They did not stop, get out, or even wave; they just drove by and looked. But the next day local memberships in civil rights organizations would swell. The supply of demonstrators was reinforced, became nearly inexhaustible, and the more that were hauled off to jail, the more appeared to take their places.

When the arrests had reached four or five hundred or a thousand, when every possible place in which a Negro could be confined was jammed, when the expense of providing food and blankets became astronomical, police policy would change. Suddenly—unless the whites were very, very determined—the authorities began to bend over backward to avoid having to arrest the Negroes. Or those arrested were swiftly tried in mass trials and given suspended sentences or token fines and cleared from jail to make room for more. In Hannington, though, and in a number of other cities determined to resist to the death, the fines were not minimal; they were ruinous.

Finally most police, though continuing to break up demonstrations with tear gas, electric cattle prods, and fire hoses, sent the demonstrators home and took only the leaders into custody.

Meanwhile, in a surprising number of places, a ground swell of white sympathy developed. Analyzing the reasons, Huse pinpointed several. Perhaps the most important, he decided, was the fact that the Negro had begun to act like a man.

He began to realize the basis for much of the contempt whites had held for Negroes. Whites placed no value on meekness, and the Negro had been too meek. He had accepted abuse too readily, and had thanked the abuser. In white eyes, Huse told himself, that alone was enough to put the Negro on the level of a dog that, kicked, wags its tail.

Now the Negro was no longer wagging his tail when he was kicked. He was reacting like a man, with a man's indignation and determination to end the abuse, and there were people who were perfectly willing to give a man his rights who would not have offered them to a cowering dog. As soon as they saw the Negro as a man, they quit trying to withhold from him what he was entitled to; they respected him and were even more willing to associate with him.

Another factor was the pragmatic awareness of white businessmen that continued demonstrations and boycotts could wreck their profits. While demonstrations went on, business fell off sharply, not only because of Negro boycotts but because white women shoppers were afraid to cross dark picket lines or get caught in the midst of a black uprising; they stayed home, and the businessmen felt it.

Thrust came from them—and from ministers, who spoke with increasing freedom for the formation of biracial committees. The theory was that differences could be negotiated if demonstrations ceased for a while. "You've made your point," the businessmen said.

"Now give us a chance to see what we can work out." For the first time in history, in many cities, black and white sat down at the same table to try to settle their grievances.

These conferences were not always successful. Sometimes die-hard segregationists scuttled them; sometimes the very inexperience of the Negro leaders resulted in a deadlock. Unused to facing whites on equal terms, inexperienced at negotiating, some local Negro leaders equated truculence with firmness; conscious of their power, they were dictatorial, presenting not a basis for negotiation but an ultimatum which could only be rejected.

In a surprising number of places, though, barriers came down. When they went, it was not gradually but all at once, by community-wide agreement. No white businessman would desegregate unless his competition also did so simultaneously. When unanimity was achieved and desegregation became reality, little actual change occurred: whites were baffled but pleased when they were not overrun with colored patrons. Actually, price was a more effective barrier than any other: comparatively few Negroes could afford to patronize the better and more costly establishments of the whites. Still, the principle had been established, and that was what they had fought for.

But that summer of convulsion was not without its cost in blood. A white man hiking on his own self-conceived freedom crusade was murdered in Alabama; in Mississippi an NAACP organizer was assassinated; in North Carolina one white was killed and another wounded in a riot. And the bombings and cross burnings and mob confrontations and scuffles and police brutality seemed to continue endlessly. Nevertheless, neither FREE nor the other organizations slacked up for a moment. There was no way they could have, even if they had wanted to.

For now the momentum came not from the leaders but from the rank and file. There had been, throughout the past several years, intense and rarely friendly rivalry among the various organizations; now, willy-nilly, they were pushed into working together. Startled by what was under way, by the spontaneous power and strength of what was no longer a protest but a revolution, the movement's leaders worked in closer concert. Together they planned and executed the massive march on Washington that capped the turbulent summer;

and, together, when in Birmingham a church was bombed on Sunday morning and little girls killed at worship, they worked to avert full-scale race war.

It was not an easy task. The crime shouted for reprisal; Huse had never seen such an instantaneous, bitter and enraged reaction among his people. Nonviolence was in jeopardy as the cry went up for vengeance. There was a week—ten days—when the issue trembled in the balance, while Negro leaders fought desperately to prevent violence, and whites across the South, moderates and supremacists alike, confronted their own guilt, appalled. Finally the rage and grief found partial release in nationwide memorial services and in the realization that the brutal incident had earned a new increment of sympathy for the Negro movement.

Only when he had managed to bring the Negroes of Muskogee back to a dependable normality did Huse go to get Della and the children in North Carolina. It was a long round trip, a grinding drive, but it did not seem as long as it had been before. In previous years it had been a grim test of endurance, as was every major journey through the South for a Negro. There had been no place to eat along the way until they could find a Negro restaurant in some town, no washrooms in which the children were allowed, so that Huse had had to park the car along the road and lead them into the brush. And if he tired or nightfall overtook them, there had been no decent lodgings along the route in which they could stop.

Now, when they were hungry, they were able to dine at one of the chain restaurants every fifty miles along the highway and use the rest rooms. It was not much, but it made the trip less of an ordeal.

Thus, driving home, Huse was not as tired as usual, and his mind raced ahead into the future. FREE was marking time right now, but it could not do that indefinitely. He had to plan its next campaign.

There was so much that still needed doing, so many projects to choose from, that it was not a simple matter. Yet he was pretty sure that he had already selected his next target; it was one he had only been waiting to accumulate strength to hit.

"And," he said aloud, "I reckon we're as ready as we'll ever be."

Beside him on the front seat of the car, Della stirred and opened her eyes. "What's that, honey?"

Huse smiled tautly. "I was just thinking out loud about the next campaign. Making up my mind where to smack 'em next."

She rubbed her eyes. "Where's that?"

He laughed without any mirth. "Where it'll hurt 'em come next year's elections. Right square in the ballot box." He saw the tower of a Howard Johnson ahead. "You about ready for a cup of coffee, sugar?" he asked, and with a certain sense of wonder of which he could not rid himself, he left the highway and drove up to the restaurant.

8

Watching Dale Moody's gaunt form stalk back and forth across the Governor's office, Cary Bradham thought of a great blue heron wading in swamp water. He smiled at the comparison, and then his smile faded as Hoke Moody's shrunken voice said irritably, "Dale, will you for God's sake stop that damn' pacin'?"

Dale Moody halted, turned and faced his brother. "All I want to know," he said, his saturnine face angry, "is why didn't we think of it first?"

Hoke snorted disgustedly, coughed a little, leaned forward and spat in the cuspidor by the desk. "Hell, I thought of it," he said. "We talked about it back in 1948, remember? Well, I don't have any more idea of goin' for it now than I did then—it would just be cuttin' off our nose to spite our face."

Mitch Moody uncrossed his legs and flipped a cigarette butt into the cuspidor. "We may not have any face left to spite," he said, "after Morrison gets through with us."

"Don't worry about Morrison," Hoke said irritably. "Cary will beat Morrison. Cary can't help but beat Morrison. Everything's all squared away for Cary to beat Morrison. Who the hell is Morrison, anyway? Just a damn' johnny-come-lately state Senator who happened to run across money enough for the primary filin' fee in a pig's track somewhere."

Powell Bradham's face was grim. "That's what I said about a fellow named Hoke Moody one time."

Hoke Moody laughed, his once-deep laugh less masculine now. "Alec Morrison ain't a Hoke Moody. They don't grow on every bush." Then his shrunken face went serious; a flash of the old fire came back into his blue eyes and his voice had bite to it.

"There's no call for you-all to git your bowels in such an uproar. I've been handling things for better'n thirty years now and I haven't made a mistake yet. I'm not makin' one this time. Alec Morrison!" He snorted. "That guff of his sounds good, but nobody's going to go for it."

"Nobody except the voters, maybe, Uncle Hoke," Mitch said.

"I'm tellin' you," Dale Moody added quickly, "we have got to break completely away from the administration, Hoke." His voice was earnest. "You're tied down most of the time. It takes all your strength just to hold things down in Washington. You're losin' touch with how people feel. All this goddam civil rights stuff has got 'em to the point where the name of that so-and-so and his damn' little brother is just like poison. They're hated bad enough so they could cost us the election just by bein' associated with 'em." He hit his bony thigh with a clenched fist. "If you try to keep us wrapped up with them, Cary don't stand a chance. We've got to come out for un-pledged electors just like Alec Morrison has!"

"Horseshit," said Moody bluntly. "Listen, let me tell you some-thing, all of you, before this unpledged-elector fairy tale goes any further. If we wanted to ruin Muskogee forever, that would be the way to do it. Hell, yes, it sounds good to stand up and wave the Confederate flag and give the rebel yell, and we'll do our share of that. Nobody hates that crowd's guts worse than I do. But you know something? Bad as I hate 'em, they got the power. And they'll use it on us if they take a notion to, and those boys—when they use power, you know it's been used. Now, let's all get some sense. Even if we did join Mississippi and Alabama with an unpledged slate, we wouldn't be able to throw the election into the House. And suppose by some miracle we did? Well, the House has got to pick either a Republican or a Democrat. So what difference does it make? They're all going to suck up to the nigger vote, either one of 'em. We wouldn't be any better off than we were before—a lot worse. As it stands now, we got something both parties want, our electoral votes. If we announce beforehand that we're not going to give 'em to either candidate, how much consideration do you think we'll get from anybody? How much influence do you think I'll have then? We'll be isolated—*I'll* be isolated in the Senate. The way it is now, I can make deals. But this damned unpledged crap, that would cut the ground right out from under me." He paused. "Those boys up there aren't the only ones that understand power or how to use it. You don't use it by going off in a corner and sittin' on it and sulkin'. You use it by wigglin' the carrot here and frammin' with the stick there, and I don't aim to throw away my carrot and be left with nothin' but a stick. Because their stick's a lot bigger. Now, let's cut out this nonsense about unpledged electors."

He turned to Cary. "You're the one who's got to make the race. Do you agree with me?"

"You pick the platform," Cary said, unable to keep a certain weariness out of his voice, "and I'll run on it."

His father snorted. "You won't get very far if you don't show more spirit than that." Bradham stood up. "All right, Hoke," he said. "What you say makes sense. We've got to think about after the election as well as the election itself. We can't cut ourselves off from Washington altogether. But if that civil rights bill gets passed, even if they just keep pushing it like they have, Alec Morrison is not anybody to be ignored."

"The civil rights bill ain't going to be passed," Moody said quickly. "Not this session, that's for sure. I can promise you that."

"Whether it is or not, we'd better start acting like we've got a race on our hands."

Moody looked at him. "So?"

"So the first thing is, we don't dare give another inch to Houston Whitley and his crowd. We let that nigger in college, we threw Sam Deal to the wolves—"

"Sam Deal was a fool," Moody said sharply. "And you were a fool for encouraging him, Dale. If I'd known what was happenin'— Well, that's too far gone to worry about now, but if Deal had shown half the sense Clancy Moore did, the niggers would still be wondering what hit 'em."

"Be that as it may," Bradham said, "we've still retreated just as far as we can retreat. Otherwise we'll be handing this state over to Alec Morrison. We've got to show we're just as concerned for Muskogee's integrity as he is. We've got to stop this business of running things by expediency, of backing down every time Washington cracks the whip. Nobody's going to respect us if we don't show we're master in our own house."

"I think we've shown that pretty well," Moody rasped. "What have the niggers got out of Muskogee so far this summer, for all their snortin' and gruntin'? Not a damn' thing that they didn't have before they started. Oh, maybe a five-and-dime lunch counter here, a chance to sit with white folks in church there, but nothing to amount to anything, nothing anybody can point at. Sure as hell nothing we've given 'em. Even Alabama and Mississippi have had to yield a little bit. We haven't yielded any more than they have."

"The first little bit is too much," Bradham said. "Morrison can say that if he'd been in, they wouldn't even have had that much."

Moody was silent for a moment. Then he said, very quietly, "You sound like you'd make a pretty good Morrison man yourself, Powell."

Bradham's face went white; Cary sat up straight. But Bradham just said, in a voice as calm as Moody's, "Cary's waited a long time for his chance. I want him to win."

Moody half rose out of the chair; he did it awkwardly. He seemed to freeze halfway up. "Umpf," he grunted. "Mitch, come give me a hand."

His nephew was at his side in an instant, helping him gently. When Moody was erect, Mitch said solicitously, "You okay now, Uncle Hoke?"

"Need some Indian skunk oil for my joints," Moody said with a wry grin. He looked at Bradham. "Don't worry," he said. "I don't care how loud Morrison hollers nigger or how much he waves the bloody shirt, nobody's gonna break our organization. Don't you worry about Cary winnin'. You leave that to me. Mitch, gimme a hand out to the car, will you? I'm tired, and I'm going home and take a nap."

When Mitch had helped the old man out, Dale Moody let out a gusty sigh and sat on the edge of his desk.

"Senile," he said bitterly. "Hoke's done lost his grip and he's gettin senile."

Bradham was looking at the double doors Moody had closed behind him. "I'm afraid you're right, Dale." Slowly, none too spry himself, he turned to Cary. "I don't care what Hoke says, you're going to have to run scared. If he won't let us loose from the administration, you're going to have one hell of a primary fight on your hands and then maybe one in the general election, too. It's going to take everything we can throw in to knock Morrison. Hoke may write him off, but I remember what Hoke did to me in 1932, and Morrison's got an issue just as hot."

Cary nodded. "All right," he said. He tried hard to put some enthusiasm in his voice and knew he had failed miserably.

Bradham stared at him. "Boy, what's the matter with you? You're behaving like you don't give a damn."

"I give a damn!" Cary flared. "I'm going to win your goddamned election for you. Just lay off of me. Settle your argument with Hoke Moody, tell me how to run, and I'll run that way."

He saw the alarm flare in his father's eyes—alarm and hurt. He saw his father's quick glance at Dale Moody. Moody was staring at Cary speculatively. The flare died in Bradham's eyes.

"Sure," Bradham said easily. "Sure, of course. You'll win all right—won't he, Dale?"

"Maybe not," Dale Moody said, and then his next words came out slowly, distinctly. "Not as long as he's sleepin with that Yankee woman, he won't."

At first it was exactly as if someone had hit him in the pit of his stomach. He could feel the blood draining away from his face as he turned toward Dale Moody. "What was that you said?" he whispered.

He heard his father sigh. "All right," Bradham said softly. "Now, you just settle down. This is something that might as well be got out of the way now."

Cary turned to him. "Got out of the way? Now, you listen—"

His father held up a hand. "I'm not trying to pry into your life. I've kept my nose out of it so far, and I wouldn't poke it in now if I didn't have to. But Dale's right. We—you've got to do something about that Jessup woman."

"I'm not even going to talk about this," Cary said bitterly. "This has got nothing to do with me running for Governor."

"It's got everything to do with it," Bradham said, and now his voice was sharp. "Listen. If this mess hadn't come up, if we'd been able to beat Morrison to the draw with the unpledged-elector thing and never let him get his head up without knocking him off, you could have twenty fancy women and I wouldn't care; it wouldn't make any difference. But things aren't that way. You've got opposition we didn't count on, and it's opposition that'll fight dirty. Now, I don't know whether Morrison knows about Maggie Jessup yet or not. But if he doesn't, he'll find out. It might be the damage is already done, but one thing I know for sure—you've got to be free and clear of her before campaign time comes. It's bad enough to be caught with any mistress during a campaign; it'll be even worse when the word gets around who that mistress is. All Morrison has to do is trot out some of that tripe Burke Jessup used to write and link you directly with it through her and you're finished. I've hated to have to bring it up. I've put it off and put it off, but since Dale's spoken the first word, you might just as well know. You can't have the governorship and your fancy woman both." As if there were no question of choice, he finished reasonably. "So you've got to get rid of her."

"Oh," Cary said with an evenness that surprised him. "Well, what am I supposed to do with her? Just drown her in the creek in a croker sack like a stray kitten?"

"Send her back North," Dale Moody said sharply. "Send her back where she belongs."

"That's right," Bradham said. "Something like that. Look, if it'll take money—"

"It wouldn't take money," Cary said. "Don't worry about that."

He turned away from them both for a minute. He had known all along this was coming. Had known it was inevitable. But he had refused to face up to the fact; he had tried to keep it not only from Maggie but from himself. Its effect had been gnawing at him, though. Slowly, as the time drew near for the official announcement of his candidacy, he had become more and more depressed. While his father seemed to shed years, to paw and snort like a fire horse at the clang of a bell, Cary had felt only a growing sense of frustration, of hatred for the injustice of it. Maggie was the only happiness, the only real happiness, he had ever had. He was entitled to Maggie. More important, he loved her, loved her exactly the way he had hoped to love whatever woman he would someday marry and had not been able to.

And now they were telling him that he would have to give her up, and he knew that what they were saying was true. But he did not see how he could do it; he just did not see how he could do it.

He felt his father's touch on his arm. His father's voice was gentle. "Son, I'm not a blind man and I'm not a fool. I know Mary Scott and I know Maggie Jessup a little bit, and I can pretty well guess what's going through your mind right now. But you've been playing a risky game all along; it's just God's blessing that Mary Scott never found out. If she'd taken a notion to divorce you, that would have finished you right then and there. Or even if she just turned the Butler family against you. It's a risk that simply can't be taken any longer. I'd rather cut off my right arm than make you unhappy; although I can't say that I approve of such goings-on, I know how these things happen and that they're harder to get out of than into." He could almost feel the hidden meanings throbbing in his father's voice, veiled before the Moody at the desk, but there. "You have a duty, an obligation, that can't be ignored. And as long as you're connected with her, you jeopardize carrying out that duty."

"Duty," Cary said bitterly. "There are times when—"

His father squeezed his arm warningly.

"All right," Cary said. He went to the hatrack and got his hat. "I'll think it over. Right now, I've got to go."

"I'll walk along," his father said.

When they were well clear of the capitol building, his father stopped. "Turn around here, son," he said, "and look at me."

Cary turned. His father's eyes and his own met levelly; he could see the distress on his father's face.

"I know how you feel about it," his father said. "But that's the difference between a Bradham and anybody else. That's the only entitlement a Bradham has got to setting himself above opportunists and trash like the Moodys. You either do what you have to, whatever it costs you, or you're nothing." He broke off. His voice was bitter when he resumed. "I didn't want to have to subjugate myself to Moody for thirty years, to be his dog robber and his lackey. But it was my duty, and I didn't have any choice. Now I don't see how you have any. We can't let this state fall either to Alec Morrison or Mitch Moody, who'd be the candidate if you . . . bow out. But I'm not going to push you. You know the situation. You know what I have done and you know who you are. So you're the one who's got to make the choice." He turned away quickly. "Now I've got to get along home," he said in a different voice. "Your mother wasn't feeling good today and I told her I'd come straight back." He moved stiffly across the parking lot toward where the chauffeur lounged by his car.

Cary stood there, watching him go. He raised and dropped a hand helplessly, and after his father had got into the car, he turned to his own vehicle.

He should have gone back to his office, where he had a great deal to do, but he did not. Instead he drove across town, toward the rather sad and isolated enclave in which Maggie kept her apartment. It was a section of old women in old houses, mostly. It had been fashionable many, many years before but was now obsolete. As the old women who had outlived their pasts died one by one, their houses would die, too, bulldozed away to make room for service stations or taverns; the antique dealers would get their furniture, the marble fireplaces and marble lavatories and magnificently carved mantels would sit out in the weather under the big trees, which would finally be cut down too, and if not bought by passersby would go to secondhand stores and junk shops, where they would be ranged alongside salvaged water closets and rusty used filing cabinets. Even now, while the old women lived, in their closed and cluttered parlors, the city had already surrounded them and was waiting hungrily, the freight yards not far away on one side, a new expressway close enough on the other so that they were penned between the rumblings of boxcars and of trucks. Because it was such an outmoded and useless island where nobody ever came to see the old women, he did not have to worry about being embarrassed by meeting anyone he knew. It was a hiding place; and it had become the most important place he knew, his only sanctuary.

He parked his car behind the old brick building—which had created a neighborhood uproar when it was constructed forty years before—the first intruder, the first invader—and climbed up to Maggie's apartment (there was no elevator). When he let himself in, he realized for the first time that he was early; she would not be home from work yet.

He closed the door behind him and looked at the disorder in which she had left the place. She was a clean but not a neat person, and there were magazines and a sloppily folded newspaper on the floor and a used coffee cup on the breakfast table, the dregs still in it. He went to a kitchen cabinet and got the whiskey, helped himself to ice from the small, sparsely stocked refrigerator, and made himself a drink. With it in his hand, he walked around the apartment aimlessly.

The shades were drawn in her bedroom; the bed had not been made. A pair of stockings, discarded, lay across the foot of the bed; he picked one up and rubbed the sensual texture of it between his fingers. The bedroom smelled of her, the scent of woman, an earthy body smell and the interwoven lingering fragrances of her cosmetics; it was a smell he knew well from holding her tightly, one that stirred him.

He drank half the drink and went back into the living room. There was something poignant in her absence; he felt as if he had caught her unguarded and helpless. As the whiskey caught in his brain, it occurred to him that he had always thought of her in terms of his need of her: what, he wondered, was her need of him?

He was not sure about that. She seemed strong and self-contained, and yet she must have her fears, her despairs and frustrations too. What did she dream about when she dreamed? What were her wants, too secret to be voiced? Now, in her absence, he seemed to be able to see her more clearly than if she were here, and he felt a surge of compassion and of protectiveness and a fervent wish to make her happy. It reassured him: yes, he really loved her, in a way that was reinforced by desire but not dependent on it.

He freshened the drink and sat down on the sofa to wait. . . . And they wanted him to throw her away. Its effect on him aside, what would be the effect on her? How deeply did she feel bound to him? What could he offer her in compensation? She had always refused to take money from him; she supported herself entirely. She made no claim on him; she had never even mentioned marriage, both of them knowing that it was impossible. Yet, surely, what she had could not be enough for her—unless she were abnormal, how could she be satisfied with it? So how much value did she place on it, on this jerry-built relationship that was tailored all for his benefit and, unfairly, with no consideration for hers?

He could not guess; but as he drank he began to be angry again. What did they think he and Maggie were, anyhow, chess pieces, livestock? Forget its unfairness to him—what about its unfairness to her? That kindled the rage and bitterness in him to a higher flame. He could at least count some compensatory gain for himself by discarding her; there would be no gain at all for her—a woman nearly forty, long widowed, with a minimal income. He was all she had. He got up and poured himself another drink, and it was half gone before she came in.

She smiled at him, tossing her handbag on the sofa. She was wearing a trim, belted jersey dress, beige; she looked neat and cool, despite the fact that in October it was still cruelly hot outdoors. "Hello, darling," she said. "You're here early." He got up and came to her, held her tightly and kissed her hard. When she pulled her mouth away, she said, "Gosh, are you geared up!" When she saw the expression on his face, her smile faded. "What's wrong, Cary?"

"Nothing," he said. "I'll fix you a drink." He went into the kitchen and she followed him. She looked at the whiskey bottle and frowned, but she said nothing as he mixed a drink for her and freshened his own. They went back to the living room, and she sat on the arm of his chair. Her hand moved across his temple, stroking.

"Rough day?"

"Yeah," he said. Then he pulled away from her, stood up, walked to the center of the room and turned and faced her. "What would you say," he asked fiercely, "if I told you we were through?"

He saw her face go white and sick, her body tense. She put her hand to her throat. "I don't know what I'd say. Are . . . we?"

"No," he said. "Hell, no, we aren't." He went quickly to her and held her, kissed her again. "We're a long way from being through." He reassured her with his hands and lips. When he let her go, she patted her hair.

"That was a not very funny joke," she murmured. "What brought that on?"

"Never mind."

"Cary, Mary Scott hasn't—"

"I told you, Mary Scott doesn't give a damn. I don't think she knows, but if she does, she doesn't care."

"Then what?"

"Nothing," he said. "I was just teasing. Nothing. Don't worry. Don't you ever worry about that. I love you."

"That's good to know," she said, but her face was still pale. "Because I love you, too. You couldn't guess how much." She licked her lower lip nervously. "Please don't say anything like that again unless it's the truth. It scares me."

"All right," he said, whispering now. "I'm sorry." The hell with them, he thought. I've got rights, too, and so has she. I don't care what they say, I've done my part and I'll keep on doing it. But this isn't in the bargain, not this.

Because they had been together so many years there were many times when he came here that he did not want her, except for her company; but now he felt a bold, almost defiant surge of desire. He put his mouth close to her ear.

"Come on," he said. "I want you. Let's go to bed."

9

Except for the long, uncluttered desk, the office of Hall Kurtzman, executive vice-president and chief administrator of the Gosnell Foundation, did not look like an office at all. With its grand but useless fireplace, its grouping of easy chairs and sofa, its extensive bookshelves, thick carpet and tasteful expressionest paintings, it could have been a living room furnished in excellent taste and without regard to expense. Houston Whitley, thinking of his own stark cubicle on Grade Street, smiled wryly, wishing he had the cost of the decor of this room added to the grant he was seeking. Then he brought his attention back to Kurtzman's soft, almost shy voice.

"Won't this to some extent duplicate other efforts along the same line?"

"I don't think you can speak of voting registration in terms of duplication," Huse said. "There's simply too much to do. Yes, the Southern Regional Council in Atlanta is working on it. So are most of the other civil rights organizations. We've had our own program for years, ourselves. but it hasn't seemed that the time was ripe to push it until now."

"Why not?" Kurtzman was small and pink; he sat up a little straighter in his chair and looked at Huse with soft, watery eyes which Huse knew masked a brain like an electronic computer.

"Because it is the very toughest nut to crack of them all. Because it's the keystone of the whole thing." Huse leaned forward, knuckling the top of Kurtzman's desk to emphasize his points. "If you think we've had resistance from the white supremacists before, you wait until you see what we'll get when they realize we're trying to get our names on the registration books. Until this summer there wasn't the Negro support or enthusiasm or experience or even desire for a massive voting registration drive. I knew that it was the one area in which the whites would stand and fight, and I didn't want to go up against them with a slipshod, scratch campaign, a bunch of people who were lukewarm or scared. But I've got plenty of people who aren't either lukewarm or scared now, and I'm ready to tackle them. It's the psychological moment."

"Why? I don't want to seem obtuse, but I want to understand your thinking thoroughly."

"Certainly," Huse said. "Right this minute there's a civil rights bill in Congress. It doesn't have a prayer of passing this year, and maybe not next year either. If it did, it would give us in one stroke a great deal of what we've had to scrabble for, bit by bit.

"If we were already registered, if the Southern congressmen knew that they were going to have to account not only to white voters but to Negro ones as well, that bill would go through. But no bill is going to pass until we *are* registered, until we are voting, until we can exert pressure. And we need that bill badly."

He broke off, took a moment to light a cigarette.

"We can't go on indefinitely trying to win our rights by demonstrating and picketing and sitting-in. Nobody believes in nonviolence more than I do; nobody is more aware of its tremendous power. But the law of averages and common sense says we can't go on this way forever. It's too risky; it's like walking a tightrope. Sooner or later there's going to be a flare-up, a bad flare-up. My people are nonviolent, but they aren't saints. There'll be trouble, and if there is it'll start a chain reaction. The white South is more bitter than ever; this civil rights bill is a red flag waved in its face. Believe me, there are three or four states down there that would secede from the Union again if they thought they could get away with it; Muskogee's one of 'em. Another season of demonstrations like the ones we had this past summer, and there may be fighting. I don't want to risk that. Nonviolence would be discredited, and outfits like the Black Muslims with their hatred and black supremacy and their strong-arm

Fruit of Islam boys would move in and take over. And if the situation once degenerates into pitched battle, we'll be set back another hundred years."

Kurtzman nodded. "So you want to stage this one last campaign. Get your people registered and fight it out at the polls from now on."

"That's right. We've got to make that shift in emphasis. Civil rights will be the main issue in next year's elections. We've got to be voting by then. But time's even shorter than that. There are several states that have primary campaigns coming up next spring. And you know Democratic primaries in the South. They're the real elections as far as governors and congressmen are concerned. We've got to move fast if our weight is going to be felt in them."

He paused. "Only twenty-five per cent of eligible Negroes are registered to vote in the South right now—as opposed to sixty per cent of eligible whites. And actually, in nine states of the old Confederacy, including Muskogee, there has been a decline in Negro registration in the past several years. In the states that have primaries next spring, there will be a general registration this fall. I want to hit the registration places while that's going on, and I want to keep up pressure on the registration books afterward. We've laid the groundwork: our Better Citizens Schools have been educating our people in the South for two years now on their voting rights and how important they are, and we've covered a lot of territory. But it's still going to take full-time workers to go out and beat the bushes, to organize, to make sure that every Negro from the highest to the lowest knows how important this is and has a chance to register."

He stopped and grinned ruefully. "As a matter of fact, I'm not registered myself."

"What?" Kurtzman sat up straight.

"I'm not registered myself," Huse said again.

"Why not?"

"Because I couldn't pass the Muskogee literacy test," Huse said dryly. "All I have is a master's degree."

"That's outrageous!" Kurtzman snapped, his soft voice taking on an edge.

"Of course it is. But it's all in the registrar's hands. He's the supreme authority. You go in there to register and he may ask you to write the whole Constitution, word for word from memory, to prove your literacy. If you leave out a word—or even a comma—you flunk."

Kurtzman stood up, walked to the fireplace. "Most absurd thing I ever heard of!"

"Of course it's absurd. This whole business is riddled with absurdities. If it weren't all so painful, sometimes I'd break down laughing, not only at the whites but at us. We fight their absurdities with absurdities of our own. But it's better than using guns—so I reckon both sides are going to go on being absurd for a long time."

He ground out his cigarette, pushed back his chair so he could face Kurtzman.

"The literacy tactic is only one gimmick. In some places it's more brutal than that. There are still plenty of counties down South, Mr. Kurtzman, where a Negro who goes to register lays his life on the line. Period."

Kurtzman nodded, his soft mouth stretching and setting grimly. He was silent for a moment. Then he turned to Huse. "All right. Suppose you do get your people to the registration places. What then? What are you going to do when the registrars find them unqualified?"

"I've made arrangements for that," Huse said. "Tentatively. As far as possible, I want to take this thing state by state. There are some states where we expect very little trouble. But in the Deep South we expect to meet the toughest resistance ever—Muskogee, Alabama, Mississippi, parts of Georgia and Louisiana, some sections in upper Florida and in a good deal of South Carolina. But I think, by and large, Muskogee will be the toughest. And I want to make an all-out effort to crack that first. I think it's going to be possible, by concentrating on a state at a time, to arrange for observers from the Department of Justice and the Civil Rights Commission to be on hand at the real trouble spots. If their presence doesn't stop the unfair practices, then we'll be in a position to file suits and obtain injunctions." He stood up. "Believe me, Mr. Kurtzman, this is the most important part of the entire civil rights movement. It's the only way we'll ever safely secure real permanent benefits. And if we can crack Muskogee, if we can win there—well, then, I believe we can win anywhere."

Kurtzman nodded. "Of course we have our usual procedures and our usual red tape. But I think I can safely promise you the financial support you say you need." He smiled. "Your prestige is pretty high right now. That helps a lot, you know. When do you plan to run for public office, by the way?"

"What?" Huse said, startled.

"Surely, after you've accomplished your registration and voting objective you're not going to throw away the support you have among your people? All the publicity you've had? You know, you have considerable backing here in the North among the white liberals and intellectuals. It would be a shame to see all that tossed aside. You might break new ground in American politics."

Huse shook his head. "Mr. Kurtzman, I don't have any political ambitions at all. I don't know how a man could be any more frazzled out than I am. If I ever—if I just ever succeed in getting the Negro his fair share of America—his right to be whatever he has within him the capability to be, no more, no less—if I just ever get that, all I want to do is rest. I've lived with controversy, hatred, injustice and scheming for so long that I—well, there's just no way to explain how *dirty* you can feel, not because of what I've done or what my people have done, but because of the insights you get into the bigoted mind in a position like this. I've had enough filth thrown at me to last me a lifetime. No, sir, when the time comes that I can safely quit, that's exactly what I'm going to do."

"It seems a waste," Kurtzman said. "But, of course, I can imagine the demands it's made on your stamina." He smiled. "Do you think you can stand one more demand?"

"I reckon so," Huse said, grinning.

"Perhaps this won't be so terrible. Ever since word got out that you were coming to see us, I've been under terrific pressure from a lot of people who're very anxious to meet you." He smiled. "Including my wife. Would it be a great imposition on you to ask you to come and have cocktails with us and stay for dinner afterward? I think you'd find the people we're having in very interesting. Do you know Jack Rimmer?"

"No, I've always wanted to meet him. I've enjoyed his books—and we're tremendously indebted to him for the interest his writings have stirred up."

"Yes, well, he'll be there. And you'll want to meet Harold M'boto, too; he's the delegate to the UN from the Republic of Kaole, just admitted this year. And there are a great many others."

"I'd be delighted to come," Huse said. "Thank you for asking me."

"Thank you for coming," Kurtzman said, grinning. "Although I think I'd better warn you, if you stay in New York too long, you'll be in danger of becoming the lion of the social season."

Huse shook his head. "Can't afford that," he said. "Got to get back to Muskogee. Got too much work to do back there."

He had liked Jack Rimmer. The novelist was an incredibly tall, incredibly thin brown-skinned man with an enormous zest for life and an acid tongue. He had evidently gotten drunk fairly quickly, but he was entertaining when he was drunk.

"Man," he'd announced, clapping Huse on the shoulder, "you don't have to worry about a thing any more. From now on, it's all downhill. You got it made, dad."

"Is that so?" Huse asked quizzically. "How come?"

Rimmer grinned, showing big, yellow teeth. "Because you're fashionable now, pops. Everybody digs the freedom bit now. That's how you can always tell when you're winning. When the publicity hounds come over to your side. When the movie stars move in on you, you know you got it locked. When the Neanderthal men down South finally get you and you're six feet under, they can engrave it on your tombstone: *He Made Being a Nigger-Lover Popular*."

Huse laughed. "You've done your share."

Jack Rimmer sobered a little. "I've tried to. You know, it's not easy to break away from the old literary convention."

"Which one? You mean Uncle Tom?"

"No, hell, no. Uncle Tom was dead in literature a long time ago. No, I'm talking about the Negro as a patsy. The Erskine Caldwell, Lillian Smith, even Richard Wright Negro. The Negro as the man-who-can't-win, even when he fights. The victim of the system. The guy who always gets the block dropped on him." He paused, snatched a drink from a tray a maid carried by, and swallowed half at a gulp. "Then we've had the Negro-withdrawn-from-society. The Negro who says, The hell with it all, I'll opt out. I'll disengage. And so who, to show his disengagement, turns homosexual or something. Uh-uh, not old Uncle Tom. Uncle Tom did us less harm than any of the others." He finished the drink. "Now we're coming, though, to the

Negro as an American, the Negro as an *engaged* American. Being either one, American or engaged in it, hasn't been very popular in literature since the war."

"Actually," Huse said, "I guess all the images from Uncle Tom on have their validity. Somewhere along the line we've all gone through those stages."

"Ontogeny recapitulates phylogeny," Jack Rimmer said. Then he smiled widely at somebody behind Huse. "Do you know my friend, the honorable Harold M'boto?" Huse turned to see a broad-shouldered, very dark man in his early thirties. "Harold here," Rimmer went on, "has gone through one phase of development we missed. In his country they had a fad for a while of hacking white people up with *pangas*. Dr. M'boto, I'm sure you've heard of Houston Whitley."

"Long before I came to this country," M'boto said, smiling and putting out an immense, hard-palmed hand. He had a smooth, melodious English accent: Oxford, Huse guessed. "We have watched the ups and downs of your crusade with great interest, Mr. Whitley. Although for a long time we were engaged in one of our own."

"With slightly different tactics," said Rimmer, and he drew a finger across his throat.

Huse was watching to see if M'boto would be offended, but the dark man just nodded. "We have won our battle, Mr. Whitley, but yours seems still to go on. Mr. Rimmer likes to joke about the violence which we found necessary as part of our overall plan. Nobody regrets it more than I do. But with a large proportion of our population unacculturated, if I may use one of the sociologists' favorite terms, it was not feasible to use a completely sophisticated approach to our problems." He sipped from his drink; his suaveness vanished for a moment. "I wonder if a touch of the *panga* wouldn't have a salutory effect in your own program," he said, his voice crisp.

Huse shook his head, something in the man's eyes touching his spine with chill. "No, I don't think so," he said. "Our problem is different from yours, Dr. M'boto. It was *your* country; you were faced with the problem of driving out white interlopers and reclaiming it. But this country belongs exclusively neither to black nor white. All we want to do is work out some sort of *modus vivendi* for sharing it."

M'boto shrugged. "As you say . . ."

"But I do want to say this," Huse went on earnestly. "The rise of the black nations in Africa has had a tremendous effect on the morale of American Negroes. It's given them a racial pride they've never owned before, a feeling of global identity. Frankly, there was a time here in America when one of the worst insults one Negro could hurl at another was: *you black African!* But there's been such a tremendous surge of pride in what you people have accomplished that American Negroes are falling all over themselves now to reclaim and repossess their African heritage."

"That's very encouraging," M'boto said. "Of course, we face a frightening task. There's only a very small cadre of us bearing the burden of bringing our country into the twentieth century almost by main strength. We have problems of poverty, illiteracy, and tribalism beyond anything you can imagine. We're going to make mistakes, I daresay, but we hope eventually to prove to the world what you and I are both trying to say in our own diverse ways: that we can stand alone if the whites will just let us."

"Yes," Huse said. "I guess that's it."

"I wonder," M'boto went on, "if your Southern Ku Klux knows just how much effect its actions have on the image of your country abroad. We have had overtures from your State Department, but how could we explain it to our own people if we publicly aligned ourselves with a country where the very principles we ourselves fought for are still in doubt?"

"Well, of course," Huse said, "part of the impression you get of us is probably erroneous. Not all Southerners are Ku Klux by any means. Or even rabid white supremacists. Frankly, if it hadn't been for the help of a great many whites, we might not be as far along as we are. A case in point: we have what we call the Better Citizens Schools. We train teachers to go out and organize schools among the illiterate Southern Negroes, teach them how to read and write and take political action. But we've found out that it's far simpler to organize these schools in most sections if we can get some local white person to take part, too. Otherwise the local Negroes won't participate. There seems to have to be a white person involved before they feel that they can fully trust us. And as for the Ku Klux, they're a minority, a lunatic fringe. The only danger from them is the initiative they hold—of course, it's not inconsiderable."

"What do you mean, initiative?" Rimmer asked.

"I mean that they're the people who can light the fuse. The crackpots, who'll stop at nothing. That gives them a sort of initiative far beyond their actual numbers. With one bomb they can blow hours, days, months of negotiations apart. With one bomb at the wrong time, they could blow the whole nonviolent movement apart. But it hasn't happened yet; let's pray it never will."

"The generosity of your heart," M'boto said, "is refreshing, but I find it a little naïve." His eyes dulled. "Or perhaps I myself bear too many scars." He let out a long breath, then brightened and smiled. "Been awfully nice talking to both of you. See you again later; there's someone over there I simply must speak to." He turned away.

When he had gone, Rimmer said quietly, "Man, yonder goes what I would call a cool cat."

After M'boto, there had been the usual blur of the sort of people Huse had come to expect at functions like this. The passionate liberals denouncing the white South *in toto,* a little taken aback upon meeting Huse to find only a mild-mannered colored man of medium height, not a dark John Brown ready to slash his way to freedom with a flaming sword. The admiring, usually middle-aged women who clustered about him and tried to sound *au courant* and who sometimes had a hunger in their eyes that embarrassed him. And the encouraging middle ground, the well-informed people of good will whose presence reassured him, even if their numbers were not overwhelmingly impressive.

Afterward the dinner had been excellent and he had been the center of attention, and, all in all, it had been a satisfactory evening. Now, stretched out on the bed in the hotel room, he was sorry that it had ended. He had another two days in New York, and he knew that he could not spend that much time here without something stirring in him that he had managed thus far to keep suppressed. In the loneliness of the room, with nobody to draw his thoughts outward to immediacy, it almost immediately began to bear in on him. He thought of Virginia.

He was still thinking of her after he had undressed and climbed between the sheets; as if he had conjured her out of thin air by the force of his own will, she called him on the telephone next morning.

10 The phone rang and he thought it was the desk with his call for the morning. He groped, found the instrument, dragged it to his ear. "Houston Whitley," he said.

There was an instant's silence; he could hear breathing only; it sounded heavy. Then a shaky voice said, "Huse! Do . . . you know who this is?"

He knew immediately; it was if he had heard that voice only a moment before, and he came wholly out of sleep without any lag. "Yes," he said, and his own voice shook. "Yes, hello, Virginia."

"Hello," she said. "Hello, Huse. How are you?"

It was like a phone call across an ocean, he thought. A call you waited forever to get put through and then when it came you couldn't think of anything to say.

"It is you, isn't it?" he said. One hand scrabbled for the pack of cigarettes on the chipped nightstand.

She gave an unsteady laugh. "Yes, it's me, aren't you surprised? I heard that you were going to be in town; I thought maybe you were staying there. Isn't it an ungodly time of morning for me to call? I set my alarm clock especially so I could catch you before you got away."

"Well," he said again, getting a cigarette into one corner of his mouth, "this is a surprise. How are you?"

"I'm fine. I'm in town to talk over a part in a musical; I've never done a musical before."

His hand shook as he got the lighter into flame and brought it to the cigarette. "Well," he said, squinting against the smoke.

"I've been reading all about you," she said. "For years now. I'm so proud of you."

"I've been reading about you. And seeing your pictures and your programs."

"Did you really? Did you see my pictures?"

"All of them," he said.

He heard her sigh as if in relief.

"Where are you?" he asked. "Where are you staying?"

"A friend of mine has loaned me her apartment. It's on Sutton Place."

"Oh. Sutton Place. High cotton."

"Yes," she said. "High cotton." Then, "Huse."

His mouth was dry; he licked his lips. "Uh-huh."

"It's funny," she said, "my hands are perspiring all over the telephone. I— Huse, we can see each other, can't we?"

"Of course." He realized that he was trembling slightly all over now. It was excitement, but it was fear, too. "I mean, I've got to go back to the Gosnell Foundation this morning. And there are some NAACP people I promised to have lunch with. But—"

"You're free for dinner, aren't you?"

"Yes," he said.

"Then I can make reservations for us at—"

"Virginia," he cut in.

"What's the matter?" Her voice sounded apprehensive. "It's all right, Huse. I . . . times have changed." She gave a faltering laugh. "I know what you're thinking. But actually it would be good publicity for me, not bad. I—"

"It's not that," he said. "It's that I don't want to be seen out in public with *you*."

"What?" she said, startled.

"Not just the two of us. I know how those gossip columnists follow you; they've started to follow me, too, and I—"

"That's right," she said dully. "Of course, you're married, aren't you? And it's two children, isn't it?"

"Uh-huh. But it's not that. Look, I've got a certain . . . well, image to maintain. Dining tête-à-tête with you is not part of it. In a crowd, a party, yes, but . . ."

"I don't want a crowd or a party," she said, her voice hurt. "I just want to be able to talk to you."

She was silent for a moment. Then she said, "You're still angry with me, aren't you, Huse?"

"Angry?" It had not occurred to him. Angry? With his heart feeling as if it wanted to hammer its way out of his ribs? With his body still trembling with excitement?

"You know. Because of Hannington. And because I never wrote you. I meant to send some money to FREE, I meant to tell my business manager . . ."

"It's all right," he said. "No, I'm not angry with you, Ginnie. God, no. I want to see you. I just don't dare risk giving anybody anything to use against me, doing the slightest thing to injure the . . . faith people have in me. Hell, what I'm trying to say is, I can't afford for it to look like I'm living high, carousing around. What about your apartment? Can't you feed me there?"

"I don't have a cook. And I'm not very good myself at—"

"Order sandwiches, then. I don't care. Just tell me the address and what time you want me to come."

She told him. He found a pencil in the drawer of the nightstand and wrote it down carefully. "About seven."

"Earlier," she said. "Earlier, if you can."

"I guess that'll be about it."

"Wonderful," she said. "Oh, Huse, darling . . ." Her voice trailed off.

"Yes," he said.

"I do so much want to see you." Her voice was very soft and low; it stirred him in a way that he had almost forgotten. "I have missed you so much," she added.

The apartment house doorman gave him a sullen, suspicious look as he entered and seemed about to halt him. Huse had an extreme sense of being out of his milieu; this was Virginia's sort of place, not his. Though continuing to glare, the doorman offered him no hindrance and Huse thought dryly as he found the elevator: He stays up-to-date. He knows this is a fashionable color.

As the elevator rose, he thought about what he knew of Virginia's career, which was almost everything. She had been married twice, once to an actor—a publicity gimmick, everybody had said; the second time to a California real estate man who had divorced her three years before to marry a twenty-two-year-old second wife. There was not much about Virginia in the fan magazines now, though she still occasionally made the gossip columns of newspapers.

He got off the elevator and paused in the corridor for a moment. Then he searched for the door and found it.

She must have been waiting for him, because as soon as he knocked, the apartment door swung open and she was standing there, wearing a simple white dress of the sort that she had liked so long ago.

"Huse, darling!" she said; but he just stood there for a moment looking at her.

First of all, she had dyed her hair—a dark rich red. The effect was flattering, but it was not what he had expected, and it threw him off balance for a moment, that lacquered swirl of deep bronze in place of the long, soft black he remembered. Then she took his hand and pulled him inside, and he saw what else the years had done to her that cameras had disguised. The line of her profile as she turned her head was still sharp, but there were crow's-feet at the corners of her eyes, and a suggestion of sag beneath her chin. Her body had not thickened at all.

When the door swung shut behind them, she said, "Oh, Huse," and took his other hand, too, and moved close to him and held up her face.

She was so white now, so utterly and completely white, so divorced from her roots, that he knew a moment of hesitation, guilt, and a kind of panic before he bent and kissed her. Her mouth worked at his, but he made the kiss a brief one, pulling his own face away; and then he stepped back, his hands sliding out of hers. "Hello, Ginnie," he said. He was not meeting her eyes, still off balance, finding it impossible to think of her as a Negro.

She laughed nervously. "Sweetie," she said; it was not a word he remembered her using. "Oh, sweetie, it's so good to see you. Come on in and . . . I've got everything ready for the drinks. Let's have a drink or we won't know what to say to each other."

"Sure," he said, smiling at last. "Let's have a drink." He followed her into the small, feminine living room and she took his hat and put it somewhere and he sat down on one of the two sofas. Coming back, she confronted him, rubbing the palms of her hands together nervously, smiling, and said, "You'll want bourbon-and-water."

"That would be fine."

She did not move.

"Or maybe . . . you'd just like a Coke like we used to drink at Johnson's after the workshop." She laughed shrilly.

Huse's laughter joined hers, but he still could not make the connection in his mind that she so obviously wanted him to. "Maybe we'll have the Coke later. Bourbon now, huh?"

While she was mixing the drinks at the portable bar, she said, "You know, I'm so proud of you."

"Nothing to be proud of," he said.

"Yes, there is. You've accomplished so much. Who would ever

have thought—" She came toward him with the drinks. "I've told my business manager to write you a check," she said. "It's not a large one—I can't afford a great deal unless this show clicks—but—"

"All contributions gratefully accepted," he said, taking the glass. Then there was silence between them. She sat down on the floor at his feet, and the silence dragged on. She cleared her throat.

"Well," she said at last, "aren't you going to ask me how I've been?"

"I know how you've been," he said. "I've read all the publicity about you."

She looked down at the carpet. "That," she said. Then, "Huse."

"Yeah?"

"I'm sorry." Still she was not looking at him. "I really am."

He drew in a deep breath. "No call to be sorry," he said. "You did the smart thing. Otherwise, you never would have had a chance to do what you were born to do."

Her voice was ruefully bitter. "You sound so damned philosophic about it. I'm beginning to think you didn't miss me at all."

Huse closed his eyes for a moment, shook his head. When he opened them, she was looking at him intently.

"I missed you," he said. "I thought I was going crazy, I missed you so much."

She said in a relieved voice, "Good," and she arose gracefully and sat down beside him on the sofa. "That's much better," she whispered, and her hand touched his arm.

It was such ambiguous ground on which they met that despite everything either of them could think of, strain persisted until after the second drink lent them a measure of relaxation that passed for assurance. Then, at first slowly and with forced awkwardness, gradually loosening and quickening, they began to talk, until at last they were going on greedily and with tremendous speed, as if each desperately wanted to fill that seventeen-year gap by telling the other every event, every emotion, of the interim.

He noticed that Virginia drank quite a lot, more than he did. The whiskey seemed to make her bitter.

"People are fools," she said, "idiots, to want success. Because after you get it, you've got to hold onto it, and it's like trying to hold quicksilver. You start out an amateur and then suddenly find out you've become a professional and you can't make excuses any longer. From then on, you've got to deliver or else . . . and somebody's always looking down your throat and all of a sudden you find out you're not even a person any more, just an enterprise, a business, and you don't dare fail. . . . And you can't keep track of yourself in all that, it's so hard to find out what became of you, and after a while you realize that maybe there's not really any you left at all." She gestured wildly with her glass. "You know what I said once? I said that I wished I'd been born black as the ace of spades at the end of a corn row." She drank deeply from her glass. "That still holds."

"No, it doesn't," he said.

They were sitting across the table from each other. She had had an excellent dinner sent in, but she was not eating any of it. She was just drinking and talking. Especially talking.

"Yes, it does," she said. "Because then I'd know exactly who I was." She pointed at him. "Look at you. You didn't try to escape from what you were, and—"

"You think I didn't?" he said. "You think if I'd been born your color, I'd be in all this? I'd have done just what you did, passed, looked out for myself. But I was too dark."

She got up from the table and came around to where he sat. She knelt beside his chair and took his hand.

"I love your darkness," she said. "I've missed it."

Her voice trailed off. He looked down at her. Under the makeup her skin was getting grainy, there was slackness and crepiness around her eyes, lines at the corners of her mouth that were too deep. But that was not what made him shove back his chair. He did not know what made him do that, because he wanted her very much.

"No, Ginny," he heard his voice say, and it seemed to come from a long way off, surprising him as much as her.

She let go of his hand and stood up. She blinked her eyes. "What?"

Huse was aware that he was trembling. He drew in a long breath. Again his voice seemed detached from him. "No," he said, "it isn't going to work."

"What?" she said again in a shriller tone.

"It isn't going to work," Huse said. His hand flailed the air. "Maybe we've both lost something," he said. "But it's too late to find it now." He hesitated. "You thinking you are going to use me to find out who you are, and me thinking the same thing about you. Both of us looking for ourselves in each—it isn't going to work."

"Huse," she said numbly.

"I'm not sure if I can say it." The words came tumbling out of him. "I mean, you passed over. You moved into that other world and then you didn't find anything in it to hang on to, and now you're trying to come back and find in your old one what you couldn't find in the new one. But it's too late, don't you see? You've got to be one thing or the other. Maybe you could come back, but you'd have to come back all the way, and you don't want that, do you? That would be mighty rough, coming back all the way."

Her eyes were enormous, looking into his. "Maybe I wouldn't have to come back all the way," she whispered. "Maybe I could bring you partway into my world." Suddenly she was against him, putting her hands on his arms. "Times are different now." Her voice trembled. "This isn't 1946 any more. Huse, we could . . ."

He had never done anything that cost him more, but he took her hands and moved them away; and he knew that what he was saying was true and right. "No, we couldn't, Virginia. I've got a wife, you know. And children."

"A wife," she said. "I've had two husbands. A wife isn't—"

"Oh, yes," he heard himself say, as if a part of him that he had never known existed were talking. "Oh, yes, she is important." The words echoed strangely in his head. *She is important.* Then he went on. "Ginny, you can't have your cake and eat it too. You want to find what you're looking for, you'd have to jump all the way back across that line." His eyes met hers, directly and unwaveringly. "You'd have to have the guts to stand up in meeting and say, *I am a Negro and I am proud of it.*"

For a moment she returned his gaze; then her eyes slid away and she lowered her head.

"You see?" he said quietly.

"Can you say that?" she asked in a strangled voice. "Just now you were saying you settled for second best."

"There isn't any second best," he said. "There's only different best."

Somehow he managed a faint smile. "You wouldn't like my life anyhow," he said. "It isn't all dinners and speeches and cocktail parties. It's Little Hammers, too, and Harlems and South Sides. It's the insides of jails, and lying awake listening to every car that passes your house in the night, wondering which one of them is toting the dynamite. Or standing on a platform at a mass meeting and knowing what a good target you make for a sniper. . . . But I've got my hand to the plow and I can't turn loose, so I can't go into any other world. Do you *really* want to come back into mine?"

She turned away, and her head was bent and her voice muffled. "No," she said. "No."

He stood there a moment longer. It was all he could do to keep from going to her and putting his arms about her. But instead he said, very softly, "It's getting late. I guess I'd better be getting along. Somebody sees me coming out of here as it is, there might be a scandal neither one of us could afford."

Still she was not looking at him. "Maybe you're right," she whispered.

He turned toward the door. "Goodbye, Ginny."

Her voice rasped with the control she was exerting. "Goodbye, Huse." Then she raised her head, and though her eyes were glistening, she was smiling. "I—I'll tell my business manager not to forget that check to FREE."

"We thank you," he said gravely, looking at her, and he opened the door.

"Huse!" Her voice was strangled, imploring.

"Good night, Ginny," he said quietly, and then he went out and gently shut the door behind him.

11   Cary Bradham broke the double-barreled shotgun to make sure it was empty and slid it into the back seat of the car. Then, his hunting coat pocket heavy with quail, he turned and looked at The Place as if reluctant to leave it.

Truly, he was. Working the dogs across the thick sedge in the pine flats and around the edge of the swamp, he had been able to forget for an afternoon the pressures that seemed now to be tightening on him like the jaws of a nutcracker. He was not anxious to go back toward Hannington; it meant going back into the nutcracker.

At last, though, he slid behind the steering wheel and started the engine. He turned the car around, and as it began the long, bouncing journey up the unpaved drive to the main road, his mind, though he tried to prevent it, insisted on beginning to chew on his problems.

Everything was coming at him all at once. He was going to have to make some decisions and must not be long about it. Damn it, he thought, seventeen years: Hoke's shuffled governors in and out of office like a man playing with toy soldiers. Now, when it's finally *my* chance, after all this time, why does somebody like Alec Morrison have to come along? Why do I have to be the one out of all those who has the opposition?

Morrison and Houston Whitley, he thought: they were the two jaws of the nutcracker, bearing down on him harder and harder. Morrison, off and running early, when he, Cary, hadn't even announced his candidacy yet, Morrison already stumping all around the state with his promises: *There will be no more integration in Muskogee. . . . We will yield not one inch. . . . They will have to arrest or shoot me before I let the Yankees usurp any more of our rights. . . . Muskogee will join with Alabama and Mississippi in voting for a slate of unpledged electors. . . .* And the red-necks were eating it up.

And, in direct opposition, Houston Whitley and that damned voting campaign of his. *We will make a massive assault on the registration books and on the polling places. . . . This is one election in which we must make our weight felt. . . . I will put ten thousand new voters on the registration books the first day. . . .*

To anyone unversed in politics, the two forces would seem to cancel each other. Certainly, given a choice between him and Morrison, the Negroes, even if they did achieve their massive registration goals, would spurn Morrison, turn to him as the more moderate of the two. They would not have anywhere else to go.

Nor could Morrison, maverick that he was, hope to win simply by arousing the common voters. Nobody won in Muskogee without control of the Democratic organization—that carefully constructed, firmly interlocked, and intricate combination of ratchets, pinions and cogwheels powered by patronage, oiled by mutual interest, and sometimes supercharged by intimidation. And the controls of that machine were firmly in the hands of the Moodys—and of Powell Bradham.

So you'd think I'd feel safe, Cary thought. But he knew Muskogee too well for that. The trouble and danger to himself and to the Moodys lay not in the major workings of the machine, but in its minor parts, the cotter pins and nuts and bolts that held it together, for the people in the black counties of the state were afraid.

They were empires, those sixty out of the state's ninety counties —empires where white emperors had held power and ruled supreme since time immemorial. The chief concern of each of those emperors was survival. As long as Moody could assure them survival—the county commissioners, the mayors, the councilmen, the hundreds of elected officials who drew nourishment and sometimes wealth from public office—as long as he could assure them survival and the continuing profitable rule of their own satrapies, then they were his men, part of his machine.

But they survived because in their counties only twenty or maybe thirty per cent of the inhabitants could vote. Because power was concentrated in white hands, the hands of the white minority. Now Houston Whitley was threatening to dilute that power, maybe wrench it away from them entirely, give it to the black majority—and they knew, those emperors, what would happen then, and if Moody did not keep it from happening, they would turn to someone who would.

Because, thought Cary, that was what it all boiled down to when you backed off and looked at it. The whole thing—all the marches and slogans and pitched battles and good intentions and shouts for freedom—underneath, basically, was just a struggle for power. The whites had it and the Negroes wanted it and the whites were not going to yield it willingly any more than the British had in 1776 or than the slave states had in the 1850s and '60s, or than the Radical Republicans had in Reconstruction days. Nobody who had power ever turned it over to anyone else without fighting to keep it as long as he could. Neither would the ruling minority of whites in the black counties.

So there was a chance that by assuring them no diminution of their power, by promising them that he would stand between them and the wave of black votes with which Houston Whitley shouted he would overwhelm them, Morrison could pry the whites in those black counties away from the Moodys and the Bradhams. Rationally, they should know that there was only a certain amount that anyone could do without ripping the state out of the Union altogether, but they were scared to death and in no mood to be rational. And if they turned to Morrison to save them, that would be a serious matter, perhaps a fatal one. . . .

Cary cursed softly under his breath. The irony of it, he thought, was that the more Houston Whitley put on pressure, the more likely he was to be the chief factor in electing the worst segregationist of them all.

He reached the wide dirt road and turned on that toward the paved highway. He saw that his gas was low and made a mental note to stop at the store in Troublefield and get the tank filled.

The terrible part of it, what made the pressure on him so excruciating, was that there did not seem any way to keep Huse from actually registering a tremendous number of Negroes. Announcement had already been made that on the three general registration days next week, the Federal government would have observers checking registration books all over the state, scrutinizing registration procedures. If they found discrepancies, there would be injunctions and Federally appointed referees. Everybody had counted on Hoke Moody to keep the observers out of the state, to pull the strings and exert the power of which he had boasted, but Hoke was grown old and senile and ineffective, and he had not, for all his bragging, been able to block their announced intention to come.

So that Morrison would already be making gains; and he himself could waste no more time making his own announcement and getting into the battle. Every day was precious, and his father and Dale Moody were hammering at him remorselessly.

But he had fended them off, fighting for time. They were right, of course: move, and move now. But he felt stricken, paralyzed, hoarding every moment of delay.

For, he understood clearly, despite all his bravado and determination at first, once he was in the battle there was no way he could keep Maggie; he could not afford her if he intended to win. He could not afford any handicap at all, and she made him vulnerable.

And though time was running out, he would cling to her as long as he could, because he did not know how he could live without her.

He hit the paved road, driving faster than he should have, as if somehow the frustration and indecision he felt could flow out through the accelerator. After a while he saw ahead of him the scattering of buildings, the glinting high sheet-iron façade of the cotton gin, that was Troublefield; and he remembered the gas.

The store had not changed much in all these years; it was still the long, cavernous, wide-porched wooden building plastered with tin signs; only the pumps outside were new, squat and modern. He was a little surprised at the number of cars parked on the driveway and the size of the group of loafers on the steps this early on a weekday afternoon. Swinging in beside the pumps, he stopped and got out. There would be no attendant leaping forward to fill his tank and clean his windshield; he would have to go inside and get Clete Daniels and maybe wait until Clete got through with whatever conversation he was engaged in or customer he was serving.

The loafers made room for him to climb the steps. He looked at them curiously, finding it odd that he did not recognize a single one of them, though they were all country-enough-looking men. It puzzled him, and he thought about it as he crossed the porch.

I reckon I'm getting out of touch, he told himself. Time had been when his father and then himself had known just about everybody who came to the store. That was part of the politician's art, and a part his father had not let him neglect.

Clete Daniels was a muscular, open-faced man in khakis, a leather change purse on his belt. Two generations of his family before him had tended store here. He and Cary had hunted together once or twice in their teens; they were on terms of easy familiarity. Daniels was ripping open cases of canned coffee with a hawk-billed knife; when he saw Cary, he smiled and straightened up.

"Hello, Gov."

"Not yet." Cary grinned.

"Okay, Loot Gov, then," Clete said. He patted the bulging game pocket of Cary's coat. "Looks like you had some luck."

"The dogs were finding good today."

"Where at you go?"

"Down there in those pine flats other side of Beech Creek and 'round the edge of the swamp. Put up a half-dozen coveys, all big ones."

"Good deal," Daniels said. "You don't mind if I take my dogs down in there, do you? Birds are kind of thinned out on our place."

"Help yourself," Cary said, going to the drink box. "You know you're always welcome." He got out a Coca-Cola and snapped off

454 · LOOK AWAY, LOOK AWAY

the cap. "When you get around to it, any chance of talking you out
of a tank of high-test? I'm running on the fumes."

"Sho," Clete said. He went behind the counter and put away the
hawk-billed knife. When Cary tried to hand him a dime, he waved
his hand. "Drink's on the house, might buy me some political influence."

"Pay for your birds, anyhow," Cary said. Then he lowered his
voice. "Clete, who's all that sitting on your porch out yonder? I
thought I knew everybody around here at least by sight."

Clete's smile faded as he came around the counter. "Damned if
I know. They don't live around here. But they've been hangin around
since dinnertime. Come in in two cars, one with a Muskogee plate,
other with a Texas plate. I reckon they're boomin through headed
for some sort of construction job or somethin. I'm kindly keepin an
eye on 'em." He started for the door, and Cary followed him.

There was nothing at all out of the ordinary about the half-dozen
men on the steps. They looked up in friendly enough fashion,
nodded, as Cary stopped on the porch.

"Howdy," Cary said.

"Howdy," one of them said. He was thin, with a red, freckled face
and bad teeth. "Look like you been bird huntin."

Cary nodded. While Clete filled the tank, he squatted down,
propping his back against the front of the store, and drank the
Coca-Cola. The men were silent, as if he had interrupted their conversation. After a while the thin, red man stood up, yawned,
stretched. "Well, I reckon we'd better be gittin on," he said.

Cary frowned slightly. He had not missed the bulge in the thin
man's left armpit, though it had shown only faintly against the coat;
the man was wearing a shoulder holster.

He watched them amble across the yard to the pair of cars parked
there. As Clete slammed down the hood of his own vehicle, they
got in and started engines; then the cars wheeled out of the yard and
drove off toward Hannington. As Clete had said, one of them had a
Texas license plate.

Clete came back up on the porch. "Well, I see my company's done
gone and left me. I'm just as glad. They kindly made me nervous.
One of them cars has got a rifle layin across the back seat; I seen it
a while ago."

"Maybe they're going hunting."

"With a Springfield thirty-aught-six?"

Cary stood up and took out his credit card. "True," he said. "It's against the law to hunt with anything but a shotgun down here, but maybe they're passing on through to another state."

"Might be. Anyhow, I'm glad they're gone." Clete looked serious. "There's likely to be trouble enough next week as it is, if any of these niggers around here come to register."

Exactly at the same moment that the little slide on the automatic credit-card ticket imprinter clicked, something clicked in Cary's brain. He said, "That's right. You're the registration and polling place for this township, aren't you?"

"Yeah. And I don't need no people hangin around with high-powered guns." Clete handed back the credit card. "They send one of those damned Civil Rights people down here to hang around and spy, I'm liable to hang me a Yankee hide right on the barn door, but I don't want nobody else shootin up the place. I reserve that right for myself." He paused. "Cary, goddammit, you people better git off your ass or the niggers are gonna take over this state."

"Don't worry about that," Cary said quickly and with a flare of anger. "We aren't going to let that happen."

"Well, this Houston Whitley stomps and hollers and yells about all he aims to do, and we don't hear a cryin word out of you people. You better git yourself in gear or Alec Morrison's gonna walk all over you."

"Alec Morrison's not gonna walk over anybody!"

"Okay, okay." Clete raised a conciliatory hand. "I'm just tryin to give you some friendly advice."

"Sure," Cary said in an easier tone. "I didn't mean to fly off the handle." He made his voice deep and confident. "Don't worry, Clete; you stick with us. We've got plans to take care of the situation. Alec Morrison's nothing but a bag of wind."

"You know that and I know that," Clete said, "but a lot of people don't. What he says sounds like it makes sense and like it's needed sayin for a long time. We've et too much shit from that damn crowd up yonder. It's time to stand up and put an end to it." Then he grinned. "Which end of the swamp are those covies usin?"

"Go up to where Spring Branch runs into the creek and work the fork," Cary said. "I found 'em right on the edge of the cane." He put the credit card in his wallet and his wallet in his pocket. "Don't worry about the niggers, Clete. The Moodys and the Bradhams, we'll take care of the niggers for you."

"Somebody better take care of 'em," Clete said, and he flipped a hand as Cary went out. "We'll see you," he said. "Come back soon."

His mother was very glad to see him, though she tried not to look at the dead birds he laid out on the kitchen table, and it took several moments of aimless chatter before he could get away for a few minutes with his father. They went into Bradham's office and Bradham poured two drinks.

"You found a lot of birds today," Bradham said, and his voice was wistful. Cary thought with a pang how much his father must miss the outdoors. It occurred to him for the first time that perhaps the mind did not age at all; maybe in men like his father only the body did, so that there was a strong, lusty mind trapped in an old, rickety body. That, he thought with compassion, must be the worst torture of all. To be old and not to be senile. . . .

So instead of getting to it directly, he told his father in great detail all about the hunt, how the dogs had worked, where he had found the coveys, how many doubles he had scored; and his father listened avidly, eyes gleaming. At last, by logical progression, he worked up to the point where he had come to the Troublefield store, and told his father about the men.

"You know what it made me think of?" he said casually. "It made me think of that guy Whipple. That crazy army colonel."

His father had listened to that part of it intently, not speaking. Now he nodded. "Yes, I can see how it would." His father got up and freshened his glass but did not take any more whiskey himself. "But you heard what Hoke told him last time. So far as I know, Hoke hasn't changed his mind."

"I hope not," Cary said with a little more sharpness than he had intended; he was beginning to feel the whiskey. "I'd hate to think Hoke or anybody else would do anything like that without talking to me about it. After all, this is going to be *my* campaign. And it either *is* going to be or there's not going to be any campaign as far as I'm concerned. For all I know, these fellows were bound up to the mountains bear hunting, but they made me think of Whipple. I don't want him in here. *I* don't want him in here, *I, me*."

"All right," his father said with a trace of irritation. "Don't get so excited. Hoke Moody—or Dale either—is not going to do anything behind my back. I know everything that goes on. You've had enough," he said as Cary started for the bottle again. "Now sit down and listen to me."

"Yes, sir," Cary said intractably.

His father's voice changed. "Forget about those men. We've got other things to worry about. Son, we've got to get moving. We've got to make a formal announcement. And we can't do a thing until you"—he lowered his voice, though no sound could have got through the big closed doors—"get rid of that woman."

Still feeling rebellious, Cary looked at him a moment. "Suppose I don't get rid of her?"

"Now, look," his father said, with great control.

"Suppose I love her," Cary said. "Wouldn't that make any difference to anybody?"

His father stood up. "You're a married man; you've got a wife."

"Mary Scott—" Cary began and then he said, miserably, "skip it."

His father turned his back on him, fiddling with the bourbon bottle. "I don't want to see you hurt." His voice seemed muffled. "I don't understand this . . . this kind of . . . affair, but the main thing is you know I don't want to see you hurt." There was a pause. "But you've got to choose," his father said at last. "You've got to make up your mind one way or the other. Do something, but for God's sake, don't keep me hanging on the edge. I've hung on the edge for thirty years; that's long enough. If you're not going to make the run, I've got some quick patching up to do somewhere, somehow. So do something, let me know."

"Dad—" Cary said, torn and anguished.

"Are you or are you not going to run?" Still his father's back was turned.

Are you or are you not?

Cary stared at the old man's back.

It was the first time it had ever been put to him as a choice; his mind flailed, trying to grasp the implications of that phrasing. Suppose I don't? he thought, shaken and frightened by having dared think it. Suppose I don't?

He stood there for a moment, appalled by what was running through his mind.

His own voice sounded strange to him, and it came without his having anything to do with it, or so it seemed.

"I'll let you know," he said quietly, but without subservience, and then he turned and went out.

When he got home, Mary Scott was on the telephone. She stayed on it for a half hour, talking to somebody about a fashion show the Woman's Club was giving. Cary used that time to strip out of his hunting clothes and shower, taking a drink into the bedroom with him.

Mary Scott's voice bore in on him inexorably.

". . . if you want to know what I think, well, frankly, I think that Sylvia Ginsburg is just trying to take over the whole show. You know what an inferiority complex she's got and this is just what she's been waiting for, with Fred furnishing everything, you know, and she thinks that gives her some kind of special authority, makes her real big, and honestly, somebody ought to talk to her. Oh, it would be for her own good, I don't think she even knows how much everybody resents that bossiness of hers, and, of course, it all comes from that inferiority complex, looking back on it I think it was a mistake not to have approached Carter-Merriman first, but, of course, with Sylvia right there in the club I guess it would have looked like we were bridging her nose, but . . ."

For God's sake, Cary thought. It was impossible to think; the pitch of her voice carried even through a closed door. And he had so much to think about. After he had finished showering and had dried, he stalked restlessly about the bedroom with a towel snugged around his waist and the drink in his hand. Finally he heard the rising inflection that meant, just possibly, that Mary Scott would be through in perhaps five minutes. He began to dress. As he was tying his shoes, the voice rose even higher and then said, "Bye-bye," and after that there was a blessed silence.

She came into the bedroom. For an instant he was afraid that she was going to recapitulate the entire phone conversation, but she did not. She was on the threshold of her forties, and her body had thickened a bit; her face, always round, was becoming a moon, bereft now of youthful redeeming kittenishness, so that she was no longer pretty. He supposed that if he had loved her, he would not have noticed that.

She looked at the drink in his hand in a way she had. Then she said, "Did you have a nice hunting trip?"

"Fine, thank you." He took a swallow from the glass, set it down on the table, and went back to the shoelaces.

"That was Grace Dabney on the phone."

"Uh-huh," he said.

"She asked when you were going to make a campaign announcement."

He raised his head. "When I get good and ready," he said.

"She said Mark certainly does like the way Alec Morrison talks."

"Mark can go take a flying leap at the moon."

Mary Scott was silent for a moment. "Well," she said at last, "when are you going to make an announcement? Everybody keeps asking me, and I don't know anything to tell 'em. It's real embarrassing."

Cary stood up, finished the drink, shook a cigarette out of a pack, put the pack in his pocket and lit the cigarette. He took it from his lips and blew a plume of smoke and looked at Mary Scott.

"Suppose I don't make an announcement," he said. "Suppose I change my mind and decide not to run for Governor?"

She stared at him, her blue eyes getting huge and round. Then she laughed shortly. "Have you gone out of your mind?"

"No," said Cary bluntly. "No, I don't think so. It's just that I may decide not to run."

"Well, of all the foolishness." The wide eyes narrowed. "What's got into you, anyhow? You're not serious."

"Nothing's got into me. There's no law that says I *have* to run, is there?"

"But . . . but everybody's always known you'd be Governor someday. *Everybody* knew that."

"Sure," said Cary bitterly. "Everybody. You, Dad, Hoke Moody, the whole kit and biling of you. Each one of you workin' out your little bit of my life so that there was nothing left for me to do. Damn nice of y'all, wasn't it?"

Mary Scott's mouth set itself. "Well, this is certainly the most foolish thing *I* ever heard of, and I've heard some foolish things from you in my time. Does Daddy Powell know about this?"

"No," said Cary in biting mockery of her high voice, "Daddy Powell doesn't know about this."

"Don't you mock me like that!" she flared unexpectedly. Then she smiled. "I'll bet when Daddy Powell hears you talking this kind of foolishness, he'll set you straight in a hurry."

"I'll make my own decisions," Cary said.

"Oh, yeah, sure, you'll make your own decisions." Now she was mocking him.

Cary turned away from her and began to scoop his wallet, keys and change off the bed and stow them in his pockets. Behind him Mary Scott was silent. But she was seething; he could feel that in the silence.

Then she said viciously, "Maggie Jessup put you up to this, didn't she?"

Cary jerked erect and whirled.

"What?" He was ashamed of the tremor in the word: it's not guilt, he thought, just surprise. Since Burke's funeral Mary Scott had given no indication that she knew Maggie still existed.

"I said that Jessup woman put you up to this, didn't she? It sounds like her Yankee notions."

Cary looked at her. He had not suspected that her face was capable of becoming so hard; beneath the roundness there was a separate frame of muscle, as if her real face lived in a shell. He let his own distaste for her armor him against his guilt.

"You're talking foolishness," he said.

"Oh, am I?" Her voice rose, not yelling, but just increasing in pitch like a saw blade coming against a knot. "You think I haven't known about it all along? You think I didn't see you start sniffing after her from the first minute she set foot in this house? Burke was your good old friend, wasn't he? But you couldn't hardly wait for him to die so you could go hop into bed with her! Hell!" Her use of profanity startled him. "Do you think I'm a blind woman? Do you think a man in this town can have himself a . . . a slut on the side without his wife knowing about it?" She broke off, sucked in a gulp of air that made her wheeze. "Of course, she's lucky. You haven't got her pregnant yet. When that happens, you'll drop her like a hot potato, won't you?"

"All right," Cary said calmly, a sickness in the pit of his stomach, but knowing there was no way out of this. "So you know all about it. I'm sorry if it upsets you—"

"Upsets me? You think that could upset me now after all this time? You think after the way you've treated me ever since we were married, that would upset me?"

"Listen," Cary said harshly, "don't you try to be a goddamned martyr. You never loved me, either. You set out to trap yourself a goddamned Governor just like you'd trap a coon. From the time I first knew you, that's all that greedy little mind of yours could think of, wasn't it? And everything I wanted, everything I had planned for myself, that could go to hell, couldn't it? Don't you come martyring around me; I'm not going to fall for that crap."

She laughed, a high, ugly sound. "Boy, have you got an inferiority complex! Did you ever stop to think, with all my daddy's money I didn't have to marry a future governor? I could have married an ambassador or a prince or something. And you talk about me trappin' you—well, my name's Mary Scott, not the Virgin Mary, and I wasn't there all by myself, Mr. Bradham, when I got pregnant! But you've treated me like dirt under your feet all this time except when you wanted to impress somebody for your political career and I went along with that, I let you walk all over me and have your whore on the side because I knew there wasn't anything in the world I could do about it, but I'll tell you now—yes, I want to be the Governor's wife. Because I've got something coming to me after putting up with the way you've treated me all this time, I'm entitled to something out of this mess, and I'm going to get what's coming to me, because that's all I *can* get. And if you think you're going to cheat me out of that too, after everything else you've cheated me out of, you've got another think coming, Mr. Cary Bradham!"

He had never seen her like this, not in all the time they had been married. She had been such a vegetable, even her nagging a slow, constant drip of remonstrances seemingly without anger, as if she just had to have something to say and did not really care. But now he was seeing into a swirling depth within her that frightened him, and he blustered in return.

"Listen, if I decide I don't want to run, there's nothing you or anybody else can do to me. All of you goddam people trying to live my life for me and I've never had a chance to—"

"You've never had a chance?" she screamed. *"You've* never had a chance?"

"No, and if I make up my mind to say the hell with everything else and try to get a little happiness, nobody's going to stop me."

"All right," she said, and suddenly her voice was low and knife-edged. "All right, nobody's going to stop you. But I can make life as miserable for you as you've made it for me. I can sue you for divorce and drag it all out, every bit of it, and ruin you and your daddy and your family in this state in politics forever. I can make sure not a penny of Butler money ever goes to anything a Bradham's connected with, I can really show everybody what a skunk you are, you and that Yankee slut—how do you know she hasn't got a nigger on the side, too? I can—"

"Oh, shut up," Cary said. He was so sick that it was all he could do to keep from hurrying to the bathroom to vomit. "Oh, just shut up."

"I'm not going to shut up, I'm not—"

He had to staunch that flow of words somehow. "All right!" he yelled. "I didn't say I'm not going to be Governor. I didn't say I wasn't going to run! I haven't made up my mind about anything yet!"

"Well, you'd better make it up in a hurry! You'd better decide what you want to do, because I've waited all I intend to wait—I'm going to do something myself, if you don't, and when I get through with you and Maggie Jessup, decent people won't touch you!"

"Oh," he said softly, "go to hell."

She stared at him, stamped her foot, her fists clenched, and she screamed, "No, you go to hell, goddamn you!" And then she whirled and ran out. After she was gone, Cary did go to the bathroom. He retched sickly over the commode, but nothing came up. When he raised his head, eyes watering, mouth drooling, the sickness vanished at the sudden realization that perhaps she had played right into his hands, that she had opened the final door barring him from complete possession of Maggie, that suddenly everything was completely feasible, if only he could be courageous enough and if he could forget about his father and Muskogee. . . .

12 Planning the registration campaign was one of the most complicated undertakings Houston Whitley had ever put his hand to. He had absolutely no idea of what to expect, either in response from his own people or in resistance from the whites. This was not like a street demonstration, where mob psy-

chology supplied impetus and there was a certain protective anonymity. This was an intensely personal matter of presenting one's self before one's enemies and having one's name recorded finally and irrevocably, with full knowledge of all the consequences to person, family and living that could result: courage in single combat. There was not, he knew, an overabundance of that. Moreover, his most reliable, courageous and determined troops—the students—would be of little use to him here; they were mostly too young to vote. This would be the final test of the depth of commitment of the rank-and-file Negro: the hope with which he approached it was thoroughly mixed with apprehension.

Clouding matters further was the uncanny silence from the enemy camp. Huse had been careful to give his intentions maximum publicity, both to stir his own people and to evoke some response from the whites by which he could measure the amount of opposition he could expect. Alec Morrison had, of course, inveighed bitterly against the whole idea, calling for maximum resistance, but it was not Alec Morrison with whom Huse was concerned. He was worried about the Moodys and the Bradhams, and they were strangely quiet.

"I don't figure it," he said to Della as they lay in bed one night. He could not stop thinking about it, planning for it—not for a waking instant, it seemed. "They ought to be squealing like stuck hogs. But all that's happened is that Dale Moody issued that statement."

It had been a shockingly moderate statement, given in a press conference: "Any citizen of Muskogee is certainly welcome to register and vote, provided only that his poll taxes are paid and he can meet the commonsense literacy requirements established by state law. There will be no discrimination in the administering of the tests and we expect complete order at the registration places. I'm all in favor of big voting turnouts."

"Maybe they know they can't get away with anything with all those government observers checking the registration books," Della said. The two of them lay very close together, the warmth of their bodies mingling, her head cradled on his arm. "Or maybe they know that we'd rather vote for Cary Bradham than Alec Morrison."

"That's not much choice," Huse said bitterly. "But I guess it's the only one we'll have this time. Just the same, it worries me. It's not like Hoke Moody to keep this quiet about something like this."

"Didn't you say Hoke Moody was sick?"

"That's what I hear. They're trying to keep it secret, but the rumor's going around. I don't know whether it's sick so much as just old and ineffectual. But he'd have to be flat-out dead, looks like to me, before he'd stay hushed up now."

"Don't worry about it," she said. "You worry too much. You need to unwind. You ain't going to be worth anything if you don't start sleeping at nights."

"I know. But this thing keeps me so keyed up."

"You've got to have a vacation. You haven't had one in Lord knows when. You just keep driving and driving . . ."

He sighed. A vacation. Even a few days with no responsibilities, no concerns, no planning or plotting to do. It seemed an impossibly alluring thought, an ephemeral goal dancing and shining in the distance. If I could just get some rest, he thought.

"We're going to take one," he said firmly, trying to sound convincing. "Sometime right after Christmas, we're going to take one."

"We can't leave the children; they're in school."

"Yeah." He sighed. "Okay, then, when summer comes. We'll send the kids to North Carolina and then you and me, we'll take off somewhere. Might even go to Europe, if we can scrape up the money. Try out France. Someplace like that, I think I could unwind."

He knew that she knew that he was building an air castle, but she pressed her body closer to his and half turned, so that he could feel her breath on his neck. "That sounds good. Are we going to fly, or we going to take a ship?"

"Let's go on a ship. I've got a bait of flying. Let's go some way that we don't have to be hustling all the time."

"Ship costs an awful lot, doesn't it?"

"Well, if we're going to do it, let's do it right. Maybe we can scrape up the money."

"All right," she said. "I'll go down to a travel agency tomorrow and get some folders. They'll give us something to look at. A trip like that, you can't start planning too far ahead. We want everything to be just right." Her voice sounded wistful.

He rolled to face her. She felt good on his arm. It was good, comforting, to have her by him in the bed. He closed his eyes for a moment, thinking of how much he loved her and how little he had done to deserve her, thinking that: Suppose she hadn't called me?

Suppose I hadn't seen her that night? Then I'd always have been discontented.

But he was not discontented now. With Della close against him, he felt instead as complete as he could ever be; there was nothing—no ghost, no dream, no haunting—blocking that sense of completion now. He loved her now as she had deserved to be loved all along, and he wondered why he had let all those other years be spoiled a little by a memory. . . . But you get older, you have got to learn something, he thought, stroking the plump smooth skin of her bare arm and running his hand down her back.

"You're tired, too," he said, with compassion. "You're bound to be, all this pulling and hauling—all this damn' strain. You need a vacation as much as I do."

"No," she whispered, "I'm all right. Don't you worry about me." He felt her lips touch the base of his throat. "I just thought of something," she mumbled, "I just thought of something might help you sleep." He felt her hand moving between them.

"Yeah," he said. "That might do it."

He strained toward her; then a hideous racket outside wrenched them apart and sent him bounding out of bed, hitching at his pajama bottoms. It was the blowing of many automobile horns in concert.

Della sat up. "What in the world?"

"Go in the back room with the kids," Huse snapped. "All the way back."

"All right," she said without protest, grabbing at a robe. He heard the pad of her bare feet on the floor as she ran out. Then the blare of horns was coming nearer, straight down the street, and he moved quickly through the hall to the living room. There were no longer guards outside his house, but the floodlights shone brilliantly on lawn and street.

Lights were coming on all through that section of Princeton. He saw a few doors open, people limned within them. He was not going to do that himself, make a target, and he stood back from the edge of the window, looking out. He could see the beams of automobile headlights, and the crash and honk and howl of horns was deafening: at a different pitch he heard Terri, in the rear of the house, cry, awakened.

The first car edged leisurely into the floodlight whiteness, a black sedan. On the side toward him, and, he supposed, on the opposite side as well, a white cloth banner had been fastened that ran the car's length. In splashy red, huge letters spelled: THIS NIGGER REGIS-TERED, and then Huse saw the man-sized dummy dragged by the hemp rope running from its cloth neck to the rear bumper of the car. The dummy bounced and flapped and dragged as the car moved through the light, and the men inside the vehicle kept their heads down and shielded their faces from the light with their hands.

Behind the first car there were eight more. They bore no legends, dragged no dummies. Their drivers leaned on their horns.

Then the cavalcade was past, the horn blasts diminishing. Huse smiled grimly. Once this would have created terror; now he saw people standing on porches in knots, talking about it, not hiding from it. He heard somebody yelling something at the taillights as they faded. It was a defiant obscenity.

Then he turned away from the window and went through the back of the house. Della was sitting on the foot of Terri's bed, holding the little girl in her lap, arms about her, rocking; Otis sat huddled beside her. Terri was sobbing.

Huse tried to keep the rage out of his voice and make it reassuring and jolly. "Now, it's all right, Terri-boo, it's all right. Wasn't nothing but some people having fun."

"She thinks it's bad people coming to git us," Otis said, wide-eyed.

"Ain't bad people, just people having fun," Huse said. He sat down on the bed, shoving between Otis and Della, put one arm around Otis reassuringly, and the other arm around Della, stroking Terri's head with that hand. "It's okay, you're all right, Terri-boo."

He saw Della's eyes looking at him questioningly, but with patience. He said, to reassure her, in an adult voice, "Just a kind of warning parade, didn't amount to anything." Then he squeezed with both arms. "Daddy isn't going to let anybody hurt anybody." Terri's sobs were quieted now. "Both you young-uns, it's time for you to crawl back in your beds."

"I'll put them in in a minute," Della said, and he nodded. He got up, patted both the children and went out, so he would not have to answer more questions. Della could say, "I don't know."

He found his cigarettes in the bedroom and lit one with short, savage motions. The rage within him was completely primitive just then: a caveman might have felt the same rage toward a saber-toothed tiger that persisted in prowling outside the cave at night, the

kind of rage that would lead a man into unequal combat to protect
his family. It shook him brutally, and he could not rationalize the
anger and the hatred. He paced the bedroom nervously, smoking
the cigarette in jerky puffs, one hand clenched and tapping against
his thigh. He cursed them softly and with every obscenity he could
think of—the whites who made war against women and children,
who left no sanctuary.

He did not hear Della come in until she said, "Darling, if you
don't simmer down, you're never going to get to sleep again tonight."

"I can't help it," he said fiercely, and he told her about the caravan
that had passed.

"You've seen that kind of thing before," she said.

"I know. But I've just had enough. Children all along this street
tonight waked up and crying like Terri. Goddamn them, goddamn
them all straight to hell."

"Huse!" There was an edge to her voice. "You know you don't
really mean that."

He ground out that cigarette and lit another one, going to the high
bedroom window and looking out at the restless neighborhood, all
lighted up now. "I'm sorry," he said. "But I don't feel very nonviolent tonight."

He paused. "There must be something about having white skin,"
he said. "There must be something about it makes 'em hate life. I
don't know what it is. But they're always fighting life, trying to rub
it out. Whoever heard of genocide before they—? Wartime, they
bomb civilians, women and children. Don't they put any value on
their own families? Or do they just think their own families are the
only ones that count for anything? What kind of God have they
thought up for themselves and decided to worship? I wonder if we
can ever get together. I don't even know whether I want to be 'equal'
to 'em if it means thinking the way they do. Maybe they've had the
power too long, the absolute power, and it's corrupted them completely. Maybe we'd be better off without them, just go somewhere,
back to Africa or somewhere and be away from 'em all."

She came to him and put her hands on his arms. "You're all
wound up and you don't mean any of that. You're tired, too. Now,
you come on to bed and get some sleep." She laid her head against
his shoulder. "We were getting along very nicely before we were so
rudely interrupted. Can't we pick up where we left off?"

Some of the tension drained away from him, some of the anger. "I don't know," he said, "the way I feel, but we can try." He put his arm about her and they went back to the bed together. As she burrowed down into his arms again, he said tautly, "I don't know what I'd do without you."

She did not answer, but he felt her hand on his body again. He relaxed and let it try to stir him, but he was wondering if it wouldn't be a smart idea to send the children out of state again right away.

The next day he made arrangements to do that, regretfully, for not only did it disrupt their school year, but he always missed them when they were gone. Then he plunged back into the nightmare of work in which he had been living ever since he had conceived this idea.

There was so much to do and so little time. There were at least three hundred thousand Negroes of voting age in Muskogee, and of those, about forty thousand were actually registered to vote—ten thousand fewer than there had been before the 1954 Supreme Court decision and the purging of the rolls. Huse guessed that out of the three hundred thousand, probably sixty or seventy thousand were genuinely disqualified because of illiteracy, felony convictions, and the like. That left an eligible balance of perhaps a hundred and ninety thousand, and of those it was his aim to put a hundred and fifty thousand on the books as registered voters.

Under the state constitution, the registration books had to be open generally in each township for three successive Tuesdays six months before the May primaries. After that, until the books opened in the townships again in April, anyone wanting to register had to do so at his county courthouse.

Huse intended to hit the township registration places hard on each of those Tuesdays. Working tirelessly, driving associates and assistants without mercy, he had set up teams in each county of the state; and the leaders of each county team had set up other teams in each township. It was a finely detailed organization, designed to hit every country store, every schoolhouse, even private homes—wherever registration places were established on those Tuesdays.

Law required the registration books to open at sunrise—about six-thirty. By that time Huse hoped to have car pools of determined Negroes moving out to register. There could not, of course, be observers from the Civil Rights Commission at every place, but they had promised that they would rove and spot-check. Government cooperation had been excellent: Huse wondered if perhaps the administration had already written off the white voters of Muskogee and was pinning its own hopes in the state on a heavy Negro vote in next year's general election.

He had thrown his greatest emphasis on two facets of the operation. The first was selectivity. It was important that all who went to register be genuinely qualified voters; he had stepped up the tempo of the Better Citizens Schools ruthlessly, trying to prepare as many as possible. They could not afford to have the clockwork operation he had projected gummed up by well-meaning but unqualified applicants; he knew too well the fine-toothed combing the white registrars would give even the best-prepared Negro.

But if he could succeed in his initial aim—if, across the state of Muskogee, he could add ten thousand new names to the books in a single day—then the movement would begin with enough momentum to insure its success. If he failed or was balked, it could die aborning, victim of fear and despair.

His second and strongest emphasis, of course, was on nonviolence. Relentlessly he hammered into his team leaders that no matter what sort of opposition or hostility they met, they must not be provoked. "If somebody tries to stop you," he said, "go through anyhow. But go through nonviolently. This state is going to be a powder keg. We mustn't take the responsibility for setting it off." His team leaders were all veterans of the summer's demonstrations; they knew the drill, understood what he meant, but he took nothing for granted. The issue was too crucial. "Don't give anybody anything they can get hold of to stop us, enjoin us, or discredit us. Demand your rights as a citizen, but demand them in an orderly fashion, as a citizen should."

Some of the team leaders were a little dubious.

"There's been some talk of men with guns down here," one of the backwoods county leaders told him. "What we do if we come up against men with guns?"

"There won't be any men with guns," Huse said. "But if there are, for heaven's sake, make sure nobody in your team has got a weapon. If you meet men with guns, you turn around and go home and call headquarters in Hannington. Don't you take the responsibility of starting a war. You just turn around and go home and if we have to, we'll find a United States marshal to take you through."

But he was more worried than he allowed himself to admit. In a few of the backwoods counties there might very well be men with guns, and if there were, he would probably have to write those off on the first day, until he could make arrangements to guarantee the safety of those going to register. But there should not be enough of that sort of opposition, he tried to convince himself, to endanger the campaign: surely the whites had better sense than that. Where the real resistance would come was in the literacy examinations; he could only hope that the presence of the government observers would moderate that.

At last he knew he had done all he could do. His teams were trained and indoctrinated. On Tuesday morning he, Jeff and Louise Marfield, and Della would go immediately to register at Washington Heights School. After that, he knew, Tuesday would not be long enough to contain all the demands that would be made on him.

By the Friday night before his big push, he was so fatigued that he felt as if he were walking in a dream.

His brain seemed to have ground to a halt; his head felt as if everything in it had solidified. He was numbly silent all through supper, aware of Della staring at him with concern.

"Honey," she said, "I want you to go to bed right after you finish eating. You look like you're about to fall over in your plate."

"I'm all right," he heard himself say. "Don't worry about me. Anyhow, I can't go to bed right away. I've got one more meeting with Jeff and Charles on the publicity arrangements for this thing. I've got to go down to the church for a little while about eight-thirty."

"Oh, no," she said. "You can't go. You're just too worn out."

"I'm not going to stay long. A couple of the network cameramen have asked for permission to ride with us when we go to register. This thing's getting pretty good coverage. The publicity's important, and I want to make sure that we get all of it we can and that it's just as favorable as it can be."

"It's not that important," she said. "You don't have to handle everything yourself. Let Jeff and Charles earn their pay. You don't want to kill yourself."

"I'm not going to kill myself," he said. "Look, honey, I'll make you a promise. This meeting tonight, then I'm going to take the whole weekend off, Saturday and Sunday both. I promise you, I'm not going to do a thing the whole livelong weekend except loaf and sleep and rest and"—he forced a grin—"maybe noodle around with my wife some."

"I'll believe you taking a weekend off when I see it," she said ruefully. "All right, go ahead with your rat killing. I guess there's nothing I can do to stop you. But don't stay out too late tonight, please. It gets mighty lonesome in this house when you and the children are both gone."

"You always got Fred Poor to talk to." Poor was the guard who had volunteered to patrol the Whitley home at night; Huse had taken the precaution of insisting that the key members of FREE have such guards at their homes during the campaign. Though they seemed more designed to intimidate and terrorize than to kill, bombings continued in Muskogee and across the South sporadically, and Huse did not discount an upsurge of them during the campaign. He no longer put anything past the diehard whites.

Della laughed. "I'll hold you to that promise about the weekend, then. If you don't start staying home sometime nights and weekends, Fred and I are liable to run off together."

"I'll take that chance," Huse said. He pushed his plate, only half empty, away. "I don't want anything else to eat. I'd rather stretch out on the sofa for a half hour before I go."

Her voice was soft. "You go ahead. I won't let anybody bother you."

"You're a good wife," he said with an attempt at lightness. "I don't know what I'd do without you." As he eased himself down onto the sofa, he thought that it was true. Lying there with his body trembling with relaxation, he remembered then that though he had been watching for it carefully, Virginia Crane had never sent a contribution to FREE.

He grinned slightly. It doesn't even matter, he thought, and almost immediately he was asleep. It seemed only an instant before Della wakened him and he arose and washed his face, brushed his teeth, put on coat and tie, kissed her goodbye, and left for Mt. Olive Church.

The conference at the church lasted until ten. They were standing in the corridor when the telephone rang shrilly in Charles Bell's office, not even muffled by the door they had just closed behind them as they left it.

Bell shook his head in exasperation. "Excuse me," he said and opened the door and went back into the office. They waited, chatting. He emerged a moment later.

"Huse," he said. "Jeff."

They looked at him. His face was ashen. Tears were streaming down his cheeks. His mouth opened and closed once without sound before words came.

"I don't know how to say this," he faltered. "Huse . . . there's been a tragedy . . . your house has been bombed . . ."

Huse just stared at him. Bell's face seemed to swim eerily; Huse was certain he felt the floor move under his feet. His throat seemed sealed tight from within; he forced out only the single whisper.

"Della?"

Bell's tongue ran across his lips, wetting them.

"She's dead," he said.

13 Maggie had never been to a funeral like it before. Della Whitley's closed coffin had lain in the narthex of Mt. Olive Church for nearly two full days. Long queues of Negroes —she thought of pictures she had seen of sightseers outside Lenin's tomb—had curled around it. Then, on Sunday afternoon, the funeral. She had not been able to sit by Cary, but he had been there too, without Mary Scott. The church had been full, packed, with Negroes. She, Cary, two white ministers, and a number of other white men were scattered through the crowd. Hemmed in by Negroes, all in impeccable, though in some cases outdated, Sunday best, she felt at once their humanity and their otherness from herself. She had always thought of them as "people just like you and me," as she had insistently maintained to Cary; it came to her now that the phrase was not necessarily accurate. She could have sized up the temper of a white crowd immediately, could have measured its anger and told its grief. But she could not take any measure of this one: the expressions on their faces, the tattered bits of conversation she heard

told her nothing. An entirely different system of cultural pressures, pressures she could not even imagine, kept them from being people like herself. She realized that though she could sympathize with them, she could not necessarily understand them. It was as if together they looked into the same mirror and saw images refracted from different angles, so that what she saw, while almost what they saw, was not exactly the same thing.

The tall, dark, mournful-looking minister—his name was Bell—spoke a funeral oration. It was long and full of feeling and contained a touch of natural poetry that moved Maggie deeply. There was singing, and that moved her, too. She had expected spirituals; but these people sang out of hymnbooks; they sang only one spiritual. She had expected something exotic, but what they sang was "Swing Low, Sweet Chariot." The thunder of all the voices, blended into bereaved mellowness, choked something within her; she could not sing with them, and she bowed her head.

She had already seen Houston Whitley and the two fine little children and the Negro men and women in the family party. While the Negroes sang, she grieved for the children. She was the kind of woman who always cried a little at funerals anyway; she had a sense of the awesomeness of death, and she cried now while the singing went on. When the funeral was over, she patiently worked her way out to the street and waited for Cary. She felt wrung out with emotion.

He caught her up and without speaking led her to his car and they rode together to the cemetery. Cary said not a word as he drove in the cortege; she saw that his face was white and drawn. At the cemetery they stood, instinctively, a little apart from the rest of the group, with an old man whom Cary had introduced *sotto voce* as Mr. Curtis McKnight. There was crying out here, crying out from the crowd as the burial service was said and the coffin lowered. Then, suddenly, startlingly, someone raised a voice from the graveside.

> We shall overcome . . .
> We shall overcome . . .
> We shall overcome some day . . .
> Deep in my heart, I do believe
> We shall overcome some day . . .

Other voices picked it up.

> We are not afraid . . .
> We are not afraid . . .

Maggie clung tightly to Cary, despite any scandal it might cause. The song went on and on and on. . . .

Then it was over. There was stirring in the cemetery as the crowd fragmented. Maggie saw Houston Whitley standing at the graveside, one big hand holding the hand of the little girl on his left, the other the hand of the older boy on his right. Then she looked at Cary. His mouth was set, his face gray. She squeezed his hand. It did not squeeze back: his total attention was concentrated on something else—Huse Whitley, turning away from the graveside now and walking down a slope toward an automobile.

Cary let go of her hand. His long legs drove him swiftly across the flat turf. She saw him come up to Huse Whitley and say something, saw Huse raise his head and look at him a moment, and then Whitley's voice, shaking, rang in the frosty afternoon air of early November.

"Don't talk to me. Just don't talk to me."

"Huse." Cary's voice rose too. "Huse, let me at least say—"

"Just stay away from me. That's all I want you to do, just stay away from me and let me alone. Can't you even do that?" His face was contorted, the cords on the side of his neck bulging visibly. Suddenly he wheeled, still holding the children's hands, and hastened down toward the car, dragging the children urgently but with still a kind of gentleness.

Cary stood there for an instant; in that moment another man—Marfield, she remembered; that was his name—came up from the street and took Houston Whitley's arm. Slowly Cary turned back toward where Maggie stood, his face pale, set, and without readable expression.

"Come on," he whispered, taking her arm. "Let's go to your place." He turned to Curtis McKnight; she noticed that even under such stress he did not forget those inevitable manners. "Mr. Curt, will you come along and have a drink with us?"

McKnight was looking at him in a curious, appraising manner. "Thank you, Cary, no. I'd better get on home to Washam County; my daughter's waiting in the car now." The lined old face, the soft, almost-English voice. What an absurd charade, Maggie thought. "Give my best to your daddy."

"Yes, sir," Cary said, "I certainly will," and he led Maggie down the grassy slope to where the car was parked.

When they reached her apartment, he did not even mix a drink until he had uncapped the whiskey bottle and put it to his mouth and gulped two long swallows. She watched him and said nothing. When he had set down the bottle, he turned to her, and his body shook as the raw whiskey settled into it.

"God," he said. "God."

She put her hand on his wrist. "All right," she said. "Now you just sit down."

"But did you hear it? He thinks I had something to do with it."

"Well, didn't you?" She poured whiskey into two glasses; she herself badly needed a drink. Suddenly she thought of Burke. For a moment she knew a very personal grief. Then her face softened as she turned to Cary and saw the shock that still gripped him. She touched him gently and with as much affection as she could, pushing him toward the living room. He dropped into a chair there and took the glass she handed him.

"I was sitting in the church where I could see him," he said. "All through the funeral I wasn't even listening to the preacher or the music. I was thinking about Huse. Remembering." He drank from the glass.

Then he waved it in a short, unhappy gesture.

"When we were kids," he said, "maybe ten, maybe eleven, you know what we had it all figured out we were going to do?"

Maggie was sitting opposite him. "No," she said quietly. "What?"

"We were . . . you know how kids are, silly . . . we were going to the North Woods and become great hunters and trappers. Learn to walk on snowshoes and drive dog teams and shoot a moose every day for meat and trap beaver and wolves and mink. . . . We were going to have a cabin, just the two of us, and a lot of good guns and knives and be the greatest trappers ever were." He drank again. He seemed to be in better possession of himself now. "That's what I kept thinking about all through the funeral." He swallowed the rest of the drink and got up. "I'm getting a little drunk," he said thickly. "I may spend the night here."

"What will Mary Scott say if you don't come home?"

He applied a terse obscenity to Mary Scott. "She knows all about us anyhow," he said harshly. "Don't worry, she'll know where I am."

Maggie stared at him, feeling a different kind of shock. "She knows about us?"

He had a way, when he was a little drunk, of thrusting his head forward before he spoke, and he did that now. "That's right," he said. "Of course she does. After all this time, what did you expect?" Suddenly he turned and threw the glass across the room; it bounced off the baseboard and landed on the rug intact. "Hell," he said bitterly.

Maggie was on her feet instantly. "Cary! Stop that!" She took his arm. "Mary Scott—how do you know she knows? What has she said to you?"

He turned, grinning humorlessly. "Well, you see, it's like this. It turns out you're the worst-kept secret of the decade. Everybody but Alec Morrison seems to know about us, and I don't reckon it'll take him long to find out." He went over and picked up the glass.

"But that doesn't make any difference now," he said and went into the kitchen.

She stood in the middle of the living room without moving, thinking: *Well, what did you expect?* There was a sickness in her: shame, and a kind of panic, even though she had realized all along that a great many people were bound to know after all these years. Still, being a mistress was like having a deformity; if nobody made an issue of it, it was possible to pretend you were normal. Then the rest of Cary's words rang in her mind, and when he came out of the kitchen with his glass refilled, she asked in a faint voice, "What do you mean, it doesn't make any difference now?"

He stopped where he was, swaying just a little and with his face sardonic. He lifted his glass. "Well, because," he said, "you're looking at the first Bradham that ever retreated."

"What?" she asked blankly.

"God knows how many hundreds of years of us," he said loftily. "Always mortifying ourselves with our duty and yelling *Charge!* Honey child, we are *some* family. Our feet won't go but one way, and we never rode a horse that could run backwards. Hell, I'm surprised we even allow reverse gears in our cars."

"You're not making sense," she said, worried and impatient.

"Ain't I? I thought I was the first Bradham that ever did." His voice turned brittle. "Because I'm getting out. Quitting. I've made up my mind. I'm going to found a whole new line of Bradhams, the Bradhams that worry about themselves instead of their goddamned state and their goddamned ancestors." He came to her and put his arm about her, one hand spread between her shoulder blades, and now his words came like machine-gun fire, brisk and with no trace of drawl.

"They say if I'm going to be Governor, I've got to ditch you. They've been after me for weeks to make up my mind to tell you goodbye. Get rid of you. They say I can't be elected unless I do. They've had me in a squeeze. You on one side and all this Bradham duty and state and ancestor crap on the other. Well, the ancestors and all the rest can go to hell. I pick you."

He put his face down close to hers. "How would you like us to get married and get the hell out of here?"

"Married?" she asked blankly.

"Married. It's something people do when they love each other."

"But—" He could not be serious. Oh, God, she hoped he was serious, but he was only drunk. Mary Scott—

"I know," he said. "It's a right novel idea. But it just happens to be what we're going to do. Listen, I had a session with Mary Scott the other night. She threatened me. Either I run for Governor, or she's going to divorce me. Oh, she says, she's going to make a mess, a mean mess, and I reckon she will, but I don't guess it'll kill us. It won't make my folks and the Moodys very happy, but that's beside the point. The point is, I'm past forty years old and I've never had a damned thing in my life that wasn't spoiled for me. And today, when Huse hit out at me, it just sank home. Even that. So that now every time I think of my childhood, I'm going to feel misery. All of it wrecked by this crap. Well, I'm no Burke Jessup. I'm not going to just stand and fight it and let it kill me or drive me crazy. I'm going to wash my hands of it, they can run somebody else for Governor, I'll play Br'er Rabbit about to be thrown in the brier patch and make sure Mary Scott carries out her threat, and then you and I—"

It was beginning to sink in now, and there was something beginning to flutter inside Maggie. She did not dare let it become either optimism or joy yet.

She pulled away from him. "Cary, don't talk drunken nonsense, please. Mean what you say. Don't joke or just spout. Is this something you really mean?"

"So help me God," he said quietly, and he set the glass aside and looked at her gravely. "You've never asked me for a thing," he said. "You've just given and given and given. Don't you reckon it's about time I paid you some return on your investment? That is, if you want it."

He shook his head, and his voice was even and controlled. "I'm not talking drunk talk, Maggie. This is something that's been working in me for a long time . . . maybe ever since Burke got killed. I don't know how long . . ."

He turned away from her and went to the window and looked out of it.

"I'm not a very bright man," he said. "I'm not an intellectual like Burke, I don't read a whole lot of books, I never sat around much and pondered the significance of the universe. I was born into this place and this time and into my family—and it was like you're born into your skin, it's just there and it's comfortable and it fits and you don't worry about it any more."

He took out a cigarette and went on without lighting it.

"But my skin doesn't fit any longer, Maggie. Something has happened to me and it feels like the skin I was born into is too tight and like there are sores all over it, big, mean ugly ones. My skin makes me sick now, Maggie."

His voice shook a little. "I love this country. I mean the South. You don't know how you can love it until you're born into it and have drummed into your head that loving it is the most important thing you can do, and that begins, if you're my age, when you're so little you can barely understand. But you sit around and you hear the old folks talk. The very old ones, like my grandmother, like a great-uncle I used to have, who actually lived through the times when people fought and died because they loved this place so much. What they hammer into you is that those must be your models, you must honor them and strive to be like them—and above all, you must never question what they died for."

He lit the cigarette now.

"It gets into your blood and into your bones. You grow up a little dazzled by it and still never daring to question. You can't understand what it's like, unless you've been on the losing side of a war

and the only thing you've got to compensate for everything you lost
—and it *was* just about everything—is a bunch of traditions, a lot
of legends, and your pride. And if you lose your faith in all that, boy,
you're in trouble. Because then you start to see things as they really
are."

He turned toward her; she saw misery on his face.

"I can't fight it any more, Maggie. All I want to do is get away
from it. If I stay and run for Governor, I'll be caught up in all this
insanity and I'll never get loose, and I'll wind up having to be an
accomplice . . . hell, I'm already an accomplice. Burke. And now
Huse's wife. I'm not going to be an accomplice to anything else, I'm
just going to break loose from it all."

All she could think for a moment was: So I won. I did win, after
all. Without even knowing it.

He made a confused gesture. His voice was almost pleading. "All
I want out of it is you. I love you, and if I can wiggle loose from
Mary Scott, I'll marry you, if you'll have me."

There was no doubting him now. The fluttering thing inside her
broke into freedom. In that moment she realized just how must the
prospect of having complete possession of him meant to her, how
she had hated sharing him, how much she yearned for order to come
out of the chaos of their relationship. She loved him. She felt her
eyes, foolishly, growing wet. "Oh, Cary," she heard herself say. "Oh,
my God, Cary, marry you?" She was not used to losing her composure, and she felt awkward.

But he came to her and held her, and the awkwardness vanished.
All she could feel was relief, love, and anticipation. She burrowed
her face desperately against his chest; she felt him nuzzling her hair.

"You're the only good thing that has happened to me since the
war," he said. "The only decent thing I can salvage out of all this
crap."

He was silent then for a moment, but he kept on holding her.

"It's going to take more guts than I ever had before," he said at
last, "to tell my father. But I'm not going to waste any time doing
it. I'm going to tell him tomorrow. And Mary Scott, too."

Maggie felt her euphoria begin to fade; she pulled away. "Cary,"
she said, making her voice as serious as she could, looking at him
gravely, "you'll be throwing away everything you've got. Are . . .
are you sure you want to do that?"

His eyes met hers directly. "I'm sure," he said. "I'm going to tell them all, tomorrow. And then to make it official, I'm coming here tomorrow night . . . and this is where I am going to stay."

14 The rain began falling during the night. When Jeff Marfield came out of his house at eight o'clock Monday morning, it was still coming down, a steady, thin, cold drizzle. From the looks of the low, even, unbroken blanket of lead-colored sky, it was raining all over the city, the county, maybe all over the state. Good, Jeff thought, welcoming the rain. Maybe it will help damp things down.

He got into his car and drove through the streets of Princeton toward town and the office on Grade Street. He passed the splintered ruins of what had once been Houston Whitley's house—and Della's. Now it was a shell, like a child's dollhouse, its front ripped away, its back rooms exposed with doorless, obscene flagrancy. He grieved for his sister, as he passed the house, and then tried to bury the grief, for there was still so much to do.

It had been a narrow thing, he told himself. It was still a narrow thing. Not since the Birmingham bombing in September had the whole region teetered so precariously on the brink of war. It would have exploded, would have blown apart immediately in raw and brutal violence, if it had not been for Houston Whitley.

Jeff remembered too well his own immediate reaction, once his mind had comprehended the incomprehensible. It had been a hatred that washed away all the checks and controls of reason or civilization—a simple, primitive need to seek direct revenge with his own two hands. The South, he thought, could thank itself that Houston Whitley, not himself, had been the leader of FREE in that moment.

He knew that Huse's reactions must have matched his own, probably had been more violent. But Huse had acted reflexively: as soon as he was able to speak, he had said, "We've got to keep the peace." Jeff knew how much Huse had needed Charles Bell in that moment, but even before they left the church, Huse had given Bell his orders. "Get in touch with people and have the word passed to every team leader. Tell them that revenge and violence would profane her memory. Tell them I said that. Tell them that I personally plead with them to keep calm." His voice had shaken. "And to pray for her," he had added.

Jeff had looked at him in awe, his own rage beginning to ebb. Huse's features were composed now, like iron. His voice was steady as he said, "Do that for me, will you, Charles? I'll talk myself later on."

The body had been in a closed coffin. She had been sitting in the living room, had been in the full force of the explosion. So that neither of them had seen her afterward, only the metal shell that held her. But that, in a way, had been its own consolation: at least she had never known what hit her.

But even seeing the coffin that night, knowing his sister was inside it, Marfield had felt the rage coming back on him. The need for vengeance was like the need for breathing. He watched Huse go to the coffin, where it sat in a room of the funeral home to which she had been taken immediately. Watched him put his hands on the cold, round bronze and stand there for a few moments looking down silently at the coffin, his face impassive. He had taken that much time to grieve; then he had begun to fight desperately to prevent Della's death from triggering another and more frightening explosion.

Somehow he had succeeded. The press associations had distributed his short, dignified statement, along with shocked expressions of regret from the city authorities, promises that the bombers would be apprehended. Huse's statement had only asked that Della's many friends express their grief in prayers for her and honor her memory by maintaining a Christian attitude of love and forgiveness.

The "lying in state" of the coffin, too, had helped, had diverted interest from revenge and had provided an outlet for grief, as had the countless memorial services in the black ghettos of the nation. Jeff hoped now that the worst part was over. Fully returned to rationality himself, he even dared hope that Della's death had not been entirely without purpose. Perhaps it was part of a pattern Huse, but not himself, could comprehend. Huse had pointed that out.

"This is bound to teach them a lesson," he had said. "And maybe now they won't oppose the registration drive. If Della's death sobers them—if it makes them less determined—well, a hundred and fifty thousand voters will make the kind of monument she would have wanted."

That was the way he had been the whole time. Cool, controlled. Uncannily so, almost frighteningly so. Only at the funeral, when Cary Bradham approached him, had that iron self-containment cracked, and Jeff had been glad to see it happen, had hoped Huse would vent then some of the rage and grief that he would have been less than human if he had not felt.

But it had not quite happened; Huse had recovered his control, and whatever he felt stayed locked up within him. Jeff had immediately sent his own wife and children away and had asked Huse to move in with him and share the house, but Huse had chosen to go back down into Little Hammer, to move in with his mother in her rickety shack. "I'll stay here," he had said, "until it's safe to bring the children back."

Now, as he turned into the parking lot behind the building on Grade Street, Jeff saw that Huse's car was already there. He wondered how long Huse had been in his office. He hoped that after this was over, he could persuade Huse to take a long rest. A man could take only so much, and he did not know what the rest of them would do if anything happened to Houston Whitley.

The rain was falling harder as he got out of the car and hurried across the lot into the back door of the building. The secretaries in the various cubicles nodded at him as he came dripping through the corridor. He shrugged out of his raincoat in his own office, hung up his hat, and was about to sit down at his desk when he heard a sound coming from beyond the door that connected his office with that of Houston Whitley.

It was not a sound that he could immediately identify, and for some reason it alarmed him. He went quickly to the door and was about to open it when some warning signal springing from his subconscious made him hesitate.

He stood at the door for a moment, listening, and then he turned away, his face grave.

He knew what the sound was now, and there was no need for him to go into the other office.

The man in there was crying.

From his office in the Law Building, Cary Bradham watched the rain fall on Hannington. It was late evening now, and the city had blossomed into a misty spangle of illumination. The rush-hour traffic had dwindled; his own secretaries had gone home, and he was alone here.

He stood at the window with one foot propped on the cast-iron radiator, a burning cigarette unnoticed in his hand, and stared out at the drizzle-blurred pattern of yellow that was the city. He was, in this moment, trying to summon the full measure of resolution he knew that he would need to go see his father.

He had meant to tell Powell Bradham here at the office. Had meant to charge in first thing, confront his father, say it, and say it hard and quick and without hesitation, to get it over with. But his father had not come in today, and that had thrown him off balance, and before he could revise his plans he had been caught up in the meshing gears of office routine, and with every hour that had passed, his courage and resolution had dwindled and his dread of the confrontation had increased.

Not that he would change his mind. He was sure of that. It was only that this was the hardest thing he had ever had to do. He was going to make a mockery of all the love, pride, perseverance and devotion to that worshiped idol Bradham called duty that his father had so doggedly built his life around these past thirty years: he was going to wipe out a thirty-year dream in one night and leave his father nothing to replace it, and it was not an easy thing to do.

Just the argument about his attending the funeral had been fierce enough. His father had not wanted him to go. "Are you deliberately trying to commit political suicide?" the old man had stormed. "Don't you know what Morrison will say when word gets out that you went to that nigger's funeral?"

He had faced his father down then, for what was really the first time. "I don't care," he had said, wondering at his own defiance. "Houston Whitley is—was my friend."

"Your friend!" Bradham had snorted. "A little nigger boy you used to play with. By God, if I had known then what I know now—"

I guess if you look at it one way, Cary thought, he's right. Just a little nigger boy I used to play with. Everybody has 'em. I had a pony, too, but I outgrew it. . . . He watched the rain beat against the window. After a moment he took his foot down from the radiator.

"Goddamn it," he said aloud, "why does everything always have to get spoiled?"

And that brought the resolution back within him. There was only one thing left unspoiled—and that was Maggie. And whatever strength he had, whatever will and courage he owned, he was going to devote now to keeping, cherishing, guarding, that one unspoiled part of his life. What he had to do tonight would not be easy. But it would be worth it.

He walked to his desk, ground out his cigarette. "And there's no point in putting it off any longer," he said heavily, still aloud, and then he got his raincoat from the rack.

When he went outdoors, the rain was cold. He turned up his coat collar and pulled down his hat and hurried to where his car was parked. His trouser legs were wet beneath the coat's hem when he reached it. He got in, started the engine, and pulled it out of the lot, away from town, toward Mercy Street.

The windshield wipers made steady, rhythmic clicks. As he drove, he tried to project his mind past the session with his father, skip that and go beyond it. He would prolong nothing. Once he had told Bradham, he would go home. He would tell Mary Scott. He would not ask her for a divorce. He would let her throw that at him, let it be her weapon. He was not worried about getting it any more. He knew her too well to think that she could refrain from striking back. That part of it would be ugly; but it would have to be endured.

After he had told her, he would leave the house. He would go to Maggie, and that was where he would stay. With her. As soon as he could, he would make arrangements for them to go away, somewhere . . . well, North. Maybe Philadelphia. Or maybe farther. The farther the better.

None of it would be fun, none of it would be easy, but he would do it all quickly. He remembered a sergeant he had been instructed by in basic training, a tough old Regular. Sometimes, the sergeant had said, an amputation is better than a weeping wound.

He hoped the sergeant was right. Because that was what he intended to do. Amputate himself from everything but Maggie.

Still, driving through the night with the windshield wipers clicking and the rain sliding down the windshield and the heater purring softly, he could not shake off a feeling of unreality. How did I come to this pass? he wondered. How did we all come to it? How did this sickness, this ugliness, grow in what we used to think was a kind of heaven? Is it something new? Or has it been here all along and we just hid it from ourselves? And is there anywhere you can really go to get away from it?

He did not know. For a moment, for just one fleeting moment, he wished Burke were alive, so he could talk to him about it. Burke thought out things like that; Burke had been able to give answers.

But he himself had no answers. All he wanted to do was run.

Then he saw ahead of him through the rain the lights of the Mercy Street house. They looked warm and beckoning. He tried not to look at them. He turned the car into the long drive, the rain splanting in his headlights. As he neared the end of it, the yellow beams picked up reflections off the chrome of two cars parked under the porte-cochere at the side entrance. There was company; he was not pleased about that, but he would not let it stop him, either. He could not delay another moment.

It would be so easy, he thought, if I didn't love him too.

He turned the car into the part of the drive that circled the house and parked before the front steps. He sat in the car for a moment, breathing heavily. Then, slowly and feeling as if every limb were weighted, he got out.

In the rain he climbed the high front steps. At their top he paused and, as if it were a pet, stroked the cold, damp ears and back of one of the pair of great cast-stone sphinxes that guarded the porch. Then he went to the front door and without knocking or ringing the bell, went into the house.

He did it quietly, almost stealthily, as if he were an intruder. The stern, gray-uniformed man in the portrait in the vestibule seemed to be looking at him as he closed the door with guilty softness.

No one came to meet him. His mother had not been well; she, he thought with a pang, would be upstairs in her bed. Probably the cook who had replaced Lucy would already have gone. But his father would be around somewhere. Likely in the room he called his office.

Cary went to the big double doors beside the beginning of the massive stair. They were closed. But a voice came from behind them and he recognized it after a moment as belonging to Dale Moody.

All right, he thought. It's just as well. Let them all have it at once.

He was tightly drawn in every muscle, and his stomach was knotted almost painfully. He remembered that he had felt this way before flying his first combat mission. But as soon as he had actually been airborne, he had slacked off, been all right then. So maybe he would be all right this time, too, once he was doing what he had to do.

He knocked at the door, and after a second's hesitation his father's voice said testily, "Yes?"

He heard someone coming, but he took the initiative himself and opened the door and entered.

It was Dale Moody's son, Mitch, who had come to open the door. Dale Moody, Powell Bradham and a fourth man were grouped around Bradham's desk with drinks in their hands. When they recognized him, their faces were oddly startled, and his father said quickly, "Son, I didn't know you were—"

But he was not listening to his father. He was looking at the fourth man. It had been a long time since he had seen him; he remembered that then he had thought the man would have looked natural in a broad-brimmed hat. There was one beside him on the leather sofa now, a white ranchman's hat, and it made recognition easier.

His father's voice trailed off. The room was silent for a moment. Then Col. Terence Whipple grinned, none of it reflecting in his eyes. "Hello, Mr. Bradham." He unfolded his long frame, arose, and came forward with his hand out. "Glad to see you again."

Cary took the hand automatically and then let go of it. He had forgotten the men at the store in Troublefield, but now they came back into his mind. Suddenly he was afraid.

He moved past Whipple, confronted his father and Moody. Moody was smiling thinly; his father's face was impassive now.

"What's *he* doing here?" Cary asked.

"Why, I just came as an interested—" Whipple began behind him, but then Powell Bradham shook his head and got to his feet.

"I invited him," he said. "Can I fix you a drink?"

"You invited him?" Cary stared at his father incredulously.

Bradham sighed heavily. "Yes, son, I invited him."

Cary turned to look at Whipple. "What about his men?"

Whipple smiled at him wolfishly. "I thought sooner or later Muskogee would be able to make use of the Constitutional Legion. I'm happy to have the chance to help out."

Now all of Cary's dread, all of his mental rehearsals, were swallowed in a growing outrage.

"Help out?" he said blankly. And then angrily, "You told me—" to his father.

Bradham's lips clamped together. "Don't use that tone with me, Cary," he said harshly. He went to the bottle on the table and poured a splash into his glass and turned. "Now, sit down and calm down and listen—"

"Does Hoke Moody know about this?" Cary cut in sharply.

His father smiled slightly. "Hoke Moody hardly knows anything. He's so senile—"

"I think somebody had better tell him about this," Cary said. "Maybe he's not that senile."

Now Dale Moody got up out of his chair. "Let me handle this, Powell." He turned himself to face Cary directly.

"We're not gonna bother Hoke with this," he said in that twanging country whine of his. "Hoke's plumb worn out. He's goin into retirement soon, he don't wanta be bothered with anythin else. It's up to us to keep things movin. Now, we got a use for Colonel Whipple and his people and—"

"Use," Cary said, his fear sounding in his voice. "What kind of use?"

"We've let ourselves be pushed by niggers as far as we're gonna be pushed," Dale Moody said forcefully. "We let 'em boycott, we let 'em sit-in, we let that nigger in the school, and that's all we're gonna do, we're not goin one step farther. We give another inch, we give the election away to Alec Morrison. This nigger Whitley, his big talk. Well, we're gonna ram that big talk right down his throat and make him like it. And you better not stand there and look at me that way if you want to be Governor, because it's just as much in your interest as anybody else."

"But you can't use Whipple." Cary's mind was groping, trying to comprehend the tactics of it. "You—"

"Now, sir," Whipple said, "there are always ways and means. That's the advantage of having an organization of patriots from out of state you can call on." He was still smiling; but he had the coldest face Cary had ever seen, and there was a light in the back of his eyes that was metallic and frightening. "Now, yes, sir, you've got these damyankee observers at your pollin places, and that's a hard thing to get around. But we can get around it for you. I'll have flyin squads of men coverin every registration place in this state, or most of 'em, anyhow. I mean, now, you folks don't know a thing about it, this is all an action of private citizens who are anxious to preserve the Southern way of life. If they form themselves into bands and block the niggers off and chase 'em away as they come to register, what can you people do about it? Is it your fault that the niggers git turned back long before they ever get to the registration places? Is it your fault that private citizens turn 'em back? I mean, sure, your state police will be out tryin to keep order, but they can't be everywhere at one time. And maybe they catch a few—all right! If niggers can go to jail for desegregation, can't a few white men be allowed the privilege of goin to jail for what they believe?"

"You'll start a war," Cary said unbelievingly. "Goddammit, man, you'll start a war."

"Sho," Whipple said, "maybe what this country needs is a—"

Bradham said loudly, "Confronted with armed force, they're not going to register. They'll turn around and go back. Nobody'll be hurt. And we've got to do something to protect ourselves against Alec Morrison."

Cary turned to him. He looked at the lined face with the silver mustache, the eyes that were still keen and piercing, and something crumbled within him. "You told me," he said, "the other night, you—"

"I didn't say anything that wasn't true the other night," his father said, meeting his gaze. "But you've been—" He put his hand on Cary's arm. "Y'all excuse us," he said. He pushed Cary toward the door. Numbly Cary allowed himself to be maneuvered into the hall. Bradham closed the door behind him, and then he shoved Cary toward the living room.

When he got him there, his eyes were flaming; the spots that had come onto his forehead and cheeks in these past few years stood out in startling contrast to the whiteness of his skin. "Boy, listen," he hissed, his fingers digging into Cary's arm. "What are you trying to do, ruin everything I've worked for for thirty years?"

"No, sir," Cary managed to say. "But, my God, Dad, don't you see, don't you understand? You let that man and his . . . his soldiers in here and—"

"That man," his father said fiercely, "is a patriot. And so are his soldiers. That man may be the last hope of the South. We've backed off as far as we can back. Now, if to make it clear to everybody that we're through retreating we have to call on him, we'll do it." His fingers were surprisingly strong: they had a young man's strength as they gouged into Cary's arm. "And you've got to quit fussing about it, you've got to quit fighting. You've already got Dale upset, first about that woman of yours and now about this, and he's wondering about you. You've got to watch your mouth and do like we tell you to. Otherwise you're going to make us lose everything."

Cary just stared at him. He pulled his arm away. "Is it worth—?"

"It's worth anything it costs," his father snapped. "I've put in thirty years of working for it, and you've got to keep yourself quiet and do what you're told or you'll ruin it." His face was turning red. "By God, you don't know what I've gone through. They came to me and said it was either link up with Hoke or else. *Me,* Powell Bradham. After all I'd done for this state. That . . . that trash came to me and said I had to ally myself to more trash, that Hampton County trash in yonder. Eat dirt. Eat . . . eat *shit.* And I've eaten it. For thirty years I've eaten it from that trash and now the time has almost come—it's right here just about in my hand." He held out his fingers and closed them. "And you almost spoiled it. Well, you keep your mouth shut, you hear? You keep your mouth shut and do what I tell you to do—and what Dale Moody tells you to do, too—until you're elected. And then I'm through eating it. Then I'll show *them* who's got to eat it!"

Cary looked at him with growing horror. No, he thought. No. . . . But it was so obvious, so completely apparent in the glitter in Bradham's eyes, in the contortion of his face. He had, in his time, worshiped his father; he had thought of his father as the embodiment of everything he wanted to be. When he had looked at his father, he had been almost dazzled by him.

But now what he was looking at was a bitter old man, an old man of overwhelming ego, an old man whose pride had been hurt years before and who had nursed the grudge for decades and would do anything to see it settled. Even if it means blowing everything apart, Cary thought sickly. Even if it means smearing me with all this filth too. His talk about honor, pride, duty, Muskogee—Christ! Suddenly he wanted to lash out at his father, strike him. Twenty years! he screamed inwardly. Nearly twenty years of . . . nothing! Because your goddamned personal pride was hurt. Not Bradhams, not Muskogee, not anything! Just Powell Bradham!

His father was talking. "Tomorrow morning Whipple will have his people out on all the roads. Nobody—no niggers—will get through. And Whipple's people are all out of state, so that we can throw up our hands. We'll even arrest some of 'em for the looks of things. But—"

Cary looked down at the twisted, spotted, completely self-centered old face and he was sick. He opened his mouth to speak and no words came out. He backed away two paces; he raised a hand and dropped it. Then, overwhelmed by horror and a kind of panic, he turned and went so quickly that he was almost running out the front door, leaving his father standing there alone in the living room.

For a long time he did not know what to do. He drove slowly, aimlessly, around and around through the rain. He felt wetness on his cheeks once, wondered how the rain had got in, realized that it was tears.

It was never me, he thought. Never any of what he said it was. Just himself. Thirty years . . . just to get even. *And twenty of it came out of my life, and he doesn't even care!*

So he did not know what to do; his father's honor was one of the few things he had believed in, that and his father's love for him, and he drove through the rain. He was surprised when he found himself on a street lined by sad, tired old Victorian-vintage houses bulking white in the wet night like massive, scabby ghosts; and he saw ahead of him the end of the streetlamps. Below, glimmering in a pool of darkness down the slope, were a thousand rain-misted lights: he had, for some reason, come to the edge of Little Hammer.

When he realized that, he tried hard to think what had brought him here, searching his numbed mind for any purpose he might have had. Little Hammer . . . Houston Whitley . . . and then it meshed.

He sat there in the car with the engine idling. I have got to tell Huse, he thought. I've got to do at least that much, give him some kind of warning. He can't send his niggers out against Whipple tomorrow—not even knowing Whipple's there. He closed his eyes for a moment, seeing again behind his lids the old man's face, feeling the gouge of the old man's fingers in his arm: the strange old man, the bitter old man, the vindictive and selfish old man.

I don't owe him anything, he thought. I never have. And he put the car in gear and took it down the unpaved and precarious street into Little Hammer, remembering the newspaper account of the bombing that had said Huse was moving in with his mother. An invitation? he wondered. To another bomber?

Water poured down the road into the hollow in a sheet that covered the spread of his headlight beams. The wheels bounced and slammed and slid in a road eroding beneath them. The sound of his engine brought people to doors, sudden oblong squares of yellow with tense silhouettes in them. It's all right, he said to them silently, I'm not here to hurt you.

He knew more by habit than by sight when he had come to Lucy's house at the bottom of the road. There were other cars there, and he had to park a distance away. It was raining hard with a vertical, gravity-fed steadiness as he sloshed through the muddy current that sluiced about his feet, walking to the porch. He was breathing hard, he noticed, as if he had been running for a while.

He mounted the boards with their familiar give beneath his weight. Lights were bright beneath shades half pulled in the windows. He rapped on the screen door, aggressively; almost immediately the door was pulled open.

Lucy pitched her head forward at the end of her neck, blinking. "Who dat?" Then she drew in her breath. "Oh," she said, and it was the first time she had ever greeted him with anything but loud pleasure. "It Mr. Cary."

"Lucy, is Huse here?"

"Yassuh." She said it dubiously in a voice that was thin with age. Then, almost automatically, "You come in out of that wet night before you catch your death a-cold."

He entered the cluttered cube of light and warmth that was the tiny living room and she pushed the door shut behind him. "I tell him—" she began, scraping anciently across the room; he had not realized she was so very old. "Never mind," he said, and knowing where they would be, he went toward the kitchen.

There were three Negroes there. Houston Whitley and the man named Marfield sat at the table in their shirt-sleeves, coffee cups before them; a tall, slender Negro in dirty flannel shirt and jeans lounged against the cabinet behind them, a bottle of beer in his hand. As Cary's tread shook the house, Huse looked up. He seemed bigger to Cary without his coat on, the thick, wide shoulders straining at the shirt seams, the forearms heavy and roped with muscle and veins beneath the rolled-up sleeves. His eyes were expressionless at first; then they were stained with slow fury. He stood up, and his voice was rough.

"Huse," Cary began, but before he could say anything else, Huse's words stopped him.

"What the hell you want, you white bastard?"

Marfield scraped back his chair, jumped to his feet. His face was startled. "Huse." He put his hand on Huse's arm. Huse shrugged it off.

"Let me go, Jeff." His teeth were showing between thick lips. "This is one man none of it applies to."

The man with the beer giggled. Cary recognized him now— Robert.

Huse's hands were knuckled, bearing his weight on the table as he leaned forward. "I said, what the hell you want?"

Marfield's hand clamped on Huse's shoulder. "Now, easy," he said, and he was polite, turning to Cary as he pushed Huse back down in the chair. Polite, but not hospitable. "What can we do for you, Mr. Bradham?"

"I want to talk to him if you can get him to listen," Cary said. "It's important."

He heard Huse let out a long, shuddering rasp of air. "I'm listening," Huse said.

Cary licked his lips. "You can't go through with this registration thing of yours the way you've planned," he said. "If you do, somebody's going to get hurt."

Light gleamed from the whites of Huse's eyes. "Oh?"

"Listen," Cary said urgently, leaning over the table toward Huse. "Damn it, now, you listen to me. I know what's going on. There has been a bunch of armed men brought in from out of state. They're making up patrols to roam the roads tomorrow and cut your people off from the registration places. You'll never get near 'em, Civil Rights observers or no. This is a private army, Huse, and it's out to make sure you don't get through, any of you. They'll use any force they have to, and they're going to be all over the state, more than five hundred of them."

Marfield was looking at him narrowly. "Ku Klux?"

"The same thing," said Cary.

Houston Whitley's face had not changed. He looked at Cary stonily, without speaking.

Marfield said tensely, "Huse?"

"I wouldn't believe him on a stack of Bibles," Huse said slowly. "He's the worst one of them all." Suddenly he dropped his head and looked down at the table. "All right," he said. "We can always change our tactics. That's all. Let your armed men come. We'll just change our approach."

Marfield was staring at him.

Cary felt shame and disgust with himself that he should be standing here enduring abuse from a Negro, pleading with one. He started to leave, simply to turn and walk out, but something held him; he did not know what it was. Maybe it was— He heard his voice going on with urgency.

"Huse, you've got to listen to me, trust me. My people haven't got any idea I'm coming here. I'm trying to keep everybody from getting hurt tomorrow. I'm asking you to call off your campaign—at least until I can do something about clearing these people out . . ."

"No," Huse said.

"Dammit, Huse." His voice was begging now; he heard the tremor in it, and suddenly he didn't care. "Damn it, believe what I say, trust me. I'm your friend. I always have been your friend. My God, don't you remember all the things . . ." His voice pinched off. "You ought to remember," he finished tiredly, ineffectually, heavily.

Huse scraped back his chair and stood up. "I'll tell you what I remember," he said, and his eyes were blazing. "I remember my wife lying there dead in that coffin, and that if I hadn't sent my kids away, they would have been there, too. That wipes out everything else I can remember."

He stopped; his barrel chest heaved as he drew in air. "Now you've got more men with guns out," he said thickly. "You come here and tell me that if we go to register tomorrow you're gonna shoot us. All right." His voice picked up intensity. "All right, you have your white men out there tomorrow, you let them get in our way." He was beginning to yell now. "But before you send 'em out, you take a good look at *me*." He slammed a hand against his chest. "You know who I am? You know what my name is? I'll tell you—my name's Houston Whitley! Take a good look at me, Cary Bradham, white Cary Bradham, because you never saw me before, and neither has anybody else ever seen a man like me. There never has been one before, because I've got the power—and from now on you had better begin to learn to tremble at my name!"

He flung out his arm in a wide gesture. "I got more power than you and all the Moodys put together. For the first time, white man, there's a Negro that can say, Don't fight, love—and thousands, maybe millions, of Negroes bow their heads and love. Or that same Negro can say, Don't love—fight! And what do you think they'll do then?"

He leaned forward, his voice rasping, his eyes wide and shining, his words lashing across the table at Cary.

"What do you think we are? Do you think we're dogs to turn our tails and run because somebody shoots at us? Why, all I've got to do is say the word, snap my fingers—and all over this state, all over the South, all over this country, Negroes will pick up their own guns to get their rights!"

He slapped the table with his open palm; it made the whole house jump. "Go ahead!" he roared suddenly. "Let 'em come! But tell 'em they come at their own risk! You bastards call us savages—we'll show you just how savage we can be! White men die just like us, like Della—"

His bellow chopped itself off; the room was ringingly silent except for his loud breathing, and he was still staring at Cary with his face twisted with hatred.

Cary stood there, knowing it was useless now. "All right," he said at last, quietly. "All right, I—" He started to turn away, then half turned. "Damn it, why can't you listen? Why can't we at least talk together? When will we be able to talk?"

Huse turned his back, quickly and with finality. Marfield stood frozen for a moment, and then he came around the table. "Mr. Bradham." He was pushing Cary gently toward the door, and, feeling empty and burned out, Cary yielded to him.

Then they were on the rickety porch in the cool air, with the sound of the rain around them.

Marfield's voice was shaky. "Mr. Bradham, you . . . you've got to forgive Huse. He's been all right up to now, but he's been under such a strain. And then, when you walked in, it was like something must have snapped in him— I don't understand it—like you triggered him off."

"I'm sorry," Cary said.

"Not your fault, but . . . was that the straight goods? That stuff about the armed patrols?"

"It's straight," Cary said. He was now very tired; he did not even feel as if he could stand here any longer. "I can't tell you much about it except that they'll be there. Away from the registration places, between you and them. But they'll be there and they'll have guns and some of 'em will probably use 'em."

Marfield sucked in a tense breath. "That's bad." He was silent for a moment. Then he said, and there was no doubt of the sincerity in his voice, "Mr. Bradham, we appreciate this warning more than I can tell you. Anything you can do to help us in this situation, we'd thank you for that, too."

Cary raised a hand and dropped it. "Just stay home and don't go to register. That's all the help I can give you now. That advice."

Marfield shook his head, and there was a touch of regret in his voice. "You know we can't do that, Mr. Bradham."

"No," Cary said, "I reckon not." He turned and started down the steps.

"Good night, Mr. Bradham," Marfield said from behind. "And thank you again."

"You're welcome," Cary said, but he doubted if Marfield could hear him for the rain.

15 When Marfield went back into the house, he passed Robert, wearing a slicker, coming out. Robert giggled and punched him on the arm. "Man, Huse sho told that sonbitch off, didn' he?"

Jeff looked at him in disgust.

Robert lowered his voice. "Lend me a coupla bucks. I'll run out an' git us some beer."

Marfield wanted no beer. But it's worth two dollars to get him out of here, he thought, and he dug in his pocket. Robert took the cash and hurried into the rain, and Marfield was perfectly aware that he would not be back until the two dollars was gone.

"That kind—" he said savagely, under his breath, and then he closed the door and went back to the kitchen. Huse was still sitting at the table, the empty coffee cup before him. There was no sign of Lucy.

"Where's your mama?" Jeff asked.

"Upset," Huse said tonelessly. "She's gone to bed."

Jeff looked at him, and it was like looking at a stranger. He began to feel cold and afraid.

"That stuff you yelled at Bradham. That stuff about guns. You didn't really mean that stuff, I know."

Huse looked up at him slowly. "Didn't I?"

"Now, wait a minute." Jeff sat down at the table. "Now, wait, I don't understand you. What's got into you? You were all right, you were doing fine until he came in." He shoved his coffee cup nervously. "You know we can't use any guns. It would tear apart everything we've built up. We'd lose everything we, any of us, ever gained. All we've got, it's been got by nonviolence. Blow that and you blow everything. Now, you ease off."

Huse did not look at him. "Maybe," he said flatly, "we've got all we're going to get by nonviolence. They aren't going to stop until they get what they're asking for. That man from the UN I met in New York was right. Only language they understand is force. We're men, and it's time we acted like men. Try anything else and they think you're scared. I'm through being scared."

"Huse, if Della could hear you—"

Huse turned his head. "Della's dead," he said.

He pushed back his chair and got up then. "I'm tired of it," he said. "I'm tired of sending men armed with nothing but love up against men with guns and bombs. I've got to think about those people."

"No," Jeff said quickly. "No, you aren't thinking about them. You're thinking about your own self. How bad you want your revenge."

"All right," Huse said. "I'm thinking about that, then." His voice shook, suddenly clogged with grief. "I tried it, damn it, I tried it from the minute they told me. My first thought was: Oh, God, now I got to go out and kill some of those bastards. But I never let myself say it again, not to you, not to me. I said, Let's forgive them. Let's love them." His big right hand opened and closed. "And all the time what I wanted to do—" He shook his head, and he was gulping as he spoke. "I've tried all I can try, I've held it bottled up in me, but now I can't hold it any longer. There ain't any love left in me. There ain't anything left in me, except I just want to—" He strode from the room. Jeff, sitting racked, all nerves strung excruciatingly, heard a drawer open and close. Then Huse was back.

He dropped into his chair and laid the pistol on the table beside his coffee cup. "I'm glad Robert didn't take it with him," he said. "It's got a full load."

He swung his head and looked at Jeff, and Marfield thought: He's crazy. He's clean out of his mind. Suddenly he was terrified.

"I'm going out tomorrow morning early and register, just like we planned," Huse said quietly. His big hand dwarfed the pistol as he laid his palm over it protectively. "There just hadn't better be anybody trying to stop me."

"All right," Jeff said, his terror sounding in his voice. "All right, you take that thing and use it, you know what will happen?"

"Of course I know," Huse said.

"All those people, all those cars we've got going out. When they meet those armed men, they'll either turn around or try to go through nonviolently. But if you take that, if you use it—"

"Yes," said Huse.

"They'll go home and get theirs and come back and shoot *their* way through if they have to. Goddammit, Huse, come out of it! Wake up! You can't go out of here with a gun and intending to use it! Don't you know what you'll set off? Don't you know who you are?"

"Yes," he said. "I know who I am. And they're going to find out, too."

"All right," Jeff said. "And then everything goes down the drain. Huse, we can find some other way. We've come this far without a bloodbath—"

Huse nodded. "Maybe it's time for one," he said calmly. "Maybe it will wash away a lot of filth."

Maggie Jessup paced the confines of the small apartment nervously; sat down, picked up a magazine and tried to look at it, tossed it aside, and got up and began to pace again. Oh, she thought, oh, please God, let him do it. Let him do it exactly like he said he would. Let us out of this place. Please . . . give us some sort of chance.

She had not really allowed herself to know, until he had said it himself, how much she wanted what he offered her. She had tried to convince herself that she was different from other women, that she could get along very well the way they were going; but, of course, it had been a lie. She was not that different—she felt just as incomplete, just as insecure and always a little frightened, as any woman loving a man and yet having no claim on him except that of love would have felt. She had accepted a situation as hopeless and had thought she had contented herself with it, and when she had found out it was not hopeless at all, her contentment, her adjustment, had vanished. Now everything in her was focused on the one ultimate goal of marrying him and trying to achieve some normal, quiet, and sane pattern of life.

And he said we would get away from here, she thought. That was the best part of it all. She rubbed her face with her hands, thinking: Now, I'll have to fix my makeup. She wanted to look her best when he came; she wanted him to be sure she was worth it.

Get away from here. . . . She had never got used to this place or these people. It was like living in a madhouse inhabited by charming, deadly schizophrenics. They were generous, courteous, intensely Christian—and they were violent, paranoiac, hating and ruthless. She could not make sense of their contradictions, and her brain was weary from trying. She yearned for a place of logic and of harsh, clean, cold winter. She had been an outsider, an intruder into the asylum, for eight years; she was tired of being that and she wanted to go with Cary among her own people, where she could relax and feel understood and capable of understanding. . . .

What is he doing? she thought, afraid. What's going on now? What kind of battle is he fighting with his father or with Mary Scott? Is he winning?

She was afraid, she knew, because it took tremendous courage, tremendous strength, to do what Cary was attempting. More than she would have had. And she was not sure that he had enough either. Oh, please let him have enough, she prayed as she applied her makeup with hands that trembled. If you know how much this means to me, please—

Then she heard somebody in the corridor. She sprang up from her vanity table and hurried into the living room. Suddenly she desperately wanted a cigarette, and she lit one as she heard the knob turn. She snapped out the lighter just as the door opened and he came in.

There was a moment then, as she looked at him, trying to read a face that was only pale and very tired, when time seemed to have ground to a halt, when every cell of her body seemed suspended in its function. Then she felt herself smile, she heard assurance in her voice, as she went to him. "Cary. Darling, I've been waiting—"

He did not move to meet her. He just stood there in the middle of the room, as she came up to him, and his face did not change.

Then he said, "Maggie, I'm going to have to run for Governor."

She stopped where she was, not touching him. She looked at him, stunned for a moment and not believing it. "No," she said. "No, you promised . . ."

He came on across the room now. There was misery on his face. "I know I promised. I thought . . ." He made a helpless gesture. "Things have changed."

Grief and disappointment made her voice sharp and bitchy. "What's changed? You lost your nerve."

He shook his head. "It isn't that," he said, rubbing his face.

"Cary, for God's sake—" Her voice rose, trembled, almost squealing on the brink of hysteria.

"Please," he said. "Just listen to me." He lit a cigarette with the slow motions of a man who was stunned. "I didn't lose my nerve. I've been driving around for half the night trying to make a decision."

"A decision? You made a decision—"

"I went to my father's house," he said. "I was going to tell him. When I got there, I found a man there who has a private army. Something called the Constitutional Legion, and it's from Texas. They've found a way to keep the niggers from registering after all. They're sending out these men with guns to turn them back before they ever get to the registration places, and, of course, the state police aren't going to be able to find 'em. I don't know what's going to happen tomorrow . . ."

"Well . . ." She did not understand, and this was not what she wanted to hear. "Can't you stop them?"

He shook his head. "Nobody can stop them except Dale Moody and my father and the state police, and they aren't going to. I could phone Washington, but there'd be nothing Washington could do.

I'm just the Lieutenant Governor; they would check with the Governor before they did anything, and he would deny the whole story, and anyhow, it's too late. No, there's nothing I can do tonight or tomorrow."

"But what about us?" she cried.

He did not even seem to hear her.

"I tried to make my father call them off," he said. The flesh of his face seemed flabby, seemed just to hang loosely from its bone structure; his eyes were circled and pouchy. "But, of course, he was the man who brought them in in the first place."

He turned away from her. "All my life," he said, "all my life, I listened to him talk about honor and duty and pride, and it was all a fraud. He didn't mean any of it. What he meant was power. That's all it was, talk to cover up how much power meant to him. He . . . he's washed so many years of my life down the drain with that talk, and I let him do it and I never even realized who he was or what he was until I saw him tonight. Just an old man who can't live without power and who'd do anything to get it, including taking away everything I was ever entitled to. Just an old man who hates everybody who's got more power than himself, who's built a whole life around hate."

He turned back to her, his face stricken. "Tonight I went to see Huse. He's full of hate, too." Cary licked his lips. "The haters are moving in, Maggie; they're taking over. I'm talking about the kind of haters Burke meant. The ones who don't value anything except their own hate, the ones who'll blow up women or children or shoot men or stomp them to death, all in the name of patriotism and the country's welfare. We've never had anything like them before . . . and—"

He stood there a moment. Then he said, "My father was right in one thing. I'm a Bradham and I've got a duty to this state, and I can't duck out of it. He's taught me that ever since I've been alive. But I never really realized what it meant until I was driving around out there tonight by myself. I *have* got a duty, Maggie, and I've got to be Governor, because if I'm not, the haters are going to take over completely, and then this won't be Muskogee any more. It won't even be part of America; it'll be something different, and I'm not going to let that happen."

"What are you going to do?" she asked in a thin, dead voice, thinking in grief: Well, I won all right, I certainly won, didn't I? I changed him, didn't I, Burke?

"I'm going to run for Governor," he said. "Just like they want me to. I'm going to put on the roughest segregationist, lost-cause, nigger-hating campaign anybody ever waged in this state. I'm going to make Alec Morrison look like an abolitionist in comparison to me . . ."

"Cary," she said, unable to grasp what he meant.

"It's the only way I'll ever get elected," he said. "And if I don't get elected, it's either Alec Morrison on the one hand, or my father and the Moodys on the other—and either way, it'll be the end of Muskogee. And no matter what it costs me, that's the one thing I can't see happen, because my father was right: it's my duty."

"I see," she said, desperately trying to keep her voice steady. "And . . . and all this means more to you than I do . . ."

"It has to," he said; she heard the anguish in his words. "Oh, my God, I love you, but— Don't you see? Somebody has got to do it. Somebody has got to put this state back in America after a hundred years, more, of being out of it. And maybe I can do it. There's nothing wrong with the people. What's wrong is with the leadership. For a hundred years their leadership has kept the people so smothered in the Confederate flag that they couldn't even see the daylight of the twentieth century.

"So they've got to have different leadership. And where is it going to come from? Not from somebody who stands up and yells at 'em that they're all wrong, that overnight they've got to stop believing everything they've believed for over a century, that their grand-fathers died for—or that they think their grandfathers died for. Or from Alec Morrison or Powell Bradham. It's going to have to be somebody who talks their language and who knows how they feel, but somebody that knows too that if you keep on living in the past you die. Somebody's got to bridge that gap, and I think I can. . . . I . . . I think it was you and Burke that taught me how. But before I can do it, I've got to be Governor, and I'll be Governor if I have to scramble over the bare bones of a hundred years, if I have to suck up to Dale Moody and go back to Mary Scott, no matter what I have to do, because he was right, I'm a Bradham, and it's my duty, and there isn't any way I can get loose from it."

"Yes," she said in a faint voice that she hardly recognized as her own. "I guess you have. Even if it means giving up me."

"Even that," he said. "Because somebody has got to do something. I can't do anything about what happens out there tomorrow. What happens out there tomorrow depends on Houston Whitley. But maybe what happens two years and four years and maybe even twenty years from now . . ." He drew in a deep breath. "Maybe that depends on me."

Maggie sat down. "But in four years," she said desperately, "in four years, you could . . . If I went somewhere and waited, you . . ."

"Four years," he said, coming and kneeling beside her, "won't even start it. It's been going on ever since they invented the cotton gin. It may go on that long again, and as long as it takes, I've got to use whatever power I can get my hands on to do what I can."

"I see," she said. "The Butler money, that's power, too, isn't it?"

"Yes," he said.

"And you'll need it."

"I'll need it."

"But you love me." She put her hand on his.

He was silent for a moment. Then he said, "I love you."

She stood up. She did not know how long she was going to be able to keep her control. "All right, then," she said, and she was surprised at how steady her voice actually was. "Then let's end it now, here, clean," and she started toward the bedroom door.

He was on his feet. "Maggie—"

She paused at the threshold and said, "Good luck, Cary," and then she went into the bedroom and closed the door behind her. She heard him call her name again, and she did not answer.

After a while he went out.

16 It was nearly sunrise now, and they had been up all night. Jeff Marfield's eyes felt seared, his face a greasy mask, his throat worn out with talking, his mind and spirit empty of any further arguments to use on Houston Whitley. Now he sat slumped in a tilted-back chair, watching Huse at the table, sitting there, his face like something carved from wood, his hands playing

interminably with the pistol, spinning the cylinder, his eyes fastened on the bright wink of the brass bullets as they went round and round.

And so this is where it all ends, Marfield thought sickly. Began with him, ends with him. People been looking for an answer, a hope, all this time. He gives 'em one, and now he takes it away.

In a little while it would be time to go. And Marfield no longer knew anything else to try. Once, he had thought: Maybe Charles Bell could . . . But he knew that was useless, too. Nothing could.

Stiffly, he got up and went to the door, opened it and looked out. It had stopped raining sometime around midnight; in the first gray dawn he could see puddles standing in the muddy street. In a little bit, they would get in his car and drive from here to Washington Heights School. His only hope was that nobody would try to intercept them.

But even if nobody did, if what Bradham had said was true, others would be intercepted. And they would be waiting for Houston Whitley to speak, to tell them what to do. And— Jeff turned, the dry, whirring click of the cylinder of Robert's gun abrading his nerves. "Will you stop doing that?" he snapped.

Houston Whitley looked at him and nodded and laid down the gun, but he kept his hand on it. It had not been out of his hand all night.

The worst part of it is, Jeff thought, I know exactly how he feels. I want to pick up a gun, too. But I don't dare to. Christ, if I got my hands on one— He shook that feeling away from himself.

"You can't do it," he said, knowing this was the last time he was even going to try. "You just can't take away from everybody what you've already given them. You haven't got the authority."

Huse stood up. "I've got the authority," he said. "And I'm going to give them something new. Isn't it about time to go?"

"I reckon so."

"What about the reporters and the television people?"

"They'll meet us up at the paved road. Up in front of Bish's place."

Huse smiled faintly. "Good. I want everybody to get an eyeful if somebody tries to stop me."

Suddenly Jeff heard himself almost screaming. "Damn it, Huse, you can't do this, you got no right to do this! You said it yourself: love, not hate; forgiveness, not revenge. Now you can't—"

"Yeah," Huse said. "I've said a lot of crap in my time. I'm through talking crap now. Get your coat."

"In Christ's name," Jeff pleaded. "She was my sister, too. But I'm not—"

"You're not Houston Whitley," Huse said.

"Ahhh—" Jeff said, and his shoulders slumped. He turned away.

Suddenly the house shook as if it would fall. There was the sound of many heavy feet on the porch; the door scraped open; all at once the living room was filled with people. Jeff heard a giggle. "Awright, boys, don't knock thangs over, Mama have yo' hide." Then they were filing through to the kitchen. He and Huse turned together, as Robert appeared in the kitchen doorway.

He stood there, very drunk, swaying slightly from side to side. His bulging eyes were muddy and bloodshot, his lips curled away from yellow teeth in a grin. He had not shaved for several days; sparse whiskers were matted on his upper lip and chin. His clothes had been wet during the night; not entirely dry, they sagged shapelessly, and Jeff could smell the stench of them.

There were five men behind him. Jeff stared. They were all as drunk as Robert, and they were armed. He saw the barrel of a shotgun waving aimlessly.

Robert himself had a knife. It was a switchblade. As he stood there, he clicked it open and closed, open and closed, the blade winking in the light.

Jeff raised his eyes from the winking blade. "What's all this?"

Robert came unsteadily forward into the kitchen, the others crowding behind him. "Why, hell," he said, his voice thick. "We come to take you to regisher. Come to keep th' white folks from gittin ya." He took a step toward Huse, grinning at him. "Come awn, ole bubba, less us go kill ourselves a mess of ofay motherfuckers."

Huse stood very still, staring at Robert.

Robert's eyes went from Huse to the gun on the table and then back to Huse, and his grin broadened. His voice dropped, with more edge to it.

"Thass right, bubba." He gestured with the knife. "Now you talkin. The Man's waitin for us out there, somewhur. Okay, we goan out there an' say hello to The Man. You come wid us—we goan see if The Man's white hide'll let a bullet through same as ourn."

Huse said nothing. One of the men behind Robert was so drunk he could hardly stand. He waved his shotgun around wildly. Jeff moved toward him, pushed the barrel away. "Put those guns up!" he snapped, full of fury. "You hear me, all of you? Put those guns up!"

Robert turned toward him, not grinning now. His hand moved too swiftly for Jeff to dodge: Robert's open palm crashed into his face with terrific force, sending him sprawling back over a chair, blood trickling from one nostril. He slumped there, half dazed.

"Shut up, you chickenshit Uncle Tom," Robert said. He went around the table and came up to Huse. Huse stood without trying to draw away, as Robert put his arm about Huse's shoulders, waved the knife back and forth in front of Huse's face.

"Know sumpin?" Robert mumbled, grinning. "I always figured you chickenshit, too, ole bubba, till I heerd you stand up to 'at Bradham tonight. But looks like I wrong, you a real brudder after all. By God, you got balls on same as us. Less us go kill us some ofay bastards."

Jeff forced himself to his feet, dragged his hand across his bloody face. He was shaking all over, not from the blow, with fury. "All right," he said fiercely, turning to Houston Whitley. "All right, go on with him. Because there's your new leadership, Huse." His voice was a rasp of contempt. "We can match anything the whites've got, can't we? Go ahead, Huse, go with 'em, get used to 'em. Because they're what you'll be working with from now on. You take that gun with you, it'll be their party from here out. Meet the new Negro, Huse." He pointed at Robert with a thrusting gesture. "Meet the new Negro—designed by Houston Whitley to supersede the old model—"

"Sheeut," Robert said. "Huse—"

Jeff braced himself on the table. He saw Huse looking from him to the armed men. He saw Huse draw in a deep breath. Then Huse reached up and took Robert's arm from his shoulder and moved a step backward.

"Put those guns away," he said.

Robert blinked at him. "Huh?"

"Get out of here with those guns and put 'em up."

Robert waggled the knife. "But you said—"

Huse's voice was quiet. "I know what I said. And I know what I'm saying now. You put down those guns and get out of here, or I'll turn you over to the white law before you can blink your eye."

"Well, I be damn," Robert said. "Well, I jes' be damn. You are chickenshit after all, ain't you? After all your big talk to Bradham, you jest as scared as you ever was, ain't you?" His lips curled. "Awright. Well, us go to regisher ourselves. Us'll go and hope The Man tries to stop us—"

"No," Huse said sharply. "No, you won't."

"The hell you say. I don't take no orders from you. These my boys an' I *give* orders, I don't take 'em. You may be a leader to some, but you ain't nothin but a brother to me, a brother The Man done got scared plumb to death—"

"Yes," said Huse. "A brother." Then he moved, with lightning precision. His hand clamped on Robert's wrist; his forearm bulged as he jerked the wrist around. Robert howled and the knife dropped and Huse let go the wrist and crashed the back of his hand across Robert's face. Robert rolled backward and brought up against the cabinet, hanging to it, stunned.

Huse's voice was thick with contempt. "Did you think I'd be non-violent with *you?*" He whirled toward the others, and his eyes were alive, commanding. "Lay those guns down," he snapped. "Lay 'em down right now. Then get out of here, the whole lot of you, and take him with you. And you better believe me, if any one of you fires a shot today, so help me God—"

Jeff held his breath. The drunken men looked at Huse. There was some mumbling. Then the man with the shotgun leaned it in a corner. Jeff watched the rest of them lay down their weapons. Huse stood tautly, watching them closely.

Then they were gone, taking Robert with them; he was holding his swollen face and cursing steadily as they led him out. When he was gone, the house seemed very empty, very silent.

"Brother," Huse said at last. He was trembling slightly, as if shaken by something he had seen in Robert's face, Jeff thought— perhaps a reflection of himself? Huse turned his back on Jeff. His hands hung at his sides, clenching and unclenching. After a while he turned around again.

"Christ," he said in an anguished voice, "I don't know."

Jeff looked at him. "It's time for us to go," he said.

Huse closed his eyes for an instant, then opened them, and said, "Yes. Yes, let's go."

Jeff reached over and picked up the pistol on the table. He held it out. His eyes bored into those of Huse. "Do you want to take this with you?"

Huse's eyes dropped to the gun and he stared at it for a moment. Then he shook his head.

"No," he said with weariness in his voice, "I reckon not. Come on and let's get going."

17

They went together out of the house into the cool, gray air of dawn and got into Marfield's car. The rest of Little Hammer was just beginning to stir. As Marfield cranked the reluctant engine, Huse sat stiffly.

They would be moving out now, he thought, just like this. All over the state, carloads of them. Moving out at his command. To what?

He did not know. All he knew was that they all had to try. And try again. And again and again and again, if it took that. Until they had worn down resistance as water wears down a stone. Until they could walk anywhere free men could go, with their heads up.

Marfield idled the engine, letting it warm. After a while he put it into gear, and drove away from Lucy's house.

They had gone only half a block when the other cars came into the street: two of them. And they stopped flank by flank, blocking completely the narrow roadway between the sad gray shacks.

Marfield slammed on the brakes. "Look yonder," he said. "Bradham wasn't lying."

"No," Huse said. "No, I never thought he was lying."

White men were getting out of the two cars. Huse saw that two of the six of them had shotguns cradled in their arms.

Marfield cursed softly, viciously. He backed the car, ran its wheels into a front yard, turned it around smoothly, and started in the other direction.

He was too late. A pair of cars had come in behind them there, and that way was blocked off, too. Huse saw a party of five men coming from that direction. He saw guns. He saw that their leader was a tall man with a military bearing; he wore a broad-brimmed hat, like a cowboy's.

Marfield's voice was unsteady. He raised his hands from the steering wheel, dropped them back, and said, "They got us. Come on, let's get back in the house. I'll call up there at Bish's. Maybe there's somebody there. They can send the reporters and the television people down here and then we'll be safe. They won't dare try anything with them watching."

Huse was afraid, too. His mouth was dry with fear, his palms were sweating. "No," he said. "No, all those others, they have no reporters and television cameramen to holler for." He put his hand on the door handle. "You go inside and call and see if you can raise 'em. I'd like to have 'em down here, I'd like to have pictures of this. But I'm not going to wait for 'em."

Marfield looked at him. "What do you aim to do?"

"Well," said Huse, "I'm going to try to go on through 'em." And he got out of the car.

The men were closer now. He could see the cold grin on the face of the man in the big hat. He could hear the man say, "That's him. I know him from his pictures. That's the daddy rabbit of them all."

"Huse," Jeff said, and then he got out of the car and hurried into the house.

Huse walked to meet the men. When he was within ten feet of them, they stopped. The man in front tipped back his hat. Huse saw brass knuckles gleaming on the hand he used to do it with.

"Hello, nigger," the man said, still grinning that cold grin. "Where you think you're going?"

Huse drew in a deep breath. "It's registration day, mister," he said. "I'm going to get my name on the books."

"Oh, no," the man said. "No, you don't want to do that. You just turn around and go on home, like a smart nigger."

Huse looked at him for a moment. Then he shook his head. "No, sir, I can't do that."

He was afraid, terribly afraid. He thought about the weapons in the house, only a few paces away. He could turn back there and—

He said, "Would you please get out of my way? I've got to go register."

The man in the big hat just grinned. In the distance Huse heard the sound of cars coming down a rutted street. That would be the reporters, he thought, the television men. Now there was no possibility of his turning around. Whatever he did would be recorded, broadcast; they would all see it, the people out yonder who were going up against this, too. It wasn't his choice to make; he knew now it never had been.

He waited a moment longer. Let them get in place, let them tell everybody about this, let the whole country, the whole world, see it. . . .

Two of the men had taken out blackjacks and were slapping them across their palms. They were grinning, too.

Huse thought about Terri and Otis. But it's not fair to them, he thought. They just lost their mother; they need me.

"Come on, nigger," the man in the big hat taunted.

But maybe, Huse thought, feeling his legs beginning to push him forward without his will, they need me more this way than any other. He thought of himself and Cary, not as they were now, but as they had used to be, when they were unaware of anything to divide them. What was it Cary had said last night? *When will we be able to talk?*

He did not know. But, he thought, maybe at least the children— Maybe them— Then the brassbound fist of the man in the big hat was driving at him, and there was not even time to raise his hands.

ABOUT THE AUTHOR

Ben Haas was born in 1926 in Charlotte, North Carolina, and educated in the public schools of that city. He was inducted into the army when he was eighteen and served for two years in the Philippines. After his discharge, he worked at a variety of jobs, writing only as a hobby. He has been a clerk, proofreader, salesman and structural-steel estimator. In 1960 he determined to make writing his profession. Two years later his first novel, The Foragers, *was published.*

Mr. Haas is married to the former Douglas Thornton Taylor. They live in Raleigh, North Carolina, with their three sons, Joel, Michael and John.